WHERE THE OCEAN MEETS THE SKY

A.R. HADLEY

Editors:

Monica Black http://www.wordnerdediting.com/

Jenny Andreasson Babcock

Proofreaders:

Devon Burke https://www.joyediting.com

Judy Zweifel https://www.judysproofreading.com

Cover Designer:

Emily Wittig Designs https://www.emilywittigdesigns.com

Cover Image:

Unsplash. Used with permission.

AUTHOR NOTE

Previously published in 2018 as The South Beach Connection Trilogy: *Landslide*, *Wanderlust*, and *Continuum* — *Where the Ocean Meets the Sky* combines those three books into one, as the author originally intended. Although heavily edited, combined, and relaunched since their initial release, the overall story remains. Literary fiction meets contemporary romance — a love made in the stars. A connection not to be forgotten.

*for the boy who taught me patience
and the girl with magic in her heart*

She no longer needed to be a square peg trying to fit into a round hole

PART ONE
LANDSLIDE

PERCEPTION

THE WAY WE SEE THE WORLD

double doors
revolving doors
movement
change
paradoxical shift
universe tilts
I glide down the star slide
and land
at your feet
on my feet
riding on the tail of a lackluster comet

ONE

Keep Calm.

The dice hanging from the rearview mirror of the cab mocked her without mercy. How many times had she read those two words? A million.

She could not keep calm. Calm was bullshit. A lie.

She hated labels, but the complacent doctor had slapped her with one anyway. Two awful words encompassing a mess of complications:

Panic. Disorder.

It sounded like knots tangled up inside a dirty throw rug.

The cab was dirty and small, or she was shrinking, scrunched down, jeans tight against her thighs. It smelled too, like the waiting room of a doctor's office, latex and sanitizer trying to mask people's filth.

She stared out the window.

South Florida whizzed by as she twirled a piece of hair around an index finger. The noises inside her head grew louder than the traffic.

I am afraid...

Afraid if she put away the phone clutched in her palm — the device both a comfort and a distraction, a child's favorite blanket or a smoker's pack of Marlboros — she would think...

Of anything.

Of everything.

Thinking was out of the question. Thinking led to feelings. A friend once told her every thought was derived from a single feeling. So, which came first: the thought or the motherfucking feeling? Maybe this was only the perception of her feelings anyway, her unique interpretation creating her reality.

There was no reality. And perception was a dream.

It was all a dream.

A Dorothy-in-the-Land-of-Oz, house-spinning-inside-a-tornado, hypnotizing dream. If she closed her eyes, she could see her there, sitting on her left. Not Dorothy Gale, but her mom, Beverly. Her dad on her right. She'd been sandwiched between her divorced, but somewhat amicable, parents in the backseat of a New York City cab less than a week ago.

"When are you going to Miami?" Beverly asked, stale cigarette smoke from her mom's clothes wafting into the graduate's nose.

"I told you, Mom. A million times. Friday."

"This Friday?"

"Yes."

"You've asked her enough questions, Beverly," Albert said, squeezing his daughter's hand. *"Let her be. It's Annie's day."*

The college graduation, celebration, and congratulations hadn't been able to drown out the regrets, the what-ifs. The death. It hadn't obliterated the passive-aggressive behavior of her mother or the sadness still palpable in the grip of her father's palm.

Every conceivable emotion had taken over the empty space of that cab days ago. And they consumed her again now in the seat of a different taxi, filling the vat no one spoke of.

The pores. The tiny holes.

The inconspicuous places in and all around, between the handshakes, the glances, the *hellos* and *hi, how are you*s, making innocuous replies to friends and strangers with the infamous line, *"I'm doing so fine,"* for the hundredth time, I think I'll puke.

And she had puked.

Plenty.

She'd secretly puked and perspired and gone nearly crazy for months before the ceremony. But she'd had to make college graduation.

Had to.

For him.

A ghost.

Did he still know her? Could he see her? Did she even know herself? Who was she?

She thought she knew who she was. Always. She was nine going on forever. She was resilient. Iron. Steel. Until death had broken her. A measly little shard of kryptonite had split her open and exposed her. What a joke.

Life.

Reality.

Perception.

Who was she?

Annie Baxter.

The dreamer. The romantic. The optimist. The born photographer. A daughter. A sister. The sky. She was blue. Blank. She was broken.

Nothing but atmosphere kept her from floating off into an endless, oxygen-deprived universe.

"Miss?" The driver cleared his throat.

Annie swallowed and looked out the window. Branches of palm trees swayed in the wind. The cab had apparently pulled into the Allens' driveway. Thank God some of the shaking had subsided. Her breathing regulated. She would disguise the panic, take back the summer. Starting now. This was her summer.

Mine.

A thousand miles from New York City. Direct, daily access to sun and surf. An immediate distraction from thinking and feeling. Except ... what good was a photographer who didn't feel? And who was she kidding? Annie felt *everything*.

"Miss?" the man interrupted again.

She peeled her eyes from the two-story brick home with frontage on the Atlantic Ocean. "*One of the few remaining places on Florida's coastal highway without high-rises or condos. Only homes,*" Maggie had informed her.

"Can I help you with your bags?"

"No, thank you." Annie smiled, stepped out, grabbed her carry-on, and slung her backpack over her shoulder.

The smell of freshly cut grass lingered in the air, mixing with the redolence of the ocean. Bees buzzed in her stomach as she made her way to the porch, ready to greet two old friends.

Friends she hadn't seen since the funeral.

Think about something else...

Pinching her lids shut, she knocked on the door, willing the optimist within her to win out over the anxiety-riddled stranger who had occupied her psyche for months.

"Kiddo," John said the moment the door swung open, a wide smile on his face, his blue-gray eyes twinkling.

"Hi." Annie grinned.

John kissed her cheek as they embraced, then he inched away, looked over his shoulder, and called out, "Mags!" as he grabbed the suitcase handle. "Come in, sweetheart." Annie had nearly forgotten the endearing sound of his voice, his drawl, the Georgia accent ever apparent — especially in his sweet sentiments. "Let me get this. Is this all you brought for the summer?"

"Yeah." Annie stepped over the threshold, backpack still over her shoulder, her eyes wide as she surveyed the foyer.

"Maggie would need several." He chuckled. "And they would all be very heavy."

"What would Maggie need?" The Cat asked as she descended a spectacular white staircase, her auburn curls dancing and hips swaying.

"Luggage. Lots of luggage," John replied. "Annie only brought one suitcase."

Maggie hit the ground floor with a bounce and a squeal. "Your hair..." She fanned out some of Annie's caramel-colored strands. "It's gotten so long. You look so pretty."

Somehow, the two of them managed to make her feel like a kid again. A *kiddo*. Nine or ten years old and squished between them on their couch watching *Toy Story* for the umpteenth time. She preferred the cowboy and astronaut to Ariel or Cinderella.

"I decided to grow it out." Annie blushed. "It hasn't been this long since I was sixteen."

"I know..." Maggie's brown eyes sparkled. "I remember."

"You still seem sixteen to me." John sighed.

"That's because you're old." Maggie winked.

Annie missed that adorable wink too, having first been on the receiving end of it *and* Maggie's devotion around the age of nine, spending afternoons, evenings, and eventually the entire night at the Allens' high-rise in Seattle.

For a time, Maggie and John had been granted guardianship of Annie. Months when Beverly couldn't be bothered to adult or had entered another treatment center — or she'd been drunk morning to midnight. Or perhaps she hadn't given a fuck. Annie's dad perpetually worked, had been on the verge of marriage number three, and never fought for custody of their only child. Albert had cheated. Her mother had won.

Thank God Maggie stepped forward when everyone else had stepped back. Almost everyone...

Annie's brother... He'd been—

"Yeah," John grumbled, tilting his head toward his wife, jolting Annie from her childhood memories. "People mistake me for her father." His signature laugh followed.

"No..." Annie shook her head. "Really? No they don't."

"It's your hair, honey." Maggie touched the tips of her husband's shiny silver locks. He'd grayed early. "I tell him all the time he looks hot."

"You both look good." Annie smiled.

"You mean *for our ages*." Maggie grinned.

"I didn't say that..." Annie mentally counted back to 1998, trying to come up with exactly how old they were now.

"You're the one who looks good, sweetheart." Maggie rested a hand on Annie's shoulder. "The year has been good to you."

Maggie spoke those words like a question or an affirmation or like some sort of dreamy consolation, her chocolate-brown eyes swinging back and forth like the pendulum of a grandfather clock.

Good to you, Annie thought. *What does that even mean*? She glanced at John, but he remained quiet, shifting his gaze to the—

No, no, no. Don't look at the floor.

The last year... What had it been? Had it been good? Annie had neglected to tend to the *good*.

The last year meant surviving, face pressed up against the glass of a passenger train window, life zooming by at the speed of light, panic and medication replacing parties and commitments, scattered ashes usurping sunshine.

Good to her?

Not if you considered pills, studying all hours of the night, hiding and escaping while literally breathing into a paper bag *good*.

Anxiety rushed in, overtaking the sensible part of her brain, constricting her stomach in the center of her friends' pretty little foyer — the exact scenario she'd attempted to avoid in the cab. Always avoiding. Until she couldn't see straight. But seeing the two of them again, John and Maggie Allen — what had Annie been thinking? Making the decision to temporarily move to Florida and exhibit her photographs. To start over.

Everything came back.

And this time, she couldn't stop it.

Acid shot up her esophagus. Her throat tightened. The day was as new as it was stale and old...

"Annie, did you hear me?" her father cried into the phone over and over and over. The sister and daughter and daydreamer stood mute and frozen in the center of Tabitha's kitchen, staring at a lamp on a table in the living room. "Annie... Annie!"

"Has it been a year?" John uttered, interrupting the horrid memory, the day her life irrevocably changed. "I wish we could've seen you sooner, kiddo. I wish we could've made it up there for your graduation."

"Maggie explained everything." Annie touched his arm, recalling John had recently attended a funeral. "I'm sorry for your loss."

"Enough of this sorry and sorrow," John mumbled, his accent subtle yet strong, imbibing each syllable with love. "Come on to the kitchen. We'll have a drink."

"I want to reimburse you for your cab fare," Maggie said as the three of them started to walk.

"No..." Annie stopped and looked The Cat dead in the eye. John coughed. "Absolutely not."

"It's bad enough you wouldn't let me pick you up at the airport," Maggie whined.

"I'm surprised she listened to you, kiddo." John chuckled and turned to his wife. "She's twenty-five now, Mags."

"I know..." Maggie sighed and linked her arm through Annie's as they began to stroll again.

Annie glanced around, getting lost in the architecture, her eyes climbing the staircase, the expansive ceilings.

"What are you thinking in that head of yours?" Maggie asked.

That she was glad she'd chosen to pay her own way here. That she was happy to be seeing them both like this, relaxed and at home. Not to mention, she'd longed for the quiet of the car after the noise of the plane ride.

"That your house is beautiful," Annie replied instead, diverting her attention to the chandelier hanging over a large walnut dining table in a room off to their right.

"I keep forgetting you haven't been here before." Maggie eyed the second floor. "Do you want to see your room now?"

"My room?"

"Yours for the entire summer."

"No, I'll wait." Annie smiled. *My room. My summer.* "I would like something to drink, though."

"That's my girl," John said as the three of them rounded the corner into the kitchen. He rested Annie's carry-on at the end of another staircase. One with rustic, dark brown steps, planks that matched the flooring. Its landing met the nook, kitchen, and an enormous open living area.

"You must be tired, getting up so early for your flight." Maggie held the refrigerator door open.

"I'm okay." Annie placed her backpack on one of the barstools tucked beneath the high countertop.

"What do you want to drink?" John asked.

"We have orange juice, iced tea, water," Maggie offered.

Annie only blinked, her eyelids flitting like the press of the Nikon shutter. The windows, the view, rendered her speechless. Not windows but walls, taking up the entire rear length of the home. The deck, the sand, the ocean, were all more beautiful than she had imagined.

"I think she wants a *drink*, Mags," John said, but Annie hardly heard a word.

She found herself in front of a set of tall French doors, warmth already covering her entire body. With no curtains or blinds to conceal the sunshine, Annie had to hold a hand above her eyes to continue peering outside.

Her camera rested in her backpack, but she wanted to see the water like this. With her naked eye first. Without a lens. Or obstructions.

"It's beautiful," Annie uttered. No matter how many times she'd seen the ocean, the majesty of it never ceased to spoon against a part of her she believed no one else could espy.

"Do you want to take a better gander?" John smiled and opened both doors. "This is all private access."

A burst of air swept in, swooshing around Annie as she stepped onto the deck and leaned into the sun, hips forward, hands in her jean pockets, the Florida heat hitting her body like a brick, enveloping her from head to foot.

She closed her eyes a moment.

Then opened them.

Her entire summer would be spent here. On this beach. Her first real summer since her brother—

No, no, no... Not. Now.

If she didn't think it or say it, he would remain alive.

Shrugging off sadness, breathing in possibilities, smelling humidity and salt and creativity, Annie cast off worry and inhaled summer's promise. The sensation traveled through her lungs violently, wildly, with a feverish independence.

Annie looked back at John and grinned. "I'd love some wine, then I think I'll take that walk."

This *had* been a good decision. Coming here. Being with old friends. Moving over a thousand miles from New York City, continuing to distance herself from her home state of Washington.

The change, although planned, somehow felt serendipitous.

TWO

Late Saturday afternoon, Annie examined the contents of the big walk-in closet upstairs in her bedroom.

Over a week had passed since she'd first arrived in Miami, and Maggie had made her feel at home — a real home, the kind with love and hugs and—

The clothing distracted her.

Annie didn't know how long she'd been standing in the closet, looking at the same selection of dresses when she knew only one would do. The white dress with the red flowers, the red belt, the slit from knee to thigh.

As Annie pulled the garment off the hanger, she eyed the multitude of empty frames leaning against the walls. Frames and dresses. Mattes and shoes. Only seven days until the gala and still so much to do.

After slinking the old standby over her five-foot-four frame, she went to the mirror. A fingernail in her mouth, she studied the creation. No more sweatpants or unwashed hair. Graduation had been the first time in months Annie had bothered much with her appearance. Tonight, would be the second.

Who am I? Annie inched closer to her reflection.

A girl, waiting to be pushed on a swing set. She shook her head and smiled, trying to recall the last time she'd allowed herself to *feel* this beautiful. And it wasn't the dress or anything she could pinpoint with thinking. The knowing came from another place — a forgotten one.

Where the magic happens.

Annie's father often said his daughter had been born with magic. *"You have a spark, doodlebug. Don't let anyone take it from you."*

Not anyone.

Or anything.

Not even death could encroach upon it.

But it had for the last year...

"Knock, knock," came a voice, mixing with the sound of knuckles tapping against the closed door, sending Annie's thoughts flying in all directions.

She grabbed some red heels and strolled toward the dresser. "Come in."

Maggie cracked the door open, batting her copper lashes. "It's almost six."

"Don't rush me." Annie grinned and lifted a brush to her hair.

Maggie flashed a smile as she stepped into the room. "You look amazing."

"You won't get me down there any faster with your flattery," Annie teased, slowly sliding the brush through several strands of silky brown hair.

Maggie joined her at the mirror. "People have already started to arrive." She turned her fair-skinned face from side to side, plucking at her auburn curls.

Annie stared at The Cat a moment, then sighed. "What is it, Maggie?" Their gazes met. "What are you up to?"

"Nothing..." Maggie smirked.

"That's bullshit." Annie rolled her eyes.

"Fine," Maggie huffed. "I'm dying to show you off."

"Ah..." Annie laughed. "*So*, the truth finally comes out. I'm your new Miami thing."

"*You are*. People are already talking of the gala."

Annie turned her attention to the window seat — her favorite part of the bedroom — and peered out at the ocean, wondering how many people *had* already arrived.

"*You* are talking about the gala, Maggie." She glanced at her friend. "You."

"*I am*. When will you be down?"

"Soon."

"Oh..." Maggie cooed and grinned, fluttering those beautiful eyelashes again, "to be twenty-five..."

"Stop it." Annie giggled and shooed her out of the room. "Go-go-go."

The moment Annie stepped into the hall, her palms began to sweat, her belt suddenly felt tight, and her heart rate multiplied, its beat echoing inside her eardrums.

People. Lots of people. Breathe.

With a loud inhale, she started to descend the wooden staircase, the sounds below intensifying with each step, like a theater audience beginning to fill an auditorium. Chatter, music, laughter. She exhaled, wiped her hands on her dress, and took a few more deep breaths. Seconds later, she stopped just shy of the bottom, thinking no one could see her on the fifth step of that staircase.

The pearls on her necklace moved through her fingers as her eyes moved over the room, scanning faces, postures, plates of food. Annie noticed things others often didn't — symmetry and angles, imperfections and lines. Then her gaze stopped on a man standing in the far corner of the living room.

Something shot up her spine.

And she dropped the pearls.

Fire.

Fire raced up her backside.

Or fear.

Someone had noticed her there.

Someone had distinguished her from all the other fingerprints and snowflakes.

A knot formed low in her belly. She perspired more.

The man's eyes engulfed her, never leaving her face. Looking at her. Or was it through her? No boy had ever sized her up with such audacity.

And this was no boy.

He was a man.

Annie tore her eyes from his. Still, a moment later, she couldn't help but look back.

The man's face was unmistakable, cut out of the side of a mountain, clean-shaven and defined. His dirty-blond hair fell neatly into place off his forehead, not combed to any particular side. Standing at least six feet tall, surrounded by a few other people, he engaged in what appeared to be lively conversation, his eyes shifting between those he spoke to and Annie — his gaze carrying an energy across the house in a wave. She could feel the water rippling up against her body even when she wasn't looking at him.

Look. Away.

She did, with effort, but quite immediately, she glanced back, meeting his stare.

His eyes.

The color was difficult to ascertain from a distance, like a welcome oasis in the desert, faraway pools with water overflowing at their sides.

They looked blue.

They looked green.

They spoke without speaking.

They were bold. Striking. They held Annie on that staircase in the palm of their hands. The man peered at her as if he knew her, or wanted to know her, but he didn't. *Did he?* He probably knew Maggie.

God, what was he thinking, continuing to examine Annie as though no one else was at the party?

She grabbed her pearls, squeezing them. The house felt devoid of people.

But for the two of them.

"There you are." Maggie approached the railing and touched Annie's wrist, snapping the daydreamer out of the stupor she'd fallen into. "There's someone I want you to meet."

Before allowing Maggie to lead her away from the protection of the staircase, Annie stole one more glance at that man. He smiled a big, toothy grin, charming the people around him. Then he looked up and caught Annie's eye again. The dimples on his cheeks faded, his expression changing, morphing into something far more complex.

"Annie..." Maggie tugged on her arm.

She cleared her throat, placed her damp palm on the edge of her fiery face, and followed Maggie into the kitchen.

"This is my friend," Maggie said the moment they met one of the high countertops, "Mrs. Sorken. She's on the board. And this," she continued, gesturing and smiling, "is the photographer I've been telling you about. Annie Baxter."

"Please, call me Betsy," Mrs. Sorken replied, the shape of her eyes calling to mind some of Margaret Keane's famous paintings. The woman fingered the aqua beads on Annie's wrist. "I love your bracelet, honey."

"I love your accent." Annie extended a hand, ready to make "normal" conversation, hoping her palm wasn't shaking.

"Thank you, honey." The woman smiled and shook Annie's hand.

"Are you warm, sweetheart?" Maggie asked, eyeballing the photographer's cheeks. "Is it hot in here?"

"You do look flushed," Betsy added.

"No. I'm fine." *Fine. Fine. Fine.* She resisted rolling her eyes. "Where are you from, Betsy?"

"I was born in Austin."

"People must ask you that all the time." Annie grinned, stuck on viewing this Texan through the lens of her imaginary Nikon. Betsy would make a marvelous subject. The angle of her large, peach cowboy hat. The pieces of hair falling across her big, brown eyes. Her hands.

"Well, I love talkin'. No matter. You don't have to worry about me." Betsy laughed. "I actually spent part of my life in North Carolina. Chuck and I moved here from Asheville."

Annie smiled. "I've always wanted to drive the Blue Ridge Parkway." Actually, she hoped to visit many new places. Explore the unknown. Take the scenic route. Miami was only the beginning. In the fall, she would travel to several destinations, rediscover magic, escape, snap pictures until her arms hurt and eyes blurred.

"Lots of galleries up in those parts, honey. People would love you. And Lord knows"—Betsy pushed on Annie's shoulder—"it's probably a hell of a lot cooler up there this summer, that's for sure."

"I'm kind of enjoying the heat," Annie replied, wondering where those interesting words had come from. The back of her neck was on freaking fire.

"You might be the only one." Betsy chuckled, fanning herself with a palm. "Whew, wait until you hit menopause."

"Maybe I should adjust the air conditioner."

"It's fine, Maggie." Annie glanced at Betsy, then behind her at the assortment of liquor bottles. "How long have you been in Miami, then?"

"Oh, I guess it's been about two years since Chuck brought me down here." The cowgirl began to chuckle again. "Get yourself a drink. I'm already on number two. You've gotta catch up."

"Yes, Annie. What do you want? I'll make it," Maggie offered.

Annie preferred to make her own cocktail, exactly the way she liked it. The way her father liked it. Albert had introduced his daughter to the dirty vodka martini with plenty of olives when Annie turned eighteen. A martini in one hand and calculator in the other, glasses at the tip of his nose, a ledger the size of a desktop filled with numbers, Annie could see him now...

"Mix me a drink," her father would say. *"Then tell me what's new with you, doodlebug."*

"I'll make it." Annie politely excused herself, but Maggie followed, cornering her before she could get to the bottles.

"What are you doing?"

"I want a drink."

Maggie sighed. "That's an important contact for you. You're somewhere else tonight." Maggie placed the back of her hand on Annie's cheek. "Are you sick?"

"I'm trying, Maggie." She shrugged off her friend, avoided eye contact, and looked around. At least eighty or more guests crowded the living area and kitchen, spilling into the den and onto the deck, calling to mind Holly Golightly's apartment — only this place was bigger, much bigger, and had no cat. Or perhaps, only a different cat lived here. A curious one on two legs with auburn hair and chocolate eyes. "This is the first time I've been in a crowd of people since gradua—"

Maggie ran a palm down Annie's arm. "You're fine." Their eyes locked. "You'll be fine."

Maggie didn't understand *fine.* Or faking it. She didn't know about the panic attacks.

"I am *fine,*" Annie retorted, then someone interrupted them. Maggie got pulled away.

Annie turned, folded her arms across her chest, and looked over the living room, fingertips grazing her biceps. Her nape had cooled down some. The man was no longer there. In the corner. Staring, peering, seeing things Annie couldn't surmise. She didn't care anymore about the martini. And maybe that magical man had left the party.

His eyes...

They were so beautiful.

But what Annie wanted was upstairs. Then outside. She desired two things:

The Nikon and the ocean.

Both beating out the man with the face carved from Mount Rushmore.

For now.

THREE

Annie joined several people outside on the deck, adults and a few children, the Nikon dangling by its strap around her neck.

Camouflaging herself with her surroundings, and after receiving the parents' permission, Annie took off, snapping picture after picture of the little ones. Dimpled cheeks, open mouths in full cry, runny noses. Laughter. A favorite blankie. Tiny fingers. Dirty toes.

She captured the adults as well. Some chatting boisterously, others talking at a whisper, their expressions reflective, happy, a buzz woven through their eyes.

She photographed objects. Shoes and candles. A wineglass smeared with fingerprints containing a few drops of red. A couple of highballs, ice melting into the liquor.

Caught up in the magic of each moment, Annie lost track of time. Only the fading daylight alerted her to its passage as she strolled to the edge of the deck, sat on a wooden step, and removed her heels. She grabbed a handful of sand and began to take pictures of the grains as they slipped through her fingers, doing it over and over and over until some white crabs off in the distance, playing peek-a-boo, entering then exiting their tiny round homes became part of her memory card too.

Then a sharp gust of wind blew, and she looked to the sky. Clouds, beautiful, never dull, wispy nothings and mighty warriors, made their way across the darkening horizon as Annie attempted to photograph each shape and size. Salt on her tongue, a breeze up her skirt, a marvelous sting in her eyes — everything felt full. Not only her camera. But her heart. Her soul.

She couldn't get enough of life.

Of magic.

Little did Annie know, while she was captivated by the beauty of the earth, the stranger, the man with the stellar eyes, had become quite captivated himself.

Inside the house, standing near the French doors, looking lean in his crisp, sapphire button-down shirt and pitch-black pants, conversing with John, he found he was unable to peel his eyes away from the girl he'd seen on the staircase. The creature. The woman. The peculiar girl with a string of pearls and a camera hanging from her neck.

Both men gazed out the window, each cradling a highball. The stranger kept a hand in his pocket, peering at that woman, staring at her the way he had when first spotting her on the fifth step of the staircase.

"Who's that girl, John?" The man tipped his head in the photographer's direction, not a care in the world.

"What girl, Cal?" John took a sip of his drink. "There are quite a few girls here." He chuckled, then came a burst of laughter.

"Mmm," Cal said, his index finger pointing, his palm around the drink, "that woman outside there, on the sand with the camera."

John squinted, scanning the deck, and replied, "Oh, that's Annie. She's stayin' with us this summer." Then he did a double take and pinched his eyebrows together. "Cal..." John tried to break the man's stare, the one Annie had surely witnessed earlier: piercing and intense, foreboding and sensual. "Annie *is* just twenty-five years old."

Time seemed to stand still a moment.

But not too long.

Cal whipped his head toward his friend, glaring at him. "Did I ask her age?"

John matched Cal's scowl, looked out the window, and shook the ice around in his glass.

Cal smirked. "I take it you don't approve."

"It's Maggie who won't approve."

"I should ask your wife's opinion on my love life, per usual."

"We've known Annie since she was a child. It's not that simple."

"She's no child."

Their eyes met, then parted. John cleared his throat. Cal took a sip of his drink.

"Don't let this stand in the way of our friendship," Cal condescended a couple minutes later, gesturing outside, then back to himself, before swallowing the rest of the whiskey.

"You're the one who has stood in the way of our friendship." John's brow furrowed again.

"I don't want to do this now. Later, when it's quiet. The two of us. Alone. We'll talk."

Without another word or glance in John's or that woman's direction, Cal stepped away to refill his glass.

FOUR

"You're still warm?"

"God, Maggie, you scared me." Annie filled a shaker with ice, alcohol, and olive juice. She had stashed her camera, eaten a plate of food, and mostly avoided people.

"I adjusted the AC." Maggie placed the back of her palm on Annie's cheek.

"Would you stop with that?"

"You're flushed."

"I was outside." She poured the cocktail into the martini glass. "I took a bunch of photographs."

"I want you to meet people."

"I am."

"Well, are you at least having a good time?"

Annie lifted the perfect martini to her mouth, touched the rim of the glass to her bottom lip, and met the eyes of the stranger. The bastard stood several feet away, in the living room near the windows, talking, breathing, *peering*.

However, Annie wouldn't turn her head toward his face. Not fully. She refused to give him the satisfaction. Nevertheless, the mysterious man had no qualms about moving his gaze on and off her as if it were the most natural thing in the world.

And she was having a good time.

"I met some fascinating little people outside," Annie replied, giving Maggie her undivided attention. "I didn't expect to see children here tonight."

"Aren't they adorable?" Maggie giggled.

Annie smiled. "What about you? Are you having fun, or are you too busy cleaning up?"

"I'm having fun." Maggie slid a towel across the countertop.

"I don't know if the same can be said of your husband," Annie continued as Maggie looked over the room. "It seems he's being held prisoner." The photographer tipped her head toward the windows, hoping to keep lust off her face and curiosity from her tone. "Who's the man keeping him captive?"

Maggie didn't cease sliding the towel over the granite, wiping spills as her eyes came to rest on two men. One of them hers. The other...

"That's just Cal," Maggie droned, as if *Cal* were some ordinary Joe. Her attention went back to the kitchen and organization of the liquor bottles.

"And ... how do you know him?"

"God, Annie, we've known Cal half our lives. We all met at UCSC. Cal and John have remained close. They're business partners now."

Annie shifted her head only a centimeter in the direction of the man, the news of the long-standing relationship between the three of them not deterring her inquisitiveness one bit. Perhaps, it only served to enhance it.

"Annie..."

"Huh?"

Maggie smiled, grabbed Annie's chin, and shook it. "Cal is forty-five years old."

"Maggie, please." Annie pushed The Cat's hand away. "Don't lecture me. I only asked about him, for God's sake."

"I'm not lecturing you," Maggie replied, but she never could feign innocence. "I want you to enjoy your summer. That's all."

"I will enjoy my summer." Annie met the man's heated gaze, blinked, then she eyeballed Maggie. "Besides, why does his age matter? We're friends, and you're..." She grinned. "*How old are you?*"

Maggie scoffed.

"You're forty-four," Annie gushed.

Maggie scoffed again, this time while tapping her fingernails across the granite. "Fine." Maggie tossed the towel onto the counter in a huff. "Let's meet him now." She looked Annie dead in the eye, straightened out her own clothing, and wiggled her hips. "Let's go."

Annie's feet cemented to the floor. Her stomach swirled. Her palms began to sweat.

"Annie…" Maggie sighed. "You are—"

"I don't want to hear it."

That she was young. That her experience with men had been narrow at best. That she couldn't handle a relationship right now. Or a man named Cal.

Fuck. That.

A rebellious glint in her eye, Annie glared at Maggie, put her glass to her lips, and finished off the martini in one ginormous sip.

Maggie smirked, grabbed Annie's hand, and pulled the young, twenty-five-year-old woman — the girl who wore her heart on her sleeve — toward Cal. "Taking the prey right to the huntsman," Maggie mumbled.

"What?" Annie asked.

"Nothing," Maggie said as they arrived at the windows, a weird grin taking shape on The Cat's face, something artificial and strained.

The men stopped conversing. Cal rested a hand in his pocket, his expression switching from amiable to serious and contemplative as he stared only at Maggie and John.

The four of them stood in a circle. John put an arm around his wife and smiled. Cal didn't even crack a hint of a smile. In fact, he still wouldn't look at Annie. Aloof yet discerning, he seemed to be taking in his surroundings: body language, the sounds, the sights. Annie.

Despite barely giving her a second glance, Cal read Annie like a beloved book. And apparently, he was already fluent.

"Honey, I thought it would be a good time to introduce Annie to Cal," Maggie began, unable to keep that odd smile off her face. Even her tone had changed. "We can never be sure when he might grace us again with his presence."

Appearing unaffected by Maggie's snide remark, Cal turned his head, pinioning Annie to the spot. Her throat went dry as he peered directly into her eyes. His were green, not blue, and they were keen and astute. Astounding. From this tiny distance, those fucking green orbs were more intense than she could've possibly imagined.

"Maggie…" John lovingly reprimanded, then he looked to his friends.

"Cal..." He cleared his throat. "This is the woman I told you about. Annie. She'll be stayin' with us this summer while she jumpstarts her career." A genuine smile spread across John's face. "Annie Baxter, this is Cal Prescott."

"God, John, you're always so formal," Maggie teased, but no one paid her any mind.

Annie hadn't taken her eyes off Cal's sculpted face, loving the way his brow crinkled vertically between his eyes.

"Hi." Annie smiled wide.

"Hello," Cal replied.

The man didn't even offer his hand for a shake. Instead, he took a neat sip of his ever-so-neat drink as he stared at Annie.

Jesus Christ.

The confidence he possessed oozed out of him naturally, the way sweat dripped from pores. Heat pulsed through Annie's body. Flashes. Like before. She started to play with her pearls, wondering how she could be so fucking hot. Cal hadn't shook her hand. Or touched her.

God, imagine him touching you.

She dropped the necklace.

The same current that had possessed her from across the room earlier now nearly crippled her as the magnets inside her body gravitated toward his, toward a stranger. A familiar stranger...

Something within her had known him before.

After a moment of uncomfortable silence, Maggie cleared her throat. "John." She tugged on her husband's cuff as Cal shifted to face the glass. "I need your help in the kitchen."

"Yes, Mags." John sighed, overacting his part. "Whatever you say."

The couple disappeared the way the sun had from the sky. Annie watched their two friends depart, leaving her and a stranger named Cal standing together and alone in a room full of people by the large windows overlooking the deck and the ocean.

Never more aware of herself, Annie waited a moment for him to speak while grating her fingernails against her palms and biting the insides of her cheeks. Blood shot through her veins at warp speed. Everything else moved in slow motion.

Everything.

Then Cal turned his entire body toward her, until they were chest to chest, inches apart. Looking into Annie's eyes, he peered deep inside a place within her she thought no one else could see.

"What career are you starting in Miami, Annie?"

She tripped over the sound of his voice.

Tripped.

It was unusual. The tone.

Mellow, relaxed, yet sharp enough to prick the tip of a finger. The man seemed to time his words. The syllables even.

"I'm a photographer." Annie smiled, circling one heel into the wood floor. "Sometimes I do freelance work for magazines, but I came to Miami to showcase my art in a gallery. My first exhibit."

Cal took a sip of his drink, sure to keep his feelings off his face, refusing to let Annie see what he saw, read, and intuited. This woman was much more than he'd imagined — and he'd already imagined quite a lot.

"I noticed you with your camera, outside with the children." Cal pointed his head toward the deck. "You were working then?"

"Yes, but it doesn't feel like *work*." Annie grinned wider. "What about you? Are you in Miami for work?"

"What makes you think I'm not *from* South Beach?" Cal smirked, the smile illuminating his greens as he proceeded to tell her a little about his job.

Annie was familiar with it. It was John's occupation. Financial something-or-other. She'd never really bothered with it. She'd been a child when her father had become John's accountant, Albert Baxter having remained John's numbers man for several years in Seattle until the Allens moved to Florida.

Numbers seemed like a foreign language.

Annie was dreams.

Photographs.

Heart-fluttering, skipping-rope dreams.

Her father was numbers.

"Do you like it?" she asked Cal.

"The work?"

"Yeah. You've told me all about it, but you haven't said whether you like it."

"It's work," he droned, shifting his weight from one foot to the other. "It makes the money."

Annie peered deep into Cal's eyes.

This man didn't care about the money.

In this one brief moment, she saw so much more within his soul than he could've realized.

She wanted to delve into his ocean.

Explore possibilities.

To know him.

He placed his glass on a nearby end table, then stuffed his hands in his pockets and looked away.

"When did you meet John and Maggie?" Annie asked several seconds later even though she already knew the answer.

"When did *you* meet John and Maggie?"

"Fine," she teased. "Neither of us wants to give away our hand." They both grinned. "Were they already a couple when you met?"

"No."

"Who did you meet first?"

"Maggie." His gaze locked onto hers, his eyes holding the heat, the intensity, Annie had seen from the staircase.

He reached a palm toward her face.

The sounds Annie now heard tricked her into thinking she was swimming underwater. Felt like it too. No noise in the room. Only that of her heart beating in her chest.

Because underwater, you held your breath.

And right now, with his hand moving toward her skin and his eyes eating her alive, she was without oxygen.

She couldn't move, but she must've flinched, because he smiled again, told her to relax, then said, "You have sand on your ear."

As Cal brushed the dirt away with his thumb, Annie leaned into his caress. But before she knew it, she found herself drifting from the warmth of his touch to the music playing over the sound system. Her eyes closed. His hand dropped. Her lips began to move.

Stretching the pearls from her neck, she whispered the third and fourth stanzas of the Otis Redding song. Opening her eyes, she released the necklace and smiled. "It's been a while since I've heard this."

"Maggie loves it," they both said at the same time.

"His singing makes me feel like I'm there," she went on. "At the dock on the bay."

Cal peered at Annie as though she were the most interesting thing he'd ever seen, his eyes darting back and forth, lighting up like a glorious electrical storm over the ocean.

"Whatever. It's silly."

"Nothing you've said is silly. Music is supposed to affect us."

"Does it affect you?"

"I first heard this song..." He grinned wide. His dimples could've powered a small town, and Annie wondered why he didn't smile more often. "Maybe I shouldn't tell you how old I was..."

"Maggie told me how—" Annie started without thinking, and his gorgeous dimples faded.

Shaking his head, Cal tipped his chin toward the floor, the look he wore the same as moments ago when Maggie had scolded him: smug satisfaction with a pinch of *I don't give a fuck*. When he glanced back up, another change occurred. His attention focused on something behind her.

"What? What is it?" Annie looked over her shoulder, but before she had a chance to move, Cal placed a palm on her back and brought her body flush against his, out of the way of the guest who'd been waiting to pass. Yanking Annie away from the waves of anxiety, safely enclosing her frame against his solid, hard-packed sand, warm from the sun shining on it all day.

Their eyes met. Their breath mingled.

Annie palmed his biceps, forgetting time, looking back and forth into his green eyes. And although she tried hard to conceal her desire, she realized Cal knew without a doubt what she felt...

What she wanted.

Him.

The reader. The man with the ocean in his eyes.

"I need to go to the bathroom," Annie muttered as she peeled herself from the forcefield, dropped her gaze, and stepped away before he could utter another word.

Once upstairs in the confines of her private bathroom, she splashed cool water on her face, then patted it dry and smirked. "My God. Look at my cheeks." Annie stared at her reflection in the mirror, pressing her palms to the countertop. "He'll think you're green."

It had been a while, months since she'd dated or flirted, but it had never been like this. Never instantaneous. Or so magnetic.

Annie had never felt such a rush.

When Cal looked at her from far away, or from only a few inches, she felt like they were the only two people in the room.

In the universe.

Nevertheless, she wouldn't let this sudden, mad desire overshadow the entire evening. She was a big girl. *Twenty-five*. Annie could handle this.

Him.

The summer.

She'd come to Miami to focus on work, and that was exactly what she would do. She splashed more water on her face. *Focus*.

FIVE

Flickering candles sat atop a few small, round tables, giving an eerie glow to the otherwise empty porch. The sound of the ocean seemed stronger than at dusk, the breaking waves mixing with the calls of Florida insects.

Annie stood at the edge of the deck, the hem of her dress and hair blowing, listening to the critters and the water, ignoring the muffled chatter behind the closed doors — the noise from the guests trying to compete with the sea.

But nothing could compete with the ocean.

Facing it and resting her elbows on the ledge, the full moon lighting a long strip of beach, Annie squinted, following the path as far as her eye could see. She barely noticed the door creaking open until the conversations grew louder for a moment, but she didn't bother turning to see who'd joined her.

"Are you avoiding me?" Cal snuck up beside Annie, and her heart stopped. Their eyes locked. His cheekbones looked even more impressive in the moonlight.

"You know, Annie," he continued, the mellifluous sound of his voice making his words feel like they wrapped themselves around her with a gentle squeeze. Or perhaps they were a warm blanket on a cold night. "There are some things you just can't avoid."

Cal pulled strands of hair from her lips, the tips of his fingers lighting a small fire as they brushed against her cheeks.

"Where are you from?" Cal shifted to face the ocean.

"Washington." Annie released her breath and tried to match his posture.

"State?"

"Yes."

"Have you ever spent a summer in Florida?"

"No."

Cal twisted his torso toward her, meeting her gaze again. "Do you think you can handle it?"

Annie smiled, biting her lip to keep from giggling. "Handle what?"

"The summer," he said as though he didn't have a care in the world.

"The summer?" Annie raised a brow.

Cal's jaw tightened, his eyes appeared both certain and limitless. "Yes. The summer." He pushed pieces of her hair behind her neck. Annie shivered, resisting the impulse to step backward. "It's going to be long ... *and hot*."

Annie swallowed. Nothing moved. Well, the strands of their hair blew. Not even the insects made sounds. Perhaps the waves continued... The serene expression on his face, his soft, seductive words, the ease with which he put his hands on her — as if he already knew her body intimately — all caused her to visibly tremble and quietly ache.

"Are you sure you can handle the heat?"

"I think I can manage," she replied, and his dimples formed peaks.

Cal placed a palm on her waist and stepped behind her, his chest now flush against her backside. A quiet puff of air released from her lungs as she gazed down at the five fabulous fingers resting on her hip. His fingers.

God. His fingers.

Annie couldn't stop imagining the spark they would ignite over her entire body, and he only touched her waist. Fully clothed.

Oh God, oh God, oh God. Maybe she couldn't take the heat.

Cal inched closer, so close, she could feel the twitch in his pants as sure as she could feel his lungs rise and his heart thump. Both of his palms now held her hips, his nails digging into the material of her dress as he lowered his face to her neck.

"Good," he whispered, his lips near her ear, against her skin.

Annie's head pushed forward some as she subconsciously tried to break free from his pull, his magnets, but it was no good. She moaned, and Cal pressed the pads of his fingers deeper into her flesh, firmer, holding her in place.

His place.

She couldn't move. Nor did she want to.

"I want you, Annie," he uttered, his voice full of a passion she'd never heard from a man's lips.

Heart pumping into overdrive, Annie gripped the deck railing as though it were a headboard. Forgetting she was outside, on a porch — Maggie's back porch — forgetting the dozens of guests, the moon, the beach, the stars, the whys, the ifs, the maybes, the hellos and goodbyes, the *I'm so fucking fine-fine-fine*, the pleases and thank-yous, their ages, the time...

She forgot ... until Cal released her.

And she grew cold.

"How old were you, Cal?" she asked a few seconds later, the moment he placed a palm on the handle of the door. "The song? 'Dock of the Bay.' Otis Redding. The first time you heard it."

"I was around seven."

"You remember seven?"

"Music is a time capsule, Annie," he said as he stepped inside the house.

Annie's head dropped. Hair dangled around her face. Her eyes expanded, combing the wooden deck, aware of the beads of sweat covering her thighs, aware of her ache — it was everywhere.

She'd forgotten she could feel such a throbbing. Actually, no one had ever made her feel a pulse between her legs with merely a brush of a touch, with a voice that could catch the wettest of kindling on fire.

God. Annie wanted him. *Now.* She must be insane.

Her consciousness floated up and out of her body, rising and hovering above her in a bubble. Suspended-like. God, Cal suspended her. His presence paralyzed her, terrified her, *and* made her come alive. Terrified and alive. All at once.

Maybe Annie was the contradiction.

Taking in several deep breaths, she gazed up at the night sky. The moonlight pacified and grounded her. The way it had earlier.

After a year of merely surviving, Annie felt like living. She felt like dreaming. Not the scattered dreaming that had her lost and grieving, nor the nightmares that woke her up drenched in sweat — no, dreaming. The kind you did when you believed in something. The dreams that had brought her to photography. Friends. Places.

Without a doubt, as she stared up at that serious moonlight, feeling the kiss of the breeze over her skin, Annie knew *this summer* would lead her somewhere magical too.

Six

"So, how are you likin' Miami?" John yawned, patting his mouth. It was after midnight. The house was quiet. The guests had left.

"How many times are you going to ask?" Cal laughed under his breath. "You need to go to bed, Jack."

"Until I get an *actual* answer, apparently."

"I'm adjusting." Cal crossed an ankle over a knee, glancing at the nearly empty glass in his palm.

"How long will you stay?"

"You know my lease is up at the end of September."

"And will you stay?"

"My life isn't here. I have to be there for my—"

"I know…" John sighed. "You needed this change, though. You told me you needed a change."

"Man, come on, you've been trying to coax me out here for the last few years."

"I wanted your assistance with several projects." John leaned forward, catching Cal's eye.

"Not in the way you implied. My work is in LA."

"*She* is in LA."

"We've been over this. I'm not getting into it again. I needed a temporary distraction." Cal looked across the den into the living room. "I don't give a fuck where she is now or—" His gaze caught on the wooden staircase.

"Is that you, Maggie?" John asked as he got up and adjusted the waist of his pants. "I'm comin' up to bed now, honey."

"It's not Maggie." Cal bit back a smile and stood.

The woman. The photographer. The girl with the forest-green eyes and skin he wanted to taste, hit the ground floor, still wearing her party dress, her hair a mess and partially in her face.

Cal wouldn't have missed the sight of her now for the world.

John clapped a palm on Cal's shoulder, startling him, and the men's eyes met. A lump formed in Cal's throat, an apology lodging there. Yet the *I'm sorry* John deserved to hear in response to Cal's former callous behavior remained unspoken. John patted his friend's back as they went toward the kitchen — toward the sleepy twenty-five-year-old woman leaning against the counter near the fridge, holding a glass of water.

"I thought you were Maggie comin' down here to drag me off to bed," John said as he reached Annie.

Cal stood on the other side of the bar, a few feet away, gazing at her bed head, those hypnotic eyes. A sly smile crested his lips. Annie glimpsed her bare feet, wiggled her toes, and tucked wads of frumpy hair behind her ears.

"No, it's only me." She yawned. "I fell asleep and then woke up thirsty. I didn't think anyone was awake ... *or still here.*" She squinted at Cal.

"We lost track of time talkin' in the den." John peeked at his watch. When he glanced back up, he cleared his throat. "Well, Cal..." His eyes moved from Cal to Annie, from Annie to Cal, but they didn't notice him. "I'll walk you to the door so I can lock up."

They only saw each other.

"Annie can walk me out, Jack. Go to bed."

John looked to Annie for confirmation, but her gaze remained fixed on Cal. "All right." He sighed. "I've locked all the doors but the front, Annie. Good night." John kissed her forehead.

"Good night." She set her glass on the counter.

The moment John disappeared, Cal stepped into the kitchen, attempting to keep a safe distance of at least two feet from the photographer.

There was no safe distance from her.

"I know ... I know," Annie mused after seconds of Cal's intriguing silence, bunching some of her knotted hair. "Now you see what I look like when I wake up."

"Mmm..." Cal grinned, his eyes sparkling like the surface of a sunlit ocean. "I always intended to see you that way."

Annie smiled and shook her head.

"Do you always do that when you're nervous?" Cal nodded at a lock of hair she now twisted around a finger.

"I'm not nervous." She stood straight and released the strands.

Cal reached for her hand. "Walk me to the door, Annie Baxter."

Tingles shot up her spine the moment his fingers slid through hers. She inhaled loudly. Cal laughed quietly. She elbowed his stomach, and he laughed a little louder as they started to make their way to the foyer.

"John told me about your event next weekend." Cal glanced at the side of her face and squeezed her palm.

"John? Or Jack? Why do you call him that?"

Cal grinned. "Look it up."

"Online?"

"Yes." He pulled a piece of hair from her lips.

"What exactly did *Jack* tell you?" Annie raised an eyebrow.

"About the gala. The time. The place."

A choice selection of her photographs would be showcased at a local gallery this Friday, and there would be a public gala to kick off the summer exhibitions. Several other artists would also have works on display.

"Will you be there?" she asked as she opened the front door. "*Cal Prescott.*"

"Maybe." He smirked and stepped over the threshold. The only place he wanted to be was with her *now*, in his bed — but he knew she was having no part in that. This photographer required more finesse.

"Oh, just maybe, huh?" Annie stretched an arm up the doorframe and returned the smile. "Okay..." She glanced at her toes, then again at Cal.

Their eyes locked.

He rested his left hand on her cheek.

"I'll be there, Annie," he finally said, a genuine kindness seeping through his velvety tone, his green eyes moving back and forth like a pendulum.

She sucked her bottom lip between her teeth, closed her lids, and inhaled. He smelled like the ocean, laundered cotton, whiskey... But the man didn't lean closer. Or kiss her. Her eyes popped open. Cal had stepped away instead.

"Annie..." Cal startled her as he came to a stop a couple feet away and turned again to face her. "What's your favorite color?"

"My favorite color?" She arched a brow, still cradling the door. "I like so many." The sapphire blue of his shirt. His green eyes. The black of night couldn't conceal the solid hold they had on her. "Pink."

Cal smiled, hoisting a finger into the air. "One more thing..."

"Yeah?" Laughing, she opened the door she'd partially closed.

"The Beatles."

"The Beatles?"

"You know them?" He tipped his head and cracked a joke with his eyes — the ocean ones.

"Not personally." She grinned.

He did too. "*Abbey Road*. Track six." Cal started down the driveway. "The lyric with the word *heavy* means substantial," he called out. "Profound."

Annie locked the door, went upstairs, and searched for the song on YouTube. Lying in the dark on her bed, twirling her hair, she listened to "I Want You (She's So Heavy)." The implication was obvious, but it wasn't ridiculous or funny or cute. The lyrics expressed something more. Like he'd promised.

How ironic.

The words and the beat had a snake-charmer effect.

Eyes on the ceiling, hair engaged about a finger, she stared. Absorbed. She sank through the mattress to the floor.

Was she the heavy?

What was Cal trying to say?

Why hadn't he kissed her? Was it her sleepy breath?

God. He was an enigma. Nothing about him made sense. Coming on so strong earlier, yet a fine-tuned sense of self-control seemed to enable him to hold back, marking his every move like a well-played game of chess.

There was more to him than this crazy fucking lust.

It was something else.

It was behind his stare, past his eyes.

Cal was a mystery.

A puzzle.

A chameleon.

The song ended abruptly, uniquely, startling Annie. She smiled, closed her lids, and shifted onto her side. The chords didn't stop playing inside her mind, though. They went on and on ... mixing with the warmth of Cal's body, his scent, his words, that voice — his sun-shining-on-it-all-day, sand-packed safety.

Cal Prescott was the *heavy*.

TO THE BEAT OF HER OWN DRUM

TO LIVE LIFE IN ONE'S OWN WAY WHILE THROWING SOCIETAL NORMS OUT THE WINDOW

a circle
round
she beat
steady
in a constant rhythm
until
someone heard her

SEVEN

"Morning, sleepyhead," Maggie chirped the moment Annie met the bottom floor with a thunk. The daydreamer donned a robe and fuzzy pink slippers. Leftover sleep crusted the bottoms of her eyelids.

"Ugh..." Annie rubbed knuckles into the corner of an eye. The light beaming through the rear windows of the house so bright, she wanted to turn around, go back to bed, and bury herself beneath the covers.

"You slept that good, huh?" Maggie laughed, ignoring the magazine she'd been flipping through while relaxing at the table in the nook.

"I did. I just want more," Annie moaned as she shuffled toward the refrigerator. She took out a bottle of orange juice, then grabbed a glass and poured. "Did you sleep?" She glanced up and over her shoulder, scoping out the adjoining rooms. "Because it looks like you already gave the house a good once-over."

"Yeah"—Maggie licked her index finger and turned a page—"what can I say? I like cleaning."

"You *love* cleaning."

"I do." Maggie grinned and started to stand. "Can I get you something?"

"Don't get up." Annie held a palm out in midair. "Have you eaten yet?"

"I nibbled on some fruit." Maggie plopped back down and gestured at the countertop near the stove. "There's plenty of coffee, and the fruit is in the—"

"I'll wait a bit." Annie yawned and stretched, then she made her way to the nook, OJ in hand, those comfy slippers whishing against the floorboards as she went. "Where's John?"

"Probably still sleeping." Maggie smiled and shook her head. Annie took a seat across from her. "He came to bed late."

"I know..." Annie returned the grin. Maggie did a double take. "I woke up and went downstairs for some water," Annie explained. "They were talking in the den. It was after midnight."

"Is that why you're still so tired?" Maggie raised her brows. She closed the magazine. "It's after ten."

Annie rolled her eyes and set her glass down. Then her gaze caught on an arrangement of flowers at the end of the table.

"Did you have these hiding somewhere last night?" Annie stood and stretched her torso over the tabletop to get a better look at the roses bursting from a beautiful etched vase. "My God..." She fingered some of the velvety petals. "They're stunning." Closing her eyes, Annie breathed in their delicious scent.

"Actually," Maggie began, "these came for you ... first thing this morning." Annie's eyes popped open. "I didn't realize anyone delivered flowers *so early* on a Sunday."

"Pink," she mouthed with a smirk, wondering what Cal would've sent if she'd told him her favorite color was black.

"There's a card tucked over here on the side." Maggie's gaze skirted to the placement of it.

Annie grabbed the envelope, sat down, and opened it.

I would love to see a picture of you with the roses.

– Cal

310-555-8255

Maggie cleared her throat and batted her lashes. "Who's your admirer?"

A grin as wide as the Atlantic Ocean spread across Annie's face. "You know who they're from. I'm surprised you didn't read the card."

"I'll read it now." Maggie winked.

"You wish."

"You must've made quite an impression on him."

"He made an impression on me."

"I know the kind of impression Cal makes, Annie. I might be married, but I'm not dead."

Annie tried to keep her mouth from hanging open. "Then why didn't you want me to meet him?"

"I never said I didn't want you to meet him. I took you to him."

"Jeez, Maggie, I'm not a sacrifice."

The maternal look in Maggie's eyes indicated otherwise as she paused, then huffed, "I don't want to see you get hurt."

"Why would he hurt me? Do you think so little of your friend?" Annie stopped short. Her gaze jogged up the staircase.

Maggie turned, glancing at John as he descended. "The coffee's waiting, honey."

Looking rested and happy, dressed in a light pink polo and dark jeans, John stepped onto the first floor and smiled at his wife, then he directed his attention to Annie. "Do you want some, sweetheart?"

"No, thank you."

"I'd like to take you girls out to breakfast," he called from the kitchen seconds later while pouring coffee into an oversized mug. Then he strolled into the nook, fingers around the handle of the cup. "Well, are y'all hungry or what?"

Maggie broke the silence. "Breakfast sounds good, honey."

Annie clutched Cal's card and stood, swooping past the two of them and disappearing up the staircase.

John took Annie's vacated seat but waited until he heard the closing of her upstairs bedroom door before asking, "What was that all about?"

"The flowers."

John glanced at the roses. "What about them?"

Maggie explained, using gestures and nods, the tells showing in the brown of her eyes and rise and fall of her lungs.

"I knew somethin' was goin' on when I saw you two." He smiled and shook his head, knowing his wife of twenty-two years all too well. "What did you say to her?"

"I didn't get a chance to say much of anything because you came into the room."

"What did you say?" John repeated.

"I told Annie I didn't want to see her get hurt." Maggie focused on the window, eyes blank, heart full of something she could never seem to articulate.

John squeezed her hand. "Annie's not a child. She didn't come here to be looked after or coddled. You'll alienate her."

Maggie's eyes blazed. She pursed her lips.

John chuckled, tapping an index finger over her palm. "Oh, Mags..." John sighed. "I told Cal you wouldn't approve."

"You talked to him ... about Annie?"

"A little. These things have never been a secret between us."

"'These things.' You mean like the *thing* he left behind in LA? Annie is not a thing."

"You're takin' it too far, Maggie. These last few years, you've pushed him with everythin'."

"He needs pushing."

"He needs understandin'."

Maggie folded her arms across her chest, expelling hot air. "This is Annie we're talking about, John. Our Annie. You're the one who keeps forgetting she isn't sixteen."

"But she isn't sixteen, honey," John soothed, caressing his wife's skin. "She's a grown woman."

"So, this"—Maggie flung a hand toward the flowers—"*this* doesn't bother you?"

John smiled and planted a kiss on her forehead. "I love you."

Maggie growled. "I'm glad you find this all very charming."

"It's you I find charmin'. As for *this*, I have to— No, I *choose* to trust our friends and leave it at that."

A door slammed and Annie bounded down the staircase, dressed in a simple, white spaghetti-strap dress, a camera around her neck, a red Yankees cap on her head, ponytail poking out of the hole in the back.

"I'm sorry for taking off like that." Annie plucked a single rose out of the arrangement and laid it on the table. Glancing at the two of them, she apologized through her lashes.

"It's okay." Maggie patted her wrist.

Annie smiled, picked up the vase, and made for the French doors.

"Where are you going now?" Maggie asked.

"I would love to go to breakfast, but I have to take some photos first. Can you wait?"

"Only you, Annie, would postpone food for pictures. Of course we'll wait. Honey, get the door for her." Maggie stood, her cup in hand.

"I won't be long."

"We're in no hurry, sweetie." Maggie topped off her coffee as Annie neared the wall of windows. "Take your time."

"The flowers are beautiful," John said, opening the doors to the deck.

"God, aren't they?" Annie beamed, inhaling their sweet aroma again.

"Have fun," he added, his grin relaying a silent message: fatherly pride.

The two of them always had encouraged her every whim.

The deck seared the soles of her bare feet as Annie made her way to the ocean, the soft sand somehow feeling even hotter. Reaching the shore was a relief.

After absorbing the magnificent scenery — the bright blue sky; the perfect waves — she put her nose to the petals...

...one ... last ... time.

Because.

The photographer had plans.

First, she placed the flowers on the wet sand and photographed them all together. Next, she separated them into smaller groups, then singles, taking extreme close-ups, the surfaces becoming nearly unrecognizable in the viewfinder. She snapped footprints, foam dotting the shoreline, broken shells, birds flying in formation, and clouds reminiscent of ones in a Monet, the painting with the woman holding the parasol.

Nothing escaped her eye.

After throwing a couple handfuls of pink pearl roses into the current, she shot frame after frame of the way they bobbed and floated, pressing the release button on her Nikon until they were drenched and her finger ached.

Still, about a dozen remained, awaiting their own watery grave. She pulled the petals off and tossed them into the ocean. Wet up to her shins, a hand resting atop her hat, Annie filled to the brim with endorphins as she observed the way they drifted apart, the sun glistening off them, reflecting perfection in the tiny droplets of water adorning them.

They looked so small in the vast Atlantic as they all finally, gloriously and completely, faded away to their final destination.

Fade to black. Or pink. Or any color.

Annie Baxter loved them all.

Several minutes later, perspiring, toes sandy but face shining, Annie stepped inside the house and set the empty vase on the table. She picked up the remaining pink rose, removed her cap, and went upstairs.

Once in the privacy of her bedroom, she sat at the window seat and combed her fingers through her hair, ready to take a selfie. Flower against her chest, thorns pricking the top of her dress and scraping her skin, she summoned a half-cocked smile and touched the capture symbol. The photo was on its way to Cal — as he'd asked. Well ... almost as he'd asked — minus a few beautiful roses.

Annie: I was compelled beyond reason to photograph the roses, all but one, as they washed out to sea. You can only imagine my ecstasy.

Cal: Only you would do such a thing.

Hadn't Maggie just said something similar? Another message popped up on her screen.

Cal: And I have imagined your ecstasy. I'm imagining it right now.

Annie: Don't let your imagination run wild. I regret to inform you our little exchange is not going to turn into sexting.

She even added an emoji — the yellow head sticking its tongue out. Cal replied with his own: head bowed and sad.

Poor baby. Well, imagine this.

She'd found him a song, had thought of it as she'd drowned the flowers. A classic full of hidden meanings. She shot off another text with a link to "Wildflowers" by Tom Petty.

The song was perfect.

It had been one of Peter's favorites. Apparently, based on his next message, Cal liked it too. He'd waited before replying, though. A sign of what? Hitting bone marrow or tissue?

Cal: I was right, Annie. Substantial. Deep. Profound. You are so heavy.

EIGHT

"They did a great job," Maggie remarked as she held the gallery door ajar, allowing Annie entrance.

The photographer stepped over the threshold into the uniquely restored building tucked amongst rows of shops across from the ocean. But it was more than "great." Everything looked beautiful. Mesmerizing. Twinkling white lantern lights adorned the tops of the walls, their subtle glow illuminating the variety of art being showcased, causing the pieces to stand out like a dream.

My dream... Annie thought and smiled. *My summer. I am a photographer.*

Then a cork popped, and Annie turned toward the sound.

Several bottles of champagne sat on ice. Dozens of leaflets lay spread out adjacent to them, brochures advertising the various artists. Maggie picked one up and began to scan its contents while Annie stepped to the side and struck up a conversation with Joseph Chung, the curator.

A few minutes later, lightning flashed, then thunder cracked. Annie jumped. Joseph laughed. Then a patron interrupted them.

Annie strolled over to the large front window alone, hypnotized by the universe's spectacular display — the flashes of light, the dark clouds, the wind already whipping water against the pane. Despite the summer rain beginning to fall, people continued to arrive, umbrellas in hand, smiles on their faces.

"You look beautiful tonight. You glow."

"Jesus, Maggie." Annie jumped again. "You're always scaring the shit out of me."

"And you're always lost in a daydream. Come on, you need to circulate."

Annie clutched her tiny, hot-pink purse and glanced around the room. More people. Less space.

She tried to absorb the moment.

To feel the glow.

I am a photographer, she repeated silently to herself.

This was real.

This was happening.

Breathe.

"Annie." Maggie grabbed her hand. "Have you heard anything I've said?"

Their eyes met. Annie tried to smile. Then she tilted her head down, toward her wrist, gazing at the bracelet encircling it. She turned the beads over and over as she fought to contain her emotions.

Maggie squeezed her palm. "This dress you found is fabulous. Your photographs are breathtaking." Maggie's chocolate eyes lit up. "Go show off."

"You like the dress?"

Maggie stretched Annie's left arm out to the side. "I love the dress."

Annie loved it too.

Vintage black. A pleated chiffon skirt. A modest bow at the waist. Sheer, black lace netting from bodice to collar, the same at the sleeves. On her feet, she sported black-and-white polka-dot pumps with cute little bows at the tips, their color matching her purse.

Annie grinned. "I wish John were here."

"I know, sweetie. He wanted to be here. You know that." Maggie stroked Annie's bicep. "Did you message your father?"

"Yes." She swallowed.

Annie wished her dad could've been here as well, but John would've been the perfect substitute — the closest thing to having her actual father present. But she understood John's predicament. Having to go away for business. Albert not replying to her text message on her big night, however, was another story. *Peter would've been here,* Annie thought. *He would've flown to Miami to see me.*

"Let's grab some champagne now." Maggie winked, interrupting Annie's thoughts. Refusing to queue, she snuck to the rear and swiped two full glasses.

"You're awful." Annie rolled her eyes as Maggie handed her the flute.

"I'm clever." The Cat winked again. "Drink up, then go mingle."

After finishing the bubbly and getting rid of the empty glass, Annie wandered toward the center of the gallery and lost herself again. This time, in the people. Their clothing. Their shoes. The way they gestured, held their drinks. The varying distances at which they stood while viewing the pieces of art. Then she spotted a man, a hard-to-miss older gentleman, standing a few feet away, conversing with someone.

She had his profile. And the angle highlighted the sharp slope of his nose, his long gray hair, his calloused hands. He would make a fantastic subject. She sighed. But the photographer had left her camera at Maggie's for the night.

"Hello, Annie," that same man said as he approached, speaking in a broken German accent. The other guest he'd been talking to had apparently departed. "I was wondering when you might introduce yourself."

Annie glanced around, then smiled. "You found me."

"I suppose." The man motioned with his hand for her to follow. "Come."

"How do you know my name?"

"I'm Dimitri." He gave her a sideways glance as they strolled. "I always read up on my fellow artists, and I've met everyone but you. You're not a shy girl?"

"No." Annie blushed as they came to a stop in front of several beautiful paintings. "Is this your collection?"

"Yes." He nodded at a piece. "Tell me ... what do you see?"

Annie inched closer to an enormous acrylic depicting a dirt road flanked by the most astounding trees bursting with cherry blossoms — the pinks, whites, and reds raised off the canvas, reaching the top. The sky.

"I see magic. Like I could jump into the painting the way the children did in *Mary Poppins*."

"Ah, I should write that in my artist's bio." Dimitri chuckled, but then his expression changed from jovial to pensive. "You know... That one almost didn't make it."

"No?"

"I had trouble finishing it." He cleared his throat. "My wife had recently died."

"I'm so sorry."

"She helped me," he uttered. "Not with the painting, but the finishing of it. It began as one thing, and after she passed, it *became* Ida." He sighed. "Still, I almost didn't finish it. I think I was afraid."

Annie itched to wrap a finger around several strands of hair, but it was pinned up, only a few wisps curled near her ears. But they would do. Resisting toying with them, she instead focused on the textures and colors of Dimitri's trees.

"No, you're not shy." He touched her shoulder, and their eyes locked. "You're afraid ... like me."

"You don't know me." She squeezed the clasp of her little pink clutch with all her might.

"I saw your photographs." He nodded toward her display. "Only someone who is a *fraid* can be brave enough to showcase art like that."

Annie dropped her chin, but couldn't fight a smile.

"Ah, that's better. You remind me of someone." Pausing, he inhaled. "You know, I'm seventy-seven."

Annie lifted her head and raised an eyebrow.

"It is true. I'm an old man. I spent much of my life not doing what I truly love." He eyed his work. "Can you imagine not taking your photographs?"

Annie shook her head.

Ever since she could remember, there had been cameras and photographs, magic and dreams. Her heart suddenly ballooned with affection for a man she didn't know but felt akin to, and she felt sorrow for what almost might not have been but elation for everything that had come to fruition.

"Why did you wait?" she asked.

"There was always something else. A job. Family responsibilities. I couldn't see what I needed. My wife — she knew. That's why she helped me. I proposed to her on that dirt lane."

Dimitri's painting blurred in her vision. *Imagine not finishing this.*

"You have been somewhere else tonight," he interjected. "I saw you ... by the window."

She *was* somewhere else. Had been for a year.

Annie searched every line on his face. For a moment, she considered brushing off his concern. But then she met his discerning gaze, allowing him to see her openly.

"Be present, Annie," he whispered and grabbed her palms. She pushed the veins in on his wrists with her thumbs. "You're so young." He nodded. "Be present. Here, now, with all this." He squeezed her hands. "Don't chase the past, and don't miss out on what your heart speaks to you."

Her eyes began to well with tears.

"Don't be afraid of fear."

"A tall order," Annie choked out, wiping beneath her lids, smiling some.

"I know what it is..." Patting her biceps, he grinned. "You remind me of my granddaughter."

Annie planted a kiss on Dimitri's cheek, then another guest pulled him away from her.

Spellbound by the colors and shadows, Annie lost herself in the painting again, imagining the love shared on the dirt road: the proposal, the kisses, the teary-eyed smiles, the scent of the blossoms.

Then the hairs on the back of her neck stood.

Her skin tingled.

She placed a palm on her nape, looked left, then right. The wind seemed to have shifted direction, blowing across her back, causing her to shiver.

But there was no wind in the building.

No breeze.

Annie scratched at her neck and looked around again, but things seemed the same. Same people. Same pictures. The same champagne-induced laughter.

But something *had* changed.

She turned and faced the door, twirling one of those wisps of hair between her fingers, her eyes moving across the front of the room until they stopped on a man.

The shift in the wind. The sixth sense over her skin.

Mr. Prescott had arrived.

Several feet away, with dozens of people between them, Cal stood near the entrance, his eyes on Maggie. She had cornered him, and they were talking.

Cal looked amazing.

Unique, posture certain, reflecting a definitive kind of poise, an elegance — as though he belonged in the center of the gallery, not by the door. Sleek and fit, he wore a crisp, gray button-down shirt and dark pants, a belt but no tie, phone in one hand, his other sliding front to back through his dirty-blond hair. Somehow, he'd managed to stay dry despite the rain pouring down in sheets over the Miami streets.

He didn't even have an umbrella.

People began to obstruct her view. She waited, stretching, lifting and shifting her head, too paralyzed by her attraction to him to make a move in his direction. Her pulse ticked off in her ears as she waited. Her heart pounded. Then the guests finally cleared, parting like the Red Sea.

Like a camera zooming in for a close-up, Cal's and Annie's eyes met at warp speed for the first time all week. As their gazes locked onto each other, a few seconds of staring became an age. An eternity. Cal's eyes were speaking to Annie, and at that moment, despite all the noise, they were the only sound she could hear.

———————

"Thank you all for coming and making this night a success!" Joseph said after quieting the room. Nearly an hour had passed in a flash. Everyone clapped. "Please stay and meet the artists if you haven't already," he continued, and Annie flushed. "And enjoy the rest of your evening."

The moment the crowd started to roar, Annie made her way over to her cubicle, needing the comfort only one image could provide.

The beginning.

The dream.

A time she'd only known magic and innocence.

The photograph was of her father and his wife, Susan, showcasing their wedding bands — only their hands, parts of their wrists and the landscape visible. Annie had taken it at age nine with her father's camera. He'd entrusted it to her for the first time at the ceremony, knowing his young daughter's curiosity surrounding the Nikon was far more than idle. Of course, he'd also wished to distract her from the changes: his marriage and new stepmother — wife number three.

The picture was Annie's touchstone. She'd kept it small for the exhibit, four by six, but encased it in a very large frame. It was her favorite on display. That and the cove. Her eyes skirted to the black-and-white photograph of a treasured spot on the West Coast, blown up and life-size at twenty-four by thirty-six.

Then the hairs on the back of her neck stood on command again.

"I've been looking for someone," a man said, his voice dripping like honey from the comb, his body hovering behind hers.

Annie shut her eyes, willing herself to remain still, concentrating only on the sound of his breathing. On how he felt as he stood behind her. She escaped into his smell too: fresh clean cotton, the ocean.

"Maybe you can help me find her," he continued, and she smiled, shifting her face to the right. "No peeking now." Cal nipped her earlobe.

She shook.

"You might know her..." he went on, that voice like nothing she'd ever heard — slow, methodical, Zen-like. "Her hair is up"—one of his fingers dipped below her chin, skipping over her throat—"highlighting her exquisite neck." His hand traveled to her shoulder. "Her dress is timeless ... like her eyes." His palm skirted to her thigh, and Annie giggled, goose bumps popping all over her skin. "People are talking. I hear she has stunning photographs up on these walls tonight."

Squirming, Annie lifted her head toward the ceiling and grinned.

"Open your eyes," he whispered, and she spun, coming face-to-face with Cal for the first time since Maggie and John's party.

"Congratulations, Annie." Cal stared into her elated green eyes as he reached for her hands. "Your photos are beautiful."

"Thank you."

Cal squeezed her palms, then he released them and put his hands in his pockets. "Where was this taken?"

"Which one?"

"This one." He nodded, not taking his eyes off the large print.

"Pfeiffer Beach."

Cal peered at the tunnel of rock with the spray and ocean surrounding it. He inhaled a deep breath.

"Are you from California? Have you been to that spot?" she asked, but he provided no answer. "I took this when I was seventeen." Annie eyed the side of his face, watching the image flicker inside his pupils. "I was visiting family. Is this beach near your home?"

"I don't have a home." Still engrossed in the photograph, Cal stepped forward, lost in the light and symmetry, lost in the enclave.

"Cal..." Annie touched the small of his back. "Really?"

"You guessed correctly." He smirked. "California is my home."

"What part?"

Cal turned from the engaging picture, away from the photograph of a childhood memory he'd forgotten, and pushed a stray wisp of hair off Annie's cheek, tucking it behind her ear. He gazed at her with the same observant expression he'd had for the photo, except now he searched the contours of her delicate face.

"Tell Maggie I'm going to drive you home."

Annie smiled so wide her cheeks hurt. "Maybe I don't want you to drive me home."

"You're saying you don't know what you want?"

She glanced at the floor, her shoes, the picture, then back at Cal. Her smiled faded.

"Look at your photograph."

"I've seen it."

"Look again." Those ocean eyes brokered no room for argument. "Is the woman who captured that unsure?"

Annie's upper lip began to burn and perspire. First, Dimitri, now, Cal. Was he reading her? Reading her the way he had the first night they'd met — the book Cal was fluent in.

No, he only wanted to sleep with her.

And he did want to sleep with her. He wanted her. He would probably say anything to get beneath her skirt.

"What are you afraid of, Annie?"

"Everything," she whispered, falling so far into his ocean it was all she could do not to be swept up in the current.

"Tell Maggie I'm driving you home." Cal stepped closer.

"Where?" Her eyes danced. "To Maggie's home, I hope. Not yours."

"Have I invited you to my home?"

"Wait," she quipped, "you don't have a *home*."

Cal smiled, and the indentation the dimples made in his cheeks could've surely held her for safekeeping.

"Would you like to come to my home, Annie?"

"Is that an invitation?"

"Yes."

Annie paused, looked over the room, then gazed at Cal, who was still grinning. "Not tonight." She tried to hold tight to her exhale, but it escaped quietly with those somber words.

"Why. Not. Tonight?"

Her eyes bounced around. She took his hand and played with his fingers. "I'm not ready, Cal."

"To leave?"

"No. I mean, yes, I'm ready to leave, but I'm not ready to come at your house," she said, and Cal laughed. "To go! I'm not ready to *go* to your house."

Laughing and comfortable. Safe. Annie could get used to these feelings. They were forgotten. Being here with him, *simply being*, was the most relaxed she'd felt all night.

***

After Annie made another round, saying her goodbyes, she stepped outside with Cal. The rain had stopped, but the pavement remained shiny and a tad steamy. The smell of the water on the asphalt lingered, tickling her nose.

"Fuck." Cal peered at the vibrating phone in his palm. "I have to take this, Annie."

"It's okay."

Leaving Cal to his call, she turned and faced the gallery window, peeking into the building the way a curious child might look inside an ice cream shop. The best flavors coated the walls, and one of them was her very own confection.

Overcome with gratitude and humility at seeing the scene from a distance, Annie tried to allow the night's events to soak into her soul the way the water had lapped her shins when photographing those roses.

She did want to be present, like Dimitri had asked. Why was it so difficult?

Let it in... she thought. Then a door shut and Annie turned, surprised to see a white four-door sedan with dark-tinted windows within yards.

She'd never even heard it pull up.

A man appeared at the back passenger door. Late fifties, a toothpick hanging from his mouth, wearing an adorable hat — straight out of a Humphrey Bogart picture. Annie wandered to the rear of the vehicle and inspected the engraving.

"Miss," the man called as Cal took her hand and led her to the open door of the Tesla Model S. Bogart tipped his head, motioned with his arm, and Cal and Annie both climbed into the backseat.

After Cal gave the man directions, the three of them were off. Cal still on the phone. Bogart driving. Annie daydreaming and looking out the window. People on the streets, buildings on the horizon, South Beach zooming by in rainbow-colored streaks.

A few minutes later, Annie pushed the circle on her phone, lighting up the screen in the palm of her hand. The time and date stared back at her.

June 20, 2014.

Her first exhibition.

A smile came, causing the muscles in her cheeks to twinge with a most pleasant hurt as she thought about the photos hanging in the gallery and the joy she'd experienced taking them.

Then she glanced over at Cal.

She stared a moment at those cheekbones, those lips, those eyes. An exhibition all right. A public display. The man who wanted no attention but received it anyway. Annie could hardly contain her thoughts.

There were too many to articulate.

Humility and pride. The anticipation of unwrapping a present she wanted to squeeze between her thighs. Sitting comfortably next to a stranger who never felt strange.

Did Cal know what she was thinking? Could he read her mind?

Listening to the sound of his voice as he talked on the phone filled her soul the way listening to a beloved singer might. Head resting against the seat, eyes closed, her hand in his, her ears perked up as he spoke of unsigned contracts, clients overseas, and land near the ocean — not this ocean, but Malibu.

His tone was unlike anything she'd ever heard.

It matched his eyes.

In intensity and distinctiveness.

Each trademark feature different, full and cascading, poetic — almost juxtaposed to the confidence he possessed.

The melody kept her occupied, content and occupied. Still, a world of butterflies swarmed inside her stomach, and her heart thumped frantically against her chest. Annie shivered, trailing her palms over the goose bumps now covering her arms.

Cal tilted the phone away from his mouth, looked in the rearview, and said to the driver, "Annie's cold."

"Sorry, Mr. Prescott. I'll adjust it."

"It's Cal, Carl." Cal returned to the call. "I apologize, Bill..."

He took Annie's hand in his, his conversation becoming livelier, his inflection increasing. Letting go of her palm, he gestured wildly with an enthusiasm she was ecstatic to see him brandish. Annie suppressed a giggle.

"Well, call me when you know." Pause. "You interrupted my plans tonight, man." Pause. "Bullshit." *Laughter.* "Sure, Bill. Get it done."

Cal pushed "end" and immediately grabbed Annie's hand again, holding it tight as he stared out the window.

The twisted butterfly knots in her stomach and her heart pumping into overdrive ceased. This felt very normal. They were two normal people, on a normal drive, doing normal things.

Ping. Annie looked down at the new text message.

Dad: The first picture. The one that started it all for you. Where is a photo of you? Send me one. I know you were the most beautiful sight there. Picture perfect. I miss you, doodlebug.

Annie clutched the phone to her chest, blinking back tears. Then she replied, telling her father she would phone him in a little while, as the car came to a stop in the Allens' empty driveway.

"May we please have some privacy, Carl?" Cal met the driver's eyes in the rearview. "I'll text you when I'm ready."

Carl nodded, put the windows down, and turned off the engine. Cal undid both his and Annie's seat belts the moment Carl stepped out and closed the door.

"The breeze feels good." Annie watched the palm fronds blowing outside Cal's window.

He glanced at them, then moved his gaze back to Annie.

"I love the trees here," she went on, acutely aware of his body and its proximity to hers.

Cal took her hand.

"But I miss the trees back home."

One by one, Cal played with her fingers, staring at them as he did.

"You haven't been home for a while?"

Cal looked up. "Not since I moved here."

Annie waited for him to share more, her eyes darting back and forth, her breath growing shallower by the second.

"I'm from Ojai, Annie." He smiled. "Does that make you happy?"

Indeed, Mr. Prescott. It does. Annie grinned. "That's near LA?"

"Ventura," he replied, peering at a few wispy pieces of hair covering her neck.

"Did you recently move"—Annie cleared her throat and wiped her palm on her skirt—"from Ojai?"

"No."

"How long have you been in Miami?"

"Since March."

Annie didn't mind his quiet, his lack of speech, the way he considered each word. It added to his mystique. But after several more seconds of silence, she pushed her hand against his knee, smiling. "Are you always so talkative?"

"I say what's necessary."

"I bet."

They stared at each other. Cal like steel. Annie swallowing and swallowing.

"Take it down." Cal tugged on a strand of hair dangling near her ear — the piece her index finger tangled around.

Even though her chin had dropped, she peered at him as she removed the hairpins, wondering how and why she listened to him without hesitation or trepidation. She'd known this man barely a week and it felt as though she was always letting him lead.

"Come closer," he uttered, watching the caramel layers fall.

Annie put the pins in her purse, then shifted her upper body toward him as she peered at his chest, his lips, his cheekbones.

Cal combed his fingers through her hair with the same concentration he probably gave a contract, massaging it with the skill of a masseur. Annie closed her eyes and made little sounds.

"You're tense."

She released a loud sigh and allowed her forehead to make contact with his, allowed her palms to hold his biceps.

"It's hot," she moaned.

"A moment ago"—he moved his mouth to her ear—"you said you were enjoying the breeze."

"A moment ago, I wasn't this close to your skin." Annie scooted back some, then looked away.

There weren't any trees on this side.

Cal trailed his fingers through the back of her hair. "What is it?" He tried to meet her gaze. "I told you I only wanted to drive you home."

Annie whipped her head in his direction and gaped at him. "Don't laugh." She slapped his thigh.

"You don't believe me?"

"I think you mean *I* only wanted to be driven home."

"Then what do I want?" Cal slid a single knuckle across her cheek.

Annie shivered, glanced out the window, and exhaled. "I've..." She shrugged her shoulders. "I've never done this before, Cal. I'm... I'm not what you think. I'm not like other girls you've—"

"I know."

God, if he knew anything, it was that. No, Annie Baxter was not like the others. *Maybe like only one other*, he thought.

From the first moment they'd spoken, Cal had ascertained that. She was different. *Heavy*. Annie thought about what she wanted and why. Which made him want her all the more so. Cal was amazed he wanted to wait for her, that he was eager to wait for her, and he was astounded at how much she had occupied his thoughts all week.

But now, as he considered what she'd said, he had another concern, and it showed on his face. "What does that mean, Annie? Are you a virgin?"

"God, you always cut right to the chase, don't you?" Annie laughed. "No, Cal..." She bit her bottom lip. "I mean ... I've never been with anyone I just met." Her stomach constricted, and she glanced away. "And I've never been with anyone so ... so much older than me."

Cal attempted to meet her gaze again, but Annie kept it on the palm trees behind him.

"Does my age bother you?" he asked.

"No."

"No?"

"No. Does it bother you? Mine?"

Of course not, she thought. He didn't need to actually answer. Cal had already proven to be skilled at circumventing her questions.

"Annie, you brought up our age difference. Are you sure about that?"

Or maybe it did bother him. Maggie had pointed it out at the party. Perhaps Maggie had mentioned the age gap to him at the gala. Because even though Cal had insisted on driving her home, Annie sensed his restraint. Felt his self-control. Nerves began to knot her stomach again. The butterflies returned.

She ran her thumb along the hem of her skirt and inhaled. "When I look at you, our ages ... everything, it all fades away."

This felt like the same *everything* she'd whispered about to Cal in answer to his question at the gallery — the one he'd asked only a little while ago when they stood in front of her photograph of Pfeiffer Beach.

Why had she said that to Cal?

She wasn't afraid.

Dimitri had said she was afraid.

I am afraid.

Cal shifted his eyes. "I don't play games, Annie. I've told you what I want."

Yeah. Me. Naked. Served up on a platter. "Do you always speak to people like that?"

"Like what?"

Annie smiled despite her irritation. "Do you always get what you want?"

"No." The truth in his tone blew across the car like the wind through the palm branches. "But I do know."

"What do you know?"

"What I want."

"You're impossible." Grinning, Annie grabbed her purse and reached for the handle.

"Be that as it may, I'd like to walk the star of the gala to the door." Cal touched the tip of her chin. "Wait there."

Seconds later, Cal opened her door, held out his hand, and lifted her weight. Nervous, but he kept it off his face. Always. Everything off his face. Except for his smile. A crown jewel of smiles, giving away his delight. The moonlight hit his dimples.

"I'll be out of town for a couple days," he said as they strolled hand in hand toward the porch, their fingerprints communicating intimately, the same as they had last week. "But I would like to have dinner with you Wednesday when I get back."

Annie glanced at him, cocking a brow. "A date?"

"Yes." Cal smiled, took his phone from his pocket, and typed out a message. "That's quite a talent you have there."

"What?"

"The trick ... you do with your eyebrow."

She raised it again, then switched, doing it with the other one. He laughed.

"I have other tricks up my sleeve." She grinned. "My father always said I was magical."

"Oh yeah?" He smirked. "What other tricks do you have, Annie?"

"I can tie a cherry stem with my tongue," she quipped, and Cal's pupils dilated. Although, that technically wasn't the *magic* her father implied she possessed. "Forget I said that." She cleared her throat. "What time Wednesday?"

"I'll message you the time and place." He began to walk away.

"Cal..."

The man stopped and turned, the two of them now facing each other from several feet apart. Cal's expression inscrutable. Annie's the complete opposite.

"That's it? You're leaving. Just like that."

"Do you enjoy teasing me?"

"I'm not a tease. Maybe I want a kiss goodnight. Why haven't you kissed me? Not tonight or last week."

His eyes narrowed. His lips formed a hard line. Cal was starting to think Annie was a puzzle. One she didn't want him to solve. God, she must've known why he hadn't kissed her.

"Annie..." Cal marched toward her, rooting her to the spot with a stare so intense, it would surely make her crumble. "If I kiss you..." He placed his hands on her hips and nudged her backward until there was no more space — until her ass hit the front door. "I will have to have you"—Cal slid a hand into the back of her hair and fell into her eyes—"right here and right now."

"Hmmm..." Her face lit up with her smile. "What about what I want? You would have your way ... right here, on the front porch?"

Madness flickered across the beautiful screen of his eyes. Annie swallowed, practically choking on her spit.

Bunching some of her hair in his fist, he pressed his hard evidence against her pelvis. "Would you like to test my theory?"

Annie couldn't breathe or think or speak.

"Tell me," he continued, his voice gruffer, his insistence stronger. "Tell me you don't want me as much as I want you — right here, right now, on this porch — and then I will kiss you goodnight."

Annie stared into his eyes, her mouth parched, her heart beating frantically, as she fought every impulse she had to put her lips on his. The warm, sticky outside air wasn't helping anything either. The ache between her legs roared.

"I can't tell you that," she finally uttered, her eyes moving back and forth, her lungs about to explode. "I'm sorry if you think I'm teasing you. I'm..."

I'm lost. I've lost my way. I've been on the edge of a panic attack for weeks. I've had several panic attacks in the last year. And now this... I look at you, and I can't fucking think or breathe or apparently move. Can you see all of that, Cal Prescott? Can you read me?

Cal released Annie, but not before leaning down and kissing her forehead. "Don't be something you're not." He ran his knuckles over her cheek, then gave her some space. "This is why I like you." He exhaled a shaky breath. "You're real."

"You like me?" She smirked.

His dimples reappeared. "Good night, Annie." He began to walk away again. "I'll sext you tomorrow."

"Ha-ha. Very funny, Prescott."

Annie touched the door handle. But right as she put the key into the lock, Cal snuck up behind her and nuzzled his face into her hair, his nose making a trail of fire toward her neck. Hands ran down the sides of her body, shoulders to thighs, finding a landing strip on her waist.

Annie breathed in the smell of the ocean.

Cal's lungs filled with tangerine blossoms.

Annie's head dropped. Her heart pounded. She shifted her face a little to the right. It was all she could do not to turn around and give herself to him.

Fully.

Now.

On the porch.

In the moonlight.

Against the door.

"Cal ... please ... go," she whimpered.

His phone pinged, the faint noise breaking his concentration and determination.

"I'm..." Cal began and immediately took his hands off her. He didn't finish his sentence. Her scent alone was enough to make him fucking crazy. Cal didn't know what it was about this girl, this creature, this photographer, that made him feel like he had no self-control. God, he wasn't an animal. He didn't lose control.

"Good night," he said instead, then kissed her temple. "*Heavy.*"

Annie opened the front door, stepped inside, and glanced over her shoulder, catching sight of Cal as he took his place in the backseat of the Tesla.

Had she made a mistake?

The heart pounding in her ears and throat wouldn't quit. The sensations followed her up the stairs and into bed.

Alone.

NINE

"Morning." A satisfying, eye-watering yawn escaped as Annie made her way into the kitchen, toward the smell of sizzling bacon.

Maggie looked up from the stove. "You're up early."

"Yeah," Annie grumbled, taking a mug from an upper cabinet, "and I'm still tired."

"Top mine off, please." Maggie batted her lashes and nodded toward her coffee cup. "You're always tired."

"I like my sleep."

"Uh-huh."

"You must have stayed late last night." Annie placed Maggie's full coffee cup next to the stove and yawned again. "I didn't even hear you come in."

"I got to talking. I had a little more champagne... I think the alcohol helped me sleep." Maggie flipped the bacon over in the skillet. "I usually toss and turn when John's out of town."

"When does he come back again?"

"Monday."

Perhaps John would return as Cal was set to leave. Or maybe Cal had already left. Maggie went to the fridge and took out three eggs. Annie met her at the counter, holding a bowl and whisk.

"How did you know I would scramble them?"

"Because I know you." Annie bumped her hip. "This was our ritual back in the day. Three eggs scrambled with cheese — one for you and two for me."

Maggie smiled, then tipped her head toward the fresh loaf of sourdough. "Do you want some toast?"

"Is that an actual question?" Annie grinned.

Maggie cracked the eggs while waving her off. She always could do it one-handed.

A few minutes later, after buttering the golden bread, Annie took the plates back to the chef. "I love the way you cook."

"It's only breakfast." Maggie slid the eggs next to the toast.

"Since when are you modest about cooking?" Annie placed some bacon on their plates. "Nothing you make is *only* anything."

Maggie smirked. "I can teach you how to cook while you're here this summer."

"I can cook." Annie picked up the dishes and made her way to the nook. "A little."

"God knows you didn't learn many skills from your mother." Maggie brought the coffee cups and silverware to the table.

"I'm not sure I learned *anything* from my mother." Annie took a seat. "Maybe lessons in what *not* to do."

"How is she?" Maggie sat across from her, facing the windows. Annie had her back to them.

"You mean she's not calling you every hour to check in on me?" Annie rolled her eyes.

Maggie smiled. "I talked to her a few days before the gala. Beverly seemed a little..."

"Distracted? Hard to get a word in edgewise? Drunk?"

"Is she still drinking?"

"I don't know..." Annie sighed.

Maggie's phone buzzed. She pulled the device from her pocket and glanced at the screen. "It's John." She winked. "He's asking about the event."

Annie grinned.

"It was wonderful, you know?" Maggie reached a hand across the table and jiggled Annie's wrist. "People were really excited about your photographs."

"Everyone's work was..." Annie picked up a strip of bacon and looked off into the distance. "Gosh, the pieces blew me away."

"Is that what I should tell John?" Maggie began to tap the screen. "How about ... 'Annie was best in show'?"

"Stop." Annie blushed. "You're biased. Besides, *you're* the one who helped me get my foot in the door."

Maggie glanced up. "*You're* the photographer."

Smiling, Annie grabbed her fork and scooped up some eggs. The two friends spent the next several minutes gabbing about the art and the artists, the summer rain and the heat. Somehow, they managed to finish every last morsel without a mention of Cal. But that was about to change. Maggie was, after all, a cat.

"Did you have a nice drive home?" Maggie pushed her empty plate aside, her tone lacking for nothing. The word *nice* could've meant anything.

Round one, Annie thought, suppressing a giggle. "It was *nice*." *Over to you...*

Maggie smiled, but her lips smacked of holding something back. Her entire face did. She was probably dying to know if Cal had come inside the house. *Her house*. God forbid.

"John's not here to interrupt us today." Annie straightened her spine. "Let's get this all out on the table." *Round two*. "Right now."

"What do you think we need to *get out on the table*?"

"Are you kidding?" Annie huffed, eyes rolling and rolling. "Maggie, *please*, even when you aren't saying what you think, it's written all over your face. I want us to be able to talk about this sort of thing ... like Cal is anybody."

"But Cal isn't just *anybody*, is he? You're finding that out for yourself?"

No, Cal Prescott wasn't like anyone Annie had ever met...

His eyes. His voice. His skin.

Shake it off, Annie. Get back in the ring.

"Is there something you want to tell me about Cal, Maggie?"

"I won't be in the middle."

"You're putting yourself in the middle," Annie guffawed. "You love the middle."

"If there are things you want to know about Cal, you should ask him."

"Then stop hinting around."

"Annie, you're young. You have—"

"See, there you go again. *Hinting*. He doesn't see my age."

"No, I'm sure he doesn't," Maggie teased.

"Do you? Do you see my age?"

Annie wanted to be seen as a woman.

Not a little girl.

As a person who had worked hard to graduate college after postponing enrollment, having taken responsibility for her alcoholic mother for years.

Why, for God's sake, couldn't she date Cal?

Annie could handle him. She'd told him so on the deck. *Fuck.* Annie shivered. *The deck...* Whatever... She could handle Cal.

Maggie stared at Annie for a long time. "I see you," she finally uttered. "Not your age."

"Really?"

"Yes."

"Then maybe Cal sees me too. For who I am."

A snide smile spread across Maggie's face. "He sees you with his penis."

Annie raised an eyebrow, then the two of them cracked genuine smiles.

"Maybe..." Annie laughed. "And maybe I need that right now."

Maggie's eyes expanded.

"All of it," Annie continued, waving her hand in the air. "Not just his ... his ... penis."

"What a ridiculous word," Maggie balked.

"Would you rather *cock*?" Annie blushed.

"I'd rather not talk about this with you."

"You brought it up." Annie stood, folded her arms across her chest, and turned toward the window. Outside, the sunlight hid behind clouds.

"Do you know...?" she began a couple minutes later, her voice cracking. "I haven't been on a date since...?" Her head dropped. The familiar shaking started, first with her hands. "It took all of me to graduate." She glanced back at Maggie. "Everything I had."

Maggie joined her at the window, placing a palm on the photographer's back. "I know, honey."

"I did it for *him*."

Peter, Annie thought. *Fuck.* Why couldn't she say his name?

"I pushed myself..." Annie's jaw clenched. "This whole last year. It's... I need this right now." Her eyes found Maggie's. "The attention ... from Cal... I like it. I need it. I need this summer with you and John too. The possibilities. The inspiration I feel here..." Annie inhaled, then looked outside again. "I need all of it."

"But it's only one summer, honey." Maggie brushed some of Annie's hair off her forehead. "You only plan on being here with us for a few months. Have you thought about how you're going to feel when you move away in the fall? Or how you might feel if Cal is ready to move on before you leave?" Their eyes met, then departed. "I can't bear to watch you go through another heartache."

Watch me? Annie thought. *Who watched me? Tabitha. That's who. I watched me. Only she and I know what I went through. A laundry list of shit.*

God. The list. Annie would rather forget it...

The attacks.

The pills.

The side effects.

The day she misplaced the bracelet Peter had given her...

After looking for the piece of jewelry for what felt like hours, Annie had gone berserk — actually fucking berserk — until she finally fell asleep. When she woke up from her nap, she found the bracelet exactly where she'd intentionally left it: on the counter, behind the sink. She had removed it before her morning shower.

Any so-called "normal" incident was viewed under a magnifying glass. Things looked huge there, intricate. A person could see every detail. All the lines and pores and faults. Annie's coping mechanism had malfunctioned. Constant headaches. Loss of memory. Barely an appetite. Sweating, sweating, sweating. Brain spasms pulsed through her like a form of legal electrocution. If someone had told her brain spasms might've been possible *before* her experience with the anxiety medication, Annie would've laughed.

But heartache.

Heartache.

Maggie wanted to equate dating Cal to Annie's brother dying.

That was unacceptable.

When Peter died, Annie died.

Not a little piece people talk about either. *They took a little piece of me when they left this earth...* No, Annie's entire fucking soul had disappeared.

The magic she'd been born with.

Everything she'd ever known.

Annie couldn't stop the tears now. Drops slid down her cheeks in succession, one after the other. Reminders of the pain. The empty. Of never seeing him again.

I'm alive. Me. Not him.

Maggie leaned in for a hug, but Annie pulled away, straightening up and stiffening, wiping beneath her lids.

"This summer..." She sniffled. "This is *the summer*. It's the first time I've really felt like I can allow myself to be happy. And I'm not talking about Cal. I mean happy with everything — *with me*."

"Annie, slow down. Catch your breath."

"I can't! It's the first time I haven't felt a load of guilt weighing down on me for wanting to feel something other than sadness."

Annie scooped away tears, gazing at Maggie through the blurry haze, the familiar ache in her chest making it hard to breathe.

"The real heartache, Maggie..." Annie swallowed and swallowed. "The real heartache would be giving up. Refusing to live."

Heavyweight champion, Annie Baxter.

She felt the implications of the title too.

The heavy.

The weight.

And she would do everything in her power not to be crushed by it.

GRAPPLE

WRESTLING; COMING TO GRIPS; BINDING CLOSELY

I do what you ask
without even knowing
you guide me
your gentle arm
strong
harsh
unyielding

do I practice
what I know not
do I say
what I dare not
do I risk
did I find
a slice of wonder
on the sand
in my hand
holding my beloved camera

sky
call back

sea reclaim
meet me
at the point in the middle
hands over mine
on the capture button

TEN

Monday morning hit with a bang. Actually, it hit with a ping. An iPhone ping. But Annie didn't hear it or the birds chirping in the distance because she was asleep. Not even the rays of sunlight creeping around the blinds existed in the comfort of her bedroom.

Ping.

Vaguely aware of it all — the birds, the sun, the notification — Annie stirred, pried her lids open, and grimaced at the bright light emanating from her cell phone. Grabbing the contraption, she slipped under the covers and squinted at the time before reading the message.

Six fucking fifty-nine in the morning.

Cal: Dinner Wednesday @ 7. Directions to follow.

I. Am. Sleeping. Mr. Early Bird.

Birds. Birds. Shhh.

She dismissed the text, rolled her eyes, then closed them, clutching the warm screen to her chest. It buzzed again.

Cal: Good morning.

Annie smiled. *Yeah. Good morning.* She couldn't imagine the phrase coming out of his mouth. He didn't do *good morning*. She started to type something when a third message appeared.

"For God's sake," she muttered out loud to the empty room. "Let me send you a reply, man."

Cal: Don't wear panties Wednesday.

Jesus Christ.

Annie sank beneath the covers, all the way to her chin. She slid a hand down the front of her body until she reached the spot. *The spot*. She cupped herself, phone in one hand, a mound of horny nerves in the other.

God. God. God. She had no trouble imagining the tone of his voice now.

Velvety. Sexy. Demanding. God.

Two days since she'd seen him. Two more until she would see him again. How much longer would her hand do? It wouldn't. Still, she held it there, over her panties, holding, holding, holding ... the exquisite pressure drowning out the endless thoughts.

Almost.

ELEVEN

Sitting astride a man.

Faceless. Without definition. Riding him. Nipples hard. Thighs clenching.

I slapped him.

Three times.

Right across his nameless, undefined face. Then I ran down the hallway. Cold and narrow. A light at the end. I couldn't decipher whether it was my salvation or the end-end. I couldn't fit inside the concrete tunnel. It wasn't small. I was too big.

Nothing about me fit.

Sweating everywhere, panties and T-shirt drenched, Annie woke with a start from the recurring tunnel dream. The nameless, faceless man was new.

She grabbed her phone and lit the screen.

5:37 a.m.

Wednesday.

Right.

No-panties day.

She sat bolt upright and stared out across the dark room. What if this was all a mistake? All of it. Being here. This summer. Maybe it wasn't *her* summer after all. It was all daydreams and fantasies. That was all she'd ever been and all she would ever be.

Cal could be a minefield.

She was walking into a freaking minefield. A sexy, six-foot, blond-haired, green-eyed, control-freak, hot-and-cold minefield.

She might as well get up. She would never go back to sleep now. The nightmare was her fucking curse. The faceless man could be...

She opened the weather app. The sun would make its appearance soon, and she wanted to watch it rise for the first time on Golden Beach. Better yet, she would photograph it, drown all thoughts of mistakes in it.

The beach glowed, lit like embers left over from a dying fire. The sun hid behind clouds and the horizon, waiting to make its debut.

Annie strolled for a while, camera around her neck, dragging her bare feet across the white foam bubbles at the shoreline, occasionally slowing to squish her toes into the sand.

It is my summer. My beach.

Nostrils flaring, she inhaled salt, wind, and boldness. She exhaled nerves, anxiety, and sex. She had to consciously exhale the sex. Cal made her want to throw it all out the window.

It had been too long.

No one had touched her in months.

Life had, though.

Life's unexpected twists and turns had stuck a knife into her heart. She'd become quite adept at disavowing her true feelings, her sexuality practically dormant. Her mind had chosen grief over pleasure.

And she'd had enough.

Celibacy by force was officially over.

Or it would be.

Soon.

But not tonight.

Annie brushed her toes along the moist sand, painting its canvas, creating wide, circular patterns. The indentations disappeared faster than she could scrawl them. Still, it didn't stop her from photographing the figure eights, lopsided hearts, and abstract squiggles. She also snapped the effects of the wind — the white skirt of her dress blowing, the corners flipping upward without warning. She didn't fight the wild breeze. Or anything.

She let all of it envelop her. To do as it pleased.

Time ticked off endlessly as the sun began to climb, inching up-up-up until the sky exploded into orange, pink, and purple hues.

Annie took photographs on automatic now. Stopping and going, observing the strangely calm sea with her naked eye, then switching to the lens, photographing the magical point where the sky kissed the ocean, made love to it — where peace met tranquility.

The other side of a rainbow. A horizon she met. Only in her lens. Only in her imagination.

Seagulls flapped their wings, chasing a meal. A few jellyfish lay dead, indented into the sand. No more meals for them. Dozens of seashells lay cracked and tattered, a few whole, scattered. Two early-morning joggers passed, running alongside one of the best backdrops on earth.

All of it became a still frame in time. A moment. Soon to be a memory.

Moving along, leaving the tripod, in no hurry, she came upon an older couple walking hand in hand barefoot by the water, their slacks rolled up above their calves as they whispered into each other's ears, pointing out to sea.

After asking permission, she photographed the two seventy-somethings' feet: old and worn, veins like vines, soles pressing into the soft sand, resembling hands pressing into the clay of a potter's wheel, except they were feet — and behind the camera, even feet and toes became divine. Small became big. Poor, rich. Sadness existed but seemed insignificant.

What she captured would render the emotions people had a hard time articulating tangible. Through the lens, Annie took control. She owned the feelings. She snapped them, projected, and framed them. Through the viewfinder, she made the rules.

Memory card filled — Annie filled — she smiled, a palm cradling her camera, the other over her eyes like a visor, and waved goodbye to the toes and the feet and the couple who seemed to defy divorce and aging.

Plucking the legs of the tripod out of the sand, she headed in the direction of the house, moseying along, watching the waves pick up, beginning to pound.

The consuming energy of nature was all she could feel now.

It was her summer.

Minefield or no minefield.

Dreams. Faceless man. Tunnels. Expectations. Mistakes. *Magic.*

Everything was hers.

TWELVE

The car dropped Annie off at one end of the street. The lane, actually. Quaint and closed off to vehicles, a hopping Cuban eatery sat on the north corner and a Mexican place occupied the south.

Annie enjoyed the stroll, fingering the skirt of her dress, her pace on par with a snail's, her eyes skipping over the architecture and the people while her thoughts kept drifting somewhere else...

To her thighs.

And the nude space a little higher.

No, higher, yes, *there*.

The place where she wasn't wearing underwear.

Earlier, not long after her phone had alerted her to the driver's arrival, Annie raced down the spectacular white staircase, ready for her date.

But...

She'd forgotten one important detail: the chameleon's command.

Don't wear panties Wednesday.

After asking the woman to wait, she bolted back upstairs, landing out of breath and in her bathroom. She turned on the light, stood in front of the mirror, and leaned forward. Looking into her eyes, she panted and purred like a lioness.

Who was she tonight?

And how in the world had she forgotten to take off her underwear?

Lifting her dress, she pulled the undergarment down, guiding the lace around her heels. The soft, vacated skin was replaced with a prickly heat — pine needles crackling in a fire.

Her face flushed thinking about Cal's hands.

How they would feel.

On her body. On her skin.

She shivered.

It wasn't happening tonight. Not tonight. Was it?

Taking a deep breath and leaving the underwear in the dust, she bounced back down the stairs like Cinderella. Except the prince would find panties left behind instead of a glass slipper.

And her prince was a chameleon.

Where was he anyway?

Annie stopped at the other end of the lane in front of the Italian place he'd chosen and began combing the outdoor tables — each adorned with red-and-white checkered tablecloths and burgundy patio umbrellas — searching for his stellar face.

Then she spied a man alone at a table for four, the farthest from the street, against the window of the building and under a green-and-white striped awning decorated with dangling white Christmas lights.

His wind-blown hair peeked over the top of the menu, and it was gorgeous. Strands the color of sand. Golden Beach sand ... or the Hamptons'. Or West Coast sand back home. Or perhaps his hair was made of sugar. The natural kind, not bleached, but pristine and fine, glistening. Annie longed to run her fingers through his dirty-blond hair and—

"Miss," someone interrupted, "can I help you find a table?"

"Thanks," Annie replied to the hostess as Cal lowered his menu and glanced up, "I'm meeting someone."

Five seconds later, she was there, smiling and peering down at him, but before she could take a seat, he stood.

"Annie, you look..." Cal pushed the bridge of his metal-framed glasses up his prominent nose as he pulled out the chair across from his.

"What?" Grabbing a few ends of her hair in one fell swoop, she flung them over her shoulder toward her collarbone. "You like my dress?"

"Mmm..." Cal scooted her chair in as she sat, then he leaned down and kissed her neck. Suddenly, he was running through the tangerine fields, inhaling grass and honey, lost in a memory, her natural scent eclipsing the aroma of homemade Italian food. "I do. I like it very much."

Annie liked it too.

Her proximity to his person *and* the dress.

Well, it was vintage, after all.

A gorgeous mint-green, short-sleeved 1960s original. Fuchsia flowers outlined in white covered the silk material, and two large hand pockets with petite bows added to its uniqueness. Her favorite part of the dress, though, and quite possibly Cal's, was the back. Open and wide, with only a tie between her shoulder blades, its connector was shaped like the wings of a butterfly, resting where a bra strap might, but Annie wasn't wearing a bra. She didn't need to. At twenty-five, her nipples pointed up and out, and her breasts were firm in all the right places.

"Have you been here before?" she asked.

"No." Cal kissed her neck again, then her cheek, and she shivered. He grinned and took his seat. "John recommended it. I've been meaning to check out this section since I moved."

"I can see why." Annie peered down Española Way to the west, then shifted her gaze again to the east. "I love it here."

"You just arrived."

"I know, but the energy ... it's ... it's so inviting. I'm glad you chose a table outside."

"What else can you sense, Annie?" He arched his brows. "Maybe you are truly magical. Can you read my mind?"

"I know what's on your mind, and we are going to talk about something other than sex tonight, Mr. Prescott."

Cal smiled, and the way those dimples made her feel had her glowing like a lightning bug on steroids. "Did you order any wine?"

"I was waiting for you."

She began to read the selections. "What looks good?"

"You, Annie. You look good."

Tapping his shin with her shoe, she started to perspire. "I'm in the mood for red."

"I can see that. You haven't been using sunscreen?"

Annie touched the tip of her sunburned nose. "I was in a hurry."

"To sunbathe?" He grinned.

"No." She paused, feeling him reading her insides. Her everything. "I woke up early and decided to watch the sunrise. I didn't think I would be out so long."

"What were you doing?"

"Taking pictures," they said at the same time, both with a tinge of pride, only Cal was smiling like an idiot.

Annie pushed her foot against his shin again.

"Have you been to the beach for just fuck's sake? For fun?"

"Photography is fun. What about you? What do you do for *fun*? Have you seen the sunrise?"

"Yes."

"Here?"

"Yes."

God, he was so quiet, even when speaking. Quiet, yet steady and sure. The need to not say more than necessary lined his posture, filled his gaze, colored his beautiful face. Cal Prescott was the steadiest man Annie Baxter had seen in a long, long time. And he'd watched the sunrise on South Beach? Alone?

"It's breathtaking," Cal added, then his eyes fell to Annie's biceps.

Goose bumps had popped all over her skin. She ran her palms slowly up and down them.

"Are you cold?" He smirked, then the waiter appeared.

Cal chose a vintage Paola Sordo Barolo. "I think you'll like it," he said to Annie, and she probably would.

Her favorite reds came from a winery in her home state, and she proceeded to tell Cal all about them — the vineyard, their wines, the beauty of Washington — then they placed their dinner order.

"What else do you do for fun?" Annie asked as she brought the rim of the glass to her nose and inhaled. Ripe strawberries, licorice, and something she couldn't put her finger on filled her nasal cavity. "Other than work and watching the Miami sunrise?"

At first, Cal's eyes opened only a little wider, but she could see the smile there as his smirk grew larger and larger.

"Besides that!" Annie gushed, her crossed leg swinging back and forth.

"I run." Cal leaned back in his seat.

"You run?" She raised a brow. "You do marathons?"

"No. Not anymore. I still do the occasional 5K."

"What else?" Annie drank some of the red, patiently waiting for the quiet man to reply.

"Surfing," he finally said.

"Something else I wasn't very good at."

"It doesn't matter how experienced you are. Not to me. The joy came from the way it made me feel. Being out in the ocean, over the board..."

"Where do you like to go?"

"The waves aren't too great here."

Although Cal seemed to have mastery over prohibiting certain expressions from crossing his face, Annie had caught the bullshit inflection in his tone. She could feel his regret, his longing. Even if he wouldn't show it. If waves weren't "too great here," he could find better ones at a nearby beach. This was Florida, after all.

"When was the last time you surfed?"

"I don't remember." Cal lifted his glass and guzzled some of the wine. But he did remember... His mind drifted to California, to the Pacific, to a long time ago. He couldn't pinpoint the last time he'd surfed exactly, nor could he believe he'd let it go.

"Why don't you surf anymore, Cal? It's not the waves."

"Don't you have something you've given up?" He shifted his gaze, then those fierce eyes landed back on her. "I thought this was a date, not an inquisition."

"I don't give up." She sat up taller. Refusing to bite her lip or twirl her hair. "And I don't believe you. You haven't given it up. It's a part of you."

"Work took over, Annie," he droned.

A second or two later, the waiter arrived with dinner. Annie cleared her throat. Cal splayed a napkin across his lap. She wasted no time stabbing her fork through the middle of a homemade, moon-shaped ravioli stuffed with ground sirloin, onions, garlic, and mozzarella cheese. As she blew on the concoction, the scent filled her nose, her irritation being replaced with pleasure.

"You have to try this," she sang, mouth partially full of cherry-tomato-sauce-covered pasta. She held her fork toward Cal. "It's so good."

Cal smiled as he twirled his fettuccini. "I'm a pescatarian."

"A pesca-what?"

"A pescatarian."

"What's that?" Her face scrunched up.

Grinning, Cal leaned closer to the center of the table, like he had a great big secret to tell. "It means I do not eat meat."

Annie glanced at his plate. Calamari, baby clams, and mushrooms bathed in the noodles.

"I eat seafood," he said.

"I see that."

"I only eat seafood. No red meat, no pork, no chicken."

"You *only* eat seafood?" Her eyebrow shot up. He smirked. "You're an interesting man, Prescott." She tapped the tip of her shoe against his shin.

Annie wouldn't have pegged him as a pescatarian, a surfer, or a runner. And she wanted to know more. With one glass of wine down and another poised, she readied herself to hit him with the hard stuff.

"Have you ever been married?" Annie took a sip of the Barolo.

Cal slowly dragged his napkin across his mouth. A boyish grin appeared in its place. "No, Annie. Have you?"

"No, God no!" She choked, patting her chest, the wine practically coming out of her nose.

"I'm surprised you never asked Maggie if I married."

"I wanted to ask you personally."

"Is it because of my age?" He laughed. "Why aren't you married?"

Heat crept up the back of her neck and danced across her spine. "I don't want to get married."

"Come on, Annie, every girl dreams of getting married."

"Now who is doing the assuming? Every girl? Really? I'm not every girl."

"I've noticed." Cal swallowed more wine, adopting the oh-so-comfortable position he seemed to favor, pretending nothing affected him.

"Actually"—Annie smiled—"I thought I might get married. Once."

Cal peered at his plate, wide-eyed, holding back the laughter. Forking some food, he timed his next remark perfectly, like a well-trained comedian. "In your younger, more carefree days?"

"You're the worst." Annie rolled her eyes. "I'm serious, Cal."

"Mmm, seriously, then... This suitor..." He laughed again. "Was he a strapping young man?"

The worst, she thought. *The absolute worst. And I like him anyway.* A lot.

"Okay, then," he continued. "Tell me."

"Tell you what?"

"You said you wanted to marry him. Did he get down on one knee and propose to you?"

"I said *I thought* we would marry. We talked about it." Her cheeks had to be turning the color of the stupid cherry tomato sauce. "His father wanted him to marry me."

Cal flinched, recovered, then pressed, "What about you?" Yet his eyes appeared flat and calm, like the sea before a storm. "What did you want?"

"I told you. I don't... I didn't want to get married."

Cal smiled and shook his head, his attention returning to his pasta.

"Why haven't you married?" she asked. "Haven't you been in love?"

The second Cal glanced up, his gaze cut her so sharply, Annie could feel the blade swiveling in the air between them. Instead of cowering, she held herself ramrod straight, glaring at him.

Pushing his plate aside, he leaned forward and rested a forearm on the table. "Don't think you can know me in one night."

Annie bit the insides of her cheeks and stared past him, willing her eyes not to water.

Fuck. Him.

He had no reservations whatsoever about wanting to know every part of her body in *one night*. And at the rate their sparse topics of conversation had been going, knowing him in any other way might take months.

Fuck. Him.

Annie's right elbow hit the table as she stretched her forearm toward his face, index finger pointing, practically growling, "*Don't* avoid my questions."

Cal snatched her palm, tightening his fingers around it. Their elbows locked. Her nostrils flared. But neither of them would give. Seconds later, he applied a small amount of pressure, ready to bring her arm and knuckles to the table. Except she fought him, squeezing his hand, flexing her muscles.

Cal smirked.

He only applied a little more pressure, and the *fuck you* in her eyes changed to a *please fuck me*.

Still, she fought him.

The moment seemed to last forever.

Eyes full.

Neither of them bending.

Until he finally uttered, "God," with an aching in his voice that made her quiver.

Cal released her palm, causing her arm to stop shaking and her expression to soften. Then he slid a finger from her elbow to her wrist, watching a trail of goose bumps pop. "Do you even know what you do?"

"What do I do?" she asked, her words nothing more than a cracked whisper.

She hadn't asked him to stop.

Nor had she given up.

Instead, she arm-wrestled him in the middle of their fucking dinner.

And it more than pleased him.

Most women Cal encountered could never forgive him for being male — in every way he thought a man should be.

"I've been in love, Annie." Cal looked up while continuing to drag a finger across her skin. "Twice. Both times, madly and deeply. Forgive me if I don't want to speak of the past tonight."

An arm-wrestling match, an apology, and an aching to have him inside her. Right. Now.

Jesus Christ. He knew what he was doing.

Speechless, mouth parched, her eyes darted around the restaurant with the precision of an eagle.

Then the waiter appeared.

Cal eased back against the seat and ran a hand through his hair as he politely answered the server's questions. Annie fell against her chair, exhausted, eyes glazing over as if she'd reached a climax.

"Would you like to take a walk?" Cal reached a hand out and played with some of her fingers. "After we finish?"

Annie smiled, stuck a fork in a moon, and nodded.

The sun had set, but the lights from the buildings and passing cars were vibrant enough to make a person forget time. Cal laced his fingers through Annie's as they walked the neighborhood, eventually making it the few blocks east to Ocean Drive.

The city pulsated. Vibrated.

South Beach seemed a separate entity from the rest of the state. A place where cultures met, coexisted, shook hands.

Cal pointed out the path in Lummus Park where he typically jogged, showed her places he'd eaten, mostly takeout, and Annie listened while framing photographs of the skyline in her mind's eye — the hotels, the palm trees, the neon signs, and of course, the people, Cal included.

Even while strolling alongside his profile, she coveted his backside. Strong, lean, a dark blue button-down shirt covering his able-bodied shoulders. She wondered what he looked like underneath the clothes. What it would feel like to run her fingers across his naked spine.

"Do you always wear long sleeves in the summer?" She tugged on his cuff with her free hand. "Do you have tattoos hiding under there?"

"No." He put his lips to her wrist. "And no."

"Thank God." She pinched his waist. "About the long sleeves, I mean. I'm hot just looking at you."

Cal's dimples formed peaks, stopping her stride. "I thought you said you could handle the heat."

"Funny, I thought that was one of your lines." Using her weight, she pushed against his shoulder. "And I'm handling it." Yanking a little on his palm, she began to walk again.

But he didn't follow.

"Did you hear that?" Annie glanced up at the sky as though looking for the origin of that thunder.

Dark clouds rolled in. The wind picked up. Her arm remained stretched out between them like a live wire full of electrical current.

Lightning would surely strike at any moment.

Cal guided her toward him. Until they stood face-to-face on the sidewalk, people passing on their left and right, streaks of headlights whizzing by in slow motion, the air eerie with the threat of rain. A tepid breeze blowing. The haunting atmosphere overtook Annie the same way Cal's eyes did.

"It's going to rain," she muttered, barely. Because her dress and chest pressed against him. Her muscles went into hibernation.

Laying his cheek against hers, he bunched her hair, massaged her scalp, and slipped his other hand beneath the butterfly wings of her dress.

She gasped.

"Shhh," he breathed near her ear, running his day-old stubble across her jaw.

The touch of his skin against hers calmed her immensely, causing Annie to feel the same odd sense of security she'd felt with him previously. The protection, the safety, like warm sand on cold feet.

After an age of only brushing his lips over every contour of her face, Cal finally moved his mouth toward hers. She opened, and in a split second, Cal kissed her. He kissed Annie for the first time on that South Beach sidewalk for the entire fucking world to see.

What began as soft grew harder. Harsher. The rain was about to fall in exactly the same manner.

The wind tossed Annie's skirt and hair, yet the two of them stood, unencumbered, locked together and unaware of anything but themselves. Tongues intertwined, mouths and nerve endings dancing, devouring each other as if they'd been starved.

Cal slid a hand past the small of her back and inside the skirt of her dress, running his palm over her derrière. Annie opened her eyes, conscious again of the impending storm, her never-ending ache, the taste of ripe strawberries on his tongue, how his fingers tickled, then squeezed her bum — conscious again of the entire fucking universe.

But Cal did not desist.

Pulling her hair tighter, causing her head to point a little toward the dark sky, he continued kissing her without letup, kissing and tasting her with the vigor of a man she'd forgotten existed.

Or maybe she'd never known a man like him existed.

Virile. All-encompassing. Determined.

Controlled.

Annie closed her eyes again, relenting, giving herself to the bulwark of a man. She sank against him, moaning and whimpering, cradling his face as he swallowed her desperate sounds, knowing full well now why he'd opted not to kiss her on the front porch of Maggie's house — either time. Because Annie wanted him now. *Now.* On the fucking sidewalk.

Rain began to fall, in sprinkles at first, wetting their hair and clothing. Droplets crept down their bodies, turning their skin into silk, making their mouths more eager to explore every possible place they attempted to keep hidden.

Then a loud crack of thunder split them in two. Hands clasped, they hurried over to a closed business and huddled beneath its awning.

"Are you okay?" Cal pushed pieces of matted hair off her forehead.

"Yes." She grinned, mesmerized by the way the rain fell only a few feet from them.

Wrapping an arm around her shoulder, Cal pulled her closer. "Where did you park your car?"

Annie hadn't heard that phrase in a while.

Your car.

She didn't own one. Hadn't for over two years. Her last car, her *only* car, had been a sweet-sixteen present from her father. Albert Baxter was a bit of an eccentric when it came to certain things in life, and it had been his idea to buy his daughter a vehicle manufactured in the year of her birth. A 1989 BMW 325i. Red, two-door, screaming for the attention she constantly fought.

Nevertheless, one of Annie's favorite pictures had been taken inside it.

I think it's still in my wallet, she thought.

Peter had snapped the impromptu photo one morning as they drove into Seattle. She remembered the look in his eyes after he'd caught his sister by surprise behind the wheel, her hair blowing across her face, a smile lighting her cheeks. He'd used Annie's camera, against her will, but she'd secretly loved every minute of affection her older brother showered upon her.

More memories came...

Peter and his priceless expressions as a passenger.

His smile.

The face he made the day they'd gotten wet from an unexpected rain shower because Annie hadn't been able to close the convertible top fast enough.

Like now.

Caught in a downpour. Always having too much fun to come in out of the rain. *What's that line?* Annie wondered. *Some people feel the rain. Others just get wet.*

"Annie?" Cal squared her shoulders.

"What?"

"I asked you a question." He searched her face. "Where did you go just now?"

She wiped a drop off his chin. "I took a cab." She grinned. "Well, that's not where I went right now..."

Cal shook his head, then narrowed his gaze. His eyes always seemed to ask the questions *and* provide the answers. Apparently, they contained the codes to nuclear weapons, the solution for world peace. Scratch that, his eyes held dominion.

In spades.

"I already had this discussion with Maggie."

"I imagine you did."

"I want to do things on my own dime." Her chest and chin puffed out. "On my own."

She also didn't want the use of the Allens' vehicles to turn into a right to set rules, boundaries, or curfew. Maggie could make her feel like a teenager again in an instant. A car would be leverage. Annie wanted to be far from middle ground. Common ground. She wanted freedom. Miami was it. Cab fare was worth it.

"I know," he replied.

"What do you know, Prescott?"

"That you're stubborn. I would've picked you up had you only asked."

"What? You would've come to the door wearing a tux and bearing a corsage?"

"I bought you flowers already."

"Oh, so it's a one-off, huh?"

He shook his finger. "I haven't forgotten your idea of chivalry or ecstasy."

"Chivalry?" She raised an eyebrow. "And, you know, that was the point." To drown the flowers. To feel a reckless abandon. She smirked. "And don't you mean you would've sent Carl to pick me up?"

"Not necessarily. It's my car."

"It's yours?" She coughed. "The Tesla?"

"Yes."

"Why don't you drive it, then?"

"Traffic. Work." He raised his palms and wiggled his fingers. "I need the use of my hands."

Before she could think or speak, Cal slipped those useful hands around her waist and pulled her against him, sliding his fingers over her delightful curves, palming her bottom. It happened so fast, she fell into a trance. Her breathing hitched. Every cell in Annie's heated body attuned itself to the station Cal broadcasted.

Afraid to meet his gaze, she kept the crown of her head below his chin, her eyes downcast, refusing to grant him access to her lips. Otherwise, Cal might swallow her whole. Or discreetly take her now under the awning and against the wall. Maybe indiscreetly. All she knew was that without her underwear, it was extra incentive for him to push her dress up and slide his cock where she wasn't ready for it to go. *Oh God oh God oh God*. She was so ready.

"You listened to me," Cal whispered as he squeezed her cheeks, cupping her ass over the dress.

"Yes..." she choked out, resting her forehead against his neck. Her face fit perfectly there, in the little crook, safe and warm, centimeters from the taste of his skin.

The taste and the smell...

The rain mixing with his perspiration gave him a unique scent. Musk, cloves, earth. His ocean. She wanted to bury her face there, in the nook of his neck and wall of his chest, and only breathe.

Instead, she glanced up and said, "You knew I would."

Bunching the hem of her skirt, Cal lifted it past her thighs until his fingernails stabbed at the precipice of her magnificent ass.

"Cal..." she whispered, back arching, knees buckling, only hearing the sound of her breath along with the faint pitter-patter of rain.

The moment his fingers slid higher, the second he gripped her tighter, she scooted away from the protective, secret place of his body and placed her palms flat on his shirt.

"Cal..." she repeated.

And a spell broke.

He dropped the material and pulled away, resembling a statue. Tall. Unaffected. Aloof.

"I'm... I'm—"

"I know, Annie." He pinched the back of his neck. "Please don't say the words again."

She nibbled the insides of her cheeks and looked away, a whirling beginning in the pit of her stomach. This was nothing — probably nothing to him. A casual fling. And look what it was doing to her. Look what *he* was doing to her.

"I'll have Carl drive you home," he said and took out his phone.

"Our date is over?"

"I can't control the rain."

"Will you ride back with me?"

"Not tonight." Cal tapped out a text.

A few seconds later, Annie put her hand on Cal's cheek, wanting him to know *his* heavy wasn't burdensome, but he wouldn't meet her gaze or shift his head in her direction. The rain lessened, becoming dull drops falling from leaves and rooftops, sprinkles on the concrete.

Cal slipped his phone into his pocket. "You'll have to take a warm bath when you get home. Maggie will probably throw a fit." He finally turned toward her, twisting pieces of her damp hair between his fingers. "God, you're so sexy." Their eyes met. "I came on too strong."

"No..." She smiled, shaking her head. "But fuck the warm bath. We need cold showers."

Cal dropped his chin, exposing a charming, defeated-like grin. Annie ran her knuckles along his cheekbone, pulling his gaze back to hers.

"What is it now, Annie? More questions?"

The moment she began to chew on her lower lip, Cal touched it, sliding a finger along the edge. "You're going to bruise it, biting it like that." He inhaled, then exhaled, his breath shaky. "I want to be the one to bruise you."

"Fuck, Cal..." Annie moaned.

His fingertip slipped inside her mouth, and she found herself wanting him to do it, to bruise her. She wanted to take his finger to the back of her throat and... Fuck. Maybe she was a tease. Instead, Annie kissed his nail, brought his hand to her side, then squeezed it, a nervous smile playing upon her lips.

"I've only been with two guys in my entire life, Cal." The wet from the rain made her eyelashes heavy. "Relationships." She sighed. "It's never been only about sex for me. I don't know what this is."

And it was three. Three guys if you counted the first. She did not. Less than a minute of penetration. A moment of weak curiosity. Loss of virginity in a split second. She shuddered to think of it. So, it was two, two guys in her repertoire. Cal would be the third.

God, she'd known it the moment he'd first spoken to her.

"Hey..." Cal touched her cheek, turning her face to meet his. "Did these two 'relationships' have pimply-covered faces?"

"'Hey' yourself"—she stepped on his foot—"asshole!"

"So..." Cal laughed and pinched her waist. "You've been with two boys, Annie?"

When he tried to grab a piece of her hair, she slapped his hand away, causing him to smile wider than she'd ever seen.

"I didn't say *boys*. You did. And I imagine you were once also a boy, so stop making fun of me."

"I'm not making fun of you. I'm making fun of your boys and their unpredictable, uncontrollable dic—"

Annie covered his mouth. "You really are the most conceited man I've ever met in my entire life."

Cal was a little over the moon with self-righteousness. Now, he wanted to please Annie sexually in a way he hadn't anticipated. He wanted Annie to be the one going over the moon. Howling.

He took her hand and kissed her knuckles. "I think my confidence is what you first liked about me."

"What makes you think I like you?" And it was his eyes. Like the ocean. Deep and mysterious and beautiful.

They both smiled.

Annie glanced at the rain as it tapered off the front of the building, aware of the calls of the frogs and the pounding in her chest.

The water mesmerized her. Water always did.

She put her hand out past the awning and caught a couple of droplets, watching the way they rolled around her palm. Then she lifted her head, looked at Cal, and swallowed.

"On our next date," she began, and he grinned. "Yes, another actual date, like this one — with food and talking..." She made a fist around the beads of water and held her breath. "I want to be with you."

Desire snaked through Annie's body. A slow rush. A burn.

Cal combed five fingers through her hair while placing his other palm flat against her back, touching her bare skin. "Have dinner with me Friday, at my apartment."

She stared at him. Into his ocean. His gaze seared across her sky.

"And stay the night with me."

Annie only nodded, her eyes now falling to his shirt as Cal slipped those fingers inside her dress, caressing the top of her tailbone.

"I have a conference call, a meeting tomorrow night with LA I can't reschedule." He massaged the nape of her neck, his fingers tangling in her hair. "Look at me."

Their eyes locked.

"Otherwise, I wouldn't let another day pass without being inside you, Annie. I want to make you feel things you've never felt before."

Mission. Accomplished.

Because the precise, skilled use of his tongue for only speech was almost enough to make her come.

Overwhelmed, she dropped her chin and concentrated on the sole task of breathing. Pushing her nose into his chest, she rubbed her head side to side over his shirt, her pulse not ticking, but throbbing, the sensation traveling through her entire body.

Little did Cal know — *or did he know?* He knew everything — he already made Annie feel things she'd never felt before.

CHANCE

THE POSSIBILITY THAT ANYTHING CAN HAPPEN

unguarded
defenses down
would you still want me
if you knew
I'm not ashamed
of myself
I protect
what is mine
I don't know
who you are
except
I do
I protect frames
I capture moments
I save myself

THIRTEEN

While sitting at the window seat in her bedroom, sun at her back, computer in her lap, Annie reached behind her shoulder and gave the nagging morning itch a good scratch. The moment she heaved a fantastic sigh of relief, someone knocked on the door.

"Come in." Annie yawned and closed the laptop.

"Good morning," Maggie chirped, stepping into the room.

"What time is it?" Annie stretched her arms toward the ceiling. "You look pretty."

"A little after eleven." Maggie grinned as she took a seat on the bed, laying a floppy lavender hat beside her. "I thought you might still be sleeping."

"How was the movie last night?"

"Excellent," Maggie replied and paused, peering at Annie with those curious cat eyes. Or were they catty eyes? Either way, Annie got them. Full on. "We didn't get in until almost midnight." Maggie's simple statements managed to sound like questions, prying without being direct. "Why haven't you come down? Aren't you hungry?"

"I started returning emails and editing." Annie twirled pieces of hair around an index finger. "Mmm, I talked to Mom. She called around nine. Couldn't sleep again. Has she mentioned the insomnia to you?"

"No. I haven't spoken to her since before the gala. And she doesn't get too personal."

"Only personal when it comes to me, right?"

"She loves you."

Actually, Annie thought, *Beverly loves Beverly, cigarettes, alcohol, and a pug named Barney.* "She didn't even ask about my photography. Well, unless it included her, and me moving back home."

"How's your work going? Have you made any plans for the fall?"

"I haven't sold anything yet."

"You will."

"I want to go back to the city for a few days and see what kind of contacts I can drum up."

She had failed to network while actually living in Manhattan. Between work and school and taking photographs, she'd been exhausted. Plus, she had assumed she would've had more time to meet people, to scout for places where she might exhibit her art.

Then the day arrived when the clock stopped.

Everything stopped the day he died.

The day she received that dreaded phone call.

Annie no longer cared about putting her career first. She quit her waitressing job. Lived in sweatpants. Her boyfriend left. Breathing and sleeping were her sole focus. Sleeping had been the *only* solace — that and her camera. When her eye was in the viewfinder, she was *somebody* — or someone else.

She'd become what she needed to be in order to live.

But it was only existing.

There was no life.

Living at the bottom of a prescription bottle until even that ran out. It all fled like the sunset bleeding across the horizon, setting, then disappearing.

Time...

Life...

Her dreams...

All gone. She'd watched them fade away during the nightmare of her senior year. Breathing became a luxury, eating an enemy, sleeping the altar where she worshiped.

"Did you purchase your ticket yet?"

"I was checking the fares when you came in."

"Let me buy it for you."

"Stop with the charity. I can afford a ticket."

"It's time you don't get back, Annie. One day, it's bills, a husband, kids."

Photography. "I know about responsibility."

"I know, sweetie. I mean it's different." Maggie swallowed and looked away.

It had been a while since Annie had seen that expression on Maggie's face: the Peter Pan searching, the regretful longing. Without kids by fate, and without kids by choice, forced by happenstance to give up her uterus and choosing not to adopt — that was Maggie Allen. Still, she seemed to understand the major shift in life that occurred once children entered the picture, even though she hadn't raised any of her own.

Except for Annie, of course.

"Well…" Annie dragged out the word as she met Maggie's gaze. "I'm focused on work right now. And I'm excited to be with you this summer. I hope New York is only the beginning of traveling."

"Where else will you go?"

"God, I don't know. California, for sure. And…" She lifted her chin, her eyes expanding. "The Grand Canyon. Santa Fe…"

"Your face…"

"What?"

"I haven't seen it light up like that since you arrived."

"I'm excited."

"I can tell." Maggie held a hand above her eyes, squinting, and Annie pulled the window shade partway down.

"You didn't have to do that." Maggie stood. "I have to get going anyway. I have a luncheon."

"So, that's the deal with the hat, huh?" Annie grinned.

"Shush. It's Florida, and I have fair skin."

"And you like the attention."

Maggie smirked. "Come down and eat."

"I will."

"You know…" Maggie began as she went toward the door. "I thought maybe you hadn't come downstairs yet because you were avoiding us. I know it might be a little awkward."

"Why would I be avoiding you?" Annie stood.

Maggie glanced out the window, beneath the shade. "Looks like rain."

Annie eyed the ominous clouds now obscuring the sun, then she turned her attention back to Maggie, but her friend's gaze remained fixed on nature. So, Annie strolled toward the dresser and pulled some clothes out.

"Did you have a good time last night?" Maggie finally asked a few seconds later.

"Yeah." Annie smiled.

"Where'd you go?" Maggie moved toward the mirror, put the hat on her crown, and fidgeted with the rim.

"I can't remember the name of the restaurant." Annie smiled wider. "Umm ... it was right in South Beach. On Española. A yummy little Italian place. Then we took a walk and got caught in the storm."

"*Cal* got caught in the rain?"

"Yeah." Annie grinned. "And he..."

"What?"

"He kissed me." Annie's cheeks hurt from all the smiling.

Maggie looked away, back into the mirror, and started to fidget with the fucking hat again.

Annie rolled her eyes. "You look fine. I need to dress."

"Are you kicking me out?"

"Unless you want an eyeful?" Annie teased. "I'll come down in a bit. I want to get more work done this afternoon."

"You mean you don't have a date tonight?" Maggie batted her lashes.

"No, not tonight." As she slipped her shorts on under her nightgown, Annie could feel Maggie's gaze burning a hole through her backside. "What do you want, Maggie?" Annie turned around. "Say it."

Maggie tapped her fingernails over the top of the dresser. It must've been some sort of Morse code signal.

"God, you are crazy."

"Had you forgotten?"

"No, but I've never dated your best friend either." Annie faced the bed, removed her pajamas, and slipped the tank top on.

Maggie seemed to stifle a scoff. "Well...?"

"We're having dinner Friday. He has to work tonight. So do I."

"Do you know where he's taking you? I could make some great recommendations."

Annie attempted to hide her smirk because the place Cal planned on taking her wasn't anywhere Maggie could recommend.

"I'm having dinner at Cal's." *Or is he having me? I'm having sex!* "I'm spending the night. I'm not taking the car."

The two of them stared at one another.

Then Maggie forced a smile. It was pity or empathy or defeat. "I'm going to be late for my lunch." She went toward the door.

"Maggie, wait. Why do you do this to yourself?" Annie sighed. "If you have some sort of vendetta with him, please, work it out."

"Has he talked to you about—?"

"No. You know him. It's like beating a steel door down."

Maggie smiled, her lips spreading with fond memories. Peanut butter smothered on bread.

"He hasn't said anything," Annie continued. "It's you. You say it all. With your words and tone. To me and him. I'm not oblivious."

"I wish you would take the car."

"You're ridiculous." Annie smiled and waved. "Go to lunch. Give Joseph lots of air kisses for me."

"Love you." Maggie leaned closer, kissing the oxygen next to Annie's cheeks. Lips smacked. Giggles followed. "There's plenty of stuff in the fridge. Or I can bring something home." Maggie grabbed the door handle and glanced over her shoulder. "Text me."

"Okay. Goodbye already." Annie laughed, but the second the door closed, her expression changed. She stepped in front of the mirror.

Staring into her green eyes. Looking at her sharp cheekbones. Gazing at the messy strands of her long hair.

Nine years old going on fourteen, going on thirty. All grown up. Twenty-five. No longer sixteen. Certainly not a virgin. Annie laughed, remembering Cal's face when he'd asked her *that* question.

Even though she sometimes still felt like a little girl, Annie Baxter saw a woman. Holding her own. Ready for anything.

Including Cal Prescott.

FOURTEEN

Annie spent much of the next day doing the same thing, sitting at the window seat, laptop open, editing photos while music blasted through her earbuds.

Closing her eyes, she sang along with Ann Wilson to "Alone," readying herself to play the imaginary drumsticks.

One. Two. Three. Now.

Arms raised, she beat the air in rhythm to the song, but then Heart's ballad was interrupted by a buzzing sound. Tabitha's name lit the phone screen.

"Hey!" Annie answered.

"Finally! I can talk to you. How the fuck are you? What's new?"

Everything. Nothing. The usual. "I'm editing." Annie saved her work, then set the laptop aside.

"Of course," Tab said, and Annie could hear the smile in her best friend's voice. "Well, I have the morning off. And it's Friday!"

"I miss you," Annie said as Tabitha's dog barked. "I miss you too, Marlon. How's my big boy?"

"He's fine. Aren't you, boy?" Marlon barked again. "I should've walked him before I called you."

"It's called a mobile phone for a reason."

"Shut up, bitch."

Annie laughed. "How's the play?"

"Fab. Don't forget it wraps a week from Sunday. Did you get your plane ticket?"

"Yeah. I bought it this morning. I'll arrive that same Sunday."

"In time to see the matinee?"

"No, but I'll make the finale."

"You better."

The brief pause in their conversation needled Annie. Even the dog was quiet. Annie itched to tell Tab the details. The things beyond the *"I'm fine, fine, fine."* Normal stuff, but feelings Annie didn't easily share with others.

She could share with Tabitha.

Tab, or T for short. The friend Annie had made her first year of college. The actress with the crystal-blue eyes and waist-length inky hair. Tab had a husband named Tom, a golden retriever named Marlon, and the three of them shared a small apartment in the West Village.

"I…" they both began at the same time, then laughed.

"You go first," Tab replied.

"I have a date tonight," Annie gushed.

"What?" Tab gasped. "Like with an actual man?"

"Well, I don't know if it's exactly dating…" Annie grinned. "And yes, with a man."

"God, Annie. That's great! Who is he?"

"Don't go getting all excited."

"Uh-oh…"

"It's not bad."

"Spill it."

"He's…" Annie trailed off, remembering Cal's lips and hands, the way his fingers had skirted beneath the material of her dress, sending tingles to all the places lying dormant. Or the ones never properly roused.

"An ax murderer? Living at home with his ma? Sending you ridiculous pics of his dick?"

"No." Annie's belly buckled. "He's…" Her cheeks ached from smiling so much. "He's older than me."

"Like how old? George Clooney old? Or like Father Christmas, white-beard old?"

"Stop. You're making my stomach hurt."

"Does he have children?"

"I don't think so." Annie bit her lip. "He's forty-five."

"You're mumbling. What?"

"He's forty-five," Annie announced as she clapped a palm to her mouth and glanced around her empty bedroom. "Shit. I shouldn't be so loud. I don't know if anyone's home."

"What are you, like, twelve?"

"Shhh..."

"They can't hear me, genius."

"It's Maggie," Annie whispered. "She's been kind of weird about the whole thing."

"What do you mean?"

"She's known him — well, her and John, they've known Cal for, like, twenty years, and she keeps hinting and insinuating that—"

"Did she fuck him?"

"Tabitha, she's married."

"So?"

"So, your mind is always in the gutter. Too many scripts and soaps and plays."

"I know women when it comes to men. If she's weird, she's jealous."

"You don't know Maggie." Vicarious, maybe. But jealous?

"Whatever, Annie-pie, tell me about him. The guy. The old fucker you want to fuck."

"Shhh." Annie laughed again.

"What's his name? Cal what? I'll Google him."

"No."

"Haven't you Facebooked him?"

"No. I don't think he's even on there."

"Are you? Have you created your work page yet?" Tab asked over a shroud of silence. "Annie..."

"I will."

"Yeah, you will, when you come up here. Once and for all. I'm making you. People want to see your stuff online. They'll want to see you, the face of the photographer."

"Drama is your middle name."

"Yeah, and yours is Daydreamer."

The dog barked three times in succession, snapping Annie back to the past. To how she felt that day in Tabitha's apartment.

"Well, now it *is* quiet," Tab said a few seconds later. "Did someone come into the room?"

A ghost had entered the room.

"Are you there, Annie?"

Annie swallowed, her eyes welling with tears as she replayed the scene in her mind…

"Annie, did you hear me?" her father yelled into the cell phone over a year ago. *"Annie!"*

"Annie…?" Tab repeated.

"I'm…" Annie's voice cracked. She was cold despite the sun shining on her back.

"Hey…" Tab's tone took on the pity. Oh, the pity. The carousel of pity. Pick a day. A week. A pill. "I thought things were going well. You sounded so upbeat."

"I am." Annie scrubbed beneath her nose. "They are."

"Then why the tears?"

"It's you."

"Gee, thanks."

Annie laughed some through the sniffles. "It's your voice. Your familiarity. I don't know."

"It's only been a few weeks since I've seen you, hun."

"Yeah, I know."

A few weeks of change. Incredible change. Well, incredible enough for Annie.

A new state. A new house. The gallery. Old friends. No regular routine other than eating and brushing her teeth. No alarm clock. No steady job. No tables to bus or wait or drinks to make. A couple of magazine deadlines, but no project-due-yesterday pressure. No classes. No boyfriend or his friends, his video games or his endless family to impress. No Tabitha forever offering Annie a ride in the front seat of her car, next to her freckles and charm, her loyalty like the Queen's guard.

And then there was Cal — the old fucker she wanted to fuck.

Annie smiled. "I am good. It's good."

"That's what I want to hear. That, and when are you actually going to get laid?"

"How do you know I haven't?"

"Do you hear yourself? Because it's been like a million years."

Silence fell over the phone.

"Annie, are you crying again?"

"No. Shut up..."

"Then what?"

"It's him. You don't know."

"No. I don't. You won't tell me anything. You won't even let me Google the bastard."

"He's blond. Okay. Dark blond."

"Yes."

"He's tall. He has green eyes."

"Yes. Yes."

"He's..."

"What? What? What?"

"When I walk into a room with him, I feel like..." *Like I do now. Air leaves my lungs. I'm deprived of all oxygen. He steals the breath from me and resuscitates me all at once.* "I've never felt like this before."

"Like what? You're not 'splaining, Luceee."

Annie giggled. "How did you feel when you met Tom?"

"When I first met Tom? You know what I was like. I wanted to fuck—"

"Tab!"

She laughed. "You asked."

"When Cal looks at me..." Annie swallowed, her skin clammy, her heart racing. "When he looks at me, it's like I'm on fire." She glanced out her favorite window. "God, it's more than that. I'm not explaining because I can't explain it." She stood. "I feel like I'm the only woman in the room with him even when we're surrounded by other people." Annie put her thumb and index finger into the corners of her eyes. "I want him so much, Tab, that I feel like I can't breathe thinking about it. And the really strange thing is..." She started to pace. "What freaks me out big-time is ... I feel like I know him. Like I've always known him." Annie twirled several pieces of hair until her fingers became stuck in the strands. "This is crazy, right? I'm officially crazy!"

"You're not crazy, Annie," Tab soothed. "You're amazing. Your old fucker has obviously noticed that."

Annie wiped her eyes, placed a palm over her stomach, and giggled. "Do you always have to make me laugh?"

"Yes. Listen, I've gotta go walk Marlon Brando. When is your date?"

"At seven."

"Promise me something?"

"What? Have sex?"

"Yes, but don't overthink it, okay? Have fun. Get laid."

Don't overthink it, Annie thought. Easy for Tab to say. Thinking and feeling were two of Annie's best assets.

"Oh..." Tab laughed. "And don't forget to call me when the deed is done."

"I will not."

"Text me the details, then."

"You're the crazy one."

"Crazy and fabulous," Tab replied, then they hung up.

Seconds later, Annie climbed back onto the window seat. On her knees, nose pressed to the glass, she looked out at the ocean, imagining what life felt like before she understood what it meant to experience anxiety and panic and unending grief.

She closed her eyes, inhaled, and summoned the magic.

And when she opened her lids again, Annie felt a hundred tons lighter.

Like a weight had been lifted.

As though clouds had parted.

She could breathe.

Palms on the warm glass, staring out at the water — this was how she felt when near Cal. A comfort that couldn't be described. No thoughts. No questions. No resistance. Only stillness. And ocean. And sky.

RELEASE

RELIEF FROM RESTRAINT AND PENT-UP
EMOTIONS; FREEDOM FROM BURDENS OR SADNESS

inside me
pent up
you escape
on my wings
I become
what I knew I could be
or what I never ceased to be
I am
The One
who
belongs
where
near
safe
on the summit
across your shoulder blades
on the tip-tip-tip of my tippy-toes
I will outrun the avalanche
I will become the snowflake
look closely
no two are alike

FIFTEEN

Annie arrived at Cal's around seven.

She made her way through the open iron gate, past the tall, skinny palm trees, toward the first place on the right inside the courtyard. A window took up the corner of the white two-story apartment on the end.

Cal's corner. His home.

Stopping at the door, she hoisted her backpack over her shoulder and slipped a thumb under the strap.

But she didn't knock. Not yet.

A few short blocks from the beach, Annie looked toward Meridian Avenue, never tiring of being so close to the ocean. Faint bursts of light streamed through the Florida sky, and the breeze from the nearby water swam up her dress and around her thighs, cooling her anticipation and urgency.

Right. Now she felt an urgency. Who was she kidding? She'd been thinking about getting underneath Cal's clothes for almost two weeks.

Still, the neighborhood distracted her. Thin, sheet-like clouds took up the opening between the tops of the trees, creating a portal to the sky. And *tons* of trees lined the street, creating canopies, making the avenue unique from the others adjacent to it.

She looked left and right, framing shots in her mind, wondering if she had time to take out her camera, considering a quick leave to shoot the trees, the road, the cars, the homes — anything pulling on her whimsy.

Oh, there were plenty of possibilities.

But Cal was a sure thing.

Opting not to launch an impromptu photo session, Annie dropped an arm to her side and began to fidget with the aqua bracelet encircling her wrist. The sparkly beaded bracelet — the only jewelry she wore — had been a birthday gift from Peter the day she'd turned sixteen. The time spent with her older brother had been some of the happiest Annie could remember.

He was the reason...

God, there still had to be a reason.

Running her fingers over the smooth aqua beads, she exhaled, then knocked on Cal's front door. Her heartbeat ticked up several notches. The texture of the bracelet and its significance pacified her, giving her strength.

Reason.

Was that why she carried it with her wherever she went? In her purse, on her wrist — everywhere.

She couldn't let him go. Ever.

Fuck. She stared at the closed door. *Breathe*. There was more to life than death.

There is this, she thought.

It didn't matter. Death crept up at all the wrong times. Fresh, always pushing. One moment, she could be fine... Right. Not fine. She was never fine.

Fine, fine, fine.

Fine was for other people now. Normal people. She could survive without having to think or be reminded for once, though. Maybe she wanted to be reminded. She wasn't without the bracelet or the memories.

How long would it take to move on? Not to cry. Not to seize in the middle of a crowd with a pocket full of grief so large, it was enough to make her double over with panic.

People said time eased sorrow, but she had no concept of clocks anymore. She had zip-lined her way to Florida, to this street, to Cal's door.

Each thing was new:

The state.

The beach.

The lip gloss.

The shoes.

The dress. Well, it was old, but new, forgotten in the bottom of her suitcase.

Life had been sweatpants and prescriptions.

Damn it. Stop thinking.

Did normal people actually know what it was like to always be thinking?

This was why people drank or...

Cal swung open the door. *Goodbye, thoughts — hello, sexy motherfucking freedom.*

Freedom wore a dark-blue, button-down, long-sleeved shirt. It hung over his faded blue jeans, not tucked in. Annie had never seen him look so casual despite the collared shirt screaming, *"Proper!"* His bare feet stuck out like a sore thumb.

"Were you expecting someone else?" He cradled the door, waiting for her to finish framing the barrage of images probably flooding her mind.

"I was admiring your street."

He peeked outside. "Yes. I did have it structured only for me."

She wouldn't have been surprised. *Cal Avenue.* Annie smiled, ripping her eyes from the magic of the neighborhood as she stepped over the threshold.

"I wish you would've let me pick you up." He slipped his fingers under her backpack, lifting it off her shoulder.

"In what?" She smoothed her hands over the front of her red baby-doll dress. Her heels matched the beads on her bracelet. "I didn't see your car outside."

"Carl keeps the Tesla." Cal dropped her bag on the desk in the foyer, stepped behind her, and put his hands on her waist, craning his neck toward her ear. "He charges it for me."

Annie's eyes closed, her back arched, and she moaned, sliding her palms over his wrists and through his fingers. He kissed her neck, and the pulse there beat so fast she was certain Cal could feel it against his lips.

"Breathe," he whispered.

The air expelled from her lungs like a sharp gust of wind parading over open water. Cal laughed. Annie gently elbowed his stomach as she managed to break away, stepping farther inside his modest apartment.

A simple staircase on her left led up to what appeared to be a loft, and across from the landing was the living area. Although, Cal's idea of living meant exercise equipment, a shelf full of books, two dark brown leather chairs, and a floor lamp. No television. Everything looked modern and, of course, as she'd imagined, clean. Very clean.

Art hung on the walls. Everywhere. His taste was eclectic, varied, and surprising. Matisse, Kahlo, de Kooning, and perhaps some local or up-and-coming artists — pieces she didn't recognize.

"Did you make dinner?" she asked, moving toward the open kitchen. "It smells good."

"No." Cal snuck up behind her again, wrapping his arms around her waist, his lips tickling her ear. She breathed in his crisp, clean, cotton scent. "I had it delivered from a place around the corner." His nose trailed along her earlobe, her jaw, her neck.

"Stop that." Annie giggled, trying to wrench herself from his grasp. "You make me feel naked when you breathe all over me like that."

"That's a first." He smirked and released her, following behind as she took a few more steps.

Mesmerized by the way her hips shook, the curvature of her spine, the way those fucking shoes accentuated her calves, Cal couldn't stop staring at Annie. At the layers of beautiful, caramel-colored hair, the ends curling a few inches above her tailbone, strands he wanted to grab, pull, bind... Fuck. He needed to snap out of it if they were going to make it through dinner without him throwing her over the—

"The table is beautiful." Annie smiled, her fingertips grazing its top.

Flowers and candles sat in the center, complete with cloth napkins and alabaster plates at each end, no tablecloth. The dark wood felt smooth against her skin.

Cal smiled as he proceeded to remove a cork from a bottle of wine. "Do you always wear dresses, Annie Baxter?"

"Do you always ask such odd questions?" Grinning, she placed a hand on his back and ran her fingers along him in soft, sweeping motions. "I made this dress." She glanced down at it. "I used to make a lot of my clothes. Several years ago."

He handed her a glass of wine and cleared his throat. "Your mother taught you?"

"No." She laughed, then put her nose to the rim, inhaling what smelled like berries with hints of plum. "Beverly didn't teach me those kinds of things." She took a taste of the red. "God, this is really good."

"Do you recognize it?"

"Should I?"

"You said it was your favorite."

"When did I say that?"

"At dinner Wednesday."

Annie tilted the bottle back to get a better look at the label, then she glanced at Cal, her eyes wide, her mouth hanging open. "My God! Where did you find this?"

"I found it online." He put a hand in a pocket and took a sip. "I thought you might want a taste of home."

Crushed grapes from her home state.

A red she'd first sampled in Yakima, a town about one hundred and fifty miles southeast of Seattle. The wineries there were quaint, the people friendly, the valleys breathtaking, the views plentiful.

He must've overnighted the bottle, Annie thought as she closed her eyes and inhaled its delightful aroma for a second time. When she reopened them, she felt alive. Comfortable. The Syrah making this new space seem familiar, like she'd come home again. "I can't believe you remembered."

"It was only two days ago that you told me."

"Thank you." She blinked, then grabbed their glasses and placed them on the table. Making a beeline for his chest, she planted her face there, stretching her arms up his backside. Holding his shoulders, her nose found that wonderful little crook of his neck. Her crook. The one she'd discovered or had always known.

God, he was warm.

Solid like a sequoia tree. Secure.

Was he?

Annie had felt safe with him from the moment they'd met — the same sensation she felt when staring at the ocean, when with her camera.

"Thank you," she repeated, her voice muffled by his shirt. Cal ran a hand over her hair. She sighed. A minute or so later, she popped her head up. "Did you have a good day?"

"I worked."

"Well, was it good?"

"It was productive."

"And your meeting last night? *Was it productive?*"

"I would've rather met with you." He smirked. "I think we could've been much more productive."

"Oh, you *think*, huh? You mean you aren't sure?"

They both laughed.

"Seriously." She took a swallow of the wine. "How did your meeting go?"

The light left his eyes. "A buyer backed out at the last minute—"

Annie raised an eyebrow, waiting a few seconds for him to say more, then she smiled ridiculously when no words followed. She sipped her well-traveled wine and brushed her fingers along the side of his crisp shirt.

Their eyes met. Locked. Staying like that for so long, Annie began to perspire. She had no doubt Cal could see right through her. Beyond her dress. Straight to her core. Everything inside her body liquified. She took another sip, then another, but the man would not desist with the staring contest. So, she peeled herself away from his heated gaze and moved farther into the kitchen.

Pictures on the fridge caught her attention. At least a dozen photographs, ranging from old to new, lined the door, attached by magnets. Images that would tell her a story or two about this mysterious chameleon. Pieces of his life.

Who are you, Prescott? Annie fingered the edge of a perfectly square black-and-white. "She's beautiful, Cal."

"She's young there." Cal's voice dropped. His face remained placid. His eyes traveled somewhere far away.

"She's your mother?" The woman appeared to be in her twenties, wore no smile, and her eyes ... they were possessed.

Like Cal's.

He snapped back to the present but shifted his gaze.

"I'm sorry." Annie ground one of her heels into the flooring. "Did I say something wrong? Did she...? Is she...?"

"No." Cal glanced at the picture, then back to Annie. "My mother is alive and in Ojai."

Annie swallowed. She rested a palm on his face. "You can give me more than that, Cal. You can talk to me."

"I don't have to give you anything, Annie." Cal removed her hand.

Turning, she bit the insides of her cheeks, wondering what the fuck he'd been thinking, buying her Yakima wine, wooing her, then simultaneously shredding her insides to pieces.

She wanted to deck him in the face.

Hot. Cold.

Contradictory.

A chameleon.

Except...

He wasn't cold.

Cal had tried his best to sound coarse, smooth and calculating, but his eyes were misleading. Because the way he looked at Annie now told her he wanted to give her everything.

Annie touched Cal's back. "Should we get the food out?" Her palm remained there as she gazed at his profile. "I'm really hungry."

Cal finished off the red in one long swallow while Annie stepped closer to the stove and started taking items out of a brown paper bag. Seconds later, he joined her, but she wouldn't look at him. His hand met one of her wrists. His fingers slid between hers.

"You don't make getting to know you very easy." She sighed and glanced at him. "Do you even want me to know you?"

"Annie..."

"Don't..." She shook her head. "Don't answer that question."

Cal dropped his nose to her neck. "I'm a much better listener." He tenderly bit her skin. "I'm much better at many"—*nibble*—"other"—*nibble*—"things."

"I'm sure." Annie giggled, pushing him away at his chest. He smiled, grabbed the boxes, and walked them to the table. The two of them sat at opposite ends, Cal facing the sink, Annie's view a closed door.

"What was your day like?" he asked while opening the containers of Chinese food.

"Oh, so now you want to know about my day?"

"Well, I do recall you mentioning the other night that we needed to have polite dinner conversation about something other than sex."

Her throat closed. Air left the room.

She could smell the sex. Could taste it. The dinner conversation was the only thing standing in its way.

"Annie?"

"What?" She cleared her throat.

Seconds later, she proceeded to tell Cal about the last two days while multitasking, refilling their wineglasses, chatting about her upcoming trip to New York, her best friend, her best friend's husband, and their dog, Marlon Brando. She also spoke a little of art school.

And true to his word, Cal listened, intently too, smiling often with not only his lips, but his eyes.

"How long have you known Tabitha?" he asked as they finished up their meal.

"We met my first year of college."

"The way you spoke of her"—his eyes twinkled—"I assumed you'd been friends much longer."

Annie shook a little, running her arms over her biceps. Gooseflesh present there, heat everywhere else. "Tell me about *your* friends."

"You know my friends."

"What about in California?"

"The kind of friends we're talking about, friends ... like family..." he said, his velvety tone thick with emotion yet full of certainty. "It's always been John and Maggie."

"I met them"—she squinted—"in 1998."

"I don't even want to think about how old you were then."

Annie smirked. "Maggie took care of me."

"What do you mean?"

"My mom..." Annie paused and glanced away, her voice cracking. "My dad remarried, and my mom..."

"You don't have to tell me." Reaching an arm across the table, Cal touched her hand. "If you're not ready." His fingertips danced over her skin while his eyes held something she'd never seen: an apology, an understanding. "I didn't exactly tell you about my mother."

Annie inhaled a shaky breath. "My mom's an alcoholic." She glanced quickly at Cal, touched her throat, and massaged the skin there. "Maggie was the one... She was there every day for a while, with me, taking care of me. She kind of took over."

"That sounds about right." Cal grinned, retracting his palm.

"You know, Maggie's very secretive about you. *You* are very secretive about you."

"I don't hide." Cal's eyes morphed back into steel.

Annie flicked a glance to the foreboding door, then flinched.

"Are you nervous?" Cal smirked.

"No." Her gaze remained on the door.

"Why are you nervous?"

"What makes you think I'm nervous?" She twisted the sides of her heels toward the floor. "I just told you I wasn't nervous." As she twirled the bracelet on her wrist, his eyes burned holes right through her skin. "Stop staring at me like that and maybe I won't be so nervous."

His gaze fell to the aqua beads she played with, then it climbed back to her face, pinning her to the chair with his blinding stare. "Why?"

"I've told you. It's been..."

No, no, no, she thought. *Don't tell him how long it's been since you've done this.* Thirteen fucking months. Cal already knew too much of her history. And the knowledge had caused his brain to swell to rather epic proportions.

"Annie, I'm going to see you, all of you. I think you can say a simple sentence to me."

Despite the apology she'd seen in his eyes moments ago, Annie wondered if Cal was even aware of his contradictory nature. Nevertheless, her mind was stuck on his last two statements — he was going to see all of her. So she would tell him what was pounding at her heart so he could see even more.

Annie looked him square in the eye, bridling her trepidation — her *nervousness* — with a mighty force, preparing for the words to slide off her tongue with complete sophistication. She could speak smoothly too.

He liked to look at her. To see her.

Well, watch me, Cal.

"I've never met anyone like you." Her words flew out, nosediving like a distressed airplane. "I've never felt what I feel when you look at me the way you are right now." She tilted her head down and almost laughed, thinking of how she must've sounded to him. Or maybe it was the wine making her want to giggle.

Annie looked back up, her flicker beginning to flame, lighting her cheeks, traveling to her thighs and between her legs, but her smile faded.

It wasn't the wine.

"I've never been with someone who actually knows what they're doing."

And God only knows what he's going to do.

He'd already dominated her in ways no one ever had before: restricting her movement on Maggie's porch, twice; smothering her with his body, his choice of words, his velvety tone; pulling at her hair; arm-wrestling her at Wednesday's dinner; giving her sly commands; still pinning her to the chair right now with no more than a stare.

She allowed it.

She enjoyed it.

And she knew he knew it.

"You mean your *boys* didn't know what they were doing?" Cal laughed.

Annie sighed. "Stop calling them boys."

But they were.

The last one, Daniel Westerly, twenty-two and spoiled rotten to the core, had proven he certainly was no man.

Annie stood and picked up Cal's plate. While he stayed in place, quiet again, hands in front of his face, fingertips touching, making a steeple. Not moving. Concentrating. Contemplative and sexy. Annie never realized quiet contemplation could look so sexy.

The nerves multiplied in her gut as she watched his wheels turn. She could only imagine what he was thinking as she waited for a response, his reaction — anything. But he only leaned back, stretched his legs, and looked past her, his gaze jogging around the room.

After several more seconds of silence, she rolled her eyes and tossed the silverware, napkins, and empty containers on top of their plates. As she walked toward the sink, she heard Cal moving glasses, candles, and flowers. Annie turned on the faucet, keeping her back to him.

"Leave the dishes," he said, his edict loud and clear over the running water.

She obeyed, then dried her hands.

"Turn around."

After cutting the light, leaving the burning candles to create shadows and shapes up the walls, Cal unbuttoned the cuffs on his shirt, rolled them to his elbows, and made his way toward her. Blistering heat filled her body from head to toe, spreading over her like wildfire incinerating a dense wood.

"If there's anything I ever do to you that you don't want me to..." he began the moment he reached her, "all you have to do is tell me."

Already, his movements, or lack thereof, had become a delicious affliction she never wanted cured — like nothing she'd ever experienced. She didn't think there was anything he could ever physically do to her she wouldn't desire.

Cal stood, almost passive, still contemplative, absorbing the moment, looking at her the way Annie might frame a photograph, checking angles, composition, colors. Except Cal set the scene of how he would devour her body.

Her soul.

Her person.

"Your skin..." He exhaled, glanced up, and met her eyes. One of his hands trailed from her neck to her hip. The other gathered up several strands of her hair.

My skin...

Did it feel the way his felt to her? Like a destined collision, a beautiful hurt.

The space between them closed.

Chests touched.

Heartbeats fluxed.

She ached and ached and ached.

This was it.

The beginning of the end. Or the end of mindless thinking.

Fuck thinking.

Cal plied her with kisses, soft and wet along her jawline, her neck, her cheeks — each one custom-made for Annie, leaving an imprint. Then he slid his mouth toward her lips. But he didn't kiss them. At first, he inched back and only stared at them, touched them, ran a finger along the edges.

Seconds later, their mouths danced, his lips drawing closer to hers, hovering there for an excruciating long time, before skirting away, doing so repeatedly, only playing, caressing, nibbling the corners, never claiming them.

Then Cal withdrew his lips from her face altogether.

Annie froze.

Well, her chest heaved. Her nostrils flared. Her knuckles went white against the countertop.

The man slid down her trembling frame, his face coming to a stop below her belly button as he moved his head side to side over the material of her dress. Annie squirmed, gyrated her hips, and groaned, sounding as though she were hyperventilating. She mussed Cal's hair, pulling on his locks, waiting for his well-timed movements to gain momentum, waiting for more contact.

Cal removed her shoes, one at a time, then his hands went up her legs, under her dress, until he found the elastic of her underwear.

"Breathe, Annie," he whispered as he pulled her panties to the floor.

As Cal stood back up and put his palm on her cheek, his fingertips threading through her hair, Annie dropped her chin, refusing to let him see inside. Refusing to let him view the broken places. Pinching the sides of his shirt, she leaned her head into his chest, avoiding his gaze. She wasn't having it.

The emotion.

The sex without ... what?

There was no empty in their fling, no empty in his eyes.

It was all there, so she avoided it.

How could she look at him and keep her heart intact, keep her mind from falling for a masquerade? If she met his eyes now, she might implode, explode, or maybe even come, ass against the counter, body answering his every silent question.

Cal yanked her head off his chest by her hair and looked into her soul with the intention of a madman. Back and forth, his eyes ticked, then his gaze wandered to her lips.

He kissed them.

Cal kissed Annie.

And she whimpered, surrendered, gave him all she had to offer in return, swirling her tongue around his, burying herself inside his warmth, savoring the feel of his cheeks against hers, his skin on her skin, inhaling the smell — the ocean and the cotton and the wine. Nearly bruising from the force of it.

"You taste amazing," Cal uttered between kisses.

Annie moaned.

Panted.

Wrapped a leg around his thigh.

The two melded together, bodies rocking into the countertop, Cal ramming her against it until her ass and back felt sore.

The room became a blur.

Several minutes later, he stopped, pulled back, and stared into her eyes, seeing all the way to her insides. A merry-go-round that had been spinning sixty miles an hour came to a sudden halt as beautiful shades of green tempted Annie's dizzy heart, obliterating the word *fling*.

The stare increased, becoming liquid and ocean and moonlight. His eyes held an intensity she hadn't seen all night. Missiles departing their silos, wishing to rip her apart, but Annie was together, more whole than she'd been in a long time.

Not taking his eyes off her face, Cal picked her up and carried her to the table, placing her at the end where her plate formerly rested.

"Lean back, Annie." Cal kicked the chair away, then tugged her dress up her torso, alternating between looking down at her body and watching her wide-eyed expression. He undid the buttons of his shirt. "I want to taste you."

Her limbs shook as she eased back and propped herself up on her elbows. Cal lost his shirt, spread her legs, and breathed against her inner thighs.

"Oh my God," she whispered before his tongue ever made contact, thinking her words had remained inaudible inside the bubble of her mind.

"You like that?" He smiled, then licked her folds, her clit, kissing and sucking until she dropped her head flat against the table and squirmed, trying to get away from the onslaught of pleasure. "Your pussy tastes as good as your fucking tongue."

"Fuck, Cal..." She lifted her head, gazing at the man between her legs.

His breath over her skin.

His fabulous tongue flicking her clit.

A mouth hungry.

For her.

She squeezed her breasts over the clothing, thumbing her nipples, continuing to moan up a storm.

"You're close," he said a few minutes later, a palm over her stomach, feeling her tremble.

"Oh God." She shifted her head side to side, arching herself toward him.

Cal grinned. Nuzzling her thighs, he slid his nose along her skin, kissing her folds the way he first had her face. Barely touching her, making her wait. Drawing near, breathing, nibbling, inching away, then closer, licking her only a little, but exquisitely, making her writhe.

Then he pulled away.

Again.

"Oh God, Cal. No." Annie gripped the edge of the table as he continued to bring her to another kind of edge.

He licked. Then stopped. Licked. Then stopped.

"No," she begged, panting, hardly able to lift her head now. But she shook it. "No."

"No, what?" He smirked, using the same tone he had in the car on the phone after the gala, the same tone he'd used with her on the street. Now, the dominance and its timbre drove her even more crazy with need.

"*Don't stop, fuck, please.*"

"Not yet." He slipped a finger inside her warmth, and she groaned. "It's not time."

"Time?" Every word became a struggle. "For ... what?"

"For you to come." He kissed her clit, moving his finger in and out of her. "I'll tell you when."

"How can you...?" She didn't know how she continued to speak, each syllable a fragile whisper. "Aren't you...?"

"You'll come when I tell you to."

"I can't wait." She squirmed.

Cal removed his digit and grabbed her hips, clamping her body to the table. Using his head, he spread her legs wider, then he bit her thigh.

Annie yelped, choking on the new sensation as he bit her other thigh, her conscious thoughts fleeing, running away with his teeth. Cal caressed what he'd bruised, soothing the sting and ache with his lips. Then he put his mouth back on her pussy, pushing his tongue inside her hole. The noises she made increased, her satisfaction sounding like both an exorcism and an awakening. Annie was awake and alive and close. Gripping the table, she lifted her bruised thighs and started to ride his face.

Then the bastard stopped on a dime. Again.

Annie's eyes popped open.

"I want to be inside you." Cal stood tall, wiping his mouth. "Now." He took her palm. "Sit up."

Annie scooted to the edge, wrapped her legs around his waist, and slid her hands up his backside, her face she buried against his chest.

"In my bed, Annie. I want you in it right now."

Squeezing his shoulders, she inhaled shaky breaths as she peered into the melting green of his eyes, looking into him the way he often managed to stare into her.

Afraid and petrified, trembling and elated, Annie's heart swelled. She wanted Cal in a way she'd never wanted anything before. She cupped the back of his neck, pulled his face toward hers, and kissed him, tasting herself on his tongue, smelling herself there.

"Take me," she whispered against his lips. "Take me now."

Cal took her hand, grabbed the bottle of wine, and led Annie to the bedroom, prepared to continue making her feel the blinding necessity that had strangled his common sense since he'd first seen her — since they'd first spoken — since they'd first kissed.

Once they reached the bedroom, he took a swig of the wine straight from the bottle, kicked the door shut, and finished off the warm, red liquid. Then he stared into Annie — his eyes full of passionate dictation she couldn't transcribe fast enough — ready to finish her off too.

Sixteen

"Wait here," he had said. "Don't move," he had said, leaving her alone near the foot of the bed.

So much for wanting her in his bed. *Right. Now.*

The breeze of his breath still blew across her body as she stood barefoot, dressed and alone, knees wobbly, thighs and folds sticky from the mind-bending assault on her lower extremities that had occurred only moments ago.

The second Cal came out of the bathroom, Annie's gaze wandered from the few stray locks of hair falling across his forehead to the softer-looking hairs on his chest. Darker and perfect, they created a faint line toward his navel, a trail Annie wanted to lick.

Then her gaze dropped lower.

The nightlight coming from the bathroom illuminated his pants in the otherwise dark room, the outline against his jeans appearing suffocating and large. Flawless. She couldn't tear her eyes from it. Her neck flamed as she nibbled her bottom lip.

"What are you looking at, Annie?"

She glanced up, found his eyes, and shivered.

"Don't," he commanded as she reached behind and began to tug on her zipper. "I want you to leave the dress on."

She twirled the bracelet on her wrist as he stepped closer, splitting open the chasm of her ocean floor. Did he know her throat was closing? That she was quaking? That her thighs were still shaking? Did he know the dull ache he'd caused on the table hadn't subsided?

The moment Cal reached her, he smirked, kissed her neck, and closed the zipper, sure as fuck to breathe against her skin in the process.

"Do you plan everything, Prescott?" Annie exhaled, kept her palms at her sides, fingers wiggling.

Of course he had a plan. The man always had a plan.

He wanted to have her in her dress.

Fuck.

He wasn't speaking.

It was really starting now. The table had only been an appetizer.

"Making you come is my plan," he finally whispered as he slid his hands over her waist and squared her hips.

"Are you sure I'm allowed to come?" Annie smiled, but it was quickly replaced with a shiver, the chill climbing her spine as the tips of his fingers caressed her ass. "You told me not to a few minutes ago."

"Do you remember what else I said to you in the kitchen?" His nose fell to the scoop neck of her dress. He ran his face across her breasts, nibbling her nipples over the material.

"What?" Annie whimpered.

"Do you trust me?" He lifted his head and met her eyes.

No, she thought as his hands continued roaming her ass, his touch striking her like a series of powerful lightning bolts. *God. Maybe. Yes.*

"Annie," he uttered near her lips, "I said if there was anything I ever did that you didn't—"

"Want me to," she took over, her words barely audible, her pulse pounding. "What ... are you going ... to do?"

The dress, he bunched above her waist. A hand cupped her sex while a single finger found its way inside her body. She gasped. Another one of his fingers strummed her clit, caressing her as if he'd watched her touch herself — as if he knew.

Pulling her head off his chest by her hair, he pressed his cheek to hers, both of them breathing heavily. As Cal fingered her. Watched her. Annie writhed and moaned, fucking his hand while attempting to kiss his lips.

But he wouldn't allow it.

Like before.

He made her wait.

For everything.

Almost as though Cal had wanted her to know how he'd felt these last two weeks. What it had been like to be aching and aching and aching to have her, thinking only of filling her completely. To kiss her. To touch her. Like this.

"Cal," she whispered, yanking on his hair, pulling his lips toward hers. "*Please...*"

His tongue went into her mouth immediately, the intensity picking up, quickly becoming harsh and swift, Cal consuming her as if she were the only one.

The only one, he thought. She was his.

He became so vehemently focused on the way she felt in his arms, against him, near him, how her lips tasted, how her skin smelled — like those fucking tangerine blossoms — that he stopped touching her below the waist. Taking her face in both of his hands, the smell of her pussy lingering on his fingers ignited him, causing him to pursue her more and more and more, her taste extraordinary, something he'd never encountered before.

Then.

Somehow.

He managed to reel it all back in, bridling the emotion, switching on the self-control.

Easing away from her lips, his nose he kept against her cheek, panting, recovering, thinking as the two of them stood stock-still, the beating of their hearts increasing. Seconds passed, time the two of them spent inhaling only tangerines and ocean.

Then Cal pulled back, stepped to the side, and smirked.

"Lie down. On your stomach. Leave the dress on." He didn't flinch. His commands sounded richer, stronger, complementing the chiseled features of his face — all of them a brick.

Aware of the thump in her chest and never-ending ache in her groin, Annie glanced at his profile as she climbed onto the king-sized bed. She positioned herself flat on her stomach, elbows bent near her ears, head to the side as Cal pushed her dress above her waist and straddled the backs of her knees.

"Let go of everything you think you know, Annie," he exhaled, his hand traveling down her spine, tickling her.

What did she know?

Cal's hands. His voice. His safety.

A palm now on her nape, he held her there, gently restricting her, revving every emotion within her without uttering another sound while his other hand and its five amazing fingers swirled across her tailbone.

He was watching her. Simply watching.

She knew he gazed at her curves, her ass, the same way he'd studied her in the kitchen. Fuck. It was hot. She couldn't breathe, tangled up in his touch. She managed to wiggle a little, but his palm insisted she stay put, remaining pressed against the back of her neck as she squirmed. And she couldn't help but squirm.

His other hand slipped between her legs, and she accommodated him by slightly raising her hips. He spread her folds, making her wetter as he began to rub her clit. After only a few seconds of featherlight touches, Annie was on the edge again, trying to fuck the mattress. Then one of her legs flew up from behind, causing a foot to meet his backside.

She dropped it on the bed and shifted her hips, determined to hold on yet wanting to force something from him.

And she did.

She basked in the sting before she could process what had occurred. Then it happened again. And again. His palm, slapping her ass. Hard. She gasped and moaned, twisting her lower lip between her teeth as his fingernails bit into her skin, massaging her. Two of his other fingers disappeared inside her warmth.

This went on for some time. A few smacks. A caress. The fingering. Annie lost count. Then Cal scooted aside, opened her legs wider, and played with her some more. A cheek against the sheets, she writhed, pinching the fibers, barely able to make sounds.

"Don't move, Annie, or I'll have to spank you again."

Full of his fingers, three now, swelling and tight, Annie struggled to catch her breath. His determination rendered her practically mute as he moved the digits in and out endlessly, the necessity of his touch communicating what she knew he would not say aloud.

That he wanted her.

This. Now.

That he somehow needed it.

Whimpering, Annie bunched the sheets, bursting with pleasure she'd never felt. Her hips gyrated, wishing for his palm to meet the warm flesh of her ass again. Wishing never to remember what she thought she knew. Wanting only to know this moment, these fingers.

Then Cal stopped.

All of it.

For a few seconds, she only heard him breathing. His lungs sounded almost as labored as hers.

Cal brushed knuckles along her jawline, tucked strands of hair behind her ear, waiting for her breath to calm, her eyes to close. Resting a hand on the small of her back, he listened to her heart beating as he swayed the tips of his fingers over her skin, the motion like a swoosh of a gentle breeze.

Peering at her backside, he palmed her ass cheeks, squeezing and kneading them, then he shoved two fingers deep inside her hole, causing Annie to cry out.

Beautifully.

The moaning like nothing he'd ever heard, like sounds he always wanted to know. The moment Annie lifted her hips, then thrust them down, trying to fuck the bed again, Cal struck her butt cheek, then stroked her clit, sliding a finger up and down her smooth slit. Annie reacted to everything with a chill, a moan, a tremble. It wasn't long before she started squirming out of control, broken syllables pouring from her voice box.

Sounding desperate.

Exasperated.

Perfect.

Cal could listen to and watch her body all night.

"Don't move," he growled as he unzipped her dress, then stood, taking a condom out of his front pocket.

After losing his pants and putting it on, he resumed his position, only now, he teased her entrance with the tip of his dick. Bucking against her, slipping it along the wet line, watching her grunt and writhe.

"Relax," he whispered, stroking her hair and spine. "You're exhausting yourself." Annie released a breath, then sighed. "That's better." Cal kissed her backside, dotting his lips between the opening of her dress.

Annie wiggled those hips, pushing back against his welcomed intrusion, both of them enjoying the rhythm their bodies had found — and they hadn't even begun to fuck.

"How do you want this?" he breathed across her beautiful skin.

Annie heard his question as if in a dream, her mind blank like a canvas waiting for paint. Mouth parched, nothing came out but the sounds, the whimpering, the groaning.

Lifting his upper body off her some, Cal slapped her ass again. "Godammit, Annie, you're making me fucking crazy." Then he gave her an inch or so of him. "Tell. Me."

"Tell you what?" she uttered, glancing back. Already she'd granted him permission, willingly giving him what no other man had asked for. In this moment, she was his. He could have her any way he pleased.

Cal spread her cheeks, pulled out, then stroked his length along her folds.

"God, what are you doing?" she cried, pushing backward, trying to swallow him whole again. "I need to come." Reaching an arm around to his thigh, she attempted to pull him even closer, but he smiled, not budging.

"Do you need *this*?" He slid back in, this time farther. Much farther. Her eyes rolled so far into the back of her head she didn't think she would be able find them. "Do you want me to fuck you?" He moved in and out, painfully slow. "From behind?"

"Yes!" she wailed through clenched teeth, ramming her ass against him again, trying to force him all the way inside.

But he was resistant, resilient. The weight of his body captured her. Then Cal surged forward and bumped her cervix so hard, she felt it in her throat.

"Yes, what?" he asked as he pulled out.

She struck the bed with a fist. "Yes. I. Need. You."

"What do you need, Annie?"

"Goddd, Caaal."

He filled her up again, held himself there, and she sagged in relief. "You need God?" He laughed a little and pulled out.

"Argh!" she roared, grabbing and bunching the sheets.

"Say it," he gritted. "Tell me to fuck you." He lowered his lips to her neck, pulled her hair, and held her down, sliding his girth over and over her slit. "Tell me you need me to fuck you."

It was hard. The word. The stupid little word she'd already moaned a fucking million times in her head was hard to say out loud. In bed.

F-U-C-K.

Harder than his cock.

Her chest rattled. Her thighs shook.

"Tell me, Annie."

"Fuck me," she burst, and he pulled her hair tighter. "I need you. I need you to fuck me. Now!"

Cal shoved inside her body, stealing the breath from her lungs, completely sealing up any remaining space between them with his cock.

"Tell me ... if it's too much," he uttered, his breath shaky as he lifted her hips, pulled her closer, and pounded her body relentlessly from the start.

Like she could run from him and he had to hold on.

Secure her to him.

Fuck the reason for everything into her. Make sense of nonsense.

He slid in.

Then pulled out.

Pounding.

The bed shook.

Annie sat on all fours, trembling, breasts bobbing inside the loose dress, hair bouncing, eyes opening and closing, choking back the wild sounds, then releasing them with each thrust, the two of them rocking in perfect motion.

Cal could feel the rise.

Her breathing changed.

He massaged her clit.

There might've been words they wanted to say but they wouldn't form on their lips.

"Come for me, Annie." Flattening her body against the bed, causing her to flatline, Cal thrust himself inside her so deeply, so perfectly, pulling slightly back, then going deeper, until he could feel her insides latch onto him, pulsate around him, electrify him.

After pumping into her one, two, three more times, Cal released his own everything inside her, attempting to quell what he'd started that night on the deck at the party, realizing, without a doubt, what he was starting with this beautiful woman was far more than a fling or a fuck or something passing or fleeting.

He released.

Cal collapsed beside her and kissed her cheek, removing the emotion from his eyes. Annie peered at him as though in a stupor. She pressed herself against his side, nuzzled his neck, and closed her eyes.

After a few moments of unwanted throat-stinging bliss, Cal got up, slinked the dress off her body, and covered her with the sheet.

He took a shower.

Annie lay fast asleep.

MYSTIFY

BEWILDERED BY AN OBSCURE PUZZLE

a gentle intrusion
a monumental fear
eclipsed
by bravery
strung out on mirrors
and green eyes
hold my hand
to the finish
until
the summer expires

SEVENTEEN

Cal had been awake for at least an hour, leaning against the headboard, glasses on, typing at his laptop.

Scratching his bare chest, he let out a yawn and looked over at Annie.

She lay fast asleep in his bed.

A woman.

A beautiful woman.

He hadn't told her that yet. He hadn't told her half of what he felt. How could he? Should he? She would only be here for what? A couple months? And so would he. Maybe three, tops. Bullshit he didn't need to think about.

Cal wanted to simply enjoy having her in his bed as she was now, actually sleeping. Although, he hoped to enjoy more of her like he had last night, but she probably wasn't up for another go, not at delaying her gratification anyway. She did seem to like the edge. He sure as fuck did.

When was the last time a woman had given it to him? Trust without contingencies? When was the last time someone had slept in his bed?

He couldn't remember. Or didn't want to.

Scrubbing his fingers beneath his chin, he smiled, recalling all they'd done the night before — the allowance, the ease, the comfort. It wasn't just the sex. It was her and...

A gentle knock put a stop to his annoying sentimental conjecture.

Thank fuck.

The door cracked opened. A woman peeked inside before proceeding to enter without waiting for a reply. Cal glanced at her, then went about his business without a word.

"Good morning," she hummed, her English thick with the tells of her Guanajuato accent. She carried a glass of fresh-squeezed orange juice in one hand and the day's newspaper under her arm. "I've got breakfast almost ready." She set the OJ on the nightstand, then raised the blinds. The single partition snapped up, allowing light into the formerly dark room. "Did you already go for your run?"

"I'm not going for a run, and you'll need to have breakfast ready for two." Peering at her over the rims of his glasses, he picked up the drink and guzzled it in one long swallow.

"You're expecting company so early?" The woman stood at his side, shifting her weight from one foot to the other. "Who is coming?"

"My company is here."

"Who is here?" The R rolled off her tongue in a beautiful, flabbergasted symphony. "At this hour?"

After closing the laptop, he pushed it to the foot of the bed. Cocking his head to the side, he whispered, "My company is still sleeping."

Feet extending past the blanket, Annie stirred, more of her hair and part of her face appearing on the pillow.

The woman's onyx eyes opened wide, and her lips curved into an embarrassed smile. She took the newspaper out from under her arm and swatted him with it several times while spouting out a few denunciations in her native tongue.

Laughing, Cal stood, grabbed the paper, and shooed her out of the room with it.

"Who was that?" Annie mumbled the second the door clicked shut. As she sat up on her elbows and rubbed an eye, the blanket slid down, exposing her breasts.

"That was Rosa." Cal took a seat beside her and tossed the paper on the bed, sure to give the sheet another tug in the right direction.

"Who's Rosa?" Annie grumbled, yanking the covers up and pushing against him with her toes. "And why the hell is she here so early on a Saturday morning? God, what time is it?"

"Now, now. There's no need to address me as God. You tried that last night." He laughed. "Show me your tits again"—he extended an arm on either side of her hips—"and maybe you'll get some answers."

Narrowing her eyes, Annie tried not to crack a smile. But it was impossible, what with his sharp intake of breath, his chest rising above hers, the smell of his skin swallowing her whole. The bed was turning into a whirlpool, and she was apparently going to be its next victim.

"Ass," she hissed, dropping her head against the pillow.

Cal snatched her arms, pinned her wrists above her head, and pelted her with that look — the one he must've spent years perfecting: an ornery, misbehaved child-turned-man who couldn't comprehend not getting exactly what he wanted.

Planting his face in her neck, he nibbled her skin until she squirmed, then he used his teeth to drag the sheet to her waist. With her arms trapped and her back arched, her lungs rose and fell, leaving her chest, bare and exposed, only inches from his face.

She wanted him to take a taste.

Instead, the man looked into her eyes, showing off the self-control he seemed to enjoy testing at a moment's notice. It was clear he wasn't going to simply give her what she desired.

That would've been far too easy.

"Look who wants to have an orgasm already this morning." His nose trailed through the middle of her breasts.

Heart beating practically stronger than his grip, she wiggled her arms and pushed her knees against him.

"You can't hide, Annie. It's in your eyes."

And across her sleeve. It was no secret people could read her. And Cal seemed to be an expert.

"You mean you will *allow* me another orgasm? You won't deny me? Over and over..."

"You enjoyed it." He grinned. "I heard you make lots of sounds but no complaints." His tongue trailed across a nipple. "Do you hear yourself?" He licked until it pebbled in his mouth. "Your body"—his lips met her neck, his bare chest brushing against hers—"is so responsive."

She moaned louder.

"I wanted you to experience prolonged pleasure."

"I thought I might die."

Cal lifted his head, let go of her hands, and let out a belly laugh. Annie's eyes went wide at the sound and the freedom he displayed in expressing it.

"You were very much alive. Did it scare you? Any of it?"

"No," she whispered and swallowed.

A sudden unpleasantness marred his handsome face — a mask to hide what Annie had already witnessed last night. Several times.

"I'm going to take a shower." She swung her legs over the side of the mattress and sat up.

"Stay for breakfast." His eyes twinkled once again. "You can meet Rosa." Grinning, he picked up the newspaper and headed for the door.

"Oh my God, Cal!" Annie ripped off the sheet, pointed, and covered her mouth. "My underwear!"

"You best"—he nodded toward her breasts—"cover up if you really want me to leave."

"Shit, Cal. I want you to get my underwear. It's... They're on the floor. With—"

He laughed and made his way back over.

"I don't see what you think is so funny," she said. "I want to make a good impression on this mystery person."

Cal lowered to his haunches, placed the tip of his index finger on her chin, and slid it down her neck, between her breasts, stopping at her navel. "I retrieved your lovely panties last night, along with your bag and shoes." Cal tipped his head toward the bathroom.

She eyed her backpack hanging on the doorknob, her shoes on the floor.

"And, Annie," he continued and stood, "you always make a good impression."

"Do I?" Annie got up and started to prance toward the bathroom, stark naked, her hips shaking. "What kind of impression do I make now?" She glanced over her shoulder, all smiles.

"A very fucking naughty one."

Eighteen

After setting the newspaper on the table, Cal made his way into the kitchen, wearing only the comfortable blue pants he'd slept in and the smile Annie had gifted him.

He retrieved a glass from a cabinet and proceeded to pour himself a tall drink of water.

Rosa opened the fridge and grabbed the eggs and strawberry jam. After the door closed, she looked at Cal's profile, holding the items near her chest. "You want to give an old lady a heart attack this morning?"

Cal tried not to grin. "You are not a lady."

"Oy." She tossed her head, put the eggs near the stove and the jam on the table, then she wiped her hands on her floral apron. "Why have I not met your girlfriend before now? What is her name?"

Cal glared at Rosa. "Her name is Annie. She's not my girlfriend."

"Hmmm..." The clicking sound she often made with her tongue against the roof of her mouth had already begun, the noise most often denoting her disapproval, the characteristic he'd heard a million times.

"You mean to say"—she poked his bicep—"you asked a woman *here*." She pointed to the floor. "To your home — something I have not seen you do since I do not remember when — and you do not wish me to say *girlfriend*?" Rosa's petite hands rested on her curvy hips, nails tapping against her capris. "*Well*?"

Knowing without a doubt she would see what Annie meant to him splashed all over his face, Cal looked away. But nothing slipped past Rosa. He'd been unsuccessfully trying to pull the wool over her eyes since the age of five.

"You think you will do your no-talking bit to get out of this one?" Rosa chuckled. "A woman — in your bed."

"We just met." Cal hoped to sound casual. Unaffected. But it didn't matter. Rosa always saw through his bullshit. With those three simple words, he'd said too much. He knew Rosa had already seen the *too much* in the bedroom earlier. In his eyes. The vulnerability he mistook for weakness.

"Ah, yes." She smiled. "Yet she's in your bed. Why are you denying this?"

Cal had been attempting to deny what he'd seen in Annie the first time he spotted her on that staircase.

The photographer.

The artist.

The beautiful woman who'd dusted cobwebs from his heart.

Shit he'd been trying to avoid ever since he'd looked into her forest-green eyes. Damn her eyes. Why had he brought her here, to his home, knowing he would surely face an inquisition?

Because he had to have Annie.

Had to touch her, taste her, smell her. Had to fuck her in his own bed. Wake up beside her. Those were the reasons. The end.

"Oh…" Rosa sighed. "What are you doing, *mi querido*? You lie to yourself? You—"

"What am I doing?" he interrupted, sarcasm coating his tongue. A fake laugh followed.

Fuck.

He didn't even know.

How was that possible?

The man who always had a plan — his entire life made up of charts and graphs and tally marks — had no fucking clue what he was doing.

But he would pretend he had everything under control — including his emotions. That wasn't new. He was an expert at shielding and burying and moving forward.

Lines stretched across his forehead. Unyielding dissatisfaction colored his next words. "I'm getting through these next few months. Annie will be *here*. *In my bed*. That's all you need to know."

Rosa went toward the sink, and Cal went toward his room, but the moment he opened the door, he stopped, discerning the soft mutterings coming from a beloved old woman. Not old to him, though. Never.

"*Mentiras a él mismo. No a mí. Yo lo conozco. Mi muchacho ... tu has olvidado lo que es amar.*"

Cal couldn't make out everything she mumbled over the running water, only bits and pieces: a lie, a boy, and love.

NINETEEN

Palms pressed to the top of his dresser, Cal stood there a moment as though his body were an anchor dropping weight. Avoiding his face in the mirror, because he refused to see Rosa's truthful words light up his eyes like the pop from an old-time flashbulb.

A lie, she had said.

Sure.

Cal had been lying to himself for several years.

Maybe longer.

Morphing into the man he'd tried to avoid, the one he once told a lover he would never become. Cynical. Worn. Hiding behind a façade women loved. Searching for what he lacked had made him tired and weak.

Burned out and done.

Cal wished to deny himself the pleasure of thinking about his life and his plans, about his mother, about his endless bitter bullshit, but he was always thinking — even when drowning in drink or work or pussy.

Now, he was thinking of Annie, the girl who was never supposed to be part of this summer. Miami was meant to be a distraction. Annie would be a temporary distraction. A fling.

This was a fling.

Cal thought he knew what he was doing. He would have her, then push her away. Or she would leave him first. Either way, it was two months, right? Two fucking months. If it even lasted that long.

But Annie was different.

He'd noticed the first night.

The grip of her hand. The smell of her skin. The way she submitted to his subtle commands. How her green eyes read, studied, and pleaded with him to open. She had character, strength, the kind of earthy, gritty, toes-in-the-sand real he hadn't met in a long, long time.

Fuck.

Annie made his throat ache.

That couldn't be right — his throat would not ache, not for a twenty-five-year-old, dreamy, muddy photographer who would leave in two months to go God knew where.

So, he found himself standing at the mirror, questioning whether he actually did know what the fuck he was doing.

It had been a while since Cal had allowed himself to feel anything other than lust for a woman. Or pity. Or a desire to sate the loneliness. And he was conflicted. All he knew for sure was whether she was near or far, Cal ached for Annie in a way that seemed almost foreign to him. She awakened things within him he'd forgotten he could feel, and he didn't much like it.

Like the damn throat aching.

He wanted to ignore it. To pretend it was only about sex.

This *was* sex.

Nothing more. End of conversation. He would not be conflicted.

She was a fling.

She was the summer.

She was a beautiful distraction in his shower.

Cal became acutely aware of that distraction as he honed in on the sound of the running water while gazing at himself in the mirror.

Then a change occurred.

His eyes showing the force with which he buried his emotions.

Scrubbing his knuckles over his jaw, he continued to imagine the way the water must've looked as it fell over Annie's naked body. Over the curvature of her hips and the tiny birthmark on her upper thigh. He imagined the surrender in her eyes that he'd hung onto last night.

His pulse raced.

He was sure, confident he knew exactly what he was doing, and in this moment, Cal Prescott knew precisely what he wanted to do next.

TWENTY

"I'm almost done," Annie called out as she pushed water away from her face, her hands mimicking a proficient windshield wiper.

Cal put a palm into the stream. The tiny, wet droplets cascading down her neck made her body look like a graceful statue come to life in the rain.

"Didn't you shower last night?" Her eyes opened as she flung him with spray.

He stepped closer and wet his hair.

"You're infuriating," Annie huffed and turned to exit, but Cal reached for her hand, tugging on her fingers.

Stopping, she glanced over her shoulder, frustration fading. Every cell in her body flooding with a need only he could placate.

Annie filled with Cal's energy as if she hadn't had him last night. As if he hadn't fucked a million reasons into her, as if he hadn't denied and tortured her with the strokes of his tongue, the palm of his hand, with his lips and his cock.

The sound of the water became deafening as she waited for him to move or speak, the drops seeming to fall in slow motion. Finally, Cal inched her toward the wall. Annie's mind couldn't keep pace with the passion emanating from him, and before she knew what was happening, his fingers were inside her body.

Water bounced off their skin, splashing Annie's face as she turned her head to the side, closed her eyes, and moaned. Biting her lower lip, she pressed her palms against his chest and pushed. But he did not desist.

Cal's stance was intense, insistent.

She felt wet *and* dry.

She felt wet...

She slid a palm to his dick.

"No touching, Annie," Cal breathed against her neck. "Hands on the tile. If you try to touch me again, I'll pin your wrists. Do you understand?"

She nodded.

He removed his fingers. "Do you?"

"Yes ... *please.*"

Annie gasped when he shoved two back in. She swallowed water, nearly choking on it, as he found cushion, tapped and pressed until nothing mattered but his rhythm, the sensations. The way he drowned all her fears.

She pinched her eyes shut again and made sounds. Had she ever made so many noises? Incoherent mumblings, grunting. She couldn't really hear herself, though. Static played between her ears as Cal played between her thighs. Then without even thinking, she had done it again — she'd touched him. He felt divine.

After slapping her hand to the wall above her head, he removed his fingers and played with her breasts.

"Please," she begged while he licked one nipple, then the other, sucking them until they ached.

Annie reached between her legs to compensate for the loss. Once he noticed, he pinned that limb above her head too, grasping both wrists with a single hand, using the other to finger-fuck her again.

"God... Mmm... Please."

Slipping them out, he caressed her clit. "Please what?"

"Let me come. Please, not like last night."

"No more talking, Annie." He circled her bud, barely touching her skin, only rubbing her enough to cause a burn, not enough to light a fire.

Biting her lip, she closed her eyes and began to moan in earnest, the cries echoing across the bathroom. Three of his fingers now pushed inside, fucking her with abandon. Her hips joined the motion, her breasts bobbed, and if she chewed on her lip any more, it might bleed.

Then he slowed down. Way down.

Slipping his digits out, he rested them on her folds, massaging her there, before moving to her hole. Up and down, over and over.

Her chin dropped, and she watched. Both of them did. The ache to come was painful. The wetness over the whole of her body, wonderful. The nearness of his skin, electrifying.

Seconds later, two of his fingers plunged deep inside her warmth, and she pinched her eyes shut.

He fucked her.

God.

He fucked her.

So fast, so hard, she could feel it in her teeth.

Fuck... God, God, God...

She couldn't speak.

Couldn't beg.

Couldn't touch him.

She couldn't come.

Everything kept her there. The water, his hands, his demands. All in a safe place — a zone she allowed him to control. But then came an edict she didn't think she could follow.

"Look at me, Annie," he said with the same gruff determination with which he fondled her.

Annie opened her eyes, but she wouldn't meet his gaze. She shifted her head to the side. God. He was fucking crazy.

Looking at him now would be like running the length of an entire football field. Looking at him would be insane, and she was already insane with his fingers pulsing inside her, pressing, pressing, pressing.

Moaning, she closed her eyes and gyrated her hips against the wall while silently chanting — *he's crazy, crazy, crazy* — in beat to the massive finger-fucking taking place.

"Look at me," Cal repeated with heavy breath.

This time, Annie listened without thinking. Without hesitation. She opened her eyes. Found his gaze. In an instant, crossing the football field, reaching the goal, meeting him in the moment.

Piercing green and insistent like his fingers, Cal's eyes were so close to her skin, delving inside her, seeming to be concerned with only one thing: making her come. Annie heard the words he'd uttered from the night before on replay,

"*My plan is to make you come,*" hammering into her skull with the sharpest of nails.

She wanted to turn away but didn't.

She continued gazing and aching, everywhere aching until Cal released her wrists and slipped five of his fingers through hers, holding her palm against the tile while keeping his other digits busy inside her.

"Come for me, Annie."

She heard his delectable words as though in a dream, the way she had last night, as she watched his expression, his lips, his eyes. She stared at him forever. God, it was all too much.

Those eyes.

His face.

The drops of water.

His unwavering, dogged persistence.

She blinked and blinked as she began to rise.

"That's it," he groaned, pumping her, staring at her, never desisting. "Let me have it."

Millions of minuscule feelings rushed in, across the football field, pouring over Annie the way the water did, dripping, flashing, a life-before-death streak, millions of everything, all sorts of jumbled, mixed-up feelings, not just sexual ones, but feelings, oh-my-God-feelings, making her whimper, the whimpering turning to sobs, shivers, cold and wet, damp, then warm, wetter, warmer, and still, she looked at him, at the crushing weight of his gaze, his eyes pulling her forward, up and out of herself — she kept staring at him, heaving, suspended, transfixed...

Then it was coming. It was really coming. She was coming.

Her insides met a precipice. Her mind became quiet. Her eyes glossed. Her sounds became subdued. Her grip in his palm relaxed, her toes curling — always in the toes, always the toes curling, up, up, up, then ... releasing... Releasing and pulsing, throwing herself over the edge.

The aftershocks quaked all over his hand. He smiled subtly — the satisfaction mostly in his eyes, not his lips — then he slowly removed his fingers from her body, kissed her cheek, and slid his face toward her chest.

Annie remained against the wall, throbbing, narrowly breathing, watching as Cal stood tall and began to rinse off.

She stared at him.

Unable to speak.

Quiet because her throat was closing. Still pulsating with the most intense orgasm she'd ever experienced.

Annie began to tremble as he turned and exited, his cool-and-collected demeanor perfectly juxtaposed to her untamed, out-of-control quivering.

Turning, she faced the nozzle, stepped into the warm stream, and placed her forehead against the tile, letting her body go limp. Eyes wide, water dripping off her lids, thinking of the way he'd asked her to look at him, hearing his damn persistent voice in her head, then envisioning the way he'd walked away, exiting the shower with the same decisiveness with which his fingers had entered her body. Only now, she was left frustrated and alone.

No sound but the water, her eyes welled with tears. Full from the orgasm — full, full, full, oh-my-God full — and then, what? Empty? From his leaving? She was confused, wanting him, needing him — all of him.

The word *primal* took on a whole new meaning.

Crying, she released another something: the promise she'd seen reflected in his beautiful eyes. The tears and unspoken possibilities of their summer ran down her face, mixing with the shower droplets.

Annie couldn't tell where her tears began or ended. The water, along with the risk she'd taken in opening up her heart again, escaped together into one big puddle of confusion down the drain.

TWENTY-ONE

Cal finished buttoning his shirt, checking his face in the mirror, contemplating whether he should shave, when Annie joined him at the double sinks.

She unzipped her backpack, not even glancing in his direction.

He looked at Annie, though. Studied her reflection as she took her undergarments out of the bag. As she removed the towel and began to put on her bra and panties. He also tried to focus on combing his wet hair.

Annie concentrated on dressing, ignoring the way Cal's eyes frisked her. The confusion she'd wished to wash away clung to her skin, her face, her psyche.

She couldn't hide.

She thought she could let go of her big-girl ideas about what sex with Cal should be like — what sex with a virtual stranger should be like — but she couldn't.

The heart ... the sleeve... They took over.

Was this a fling?

Raw, vivid, amazing sex.

Was this the way it felt to just screw?

She'd loved, or believed she'd loved, and no one — *no one* — had ever made her feel like that with a mere look.

"How do you do it?" she finally asked, stretching forward, her palms on the vanity as she glared at him.

Cal leaned his ass against the counter and stared into her eyes, attempting to avoid the way her tits filled out her lacy peach bra.

"Do what?" That dapper, dubious, irresistible grin smacked his face.

Annie wanted to slap it right off him.

"Separate yourself"—she took the comb he'd set aside and pointed it toward the shower—"from what happened in there?"

Cal stood tall, came closer, and tucked some fingers under her bra strap. "What happened in there, Annie?" He tugged the nylon.

She thought about what had, indeed, happened. Except she didn't have to actually think about it. She hadn't been able to stop thinking about it — the mad rush of feelings, the insanity, the insisting.

His eyes.

It was all over her again in a flash, zipping through her, spreading out of control. Her throat became tight. Her eyes welled with tears. She attempted to focus on Cal, but he was a blurry haze. The hold he had was more than his actual hand tugging at her bra strap.

Cal held her.

He tugged her.

She was his for the taking.

But she wouldn't let him see her cry. She straightened and tried out her own dominant voice. "You. Tell. Me."

"I think"—he let go of her strap, enjoying the sound it made as it struck her skin—"I finger-fucked you to orgasm. *I think* ... you came. Hard. On my hand."

And now, she might come again.

Smiling despite herself, she tilted her head toward the floor and tried to hide her amusement, then she pushed against his chest.

"Annie..." He lifted her palms and kissed them. "Everything we do together doesn't have to be held under a microscope."

No. No. Of course not, she thought. That was the way he wanted it. But she'd already seen him through the lens of a microscope. From the moment they'd first met.

She was looking through a microscope now.

The effect he had on her, the way she felt in his presence, had nothing to do with the orgasm.

God, her orgasm.

He surely must've seen in her eyes, in that moment, all she felt. It was more than the force with which he touched her. He'd looked into her eyes as she came like *he was* looking through a microscope, studying her, examining her, giving her a place to safely release her fears.

Or helping her come to know parts of herself she'd abandoned.

Annie turned, sighed, and dug a white sundress out of her bag. While slipping it on, she began to wonder what in the hell he was actually thinking...

Cal was thinking he didn't need to have this conversation. He didn't want to have it. He had wanted her, had her, and he would have her again. And again and again. He was ignoring her aggravation in order to avoid his own. He would distract the distraction. He would show the girl who had only been fucked by two young men *fun*.

"I have to get some work done today." He leaned against the counter again, arms folded, biceps outlined to perfection in the white, collared shirt he sported.

Annie collected her thoughts and tried to switch gears. The conversation she wanted to have was apparently over. She put her semi-wet hair up in a clip, then dotted balm across her lips with a pinky. "Should I still stay for breakfast?"

"Yes."

She pressed her lips together, tossed the tube in the bag, and zipped up the backpack.

"Rosa probably has it ready." He grinned. "I wouldn't doubt she's out there right now cursing me for not coming out sooner."

"Then I will stay and meet Rosa."

"Good." He grabbed her hand and tugged, starting to lead her out of the bathroom.

Annie squeezed his fingers and came to a stop. "What about you?" She stepped forward, wrapped her arms around his waist, and ran her palms over his ass. "Don't you want to come?" She glanced up at his chin and kissed it.

"It doesn't work like that."

Of course it worked like that. In fact, it usually worked quite the opposite — Annie being the giver without receiving.

Cal pulled his head back and smirked. "And you're not ready for what I have in mind."

Annie started to cough, which only caused Cal to laugh. She slapped his chest. "Do you always get off on ... on...?"

"Subjugation," he said, still laughing.

"Mmm. Nice, Prescott."

"I don't define what I do in the bedroom, Annie." He'd also never wanted to push a woman's boundaries so hard and so fast.

What he wanted either happened or didn't.

Or perhaps that was a lie too.

She listened naturally, though, naked or clothed. He forgot himself with her. Found he wanted things from her he hadn't often asked of other women. Because she would give them to him. Not out of pity or spite or obligation or even love, but because she needed what he offered as much as he needed to provide it.

"You defined the shower pretty well." She waggled an eyebrow. Maybe she didn't need to label or define what they did either.

She liked it. All of it.

The biting, the bruising, the spanking, the hair pulling, the denial of her orgasm, the commands.

Annie would trust him.

She did.

At least with her body.

Could she trust him with her heart, though? Could she handle what he had in mind?

Jesus. What did he have in mind?

Surely this.

She attempted to unbuckle him, but he laid a hand on her wrist, stopping her.

"What?" she asked.

Cal cupped her face. "I said not today."

Annie had already given him what he'd wanted the moment he'd stepped foot into the shower.

Cal wanted her to be satisfied in ways she never had been. He wanted to behold her face and stare deep into her eyes as she came. He needed her responsiveness, her willingness — her subjugation.

Needed? he thought.

That was bullshit. Women didn't need him. Therefore, he refused to need women. What had changed, then?

A dreamer named Annie...

"You already gave me what I wanted this morning," Cal said, his voice tender, his eyes wide.

The tone reminded Annie of the way he'd spoken to her the first night she'd met him. Not on the back porch in the moonlight, but when standing outside Maggie's front door before taking his leave. It held a soft reassurance. A solace. Telling her things he wouldn't articulate. Who he was inside.

It held a promise.

The need she had to tear his pants off and put her mouth on him took second place to the loving glow in his gaze, and she basked in it.

Cal glanced down at her décolletage, then back into her eyes.

Despite his denial, his pact, his lie, his throat ached at her beauty — the beauty he saw deep within her — always. The beauty he'd seen in the shower, against the wall, his fingers inside her warmth, her body pulsating against him, taking his pulse, keeping his heart beating, making him come alive.

Did he believe in that shit?

Anymore?

Ever?

What did he believe in?

Her lips. Her pouty, sexy-as-fuck lips.

Cal kissed them.

Then he took her hand and led her out of the bedroom, both of them quiet, both awake.

Both awakened.

TWENTY-TWO

"Oh," Rosa exclaimed, patting her chest and chuckling as she stepped off a small wooden stool, the cross around her neck swinging a little as she went. "You two startled me."

Annie found she was a bit startled too.

The mysterious woman standing in Cal's kitchen had taut cheeks, comely age lines across her forehead, and a few beautiful wrinkles resting in that little hollow in her neck. Yet ... her age seemed hard to define. She appeared to be about sixty-five. Petite, a couple inches shorter than Annie, she had cropped, dark hair, chunky curls she'd tucked and pinned.

She would photograph like a dream.

"That's two heart attacks today, *mi hijo*." Rosa raised two fingers in the shape of a V and eyeballed Cal. "Two."

He took note of Rosa as well, not her words but her eyes: black as night, loud and clear, reprimanding him yet holding concern and a twinge of hurt.

"I didn't know if you two were ever going to come out of that room." Rosa winked.

Annie blushed.

"This is Rosa, Annie," Cal said, stuffing aside the regret he felt over his abrasive attitude from earlier. "And this is Annie," he continued as he started to laugh. "The *company* in my bed."

"Hi." Annie extended a hand.

"He's *muy travieso*." Rosa's onyx eyes danced as she gave Annie's palm a firm squeeze. "Very bad."

"Yes. He is." Annie eyeballed him.

Rosa pointed at the table and shook her arm. "Sit. Sit. I've had breakfast waiting." She hustled over to the stove.

The two of them promptly obeyed.

"Do you always spoil him like this?" Annie teased while fiddling with the silverware. She sat on Cal's right.

"You both keep talking about me like I'm not in the room," he grumbled.

"Shush, Calvin," Rosa replied, and Annie whipped her head toward him, peering deliciously at ... Calvin.

He peered back, his gaze intuiting, *Don't you dare*. But Annie would, just not right now...

"Oh, yes," Rosa answered. "He's spoiled, Annie, but he's worth the trouble."

"I'm not so sure." Annie smirked, tapping Cal's shin with her bare foot.

Rosa laughed. Cal slipped on a pair of eyeglasses and spread open the front page of the newspaper as Rosa placed two plates in front of them full of scrambled eggs, sautéed potatoes, onions, peppers, mushrooms, and freshly grated white cheddar cheese.

"God, that looks good." The bottom of Annie's feet caressed the cool floor. "Can I help you with anything?"

"No, *mi querida*. You relax." Rosa glanced at Cal. His eyes were on the ink. "Enjoy your morning."

"Did you eat?"

Rosa grabbed a plate of toast. "I eat very early." She set it in the center of the table.

"Do we have any other preserves?" Cal asked.

"I'll look." Annie stood.

"If we do, they would be on the door. He likes orange marmalade. I think we're out."

Annie scanned the fridge. "I don't see any."

"No, no, we must be out."

As Annie returned to her seat, Rosa nodded toward Cal. "Don't mind him, Annie ... with this paper. He has to do this. It's like a ritual."

Annie smiled. She wanted to learn his rituals. And silence could be good. His quiet was comfortable, not awkward.

"Do you drink coffee?" Rosa asked.

"Sometimes." Annie buttered a piece of toast.

"Would you like a cup? This one," she said, pointing her head toward Cal, "doesn't drink it."

Annie looked over the kitchen. "Do you have a press?"

Cal lowered the newspaper. It still concealed his lips but not his eyes. The green missiles were astute over its top, attacking her senses. Bolder and brighter through his lenses, and they teased her mercilessly.

"No, Annie." Rosa chuckled. "It's only a regular old coffee pot. One I picked up when we moved. No Keurig. No press."

Mouth full of buttery strawberry toast, Annie replied, "I might grab a coffee in a little while when I go out."

"Will it be from a *press*?" Cal asked.

Annie shoved her foot against his shin again, her cheeks turning the color of the jam.

"Where are you two going?" Rosa called out as she began to wash dishes.

Annie eyed Cal, but his mouth was full. "It's me. I'm going out ... by myself. I'm going to take some photographs. Cal has work."

Rosa turned, wiped her hands on her apron, and looked at them.

"Annie's a photographer," Cal said.

"This is your job?" Rosa asked.

"Yes."

Annie didn't know why the title hadn't completely sunk in. Despite the four years of college, her accomplishments, the congratulations, despite knowing in her heart she was an artist and always would be.

"I would like to see your work someday," Rosa said, coming closer and inspecting the table, checking each detail with the care of a craftsman.

"Speaking of work..." Rosa turned her attention to Cal. "Why are you working and not spending the day with this young lady? It's beautiful out."

Cal glanced at Annie. "I'm going to London on Monday." He turned back to Rosa. "I have to work today or I won't be ready."

Annie's gaze fell to her plate. She stared at the food, shoveling the eggs around. Her toe knuckles curled into the floor, and she began to twirl a few locks of hair that had resisted the clip with her free hand.

"You didn't tell me you were leaving," Rosa said.

"I found out it was definite yesterday."

"How long will you be gone?" Rosa asked.

"Almost a week. I'll be back Saturday." Cal smoothed a finger down the strands of hair Annie twined until she loosened her grip and dropped them.

Rosa mumbled under her breath in Spanish as she went back to the sink and turned on the faucet. Cal raised the front page and continued to eat.

Annie liked observing the side of his face as he read. His strong jawline. The solid sequoia tree. She loved the way his eyes looked through the lenses of his glasses. Somehow greener, brighter. More intense. She sighed, grabbed a section of the newspaper, and stuck a fork in her eggs. Wondering if she would see him again.

After breakfast, Annie collected her things then exited the bedroom, her damp hair now out of the clip and combed as she hoisted the strap of her bag over her shoulder. Cal hadn't moved from the table. Or stopped reading. His back was to her.

Rosa was about to clear away his plate when she noticed Annie. "You're leaving?"

"Yes," Annie replied, but the de Kooning print hanging nearby gave her pause. An abstract she'd recently seen in person at a museum. The name of the painting had stayed with her: *Garden in Delft*.

Rosa joined Annie. "We're lucky he brought these when he moved." Her eyes darted around the house. "I was surprised he packed them. But these few..."

Cal snapped the paper open, and the timing of the interruption did not feel like a coincidence. Rosa smiled, but it failed to reach her eyes.

Annie stole a glance at Cal over her shoulder, then Rosa patted Annie's arm and said, "I like you."

"I like you too." Annie smiled, giving Rosa a little squeeze around the waist. "You know"—she directed her attention back to the print, carefully going over de Kooning's brushstrokes—"he continued to paint even with Alzheimer's."

"Yes," Rosa stuttered, cleared her throat, and looked at Cal. Well, at the back of his head.

Annie followed the motion. Something in his posture had changed. Shifted. The paper was still in his hands, but it had become a prop to conceal his thoughts, to hide his intentions.

Or maybe that had been its purpose all along.

Rosa sighed. "I have things to do today as well." She smiled, the skin around her eyes crinkling "*Eres bella.*"

The moment Rosa disappeared, Annie stepped behind Cal's chair, rested her forearms over his shoulders, and let her fingers slide down his chest.

Had he heard every word of their conversation?

She bet he'd even understood the Spanish. She was the one who would have to brush up on it, and she would, because when Rosa had uttered those last two words, Cal had flinched.

Annie ran her nose along his neck. "I'm leaving." She nibbled his ear.

He took one of her hands, held it, and shifted his head to the side. Her hair dangled down the front of his body. Removing his glasses, he set them aside with the newspaper and stood. Stretching his arms, Cal looked at Annie, but didn't speak.

The quiet man.

The regal, understated man.

Annie smiled, shook her head, and made her way to the foyer. Cal followed. He stood near the closed front door, one hand in his pocket, the other on the handle.

Annie moved a piece of hair away from her lips and stared at him. This felt like the first time. On Maggie's staircase. All. Over. Again.

He merely stood there, making no attempt to embrace or kiss her.

Nothing.

And that was all that was required.

Affecting her without words or movement. Nothing.

Yet, his *nothing* was like that de Kooning painting. Seemingly calm, neutral, squiggles and lines, odd shapes. However, if you stared at it long enough, or maybe even only for a few minutes, the shapes and colors would strangle you until the emotions it sparked couldn't even be defined. The creation taking over the observer, all while being still, motionless, beautiful.

The way Cal Prescott took over a room.

He mystified Annie.

Captivated her.

Enchanted her.

He was a constant contradiction.

A chameleon.

Being with him distracted her from the anxiety she'd come to rely upon.

The obsessive thoughts that had helped her cope since the funeral ... or maybe they'd only served to slow her down.

The way Cal made her feel terrified her. The very things that turned her on the most about him were the same that practically paralyzed her. Annie didn't fear Cal. She wasn't afraid of him. She was afraid of her own feelings.

"What are you afraid of, Annie?" Cal had asked the night of the gala.

What is it? Right now. Define it. While he stands here staring at you.

I'm afraid I really like him.

I do.

I'm afraid of people telling me I shouldn't really like him, not only the people who know me but strangers.

I'm afraid people don't see him the way I do.

Rosa does.

I'm afraid of failing. My parents ... the gallery.

I'm afraid of the end of summer. When this is all over. Not only him but me.

I'm afraid of settling for a life my mother picked out of a catalog — the way she shops for things.

I'm afraid of walking out this door and forgetting how every nerve ending in my body comes alive in his presence.

The dark side of the moon existed beyond the other side of his front door. Annie had sheltered herself after her brother died, had forgotten what it was to feel. Or maybe she had never known. Cal had been coaxing her out of a self-induced coma.

There was something between the two of them, though.

Did Cal even realize how dead she'd been? What a waste of a year. Alive but dead.

She stared into Cal's possessed green eyes, knowing without a doubt she'd never experienced the kind of alive she felt right now. She came alive when taking photographs, when hunting the subject, when craning herself into the strangest of positions to get a shot, but this kind of alive was apples to oranges in comparison.

This was different.

When Cal looked at her the way he was right now, the way he had in the shower, on the porch, the way he'd looked at her photographs on the wall at the gallery, it was incredible, euphoric, addicting.

It made her throat swell.

She touched Cal's face.

The flecks in his eyes glistened with a hope she'd gotten used to replacing with manufactured sunshine.

She kissed his cheek.

No more thinking. Please. Shhh. Quiet.

She held her face near his for a moment. The magnets in their skin twisted and pulled. Then she inched back and looked into his eyes.

He matched her gaze.

They matched. He was a match.

Even though he still avoided embracing her, she could feel his calculated restraint. Everything he needed to say, he communicated through those flecks of hope and his one-of-a-kind posture.

Her hand slid from his face. Cal opened the front door. Rays of sunlight burst in a pattern of lines across their faces, bodies, and the floor. The humidity closed around them like a fist.

"It's going to get expensive," he said, and despite the heat, a chill ran through her, head to foot. "Coming here."

"First, you withhold orgasm. Now, you want to charge me to come?"

"You're a naughty girl." He leaned toward her mouth.

"No kisses." She beamed, inching away from him, that feisty smile lighting her eyes and curving her lips. "Kiss me and I'll have to have you ... right here, right now."

"I hope you liked the spanking, Annie, because it's all I can think of doing to you when you run that clever little mouth."

Annie grinned wider.

"Text me when you're done gallivanting around." Cal made a gesture. "I'll have Carl drive you back."

"Come with me. Bad choice of words," she quipped, and Cal laughed. "Hang out with me today."

"I've got a whole shit list to do." He paused. "Tomorrow..."

"Tomorrow, what?" she asked, a hand on her hip, eyes wide and curious.

"I'm picking you up."

Annie stared at him. He didn't blink. Didn't flinch. Tall, aloof — the most infuriating thing on planet Earth — scratch that, the universe. "Maybe I have plans..."

"Be ready at eight."

"In the morning?" She gawked up at him.

"Yes, for fuck's sake. You can get up early. Set an alarm. You do know what that is?"

She shoved his arm. "Where are we going?"

He smiled. "It's a surprise."

"What should I bring?"

"A bathing suit. A change of clothes."

Annie grinned. "Eight."

"Eight." Cal leaned against the doorframe, squinting from the bright sun, and watched her leave, until he could no longer even make out the faint outline of her beauty.

SENSE

A KEEN INTUITIVENESS OR AWARENESS

a whiskey neat
a special rapport
a different beach
a sequoia tree to explore

capture me
frame me
remember me

I will extend patience to you
I will not ask for favors

Twenty-Three

The dark side of the moon on the other side of Cal's door turned out to be the sun. Eighty-nine degrees of it, but the humidity made it feel even hotter. The nape of Annie's neck, her thighs, were already slick with a fine film of sweat as she trotted due east, backpack and camera in tow.

After putting her hair into a ponytail, she stopped for a bit on Collins to shoot people, hotels, shops, and one particularly huge mural covering the side wall of a boutique. The two-dimensional painting stretched from ground to roof, showcasing huge heads with razor-etched lines drawn on faces and fists, and a man with a car driving into his mouth.

Or was it out?

Other cars, real ones, created traffic, reminding her of another city. New York. Vehicles merged and blended into lanes, made illegal turns, and honked horns. Pedestrians moved along, passing her, some in a hurry, others strolling. Tourists sat outside on the verandas of hotels and cafes. The sidewalks hummed a loud but pretty song.

Interestingly, Cal had chosen to live blocks from the melody, the madness and hustle and bustle. A rather private, guarded man immersing himself in an energy that, at first glance, might seem diametric to his own.

A place he pretended to tolerate.

Whatever. He liked it. She did.

Trekking another block east, the architecture on Ocean Drive met the heavens in Annie's lens, each building unique and independent. The majestic tops of the structural works of art kissed the bright-blue sky in pure brilliance, framing her photographs and coloring her whimsy.

Lummus Park, the place where Cal (and probably hundreds of others) jogged, was across the street. Annie made her way over, past a bike rental kiosk and a couple workout stations, stopping briefly to shoot several palm trees and women in bikinis. After following the narrow path connecting the park to the sand, she came upon people, umbrellas, chairs, litter. Children building sand-castles and dreams. Engines of WaveRunners, music, and chatter filled the air as did the smell of weed.

The sun was bright. Barely any clouds were out. Without a hat or lotion, she couldn't stay long. Or she might burn. Still, she craved the warmth the way she did Cal's certainty.

The heat was like a blanket, relaxing her from the inside out, whisking her away from the intrusive thoughts often occupying her mind and into the wonderful *other* pleasure she couldn't get enough of.

The nonsexual, sensual variety.

The ecstasy she'd texted Cal about after drowning the roses.

The high she wanted to ride indefinitely.

These were the reasons she'd become a photographer in the first place. And maybe that was why the title didn't seem like a job. Or a title.

It wasn't a job — not a traditional one. Photographer was a synonym for daydreamer as far as Annie was concerned. A perfect fit for her personality.

The camera had chosen her.

Actually, no one in South Beach had a job. Or cared about their job. Not in this moment anyway. Work meant lifting a drink, applying sunscreen, or tossing a ball. People were here to forget their daily stresses. The ocean carried their troubles away. The sun melted it off their faces. The beach was a perma-nent vacation — an oasis. No sorrow could enter its realm. Here, there was an unspoken mantra everyone seemed to follow.

Sun. Surf. Play. Swim.

Perhaps Annie could follow it too. Maybe listening to the sounds of laugh-ter, crowds, waves, wind, and music would usurp the *I'm okay, I'm okay, I'm okay*. The *everything's fine, fine, fine*.

The undertow took the repetitions and chucked them into the deep end of the ocean. She didn't give a fuck about *fine*. Not right now, anyway. She cared about taking pictures. After snapping probably hundreds, Annie felt the blistering heat on her face and shoulders. Her nose had probably already burned.

Her eyes widened as she noted the time on her cell phone. Two hours had passed since she'd left the chameleon's apartment. She quickly arranged a ride, and several minutes later, she plopped into the back of a car, dropping her head against the cushion while twining strands of hair through her fingers. Then her phone pinged.

Cal: Did you make it back yet?

She grinned and began to type with her index finger.

Annie: Shit! I forgot to text you about the ride.

She added a sad-face emoji, then sent another message.

Annie: Heading home now. I got some awesome pics.

Clutching the phone to her chest, her stomach began to churn. He wrote back in an instant.

Cal: I close my eyes and I can taste you.

The insane pile of feelings she'd managed to set aside while *gallivanting around* rushed toward her shore like a tidal wave. And to top it off, he was typing again. The ellipsis flashed. She waited, trying not to writhe her sticky, sweaty thighs against the seat.

Cal: I wish I'd put my tongue on you again so I could have your scent on my skin all day long.

The tidal wave crashed.

She burned.

Scrunching lower, phone in both hands, a gigantic smirk cresting her cheeks, the dull ache returned — the one needing release. God, there was an orange between her legs, ready to burst.

Annie: Jesus, Cal. I'm in the car.

Cal: Do you want to touch yourself?

Annie: You're so bad. Aren't you working?

Cal: Do you?

How was it she could hear the sexy sound of his voice in the plain, little words of a text? And she didn't want *her* hands. She wanted his.

Annie: I want you.

Cal: I'll text you again tonight. No cheating.

Annie: What?

Cal: No fingers on yourself until I tell you to put them there.

Annie: Where?

She grinned, then stuck a thumbnail between her teeth.

Cal: I'm trying to work.

Annie: Fuck off.

Cal: There'll be plenty of that later.

Annie stashed the phone, but her smile remained. A range of emotions rolled across the sky of her eyes as she looked at the sights whizzing by, watching the cars and trees reflect off the glass.

First emotion: elation.

The stage curtain opened. A twinkle lit her eyes, a glow, as she thought about all the ways Cal had put his mouth on her body — on her lips, her neck, her pussy, her nipples — the look she'd seen in his eyes as he gave her what she needed. The way he knew without her asking or telling — no guessing, only knowing.

Second emotion: surprise.

Her pupils dilated. Her stomach rose on its tippy-toes and did a dance. The roses. The Yakima wine. The paintings on his walls that were not happenstance.

Third emotion: excitement.

The kiss in the rain. The tabletop. The underwear on the floor. The shower. The heady *look at me, look at me*. All a carnival ride of unexpected proportions.

Fourth emotion: confusion.

Eyes flickering the way they might while watching an Alfred Hitchcock picture, back and forth, teetering on the edge of her seat in suspense. Her give. His take. The mental biting back. The guarding of hearts. The Great Wall of China. The hurt of hundreds of somethings he didn't seem to want to talk about. The way they came out of his eyes but not his mouth.

She put her thumbnail between her teeth again. A few wispy strands of hair were stuck in a loop around her index finger. Closing her eyes, she disallowed the choke she began to feel rising in her chest.

What did she want from Cal? He couldn't provide her what she needed. Could he? Could any man, really? How far would an archaic spanking go? A toe-bending orgasm? Another text message sure to wet her panties before bed?

She wanted more.

And she needed it the way she needed everything.

TWENTY-FOUR

"Is that you, Annie?" a voice called from the other end of the house as she entered the Allens' home and closed the front door.

"It's me." She rounded the corner to the kitchen.

"Make me a drink, will ya, kiddo?" John said from where he sat in the den. "Make yourself one. Yeah? Then come and talk to me."

"The usual?" She dropped her bag on a chair.

"Yes, darlin'."

After stepping into the enclave, Annie gave John a hug and retrieved his empty glass.

"You've been out in this heat?"

"Do I stink?" She lifted an armpit to her nose and sniffed. "I was at the beach."

"You smell like the ocean."

I smell like Cal, then... Annie thought.

And John, he smelled like the drink. She loved his accent, though. If liquor made it more pronounced, she would gladly refill his glass. She didn't mind. Even if it was only lunchtime. At least he wasn't like her mother. God, no one was like her mother.

Beverly Saint.

Bev.

Pixie dust reversed.

When her mother drank, she became unkind, belligerent and nasty disguised with concern.

John became sweet, sweeter, like fine wine. And Maggie ... well, that remained to be seen. Annie couldn't recall a time she'd seen Maggie buzzed. Probably because Maggie had been conscious of the bad example Annie's mother had set. No matter. Beverly drank enough for several people — a village. It was a luxury her liver continued to function. Or maybe she'd quit again.

Doubtful.

The woman had gotten plastered at the dinner celebration after Annie's graduation, embarrassing the photographer in front of her friends. Beverly loved any excuse to be sharp-tongued, and she never could hide a binge. Weren't the best alcoholics supposed to be able to conceal their stupors?

She's not your responsibility anymore. She never should've been. She's fine. Fine, fine, fine.

Two Jamesons on ice now poured, Annie made her way back to the den.

"You're sunburned, kiddo."

Annie rolled her eyes and took a seat next to John. "I know." She placed a palm on her nape. "I shouldn't be drinking either. I haven't eaten lunch. Do you think the alcohol will cure the burn?"

John chuckled. "Maggie will fix you somethin'."

"Where is she?"

"Out back ... in the garden." John swirled the ice in his glass with a finger. "I think."

"I don't want her to wait on me."

"You know she likes that kinda thing."

"Well, I think I can manage lunch."

"You do like to do everythin' on your own. You won't even use a car for your dates."

"I use the cars."

"You go shoppin'. Maggie won't bite, you know?"

Annie wondered if they were even talking about the same woman. "It's leverage."

John laughed. The loud, adorable Big Bad Wolf ha!

"It's true. I use the car to go to Cal's, and she'll think she can play twenty questions."

"How about my questions?" He sat forward, arched a brow, and took a swallow, suddenly seeming stone-cold sober.

"Oh, yeah." Annie grinned. "What'cha got? Maggie's already put me through about all I can handle."

"I don't know about that. You're a tough cookie." He paused, peering at her the way he often did. With that paternal look churning in his blue-gray eyes. That belief he always had in her.

"I'm simple," he went on, clearing his throat. "We want Cal to come for dinner Saturday, and ... well, Maggie thinks..." He chuckled. "She wants—"

"Me to ask him."

"Right."

"Why?"

"Trust me," he said and chuckled again.

Annie didn't understand what was so amusing about asking Cal to dinner.

"I trust you." She peered at John. "But do you trust *him*?"

"Cal?" He nodded. "Yes."

"Why is he here, John?" Annie tasted her foot in her mouth as she fondled wisps of hair between her fingers. "In Miami?"

"We decided to form a partnership. I've been askin' him for years. He doesn't talk much about work?"

"He doesn't *talk*. Not about himself, anyway."

John grinned. "No. No. He's a thinker. An observer. Be patient, Annie. He could use it. Believe me."

Believe me. Who could she believe? Maggie telling her *it's only one summer ... I don't want to see you get hurt.*

Annie knew how to bottle hurt.

John telling her to be patient, insisting she was a *tough cookie.*

She was strong.

Her father telling her she was beautiful, that the photographs were beautiful.

The photographs stood on their own.

Her mother insisting she move home, manipulating Annie until a rotten mixture of both duty and empathy formed.

Fuck Beverly.

Or Cal... The chameleon who drove wild abandon into her core with a look, a touch, with seemingly innocent questions:

Is the woman who captured that unsure? You're saying you don't know what you want?

Annie thought she knew what she wanted.

She did.

Only, recently she'd been riding the passive escalator to get there. At least it was heading up.

I want...

I want to breathe in and out without reminding myself to catch my breath. I want to wake from sleep and not feel like I've entered a perpetual nightmare, a world where Peter no longer exists. I want to travel and take pictures until time has no meaning.

The camera had been the only thing in her immediate focus until a certain mysterious man named Cal Prescott stepped in front of her lens.

Believe me, John had said. A whole list of other commands ran through her head...

Be patient.

Snap out of your daydream.

Mingle.

Get on top of social media.

Send me a picture.

Look at your photograph.

Move home.

Take the car.

Don't get hurt.

Enjoy your summer.

The only commands she wanted to hear were Cal's.

Listening to him wasn't a chore. It wasn't responsibility. Or powerlessness. It wasn't fear or weakness. Capitulating to him was like giving him something she desperately needed someone to hold. Except he took the burden and didn't give it back. And once she released the thing — the thing, the thing, all the fucking things — her worries, her doubts, her anxieties ... when she gave them all to his possession...

She found something few understood:

Me.

TWENTY-FIVE

Annie switched off the lamp and closed the app she been scrolling, not realizing how tired she felt until her eyes finally closed. Right as she began to hit that perfect moment, the lull right before sleep, she heard a sound.

Ignoring it, she continued drifting toward nirvana. But a second or two later, it buzzed again. Semiconscious, she reached out from under the covers and grabbed at the annoyance, blinking repeatedly at the message.

Cal: Are you in bed?

Annie: I'm asleep.

Cal: Do you want me to fuck off?

Too drowsy to completely engage, brain not quite alert, she typed out a blurry-eyed reply.

Annie: No.

Cal: Slide your hand down the front of your panties.

Fully conscious now, a sudden flare of heat pooled in her stomach and groin.

Annie: I'm not wearing any.

Cal: Did you touch yourself before I texted?

Annie: No!

Cal: Call me. Now. I want to hear you come.

Annie: I'm not alone here, remember?

Her phone buzzed, not with a text but a call. She swiped the screen.

"One hand is on the phone. Where's the other?" he asked before she could bother with hello.

"On my belly."

"That's no good." He paused, and the silence ate her alive. "Is that where I want your hand?"

"No."

"Where do I want it?"

"Lower."

"Where?"

"On my pussy." Her breath caught.

"Is it there now?"

She answered with a broken and elongated, "Ahhh."

Cal laughed. "Are you wet?"

"Yes."

"Slide a finger up and down your slit. Keep doing it." He paused. "Let me hear you."

Shallow breaths poured into the phone. Hers.

"Two fingers in. Right now."

"Mmm..." She squeaked and moaned.

"Is it good? Does your pussy feel good, Annie?"

"God. Yes," she spluttered. "Fuck..."

"Pull them out."

Annie froze, then whispered, "No..."

"Do it. Put them in your mouth."

The sound of two digits being swallowed and sucked assaulted the phone.

"That's what I taste. It's what I want. On my lips. My mouth. My tongue."

She whimpered. "I want you." Her stomach did a million somersaults. "Please..." She turned inside out.

"Put them back inside your cunt." His voice turned to heat and gravel. Power and need. "It's me fucking you. Do you understand?"

"Yes." Grunting, hips rocking, eyes closed, she imagined her two fingers were his hard cock slamming into the mouth of her pussy and then hitting the entrance of her womb. Until she cried. That was correct — cried.

She bit back the tears by twisting her bottom lip between her teeth until it practically bruised.

"Come, Annie. Fucking come."

Ecstatic stutters escaped, one by one. Ripped stutters. Held-back sobs. She lifted her hips in midair as the orgasm flew from her body like a slingshot, pulling back, then — whoosh! — gone.

Her ass dropped onto the bed, followed by a burst from her lungs. It was so loud, she was quite sure John and Maggie might've heard. As she slapped a hand over her mouth, the phone fell. She giggled while fumbling for the stupid thing.

"Feel better?"

"Much." She laughed and laughed. "I've never done that on the phone."

"There will be lots of firsts for you this summer."

"What about your firsts?" she asked. "What do you want?" The laughter in her voice died down.

The phone went silent.

Eerily silent.

Thank God she couldn't hear his thoughts...

Cal wanted a healthy mother.

He wanted a woman who took him at face value.

He longed for a moment of peace in the mirror.

He wanted what he'd started searching for at the age of twenty-one.

The water. The ocean.

Cal wanted ... to read.

"Good night, Annie. Be ready at eight." He hung up, opened a book, and read until his eyes were so tired, they ached.

SPIN

A DOWNWARD SPIRAL; A STATE OF MENTAL
CONFUSION; TO PLACE RECORDS ON A
TURNTABLE

what I thought I knew
I have no clue
what I assumed
I understood
blurred
solid lines
became dotted
then those turned to sludge
paste
swirls of white and gray
something that could be erased
by rain

music showed up
in the form of a bright orange life ring
amidst the puddles of floods on the street of my grief
I wrapped my arms around it
and held on

apply pressure

I resist
come hither, come hither
I whisper
crawling on my knees
the candle burns at both ends

TWENTY-SIX

Annie entered Cal's apartment and stretched her arms, forming a bendy lowercase T. She set her tote on the desk, slipped off her sandals and sunglasses, and scrubbed her fingers through her oily hair, careful not to disturb the flower Cal had placed over her ear earlier while visiting Key Largo, the first key in a string at the bottom of the state.

"I have to return a couple messages," he said, then kissed her cheek. "Wait for me upstairs." Cal tossed his keys on the desk and pushed off his boat shoes. "Do you want a glass of wine or anything?"

"I'll take a water." God, he looked handsome. Glowing, tanned skin, especially on his face. The shimmer highlighted the sugar strands of his hair and made his green eyes pop. "Thanks."

"Go on." He grinned, nodding toward the loft.

Annie trotted up the stairs, landing in a comfy, inviting space that looked out over the living area and kitchen and also had a great view of the front courtyard. Strolling over to the wide window, she gazed at the branches and trees and leaves and limbs covering the street.

His street. *Cal Avenue.*

Even though the sun had mostly faded, a hint of natural light still found its way into the otherwise dark room. A few minutes later, Cal illuminated the room.

Still sporting his swim trunks and shirt, the top couple buttons of the latter undone, he switched on a lamp, then set two glass bottles on the coffee table.

"You're not drinking either?" She eyed the Perrier.

"I'm drinking water."

Annie rolled her eyes, tore one of the caps off, and took a sip.

"I am your designated driver, my lady." He smirked.

Annie smiled, watching as he disappeared behind the futon. Only the top of his head remained visible over the rear. "What are you doing back there?"

"You'll see."

Several seconds later, after she'd finished about half the mineral water, familiar sounds caught her attention: a needle dropping, the crackle as it hit the dust and imperfections. The static.

Her eyes widened. She set the bottle down as Cal stood.

An old song began with a bang, and Annie wasted no time bouncing her hips to the horns, the piano, the steady beat. But it was the singer who made the tune. A gravelly, throaty voice, also familiar, clung to the walls of her chest the way the lens of her camera hugged its subjects.

She danced toward Cal. He had taken a seat on the futon, one of his ankles resting over a knee, watching her.

Not just looking at her but eating her alive.

Staring.

He cracked a smile.

Annie reached for Cal's hands and tried to pull him up, but he was reluctant, only scooting to the edge of the cushion. As he placed his palms on her waist, she swayed inches from him, cradling his face while he turned his head slightly from side to side over her dress. His nose, lips, jaw, his stubble — all of it pressed against her. Then all ten of his fingers found her thighs, pushing her sundress toward her hips, his eyes full, his gaze intuiting she was merely Silly Putty in his hands.

Grinning, she shook herself from his grasp and picked up the pace, intent on having this man move his body against hers — fully clothed and simply for the hell of it.

She wanted to see him let go. Like this. Now.

Lacing her fingers through his, she attempted to pull him up again — but to no avail. The man was dead weight.

Startling her, he yanked her toward him, but Annie resisted with all her might. For a few more notes, they engaged in a tug-of-war. Annie wanted to dance with the sexy fucking man before her. And the man ... well ... he simply wanted to fuck the woman putting on the show.

"Why didn't you have this on the other night?" Her words bobbed to the beat. "You love music."

"If I'd brought you up here, we wouldn't have had dinner." Cal smirked.

"Well, *I* would've eaten."

Annie blushed and shoved him. Except he didn't budge.

He slipped his hands under the flimsy little dress again and stroked her thighs. "I. Would. Have. Had. You."

"You have me now." She squeezed his fingers.

"You're fighting me." He pinched her butt cheek.

"I want to dance ... and talk."

He squared her hips. "We talked all day." The tone of his voice held her in place. For a moment, she couldn't move or dance or shake. Closing his teeth over the material, he nibbled her stomach. "I want to fuck you, Annie." He glanced up. "Now."

Before managing to tear herself away, she took his cheeks in her palms and smiled. "Yeah." She kissed his nose and backed up. "But I like resisting you. It's fun." She turned. "You torture me, so..." She looked over her shoulder. "This is how I torture you." The dancing kicked up a notch, the swaying, the hands in the air, the hips shaking.

The seduction.

Smiling, Cal eased back, ankle over his knee again, finger and thumb on his chin, watching her uninhibited movements, her artistic expression, thinking she looked rather ridiculous — yet mesmerizing — hamming it up to ... what? Her audience of one. An adorable kind of ridiculous. A sexy, utterly fuckable kind of ridiculous.

Reaching over, she gave his arm another good yank, enticing him all the more with her *ra-ta-tat shake*. And finally, Cal stood, allowing the wild performer to have her way. Annie grinned, placed her hands on his hips, and guided him, trying to make up for what he lacked.

Because he had to be lacking in something.

Apparently, it was this.

After a few more seconds of rocking her pelvis against his, of attempting to help him find his rhythm, the song ended, and they plopped onto the futon together, holding hands and laughing.

"I like this music." Annie puffed out, pulling hair from her lips.

"Music is a window to the soul."

"Not the eyes, huh?"

"That too." Cal reached over the back of the futon and turned the volume down.

"God, I haven't listened to anything on a record player in a long time."

"I didn't think a girl your age had ever actually seen a living, breathing record player."

She scowled and jabbed him in his side. "You know they've made a comeback."

Cal laughed. "I should've known, though ... with your knowledge of classic songs."

They exchanged a glance, smiled, then blurted, "Otis Redding," at the same time.

Cal extended his legs and slid his feet toward Annie's, grazing her toes with his. Peeking at her face out the corner of his eye, he whispered, "*Heavy...*"

Annie squeezed his hand. "My brother collected records." She gazed at their toes. "One of my earliest memories is playing some of Dad's old records on our beat-up turntable." Her cheeks felt warm. A nodule formed in her throat. "We would laugh and talk and sit for hours sometimes, listening to music."

"That old thing," Cal said and tipped his head, "was my grandfather's." His eyes glossed. "This music..." He cleared his throat. "It's his. I guess it never left me."

Annie squeezed his palm again. "What's his name?"

"My grandfather's?"

"Yeah."

"Everett." Cal swallowed and glanced away.

Even though his grandfather had died an old man, Cal missed him. The stories he would tell — especially after placing the needle on a classic. Tales about songs, meeting his wife, raising children — about carving and etching wood and what it was like eking out a living during the Great Depression.

Grandpa E.W. had become the closest thing Cal had had to a real father, and he would never forget the love that man showed him. Now, Cal played the music *for* Everett.

"I like that name." Annie sighed. "You don't often meet an Everett. It's a strong name." She peered at Cal and touched his cheek. "Like yours ... *Calvin*."

"That's what he called me."

"Calvin," she repeated, whispering his name like one might in prayer, no longer desiring to tease him over it. Holding his gaze as long as he would allow, she stroked pieces of his hair. "You love him."

Cal reached forward, grabbed the other water, and opened it. "You never mentioned a brother."

"Yeah..." As she watched him drink, she cleared her throat, then finally choked out, "Peter."

"Older or younger?" He set the bottle down.

"Older."

"Is he your only sibling?"

"Yes. What about you? Any brothers or sisters?"

"No. My mother never remarried. I don't think she wanted more kids."

"I'm sure you were enough." She bumped his knee. "And your dad is...?"

"Don't remember him."

"He passed?"

"Peter didn't live with you?"

"He lived with his mom in California. He spent summers with us. Some holidays as well. Before I turned ten, though, he was on his own. He was— is twelve years older."

Cal's eyes glistened, astoundingly green. Perhaps they too had been tanned from the sun. It hurt to look into them, knowing he peered all the way inside her soul, hanging on to her every last word.

"He played guitar too." She tilted her head up, smiling. "God ... he loved the song 'One.' He wasn't a singer, but he played really well. Taught himself."

Cal stood and made his way to the rear of the futon. By the time Annie glanced over the back of it, he was already sorting through his LPs, the familiarity he had with his collection obvious.

"I think I have it."

"*Achtung Baby*? I'm not talking about Metallica's 'One,'" she said, and Cal grinned. "Is there anything you don't have, Prescott?"

Besides rhythm, she thought and laughed to herself. *He certainly has virility in profuse amounts*. She eyed his strong back and arms. His magic skin could be seen through his thin shirt. Skin she wanted to taste, a back created to take bullets, arms to envelop and warm her...

As Cal removed the Louis Armstrong record, replacing it with his clever find, and set the needle at the start of track three, the beat took her instantly, whisking her away from the shape of Cal's body and transplanting her inside a time capsule, to a place she wasn't ready to feel or absorb. Cal had been right. *Music is a time capsule; it is a window to the soul.*

She closed her eyes.

Where am I?

She opened them.

It all happened so fast. First, the conversation. Then, the song.

She hadn't expected him to have it, find it, or actually put it on. Yet, here she sat, the unique chords bringing back memories as she fought a torrent of tears, the song transporting her to a time that no longer existed.

It existed whenever certain music played. Especially a few particular songs. "One" made it seem as though Peter was still...

"Was this a bad idea?" Cal interrupted.

Annie hadn't even noticed his return to the futon. "No." She took his hand, felt the magnets and the warmth, and tried to shake away the vulture of death as best she could.

Can he see it flying overhead? she wondered as she pushed her fingers through Cal's and squeezed.

I was important to him.

I am.

I was.

He could make anybody feel special.

Fuck. I love you, Peter.

She dropped her head, and when she picked it back up, her face heated; her jaw felt like it was lined with hives. "When I went away to college, I didn't see him as much as I—"

"Annie, where does Peter live? In Washington?"

Shit... It was coming. Starting. What if it didn't stop this time? Her crown felt hotter than her face. Her stomach churned. She might throw up. *Fuck ...* she couldn't have a fucking panic attack in front of him. She couldn't have an attack. Period.

Standing, she walked to the window and looked outside, asking the courtyard, the trees, and the sky for a reprieve.

Please, make it stop. Please.

The narrow hallway of her mind shrank to the width of paper, catching in her throat, migrating to her nerves, possessing her person, throwing rationality out the window. Her head throbbed. Not with a headache, but a shake. Prickly heat replaced the blood in her veins. Tunnel vision consumed her sanity.

Doom! fuck die air paper bag death red lights breathe Doom! chase collapse nausea supernova breathe...

It isn't real. Shhh...

You're okay, you're okay. Okay! Okay!

"Annie." Cal met her profile. A hand came toward her.

No. He couldn't touch her. She gave him the cold shoulder, but he didn't desist. He wiped away the single tear suspended on her cheek and placed his hand on her back, but it only felt like an alien pod from Planet Pity had landed there.

"Please." She shrugged her shoulders, willing herself not to hyperventilate or throw up. The heat spread, clawing up her neck.

"When was the last time you talked to him?" Cal searched the side of her calloused face.

Please. Don't look at me. Don't touch me. I can't breathe.

The tunnel collapsed into nothing. Dust and ash. *Doom!* She clutched her throat, pulling at the skin there. Her hands began to shake. Violently. Actually, her entire body felt like one gigantic heart. Beating and beating and beating.

The sound was deafening.

"Talk to me, Annie." Cal used the voice. The defibrillator.

"It's been over a year," she choked out in a whisper as she brought her stupid fucking shaking hands to her lips.

"You're shaking, Annie."

No shit. I'm dying. I'll die. The world is ending. The universe is spinning. Collapsing. I'm crazy. Turning inside out. I'm a rubber band expanding. I'm being chased. Pursued. I'll die.

Die!

Don't. Touch. Me.

Cupping her hands with his, Cal tried to look into her eyes, but she wouldn't turn toward the pity or the concern. Or the make-believe safety.

Don't touch me.

I can't.

Doom!

Pound!

Shake!

Die!

No. Don't take me. I can't go. I can't do this. Not here. Stop. I need a paper bag. Stop. I need a pill. Anything. Please. Make it stop.

Lights flash.

Red.

Flash.

Green.

Flash.

Smaller...

SMALLER... Smaller... smaller.

The hole is tiny. I can't fit. It's the eye of a needle. I'm an elephant. I won't fit. I won't fit.

On a sharp inhale, she turned toward Cal and said, "He died." Nothing about her pliable, speaking like a programmed drone. "In May. A year ago, May." *Fucking Mother's Day.*

Annie shifted, giving Cal her backside. He massaged her shoulders and trailed his nose through her hair.

Don't. She shrugged him away again, and he dropped his hands and sighed. The doom had begun to subside. The urge to vomit had faded some. She felt flushed but no longer on fire. Reality started to return.

Fuck reality.

He was dead.

God, God, God.

Annie hated saying those words out loud. *He died.* Or any of them. His name. Peter. Peter. Peter! Doing so would make the superstitious superstitions true. Every time she said them, every time she *thought* them, it was a horrible affirmation of the truth.

The truth. *Right.* There was no truth.

He wasn't coming home. Ever. That was truth.

He can't call me. Console me. Smile at me. Hold my hand. Save me. His smile is ash at the bottom of a tin can.

"Annie," Cal said and turned her around, pulling her against his chest, cupping the back of her head. His eyes went wide as they scanned the space. "I'm so sorry."

Sorry is a stupid little word to excuse death, Cal thought. He wanted to kill it. Murder the son of a bitch. He wanted to quench Annie's pain with a billion gallons of water over the raging fire of death. He loathed it. The unexplained, out-of-control, shitty eventuality. The helplessness that shadowed it.

Where could he put it? Her pain. What could he do with her tears? Her sorrow.

Annie let her head remain there against his shirt for a few more seconds as he ran his hand through her hair.

But it was no good.

She stiffened. Suffocated. She pushed Cal away.

Daggers sank into their chests.

"I..." she said and sucked in a breath, "think..." She heaved. "I..." She inhaled. "Should..." She heaved. "Go."

"Breathe, Annie. Sit down. Please."

If one more person told her to breathe this summer, she was going to fucking scream. She cradled her face, partially covering her eyes, no longer sick to her stomach or shaking, but mad. Pissed. She tried to stop hyperventilating as she removed her palms and glanced up at him. "This was a mistake."

"What's a mistake?"

"Everything is a mistake! You, me, death, this, us, all of it." She went toward the stairs. "I need to be alone."

"I don't want you to be alone."

"It's not your decision." She stood at the top, ready to descend, shoulders squared.

"Don't hide from me, Annie."

"What?" Annie looked him straight in the fucking eye. "Don't hide — *from you?*" Her voice went up several octaves. "Oh, you mean the way you hide. From me!"

"I don't hide from you — or anyone."

Oh-ho-ho-ho. The master and his superlative voice have spoken.

"Bullshit!" She narrowed her eyes, the green pink from tears, her mind spent, weary from a year of her own shitty-shitty bullshit. She didn't need his shit as well. She didn't need him. Or this! The ass with his stupid ruler-of-the-entire-world disposition.

"No," Cal said with an eerie calm and a slight smile, her temper secretly thrilling him. Despite her extreme sadness, her inability to breathe, her ... panic attack? Her fire, her eyes, and the way she pushed him beyond measure enthralled him. "I've always been upfront with you about who I am. I. Don't. Pretend."

"Mmm…" A snide laugh escaped. "That's right. I forgot. Upfront about what you want"—*me, my pussy*—"but not about who you are. In here." She thumped her chest.

"Annie, this is who I am." Cal slowly moved forward.

"Don't come closer to me." She put a palm to the floor, her eyes following suit. Drops streamed down her cheeks. The girl who craved openness, the one who practically demanded it from others … wasn't going to let him in. "I have to go."

"Annie, don't," Cal pleaded as she descended a few steps.

"What can you say"— she stopped and glanced up—"that I haven't already heard a million times? What do you think you can do?"

Annie swallowed.

Cal surprised her in the middle of the staircase.

Grabbing her arm, he gazed at her, the look in his eyes the exact opposite of the severity of his grip — the same expression he'd exhibited on the couch when reminiscing over his grandfather.

"Don't go," he whispered.

"I have to," she begged. "Please … let me go."

But, it was happening.

The handing over.

The abdication.

Wiggling her arm, she fought him for a few more seconds, trying to break free from his grasp, his gaze, but she couldn't. Nothing about her wanted to be free of Cal in this moment. He was the tree. The sand. The shade. His green eyes the comfort she'd been searching over a year for. A rush of another kind took precedence, capsizing what remained of her grief and panic.

"Cal…" she uttered as he twisted her arm behind her back, leaned her body into the railing with his weight, and kissed her neck.

Starting off slow.

Tender.

His lips dotting along her face and ears, all over and back again, until the tension released, until her body seemed to lose its bones and muscles. Her breaths and whimpers, were the sweetest sounds he'd ever heard.

Lifting her into his arms, the way a groom carries a bride over a threshold — her feet dangling off to the side, her hair bouncing with each step — he brought her to the loft. After laying her down on the futon, Cal hovered over her body, his arms extended at her sides, and stared into her eyes for an eternity.

Glass cut her throat. Or diamonds.

Unable to swallow, think, or barely move, unable to contain the look in his eyes any longer — the one hitching her in place, gauging her soul, the one fucking consuming her — she pulled his face against hers and kissed him.

The sadness lingering in her heart seeped through her pores, melting into him, Cal whisking it away with each lick of his tongue and imprint from his lips. Within seconds, the actions became stronger, more insistent, nearly bruising her, causing her to mewl like a wounded animal. Or like an animal rescued by a man, this man.

God, this man.

"You smell like the ocean," she groaned, lips against his face.

"And sweat," he replied, nibbling and kissing her neck. Cal pushed her arms above her head and clasped her wrists, inhaling *her* scent — she smelled like the reason for everything.

"No," she whispered and giggled.

"What should we do with this?" Sitting up, he straddled her lower legs, took the flower from her ear, and pushed the hem of her sundress above her waist. Touching the yellow petals to her skin, he twirled them over her jawline. Annie moaned. "You like that?"

"It tickles."

He slid it under her chin, down her neck, through the center of her breasts, to her navel, twirling and swirling it around her adorable belly button. "Where do you want to be touched?"

"Everywhere."

He circled the flower over her bikini bottoms. "Here?"

"Yes."

The petals spun over her thighs, then he put the stem in his mouth. She never would've believed any man — even him — could look so fucking sexy with a bright-yellow flower protruding out of his mouth. But he did. He drove her mad with need, and it only increased as he fingered her over the nylon of her bottoms, making her back arch, doing it until she thought she might burst.

"Take them off." Wiggling her hips, she tried in vain to push the elastic down without the use of her hands.

Cal shook his palm against her wrists, his eyes smacking her into place.

His place. She was his.

He would devour the sadness. He would make it obsolete.

"I want your hands — here." Tossing the flower onto the table, he lifted her dress over her head and wrapped the material around her forearms and wrists. "I want to restrain you."

Annie's eyes closed, her mind blanked, and with each exhale, her heart expelled sadness, forcing one emotion away while submerging herself in several others. Bliss, satisfaction, elation. The feelings came together like a storm, hot weather on the ground mixing with cooler temperatures in the sky, forming a dangerous funnel of passion, picking up where the panic attack left off.

"I have you, Annie," Cal whispered, kissing her cheek, then her lips as he slid her bottoms down her legs. "Let go."

Her eyes opened.

Let go... She couldn't let go.

"I have you..." he repeated, palming her cheek, nuzzling her breasts and neck, hoping she felt the truth of those words.

Tension pooled from her muscles as Annie swam around his strength. His breath, his voice, his touch was more soothing than a thousand bits of the best therapy.

The straps of her bathing suit top loosened, the material fell, and lips, soft and warm, met her breasts, her nipples. A tongue swirled around them languidly. Everything he did put her in a trance.

Then Cal shifted and stood. He took a package from his pocket before removing his shirt and pants. Kneeling next to the futon, he resumed stroking her cheek, resolutely asking for things she wasn't sure she could give.

His green eyes glossed.

A metamorphosis took place.

Cal suddenly felt unable to move. *Fuck.* He was frozen. How many years had it been since he'd been immobilized by a woman?

He knew. He remembered.

And only one woman had ever had this effect on him.

Cal swallowed past the tingling in his throat, ignored the swarming in his gut, and clasped his hand onto Annie's bound ones, squeezing. He trailed a finger from her neck to her thigh, watching as she began to tremble, watching her lungs fall and rise.

Breath as rickety as hers, heart thumping, Cal touched her, massaging her into a frenzied mess, his thumb concentrating on her clit, listening intently as he quickly brought her closer and closer to orgasm.

"Please," she finally uttered, shifting her hips and the back of her head against the cushion.

Draping his body over hers, Cal rolled on the condom, then dipped into her opening. "I'm not going to last, Annie."

"W-what?" She blinked up at him, her throat parched, ready to unleash every bit of what he'd asked for into a tornado-like orgasm.

"I want you," he continued, choking on the words, "so much. I..."

"Take me." Annie's voice cracked. "You have me. *Please*." Wrapping her legs around him, she pulled him closer. "Don't hold back. Don't wait."

Surging forward, he pushed inside. All the way. Until there was no more room for grief. No pain. No panic. No death. He fucked away sorrow, replacing it with something else, feelings he'd refused for years to acknowledge, ones he'd forgotten existed. Or ones he didn't want to accept were real.

"I need to touch you, Cal."

"Not yet." He took her the way she'd asked, without holding back, sliding in to the hilt, staying a moment, then pulling out. She yelled and expelled with each entry, her body shaking for all the right reasons now.

"Please..." she begged moments later, "Cal... Let me touch you."

Still deep inside her, he began to untwist the dress from her wrists. "Don't wait for me to tell you to come this time."

"No," she moaned. "I want you to tell me." Grabbing his face, she thrust her tongue into his mouth in haste. "Tell me." She stroked his cheeks. "Tie me again. I don't care how you do it. Just... Please. *Please*." *Keep me safe.*

"Fuck, Annie." Her wrists, he pinned above her head. "You're so beautiful." He rattled her palms against the cushion. "*Just like this.*" He peered at her skin, her eyes, her mouth, at where they joined. "Fuck..." Bucking against her clit, he wet his cock until it was slick, driving them both nearly insane with need and want and passion. "Ready?"

She bit her lip. "Uh-huh."

"Lift your knees." Spreading them wider, he pushed back in, fucking the *you're so beautiful* into her psyche, pummeling her until all thoughts fled and only their hearts conversed.

Cal shut off the valve of grief.

Killed death.

He swallowed her whole, fucking her until he could barely hold off his own pleasure any longer. "Do you want to come?"

"Yes."

"For whom?"

"You."

"Say it. Say my name."

"I want to come." Her moans became quiet little sobs as he put pressure on her wrists like no other, as he started to massage her clit. "For you. Oh God ... Cal. For you."

"Come." He put his mouth on hers.

"Cal..." she whispered as he devoured the sound with his tongue.

Never had Annie been kissed like this. In a moment like this.

Lost in a maze of his commands, his touch, his skin, wanting to follow each in circles, never to be found. The voice inside her head continued to whimper his name on repeat.

It was the start of the race.

No.

It was the finish.

The sliding off the chasm.

The precipice.

Her toe knuckles bent. Her muscles tightened. Her eyes rolled and rolled as she shook everywhere, their tongues still touching, tasting the way they perfectly fit together on each and every groove.

She came.

Her eyes combing the ceiling, breath exorcising from her lungs, she hummed as little pulses continued to vibrate deep inside her body.

Cal kissed her neck, burying his face there, the smell of tangerines nearly drowning him, while sliding in and out of her warmth, his finish beginning as hers trailed off, his finish seeming every bit as immediate and necessary as hers, compulsory, making his own combination of earthy sounds, unable to bridle any more of his emotions — they all released with his groans, his breath. They released inside Annie.

He lasted mere seconds longer than he'd anticipated.

Wiping his brow, he watched the orgasm still swimming in her eyes, realizing more than twenty years had passed since a woman had come close to giving him a comfort like this. And to top it off, he hadn't been able to last.

What the fuck? Where was his self-control now? Gone. He was gone staring at her. His throat ached. Annie was beautiful. And despite his impulsive rescue mission...

She still looked lost.

He dropped next to her, slightly heaving, glistening with sweat, deciding against his better judgment to conceal the comfort running through his veins.

Why was he such a fuckup? Still. At forty-five. Not a fuckup, but what? The same man for the last how many years?

Nothing was the same.

Not now.

Cal found it difficult to look at her after another monumental orgasm, fearing she would see straight through to his soul. Read him like a book. She could. She had. She would flip through his pages straight to the end and be done with him.

Annie continued to stare at the ceiling, feeling a lump in her throat, death not far and somehow mixing with the tingling still running through her entire body.

Cal nibbled her ear, breaking her concentration. "I'm going to shower."

Annie didn't move. Her eyes stung.

Sitting up, Cal scooted to the edge of the futon.

She clutched his waist.

"Do you want to join me?" He glanced over his shoulder.

"No."

Standing, he picked his clothes off the floor and went downstairs.

Annie's eyes pooled, and she blinked out tears. Pulling at a mess of hair near her forehead, she squeezed the strands until she thought her eyeballs might pop out. The anxiety made her teeth clench, her stomach swirl, and it kept her fingers near her temple, pulling and pulling.

Fuck ... what is this? What are we? I can't do this. What am I doing?

One minute, mourning, having a royal freak-out panic attack and preparing to leave. The next, underneath his strength, succumbing to him, allowing him, wanting him, never wanting anyone so much, so fast or so intensely, experiencing an out-of-this-world safety.

Safety got up and left.

Safety wanted to take a shower.

Safety died with Peter.

The needle on the record player skipped.

Annie sat up, slipped on her dress, stretched, and began to twirl her hair aimlessly. She looked at the wilted flower on the table. It had been such a perfect day. It had been a lovely flower — on the bush and in her hair. Now, it was shriveling.

Dying.

"*You're stealing from nature,*" she'd said earlier, teasing him as he broke the flower from its shrub.

They had just finished snorkeling on a beach in a state park when he put the little sunflower in her hair, kissed her cheek, and for the first time told her, "*You're beautiful.*"

Thinking of it now, her stomach zipped up the fast lane to her throat. She rotated the strands of hair around her index finger faster.

"Don't move." She opened her bag and took out the camera as Cal smiled and looked away. "You're seamless right now in the light. Don't move."

She snapped him up as if he were the most fascinating thing on the beach even though they'd seen a two-foot barracuda, brain coral, and handfuls of little black, orange, and red fish.

A few seconds later, he snatched her by the waist and pulled her against him.

She giggled. "Hey, you messed up my next shot."

"I'm done being the subject."

"One more." She turned the camera on the two of them and pressed the button. Perfect. She didn't need another take. It was misaligned perfection in the lens.

It was them.

Us.

Who are we?

As she placed the needle on the holster, gazing at the record, mesmerized by its grooves, her eyes blurred.

I'm the circle. I'm spinning.

Out of control, getting nowhere.

Fast.

Somewhere.

The end of a track.

Scratched.

Her eyes centered as she heard the water shutting off below, allowing her to focus on something, anything except the black circle, anything but the look in Cal's eyes — before he'd had her, when he'd had her, the way he'd looked at her all day.

She refused to see the look that had come after the orgasm. The switch. The blank slate. The gutted, misplaced man who seemed unable or unwilling to share further intimacy.

After grabbing her bathing suit, she went downstairs, then stashed the items in her tote. Once in the kitchen, she opened the refrigerator and peered at its contents.

"Are you sure you don't want to shower?" Cal came out of his room, hair wet, blue jeans fastened, shoes on. He finished pulling a white cotton T-shirt over his head.

"No, I want to eat. I'm hungry." She closed the fridge.

"You're always hungry." He flashed a smile. "Have you been twirling your hair?" He fingered some of the strands. "It's knotted."

"Yes." She snatched them from his grasp, then opened the fridge again.

"I have to leave early in the morning for my flight. I need to drive you home."

"Okay." Bending forward, she scanned the shelves.

Placing a thumb and middle finger in the corners of his eyes, he stepped behind her. "I need to take you back now. I can pick something up for you." He rested a hand on her tailbone. "I'm exhausted."

She jerked upright and slammed the door. "Only if it's no trouble. I wouldn't want to put you out."

"It's no trouble."

Sidestepping Cal, Annie went to the desk, slipped on her flip-flops, and picked up her tote. She stood near the door, resembling a statue, a stubborn one.

"You've got to be kidding," he mumbled under his breath as he made his way to the foyer, grabbed his keys, then opened the front door.

But she didn't exit. Didn't even bat an eye. The only part of her body moving was her foot as it tapped the flooring. No longer amused by her attitude, her antics, or her roller coaster of emotions, Cal slid the keys into his pocket and faced her head-on.

"You think I don't want you here?" She. Didn't. Bat. An. Eye. "That's fucking ridiculous."

"Me?" she barked. "I'm fucking ridiculous?"

"You were the one ready to march out of this house only a little while ago."

"I couldn't leave, though, could I?" Annie moved closer to him. "Not until we could fuck! That is what you do best, right? You fuck!"

Placing two fingers on his temple, Cal rubbed his skin until it seemed it might peel off. He barely gave the front door a shove, yet it still slammed shut.

"You're going to stand here and tell me you didn't want that to happen?" He nodded toward the loft. "That you didn't need that to happen?"

"I was grieving... Having a—"

"I know."

"You don't know." She stepped aside and looked away. "You don't know what I need."

"I tried talking to you, Annie. Do you think I wanted you to walk out of here ... *alone*?" Cal stood taller, straighter. "That I would send you off into the streets at night without concern for your safety?"

"Your concern was in your pants, in your pocket."

Cal's eyes flickered, but he quickly composed himself, then he stepped into her space and met her gaze. "Why do you keep punishing yourself?"

Annie blinked. Like a deer, a fawn, caught in the middle of a road, gazing at someone's headlights.

"Do you know, Annie?" Pushing her hair back, he cupped her chin. "Do you know what you need? I gave you what you needed."

Annie could still only stare at him, her bottom lip practically trembling, her eyes on the verge of tears. Maybe she had needed exactly what he'd provided. To feel their magnets fuse on the futon. To be beneath him, secured to him.

Despite her initial playful resistance. Despite the panic attack. She had needed him.

After being together all day, his arms and chest against her for much of it, saltwater across their bodies, his eyes sparkling, his hair glistening, the smell of his skin in the Florida sun — Annie couldn't wait to be with him.

And she did punish herself.

For almost everything. For every bit of pleasure she'd felt since Peter's death. None seeming greater than sex — the ultimate physical pleasure. Satisfaction she'd denied herself for over a year, barely even masturbating, preferring to function without the biological release rather than suffer guilt.

Guilt for feeling anything other than pain.

The guilt never really went away, though. The orgasm took it for but a moment.

She peered at Cal's chest, choking down saliva, the lump in her throat ballooning. Then she glanced up and stared into his eyes. "What about after?"

"What? You didn't want to shower with me."

"Cal, please, don't avoid what I mean."

"I'll hurt you, Annie."

Something dropped to the floor. Like her heart or soul. "It's too late." She paused. "This hurts."

"Annie..." Cal sighed, taking her hand and playing with her fingers. "You expect things from people..." While staring at their knuckles, he blew out another breath. "You expect things from other people you aren't willing to give of yourself." Glancing up, he met her gaze. "You run, and I hide."

Annie searched his eyes, slowly rowing her oars across his shore.

Finally.

He admitted it.

But that meant she had to acknowledge something too.

I do run.

Nevertheless, she wanted to let him in. She wanted Cal to let her in. But how could they get to that place of no running and no hiding? Of true vulnerability. It would take more than a loaded, lock-stock-and-barrel look. More than a great fuck. It would be more than her aching to be held afterward.

It was work. Effort. It would be challenging.

Annie didn't know how much time they had to get to that place. She didn't know if the summer would last that long.

Cal pulled her head against his chest and exhaled his next two words with a sobering breath. "I'm sorry."

Stroking her hair, he held her there, understanding the art of self-affliction firsthand. He'd mastered that skill. Cal still hadn't accepted the move to Miami or his mother's disease, nor the denial that followed. He hadn't come to terms with the seven months of shame named Reegan. God, if he were honest, he had failed to fully forgive himself for letting Samantha down.

Three. Years. Ago.

He punished himself far more than Annie would ever know.

Still, Cal held her, trying to give her what she needed, a comforting reassurance, a friend, certain the things she desired would be far more than he'd planned on offering the summer's distraction.

The distraction that wasn't a distraction after all.

She never had been.

Annie was an artist, a dreamer, creating a figure through the scope of her lens. She positioned, studied, read him, and once she clicked the shutter button, maybe Cal could let go.

Of delusion.

Of what propelled him.

Of all the things he held on to.

Holding her in his arms made him understand what it felt like to truly be a man.

TWENTY-SEVEN

The ride home in the dusk was nothing like the ride had been in the sunshine on the way down to the Keys or on the way back up, chatting and relaxing, holding hands, music playing, discussing life — and it was nothing like the fabulous ride on the futon.

The argument may have finished in the apartment, but tension took up all the available space inside the Tesla as Cal flipped through the satellite stations like a drone, finally settling on "Crash Into Me."

Dropping her head against the seat rest, Annie immersed herself in the beautiful music, refusing to believe the lyrics were applicable to her, him — *to us* — but somehow, they made sense. She turned her face to the left and looked at Cal — the boy, the man — and placed a hand on his cheek, holding her palm there for several seconds as she stared at his profile.

"I'm sorry too." She exhaled.

Cal grabbed her hand, squeezed it, then rested it on his thigh. Annie's eyes glossed, and she glanced out her window at the trees and streaks of headlights from passing cars.

"I've been..." she began a couple of seconds later, taking a quick peek at the side of his face, then turning her attention to her lap. "It's been happening since he died."

"The panic attacks?"

"Yes." She removed her hand from his and began to twiddle her thumbs.

Not her hair. "Only Tabitha knows. I hid it as best I could. Avoided people. I didn't see my parents much after the funeral."

"Did you go to a doctor?"

"I took a prescription. Yes. For a little while."

Bringing her palm to his lips, he kissed her knuckles. "I had a friend, in junior high ... he had them. No one talked about stuff like this then. I didn't know what was going on with him at the time."

"I don't... I didn't want you to see me..." She swallowed and looked outside again.

"Annie..." He peered at her, squeezing her hand. "Nothing you could do, like that, would ever change what I feel."

"What do you feel?"

Cal smiled, the boyish grin with pockets for dimples. "I think you know."

She waited for a further reply, the pause beginning to feel like the length of a James Cameron movie. "The worst, Prescott!" She knocked his knee with their palms. "Don't you forget it either."

His smile grew bigger, teeth and all.

"Well, if you're not going to answer *that* question"—she cleared her throat and looked at the road—"I have another one. John and Maggie want you—"

"Jesus, Annie." He let go of her hand.

"What?" She tried not to roll her eyes. "I haven't even spit it out yet."

"You're doing her bidding."

"I am not." Annie ran her fingers through the back of his hair. "They want you to come to dinner Saturday. I do too. All four of us. Together."

"A double date?" He cackled.

"You're an ass." Smiling, she nudged his knee again.

"It's Saturday?"

"Yes."

"This Saturday?"

"Yes!" She touched the crease where his thigh met his hip — apparently, a tickle spot for Mr. Tightly Wound Spool of Perfected Restraint.

Cal suppressed a wiggle or a giggle as he shoved her hand away with a grin. "I'll be jet-lagged, on London time."

"You don't get jet-lagged." Now, she squeezed his quads.

"Do you think I'll be in the mood to see anyone?" He eyeballed her. "You're the only person I'll want to see."

"This whole situation is unnerving for them."

"This situation?" he scoffed. "For Maggie."

"Whatever. Cut them some slack, please, and come over." She pinched his crease again, except he didn't seem to find it as funny.

"Are you telling me what to do?" Glancing over, his eyes filled with the possibility of a punishment she wanted to see him carry out.

"Do you like it?"

"No."

Putting her lips near his ear, she whispered, "Fuck off, Prescott," while finding another spot on his body to taunt. And what do you know? This particular place bulged. She wrapped her fingers around him over his jeans.

"You're being very naughty." He gripped the wheel, shifting his eyes back to the road.

"You like it..." Leaning a little closer, she moved her other hand to the nape of his neck, sliding her fingers through his hair. "Cal...?"

"Yes, Annie?"

A palm slipped past the waist of his jeans and inside his boxers. "I'm asking you, Mr. Cal Prescott." She made a fist around him. "Will you have dinner with me at the Allens' Saturday night?"

"Annie." He pinched his lids shut, looking to be in exquisite pain.

"Watch the road."

The second his eyes popped open, he sighed so loud, she laughed. Even his knuckles turned white over the steering wheel.

"Annie," he repeated, this time louder, more urgently as he blew out another elongated breath.

"What?" She batted her lashes.

The word *hard* didn't even begin to describe what she touched.

How or why had he managed to disavow her the pure joy of touching him? *Fuck. Fuck. Fuck.* She hadn't touched a man since the Stone Age. Fuck. She'd never touched a man. "*So ... you've been with two boys, Annie?*" Annie needed to see it and touch it at the same time. She needed to put her mouth on him.

"Annie!"

She jumped, then giggled. This was exactly what she wanted. To hear him yell. Show emotion. Lose himself.

"Do you want me to wreck the fucking car?" Mr. Spool of Tightly Wound Restraint fidgeted in his seat, then grabbed her by the wrist.

"No, I don't." She nibbled his ear. "I want you to come to dinner."

Cal let go. "Dinner is fine!" He smacked the wheel. "Just stop jerking me off before I drive off the fucking road."

"Then pull over."

As Cal slowly turned his head and peered at her, Annie swallowed. The anger had turned to need. Heat. A few minutes later, he found an inconspicuous place to park.

"God, this is not how I wanted to do this," he groaned as she began to stroke him again, his eyes widening, watching as she undid his pants and pulled his cock up and out of his boxers.

"How do you want to do it? What have you imagined?"

Their eyes locked. Both of them swallowed.

"Tell me." She exhaled. "I want to make you feel good."

Cal grabbed a handful of her hair, pulling on it good and hard as he kissed her. "I want you..."

"Yes..."

"On your knees."

"Mmm," she moaned, her ass moving over the seat. "What else?"

Staring at her mouth, he dragged a thumb across her lips. "I want control."

"No shit," Annie whispered, trying not to laugh, and Cal smiled.

The moment he slipped a finger past her teeth, his expression transformed into something much more serious, something pained and beautiful.

Annie started to suck on his finger.

Pushing back pieces of her hair, he put his mouth near her ear. "I want control of your face and your hair. I want to hold you to me."

"Uh-huh," Annie panted.

"Force you." His thumb moved to her chin, and he pressed the pad into the hollow of her neck. "Choke you."

Annie's breathing hitched. Their foreheads touched. For a few moments, they only watched the indelible way she touched him.

"Do you want that?"

"Oh, fuck," she replied, moving her hand up and down his hard length, feeling as though she would be the first one to come. If she could wrap herself around something — his thigh, his dick, a surface, anything. "Yes, yes I want that."

"I'll..." He stopped short.

"Yes?" Her gaze fixated on his tip, the way it leaked, how her hand fit perfectly around him. "More ... please..."

"I'll fuck your little mouth until you can't breathe ... until you want to scream my fucking name."

"Jesus Christ, Cal." Frantically, she rubbed herself against the seat, wanting to scream his name *now*. She caressed his cheek. "I... I want you to do it now." She nodded. "I know we're in the car ... but make do here. Hold me to you. Please." Annie blinked up at him, sucking her bottom lip between her teeth. "Fuck my mouth right now. I'm yours."

"Jesus Christ, Annie." Clasping her nape, he shoved her head into his lap.

She swallowed him past her tongue and toward her throat with a moan so loud, it confirmed everything she'd promised: the agreement, the nod, the *I'm yours*.

And then Cal groaned. God, did he groan.

It was the most uninhibited sound she'd ever heard him make, and it was incentive. She continued to take him as far back as she thought she could go without retching. Then, she used her tongue. Licking and sucking, losing herself, gratified she pleased him, she drowned in the series of noises he made — the panting, the grunting, the "*Oh fuck, Annie.*"

Cal kept her there. He couldn't take his eyes off her. The two things were practically all he could do. With scarcely any room to move his hips, he couldn't fuck her face the way he needed to. The way he'd told her he wanted to. His pants and the lack of space constricted him. Yet this was exactly what he desired.

Because it had been given to him freely. With no strings. And with something swimming in her green eyes. Feelings he refused to acknowledge. Not right now anyway.

Cal pulled her hair.

Held her to him.

But it was *her* sounds ready to send him over the edge. She whimpered and whimpered as she sucked him, humming as though he were the best thing she'd ever tasted — the only thing she'd ever tasted — as though she might burst if she couldn't keep doing it.

"Fuck..." The one expletive was all he said as it began, as he shook, trembled, groaned in long, broken vowel sounds.

Mesmerized, Cal watched Annie drag her lips to his tip, kissing and licking as she went. Then she rose, wiped her mouth, and took a swig from a water bottle.

Putting a hand on his jaw, Annie stroked Cal's cheek with her thumb and looked into his eyes. The man couldn't get up and walk away from her now. He couldn't shower, couldn't hide. She couldn't run. They had to face each other.

However, he shifted from her gaze, tucked himself away, and palmed the wheel.

"Cal..." She rested a hand over his to stop him from reversing. "Look at me."

God, why is it so hard to look at her when it's over? he wondered.

Because he was a bastard.

Because his feelings for Annie were stronger than he could've imagined — no, he didn't need to imagine. He knew what they were. He had felt things the night they'd met that made no fucking sense. And he stupidly thought he needed to keep that from her, to protect her. From what? Himself? The end of summer?

What?

He gripped the steering wheel with both hands now. If he squeezed hard enough, maybe it would give him the answers he wanted.

"Look at me, Cal, please."

He relaxed, and as his back met the seat, he turned toward her and let her see him. Fully. It wasn't merely a mask that slipped.

A curtain lifted.

She saw him in a way she hadn't before.

Vulnerability wet his eyes, covering him in a sticky gloss, a needy sheen, a waxy goo.

She glanced away, then looked back, seeing every gamut of emotion in his beautiful soul from A to Z.

Who was he? What was he telling her? He looked like he needed her. What did she need? What did they both need?

They stared into one another in a cloak of silence for several seconds. Maybe a minute or an hour.

Her throat was parched. It swelled. It was a fucking balloon.

"Kiss me," she finally uttered, breaking the deafening fast, lost for what he wanted, needing what he offered and vice versa.

Cal hesitated.

Again.

Even though he had nowhere to go but backward — and he wasn't doing that, not with this girl, he was done with mistakes — still, he hesitated.

"Kiss me, Calvin Prescott."

Cupping the back of her neck, Cal pulled her across his lap, nudged the back of her body against the steering wheel, and planted his mouth on hers.

Panting with shock, Annie kissed him in return, his lips and tongue speaking the expression from his face: the amazing, vulnerable open theater curtain.

It was absolute.

This was absolute.

She crashed into him. Or he crashed into her. Like Dave Matthews had crooned.

After bumping against the steering wheel several times, the horn finally honked, causing Annie to jump.

"Shit!" She laughed, climbed back into her seat, and clicked her belt into place. "I'm still hungry. Apparently, I worked up an even bigger appetite."

"That was a first for me, you know?" Peeking at the side of her face, he started to reverse. "In a car."

"What?" Her eyes widened. "No..."

"I said it would be a summer of firsts."

"Yeah, for me."

"Well, you surprised me today."

"You surprised me." She took his hand. "With this little road trip. Thank you, Cal."

Smiling, Cal pulled onto the road.

She hadn't screamed his name, after all. She had supplicated him, opened him up and hooked a finger beneath his skin.

Cal drove her home, knowing Annie was what he needed, what he wanted. She was more than he could fucking handle. He drove her home, fearing he would somehow fuck it all up, that he would push her away or disappoint her. Or she would leave him first.

He couldn't... It wouldn't... Love was never enough.

Like a little boy dreading the start of school, Cal feared the end of summer already looming on the horizon.

ENLIGHTEN

KNOWLEDGE OR UNDERSTANDING; SPIRITUAL
INSIGHT

I'll fly away on a beach
wish upon a grain of sand
I'll meet you in the sky
and wait
for understanding
it cannot be a ruse
my existence
time
what I wake up for
put up with
anticipate
I'll immerse myself
in pretend
bathe my wounds
in the stars
I'll fall asleep
under
the light of darkness
taking comfort
in your branches

and the truth
bleeding from your eyes

Twenty-Eight

Saturday night arrived, and everything seemed to be in order:

The house.

The ocean.

The finished freelance assignments.

The edits.

The Nikon.

The dress.

Maggie's kitchen.

My brain.

Really?

It seemed orderly. Calm.

A man would soon walk through the door and change that. A man Annie hadn't seen in almost a week. Knees would knock. A heart would seize. The brain — *my brain* — would analyze and wonder and generally think too much about nothing and everything. Like now.

Maggie whistled, the sound like that of a construction worker, interrupting Annie's spiraling thoughts as she finished descending the wooden staircase.

"What?" Annie replied, stepping into the kitchen, a flush crawling up her cheeks.

"Foxy lady. You're going to give him a heart attack in that thing."

"It's only a dress." Annie fingered the skirt. "I've had it forever."

But she had to admit, the old *thing* was sexy. And strapless. With points near her underarms, resembling a Wonder Woman-type bodice — except it wasn't red and yellow, but daisy white and covered in vertical patterns of pastel-blue ribbons and pink flowers.

The colors looked radiant against Annie's tanned skin.

It was delicate and graceful. Understated. Well ... maybe not at the chest. Two white bowties rested smack in the center of her breasts, the ones meant to help cover the four-inch slit exposing her cleavage. She recalled the task of making the bows, placing the bows, and finally attaching them.

Now, she imagined Cal's face near them. His lips and tongue tracing an outline around them, between them, inside the opening... Yep. A coronary, all right. But the heart failure was happening to Annie — and Cal wasn't even here yet.

"Well, you know how to pick 'em. That's for sure."

"Dresses or men?" Annie smirked.

"Both. You choose the doozies."

Annie rolled her eyes. "What's in the bowl?"

"The ahi," Maggie replied as Annie grabbed the open bottle of wine on the nearby counter, then poured herself a small glass.

"I'm waiting for him to arrive first," Maggie continued. "I can't overcook it or let it sit too long after it's done. Have you heard from him today?"

"This morning." Annie glanced around the room, wondering why Maggie couldn't seem to bring herself to say the name Cal. "What can I do?"

"Pour me some more wine." Maggie nodded.

Annie picked up the red again. "This one is almost gone." She handed her friend the partially full glass. "Where's John?"

"In the den." Maggie took a sip, then opened the oven. "I shoved him out of my kitchen earlier too."

Annie leaned in the direction of the delightful smells. "Is that a hint?" As she surveyed the vegetables in the casserole dish, lying in rows of perfection, cheese melting over the top, Annie's eyelids fluttered shut. "Mmm. I'm starving." She stood tall and took a drink of the wine. "Really, Maggie, what can I do?"

"It *is* a hint. You aren't taking it. I already told you—"

"I know. I know."

"I don't want you to lift a finger."

Maggie wanted the night to be special. She wanted to play hostess. She wanted to be alone in the kitchen.

"Go keep John company." Maggie glanced at the clock. "It's seven." She flapped her hands in the air. "Go."

Annie rolled her eyes again, then made her way across the house.

"And don't spill wine on that dress!" Maggie called as Annie reached the archway of the den, a bell chiming in her wake.

"John, the door!" Maggie cried.

"Jesus," Annie said to John. "The woman's a drill sergeant."

He chuckled, kissed the top of Annie's head, then they both returned to the kitchen.

"Honey, please." Maggie stood near the stove, looking around feverishly, the glass of wine pursed at her lips.

"I'm right here," John replied.

"Then get the door." Maggie yanked her head in the direction of it as he chuckled again.

John made his way to the foyer while Annie remained on the opposite side of the bar-top counter, observing Maggie's steps:

Wineglass down.

Front burner on.

Extra virgin olive oil drizzled into the stainless-steel pan.

Salad bowl removed from the fridge.

Annie was exhausted watching her. Still, she proceeded to ask Maggie for the hundredth time if there was anything she could do.

"No, no, no," Maggie replied, continuing to multitask in all seriousness.

Yes, yes, yes, Annie thought as Cal Prescott entered the room.

Order obsolete.

Thinking obsolete.

Movement, breath — obsolete.

The changer, shifter, and disorganizer of Annie's thoughts walked along the right side of the counter directly into the kitchen. Even the way he moved was obnoxious. That sexy, purposeful gait matching his personality to a tee. She couldn't peel her eyes away from him. Her heart must've skipped a million beats. And what was that noise in her head?

Time.

Time stopped on Cal fucking Prescott. Or did it stop *for* him?

Holding a bottle of wine in one hand and a bouquet of flowers in the other, Cal kissed Maggie's cheek, smiled, and said hello.

She took the arrangement and brought the petals to her nose. "These are beautiful, Cal. Thank you." Maggie set about grabbing a vase from one of the cabinets, but not before she stole a quick glance at the stove.

"Did you sleep, old man?" John asked, joining Annie on her side of the counter.

"A little," Cal said to John but peered at Annie.

"You were *almost* on time," Maggie jabbed from where she stood at the sink, filling the vase with water.

John glanced at his watch.

Cal didn't seem to be listening to The Cat. He eyeballed Annie as he peeled the plastic off the top of the pinot he'd brought. The expert chess player contemplating his next move. The play flickered in his eyes.

But Annie knew he wouldn't force the move.

"I think there's a bottle open already, Cal, unless my wife finished it off."

"I did not," Maggie guffawed, arranging the flowers in the vase.

Cal reached for the open bottle instead, then filled a nearby glass with the rest of Maggie's red.

"Annie," John began, and she cleared her throat, wrenching her gaze from Cal as he finished sliding the cork into the empty bottle. "I think I left my glass in the den. Would you mind gettin' it for me?"

"Sure." She grinned, attempting to conceal her blush and failing. "Excuse me, gentlemen."

Upon returning, the two men were actively engaged in conversation about work.

London.

Malibu.

New York.

Miami.

Construction.

Numbers.

Clients.

Contracts.

Numbers.

Maggie never stopped working either. She set the vase on the dinner table and looked over the settings. Everything always needed to be in its proper place. Including Annie.

And she was proper and in her place.

Next to Cal.

She stood so close to him, the hem of her skirt brushed against his khaki pants. Her body temperature rose the way it had the first night she'd met him. Even with the air-conditioning blasting, the hot flashes came ... so long as she was near his skin.

Sweet. Crisp. Cotton. Ocean.

She wanted him. She wanted to touch him.

Instead, she reached for the new wine bottle. It wouldn't do much to keep the warmth off her cheeks, though. Reds always gave her heat.

Despite being engaged in an all-inclusive conversation with John, Cal grabbed the pinot at the same time as Annie, their fingers meeting as he play-fully shook it from her grasp and smiled.

Electricity sparked off the tips of their fingers. But rather than refilling her glass, Cal turned his attention back to John.

Annie wondered if he was going to treat her differently around their friends.

Maybe he had a different face for each day of the week:

Work face. Jog face. Hide face. Flower face. Song face. Chess face. Fuck face.

Cal's typical indifference was both sexy and annoying — as usual. Pins and needles. She wanted his attention. All of it. She didn't want to share him. Not with anybody. Not now. She sorely wished she had listened to Cal and planned this another night. Tomorrow, she would leave for New York. If only she hadn't booked her flight for Sunday. But she had to see Tab's play.

While nursing the last few drops of wine in her glass, Annie attempted to feign an interest in what the men discussed. Every time she thought she had something to add to the conversation, though, one of them would finish the other's sentence, then start a new one before she could speak.

She inched away about an arm's length and looked toward the rear of the house. Grayish-blue clouds streaked across the horizon. Maggie streaked between the two rooms. Back and forth. Nook to kitchen. And then Cal reached over, clutched Annie's waist, and pulled her against him.

Finally.

He kept his hand securely on her hip as he continued looking at and speaking to John without missing a beat.

How did he do it? Maggie, too? They seemed to have their own agenda. Annie had one too:

The crook of Cal's neck.

She leaned her head against his shoulder, nuzzling her face beneath his chin, against the warmth she felt there.

She closed her eyes.

Although certain they were still talking, she no longer heard any words. No contracts. No numbers. Only the comfort of Cal's embrace and the smell of his ocean.

Then Maggie broke the tranquility. "It's ready."

Annie lifted her head. The men, however, didn't flinch.

"John, could you please help me bring a few things to the table?"

"Yes, honey..." John chuckled, eyeballed Cal, then he joined his wife.

Cal opened the pinot while Annie looped the silver chain hanging from her neck around an index finger, watching as he twisted the wine key into the cork.

"Did you listen to that song?" Cal asked.

"Oh, so now you're speaking to me?"

He laughed. "Do you know why I didn't speak to you?"

"Because you're an arrogant asshole."

Cal let go of the bottle and squared her hips. Staring at the material of her dress, his thumbs traced the outline of her navel. Then his eyes climbed, traveling to her breasts, her throat, her lips, stopping on those eyes. "Are you wet?"

"W-what?"

"Are you?"

"No."

"Liar." He grinned, placing two fingers in the hollow of her neck. "The waiting increased your pulse. It had an effect on your entire body, Annie."

She glanced away. "Too bad I don't have a fondness for arrogant assholes, then."

He laughed again. "Shall we discuss the *fondness* you mentioned earlier?"

Cal referred to their text messages, the first one having arrived from him at a god-awful hour earlier this morning.

Cal: Boarding the plane in an hour.
What time is dinner again?

I need to be inside you.

She stuck to his format. A three-line reply.

Annie: Have a safe flight.

Dinner is at 7.

Absence makes the penis grow fonder.

Cal: No. It only makes it … harder.

I have a song.

Born in the USA. Track six.

"Are you blushing, Annie?" he asked. She wanted to twirl her hair, the necklace, his dick. "Did you listen to it?"

"Yes," she replied, her throat feeling like tires stuck in sand.

If she hadn't been blushing before, she certainly was now. After listening to that song, earlier in the day, she'd brought herself to climax, thinking of Cal, the chords, the lyrics, Springsteen's damn, ready-to-break breath telling her what Cal felt. A train through the middle of her head all right — the size of Texas.

Grinning, she swirled a finger across his chin. "Was 'I'm on Fire' the best you could do?"

"The best I could do…" Cal smirked. "How about…" Putting a stop to her taunting little finger, he squeezed it, then removed it from his person. "I take you back to my apartment after dinner and shove you against my desk?" His mouth caressed her ear, and she bit her lip to stifle a groan. "I'll kick your legs open, lift your dress, and I'll fuck you, Annie. *Hard*. So hard, you won't be able to board your flight tomorrow without people wondering why this poor girl can't walk — then you can ask me that asinine question again."

"Annie, we're ready!" Maggie called from the nook.

"Fucking Christ," he growled and adjusted himself. "Does she always yell like that for you?"

"No…" Annie laughed as she tilted her head toward his zipper. "Your penis. It has grown fond—"

His lips landed on hers, quieting her clever little mouth. He kissed, nibbled, tugged. He parted.

"I'll be along." He nodded, telling her to go ahead without him.

Annie joined John and Maggie. The table, normally bare, was adorned with a striking floral cloth. Cal's flowers soaked in a large, etched vase in one corner, and a few lit candles sat in the other. Silver-plated forks, spoons, and knives lay next to cream plates, Maggie's finest china with the comely white, red, blue, and purple flowers dancing along their edges. Blue cotton napkins were folded on top. And the food Maggie had worked hard to prepare took up the center.

Wine in hand, erection fizzled, Cal appeared.

The party of four had arrived.

"I opened the new bottle." He held it up. "Would anyone like a top off?"

"Oh, I left my glass in the kitchen," John said.

"Yes. Please," Maggie answered, untying her apron and looking over the table again.

"Annie," John said. "Would you get it, please?"

Cal filled the three glasses as Annie departed, mixing the old pinot with the new. No one seemed to mind. John, Maggie, and Cal took a seat.

"You sure you slept, old man? You look tired."

"I'm jet-lagged."

"I didn't realize you would be getting in today." Maggie eyeballed John. "No one told me."

"I'm fine." Cal dragged out the words, but his thoughts were elsewhere. As were his eyes. Annie had returned and was already energizing John's glass with red.

"Why is everyone so quiet all of a sudden?" Annie passed the glass to John, then glanced at each of them in turn as they stared up at her. "Do I have something on my face? *Did I spill wine on my dress?*" She looked over the sexy old thing, mortified as she spread the material apart.

"No, Annie," Maggie said, looking at Cal. "We're quiet because we're drinking in your beauty."

Cal ran a palm over his throat, but that wouldn't stop the aching. Sexy might come easy, sure. But beauty, throat-closing beauty, not so much. Annie didn't only look beautiful — she personified it.

And it had nothing to do with the dress.

Annie rolled her eyes. "Maggie..."

"Take the compliment, sweetheart," Maggie replied, "and sit down. I'm starved."

"It looks wonderful, Mags," John said. "She's been workin' on it all day."

"Not all day," Maggie huffed.

"Now who isn't takin' a compliment?" John smiled.

"It does look good, and smells good," Annie added. "And she has been working hard all day."

"Well, thank you, Maggie." Tipping his head, Cal held up his glass with one hand while placing the other on Annie's thigh.

Two by two, side by side, all four of them clanked their glasses together, then they proceeded to dish up the food.

"I hope no one minds eating in the nook," Maggie said, and Cal laughed, his body jolting forward a little, his chest knocking the table. He'd just received a firm kick to the calf. "Is that funny?" Maggie eyeballed Cal. John peered at him as well.

Annie took a generous sip of water. Cal only shook his head, smiling.

"Well, anyway, John and I love eating in here. It's like a sunroom. It has a great energy. Not that I'm into all that mumbo jumbo."

"You are into all that"—John bumped his wife's shoulder as he put some salad on his plate—"mumbo jumbo."

"I do feel something in this room." Cal turned his face toward Annie as he continued caressing her inner thigh. She wanted to kick his fucking leg again. "Don't you, Annie?"

A broad smile tackled Annie's lips.

"Are you two making fun of me?" Maggie asked, holding up her nearly empty glass.

"No, Maggie. I do love this room." Annie cleared her throat and grabbed Cal's roving fingers. "We both do." She squeezed them.

"We always eat in here," John said. "I've been threatenin' to turn that ... that dinin' room out there into a man cave."

The four of them laughed and began to eat. Several minutes later, however, Cal's hand returned to Annie's skin, her thighs. The hem of her dress was almost at her waist.

"Annie," Maggie said.

"Hmmm?" Annie had lost track of time. She could barely drag her eyes forward.

"Have you heard anything I've said?"

"No." Annie shook her head and dropped her chin. Her stomach constricted, her heart bubbled up into her throat, her face became warmer by the second.

"You haven't missed much." Cal ran his middle finger over the center of Annie's panties. Her mouth fell open. Her breath almost ceased. "Maggie can't stop talking about the past. As usual."

"You look a little flushed," Maggie said, and Annie glanced up. "It must be the wine." Maggie drained her glass, then looked at the bottle. "The tannins have always affected you."

Annie coughed, wiggled her hips, and eyed Cal. His face appeared placid. Serene. She wanted to kill him.

"Reds make you hot?" Cal shot her one of his best stares. So aloof, so resolute. So fucking sexy.

"Reds also make me mad."

"Mmm." Cal smiled. "Too bad you seem to have forgotten that I like it when you're mad."

Maggie cleared her throat. John smiled.

"What ... uh... What stories were you telling?" Annie asked as she stabbed a fingernail into Cal's wrist. The fucker barely made a sound.

"About you. When you were a kid," Maggie answered, her gaze drifting across the house.

"What is it, Mags?" John asked.

"I was thinking about when we met." She gave the three of them a tight smile.

"Us?" he asked.

"No," Maggie snorted, becoming boisterous again. "When we met Annie. She was about... God, Annie, how old were you?"

"She was nine or ten," John added, a fatherly glint in his blue-gray eyes.

"I was nine," Annie confirmed.

"We met her family through the firm John did work for when—"

"Annie told me how you all met, Maggie," Cal interjected.

"What year did we first move to Seattle, John?" Maggie glared at Cal.

"Having trouble recalling things?" Cal smirked, and Maggie scowled.

"It was 1998 when my dad met you," Annie offered.

"Cal, where were you living then?" Maggie narrowed her gaze at him, then peered at Annie.

"New York."

"I didn't know you lived in New York," Annie gushed, her eyes twinkling. A stark contrast to Cal and his serious business-like manner.

"I did. Twice."

"That's right," Maggie said. "We begged him not to go the second time."

"Why?" Annie asked.

"God," Maggie huffed. "What was her name?" She snapped her fingers, picked up the empty wine bottle, and shook it. "The girl, the bitch, the one who—"

"Honey..." John guided the bottle back to the table.

"Maybe we should tell Annie about some of the guys you dated, Maggie, before you met this one." Cal smiled, tipping his head at John.

"I don't know if my husband wants to hear about that." Maggie covered her grin.

"I want to hear about it," Annie chimed, happy to have the heat off herself, enjoying the comfort they shared — *like family*, Cal had said.

"Nonsense." John's drawl thickened. "We'd all love to hear those stories. Cal, you introduced us. Tell Annie what my Maggie was like before she met me."

"Really? You introduced them?" Annie turned to Cal.

"Yes, Annie!" Maggie burst.

"I think maybe even the two of you dated." John pointed his fork in the air, first at his wife, then at his friend.

Annie wondered how John couldn't seem to remember whether his friend had dated his wife. Had Tabitha been right? Had Cal and Maggie...?

"You know I dated some guys before I met you, honey." Maggie glanced at John and shook her head. "But no... Cal and I... No." Maggie gripped the edges of her plate with both hands, her chocolate eyes frothing. "I was the girl who always wanted to get married. And Cal"—she stared at him—"let's just say he wasn't marriage material."

Cal arched his back. Sat up taller. He removed his hand from Annie's thigh, wiped his mouth with the pretty little blue napkin, then dropped his forearm to the table, running his fingers slowly around the palm of his hand. He matched Maggie's stare pound for pound.

Annie waited a moment, hoping for a break in the tension, the aggravation, waiting until she couldn't wait any longer. "God, Maggie"—her jaw practically shook—"you're drunk!"

Silence descended over the nook. No one ate or chewed or moved.

"Not everyone wants to get married," Annie went on, steam rising off the top of her head. "Or needs to get married or plans on getting married."

"No," Maggie droned, looking square at Cal, her eyes growing dimmer, her elated high turning to a somber low. "Not everyone does."

"You two were lucky," Cal interjected, then cleared his throat, glancing at the dark sky across from him and behind his two friends, refusing to see the reflections in the window — especially his own. "Not everyone finds the love of their life by twenty-one."

"We *were* lucky," John added, managing a smile. "And Cal, here, was the best man at our weddin', Annie."

The *best man* continued to stare out the window.

The times they spoke about didn't seem that long ago, yet here he sat, more than twenty years later.

The same.

And alone.

Perhaps being alone was what he preferred. Was it his destiny? Always attracted to the wrong girl, at the wrong age, and wrong time.

The last few years, Cal had fallen into a pattern, a routine, wishing to quiet the searching, the endless climb up the hill of nothing, the one he'd started ascending once landing in New York City in 1991. No rainbow, no ocean, no dreams — only sex and work. And alcohol.

The rest would have to finally take care of itself.

Trouble was that the sex never quenched it. The hours spent on work never placated it. The nothing he searched for grew wider, bigger, until the hole in his soul became the size of a gap in the ozone layer.

"I would love to see your wedding pictures." Annie directed her gaze to Maggie as she touched Cal's thigh, snapping him back to the present.

He took her hand and squeezed it. She gave him a little smile.

"We can look at them after dinner." Maggie stood, attempting to find her footing as she started to pick up some of the dishes.

"Everything was very good." Cal eyed Maggie and forced a grin.

"Yes, it was delicious. Thank you." Annie got up and started to clear the table.

"We'll have to do it again before—" Maggie stopped mid-sentence, placing a palm over her upper lip, her eyes wandering. "We'll just have to do it again," she finished as she rushed off.

"I'm sorry," John said to Cal once both women left the room. He glanced at the empty wine bottle.

Cal palmed the back of his neck and shrugged his shoulders. "Nothing new."

"I don't know what brought on the drinkin'."

"She should've known better. Maggie is like a mother to Annie, and Annie's mother—"

John smiled, glancing at Annie, who had reentered the nook. She gathered more dishes, then left.

"Why don't you take a walk on the beach?" John nodded toward the kitchen. "With your girl."

Cal swallowed, thanked his friend, and stood.

"Did you make this dress too?" Cal asked Annie the next time she came into the room. John had excused himself.

"Yes." Annie smoothed a palm over the material.

Taking her wrists, Cal pulled her closer and peered into her eyes, then he really put his hands on her for the first time that evening — for the first time all week. Resting his palms on top of her shoulders, he began to slide them down her arms.

Annie shivered.

Once he reached her hands, he laced his fingers through hers, pushed them behind her waist, and dipped his face to her neck. Annie giggled. Cal loved her laugh, and so, he kissed her again, hoping to hear the same joyful sound.

"We're going for a walk on the beach."

"What about—?"

Cal pulled her toward the French doors. "John's taking care of Maggie." The moment he opened them, the wind blew through their hair and wrinkled Annie's skirt. "I haven't seen you all week."

After stepping over the threshold, Annie fanned out her dress and curtsied as she looked up at Cal and smirked. "Well ... here I am."

"Come on..." The dim porch light smacked Cal's irresistible dimples. "*Heavy*."

Twenty-Nine

Cal and Annie slipped off their shoes and hit the sand, the breeze still mussing their hair as they made their way toward the water, hand in hand. The moonlight and waves greeted them — no one else seemed to be out.

"How was your week?" Cal asked.

"How was yours?"

"The last thing I want to talk about right now is work."

"You talked to John about it."

"And you seemed very interested." He grinned.

"I'm interested." She squeezed his palm.

"No, you're not." He laughed. "I want to hear about you."

"I sold a piece ... yesterday ... at the gallery."

Cal stopped strolling and stepped into her space. Smiling, he tucked strands of wild, windblown hair behind her ears. "Your first?"

"Yes." She tilted her head down some while still peering up at him.

"It will be the first of many." He cradled her jaw and kissed her forehead.

A wide smile spread across her face. "More firsts..." She sighed, and they began to walk again, moving closer to the shoreline.

Upon reaching it, Annie dipped her toes through the shallow water, creating ripples as Cal stepped back and rolled up his pant legs.

Inhaling the salty breeze, she went toward him, smashed her back against his front, and wrapped his hands around her waist.

They both faced the ocean.

He smelled like the ocean.

Cal pressed his fingers into her pelvis.

With her right arm behind his head, she ran her palm along his neck, resting the back of her head on his chest as she swayed her hips. Mesmerized by the waves, the moonlight, the feel of his skin, the way the foam bubbles tickled her feet, she decided she was quite content to stay here all night.

Against him. Under only sky. Their bodies moving in perfect rhythm.

"Do you believe in God?" she whispered without turning to see his face.

"I don't know." He nipped and tugged on her earlobe with his teeth.

Sliding her palms over the tops of his hands, her body stiffened some as she looked over her shoulder and glanced at him. "What do you mean you don't know? You know. Deep down."

Cal rocked them again, nuzzling his nose through her hair. "It's not something I've given thought to in a long time."

Which was another one of his lies.

Because he did think about it: God, the universe, life. All the fucking time. But he refused to burden her with his musings. Cal wanted to be *her* rock. And, for once, it came easy. Annie's presence provided a much-needed peace. The ocean did as well. The stillness that often came while waiting for the perfect wave, riding that wave, then starting the process all over — things to be felt, not questioned — were what Cal chased.

"How can you not?" She gestured toward the water. "When you stand here and look at all this." Her eyes stung. Her throat swelled. "I mean ... don't you think about it? Don't you wonder?"

"What I wonder"—he ran his nose along her jaw—"is when you're going to stop talking philosophical bullshit and turn around so I can put my mouth on you."

Annie faced him, but she wasn't finished talking. Philosophical or nonsense or the end of the world or death or escape or everything she'd never bothered with until life had been snuffed out in an instant via a wreck on a bike on a street at night in the dark.

He wore a helmet. He was safe ... until he wasn't. He's gone. Death is warm. He's cold. I'm...

Cal kissed her bottom lip.

Thinking was all she had to get her through, to keep her going. The obsessions comforted her.

Cal kissed her upper lip.

This man did too.

"You're distracting me." Wrapping her hands around Cal's waist, she stared into his eyes, looking for answers and truth.

He kissed her again. "Is it working?"

She managed to peel her upper body from his chest, although he still held her tightly. "Did you go to church? As a boy?"

Cal smiled. Annie swayed. He tried to lean his face toward her neck, but she resisted his attempt at circumventing her questions.

"Did you?"

"We went when it was convenient for my mother, which wasn't often. My mother..." His voice trailed off, along with his eyes. "You should talk to Rosa, Annie. She believes in God."

"I want to talk to you." She walked her fingers up his chest, smoothed the pads of them over his face, and looked so far into his eyes she thought she might never find her way out.

But it was her eyes...

Her expression.

The tone of her voice.

Her tangerines.

Always stripping away his layers, gazing at him in a way that simply begged him to be honest, to level with her and freely open. She made it easier for him to divulge a part of himself he otherwise would've never been so eager to share.

Glancing heavenward, he exhaled. "I can't deny there's something bigger than me that came up with all this."

Annie stepped back, eyes wide, and stretched one of his arms out, swinging it between them. "Something bigger — *than you*? I didn't know you could grasp a concept like that."

Cal laughed. Annie dropped his hand and took a few steps toward the water. She scooped up chunks of sand between her toes. Getting lost in the sensations and textures, lost in the wind, the smell of the ocean ... lost in Cal's eyes — she could feel him watching her — she grabbed a few seashells and tossed them into the murky water. Then she turned and faced him again.

The man had his hands in his pockets.

Lips pressed together tightly.

Eyes never greener or more certain.

She stretched her arms wide, tilted her head up a little, and inhaled.

Cal watching. The entire time.

She dipped her chin while peering up at him, swallowing only wind.

"Say it, Annie."

"I need to believe all of this is for a reason." She paused, sucked in another lungful of salty air. "I need to know..." Her voice cracked as her hands fell to her sides. "I need to know that I — that *we* — have a purpose." She started to grate her fingernails against her palms and bite the insides of her cheeks.

Stepping closer, he placed a hand on her nape, gathering her hair as he searched her face. "You have a purpose."

Cal waited, willing what he'd said to sink in. Words were never enough, though. She proved him right by looking away, down at his chest.

"You have a purpose," he repeated.

She glanced into his eyes, uncertainty still plastered across her face. Death made her uncertain. Death made her doubt everything.

Nothing about it made sense.

It was completely incompatible with the life all around her. Their breath. Their bodies. The beach. The stars. The moon. A million trillion grains of sand beneath their feet.

Death was incompatible with God.

"I want to head back inside." With nothing more than a quiet sigh and a tug on his arm, she relinquished the fight ... for a moment.

"Let's sit a while," she said as they approached the house.

"I thought you wanted to go inside."

"I changed my mind."

Women always do, he thought.

Annie plopped onto the sand, but Cal remained standing, a hand in his pocket, eyes out to sea.

"Prescott." She glared up at him, and Cal joined her.

They weren't far from the Allens' yard, relaxing atop the dry sand, leaning on their hands, legs stretched out in front of them.

"What are you thinking about now, heavy?" He sighed. "More philosophical BS?"

He peered at their feet. She stopped wiggling her toes and looked straight ahead — not at the ocean, but into a void. Then she took a deep breath and turned her face toward him. "Are you seeing other women?"

First, Cal started to crack a smile, but the emotion was quickly replaced with something else... Intimidating didn't even begin to describe it. His stare resembling the one he'd gifted Maggie over dinner. His face was implacable. His body a statue.

Annie's heart began to pound.

"Why don't you ask me what you really mean?" His green eyes morphed into swords. "Am I fucking anyone else?"

Annie looked to the ocean, the sky, the stars. Anything.

"Are you asking me this because of the things Maggie said tonight?"

Sitting upright, Annie wiped sand off her hands and pulled strands of hair from her mouth. "I'm asking ... because I want to know."

Cal sat forward, wiped his hands off as well, then placed a palm against her cheek. "Annie..."

She wouldn't look at him. The wind burned her eyes. Her face flushed. Then Cal gently turned her head toward his. Their gazes locked. His thumb brushed her cheek.

"No..." His voice was like the breeze now. Soft and welcoming. "I'm not *seeing* anyone else, and I'm not going to *see* anyone else."

Annie continued staring forward, a lump in her throat the size of the moon.

"You're so beautiful." Cal traced the bodice of her dress, the points and curves, the bowties she desperately wanted him to explore. "*Just like this.*"

Their eyes met, and she swallowed.

"What about you?" he whispered. "Are you seeing other guys?"

"No..." she replied, her voice cracking.

"You're only twenty-five, surely you want to see other guys." His chin fell to her bare shoulder, his mouth moving over her skin.

"I'm not that girl, Cal." She swallowed again, blinked, jogged across a desert. Then she rested a hand on his cheek. "You know who I am."

Cal flinched.

He'd expected the first declaration but not the second, and hearing Annie utter that bold statement out loud rocked him to his core, hitting him hard — like the smack of a baseball bat blasting a homer out of the park.

"Last week, after I had my thing, my attack..." She clasped her fingers together and rotated her thumbs. Cal draped his arms over his knees and stared out to sea. "Why did you say you would hurt me? I know you wouldn't—"

"It's one summer, Annie." He looked back at her.

Right. One summer. An ordinary summer. More to follow. More girls, more work, and a series of random, lonely fucks.

Is that it, Prescott?

Cal was so inexplicably two sides of himself, Annie didn't know how he managed to get dressed in front of a mirror every morning. Or maybe that was his parlor trick — he didn't look in a mirror.

"So, that's it, huh? We're the summer." She didn't like him saying the words aloud. Making it fact. There was no such thing as *just* anything. "You put an end date on something we just began."

"Annie, you were introduced to me with an end. I have one too. This move is temporary."

"When do you go home?" Her throat became thick and pasty as she imagined the goodbyes, the entire summer, the *fling*. The sky became less of a blanket of soothing stars and more of a heavy curtain putting out a once-smoldering fire.

"My lease is up in September."

"And you'll go back to California?"

"Yes." He lifted her palm and kissed her knuckles. "Do you know where you're going to be in September?" He threaded his fingers through hers.

"I want to travel."

"See, now you're being logical," he said, but she wanted logic to go fuck itself. "You told me in the Keys you wanted to see places. I saw your excitement, the way you lit up at each new discovery on the beach and under the water. Honesty can be a bitch, Annie, and timing is a fucking whore."

"Listen to your filthy mouth." She grinned, bumping his shoulder.

"You like it."

Her smile faded. The air stung her eyes as she stared at the ocean. "I don't want to talk of the end of summer or plans or deadlines or facts or logic. Ever. Talk about something else." She turned toward him. "Anything."

Needing no further encouragement, Cal put his lips on her neck and kissed her, trailing his mouth toward her chest as he lowered them both to the sand.

Annie placed her hands on either side of his head, guiding him toward the bowties, the slit, her tits. "You think you're getting some tonight."

A hand slid beneath her dress. Teeth bit her nipple through the bodice.

"Cal..." she whispered and found his fingers, grabbing them before they reached the top of her underwear. "Fuck..."

Instead of pulling the garment off, though, he caressed her over the cotton, running a finger up and down her seam until she squirmed and whimpered and repeated his name.

"Cal..." she moaned. "I'm serious."

"You're leaving in the morning." Cal forced her gaze.

"And what? You want to penetrate me into the sand, right here in Maggie's backyard?" She smirked, but Cal didn't budge.

Annie shoved his chest and smiled, but his expression remained. His sticky body did too. Pressed over her completely, he kissed her jaw, dotting his lips to her collarbone until his mouth ended up right back on the bowties, the gateway to her breasts.

"Cal..." she moaned again.

Assuming her hesitation was haphazard, perhaps because they were on the beach, in the sand under the stars, practically up against the Allens' property, he slid that same palm beneath her skirt and squeezed her thigh.

This time, Annie tensed.

Was she still stuck on death, God, purpose? he wondered. Or was she imagining he was interested in fucking someone else despite what he'd said moments ago?

"I'm on my period, okay." She laughed and grabbed his wrist. "For God's sake, it's not happening."

"Why didn't you tell me earlier?"

"I started this afternoon." She sat up, and he followed suit. "And when should I have told you? At dinner? In front of John and Maggie? When you *also* had your hand on my leg, up my dress? I'm sorry I didn't make an announcement as we passed the bread." She cleared her throat and continued in a baritone, "Attention, everyone. I'm on my period. There will be no copulating tonight. Thank you. Oh, and please, enjoy your meal."

Never more amused with Annie than he was right now, Cal gently pushed her body flat against the sand, breaking her fall with his hands, one on her back, the other behind her head. Staring down into her eyes, he brushed her hair from her face with his nose.

"I didn't think there would be an opportunity to—"

"An opportunity to what?" He nibbled her earlobe, then made his way back to her breasts. "To make you come?"

"Fuck..."

"Yes."

"To penetrate me into the sand," she moaned.

Lifting his head, Cal stared into her eyes, his face a hard, unforgiving line of want, haste, and need. The line read:

There will always be an opportunity, and don't underestimate me.

"I just need you to..." Her eyes glossed with tears, her ache for him cresting like the waves. God, it was beyond physical. "I just want you to ... hold me."

Something in his green eyes flashed.

Cal wasted no time pulling her against him, stroking his fingers through her hair, surrendering to the smell of tangerine blossoms.

As she rested her head on his chest, below his neck, against the warm made-just-for-her crevice, his heartbeat filled her ear, the rise and fall of his lungs securing her to him with the strongest cable on earth.

They didn't speak.

They didn't need to.

Annie closed her eyes. She would always remember this moment.

His body against hers, salt in the air, waves crashing on the shore, the blanket of stars a renewed comfort, a surreal contentment. She wished upon the sea of flickering lights: *Make it last forever. I do believe in magic.*

"I could fall asleep out here, like this, with you." She propped her head up on his chest, blinked a few times, then nudged her face into him again while tucking one of her legs between his. "You feel so good."

Cal brought her closer, squeezing her tighter at the declaration of those soft, loving words. He could fall asleep with this woman too, on the beach, under the stars, without penetrating her into the sand. He only wanted her near. Wanted her close.

Every day until summer's end.

He kept the emotion to himself, but Annie had already seen what he felt in his beautiful eyes. She could already feel the emotion running through him by the way he held her, touched her. By the stillness in their souls.

After several more minutes of staring up into the sky, holding one another, trusting, woven into the sand, Cal lifted his head.

"Come on, baby. Let's go inside. You need sleep. You have an early flight."

THIRTY

Annie wiped her feet on the mat and reached for the doorknob.

"Do you kiss on your period?" Cal stood behind her, planting his face in her hair.

Annie smiled.

Except for the quick peck in the kitchen and a few more on the beach, it had been almost a week since Cal's lips had been on hers.

After turning around, she stared at him, silently begging him to take her upstairs and do as he pleased. She didn't care if John and Maggie were home. She didn't care about her period.

She wanted him to touch her.

To need her.

To want her.

Cal pushed her against the French doors, pressing his pelvis against hers as he kissed her upper lip, then her lower, until they were a complete, glorious concoction of one. Lips. Tongues. Hands. Bodies dancing and looking for a way out of cotton. The door rattled some.

"Do you want to come?" Cal exhaled, between kisses, his breath warm and heavy.

"Are you that good?" She tugged on his lower lip with her teeth and cupped his ass, keeping him tightly against her. "You can make me come with just kisses?"

"Lift your dress in the front."

"They'll see."

"Lift your dress," he repeated, his eyes much darker. "This will be quick and quiet."

The moment he slipped a finger inside her panties, she went boneless and squeaked. Cal laughed a little under his breath, then he sealed her noises off with another kiss.

"Quick and quiet, Annie." Circling her clit, building a fire, stacking wood, he slid two fingers up and down her folds, working her into his favorite kind of mess. "I need you to come for me."

Her eyelids fluttered. Her breathing increased.

"God, you're so fucking sexy." He pinched her clit but covered her mouth before she could scream.

Nostrils flaring, Annie bit his palm, seeing haze as Cal utilized the perfect amount of pressure, stoking the fire to a roar.

"Come," he ordered seconds later, his velvety, no-room-for-argument instruction sending her over the edge. "Now."

Tip. Pour.

She urged her hips forward, arching into his hand. Fogging his palm with her bated breath, she came, swallowing one of his fingers into her mouth in the process. She wrapped her tongue around it as she stuffed away the final bit of her orgasmic sounds.

Cal took hold of her chin. "I want to know your return itinerary." His lips roved over hers. "I want you all to myself when you get back." He wrestled with her eyes. "Do you understand?"

"Yes." Annie nodded, her exhale blowing out imaginary candles. "I'm yours."

Smiling, Cal reached around her waist and pulled her forward, looking deep into her eyes, then he opened the door.

John and Maggie watched TV in the living room. Cal washed up in the kitchen, then poured a glass of water as Annie made her way to the rear of the sofa.

"I hope you don't mind." She touched Maggie's arm. "I want to get to bed early."

John muted the television. Maggie glanced over her shoulder, her eyes downcast, her mouth in the shape of a frown.

"We don't mind, sweetheart," John said.

"I should go to bed too," Maggie added. However, she didn't move. "I took our album out."

Cal joined them.

"I'll look at it next week." Annie glanced at him. "I can't wait to see Cal"—her eyes widened—"at what?"

"Twenty-two," Cal replied, a mischievous smile appearing on his gorgeous face.

Annie grinned and walked around to the front of the couch.

John stood. "Have a safe trip." He kissed her temple.

"Thanks."

"Will you stay and have a drink with me?" John turned his attention to Cal, and he nodded.

"Can you walk me upstairs first?" Annie reached for Cal's hand.

"I'll be back down in a minute." Cal patted John's shoulder.

"Good night, Maggie," Annie said. "Dinner was really good. I'll see you in the morning, nice and early."

"Five?"

"God, yes, five."

"Come on." Hands on her shoulders, Cal pushed Annie forward.

With a little sass in her step and a light in her smile, she repeated herself, "Good night."

The moment they reached her closed bedroom door, Annie stopped, gave Cal her back, and glanced over her shoulder.

"You are a tease, you know that?" he said, and she turned around and grinned. "I'm not going into your room, Annie." He put his hands in his pockets.

"Afraid?" She raised an eyebrow.

"No. I have self-control."

Annie laughed. A hand-over-mouth, body-buckling laugh. No shit. And she enjoyed making him lose it too.

"I should take you in there, throw you on the bed, and spank your ass raw."

But he couldn't.

If he entered that room, he knew he would want to please her again any way he could — period or no period.

"Not tonight." She faced the door again, putting her palms against it. "Unzip me."

"You think you're in charge?" He leaned closer.

She glanced back. "Right here..."

For a change, Cal was the one sounding like he'd forgotten to breathe, his exhale loud and full of a struggle she seemed to enjoy inflicting upon him. For a brief moment, he contemplated actually following her into that bedroom.

They could fuck in the shower.

First, he would strike her butt cheeks, just enough to cause a beautiful blush, then, he would have her.

Under the hot stream.

He would show her purpose, reason. Remind her why she was on the goddamn earth. The having, taking, and fucking would wash away concern, worry, death. Overthinking. The copulation, as she had called it, would also finally relieve him of the weeklong hard-on he couldn't seem to get rid of no matter how many times he jerked off.

Christ.

He needed to get a grip. He did have self-control. Funny. She'd laughed about that. He regulated his breathing now. Slowing it way down.

No woman — perhaps only one — had ever made him so...

Moonstruck. Needy.

Out. Of. Control.

He needed control. And when he was inside Annie's body, he had it.

Did she realize what she gave him?

She'd implied he wasn't getting any tonight, but she'd already given him a little bit of everything.

Fuck.

He wanted her.

With her neck so close to his lips, the scent of the beach still on her skin, blending with tangerines — *she commanded him*. He only had to keep his hands and his dick in his goddamn pockets. That was all. Simple. No touching. No thinking. No spanking. No fucking. No needy needing.

"Annie," he finally said, hesitating.

"Do it, Cal."

Hands escaping their pockets, Cal put one at the top of her zipper and pulled, watching as more of her skin became exposed, inch by inch. No bra, pink, lacy underwear, her skin glowing and filling his nose with citrus. Jesus. He had to go or move or run. Instead, he froze. His throat tangled into a wet ball of yarn.

Letting the dress fall, Annie opened the bedroom door and stepped out of the sexy old thing. She folded the garment over her arm and turned around, nipples erect, face screwed up with delight.

"Good night, Calvin Prescott." She smiled and shut the door.

Unbelievable.

The tease, this woman, this Annie, this photographer, the soon-to-be world traveler, his heavy, the something-something-something.

The summer...

Cal remained in the hallway for several minutes, quiet and alone, smiling and thinking, ball of throat yarn shrinking. He had to wait for another something to shrink. He was aroused — again — and it was painfully obvious.

Thirty-One

"That was fast," Maggie said from the kitchen as Cal descended the staircase, her eyes brimming with sarcasm.

Cal tossed her a curt glance, then projected his voice toward the living room. "Where's my drink, Jack?"

John turned off the TV and stood.

"Argh," Maggie cried. "Haven't we had enough to drink for one night?"

The two men met her at the countertop closest to the nook.

John spoke first. "Well, we know you did, Mags. The wine really snuck up on you."

Cal rolled his cuffs up his forearms, refusing to meet her gaze. Or give her an ounce of pity.

"Yes, it did." Cradling a glass of cold water, she traipsed her thumb along the condensation. "I'm sorry, Cal"—she glanced up at him through her copper lashes—"for the things I said at dinner."

"Are you?" Cal's brow crinkled.

"Are *you*?" she huffed. "Are you sorry for never stepping foot into my home for a meal until Annie asked you?"

John sucked in a breath, then blew it out, his mouth an O, his eyes even larger Os.

"It's Annie who needs an apology." Cal slipped his hands into his pockets. "You made her think she can't trust me."

"Me? I made her?"

"Do you trust me, Maggie?"

"I trust you, Cal, but I'm not sleeping with you. It's different."

"You really are something," Cal replied, his hands now fists at his sides. "You're coddled, you know that?"

As Maggie tapped five fingernails across the granite, her gaze narrowed.

"I don't think you can actually remember what it's like to be single." Cal cocked his head toward John. "Your husband loves you, truly, more than life itself, for more than twenty years"—he pressed a palm to the countertop— "and he's there to fuck you whenever you need him to."

"Is that my only need, Cal?" Maggie scowled. "Really?"

"You two are somethin' else," John interjected. "What's this now? How many years of fightin'?"

"I'm sorry, man." Cal glared at Maggie. "She needs to hear it."

"Oh, I need to hear it? It's okay, honey. We've had this coming since—"

"Since when, Maggie?"

"Since you wouldn't step foot into my house. Since... Since Sam."

"When will you let that go?"

"That?" she spat.

"You think you have me all figured out?" Cal crossed his arms over his chest. "Have you ever even given thought to how you might feel if you had no one to meet your needs? And no, not only the sexual ones — all. Of. Them." He shook his head. "No. You don't have to think about your needs because John has already met them. Maybe he doesn't always get it right ... because all men are fuckups, right, Maggie?"

"Speak for yourself, old man." John chuckled.

Cal couldn't help but grin. "Still, he's there. John's a constant. Every day. There for you in ways no one else will ever be. Don't. Judge. Me. And don't put ideas into Annie's head. From the start, you've been inserting your fucking ideas into her head. I know how to really be with someone"—he swallowed—"when I find a girl with substance. Character. Fuck, you know that, Maggie."

"I think the substance scares you off." An ugly smile stretched across her pale face. "How do you know a woman has substance if you don't stick around long enough to find out?"

Cal slapped a palm on the countertop, and Maggie jumped. John splayed his hands in the air, feigning surrender.

Long enough to find out. Ridiculous... Women always knew where he stood. Even if it was on the fence.

"How do you find substance fucking someone who is—?"

"Who's what?" Cal interrupted, a sudden, awful heat on the nape of his neck.

"You know what I'm talking about. Or can't you say it?"

"John told you about her?" Cal's tongue felt heavy, his throat heavier. His palms grew sweaty.

"Yes." She glanced at her husband. "Why be with someone who's married? There! I said it for you."

"Maggie..." John pleaded.

Cal's gaze roamed the tips of his shoes. But the stupid black oxfords couldn't provide a reason or an excuse. The Lonely was a lame one, but it had fueled him. The familiar seven-month shame crept over him — the shame he'd left behind and tried forgetting since arriving in Miami.

"I'm sorry, Cal." John placed a bottle of Jameson and three highballs on the counter. "You know I tell the wife pretty much everything."

"You're defending him?" Maggie snapped.

"This is different," Cal uttered as he picked bits of nothing off his pants and flicked them. "I made a mistake with Reegan. Annie is different." His grip slipped...

Slip. Slip. Slipping. Gone...

The different was upstairs. Close and near. In the bed sleeping.

God, what a beautiful castle in the sand Annie had been earlier, her forest-green eyes shining in the moonlight, reflecting pieces of him he thought he'd stowed well beneath his surface.

And that look he'd seen in her eye...

Sure, she had a million, and each one pierced him, but *the look*, the base-ball-bat crack of a stare.

"*I'm not that girl, Cal,*" she'd said. "*You know who I am.*"

How much longer could he deny it? All of it. The throat-closing ache. The need to keep her safe. The endless, unfathomable pull Annie had over him.

"I know she's different," Maggie retorted. "And she's young."

Cal returned to the present with those harsh words. Back to the tension. The bullshit fight. His age. Hers. Reality.

Pinching his neck, he turned and took a few steps, giving Maggie his back-side, attempting to restrain himself from really losing his temper because

Margaret Jacqueline Oppenheimer was somehow an expert at pushing all his I-need-to-be-in-control buttons.

Massaging the back of his neck, he concentrated solely on breathing, then he turned and joined the two of them again.

"You really are on your high horse." His voice nearly splintered. His eyes blazed. Age was a fucking number. That lesson had been learned early on, at twenty-fucking-one. A number. "If all I wanted from Annie was one thing, do you really think I would've come here tonight ... to face you? You don't know how I feel. It's all I can do not to go upstairs and break down the door to be with her."

Maggie's eyes narrowed.

Cal upped her stare.

"It's not just the sex. It's her." A film of sweat coated his nape, his palms. "I want to be with *her* — all the time."

Cal couldn't stave off the nerves.

Had they noticed?

Turning from Maggie, he looked at the floor. Yes, she'd noticed, and she'd pushed him too far this time.

Too. Far.

He wanted to be with Annie ... all the time?

Cal's eyes grew wider and wider as he brushed his knuckles across his cheek, his fucking emotions agitated.

He didn't need emotion.

He certainly didn't need to show it. Not like this. Like some sort of love-struck, hormone-affected teenager.

Cal looked up, past Maggie and over at John, his next words a struggle. "I'll take that drink now, please."

"I didn't realize you felt that way about her," she muttered, an apology written all over her face.

"It shouldn't matter, Maggie. This is none of your fucking business," Cal droned, an eerie calm in his voice despite the curse.

Jameson filling the crystal became the only sound for a moment, the clank of the bottle as it hit each glass.

"Annie is my business, Cal." Maggie twirled one of the highballs, then glanced at him. "Do you even know? Are you even aware of the shit she's gone through?" Maggie clapped a palm over her mouth.

"I'm sorry." Cal brought Maggie closer, forcing an embrace, resting his chin on top of her curls. "I am aware. Annie told me about her brother's death. She told me last week."

"Did she tell you how it happened?" Maggie popped her head up, her eyes blank, her voice dull.

"We don't have to do this tonight." John reached an arm out.

"We do." She gently pushed her husband's hand away.

"No," Cal said. "She didn't tell me."

Suddenly, the man had no room inside his damn shoes to wiggle his toes. Shifting a foot, he twisted an ankle toward the floor, trying to numb the remembrance of being unable to take away Annie's pain the night they'd come home from the Keys. The panic attack he'd wished to make obsolete in the middle of his staircase.

He hadn't wanted her to leave.

She couldn't leave.

The void she carried around, the one he'd been unable to obliterate ... even as they'd made love on the futon. *Made love*?

Twist. Numb. Twist.

Cal coughed, planting that left foot onto solid ground, waiting for Maggie to fill in the blanks.

"Peter was only thirty-six." Maggie dropped her forearms on the counter. "Coming home from work on his motorcycle..." Her voice started to crack. "And the roads ... they were wet from rain." She swallowed. "No one really knows why he lost control of the bike, but it wasn't alcohol." Maggie stood tall and met Cal's eyes. "They pronounced him dead at the scene."

John rubbed his wife's back, wiped a tear from her cheek, and pulled her against him. Cal stared across the nook, his eyes climbing the staircase, initially stopping on the step where he'd first seen Annie. Then his gaze ascended to the top, landing on what looked like an apparition.

After shaking his head, he swiped a palm clear across his face, and when he looked up again, he only saw death.

No ghosts. Or shadows. No *heavy*.

"Annie was away at school when it happened," Maggie continued, a hand over her upper lip. "We flew out to Washington for the funeral. The whole family... I'd never seen Annie's father so undone... It was awful."

Maggie's gaze combed the kitchen as her hands met in a triangle below her nose. "I stayed with Annie and her mom for a few days. I tried to talk her into taking the next semester off school, but she wouldn't hear of it. She said Peter wouldn't have wanted her to stop." Maggie paused and looked at John, her eyes welling with tears.

John wrapped his arms around his wife again, and she leaned into his chest. After a moment of silence, she picked up her head and scrubbed two fingers under her nose.

"Mags, you've had too much to drink. You've worked hard all day. Let's go to bed, honey."

"I can't." Maggie removed herself from John's embrace and walked around the counter until she stood face-to-face with Cal. He set his drink down.

"You weren't around, Cal." Her eyes moved back and forth. She touched his wrist. "His passing ... it changed her."

Cal pulled his hand from her grasp and ran his fingers through his hair.

"Do you understand now? If I'm overly concerned about Annie? It's not only about you or your past. It's Annie I'm worried—"

"Annie is stronger than you give her credit for, Maggie."

Dropping her chin, she smiled and shook her head. "I am going to go to bed, honey." She stepped toward John and kissed his cheek. "Good night."

"I'll be up soon," John replied.

Maggie stopped at the bottom of the wooden staircase. Both men glanced over at her.

"Don't lead her on, Cal." Their gazes locked. Cal wanted to swallow but didn't. "Don't break Annie's heart."

She went upstairs. Cal downed the whiskey. But the fucking lump in his throat wouldn't budge.

Fucking Maggie. She always did want the last word.

John tried to ease the tension, making innocuous conversation as Cal nodded, pretending to listen, feigning a smile. But all the while, Cal's mind drifted to Annie. To the ocean. To the searching he'd begun since coming to understand there was more to life than the lies people believed in order to comfort themselves.

Where was the water Siddhartha had found? In Annie's eyes? Across her precious face? He was done searching for something he would never find.

Sure. Done.

Or perhaps Annie was the beginning of the whisperings in the water.

The night they'd met, it felt like he'd been blinded, healed, then dragged to the edge of the ocean, forced to look upon his own reflection.

And what he'd seen scared the fucking shit out of him.

Rosa said Cal lied to himself. Of course he lied to himself. He'd been excelling at that sport for years.

"*How do you feel?*" Annie had asked him in the car on the ride home last week.

"*I think you know,*" he'd replied.

The truth?

Cal did want to knock down Annie's bedroom door to be with her. To lie next to her the way they'd embraced on the beach, absorbing *her* strength, the power Maggie thought Annie didn't possess. To listen to her speak a thousand stories. To breathe her air. To smell tangerines. All. The. Time. He wanted to hold her in the sand under the stars until morning. He wanted...

A clock with no hands.

The creature with a million shards of magnets for skin, reeled him in, pulled on him, calling him home.

Home?

She provided a comfort. Lust versus throat-closing ... what? A polar pull he hadn't felt since... Since college 1991. The undeniable connection clouded his mind, strangling his normal cool, collected logic.

He needed to think.

Think.

Cal didn't want to lead her on. *Fuck.* Break her heart.

She wouldn't fall in love. Not with him. No one needed him. This was addiction. She was an addiction.

Not a mistake.

Not logic.

An addiction.

Not a choice.

Okay. Sure. Wrong. She'd always been a choice ... and somehow not a choice. A perfect double entendre. And it was too late to stop this now, anyway. It had been too late the night he'd met her.

It couldn't be stopped.

The magnets. The truth in her eyes. The tangerine fields he ran through when inside her warm body.

It was the summer. Annie was summer.

The sun.

The sky.

Truth.

A temporary distraction.

Fuck. She was anything but a distraction.

Cal needed to stop analyzing the hell out of it and have fun. Enjoy it while it lasted. Because he would leave. She would leave. That was the way it had to be. Logical, right?

Fuck logic.

Fuck the chalkboard of arithmetic he couldn't solve or delete or erase.

Cal wouldn't give up Annie. Not for Maggie. Not to avoid the reality of the future or some imagined heartache. Annie had said she didn't want to hear of plans or facts or logic.

Right?

Ever.

Well, neither did he. Summer would burn off illogical balderdash. The false addiction called Annie would become rational sense.

THIRTY-TWO

White buds tucked inside her ears, Annie lay in bed, trying to replace the ache in her stomach, the empty in her heart, trying to stop the tears from falling while replaying the pieces of conversation she'd overheard at the top of the staircase, the yelling that had made its way through her closed bedroom door, the voices that had been impossible to ignore.

Crouched in a fetal position, no covers over her clammy body, Johnny Cash singing via iTunes, his vibrato filtering through her scattered, morose thoughts, she cried the lyrics to "Hurt," salt spilling into her mouth in the process, the landslide making its way down the mountain of her heart — the way it had been for over a year.

A million cherished moments struck her brain like bolts of lightning, playing like a film in her head as the chords progressed and The Man in Black sang. Even the sepia-colored music video came to mind — Johnny's, not Nine Inch Nails'. A visceral, stunning portrayal of a man's life. A man snuffed out, gone too soon.

Like Peter.

Now, the words became her own, as was often the case with music. The listener applied lyrics to their own life, and these words were autobiographical. They were about her and him and regrets — the bottom she'd fallen into, the one she was uncertain she would ever climb out of.

She was afraid. So fucking afraid.

Her entire body shook.

Annie was afraid all the people she loved — the people she could luckily count on two hands — would leave her and go away, never to return.

Like the song said.

Peter's idol, Johnny Cash, died shortly after that video was made. Her brother loved that song. Both versions. Both renditions haunting, a slideshow of life and its many varied emotions. Peter used to play it on his guitar. She could hear him now, simultaneously with Johnny, both strumming and singing as lightning bolts electrocuted her, as memories consumed her, as tears choked her.

The song climaxed.

The tempo increased.

The melody bit into her skin.

And as the fallboard on the piano closed, Annie shut her eyes, praying she wouldn't dream of tunnels and hollows and birthday cakes.

She would claw her way up from the bottom.

She would find a way *not* to center her life around the pain.

PART TWO
WANDERLUST

BELONGING

THE SAFEST PLACE IN THE WHOLE WIDE WORLD

I visited you
in my waking sleep
nightmares
dreams
agitation
I gave birth
to fears
sucked doubt's dick
fancied nothing
sat up
played dumb
discovered denial
not far from truth
discovered
you
at the bottom
of my rock bottom

where were you
when I slipped
my fix

my hero

A group of people scared me off
noises laid claim to me
but you
you rescued me
saved me
you called me home
and missed me

THIRTY-THREE

"Miss?"

Annie became agitated in the narrow seat, her neck cramping. Reality seemed to be attempting to mix with her peaceful slumber. A birthday cake and a wish. The voice of—

"Miss." A hand shook her shoulder, breaking the notion Annie had put faith in for a moment. "Miss, wake up. You need to put your seat belt on. We're preparing to land."

Annie blinked her eyes open, yawned, then clicked the lock into place — its sole job to keep her safe from an accident.

An accident...

Rubbing her eyes, she sat forward and exhaled, blowing out the candles on the cake from the dream.

The dream had felt real. Realer than real.

If only she could bottle that hope, harness this break from anxiety, Annie would be able to carry Peter with her for the remainder of the trip — for the day, for life.

Why was her brother so vivid in her dreams?

Finding his way into small places, out of corners, into corners. The alleyways and tunnels. Peter was always alive in the dream. Someone — it didn't matter the person — would explain his presence by saying the accident had been a mistake. Sometimes no explanation was provided, but even without one, the mistake of his death was an unspoken acknowledgment.

Of course his death had been a mistake. Nothing like that happened in real life. A motorcycle crash. Pronounced dead at the scene. It had to be someone else's reality.

Not Annie's.

She was a dreamer. An optimist. A curator of magic. But the last year had caused her to stop believing in things like forever or fate. Or reasons for anything.

She hadn't lost her imagination, though. Not completely.

Staring out the plane's window, New York City, with its spiky, cerebral building tops, looked like a mirage. An invention. Annie peered through the glass, eyes blurring, until her heart reaccepted what she knew to be true. Until she could escape. She would jump through the window and fly. Create a story. Make something up through the lens of her Nikon.

Even though many things had been stolen from her that horrible day in May, Annie had something no one could take. Not even death. As she gazed down upon one of the greatest cities in the world, she smiled, knowing absolutely nothing could rob her of that birthright.

THIRTY-FOUR

The rain had started coming down in droves the moment Annie exited the airport and arrived on the city's pavement. In fact, it poured the entire drive to the two-story brick building in the West Village — the apartment where Annie's two best friends resided with their dog...

"Marlon," Tom strained, holding the dog's collar, the golden retriever's shiny black nose the first thing Annie saw peeking through the opening of the door. "Stop, boy."

"I woke you." Annie laughed, squeezing by them as she made her way inside.

"Quick, shut the door." Tom's wavy hair fell across his forehead, the chestnut strands appearing slept on, mussed, not combed ... typical and basically adorable.

Annie arched a brow. "A little grumpy today, aren't we, T?"

Marlon sniffed around Annie's crotch as she touched his furry head. Tom stared at her, his amber eyes still coated with a thick sheen of sleep.

"You're soaked."

Dropping her chin to her chest, she pinched the damp cotton away from her skin. "It's not 'wet T-shirt' soaked."

"Yeah." He snapped a towel off the kitchen counter and tossed it to her. "What would you know about that?"

She caught it, smirked, then blotted her face with it.

"It's been raining here for like forty days and forty nights." He jammed a set of keys in his pocket.

"Maybe I brought it with me from Miami." After setting the towel on the counter, she knelt in front of Marlon, giving him more attention. "Hi, big boy." Annie patted his coat. "Did you miss me? Yeah."

"Where's my hello?" Tom smiled.

Annie rolled her eyes, stood tall, and embraced the adorable, cranky man. Thomas McAlester did need his sleep, though. He worked as a nurse on the graveyard shift at Mount Sinai.

"He's the one who woke me," Tom grumbled. "I have to walk him."

Annie's gaze traveled from the boys to the couch, landing on the spot Tab had apparently already arranged for her guest, probably before leaving to prepare for the matinee. A sheet was tucked into the cushions, a pillow and a folded blanket on top. *Old times,* Annie thought as she rolled her suitcase into the living room and found a little enclave for her things.

The moment she looked up, her eyes stopped on the vintage lamp sitting on one of the end tables. It had a gold cherub for a body, complete with wings, toes touching the earth, arms reaching to the heavens.

Suddenly, Annie couldn't move or breathe.

The lamp had been what she'd fixated upon when standing in the middle of Tab's kitchen, listening to her father repeat her name into the phone.

Annie swallowed, wrenching her gaze from the beautiful angel, and stepped closer to the living room window, pressing her throbbing head against the speckled glass. Rain had fallen incessantly that fateful day in May too. Raining in New York City when she'd received the dreadful call from her father. Raining in Seattle, day after day, the week of the funeral.

The dream she'd experienced a thousand times flashed through her mind. The one from the plane...

"Annie," the familiar voice called in her sleep. The room seemed hollow. Felt hollow. Like the inside of a tree trunk. Or an underground concrete tunnel. "Come on, Annie. It's time."

The voice echoed, becoming louder and clearer with each call. "Annie. Annie. Annie..."

Except no one was there. Or she couldn't reach them — the voice with no face. Not even a hazy outline. Still, she knew who the melodious sound belonged to, but not where it came from.

A door materialized.

She opened it and stepped into a sterile room. A white box. A dark, wood table occupied the center, juxtaposed to all the alabaster.

Beverly stood behind the furniture next to Annie's father. Her parents looked artificial against the snowy walls, their faces glowing from the light the sixteen candles on the cake in front of them provided.

"Help me blow them out, Peter," Annie said to her brother, the distant voice she'd heard in the tunnel. Peter appeared instantly, as if he'd never been gone.

He wasn't gone. Peter was always there. He was here.

Right now.

Death had made a mistake. His death had been a mistake.

Everyone knew it. Annie knew it was true.

"Help me blow out my candles."

Her mother and father smiled at their daughter, then at each other, showing perfect teeth, each gesture happening in slow motion.

Then the stewardess had spoken, touching Annie's shoulder, interrupting the immaculate moment of dreamlike security where everything wrong had been made right.

The space between sleep and awake.

The minutes Superman circled the globe, took back time, and made it his, resurrecting Lois Lane.

For a few endless seconds, Peter had been alive. Things were as they should've been. The tightness in Annie's belly had recoiled. The cloud hanging over her mind had departed.

Nothing could contaminate this dream.

Except life.

Now, she had to force herself to leave behind childhood notions. She had to let them go. Watch them fade outside the window. Tab's window. Let summer run away with the idea that the world continued to spin on its axis without Peter's presence.

Annie had to acclimate to reality.

And the reality was she felt odd standing in her best friends' apartment looking out their living room window, wondering how this place could feel both intimate and fresh ... and different. Like somewhere she'd been before but couldn't fully remember.

Something *had* changed since the dream on the plane ... since the conversation she'd overheard on the staircase last night.

Annie shook off the peculiar sensations, insisting she felt safe in this home away from home. The brownstone off the beaten path on a tucked-away, one-way, L-shaped street — an alley filled with trees, the branches hovering over it like a canopy.

Reminiscent of Cal's street.

Except there were fewer trees here. Still, they were striking, with their summer leaves supplying a little shade from the heat. Perhaps a bit of respite from the storm. Annie recalled the way they looked in the winter when they didn't have any leaves — only branches, sticks ... snowman parts.

"It's hot as fuck," Tom said, interrupting her thoughts, sidling up beside her, looking out the same window. She shook a little. "Did I scare you?"

Annie feigned a smile, grimacing as she rubbed a temple.

"You have a headache?"

"Huh?"

"Some things never change."

"I don't always have a headache." But today, she had a horrible one. The pounding had started after landing.

"No, Ann," he said and made his way to the door. Marlon was already leashed. "You're daydreaming."

Palming her throat, Annie's gaze wandered to Tab's infamous collage. It covered the entire wall next to the newlyweds' bedroom. No matter how many times Annie had seen it — probably thousands — she lost herself in the images. Snapshots of family, friends, vacations.

The Wall of Life Annie always called it.

"Do you need anything while I'm out?" Tom asked, waltzing into Annie's thoughts again. Marlon barked, and Tom grabbed a large umbrella — the one Annie had bought them, the vinyl depicting Humphrey Bogart and Ingrid Bergman gazing at each other like they were the only two stars in the universe.

"You have to go?" Annie asked. "Out in the rain and everything?"

"My master beckons." Tom opened the door. "We have Advil or some shit in the cabinet for your headache. Did you eat? Do you want me to pick up a sandwich or something? You like steak and cheese, right?"

Massaging her throat again, her eyes went back to the collage, climbing photo after photo, her gaze inching up the wall like the Itsy Bitsy Spider.

"Are you sure you're okay, Ann?"

The word *okay* managed to capture her attention. "Yes, Thomas, I'm fine," she remarked in a dramatic baritone, but he didn't seem to be buying that bullshit. "I'm fine," she repeated. "Go."

"Help yourself to whatever food you can find in that tiny room we call a kitchen." He laughed.

"Hey, wait." Annie joined them in the hall. Marlon's tongue was out, his tail wagging. The leash was stretched, fully open, as was Tom's arm. "Are you going tonight?"

"No, I have to work." Marlon started to lead his subject down the stairwell. "Have to cover an early shift," Tom called out as the two boys disappeared around the corner.

The second Annie closed the front door, she rested her back against it and sighed. The first time she'd been alone in a while. Completely alone. Her palm shook as she covered her mouth and surveyed the apartment again. The collage, the window, *the lamp.*

Her stomach growled.

She'd skipped breakfast.

The headache rendered almost every other sensation into useless background fodder. Only the headache, hunger, exhaustion, and the *different* she'd felt since the plane ride existed. Nothing else.

After making her way to the kitchen, Annie opened the fridge. As she tugged her damp shirt away from her body, a chill ran up her spine. "These damn wet clothes." Squeezing her lids shut, she willed a reprieve from the throbbing. *A moment. Please.* "I need to eat."

She took out a block of cheddar, poured a glass of water, then opened a couple of cabinets. They'd moved things around since she'd last been here, Tabitha never content with the ordinary. The lazy Susan in the corner cupboard contained supplements and medicine, not crackers.

Annie scanned the labels, until one particular bottle caught her attention. She removed two pills, snapped the lid back into place, then cradled the white ovals in her fist. Her palms started to sweat as she stared down at them. 5 milligrams each. In as quick as fifteen minutes, she could feel relief...

No, this is not a good idea. A devil and an angel began to debate across the tops of her shoulders. The angel had piped up first.

Yes, you can take them. You have self-control. You're a different person now. You deserve to relax. To feel good. To eat and not have a headache. To not feel alone. To escape the different, different, different. The bullshit.

No, Annie. Don't take them.

Yes. Do it. It'll be the last time. It's not a big deal.

It's not a good idea.

It is. You need this today. Only today.

Fuck. This. Shit, she thought as she tossed them back and swallowed a gulp of water.

Done. Now, to find the crackers. Except her phone pinged, interrupting her search. Annie pulled the device from her pocket, then swiped the screen. A picture of Barney along with a message from her mother came into full view.

Mom: Are you okay? I haven't heard from you. Did you land?

Poor Barney, dressed in an outfit, rested in a pet stroller, looking ridiculous. Annie rolled her eyes, then she took a selfie, her hair slightly matted from the rain, a smile woven across her face — minus the eye-rolling. She sent it and a polite message, complimenting Barney, wishing them well, informing her mother that yes, she had indeed landed safely.

After finding some crackers and eating quite a few, Annie pushed aside the plate and fingered her hair until it looked somewhat presentable. Then she took another photo. She took several actually. Peering into the camera, eyes haunting, her mouth pursed, not smiling.

The pictures were quite a contrast to the one she'd sent Beverly. Annie texted the photo she liked best to Cal, along with her return itinerary, and then she made her way to the makeshift bed Tab had prepared and put on some dry clothes. The moment she plopped down, The Wall of Life caught her attention. Annie focused on a few pictures, remembering all the details, the timeframes, while twirling damp strands of hair around an index finger.

Life had changed since many of those — since most of those — had been taken. Everything was different. Even now, tons of change, after only a few short weeks of absence from this city.

It was a strange feeling to experience in such an intimate space.

Annie stretched out on the couch, closed her eyes, and clutched a throw pillow.

It came hard and fast.

The medication hadn't helped to contain the emotions. Not yet.

Define it. Please.

Annie didn't want to define anything. Not *it*. Not feelings. She didn't want to remember. She pushed the surge back — *go away* — into an abyss before the emotions completely engulfed her, the feelings trying to suffocate her on the pretty, made-for-her couch.

Right as the war inside her head was about to commence, her phone chimed. She glanced at the text message on the screen, but it wasn't from Beverly.

Cal: Thursday can't come soon enough. You're beautiful.

Release. Swoosh.

Water trapped behind a dam flowed.

The crying began first in whispers as Annie attempted in vain to hold back the deluge with the stubbornness of a mule, but it was no good. Everything she'd tried to quell burst forth like the shattering of the Hoover Dam in the 1978 film *Superman*.

A million tiny cracks splintering open over its surface, water went everywhere all at once. Mainly in her heart and throat. Her stomach. A mess only one man could clean up. The man with the S on his chest. The man with superhuman strength.

Another text bleeped.

She stopped up the dam. No, he did.

He flew in and made time itself obsolete.

Cal sent a link to a song. Not very subtle with this particular selection. Maybe the chameleon never was mysterious when it came to his choice of music. She squeezed her eyes shut. Leftover tears slid out. But before clicking the link, she Googled the lyrics and read them.

Medication now traipsing through her bloodstream, mushrooms began to sprout. Nerve endings waltzed across the tips of the fungus as she dwelled on the not-so-mysterious lyrics of The Rolling Stones' tune "Miss You."

The phone shook in her palm.

Definitely. Not. Obscure.

Who are you, Calvin Prescott?

Each song he'd ever shared had told her things he couldn't say aloud. Things he dared not say or was afraid to say.

Was he afraid? Waiting? Missing her?

The same sensation that came over her whenever Cal was near struck her now. Something else hit too. A good kind of nausea. Butterflies in her stomach magnified to infinity.

The feelings seemed to start in her toes or between her thighs. They were everywhere and hard to pinpoint. Similar to an orgasm, the energy ran through her completely, swirling in her middle, low in her belly, vibrating through her entire body — her veins, her muscles, her bones. Escaping through her pores as she began to dance, eyes shut. Synapses firing across the tops of the mushrooms. There were a lot of fungus now. Fat, round capped. Long-stemmed. Too many to count. Fuzzy, warm, vivid daydreams came. Unusual mind pictures. Lucidity. Problems were insignificant. A thin film of sweat slicked every inch of her body, the heat enthralling the way it might a sunbather on a tropical vacation, as she bounced off the mushroom tops in Mario Kart.

Hop. Pounce. Vault.

Dropping, falling with an open parachute, then jumping up again, up-up-up, then gliding down-down-down. Sadness, a blip on the radar. She was a balloon, a blimp, a fantastic thing in motion — untouchable and suspended — and for once, her mind harbored absolute peace, no over-thinking. Only quiet.

The next thing she knew, without having played "Miss You," without sending a reply to Cal ... Annie fell asleep.

Neither Tom's nor Marlon's return stirred her from her slumber. And when she woke up, she felt renewed. Annie Baxter, daydreamer extraordinaire, felt ready to take on New York fucking City.

Thirty-Five

Annie arrived in Midtown at the restored firehouse-turned-Off-Broadway theater minutes before curtain, dressed for the wet weather in boots and Tabitha's rain jacket.

She strolled down the center aisle, maroon seats on her left and right, until she found a single cushiony chair five rows from the stage. Crossing a leg over her knee, she peered at the people, listening to the hum of their chatter while she waited for the imminent arrival of the characters, the plot, and Tabitha — the friend she hadn't seen yet and couldn't wait to.

Annie hoped tonight would be a wonderful escape from the anxiety that had returned in spades. Although, she'd woken up from her nap refreshed — showered, dressed, and even sporting a little makeup — by the time she walked toward the doors of the theater on 45th Street, Annie's stomach had knotted itself into a million twisty little threads of bullshit.

She planted her feet on the ground. The tapping of the soles of her boots on the floor made her knees bounce. She chewed a nail. Bit a lip. Twirled a piece of hair.

She waited.

In the stillness, another feeling descended, overwhelming her ridiculously fragile nerves. Sprinkling her body the way the rain cloaked the city. It wasn't a panic attack. Or was it the beginning of one? Had the sweet-sixteen birthday dream been a prelude to a noxious, heart-choking descent through the eye of a needle?

Peter was only a dream.

She'd experienced tons of those — *he's alive, he's alive, he's alive* — dreams. What was it, then?

Something ... something...

Annie found herself longing for the peace of Maggie's home — the sound of the ocean a most-welcomed noise. She needed her room where silence was abundant. Because here, Annie felt like an insignificant grain of sand on New York City's beach. Being pelted by its surf and wind, by the millions of people walking and walking and walking — in a hurry across its shore. Annie was merely another person. A mosquito. A gnat. An insect.

I'm a bug. Trapped. In the throngs.

Fly. Flight. Flee. Leave.

She wanted to bolt from her seat, escape her scattered thoughts — Post-it notes she scrawled on and couldn't keep track of — and run from the inde-scribable, the unavoidable, the nothingness which had begun its chase at the airport. The somethingness. Something. Something. Something.

Stop!

The lights in the auditorium dimmed. The audience became quiet. The black curtain parted. An actor took center stage. *Stop.* She clenched her fists. Bit her bottom lip. *Stop. Straitjacket yourself to the seat. Don't move. Watch the play. Shut up.*

A couple hours later — a full-blown panic attack somehow averted — Annie leaned against a brick wall outside a random dressing room door after the play. Hands in her pockets, face somewhat down-turned, she observed the hustle of the behind-the-scenes action, the goings-on every bit as exciting as the show had been. The story had accomplished the task of distracting her from the cage of her mind.

"Annie!" Tab shrieked, an ink pen above an ear, her long hair pulled tight in a clip — still, pieces of the raven strands clawed her freckled face. "You're wearing my coat. Aren't you hot?" Smiling, Tab pulled at the knotted string around Annie's waist. "God, it's so good to see you."

The two friends hugged.

And even though Annie rested her chin on Tab's shoulder, smelled the vanilla in her perfume, felt a relaxing, familiar comfort in their embrace, Annie couldn't help but focus on the wall of bricks she faced.

The need to touch and photograph them, to stare at those spaces and colors until her eyes blurred — the places where the concrete created chasms — superseded everything. The gray grout along with the warm reds and burnt orange of the bricks soothed her. Made her feel safe. Gave her something to concentrate on besides the love she had a hard time accepting while wrapped up in Tabitha's arms.

Whatever it might take to deny the feelings which had consumed her since arriving. Acknowledging this moment might split her wide open.

"Did you like the play?" Tab pulled away and squared Annie's shoulders. "What did you think?"

"I did. I really liked—"

"There are so many people I want you to meet." Tab took the pen from her ear and tapped the air with it. "We're going to a great little place not far from here to celebrate."

Annie stuffed her hands back into the raincoat pockets but left her thumbs poking out of the creases as she twisted her lip between her teeth and sighed. "I'm sorry ... I can't. I'm not feeling well. Tom gave me a key. I need to go back to the apartment and lie down."

Tab's brow furrowed. She rested the back of her hand on Annie's forehead the way Maggie had been doing lately. "Are you sick?"

"No." Annie glanced at the ceiling, then at the few people still milling about. "I think I just need to rest. I'm exhausted."

"God, Annie, you know I have to stay."

"I know..." Annie paused, getting lost inside her friend's blue-blue eyes. "It's me, okay." Annie shrugged. "I'm sorry. I—"

Tab reached out and squeezed Annie's hand. "Don't feel bad. It's probably all this damn rain. You'll feel better tomorrow. I hear the sun is actually supposed to make an appearance by then."

Both girls smiled as they immediately sang the line the little orange-haired orphan made famous, the one about the sun. The *Annie* song. Tabitha, with her adoration of musicals, loved to tease Annie about that.

"I have the day off tomorrow. Remember?" Tab tugged on the raincoat belt, but Annie didn't budge. "Come here, silly." She pulled her friend in for another hug, this one deeper and longer.

"Thank you," Annie mumbled, her head over Tab's shoulder.

Those bricks had lost their appeal. Being "normal" had apparently also lost its appeal. Once upon a time, Annie actually enjoyed going out, hanging out, doing things. Now, she walked around with a wad of cotton in her throat, a bunch of shit in her stomach. She lived inside a turtle shell. Closed up and off. Broken. Not normal.

What the fuck was normal anyway?

A word. A connotation. Subjective bullshit.

A lame word designed to make weirdos feel even weirder. But she could've done without the anxiety, the running, the suffocation, the whatever-something feelings, the desire to swallow pills, the panic attacks, the blah, blah, blah. *Fuck. Me.*

"Do you need any help getting a taxi?" Tab yelled across the open space.

Annie had pulled herself together and now stood at the exit, looking over her shoulder, about to push on the fat bar to open the door. "It hasn't been that long."

"Yeah, well, cabs can be a bitch to flag down around here. Get an Uber."

"I'll manage."

All smiles, blue eyes twinkling, Tab waved. "I'll see you in the morning, Annie-pie. I'm sure you'll be asleep when I get home."

Those blue-blue eyes, the wave, the "Annie-pie," and their goodbye turned out to be the most "normal" thing Annie had experienced since stepping foot off the plane.

THIRTY-SIX

"This is odd," Annie heard Tab mutter from the kitchen.

Adjusting her sight to the glow of the stove light while sticking her thumb and index finger into the corners of her eyes, Annie groaned. It was early Monday. Tom must've still been sleeping.

"Are you awake?" Tab made her way to the other end of the counter, the prescription bottle she palmed now in plain sight.

"What?" Annie batted her lids, sat up, and yawned. "I am now. What is it?"

"T's pills." Tab hoisted them up, giving the photographer an even better view.

"Oh, I left those out yesterday." Annie grabbed some hair and started to twirl the strands. "I'm sorry. I had a really bad headache."

Tab glared at Annie.

"What?" Annie grumbled.

"You know what."

"No. I. Don't," she insisted as she looked away, at the blanket, the pillow, anything to avoid Tab's burning gaze. "Tom told me to take something for my—"

"Since when do people take hydrocodone for a headache, Annie?"

"Don't start with me. I just woke up." Annie stood and began to tool around for her things.

"I'll raise hell! We've barely had a chance to talk. And you've been strange since you got here. Is this why?" Tab's voice shook the way the little, white ovals did inside their amber prison.

There's about eight or ten left in there, Annie thought. *Eight.*

"No. And I only took two, okay?"

"Two!"

"I can take a freaking pill." She couldn't, though. She'd proven it. "I mean, you have them right there."

"Don't put this on me. These are from when T sprained his ankle. Six. Months. Ago."

"Stop treating me like a child." But maybe Annie was acting like a child. Not that she would've known what that meant, always playing the role of parent to her own mother. "Can we talk about something else, *please*?"

Nights spent on the couch or in bed, relaxed and in a fog, paraded through Annie's mind. Memories she wanted to erase mixed with the desire to swallow another one. *One.* She glanced at the bottle again. Eight left and she wanted only one.

"Promise me?" Tab pleaded, her eyes never bluer, hypnotic, begging — wet like a thousand rivers.

"I'm clean. I'm..." *Stand taller. Say it like you mean it.* "I'm never going down that road again. I promise."

"Good." Tab placed the bottle onto the counter in a huff. "Because you scared the shit out of me."

"You're the only one," Annie clipped, then covered her mouth.

"What?" Tab closed the distance between them and took her friend's hand.

"You're the only one who knew." Annie started to cry, but she sucked back the sobs, denying them release.

"Your parents knew you were on those anxiety meds?"

"That's all they knew."

"You never told your dad about this?" Tab nodded toward the bottle.

"No." She wiped away tears, sniffed, and straightened. "I'm done. With all of it. I'm done. I told you that months ago."

Tabitha squeezed Annie's palm. "I will always be the only one, hun."

Annie nodded, giving her friend a tight smile.

"Do you want to go get something to eat?"

"Not really."

"Aren't you hungry?"

"I guess." Annie shrugged.

"What's going on?" Tab asked. "If it's not the pills, then what the hell is it?"

"I don't want to go out right now … on the streets."

"Since when does the city bother you?"

"It doesn't." The bagels, the coffee, the bridges, the park and the trees, the taxicab seats. "I don't know. This visit—" Annie stopped short, shook her head, and held back another garbage bag full of tears. She never used to cry like this either. Back when she was *normal*.

"I have to take Marlon Brando for a walk," Tab said. They could hear him clawing the other side of T's bedroom door. "I want you to come with me."

Annie's best friend knew exactly when to change the subject. She knew when to push and when to wait. After all, timing was the hallmark of any great actress. Besides, Annie was like fine wine. The cork might've been removed from the bottle, but any sensible person understood the tannins needed a moment to breathe.

Bright sky, green leaves, horns and the occasional siren, greeted the three of them as they made their way onto the street. As did the heat. The temperature wasn't much different than Miami's, humidity you could slice and spread with a butter knife.

They hadn't wandered too far from the building. A few other people were out, walking their dogs, returning from the market, jogging. Nothing remained of the endless rainstorm but a few puddles … and the heat.

"It must be record temps here this summer," Annie said as they strolled, the shade from the trees doing their best to provide a little relief.

"I wish we could drive to the beach. Oh, I forgot…" Tab laughed. "You *live* at the beach."

Annie grinned.

"Are you meeting Beck tomorrow?" Tab asked as Marlon Brando casually sniffed around the girls' feet and toes, then toward the cracks in the sidewalk.

"Yeah, around noon." Beck, her pencil-thin former editor, the man with the perfectly groomed orange goatee, the one who occasionally tossed Annie freelance assignments. "How late do you work?"

"Two."

"I don't know exactly when I'll be home."

"Take your time. That is, after all, the reason you came back up here."

"I came to see you too."

"I know you did." Tab removed a section of hair hiding beneath Annie's shirt collar. "But your priority needs to be meeting curators."

"What about Wednesday?"

"I couldn't find anyone to cover my shift and I've already taken off so much for the play."

"The play was really great."

"Yeah? Thanks." They stopped walking while Marlon did his business, Tab prepared to scoop, glove on one hand, bag in the other. "What were your favorite parts?"

Annie glanced up at the sky, a palm over her forehead, blocking the light peeking around the white clouds, avoiding the wonderful scene happening near her feet. "I liked the relationship between the mother and daughter." She eyed Tab. "The actresses did a really good job — an amazing job — showing the emotions of the characters, sometimes without even speaking."

"Didn't they?" Tab gushed.

"You did a good job." Annie poked Tab's arm.

"Mmm. My part was small." Tab smirked.

"I thought there were no *small* parts," Annie teased.

"That's right. 'I am big...'" Tab began in her best Gloria Swanson voice.

"Ahh! I love that! What's that from again?" Annie asked as Tab finished the rest of the infamous movie line.

"*Sunset Boulevard.*"

"You always make me laugh, Tabitha McAlester." Annie smiled. "I've missed you."

"I've missed you, too."

The teakettle whistled. Tab lifted the pot off the stove and poured the boiling water into two mugs. Marlon and Tom slept. The girls had returned from their walk and eaten.

"You have some new pictures up on the wall," Annie said while dunking the chamomile bag into the steaming water.

"I finally put some up from our ski trip. The one we took with my mom."

"How is she? Did she have that test you told me about?"

"No, not yet." Tab lifted her mug and blew over the rim. "She's scheduled to have it Friday."

"I forgot," Annie replied, and Tab glanced off into the middle distance, the lines etching across her forehead attempting to mar her usual fearless face. "I'm sorry. I shouldn't have brought that up again."

"She's in remission," Tabitha interjected and glared at Annie. "Mom is fine." Tab swallowed. "She'll be fine."

Fine, fine, fine. You know the line, Annie thought as she made her way to the window in the living room, giving Tabitha's arm a gentle caress as she passed. Rather than looking outside, though, Annie's gaze immediately landed on a photo adorning the Wall of Life, one taken only days before Peter's accident. A picture of Annie and Tabitha in front of The Met, both grinning, arms around each other. It was uncanny. How the smile lit Annie's eyes — the way she liked to imagine it still did.

"You haven't talked about your mysterious man." Tabitha took a seat in one of the two chairs across from the couch, the window, and Annie's profile. "Did you think I forgot about him?" Tab tapped her nails on the ceramic mug and smirked. "What's his name again?"

"Very funny." Annie turned from the photo and narrowed her gaze on her friend. "You know his name."

"Are you still seeing *Cal*?"

"Have you just been waiting to ask me that?"

"You've had me on eggshells all morning. I've been waiting for the right time."

Annie placed her cup on the coffee table and her butt in the adjacent chair.

"Well, are you?"

"Am I what?"

"Annie!"

"Yes, I'm still seeing him," Annie replied as she lifted her legs and brought her knees toward her chest, wrapping her arms around them, locking her fingers together. Still dwelling on that photo and its pre-life-altering smile, her thoughts were far from Cal.

Inching closer, Tab put her hand on her friend's knee and shook it. "And?"

"And I don't want to kiss and tell. Not right now."

"*So* ... there has been some kissing to tell about?" Tab's eyebrows bounced like Tigger.

A fingernail found its way into Annie's mouth, and she nodded, but her insides frowned. Summoning any salacious detail about Cal right now seemed impossible. The man was a ladder to the stars, and Annie stood at the bottom rung.

"This is a good thing here." Tab smirked. "Don't deny yourself the fun of talking about this."

"You'll say anything to get what you want." Annie scoffed, rolled her eyes, and smiled. "Gossip whore."

"Bitch."

Annie laughed a little, but then her gaze quickly wandered to the collage again. To that picture. Back and forth her eyes darted from Tabitha to a daydreamer named Annie. From light to dark, past to present. Her stomach filled with sick. She rested her head on her knees and started to cry without making a sound.

Tabitha moved to the ottoman at the foot of Annie's chair. "I'm sorry." She stroked her friend's hair. "I shouldn't have pushed you to talk about him."

Stealing a quick peek at Tab, Annie said, "No," then sniffed. "It's not that."

"What is it, then?"

Define it, the voice said. Annie buried her face in her knees again. Define the uneasiness. The nothingness. The somethingness. The blank emotions beating a monstrous fist on the door to her heart.

Propping her head up, Annie heaved. "Being here with you"—she inhaled sharply—"in this apartment again." Her hands shook. "Being in this city"—she swallowed a gulp of air—"I can't stop thinking about Peter."

"Annie..."

"No, no, no! He's everywhere." She flung a hand out and waved it around. "The streets. The wind. He's here. I feel his death like I never did before. Did I not grieve him enough? Or ever? When will it end, Tab?" Annie stood, then sat. She wanted to pace. "My memories of being with him aren't here, in this apartment. Why can't I stop remembering how I felt and where I was when I found out he fucking died?" Her breath still came in gulps. Her eyes stung. Her throat felt like it had been cut with a razor blade. "I wasn't a good enough sister. I let him down. I should've been—"

"Bullshit. You were a good sister. You are. I don't want to hear you say that ever again."

Tears streamed down Annie's stone-like face. "I hate this." She wiped under her eyes, across her cheeks. "This is not me. I cry all the time."

"This is you." Tab grabbed a box of tissues from the end table. "Look at me. This is you. Crying doesn't make you weak."

Annie made a noise of disbelief as she took out a swath of Kleenex, blew her nose, and scrubbed her face, her chest still moving up and down in quick succession. Her heart still pounding.

Tabitha pulled the stool even closer to the seat, leaned into her friend, and pulled Annie against her, holding her until she calmed. Until her cries subsided and the shaking ceased.

"I had one..." Annie lifted her head off Tab's shoulder. "In front of him. The first bad attack in a couple of months — and it happened *right* in front of him."

"Any guy worth his salt would understand. Believe me when I tell you crying is not a sign of weakness."

Annie didn't know what to believe. She wasn't even sure where to rest her eyes. They shot around the room like loose cannons.

Was Cal worth his salt?

Was he going to put up with Annie's bullshit?

Would she put up with his?

"Where's your purse?" Tab asked, looking around. Annie pointed. "Do you still have that picture in your wallet?"

"Yes." Annie stood, dropped the crinkled tissues on the table, and retrieved the item. She kept only two pictures in her wallet: one with her first car and the other...

A photograph of a girl with her older brother.

Annie had been a teenager, braces still fastened to her teeth — a smile so bright, the sun glistened off the metal — when that picture had been taken. Peter looked the same as ever: handsome, hair the color of perfect little light brown leaves, bits of freckles on his nose and cheeks. His arm tightly wrapped around his little sister.

His smile took care of me, Annie thought. *Peter looked after me. Spoiled me. He needed me. He loved me. God, his love was unconditional. And he never feared saying the words out loud.*

Annie closed her eyes. She could hear him, his voice... "*I love you, Houdini.*"

"Why don't we take a walk?" Tab interrupted.

Annie's eyes popped open. She put the photo away, then sat on the couch. "We just took a walk."

"*Okay*... Then let's talk about your work. Show me the photographs you've been taking in South Beach. Hey, what about your Facebook? Did you do the photography page yet?"

Annie blinked and looked away.

"Annie..."

Ignoring the question, and Tab's lovely tone, Annie grabbed the laptop and opened a picture folder. For the next several minutes, while finishing their tea, she showed Tab Key Largo, the fish, the beach. *Cal.* The only photo she had of the two of them together being the imperfect-perfect selfie. Annie endured a few more of Tab's prying questions and an astonished, "Fuck, he's hot. He's forty-five? Looks thirty-five to me. Jesus, Annie." Then Annie opened a different folder ... and another ... and another. Folders full of family photos.

Annie told Tab things she hadn't thought about in a long time.

Ordinary things.

What truly mattered in life.

The way Peter loved to lick the knife after making a peanut butter and banana sandwich. How he focused with the concentration of a neurosurgeon when playing guitar chords. The way he held his hand, palm out, in a straight line when making a superfluous point. How he worked tirelessly to restore the antique bike he eventually crashed.

Times he had talked about wanting to be a father...

Annie practically choked on her own saliva.

Peter had tried for months with Trisha, his girlfriend, to make a baby — a secret not even their father knew about. Now, Tab knew. It felt good to share things Annie typically stowed beneath the surface. It was good to talk about him. The past, but in the present moment.

An old "normal" became new again.

THIRTY-SEVEN

On Tuesday and Wednesday, Beck — aka Mr. Theodore Becker — introduced Annie to several gallery owners. The curators were mostly friendly, the art on the walls beautiful, the galleries modern and sleek.

However, only one place requested her information.

Disappointment came with the territory. And ambivalence toward her work often served to encourage Annie, lighting a fire under her soul, inspiring her to try harder, to never stop pressing forward. Besides, no rejection could ever truly take away the joy experienced when capturing the images in the first place.

And that was precisely what she intended to do to lift her spirits.

Both afternoons, after leaving Beck behind, while Tabitha worked her real-world job, waiting tables at a local cafe, Annie walked the streets of New York City — alone but with accompaniment, the perfect companion hanging by a strap off her shoulder.

Block after block, Annie took photo after photo, never weary of photographing this city. No two places looked alike. The park, museums, restaurants, spots she'd seen perhaps dozens of times, shined like a diamond polished after being unearthed in a mine. There was always something new to discover, always a new way of seeing the same landscape.

Like lying on her back. On the ground.

Annie framed the sky, the sun, the clouds, walls, bricks, building tops.

Then she took extreme close-ups of stop signs, subway entrances, cracks in the sidewalks, making the obvious almost impossible to identify. Hundreds of people became her subject as well, maybe more, along with traffic lights and taxicabs, flowers and food for sale.

The people were the most engaging. Their energy contagious and stimulating, causing Annie to realize the differences we claimed to have weren't really all that different after all. Our insides were the same:

The same sadness when hurt.

The same aching loneliness.

The same excitement of the unknown.

All trapped by death and freed by life.

And nothing seemed more alive than New York City.

THIRTY-EIGHT

Early Thursday morning, the final day of her trip, Annie sat on the couch, eyeing Tabitha as she slipped out of her bedroom with a towel wrapped around her head and puppy dog slippers adorning her feet.

"He never wakes up when you take a shower, huh?"

"Holy shit, Annie." Tabitha jumped, then closed the door. "You scared me. I didn't think you'd be awake yet."

"I couldn't sleep." Annie set the laptop aside and stood. "Is Marlon sleeping too?"

"Yeah. Tom walked him when he came in from work. They sleep like babies together. T puts his earplugs in and turns on the fan. I swear, it's Marlon's breathing that keeps him dead to the world, though. They both snore." Tab imitated the sound as she entered the kitchen. "Way louder than you."

"Shhh. You'll wake them." Annie giggled. "And I do not snore."

"Oh, yes, you do. You should hear them, though. They're like a train. You'll probably hear the engine through the door soon. It's quite a scene." Tab started preparing coffee while glancing across the room. "Hey, you should sneak a picture of them."

"No," Annie replied, laughing. "I'll let them sleep. Besides, I think I took enough pictures this trip."

"You amaze me."

"What?"

"You never seem to bore of taking photos of New York. Don't you have about a gazillion by now?"

"It always looks fresh." Annie joined Tab in the kitchen, taking a seat on a stool. "There's always a new angle. The city still surprises me."

"Yeah, well, it surprised you this time for sure." Tab grabbed a bowl from the cabinet and a spoon from the drawer. Annie looked at the clock on the microwave, avoiding her friend's gaze. "Did you eat?"

"I had cereal."

"Me too." Tab picked up the box and shook some of its contents into the bowl.

"When are you going to take that damn thing off?" Annie eyed the purple towel on Tab's head.

"Don't be a bitch."

Smiling, Annie grabbed her phone from her pocket. It had just pinged.

"Is that your mom again?" She poured the milk. "Didn't she text you a bunch last night?" Tab shoved a spoonful of cereal into her mouth. "You have way more patience than me."

"It's not my mom." Annie bit the insides of her cheeks.

"Hmmm ... it's your mystery man," Tab teased, still eating plenty of the crunchy, cinnamon squares.

"Why do you keep calling him that?"

"He's a mystery to me."

Annie pushed herself up, sighed, and handed her friend the phone, leaving the message tab open. Then she strolled toward the window in the living room. The sun's rays were bright, but Annie only felt Cal's light. His strong arms wrapped around her body, his energy coursing through her, his breath on her neck. His make-believe embrace made her feel secure. Safe. She climbed his sequoia tree and stretched out on the branches. Finally, she knew what song to send in reply to his "Miss You."

"I haven't told my mom about him," Annie said, glancing over at Tab.

Her friend stood, pushed the bowl aside, and removed the towel from her head. Damp raven hair fell toward her waist as she made her way to Annie, then handed her the cell phone.

"Did you hear what I said?" Annie Googled the Bill Withers song, a classic her father had introduced her to a long time ago. "I haven't told my mom about him," she repeated as she copied the link and sent it off to Cal.

"You haven't even told me about him."

"Yes, I have." Butterflies flitted through Annie's stomach as she stuffed the phone in her pocket and sat in one of the big, comfy chairs, legs bent at the knee over an arm.

"No, bitch, I want the good stuff." Tab plopped into the adjacent chair.

"What makes you think we've *gotten* to the 'good stuff'?"

"Because I can see it in your eyes, my dear. You can't hide anything from me."

"So, you want me to give you a play-by-play of the way we—"

"Fuck..." Tab's eyes lit up.

Annie wasted no time grabbing the throw pillow from behind her back and smacking Tabitha with it a few times.

"I'm sorry," Tab said, laughing. "Is it *making love*?"

"You don't quit, do you?" Annie's eyes danced. Her heart pounded.

"No. It's been days since I've had sex, and it's always—"

"Days. Oh my God, and you haven't spontaneously combusted? How are you managing to sit here and hold yourself together?"

"Shut up, Annie. I like sex."

"I like it too."

"And?" Tab's mouth practically hung open.

"And what?" Annie shrugged.

"How is he?" Tab squealed.

"Shhh... You're going to wake up T."

"Annie!" Tab gritted her teeth, looking ready to explode. "Jesus."

The butterflies had left. Replaced with bees. They swarmed in Annie's belly. Actually, they ricocheted off the walls in there. Played ping-pong. She glanced at Tab, then at her feet. Her face surely must've been bright pink. Her heart thumped so loudly, it wailed inside her eardrums.

"He is..." Annie started, then swallowed, pausing as she went about gathering her most private thoughts. "Cal is..."

"Bold!"

Annie's eyes bulged realizing what Tab had gotten up to on the phone. "You read our messages?"

"You gave me the damn thing."

"God..." Annie exhaled and disappeared into the chair.

"What? Don't be embarrassed. You send songs. It's cute. And don't worry, I have phone sex too."

"With Tom, I hope?"

Tab mouthed, "Bitch."

Annie grinned.

"So. Cal? Bold?" Tab perched herself on the edge of her seat right as Annie's phone buzzed. "That's probably him again." Tab looked like a cat ready to eat a canary.

"I'll check it later." Annie rolled her eyes. "I don't really have anyone to compare him to, but, yeah, he is ... confident. He knows what he wants, I suppose."

"He wants you."

Annie could feel herself flushing a million shades of schoolgirl-crush red. Fuck. Fuck. Fuck. Of course he was bold. Annie had no doubt Cal would've had his way with her on Maggie's front porch the night after the gala. If she'd consented.

What would that have been like?

Sex on the porch...

God. Sex. Outside.

No one had ever wanted her with such an appetite. No one had ever made her feel like fucking on a front porch would've somehow been proper. Like something necessary. Something she both wanted *and* needed. No one had ever made her feel like she wanted to toss proper out the motherfucking window.

Cal did.

God, his hands...

They would push her skirt up and slide her underwear down, grasp her hips, throw her legs around his waist, and hold her in place. Cal would pin her body to the unforgiving door and fuck his boldness, his confidence, and his need into her over and over and over. *Oh God, oh God, oh God.*

"Yoo-hoo?" Tab waved a hand in front of Annie's fiery face.

"Sorry." Annie smirked. "We've only done it—"

"Fucked."

"Yeah, well, we've done that twice. And like I said ... I don't have anything to compare him to."

"Pfft..."

"What?"

"Are we talking about Daniel, Annie? Please. Don't even mention his name to me." Tab held a palm flat against the air. "He wouldn't have known how to fuck you even if he'd had a fucking manual."

Annie laughed.

"First-class jerk."

"Not in the beginning."

"I told you, Annie. A man shows what he's made of in times of trouble. His salt. Daniel did. Peter died, and Dan left. Now ... what did Cal do when you panicked? When you had that attack?"

"I... I shut off. I could barely talk. I took it out on him."

"And what did he do?"

"He begged me to stay. He held me. He... I tried to take off."

"Sounds like you."

"He wouldn't let me leave, though. He made love to me like..." Fuck... Annie turned her head. *Made love? Slow down, Annie.* "He fucked me like I've never been fucked before." *I felt safe.* "But then, afterward, we fought. I don't know, Tab. What does it matter?"

"Because..." Tab touched Annie's knee and paused. "It's okay to need someone."

"You don't need anyone."

"That's not true, Annie. I need you. I need T. I need Marlon Brando."

Annie couldn't help but smile. Who wouldn't *need* Marlon Brando? Tab grinned too. But what Tabitha didn't realize was that if Annie needed anyone, truly needed them, they might die. Needing someone meant they would go away and leave.

"Have you told Cal what happened with Dan?" Tab asked, her entire face crinkling at the mention of the name.

"No."

"What do you two talk about, then?"

"Cal's very private."

"Geez. So are you. What a combo."

"He's different," Annie continued, mellowing, shutting her eyes and opening them, feeling Cal close again. "He is confident, but he's not full of himself." *Not all the time anyway, and it's cute.* "He stands out in a crowd, but he really doesn't want to be the center of attention. Yet people are usually drawn to him." She flicked her eyes to Tab and smiled. "Well, I was anyway. He seems lonely too, but he doesn't want me to see it ... or know it." A rush came over Annie's entire body. Chills. Goose bumps. She hadn't even realized she'd started twirling her hair.

Tabitha only stared at her.

Annie dropped her feet to the floor, lowered her head over her knees, and concentrated on breathing.

"You've got it bad for him." Tab rested a hand on her friend's arm, and Annie glanced up. "He's fucked you how many times?"

"Twice."

"What has it been ... like, three weeks?"

"Yeah, that's me. Real hot mess. Aisle thirteen." Annie covered her mouth.

"No." Tab stared at her friend, pulling Annie's palm away from her lips. "You've been through hell, and this ... this relationship ... it's probably..." Tab trailed off, appearing lost in thought.

"What? What is it?"

"God, Annie. He's the first guy since jerk-face left and Peter passed?" Tab seemed to be getting ... what? Choked up? And she didn't do choked up — only on stage, and then the verge of tears transformed into bottled perfection.

"You know he is."

"Leave it to you, Annie-pie." Tab shook her head. "The first guy after a year to really interest you. The first guy you hook up with. Did it have to be with someone so fucking intense?"

Intense.

Now, there was a great word.

It was probably filed under "Calvin Prescott" in the dictionary.

The knots in Annie's stomach grew, tightening, traveling to her chest, her throat. Then the fucking things exploded.

"I know I barely know him. I know it's been only a few weeks, but I feel like I know him. I don't know. That's stupid." Annie fell back against the chair in a huff and glared at the ceiling. *He's different. He's confident. He doesn't want to stand out in a crowd. He's lonely. When he made love to me... Don't be a fool, Annie.* "I thought I could handle being with him. It's only the summer, you know? I'm going to travel in the fall. He's going back to California." Annie twirled hair around an index finger. "Jesus, look at me. What can I handle?" She dropped the tangled strands.

"What do you want?" Tab rattled Annie's knee. "You've always known what you've wanted. Even after Peter died, you knew."

Once upon a time, that statement had been true.

However, the moment Annie answered the phone while standing in this very apartment, in that kitchen, on that day, she immediately began to question everything — including all the things she thought she'd always wanted. Since her brother's death, Annie had been floating from cloud to cloud, waiting for a rainbow.

"That's bullshit. You saw me. You saw me come apart every single day. You saw me take those—"

"Fuck all that. Fuck those pills. You know what you want."

"I don't know. I'm still— I've lost my magic."

"Still nothing. And no, no you haven't. You're Annie Rebekah Baxter. You're amazing. Don't let your feelings for this man — a man you only just met — fuck up what you want. Your own goals. Your own happiness. You were happy before you met him, right?"

But Tab didn't understand.

No one who hadn't experienced it firsthand could truly understand. Sympathize, perhaps. But understand? No. Happiness hadn't been the same since Peter died. Happiness carried death in its front pocket.

Annie was afraid in ways she never used to be, and ironically, she was also fearless in ways she never had been. Death constricted her and death freed her. The fucking eventuality always a conundrum.

"I am happy," Annie replied, sounding more sure of herself, though she still wasn't sure. It was a catch-22. A fucked-up kind of happy. A new normal.

"Then don't lose that feeling worrying about your future with this man."

"A future? With him?" Annie laughed. And it tasted bitter. "I told you *it's the summer*. This is just sex." Her voice cracked, yet she managed to look Tab square in the eye. "It's only sex."

Liar, liar, pants on fire. How long can you do this? Go ahead. Convince yourself. That's what you do, Annie. Go on. Try.

But she couldn't.

Because as she thought of how she felt when that private, sexy, confident chameleon-of-a-man touched her, stared at her, brushed his freaking leg against hers, or held her in his arms...

She knew it wasn't only sex.

But what it meant to Cal, Annie wasn't sure. Or she denied it. The song lyrics, the flowers, the *you are beautiful*, the *don't go, Annie*, the *I'm not going to see anyone else*, the *look at me, look at me, look at me*. All of it would be a lie she would perpetuate to protect her heart from ripping open.

It would only be the summer.

He had said so. She'd confirmed it.

And she had repeated the lie aloud to Tab, hoping she could make herself feel it, believe it, accept it. Nevertheless, it was a lie ... no matter how many times she said it.

Annie took out her phone and read the new message, the one in response to the "Ain't No Sunshine" song she'd sent several minutes ago.

Only three little words constituted Cal's reply.

Cal: Who are you?

Ironically, that question held the key to everything.

Who are you, Prescott?

She scrolled up to the previous message, the one she'd shown Tab in the kitchen, the one prompting thoughts of the song in the first place, the message that had sent shivers up her spine and a heavy ball of need between her legs.

Cal: I can't wait to see you. It's cold here in the sun without you near.

After setting the device aside, she breathed, then blinked, then breathed.

Don't think.

It is just sex.

It's better to lie.

Protect yourself this time.

You don't need anyone.

You are happy.

Summer is for filling your portfolio, not your pussy.

This is a distraction. A fling. He's cold without me because his dick is lonely.

Lie. Lie. Lie.

"So..." Tab said, interrupting Annie's endless train of thoughts. "I guess I'm not getting the play-by-play on the 'he fucked me like I've never been fucked before'?"

Annie deflated, smiled, then hoisted that lovely little throw pillow up into the air and smacked Tabitha with it wildly again.

CHARGE

A FEELING OF ELECTRICITY SO STRONG IT SURGES
FORWARD; OR RESPONSIBILITY

I am
in your ring
Circle
Me
inhale me
rough me up
take me out
by the horns
Destroy
Me
before
I discover
what it all means

THIRTY-NINE

As Annie's plane descended into Miami, she gazed out the small window beside her. The late afternoon sun shined in the western sky, and the surface of the water below glistened jade green and dark blue. Absolutely magical. Flat and calm, and so deceptive from this angle.

Annie no longer wanted to fall out of the shape and escape the way she had upon first arriving in New York City.

Not now, anyway.

Relaxed and leaning her head against the seat, Annie felt like a feather, drifting from the top of one little white cloud to another. She wrapped her arms around herself. The time spent with Tabitha had been precisely what she'd needed. Tab had been the pill. The medicine.

Perhaps, it was okay to need someone.

Annie gave addiction and despair a stoic middle finger as she continued peering below at the topography. The sand, the ocean, the buildings. People were down there somewhere too, going about their business. Like tiny bugs from this distance, practically invisible. Working, learning, living, breathing.

Significant even if no one could see them.

There has to be a reason, Annie thought as she sat forward, rubbing her palms over her biceps. A purpose. If she could only focus, rediscover magic and then ignite it.

If she could only ... stop overthinking.

Unless those thoughts were about her camera or Cal or that beautiful ocean.

Maybe feelings weren't the enemy. Because right now, Annie was *feeling* pretty damn good.

———

The airport was crowded as Annie made her way through the throngs, her small suitcase in tow, her pretty floral bag strapped to her back, her flip-flops smacking the floor.

She hadn't gotten far when she heard something over the loudspeaker, the announcement causing her to stop in her tracks.

"Annie Baxter, please meet your party at baggage claim."

Annie's heart started to pound, her face heating. She looked left, then right, wondering if the chameleon was actually at Miami International. Shaking her head, she smiled and started to walk again, thinking they must've said Annie Saxon or Annie Braxton.

After stopping to get a quick bite to eat and texting her mother, Maggie, and Tabitha, Annie hopped on an escalator. Then she heard the announcement again, the same as before. The employee definitely hadn't said Saxon or Braxton. There was no mistaking what she'd heard this time: *Annie Baxter.*

With a loud exhale she stepped off the moving staircase, each foot forward hammering into the floor.

He's not here. Please ... he's not. Get a grip.

She surveyed the area. Swarms of people waited for their luggage, creating a tight space, resembling cattle in a herd — not much room to move or breathe. And Annie needed to breathe.

Desperately.

As if preparing to use her Nikon, her gaze combed each and every frame and face, scoping out the scene as best she could on her tippy-toes, looking for any sign of Cal.

Chiseled face. Steel jaw. Dirty-blond hair. Posture perfect. A man whose atoms were made up of control.

She laughed to herself.

Off in the distance, away from the herd, Annie finally spotted some people holding signs. A familiar gentleman cradled a piece of thick cardboard in front of his chest, his rotund belly poking out beneath it. As she moved closer, Annie noted two words written in Sharpie:

ANNIE BAXTER

Carl wiped his forehead with a handkerchief as he gazed off into the distance, people cutting between them. Once she approached, he shoved the sweat-stained cloth into his pocket, looked up, and visibly deflated.

"Ms. Baxter..."

"Annie." She smiled. "Please, call me Annie."

"Mr. Prescott sent me," Carl continued, sporting black trousers and a white button-up shirt; a toothpick hung from his mouth.

"Oh, he did, did he?" Annie smirked. "And where did he tell you to take me?"

"I assumed you knew." Carl coughed. "I'm driving you directly to Mr. Prescott's, Ms. ... uh, I mean, Annie. Unless he was mistaken?"

"No, no." Annie couldn't stop grinning. "There's no mistake." Even though she'd given Cal her return itinerary a few days ago, they hadn't made definite plans. "Please, take me to Cal's."

"Of course." Carl grabbed her suitcase.

"Thank you for coming." She patted his back as they started to head for the exit.

"You're welcome, Annie." He smiled.

Several minutes later, Carl opened the back passenger door of the Tesla. The Florida sun had already managed to heat the leather, making the space feel like a sauna. But it didn't matter because it looked like a dream.

This was the magic.

The rainbow.

A hundred or so roses had apparently exploded all over Cal's car. Petals everywhere. Annie could barely see the floors or seats. A variety of colors, red and pink, white and yellow, orange and purple, all floated, as if they bobbed in a giant Tesla tub of water.

Annie grinned as Carl closed the door. He had been smiling as well. No doubt, the driver had probably bought the roses on Cal's behalf and done the romantic deed himself. Although, how romantic was shredding flowers? Annie laughed. She'd done something similar, tearing petals off pink pearls, then drowning them in the Atlantic Ocean.

Is this retribution? she wondered, and laughed some more.

"You sound happy," Carl said as they pulled away from the airport.

Slipping off her shoes, Annie squished her feet into the soft petals and pressed them between her fingers, scooping them up the way a child might play in leaves. "I am. I am happy."

Carl adjusted the mirror while Annie's heart began to thump in her ears. The silky flowers covering nearly every inch of her skin, their aroma mixing with the AC, the leather, the beach, the heat — Annie wasn't merely happy, she was euphoric. The anticipation of being with Cal — seeing him, hearing him, smelling him, tasting him — made her practically dizzy as she sank deeper into the roses, sliding her hands through the petals, swimming in the floaty warm bathtub.

Annie rode those wonderful feelings all the way to South Beach, her pulse gaining momentum with each mile, her entire fucking body awash with some sort of overfull need only one man could satiate.

FORTY

After saying goodbye to Carl, Annie made her way to Cal's door and put her hand on the knob. But before turning the handle, she pressed her ear to the grain and smiled.

Music vibrated through the walls, something muffled, something she couldn't quite make out. Shaking her head and grinning even wider, Annie crept inside, feeling a little like Goldilocks sneaking into the house of The Three Bears.

Placing her backpack on the desk, leaving her suitcase next to it, she glanced up the staircase, the song blaring from the speakers one she still couldn't name.

"Cal!" Annie yelled and looked around.

Bedroom door closed.

No lights on.

Sun beaming in the front windows.

A light gray jacket draped over the desk chair.

Annie lifted the material to her nose, closed her eyes, and inhaled.

But the unique scent wasn't cologne or detergent or anything artificial. Only pure Cal: laundry hung out on the line to dry in the sun, the beach, coconuts.

The man who was nowhere in sight, seemed to be everywhere all at once, wafting up her nose, registering in that little place inside the brain where memories were stored. To one day be opened by a future trigger, perhaps when Annie was older or had forgotten this moment.

Standing on a beach twenty years from now, she would take in a deep breath and be reminded of *this summer*. Of South Beach. Of the music they'd shared. Of all the things that couldn't be properly understood but would eventually make perfect sense. The familiar song spinning on his turntable. A single scent making all of it impossible to be effaced.

After returning his jacket to the chair, Annie put a foot on the bottom step of the staircase, fingernails tapping the handrail, both appendages dancing in time to the beat of the song she knew originated from the fifties or sixties, a man crooning about staying just a little bit longer.

Stay...

Tap. Tap. Tap.

"Cal..." she called again but heard nothing except the music ending, the player going silent, and her feet hitting the wood floors as she stepped down and slipped off her flip-flops.

The second she glanced back up, she saw him, leaning against the bedroom doorframe. Motionless. No shirt or shoes or smile. Only blue jeans.

Serious.

Sexy.

Contemplative.

Cal.

He stared at her from across the space. Not much had changed. Still affecting her without words. Or touch.

"My God." Annie grinned, wanting nothing more than to bury her face against that chest, to push her fingers through those hairs. "How long have you been standing there?"

The hems of his faded blue jeans dragging on the floor, Cal started to walk toward her, his eyes never leaving her face. Her heart pounded; her body heated. But the man didn't say a word. He wasn't even smiling.

The moment he reached her, Cal placed his hands on her cheeks, brushed his fingertips over her skin, and looked deep into her eyes. Annie palmed his biceps and returned the stare.

Then their lips met.

Painfully slow and tender, tortuous, Cal kissed her until a dull ache sliced through Annie's back. Her fingers tangled through his hair, pulling and pulling and pulling as she wrapped a leg around his thigh and moaned.

Her hands moved up and down his chest as Cal's gaze fell to the hem of her shirt. He grabbed the material, lifted the tank over her head, and dropped it to the floor. Without missing a beat, they became one again, lips and tongue and teeth. Hands.

Cal pushed her against the stair railing while she shoved her pelvis against him, weaving her fingers through his chest hair, tugging at the strands, moaning into his mouth. His lips so forceful now, they nearly bruised her.

After fumbling with the button of his jeans, Annie slid a hand to his zipper, rubbing him over the material. Cal removed her palm and lifted her into his arms, her legs wrapping around his waist as he carried her to the bedroom — the two of them never breaking the kiss ... or the sharing of the pieces of their souls that somehow fit together like a puzzle.

But they didn't quite make it inside the room.

Not yet.

Pushing open the door, Cal held Annie against it — her thighs still about his waist, her feet off the floor — and plied her with kisses, tasting her neck, her collarbone, her cheeks. Kissing her until they both ached, until the stubble covering his jaw burned her skin. Cal welded her to the door as if he couldn't get close enough. Like he needed to be let inside. Consuming her as though he must burrow beneath her skin in order to survive.

Annie didn't even know how they'd arrived here — a blur of kisses, intertwined like vines, without shirts, bodies touching, magnets seeking each other out, only the thud of her spine against the rattling bedroom door proof. Like a pinch to the skin affirming a moment was real.

Not a dream. Real.

Magical.

So pleasurable, it was painful.

If it hurt, she didn't know it.

Or she desperately wanted it to.

Each time her body banged against Cal's door — exquisite. His lips — exquisite. His tongue, his hands, his scent — *everything* — fucking exquisite.

Neither of them barely breaking for air, their mouths still devouring each other, Cal pushed up her bra, exposed her tits, then lowered his head to them. She arched, wiggling her feet, pulling his hair, scratching nails over his backside as her eyes rolled toward the heavens.

"Fuck..." Annie cried the second Cal's teeth made contact with a nipple, licking, tugging, twisting. He bit the other one just as hard. Just as majestically.

"Ahhh..." She cradled his head against her chest, holding him there, yanking fingers through his hair, basking in the little twinges of pain radiating out to every nerve ending. He did it again and again and again. "Cal, Cal, Cal... Please..."

Glancing up, he smiled, and carried her to the bed. After dropping her on the sheets, he tore off her jeans and bra, then fell over her body in an instant, placing an arm on either side of her waist, looking down at her as though he had brought this creature to his castle after capturing her in the wild.

He.

Had.

Captured.

Her.

Wild, unbridled.

His.

Straddling her hips, Cal stared at Annie for what felt like days.

"I missed you," Annie finally uttered as she propped herself up on her elbows, her chest rising and falling with those three soft words.

Cal kissed her, slipping his tongue inside her warm mouth, licking her lower lip, her upper. Then he made his way to her neck, her breasts, her navel before standing, sliding off his belt and losing his jeans. When he returned to the bed, he hovered over her again, placed a hand on her cheek, and stroked his thumb across her skin, peering deep into Annie's eyes.

Her throat swelled as she soaked up the expression across his face. Her heart thumped so hard, she feared it might burst from her chest.

Then his eyes closed. Their lips met. The weight of his body pushed her flat against the sheets. Cal's kisses enveloped Annie, consumed her. His kisses were real, from the earth — the nearest thing to bliss she could possibly imagine.

The strength of his feelings poured from his lips, his mouth, his tongue. What he usually could only show by sharing a song, became clear.

Loud.

Something he couldn't squander.

Annie squirmed in near-drowning elation as Cal skirted his bristly jaw over her breasts, her stomach, her thighs, the instep of her feet. His beard was tingly, scratchy, exceptional.

She wanted him to dive inside her body and never be found.

Annie couldn't help but giggle and writhe as Cal kissed and scratched his way back up the front of her body, making her feel cherished and loved ... safe.

How was that possible?

Shhh. Don't think.

Climb his tree.

Wait. Wait. Wait.

Cal paused the moment he reached Annie's face, the same look in his eyes as before. The mist. The magic. The need.

Why isn't he speaking?

He looks pleased.

Not smug, but pleased — content, at peace.

Safe, like me.

Annie trembled watching his expression, quivering as she acknowledged the enormity of feelings she had for him.

It's supposed to be just sex. It isn't. It is.

As she touched Cal's face, ran her fingertips along his cheek, he peered deeper into her soul, seeming to fall over the edge of her skin, those green eyes reading her, observing her, seeing all the way to her underbelly, way beyond her insecurities. Past her fears.

"Say something to me, Cal," Annie uttered, surprised she managed to speak at all. Her mouth seemed to be shot up with Novocain. "Please."

Cal continued to stare into Annie's eyes.

His Adam's apple bobbed.

Then he kissed her.

His hands ran over her skin, touching her practically everywhere, until she felt his unspoken, silent words bleeding through the tips of his fingers.

His eyes were piercing.

His mouth was smooth.

His hands were all-knowing.

Annie was beginning to think Cal wouldn't speak to her aloud at all until it was over.

And it wasn't nearly over. It hadn't nearly begun. Their underwear had yet to come off. And, as usual, Cal seemed in no hurry to reach the destination so many longed for. His goal the journey. A fury of passion transpiring at his pace, under his charge.

The moment they broke for air, Annie managed to switch places. She pushed Cal down to the mattress, flat on his back, and straddled his waist. Smirking, her hair dangling all around him, caught like Velcro in his beard, she sat up tall and squeezed his torso with her thighs.

Cal smiled, his face lighting up completely.

Still boasting a most mischievous grin, Annie lifted his arms above his head, held them there, and leaned closer, her nipples grazing his skin, her silky, long hair scattering everywhere.

"Don't you have anything to say to me after almost two weeks of no sex, Prescott?"

In one swift motion, Cal flipped Annie onto her back, grabbed her wrists, and pinned them and her body to the bed.

Her chest rose. Up. Down. Fast. Sideways. Or maybe she couldn't breathe at all. That was it. She couldn't breathe.

The man stared at her with those stellar green readers. Asked questions with those freaking ocean eyes.

And Annie answered him.

Silently.

Her eyes told him everything he wanted to know. Who she was — unequivocally. Her eyes held a promise of everything Cal longed to be. Her eyes were the little white flowers on the tangerine trees. In full bloom.

"I need to fuck you, Annie," Cal breathed against her skin as he peered into her eyes. "That's what I need to say. That's what I need to do. Do you want me to fuck you?"

"Yes," she choked out, spastic. No one had ever spoken to her like that and if they had, it wouldn't have gone over.

It was him. Only him.

Cal's words were raw. His tone velvet. His gaze the hot sand at the beach she burned her toes on. His ardent insistence was blinding. And so, she shut her eyes.

"Don't turn from me, Annie." One hand held her wrists, the other grabbed her chin. "Did you lie in your bed each night while you were away and think of me fucking you?"

"Fuck…" she whispered, struggling to catch her breath.

Cal smirked as he released her, slid toward her thighs, and licked her over her underwear.

"Oh God, oh my God."

After removing the garment, he inhaled her scent, tickling her with his nose until Annie squirmed. Lying on his stomach, his face centimeters from her skin, he began to spread her wide, opening her up like the petals of a flower. The words *I need to fuck you, Annie* played over and over in her mind as he touched her, breathed on her, began to taste her.

She wanted him to crawl inside. So far inside.

It was always like this.

Today marked only the third time Cal would be inside her body, but it was always like this.

A haste, a flurry, an ocean of feelings pouring out of them.

Wriggling beneath him, eyes closed, Annie started to unintentionally scoot toward the headboard. Each time she did, Cal would pull her back toward his face. Digging his nails into her hips, he continued exploring every inch of her, his breath and tongue warm and divine.

Everything.

Annie was going to die. Thighs trembling. Chest shaking. She would die. On his perfect bed. With his perfect hands. His perfect tongue licking her seam and clit. Her hole. She would die.

No. No. No.

She bunched the sheets in her fists. She was going to come. Lifting her head, she watched his scruffy, exquisite face between her legs.

"Oh God," she cried, ready to explode, this being the first time she would climax with his tongue in her center, his tongue in her, a part of her. God, she wanted all of him.

Now.

"I'm coming..." Gripping his head, her hips rising off the bed, she writhed against his face, holding him there, taking what she wanted without inhibition.

"Yes, baby," Cal uttered against her flesh. "Come."

Her breathing slowed. Time stopped. But the man kept right on going. Kissing and nibbling and sucking, waiting out each last contraction until she begged him to stop.

"God, you did miss me," he said, nuzzling his nose over her sex.

"Shut up, Prescott. God." Annie dropped her head on the pillow and pushed pieces of matted hair off her forehead. Her eyes wandered, combing the ceiling, still floating on the cloud of her orgasm.

Cal kissed his way up her body and met her gaze. "How was your trip?"

"Fuck me," Annie whispered instead, and their eyes locked. "You said you wanted to ... that you needed to..."

Those earnest words dropped off a cliff as she watched Cal stand, lose his boxers, and retrieve a condom from the drawer. He was inside her body in an instant, her legs open and suspended on either side of him, the luscious invasion a welcomed relief from the last several days of grief.

This was what she needed.

Him. Filling her.

Fingers through his chest hair, a hand clutching his bicep. Their eyes never breaking contact. Hers begging for things she couldn't express out loud as Cal pushed in, then out.

"Do you still want to know about New York?" she groaned.

Cal slid out some, licked her nipples, one, then the other, then he teased her opening with the tip of his dick, brushing his erection against her clit until Annie was in a panic again.

"Cal," she moaned.

"What?" he asked, repeating that process several times, much to Annie's dismay. "Do you want to come again?"

Frenzied, she gripped his ass, attempting to force his hand. Endorphins piled up inside her brain, one by one, stacking themselves like Tetris blocks. Could she come again after such a short time? No one had ever tried. She'd rarely tried.

"Do you want to come again?" he dinned, breathing the velvety words against her chest, pushing his nose into her breasts. "Tell me."

"I do. I want to."

"What?" He glanced up. "What do you want?"

"I want to come. *Please.*"

"Do you need me?"

"God," she replied, eyes opening wide, hips wiggling, still trying to maneuver his fucking stubborn cock inside her greedy little entrance. His arms held her in place, though, his weight keeping her pinned beneath him.

"What do you need?" He gave her an inch or two, the control he exercised to maintain this chess game etching fine lines of anguish across his forehead.

"I need you."

"Yes?"

"Yes! I need you..." She bit her bottom lip, and Cal pulled out. "God..."

"Say it, Annie."

"I need you to fuck me."

In an instant, Cal thrust back inside her warmth, shoving all the way to her womb, causing Annie to burst with a symphony of sounds: a sob, a moan, a scream. Again and again, he rushed his full length into her body, rattling her against the sheets, giving her as much as they both could stand.

Until they might break.

Or crack.

Until they would let go of everything they held on to.

"Look at me," Cal said, stopping the feverish jolts, holding himself inside her with an intense pressure she'd never felt. She cast her eyes into his net. "Come, Annie. Again. Please," he pleaded, and she nodded, then cried. Honest-to-God cried. A tear slid down her cheek. "Come for me, baby."

Their eyes became windows.

Reflections.

Each of them peering into the other's soul.

Past all life's bullshit as long as their orgasms lasted, both of them finishing simultaneously, for the first time together.

After removing the condom, Cal curled up beside her. She laid her head against his chest, sucking back the weeping, releasing it instead with several shaky breaths. The two of them rested in the silence, the silence Cal often preferred, sharing a surreal sort of comfort neither knew how to orchestrate.

"So, now do you want to tell me about New York?" He grinned.

Annie smiled, smoothing her nails through the hairs of his chest. So soft and fluffy, juxtaposed to the strong, lean body they covered. She hoped to never tire of the electromagnetic field she felt on the tips of her fingers, on her palms, over the entire surface of their skin whenever they touched.

"No takers on my work," she replied.

"None?"

"No. One curator asked for my information, though."

"They aren't ready for you yet." He traced a finger along the curve of her hip. "*Your magic...*"

"Maybe."

"The timing has to be right."

She propped herself up on an elbow and stroked his chin. "You believe in that sort of thing? Timing? Fate?"

"I don't know that I would call it fate, but yes, I believe in timing."

Plopping back down, she fell into the crook of his neck. "Maybe they'll never be ready for me."

"Did you not make some contacts in New York before you moved, while you were still in school?"

"No."

Cal touched her waist, the soft rush of her two-letter reply telling him all he needed to know... Peter. He wished to pull her body into him farther — more, if possible — and she was already snuggled against him tightly. "I'm sorry, Annie."

She looked up at him and blinked.

"It is timing. It has to be right."

Twisting her fingers through his chest hair again, she sighed. "How old were you when you first moved to the city?"

Cal stared at the ceiling, holding back a grin. "Twenty-two."

"Was that ... the girl Maggie spoke of at dinner?"

"You don't forget, do you?"

"Was she one of your *mad loves*?"

A noise came from his chest. A rattle of laughter. Cynical, bitter laughter. Quiet too. Like him.

Annie touched his lips. "She's not one of the two?"

"No." Taking her hand in his, he kissed a group of her fingers. "She is not." It had been a while since Cal had given any thought to the woman he'd once shared an apartment with on the Upper West Side. Was Allison maddening? Yes. A mad love? No. "I don't want to talk about her. She was venom. Lethal." He laughed again, the sound like a private joke he could only share with himself.

"I don't want you to stop talking." Annie kissed his cheek. "Tell me something else."

Cal peered at Annie for what felt like days. Then he cupped her sex. "You're still wet."

She was wet. And he was—

"And you're changing the subject."

"I'm going to fuck you all night, Annie. In ways you've never been fucked before."

She sucked in a sharp breath. She'd told Tabitha he'd already accomplished that. And there was more?

"I didn't have Carl bring you here so I could spend all night talking about myself."

For once, Annie agreed, conversation might be a bit overrated...

Cal spread her legs, peered at what he wanted, needed — at what he knew how to bring to the brink again and again — while Annie lay there, open, vulnerable ... his. She didn't know how his dick could already be hard, but it was, and it pressed against her hip.

"You're beautiful," he said, staring into her eyes as if he wanted to consume the whole of her, limbs and all, starting with the area he touched. "*Just like this.*"

Eyelashes fluttering, Annie exhaled.

"Put your hands above your head. Good. Now, close your eyes."

"Cal..."

"Trust me." He kissed her cheek. "Do you even know how beautiful you are ... *here*?" Even though he barely grazed her clit with his thumb, his words and touch caused her to tremble. Everywhere.

He made her *feel* beautiful.

Lowering himself to her center, he gazed at her, worshipping her pussy. And she knew because she peeked. She saw the adulation in his eyes. Then he left the bed, and she pinched her lids shut.

"Open." His belt was in her eyeline, in his hands, near her face. "Give me your wrists." After looping the leather around them, he fastened it, pushing her arms over her head until her tits jutted out.

"I never want to wait ten days to be inside you again."

Five days in London. One day in between on her period. Four days in New York.

He took a condom from the drawer, rolled it on, and positioned himself near her entrance, nudging her clit with his dick. "Do you understand?"

She didn't. Because this was *just the summer, just the summer, just the summer.*

"Did you touch yourself while you were up there?"

"Yes."

"Did you like waiting?"

She smiled, then looked at the ceiling, but he pulled her chin back front and center.

"You know, I went without for thirteen months before I met you." Her grin increased. "I can wait."

He hung his head, then shook it.

"Didn't you ever have to wait? Or do you wait for no one?"

"I did." He smirked and glanced up. "I have. Not that long. Christ. But long enough."

"How long?" She bumped him with her knee.

"When I decided to train for my first marathon."

She laughed. "A dry spell?"

"By choice."

"Same."

"You mean no one ate your delicious pussy?" Cal inched that cock up her folds, up and down. "No one had their fingers inside you? Nothing ... for thirteen months?"

"No. Only my fingers." Legs wrapped around his waist, her ankles cradled the small of his back, trying to pull him toward her, but he wouldn't budge.

"God, Annie, no wonder you're so responsive."

"No." She shook her head and giggled. "It's you."

Smiling, he circled a finger around an areola. The second he nipped her nipple with his teeth, she made an explosive sound.

"Did you like the biting earlier?"

"Yes." She arched, willing him to repeat the action. "Couldn't you tell?"

"Close your eyes again."

The moment she did, the weight of the bed changed. Annie instinctively began to push her legs together.

"No." Cal touched her knees. "Keep yourself open to me, baby."

"Don't make me wait," Annie whined, pulling against the bindings, cocking open an eye.

"No peeking." Cal slapped her thigh. Then he shoved them both wide. "And no moving."

"Where are you going?"

"No peeking and no more fucking questions. I'm asking the questions. I'm doing the talking."

Whatever, she thought.

If she were in his bed an eternity, it wouldn't matter — she would wait. Besides, her arousal only increased with each second that passed, causing her to wonder exactly when she'd turned into a horny ball of nerves awaiting release.

When had the commands of a man made her want to come without even being touched? And when had she ever been commanded in bed?

Never.

Only by him. Cal Prescott.

The stranger. The chameleon. The ocean to her sky.

"What else did you do in the city?" He sat beside her. "Lift your head."

Something soft wrapped around her eyes. A necktie or a scarf.

"You're the worst," she said, smiling.

"You like to talk, so we'll talk." He knotted it in the back. "What did you do?"

Lost my mind. Cried a river. The usual. "I went to a play, met curators, like I told you. I hung out with my friend."

Cal hovered over her, his knees on either side of her body. She couldn't see him, but he was there. The instant the tip of his dick met her opening, a gasp escaped her lips as she uttered, "W-we... We talked."

"About sex?"

"Everything isn't always about sex," she blurted as he continued to taunt her slick flesh.

"Girls talk plenty of sex."

Cal moved in and out of her now — without much pressure or speed. Slow. Easy. Torturous. While Annie waited for the other shoe to drop.

"Tab is married," she finally said.

"So."

"So, I don't ask about her husband's—"

"Dick," he said as he thumped her cervix. "Did you talk about me?"

Back arched, fists closed over the loops, Annie couldn't breathe or think or hardly move. "God, Cal, please."

"Did you?" He was out again, his tip sliding over and over her swollen and achy folds.

"Yes."

"What did you say?"

"You're the worst, Cal Prescott," she groaned, and he moved so far away, she grew cold. "No..."

Laughing a little under his breath, Cal spread her legs and massaged her clit. "Calm down, baby." Brushing her skin as though he weren't even touching it, as if he were only stroking air, he brought her to the edge again. In less than a minute. "Talk, Annie."

"I told her this is sex."

"Indeed."

"I told her ... it's only sex."

Cal stripped the blindfold from her face, and even though she'd only been covered a short time and the room was fairly dark, Annie still squinted, trying to turn from his polarizing glare.

"Say that to my face," he said and filled her. All. The. Way. She moaned and moaned and moaned.

Then he pulled out.

"No!"

"Beg me."

"Fuck you."

"Say my name."

"Fuck you ... *Cal*." The letters shook loose from her mouth as he rocked her into a frenzy of *not waiting ten days to be inside you*, of *it's just the summer-just the summer-just the summer*, of *it's only sex-sex-sex*.

A mess was what it all was.

The leather of the belt chafed her wrists. Her breasts bounced. Each push inside her a reminder of what they were, who they were.

Then he slowed. Stopped. Slid out.

"No," she whispered, bit her lip, and yanked on the restraints.

"Shhh..." He moved his mouth to her clit, licking her. "Be still. Grab the headboard." As he pushed her forward, she gripped it. "Tell me if you like this."

"Fuck." She pulled the headboard away from the wall while wailing the expletive — the soft pad of his tongue on her clit had turned to teeth. "Fuck, fuck, fuck!"

Then he cared for what he'd bruised, gently sucking, kissing her there, barely licking her skin.

"Again," she panted, moaned, tugged.

The sadistic combination — bite, nip, suck, lick, kiss — went on and on until an explosion occurred. White streaks of pain burst into red-hot fucking pleasure. Could Annie tell him how much she liked it in words? She was past words, unable to speak anything other than animal sounds. The grunting, the broken gasps, the *mmms* and *ahhhs*.

"God, Annie..." Cal sat up tall and squared her hips. "I've wanted you for two fucking weeks." Stretching her open, he pushed one of her knees up and to the side, then he thrust inside her warmth and groaned.

Eyes rolling, she yelped, alternating between watching how and where they joined and gazing into his insane eyes.

Cal slammed into the back of her pussy. "I could barely concentrate on work... God, you feel so good." His eyes closed, then opened, painfully slow. "I'm going to fuck you all night." *Slam.* "I'll bite you." Slam. "Spank you." Slam. "I'll make it so you can't speak unless I command you." He held himself deep inside her now. "Tomorrow morning, you'll be so sore, you won't be able to fucking walk."

Shifting her head side to side, Annie shook and moaned. Everything hurt. Everything ached. Everything was perfect.

"Look at me."

Her eyes opened, lashes fluttering. "Yes?"

"Not yet." He slowed down. "You said you had patience. You waited thirteen months." He slid out. "I let you come already." His eyes swam with contentment. "Twice." The man was in his prime. His element. "Beg me for what you say is just sex." Glancing down at their centers, he rolled the tip of his dick over her wet slit.

"You're a fucker." She wrestled with the belt loop. Rocked against the steel plank of his body.

"Beg me." Sucking a nipple into his mouth, he squeezed it between his teeth.

All her muscles went slack. Her mind blanked. She exhaled. "Please..."

"Your body is mine this summer." He filled her again. "Beg," he demanded, fucking her just enough to keep her on the edge but not enough to bring her release. Then he pulled out again.

"God, Cal, please. You know I need you. I just told you that. Before. I want you. *Please.*" She closed her eyelids, sweat glistening off every part of her body, her throat aching to the point of pain. "Please, fuck me. Please." She opened her eyes again, staring so far inside him, she wasn't sure she could utter another sound. "Fuck..." She pulled on the leather belt, took a deep breath, and steeled herself against him. "I. Need. You."

Cal surged forward, sealing her to him, completely, climbing inside her body to the hilt. They were together. They were one.

One thing.

One body.

One heart beating loudly against the door to the other's chests.

"Please," he said, each letter hitching. "Look at me, Annie." Cal had worked himself up into his own frenzy. The next four words matched his thrusts. "It's. Not. Just. Sex." He nodded, and Annie knew he was starting to come. His eyes became glass. His face tensed. "Yes?"

"Yes," she agreed, practically choking on her own spit.

It's not just sex. It's not just sex. It's not just sex. The mantra repeated inside her head until the words became her undoing. The look in his eyes as his orgasm consumed him became her undoing.

His groaning, *his* unraveling — stripped her bare.

Her entire body filled with those stupid four words, his sounds, and the smell of his skin as she began to release.

A third time.

She watched his eyes glaze, his head droop, then shake. She listened to the quiet way he released his breath with each final tick of his climax, her eyes never leaving his face.

Cal unbuckled her in an instant, fell on his back, and blew out an elongated, exhausted breath. Annie stared up at the ceiling, running her fingers over her wrists.

Taking her palm, he kissed the veins and blush marks. "It's not just sex."

"Then what is it?" She turned, putting her ass against his pelvis. "Am I allowed to ask you questions now?"

Wrapping a hand around her waist, Cal pulled her closer. They spooned — cut for each other, made to fit. She smelled like home, fields of citrus, seasons, a reason. He buried his face into the tree-lined rows of her neck.

"I missed you too, Annie. We said no discussion of what-ifs or plans. Go to sleep. I want to hold you like this until you fall asleep."

Even though she'd started to cry, she somehow kept her chest from shaking. Cal wouldn't know she released tears. He couldn't.

Everything they'd done had felt good and right, fucking amazing. Physically and emotionally. The kissing, the biting, the way he'd called her *baby*. His commands, the torturing and taunting, the delaying. She'd wanted it all without knowing exactly what it was.

And Annie had never felt stronger.

They both needed this.

The sex, the snuggling, the comfort, the peace. Another few moments of only feeling, without talking or articulating or speculating. No microscope to examine every one of their hundreds of thoughts. Because despite some of the things Cal had ever told her, the way he sometimes tried to disguise his emotions, Annie knew he was as much of a philosopher as she — an old soul, maybe more so. She had noticed those deep chasms residing in his ocean eyes the very first night.

Annie wanted to swim in the pools of his greens without a life jacket.

She wanted to drown in him and never be rescued.

Everything. All at once.

No what-ifs. No future best-laid plans.

Only sleeping, spooning, coming. Only now, now, now...

FORTY-ONE

The cotton sheets felt wonderful, soft and heavy, as Annie stretched an arm toward the spot where Cal had slept, running her palm over the smooth thread count.

Still warm. Still smelled like him.

A large novel now occupied his space, and as she brushed her fingers over the hardbound spine of *Infinite Jest*, she smiled. Then she noticed her suitcase. The red thing she'd left near the front door last night was now on the floor, open, her clothes appearing freshly laundered and folded. After blinking a moment in disbelief, she heard someone ... singing?

Dressed only in one of Cal's white T-shirts, Annie cracked open the bedroom door and looked toward the kitchen. Music played from a tiny radio on the counter, and Rosa danced to the sounds coming from it, her lips and hips moving.

"Morning," Annie called out, her half-naked body partially hidden behind the door.

"Good morning," Rosa chirped the moment she turned the volume down.

"Thank you for washing my clothes."

"You're welcome, love." Smiling, she glanced over at Annie while continuing to cook. "Are you hungry?"

"Where's Cal?" Annie craned her neck around the edge of the doorjamb, the hem of Cal's shirt tickling the tops of her thighs and bottoms of her butt cheeks.

"He's on his morning run. You just missed him." Rosa placed silverware and napkins on the table. "He's usually out about thirty or forty-five minutes."

"I need to shower." Annie smelled like sex and Cal. Part of her hated to rinse him off. "But then I want to help you."

"That's okay, *mi querida*." Rosa winked. "You take care of yourself. I have this almost finished."

Fifteen minutes later, showered and dressed, Annie moseyed into the kitchen and poured herself a glass of water. Lingering at the fridge, she found herself staring at the photographs on it the way she had the first time she'd been at Cal's. People's eyes and faces — it mattered little that she didn't know them, and it scared her how much she wanted to — commanded her attention, the camera capturing things the naked eye might not notice at first glance.

The nuance of regret.

The relaxed lines of humility.

Love.

"This is Michelle and her children." Rosa joined Annie, pointing at a photo. "Cal's cousin. Ah, and this one is Constance," she went on, nodding at a print next to it, "at Cal's graduation."

The woman's eyes were stark and blue, haunting, grabbing the viewer by the throat — the same way they did in that tiny, square, black-and-white photo Annie had commented on two weeks ago. Rosa was the star of a few photographs as well, one appearing to have been taken the same night, college graduation.

"When did you meet Cal?" Annie asked after taking a drink of water.

"I met him when he was a little boy."

Annie's mouth dropped open. Her heart skipped a beat. But she managed to set her glass down and follow Rosa to the stove.

"What can I do?" Leaning forward, Annie inhaled the sweet aroma of tomato sauce Rosa poured over a pan of lasagna. "It smells so good. I'm starving."

"This is dinner. Your breakfast is over here." Rosa lifted the lid off an adjacent skillet. Now, the scent of omelets filled with vegetables and cheese took over the room. Annie's stomach growled; her eyes bulged.

"Could you please grab five or six oranges from the fridge?" Rosa nodded. "They're in the bottom right drawer."

"I had no idea you've known Cal for so long," Annie said a minute or so later, once she started to wash the fruit off in the sink. "He doesn't speak much about his family."

"No." Rosa glanced over her shoulder. "Cal is very private."

Rosa came up beside Annie and grabbed a couple of the clean oranges. "Be patient, *mi querida*. I can see you are special to him." Their eyes met. "Don't give up trying to know him."

Annie swallowed, shut off the water, and brought the remaining fruit to Rosa.

"What was he like?" Annie's eyes lit up. "As a boy?"

"Cal was..." Rosa smiled while beginning to slice open the citrus. "He was ... determined."

"Then not much has changed." Annie grinned and took a glass from an upper cabinet.

"No." Rosa chuckled. "He always was a little man inside a boy's body. That's what I always said. That's what I often told his mother."

Rosa started to juice a couple of oranges.

"How did you meet his family?" Annie asked between the buzz of the extraction.

"I was around your age and newly married..." Rosa lifted her palm off the reamer but still held onto half the orange. "I already had my first boy, Ivan. I had to find work. Times were tough, and my husband..." Rosa looked off into the distance. "Well, his cousin was an apprentice for Cal's grandfather. Everett taught him carpentry. He made the most beautiful things, Annie." She paused, glancing down at the fruit, her mind seeming to catalogue the items Everett had once carved. "We knew the family," she continued, "and Constance needed help managing the house. I could bring my son along with me too. It seems like only yesterday..." Rosa sighed. "It was good for me then, and it never seemed like a job, you know? We are family. And now ... now Cal takes care of me."

"It looks to me like you take good care of him." Annie put her arm around Rosa's back and squeezed her shoulder.

"Mmm..." Rosa met Annie's gaze. "Looks can be deceiving." Then she shooed Annie away like a fly. "Sit. I have your breakfast ready."

"I can finish the oranges."

"Yes, yes, then sit."

As Annie lifted one of the halves up to the top of the juicer, holding the handle on the machine with her other palm, she smiled. Meeting Rosa that first morning at Cal's had been a surprise. Talking to her today, a blessing. Being here felt like home. More than something familiar. Some people didn't need to have shared a plethora of words or experiences to understand they were kindred.

"Does Cal see her often?" Annie asked a few minutes later while carrying her glass of water to the table. "His mother, I mean?"

A plate full of food in hand, Rosa wasn't far behind. She placed it in front of Annie the moment the photographer took a seat. "He does not talk of his mother?"

"No." A lump formed in Annie's throat as a picture began to take shape in the viewfinder of her mind, the subject at first appearing blurry, not yet in focus.

"No, no. I suppose he would not." Rosa shook her head and made a clicking sound with her tongue against the roof of her mouth. "Cal's mother ... she..." Rosa quickly glanced at Annie, then looked away. "She has Alzheimer's, Annie."

Fork in hand, Annie froze, unable to move or speak, as pieces of that fuzzy photo came together. Clearly. The de Kooning print hanging on Cal's wall. The swimming out to sea lonely. The guilt behind his stellar grin. The pain sometimes etched across his beautiful face. The sharp remark he'd made when Annie had asked about his mother only two weeks ago. *I don't have to give you anything, Annie..."* he'd said.

It all made sense now. The snapshot was complete.

"I... I had no idea," she finally managed. "I'm so sorry."

"She's been sick for years," Rosa added as Cal stepped through the front door, slipped off his shoes, and removed his earbuds.

"Morning." He grinned, making his way to the kitchen, his hair and clothing damp with sweat. Lifting his shirt collar, he wiped his face with its fibers. "Did I interrupt something?"

"No," Rosa replied, giving him a tight smile. "Only girl talk."

"How was your run?" Annie asked.

"Good." Cal moved to stand behind Annie's chair. After placing his hands on the arms, he lowered his head and kissed her cheek. "How was your *sleep*?"

Failing to hold back a monstrous grin, she rolled her eyes as she looked up at him. The man had made good on his promise, giving her two more orgasms after the three.

Five total.

One after the power nap and dinner, and the other in the middle of the night when she'd woken to pee. She literally had died the little French death, and she was sore. She could walk, though. Barely.

"I'm going to shower." Cal rested his chin on the top of Annie's head.

"*Tu jugo, hijo,*" Rosa announced, lifting the fresh OJ into the air.

"*Only* girl talk?" Cal asked after grabbing the glass from Rosa, his brows pinched together.

"*No necesitas saberlo todo.*" Rosa filled a mug with coffee. "You know?"

Cal finished the juice in two seconds, made a loud "Ahhh," a little burp, and a thunderous, "Thank you," then he went toward his bedroom. The moment he grabbed the door handle, he fixed his sights on Annie, a smirk lighting his gorgeous face. "*Yo lo sé todo.*"

Rosa scoffed.

"Have you been brushing up on your Spanish, Ms. Baxter?" Cal asked.

Annie blushed. "You're *loco.*"

"Ah, good one, Annie." Rosa took a seat, palm around her cup, waving her other hand in the air, dismissing Cal. "He does not know *everything.*"

"I do," Cal repeated as he closed the door, but not before scolding Annie with his swell green eyes and all-star motherfucking grin.

"He acts like it," Annie said and laughed.

"Yes, and he thinks he's very good at *acting.*"

Annie smiled, brought her fork to her mouth, and took a generous bite of the omelet. "Thank you for breakfast."

"You're welcome." Rosa patted Annie's wrist.

"You mentioned you have a son." Annie scooped up more of the eggs and cheese and veggies. "Where does your family live?"

"I have four sons." Rosa lifted her brows. "Three of my children live in California, one is in New Mexico, and I have three grandchildren." She made a W with her fingers, smiling. "And my husband, well"—tapping her nails on the side of the mug, her grin faded—"he passed away a few years ago."

"I'm so sorry." Annie frowned.

"It's okay..." Rosa exhaled, her eyes bouncing around the room. "This is where God wants me to be."

"What do you mean?"

"Not long after George transitioned," Rosa continued, giving Annie a forced smile, "I started to do things for Cal — little things that turned into bigger things. And before I knew it, I'd offered to move to Florida."

"You offered?" Annie coughed, patting her chest.

Rosa shot Annie a sharp stare. "Yes."

Annie took a few more bites of breakfast, her feet shuffling across the cool wood floors while Rosa slurped her coffee.

"Luckily," she went on, "he found me my own place right here." Rosa tilted her head toward the front window.

"Here?"

"Yes, across the courtyard." Rosa chuckled. "And Carl ... well, Cal has had good luck with him too."

Luck or timing? Annie wondered as she recalled some of the conversation she'd had with Carl in the Tesla on the way home from the airport.

"Ah, yes, he told you this?"

"No, Carl did." Annie smiled. "But I told Cal we talked. He was really modest about the whole thing." Hiring a veteran, a man suffering from PTSD. "And quiet. He hasn't always been so quiet?"

"Not what I would call 'quiet.' *Pensando.* Thinking. Reflecting."

Annie reflected a moment too. Mostly on Rosa. The way she carried herself, the grace with which she held her cup of coffee, the way her eyes always seemed to do an intimate dance with her words.

"It must be difficult being away from your family."

"Cal is my family, too." Rosa met Annie's gaze again. "*Mi hijo.*"

Annie started to do the calculation in her mind, coming up with around forty years of friendship. More than friendship. *Rosa must be like a second mother to him.* Or like an actual mother to him. This woman moved across the country, thousands of miles away from her children and grandchildren, to be here — the change must've had to do with much more than taking care of the "bigger" things.

Rosa reminds Cal that he is whole, Annie thought. *Of where he comes from, of who he is. Her presence keeps him grounded. Helps keep the loneliness he hides from whisking him away.*

No wonder she needed to be with him in Florida.

Perhaps, Tabitha had been right. Maybe it was okay to need someone.

Cal loved hearing Annie declare she needed him whenever they were in the bedroom. But when it came time to admit what he needed, he avoided the conversation the way he had that night on the phone. Annie wondered why he lied to himself. To others. She could see what he needed from miles away.

Someone to care for him.

With no strings.

Or questions.

Someone he could need right back.

FORTY-TWO

"Excuse me, love." Rosa reached under the sink, next to Annie's legs, grabbed a few items, then stood. Breakfast was finished. Cal had eaten too. "I told you, you don't need to do these dishes."

"I want to."

"You're a sweet one."

Annie smiled and shut the water off.

"I'm going to get out of your way and do some work up in the loft."

"You're never in the way."

"Well, I see that look you two had in your eyes this morning, and I should be out of your way."

Cal's *look*. The I'll-be-eating-Annie-alive look. "Rosa..." Annie dried her hands on a towel. "Really."

"I remember..." Rosa set the supplies on the table. "I remember what it's like when you first meet someone. I may be old, but I remember how I felt when I first fell in love with George."

Annie's feet suddenly grew roots. *Love...?* she thought. *Fuck.* Her throat tightened. Her stomach twisted. The boy-man-guy she'd thought she'd loved, Daniel jerk-face Westerly, had never made her feel like this.

Roots. In. The. Ground.

Upside-down roller coaster.

Mind in the sky.

Stifling.

Wind knocked from her chest.

Crazy.

Unable to make sense of words or questions.

The temperature... She pulled at the neckline of her dress. Was it hot in the room?

Talk, Annie. Speak. Respond.

"Come here, my child."

Annie managed to follow Rosa's gentle command. Pressing her fingers against her skirt, she made her way to the table, terrified the four-letter word could somehow apply to their *just the summer, just the summer, just the summer*. The June, July, and August of no relationship plans or what-ifs. There wasn't any room for love. No sequoia trees. No safety. No thinking.

"George, my husband, he was older than me too, you know?" When Rosa spoke, she meant business. Her eyes told the stories. Her hands followed. "Don't let anyone give you a hard time about that."

"How much older?" Annie asked, a lump in her throat the size of those oranges she'd juiced.

"He was almost ten years older. He was..." Rosa trailed off, eyes glossing.

Annie ran her fingers across Rosa's upper arm, and the fearless woman straightened her posture and nodded.

"Mmm. My George was a pistol, and I loved him all the more for it. I was never afraid to love him. Time is precious, Annie. You will see."

"I know..." The photographer dropped her chin.

"Who have you lost?"

"My brother."

"Your only brother?"

"Yes," Annie whispered.

"What was his name?"

"Peter."

"Ah ... Peter," Rosa replied in her thick, beautiful accent, every word she pronounced sounding like a symphony. "This name means rock. He was your rock, yes?"

Annie's eyes surely gave Rosa the answer she desired. They lit up with heartache. Drowned in the ocean. They filled with all the tears she'd tried to numb with pills. They held her father's grief, her mother's faux concern. But she contained it. All of it. Behind the dam she'd built many, many months ago.

It won't break. Not now.

Rosa spoke several sentences in Spanish as she looked heavenward, her supplication so raw and mesmerizing.

"What was that all about?"

"That?" Rosa asked, pointing to the ceiling as if what she'd done was obvious. "I spoke with God. I told him how I feel about this — this senseless business of a man dying so young."

Senseless, Annie thought. *No reason.* Rosa had read Annie's mind. *Talk to Rosa about God, Annie,* Cal had said that night on the beach. But Rosa talked to God, and there were still no answers.

"You go." Rosa nodded toward Cal's closed bedroom door and smiled. "You go be with Cal."

Annie hesitated. *Go be with Cal.* Love Cal. Comfort Cal. Simple. Let him comfort you. Be patient with Cal.

It's. One. Summer.

Besides, all that jabberwocky required thinking. And she wouldn't allow herself to imagine anything beyond this summer. Annie wasn't ready to entertain the idea of making a life with someone. Not when she was too busy trying to find her own.

Right now, she only wanted her camera. She needed her camera. *It's me and my Nikon. Always.*

"Cal got a phone call," Annie said to Rosa the moment she stepped into the loft. "He's working ... has papers scattered all over the bed."

"Cal works too much." Rosa made circles on the window with her towel.

"Do you mind if I play some music?" Annie took a seat on the floor in front of the media cabinet.

"No, I don't mind." She grinned. "Some of those records are probably older than me."

They both laughed as Annie opened the cabinet's double doors and began to thumb through the albums one by one. When strands of hair fell across her face, instead of twirling them, she pushed them behind her ears.

Rosa's towel squeaked against the glass. Air squished between the jackets as each fell against the next. A smile formed on Annie's face as she fingered the vast assortment of vinyl, the smell of old cardboard mixing with a barrage of memories she didn't know about but wanted to.

INXS
Nat King Cole
The Temptations
Van Morrison
Soundgarden
The Beatles
Ella Fitzgerald
Bob Dylan
Lead Belly
The Bee Gees

Wait. What? The Bee Gees? That cannot be his, she thought, suppressing a giggle.

A few minutes later, Annie finally settled on an album. First, she held the record up and looked at the way the light streaming in from the window glistened across the grooves. She could see the imperfections, some scratches, along with particles of dust. It never ceased to amaze her how an hour or so of music could be stored on an LP or a CD — and now on a cloud in her phone.

The need to photograph Cal's records seized her. She wanted to remember his collection. This moment. What it felt like to be on the precipice of so many different things at once.

Taking her camera from its case, she began to capture the different ways the light bounced off the big black circle. She shot stacks of albums, separate and together, in the sleeves and out. Then, after photographing the naked turntable, she dressed it with her choice and carefully dropped the needle onto the track she wanted to hear most.

Resuming a lotus position, she picked up *Use Your Illusion I*'s jacket and began to read the lyrics to "November Rain." She knew the song. She knew a lot of before-her-time songs, mainly because her brother or father had introduced her to them. But she didn't know these particular words very well, and she wanted to. And after sharing songs with Cal, Annie didn't think she would ever look at any lyrics the same way again.

Especially these.

The poetry filled her mind — words she applied to Cal, herself, life. Especially the part at the end. Phrases and questions Axl would soon repeat over and over — a mantra after her own heart.

But perhaps the songwriter had gotten it wrong. Because nobody truly needed anyone.

"Is it too loud?" Annie asked, glancing over at Rosa. The woman stood at the corner bookshelf, carefully wiping around Cal's novels with a cloth, hips moving to the rock-n-roll beat.

"I like this." She grinned. "Guns N' Roses. Yes?"

"Yes." Annie laughed, lowering the volume, then she held her camera up. "Can I take your picture?"

"I'm not dressed for a photoshoot."

"You look stunning." In her orange capris, a cross around her neck, a white satin blouse. "Please."

"All right," Rosa conceded, placing her things aside. "What shall I do?"

"Nothing. You're perfect." Annie remained on the floor, rose up on her knees, and began to press the shutter button.

"Cal took me to the gallery by the beach," Rosa interrupted a few seconds later, and Annie lowered the camera. "I saw your photographs." Annie stood as Rosa finished speaking. "They're beautiful."

A clothespin pinched Annie's tongue.

Or something...

He'd taken Rosa to the gallery... Doing something so intimate with someone he loved so dearly. To see *her* photographs.

Words weren't forming.

Forget the clothespin, her tongue was a brick, and it was pasty. Thick. Nothing about her could move. No hands. No feet. No breath. Axl continued, though, singing about needs. Annie couldn't need anyone.

Cal didn't need anyone.

The eight-minute song had reached the crescendo, the climax, the part that had affected her as she'd read the lyrics. The incessant piano, the crashing, violent noises. Perfect timing. And by perfect, Annie meant *not perfect*. Singing and pleading mixed with the sounds of the instruments, making her want to believe in magic. In needs.

Rosa stared at Annie like she'd morphed into a deer caught in headlights. While Annie only focused on the song...

Axl's voice.

The shredding of the piano.

Fingers falling across several keys.

Raking-raking-raking.

I don't need someone. We have to move on. Nothing is permanent.

"Annie..." Rosa broke into her thoughts, touching her arm.

She tried to smile. "I'm sorry." *Tongue untwist. Please.* "I'm..." *At a loss for words. In shock. Making a big deal out of nothing.* "I didn't think... I didn't know he cared about..."

"You didn't think he cared about what?" Rosa moved some of Annie's hair behind her neck and cupped her chin.

"My photos." She swallowed.

"About you, Annie," Rosa affirmed, but the photographer looked away. "You know he cares for you." Rosa placed Annie's hand over her own heart. "*Here.*"

Glancing up, Annie met Rosa's onyx, truth-telling eyes, which was a terrible mistake because, now, Annie might cry. She removed her palm, refusing to shed tears, and shook her head. She stared at the floor.

It's a fling. Tab said don't overthink it. I say don't overthink it.

Annie teetered on the edge of erupting, of embarrassing herself, of crying. Instead, she held it all inside, afraid dwelling on any kind of future with this man would eat away at whatever time they had left. They had discussed this, rational and adult-like. They'd made a decision.

To be in the now. No talking of plans. No what-ifs. No future.

Only the summer. This one summer.

"He bought one, you know?" Rosa said as she made her way back to the corner shelf.

Annie tripped over this new piece of information. Her eyes bounced around the room. She clutched her neck.

"Oh, I'm always telling you things I shouldn't."

"Which one?" Annie whispered even though she knew the one Cal had chosen. *The cove...*

"The large one of Pfeiffer Beach."

"Where is it?" Annie looked around the loft despite knowing it wasn't here.

"He sent it home." Rosa's eyes flickered, saying much more than her words ever could. "It was a gift."

Annie seemed to have forgotten to breathe.

"He wanted her to see something she used to love. To be able to look at that beach every day."

Unable to keep the water at bay, Annie started to cry. Not blubbery, but quiet. Tears slid down her cheeks.

"Oh, *mi amor*," Rosa said, stepping into Annie's space. "Your heart, *preciosa*, is opening his back up. He has been waiting for you."

Annie wiped her face and allowed Rosa to pull her into an embrace. Not a second passed, and she longed to escape. But it was pointless. Useless. Her throat, tighter than ever, had sealed shut. Her body remained rigid, unsure, afraid.

Moments later, Annie's phone pinged, breaking up their exchange. Rosa placed her palm against Annie's cheek and sighed, then she whispered a few gentle words in her native tongue as she returned to the tasks she seemed to do only because she loved him.

Annie pulled up the text message.

Cal: You haven't left me?

"It's getting late," Annie muttered, phone in her palm as she walked over to the large, sparkling-clean window.

The late morning sun made its way through the trees, shining into the loft. Cal's things reflected off the glass. Annie leaned her head against the pane, closed her eyes, and simply felt the vibration of the song as it played. She didn't recognize the next track, only Axl's screech.

"Where's your family, Annie?"

"Seattle," she answered as she lifted her head and turned.

"You are from there?"

"Yes," Annie replied, and her phone chimed again.

"Hmmm," was all Rosa said, but it appeared as though dots made connection inside her mind.

Cal: I'm sorry I have work today.

Annie dismissed Cal's second message and opened the Uber app. She should've asked him to call Carl, but she needed to go — and *now* — before her feelings completely consumed the lot of her. After securing a ride, she placed the needle on the holster and put the record away.

"I won't see you the rest of this week," Rosa began while putting her things away. "I'm going home to visit my sons and their families." Rosa gave Annie's bicep a squeeze. "I like talking with you." She winked.

"I feel the same." Annie smiled.

"It's easy to tell you things. You're different than—" Rosa stopped and shook her head.

"Than what?"

"I came here, Annie, because Cal had lost the light."

FORTY-THREE

"First, you ignore my texts, and now you're leaving without saying goodbye." Cal grinned, peering at her over the rims of his eyeglasses.

The man had been sitting at his desk in the corner, studying the laptop screen the way she might observe a subject through the lens of her Nikon since she'd entered his bedroom only a few minutes ago.

"No, but I sent for a car," she replied, returning the smile as she stopped near the closed door, suitcase in tow, backpack over a shoulder.

Still grinning, he removed his frames, set them on his desk, and shook his head.

"I wanted to have my things ready and in the foyer."

"Turn around, Annie." Unflinching, Cal leaned back in his chair, folded his arms across his chest, and stared at her. No longer smiling, his eyes like laser beams.

Annie wondered whether this little show of power was her punishment for deciding to leave early. Or for not using his car. Or both. Nevertheless, she let go of the luggage, dropped her backpack, and turned around in her halter-style dress, its back open, skirt flowing while feeling a little foolish — as though she were, not the fashion model at an event, but the actual car atop the turntable.

Upon finishing the complete three-sixty, she faced him again — Mr. Serious, looking like he wanted to eat her for lunch. Chin pointing down, he peered up at her through his lashes and cracked a smile — a devious one. "You don't have to leave on account of my work."

Annie crossed her ankles. "I know, but I want to see Maggie." Her knees knocked. Her breathing changed. Goosepimples broke out all over her skin. "And I want to be in my own space. My room. I was gone for almost a week."

Cal grabbed an ink pen and began to twirl it between his fingers. "That's fine." Clearing his throat, he released the pen. "I don't know how much work I could actually get accomplished anyway after imagining what I want to do to you in that dress."

Fighting a smile, Annie rolled her eyes. "There are other things we can do."

"But we do that so well." Cal smirked and eyed the bed.

Annie dropped her chin, but she could no longer hide her big, fat grin. Hair fell around her face. Perhaps the strands would cover the heat flooding her cheeks.

"We do other things," he piped up. "Pick something. Anything. We'll do it tomorrow."

Annie studied his expression, the few lines stretching across his forehead, his self-control never more evident than right now, urgency hidden beneath a strange sort of calm.

"I'll look online this afternoon," she replied. "See if there are any local events scheduled for tomorrow."

She'd barely spat out the words when Cal's phone rang. Annie thought it might be her exit, but he simply glanced at the screen, silenced it, then turned his attention back to her.

"Does it make you uncomfortable that I want you?" Cal didn't break eye contact. His face was placid. "That I make that known." His eyes seemed to reach full charge. "You're a beautiful woman."

Annie swallowed, blinked, fidgeted with her fingers. "Uncomfortable, no." She glanced at him, then the bed. "But sometimes it feels like that's all you want. I want to know you."

"Come here, Annie." Cal patted his thigh.

"Do people always do what you say?" She stood straighter, taller. She stopped fidgeting.

"You like to listen to me."

"Oh, really?"

"You don't think I know how to pick the ones who will listen?"

Swiping her backpack off the floor, she palmed the door handle so hard her knuckles whitened.

"Annie..." Cal said, stifling a laugh.

"The 'ones'?" She whipped her head in his direction. "I'm not part of a category."

"*Come here.*"

"No."

For a time, they only stared at each other, Annie's hand on the doorknob, Cal's eyes like molten steel, her breathing labored, the whole of his gorgeous face still like the surface of water right before a storm tramples the ocean.

"You are your own category entirely." He laughed. "Now, come here."

She huffed, made him wait a few seconds longer, seconds in which he seemed rather amused — the fucker — then she dropped her bag and went toward him. With each step, the anger lessened and the ache she had for him to fill her completely increased.

"You like to listen," he uttered the moment she reached him, his voice dripping like honey as his fingers went under her dress. She stood in front of him. He remained seated. "And you like it when I lead you."

She smacked his hand away, but he put it back on her ass immediately.

"Do you want me to spank you?"

Her head fell back. Her eyes combed the ceiling. Biting her lip, she tried to suppress a moan. Two hands were beneath her skirt now, one squeezing an ass cheek, the other gripping her hip bone.

"You like all of it," he whispered.

"Maybe..." She spread a palm over his shirt. "I like this." Over his heart. "I want to know who you are. On the inside."

"You do know me." He glanced up. "We talked for hours last night."

"I did most of the talking," she guffawed. About herself, about the roses he'd somehow exploded in the backseat of the Tesla. She'd shared her favorite foods, drinks, places she'd been, stories of her mother and father. A little about her prior relationships. But there had been no talk of his heartbreaks. Only hers. No mad loves or Constance Prescott. "You listened."

"I'm a good listener."

"Yeah ... well, I want to listen too."

"It takes time, baby. Give me time."

"Time," she groaned. "What time? You said time was a bitch."

Cal laughed. "What do you want to know?" His palm trailed to the front of her panties, and as he skirted a finger over the material, Annie released a fabulous breath. "A free pass. Anything. Right now."

"Two free passes." She grabbed his forearm, but it didn't stop him from running that digit up and down her seam. "Yes?"

"Mmm..." he replied.

"Your father."

Cal stopped touching her.

"You said you didn't remember him."

"I was five when he left."

Annie stroked a few fingers along his jaw, staring into his eyes until their breathing regulated.

"I'll go easy on you now." She grinned. "What's your middle name?"

"My middle name..." Cal's expression softened. He bit her nipple through the dress.

"Cal..." Annie pushed him away at his shoulders, but her defiance only caused him to pull her body closer.

"It's my mother's maiden name." Their eyes locked. Cal squared her hips. "Warner."

Wrapping her hands behind his neck, Annie combed her fingers through his hair, messing it up some while Cal nuzzled his nose to her chest, kept his palms beneath her dress, one on the front of her panties, the other on her butt cheek.

"Don't you want to know mine?" she uttered, holding his face against her breasts as she began to ride his hand.

"Your what?" he joked as he popped his head up.

Annie shoved him, pointing a knee toward his groin.

"Yes, please." He laughed, batting her knee away. "What's your middle name?"

"It's Rebekah." She grinned, swung her legs to either side of his chair, and straddled him from a standing position.

"Annie ... Rebekah ... Baxter," he whispered, moving his fingers from cotton to warm flesh, up and down her folds, then inside her body. "You like that?"

"You're not winning today." Her back arched. Her eyes closed. She moaned and moaned.

"No?"

"No." She opened her lids. "I have another question."

Cal slid his fingers out. Her face scrunched up in pain. Then he put those same two fingers at her mouth, dotting her lips with the taste of her arousal. She licked them, sucking on them until he made his own delicious sounds.

"Fuck if I can get any work done today," he groaned, pinching his eyes shut. "That's three fucking passes..." He rubbed his forehead. "What's your question?"

"You bought a photograph."

"What?" He opened his eyes. "That's a statement, Annie."

"Pfeiffer Beach, Cal."

"Rosa..." He sighed, shaking his head.

"Don't be upset. She thought I knew," Annie said and paused, waiting, giving him *patience*, wishing to hear the story of why the picture held meaning to him to come out of his own mouth. Then his stupid phone rang ... again.

"Persistent bastard." He glanced at the screen. "I have to take it this time."

The moment Cal answered the call, Annie moved to stand behind his chair, running her fingers through his hair, scratching her nails along his scalp. Leaning down, she whispered in his ear, "I'm happy you bought the photograph."

Smiling, phone in one hand, Cal put on his glasses and quickly scribbled something on a Post-it. Then he held it up, the writing facing Annie.

Snatching the sticky note out of his hand, she smirked and pinched his waist. Squirming a little, he peeled a second piece of tiny yellow paper off the pad and held it near her eyeline.

The moment she grabbed it — shocked he'd spelled her middle name right when most people would've spelled it Rebecca — another square appeared, a third.

After swiping the last one, she slid a palm down the front of his body toward his waist. "I'll have you tonight," she whispered in his ear as she touched him over his pants. "On my knees." Her fingers pressed against his crotch. "I want you to fuck my mouth the way you promised."

Every muscle in Cal's body tensed.

Grinning, Annie stood tall without making a sound, backed away, and put her palms up in surrender.

Cal eyeballed her, shaking his head.

As she made her way to the door, she remembered something she couldn't believe she'd forgotten. His notes had reminded her of hers. Inside her back-pack, nestled at the bottom, were two gifts she'd bought in New York City.

A moment later, Cal glanced down at the white boxes tied with red ribbons Annie had placed on his desk, narrowly noticing her exiting the bedroom as his eyes became glued to the instructions written on each.

Open me first...

Open me second...

Cal no longer cared whether he pacified the persistent bastard on the line, but he persisted with the persistent bastard, making the mistake of opening the gifts while he remained on the call. After pinching his nose and pushing his glasses up it, he switched the device to "speaker," and opened the first box. A handwritten note rested atop tissue paper.

To help you find your
way back to something
you once loved.

Underneath the paper, Cal found a small container of surfboard wax. Scrubbing a palm over his chin, he lifted and twirled the jar, gazing at the label, attempting in vain to continue listening to the man on speaker. Then Cal moved on to the second gift. Another note greeted him.

The courage you need to help you value the time it will take to get you there.

Wrapped in wads of tissue paper, he discovered an old-fashioned oval-shaped mirror with a golden etched handle.

The man on the line made noises. Babbled. Spoke a foreign language. Or something.

Cal wasn't sure.

Because the chameleon had already changed from bright green to pale white as he floated up and out of his body. He tried to clear his throat, but it felt sticky, sap-like. No sounds formed. No thoughts came.

Cal was often quiet, but right now, he was simply without words. The person on the phone noticed.

"Yes, yes, I'm here," Cal finally managed, clearing his throat. But he really wasn't *here*. Or anywhere.

Did he know anything?

Holding the embossed handle of the antique mirror, he looked at his reflection, trying to conceal his emotions. But he failed. He had no choice but to abruptly end the call. His self-control had vanished. He was beside himself. Above himself. He was suspended.

Everything Annie stood for became crystal clear.

Everything she meant to him.

Cal sank deeper into the chair, his vulnerability a yoke begging to be pulled. All of it he saw in the fucking mirror. The expression on his face — worth a million dollars.

And it all scared the fucking shit out of him.

After setting the truth-telling oval down — facedown — he stood, his fingers digging into the skin at the nape of his neck.

He wanted a drink.

No, he needed a drink.

Like a lion, he paced back and forth near the foot of the bed, maybe a minute, maybe longer. Days might've passed, his eyes wide as he stared at the floor.

Annie did know him.

He knew that.

Crack of the bat, she knew him.

But Annie *wanted* to know him?

Did she need him?

The earnest looks she gave him in the bedroom — what she offered and seemed to sacrifice in the sheets — weren't without merit or truth or strength. The *I need you, Cal* wasn't a ruse, a taunt, or merely a game they played.

Those words carried weight.

What Cal had come to rely upon, what had served him well for so many years — using his sexuality to get exactly what he wanted — was no longer any good here. Annie needed more than a good, hard fuck. She needed a man who would bear the brunt, who followed through, a man who would let her truly see who he was on the inside. Fully.

Denial was over.

Lies were over.

The time they had to spend together was real — weeks of what could possibly be an endless summer.

Cal exited the bedroom and stood outside the door, eyes blurring, transfixed in thought, the need for a drink forgotten.

"Where's Annie?" he asked Rosa, his voice booming.

"She just left." Rosa's brow furrowed. "Is everything all right?"

Without responding, Cal marched toward the foyer and opened the front door. A Toyota, engine running, was parked several feet away at the curb. Annie stood at the opened rear passenger door. Before taking her seat, she glanced up.

Cal stood outside, peeking through the entry gate, gripping the bars, and stared at her.

He wanted to go to her but couldn't.

He was stuck behind the stupid gate to the courtyard. The longer he waited … the urgency faded, being replaced by suffocation. Although fully clothed, Cal felt naked, frozen, like he'd been heated up in a brick oven, then dropped into an icy ocean.

The change in temperature could kill a man. And he'd already died a thousand deaths looking into Annie's eyes. She was the sun, the earth, the sky.

Fuck him for not being what she needed.

Fuck him for not being able to move.

She knew him.

Did she know he would fail? Did she know he would leave? Did she know *she* was the strength he couldn't bring himself to rely upon? Did she know he had a sick mother to care for? Did she have the patience to put up with his astronomical bullshit?

The driver asked a question, and Annie and Cal broke eye contact, the live wire of energy between them fizzling, creating sparks on the ground.

"Yes, yes, I'm ready," she replied.

Ready for what? she thought.

The future.

The end of summer.

As the car pulled onto the street, Annie flicked her gaze once more to the man behind the gate. Messy, splotchy, colorful emotions wet his face, splattering his features as though a child had painted an open, beating heart across his cheeks and jaw and eyelids with their fingers.

Annie did know him.

Just like she knew the gifts must have reached his heart.

No one had ever affected her the way Cal did. And she suddenly found herself cataloguing all the things she'd come to know about this man...

Cal didn't like coffee, but he loved fresh squeezed orange juice.

He ran to stay healthy, to feel good. To chase away the blues or the mean reds. He ran to think, to compartmentalize, to organize. He needed to run. Had to.

He loved music. It calmed and comforted him the way nothing else in life could.

He was fluent in Spanish. And in the language of her body.

He loved shrimp any way it was prepared. He liked orange marmalade and scrambled eggs.

He smelled like ocean and sand and a bright, white towel.

He pinched his neck, his nose, or the corners of his eyes when he worried or tensed.

He needed to fuck all his feelings away, or he needed to absolutely fuck every feeling he'd ever owned into her soul — each thought and emotion he couldn't verbalize.

The tips of his fingers spoke volumes while she listened to every syllable they pronounced.

He had an eye for art, and he collected things that not only appealed to those perspicacious eyes but things that touched his heart.

He opened doors.

You do know me, he had said earlier in his bedroom. Apparently, she did. Fuck plans, right, Cal? She hadn't come to Miami in search of a man or a plan, other than the one to take photographs.

She'd come to Florida to be with friends, to rediscover the magic she'd misplaced — the life stolen from her the previous May.

It was too late for thinking now.

Or decisions.

She'd already dipped a toe into Cal's ocean. Actually, she'd dived in and hadn't come back up for air.

She wouldn't cry right now, though. Not in the back of the Toyota.

She would rest, regroup, edit. Then she would go to him later tonight and try her best to be what they'd agreed upon.

The summer.

Plenty more weeks of summer, right?

Could she manage it? Could she hide all the love bubbling out of the center of her fuck-the-depression-feel-something-you-are-not-numb-don't-take-pills-cry-for-your-brother-understand-your-father-and-mother-it's-not-just-the-summer-love-Cal heart?

She would have to try. Because Calvin Warner Prescott wouldn't acquiesce to any fool's declaration of love. He needed someone who meant what they said and followed through.

The no-plan plan had changed.

Annie had let Cal into the cracks of her heart, into the places where her wounds had begun to heal. Cal had helped to stitch them up too.

Maybe he did need strings... Sutures.

She'd fallen into him. Into his eyes, his protection, his hands. She swam in his ocean. Climbed his tree. And now, she needed to exercise patience.

But for how long?

She tapped her fingernails on the edge of the car's windowsill, counting out the remaining days of this ... one ... summer.

THE BRIDGE AND THE BLEEDING

A MEANS OF CONNECTION; ANGUISH, PAIN, OR SYMPATHY; TO SPREAD THROUGH SOMETHING GRADUALLY

I begin
where you end
never sex
only sex
and stars
folded inside clouds
protected for eternity
where nothing
can touch them
or me
where blood
becomes remedy
touch
becomes ascension
where
I float
on love
we refute

FORTY-FOUR

Annie arrived at Cal's doorstep, sweat beading over her upper lip and sticking to her thighs, with a brown paper bag full of fresh groceries on a Saturday evening in mid-August.

More than two months had passed since they'd first set eyes on each other, and despite the heat invading the dusk falling over Miami, the summer was coming to a close. Kids were starting school. Vacation was over. Annie's display at the gallery would end in a few weeks, and Cal's lease would expire in September. Nevertheless, they'd been going along as always, ignoring questions that needed answering.

But not tonight.

Tonight, would be different.

Pushing the impending conversation of summer's end far from her mind — the one she knew she was going to force upon them — Annie opened Cal's front door and made her way to the kitchen. Focused only on making Cal a meal for the first time.

As she pulled items from the grocery bag, Cal descended the staircase barefoot, wearing metal-rimmed glasses, a pair of dark blue jeans, and a white polo shirt.

The man was beautiful, quiet and stealth and flying under the radar, making a crash landing into the valves of her heart. Before she knew it, Cal landed in the kitchen, smelling like soap and wine, his hands finding her waist and his nose her face, the latter trailing along her jawline.

"I thought you said you weren't working today." She eyed a bottle of something light and golden and half-finished on the table next to his laptop and folders.

On a deep inhale, he tangled his nose through her hair. "When did you get here?"

Three seconds in his presence, and already Annie could barely concentrate. Not on the items she pulled from the bag. Or the fact that "Stand by Me" blared. After weeks of bedding him, of staring into those ocean eyes, after thousands of conversations and sharing dozens of meals — Calvin Warner Prescott still made her knees weak and her breath hitch.

"Maybe you should lock your door." She bumped his hip, then folded the empty bag. "Keep the riff-raff out."

Cal smiled, slapped her ass, then he went to the table and took a seat in front of his things.

"I bought some local shrimp," Annie called out, humming along to the chorus of the famous Ben E. King song.

"It looks like you bought a hell of a lot more than shrimp." Cal's fingers flew across the keyboard.

"And it looks like"—she eyeballed him—"you're working."

Cal glanced up, his gaze charged, his face implacable, then his attention went back to the laptop. "Do you want some help?"

"No." Annie's hips bounced as she washed peppers and mushrooms. "I'm cooking you dinner, Prescott. You keep ... *working*." Grinning, she looked over her shoulder and fluttered her lashes, then she turned off the faucet.

"I'm returning emails." His brow crinkled. "These people don't wait."

"I don't wait." Tapping a foot to the beat, Annie began to chop an onion, her eyes already watering as she tucked her hot-pink bra strap beneath her green sundress. "Did your meeting go well yesterday?"

"I thought we were going to close but they weren't ready. So that's what I'm doing, Annie. Answering questions, more questions, always fucking questio—"

"Dammit!"

The second the knife hit the floor, Cal jumped up and met Annie at the sink. Cool water washed over the cut on her index finger. Tears streamed down her cheeks. But she didn't utter a sound. She tilted her head to the side as Cal brushed drops of salt off her face, watching Annie pensively, never breaking gaze, smelling sweet-sweet-sweet like the wine he'd been drinking.

His quiet strength overwhelmed her.

His silence never stifling.

His presence never dull.

Annie loved his quiet. His smell. Loved how every moment between them felt like coming home. Or what she imagined coming home should feel like.

"Hold this against your finger and don't let go," he said after grabbing a wad of paper towels. Nudging Annie along, Cal led her to the kitchen table, and they sat down. After refilling his wineglass, he pushed it toward her. "Drink, baby."

Her eyes filled with more tears.

"Don't worry about dinner." He caressed her cheek, then stood. "I'll be right back. Stay put."

Annie took a big gulp of the pinot grigio, trying not to cry over the ridiculous turn of events. Or over the days leading up to her trip to Seattle. But her thoughts continued wrapping a fist around her heart while she pressed the gash to the towel. Pressing, pressing, pressing. Or was it the other way around? Everything she'd wished to bury these last few weeks — *love love love love love* — made her tingle and ache.

"Your eyes turn a brilliant shade of green after you cry," Cal said the moment he returned and took a seat, a few supplies in hand. "They look like bright green lollipops."

Annie swallowed, thinking it was *his* eyes that commanded her attention, his eyes that had her practically tripping over her breath. The beautiful ocean green shone keenly through his lenses. *Strong and masculine*, she thought, *even when performing the simplest of tasks.*

Removing the paper towels.

Beginning to clean the cut with cotton balls and peroxide.

Preparing the gauze and tape.

The cream.

Annie desperately tried to hang onto the emotions the wine had forced to the surface, the emotions cutting her finger had wrenched from her — because one hurt had the ability to open all hurts — but they were all about to burst.

Reaching up, Annie removed Cal's glasses with her good hand, set them aside, and peered deeper into his soul. Music played, a song she didn't recognize now. It seemed far away. Thousands of miles.

But Cal was close.

Time expired on his face. Ran out. Stopped.

They shared breath the way they shared everything.

Annie's throat swelled beyond explanation at the expression on his face, a quite readable one: vulnerability. His glasses were off, yes, but what she saw was more than his naked eyes. It was far more than an appearance of Superman behind Clark Kent.

He cares for me. He loves me.

Wait. What?

Of course she was going to acknowledge it now. Now. After weeks of denial. She'd known it for how long? She could see love all over him, and she could no longer refute it. The way he cared for her, gentle and strong, and what she meant to him.

Cal's feelings spilled onto the kitchen table the way the blood flowed from her cut: uncontrollably, real. And the only thing that could stop it was too much pressure ... or time. Or the end of summer. Or a million other material things.

"You changed my album." Cal held the clean knife, chopping away at the peppers, green and red.

The emerald skirt of Annie's dress bounced as she made her way down the stairs, faint strands of hair falling outside the clip and framing her face. "I told you I wanted to listen to something different."

"That is different."

"It's yours." She picked up her wine — actually, his wine — then emptied the rest of the bottle into the glass. "Don't you ever listen to it?"

"Not in a million years." Cal popped a slice of red pepper into his mouth.

"I saw them in concert a couple years ago. They were freaking awesome." Annie placed the glass on the counter, eyeing his back, his shoulders, the way everything gracefully flexed as he chopped.

"I saw them at Lollapalooza."

"*You* went to Lollapalooza?" She coughed, then patted her chest.

"Yes." He narrowed his gaze.

"I'm sorry." She laughed and stepped closer to him. "I'm having a hard time imagining you there."

"I went in '92."

"1992!"

Cal glared at Annie again, this time, his eyes resembling lasers. "Yes." He threw a pepper at her chest. "Not 1892."

"Hey." She caught the scrap and tossed it onto the countertop, then pushed the back of his knee in with her foot, causing him to buckle.

"I'm having a hard time imagining you at all in 1992." He smirked. "Were you even walking yet?"

"Stop it." Marrying her chest to his back, she covered his mouth with her palm, wrapping her other arm around his waist.

"Do we need to open a new bottle?" Cal mumbled, his voice muzzled by her hand.

"What? What was that?" she whispered near his ear as she removed her palm and laughed.

"Get another bottle out of the fridge."

But Annie remained at his side, arms folded, gazing at his profile. "Did you like it?"

"Like what?"

"Cal..."

He smiled. "My girlfriend wanted to go."

"Ahhh."

"There were too many damn bodies everywhere for my taste."

"I'm sure there were."

"The music was good. I've never forgotten it or the experience."

"How old were you when you went?" Annie asked as she began calculating his age in her mind.

"Mmm, I think I was about twenty-three."

"That's how old I was." She beamed.

"What are you talking about?"

"When I saw the Chili Peppers. In 2012. I was twenty-three."

"Holy shit, Annie." He laughed. "Are you trying to make me *feel* old?"

"No, I'm trying to make you see how special it is that we went at the same ages and—"

"We went twenty years apart."

"So. It's a moment we both experienced at the same age, with the same..."

"The same what?" he pressed.

"I don't know. The same wanderlust. Don't you remember what it felt like to be twenty-three?" She pinched his ass cheek.

Cal walked to the stove, tossing her the sexy, I-am-so-spanking-your-ass-tonight look, then he slid the vegetables into the waiting skillet. The savory aroma filled the air in an instant.

"I didn't know you could cook." Annie handed him a wooden spoon, and he moved the sizzling peppers and onions around in the olive oil. "Is it going to be edible?"

"I cook well," he said, and their eyes locked. "But if you're worried about my ability in the kitchen, we can skip dinner"—he nodded toward his door—"and go straight to the bedroom."

"I've seen your ability in the kitchen." Annie made an ahem sound, arching a brow. "I'm not worried."

Cal grinned and added the mushrooms to the pan.

"And, yeah, right, we're skipping dinner. I've been looking forward to cooking you this meal all week. Maggie has been giving me pointers. I couldn't wait to—" Annie stopped short, her voice cracking.

She placed a palm over her damp upper lip. Her injured finger protruded out like a stupid football-game souvenir, large and pointy.

"It's okay, Annie." Stirring the vegetables, he stroked her cheek. "We'll make it together." He kissed her temple.

"What will we make together?" She smirked. "Dinner or *it*?"

Cal grinned, showing dimples and teeth. "I can arrange *it* right now."

Annie rolled her eyes.

Cal turned off the burner, flipped her around, lifted her skirt, and spanked her ass. Hard.

Annie sucked in a loud breath.

He did it again and again and again.

"Fuck," she moaned, wiggling her hips.

"Is this what you want?"

"Mmm," was all she said as Cal started to finger her. A hand inside her panties. Two digits in her warmth. Annie was lost, already forgetting. The blood. The pain. The impending conversation.

"More," she managed a few seconds later, and Cal struck her ass until she could feel absolutely nothing but fuzz. Or sunsets. Or colors in the viewfinder. All blending together with the smell of the food, him. The sting on her cheeks. The space she could finally feel in her gut. Her heart opening up.

The next few minutes passed in a blur, Cal alternating between smacking her ass and fingering her good and fast and hard, causing her to gyrate her pelvis against the countertop. Like she needed to both run away from him and draw closer. Bending forward and coming back. She could feel his touch in her teeth, clawing at her throat.

Annie worried she could no longer stand. But right when it seemed this man was the only thing holding her up, she exploded around him. The second he removed his hand, she nearly slid to the floor, melting into a puddle of everything she'd been attempting to regulate — the emotions she'd been trying to hide from.

Cal promptly scooped her up and turned her around, kissing her lips over and over.

"Thank you for taking care of me," she uttered between kisses, palm on his collar, fingers about his neck. "And thank you for cleaning up my mess ... and for cooking."

Smiling, Cal nuzzled his nose with hers. "And thank you for helping you climb into space."

"Yes," she replied, dropping her chin and blushing.

After he removed her hair clip, beautiful caramel-colored strands fell around her face, and he touched them, put his fingers and nose through them, inhaling tangerines until the scent reached his hippocampus. Pressing his body closer, careful not to ruffle her bandaged finger, he cradled her jaw and kissed her again. As though he hadn't already done so tonight nor hundreds of times during June, July, and August.

She tasted like the first time.

She made all other women, everything, obsolete.

"Are you still there now?" Cal asked, cradling her face, sucking on her bottom lip.

"Yes," Annie muttered.

Cal laughed a little as he wet her cheeks, her eyelids, her jawline.

"Good." Picking her up, he set her on the counter and said, "I want to be inside you, baby," as she wrapped her legs around his waist and mussed his hair. "*Just like this.*"

His cheek rested against her breasts, the rise and fall of her lungs moving his head gently up and down like a perfect wave ... coming in and going out. Squeezing the nape of his neck, she pushed his face deeper into her chest while shimmying her hips to the crashing beat of the drum break in the Chili Peppers song — the sounds like nothing ever synthesized.

Phenomenal sounds, impeccably winding through them both, bringing them closer, their bodies and souls finding an amazing rhythm. The infectious beat ascended the earth, lifting Cal and Annie off the planet.

Leading Annie further out into space.

And then...

The doorbell rang.

The break in the song ended.

Cal continued his exploration, kissing Annie as if nothing else existed but the two of them.

"Are you expecting someone?" Annie panted as she slid her hands beneath Cal's shirt.

Standing between her legs, Cal nuzzled his nose into her breasts, kissing her all over, wetting her neck, an ear, knocking the dress strap off her shoulder as he shoved his clothed body against hers.

The bell rang a second time.

"Cal..." Annie moaned, grabbed his wrist, and held it.

After kissing her cheek, he gently placed her on the floor. Her skirt fell as she bit a thumbnail and shook her hair out, the room a blur. "Breaking the Girl" came to an epic conclusion as Cal opened the front door.

Annie picked up the white, paper-covered package on the counter and unwrapped the large, freshly caught Florida shrimp. She rinsed handfuls of them off in the sink, still a little wobbly on her feet.

"What is it?" she asked, glancing over her shoulder, shaking the hair out of her face, trying to remember where she'd left her clip. *Ahhh. The countertop.* He'd removed it. A chill raced up her spine.

"Annie, shut the water off," Cal said while scanning the papers in his hand, glasses on his face. "I'm going to do that."

"I can do it." She flicked the swath of hair again.

"You're going to make it worse." Cal came up behind her, tucked those annoying strands of hair behind her ear, and kissed her temple.

"It's fine." She washed and dried her hands, careful not to disturb the bandage.

"It's not fine," he huffed and washed his own hands. "If you bump it or get it wet, it's going to keep bleeding."

"I wanted to be the one to make you dinner."

"Goddammit, Annie, we'll do it together," he grumbled, cutting the water. "Did the effects of that spanking really last for, what?" He glanced at the clock. "Only five fucking minutes?"

Annie rolled her eyes and shrugged as her phone rang to the tune of "Just the Way You Are." She went to the table and glanced at the screen.

"You're stubborn," he said while grabbing the colander full of shrimp. "And you're lucky," he mumbled. Lucky the doorbell rang. Cal wanted to tie her ass to the bed and spank her for hours, fuck her for even longer. Until she could actually let go for more than five fucking minutes.

"It's my mother." She strolled back into the kitchen, phone in her good hand. "*Again.*"

"Take a picture of that almighty finger and send it to her." Cal carried the shrimp to the stove. "I'm sure *she* would tell you you're being stubborn."

"God, Cal, then you know she'll just start asking me all kinds of questions." Annie glanced at him, bit her thumbnail, then quickly looked away.

"She's your mother," Cal scolded.

Hence, the reason Annie twisted herself into a knot. Two reasons, actually. One: Cal disapproved because she hadn't told her mom about him yet. Two: *This was Beverly.*

Cal knew why she avoided it, Annie had told him plenty of "Beverly" stories, but he didn't understand what it meant to have lived with her. Daily. He hadn't witnessed Annie caring for her mom day after day, months that turned to years. The postponement of college. Resentment that grew into dysfunctional branches on their family tree. The responsibility. The sacrifice. The alcohol. The dependence.

"Yes, but she is ... she is..." Annie trailed off, now looking in the fridge for a lime. She spotted a bottle instead. Grabbing it, she examined the label on the chardonnay.

"She's what, Annie? Incorrigible?"

Annie smiled — *perfect, yes* — incorrigible. As she looked up from the Chilean wine at Cal, their eyes met, and she laughed.

But Cal glanced away. Swallowed past the goddamn lump in his throat.

His true emotions, he kept off his face, wiping them clean from his eyes, disguising the familiar doubts, the familiar sting, the self-inflicting prophecy he feared would come true.

She would leave.

Travel.

Or find someone new.

She needed to.

Someone younger.

Someone who could do more than fuck her good and hard while living in denial. Someone who wasn't fucked up and unable to tell her all the things she deserved to know. Things about his own mom.

Constance's disease made him weak, undone, out of control.

Cal needed control.

Being afraid was unacceptable. So, he shoved it all down. Taking risks never worked. Only in business. He would keep his feelings covered up, bandaged. Like her finger. He would flash a smile, fuck like a king ... and only for a little longer.

Because the summer wouldn't last forever. The dream of Annie's eternal comfort would die like everything else in life did.

Shrimp fajitas smothered in sweet onions, green and red peppers and mushrooms, Rosa's homemade tortillas, and a generous bowl of freshly smashed guacamole, the green of the avocados brilliantly speckled with red onion and tomato garnished the table. The meal had been prepared together, Cal and Annie enjoying lots of laughter and conversation while doing so.

But the mood was about to shift.

Annie finished eating first. Pushing away her dish, she set her forearms on the table and leaned forward, watching Cal dip the last bite of his stuffed tortilla into the guacamole on his plate.

"I need to talk to you about something." Annie slid her index finger down her water glass while peering up at Cal, a nervous smile flickering across her face.

"I know."

"What do you mean?"

"I mean ... I can tell something has been on your mind all night. This isn't about your cut and making dinner."

Annie placed her palm on her chin and glanced away. After blinking several times, she looked back at him.

"Say it."

She inhaled a deep breath, and on the exhale, her words chartered a supersonic jet plane from brain to tongue. Sentences came out without periods. "I'm going back home next week I have to make plans for fall and winter for my work and I need to be with my family I'll be gone at least a couple weeks."

"You already booked a flight?"

"Yes. I leave a week from Monday."

"Mmm. And you were avoiding telling me." The man peered into her spleen or kidneys — or all her organs.

"I was scared."

"Of what?" he asked, not flinching, his stare slicing her in two.

"We've never talked about this before."

"About what? You're taking a work trip."

"We've never talked about the future."

Cal laughed. Sardonically. "We have. You want to travel. I have business and family in California. I came here for the same reasons you did. To be distracted and forget. You made it clear you didn't want to talk of plans." He flicked imaginary crumbs from the table. His eyes were stones. "Ever."

"*You* listened to *me*? I didn't think you did that." She gave him the stone eyes too. Jade. "Ever."

"Okay, Annie..." Cal leaned back in his seat, using that same tone, shooting her that same stare. Both of them smooth as ice, gouging her. Even though he did his best to act devoid of emotion, she knew him better now. His impervious nature was an act. He was full of shit-shit bullshit. "What about the future?"

"Our future." *Asshole.* "I want to move back home." Her throat felt tight. Her eyes stung. "And I know your lease is up at the end of September."

"Oh, you want to *move* back home. A minute ago, you said you were going home to set up work."

Annie lifted the empty wine bottle, then set it down again. She drank her water instead, avoiding his statements — the ones that sounded like questions.

Cal remained silent.

Something forbidden pained his chest.

He hurt.

Still, he readied his chess piece, prepared to speak his next words with his typical bridled control. Without thought ... or with it. He didn't know anymore. Annie made him fucking out-of-his-mind crazy with need and passion and things he couldn't pocket or order or label.

"Annie, when you moved here, you knew it was temporary." He rubbed the tips of his fingers against his palm, his Mount Rushmorian face somehow looking like a rubber band being stretched and stretched. "When I moved here, I knew it was temporary." Stretching, ready to slingshot. "This whole damn thing is temporary."

Zoom...

Although he'd spoken the last sentence with the most harshness and insensitivity she'd ever heard leave his lips, Annie knew deep down Cal wished to protect his heart from breaking too. Fiercely. The way she wanted to protect hers. But it was too late.

He would feel pain.

Just. Like. Me.

Pressing her lips together, Annie stood from the table. "It's all temporary. That's right, Cal." An ache unlike any other throbbed against the walls of her chest. She picked up his plate and stacked it on top of hers. She wished to cry but didn't. "So why actually give a damn about anything or anybody, right?" She glared at him. Hard. "Don't be such a prick."

"I am a forty-five-year-old prick. Did you expect something different? Didn't Maggie give you fair warning?"

Annie had never expected him to be anything other than himself. Fuck age. Time. Sense. She wanted him. The prick. The man whose heart was so much bigger than he ever gave the muscle credit for.

"What did she say about me the first night I met you?"

Annie clanged stuff onto the plates — silverware, bowls, whatever. "I don't want to do this. I'll go home like I planned. We'll have one more week together — *to fuck* — and when I get back, we'll both be packing all our temporary shit up."

"Annie..." he pleaded. "Stop with the fucking dishes." He stood. "I'm sorry we avoided this discussion for so long. My business is in LA. You knew from the start—"

"So, this whole thing *is* temporary? Right. Then congratulations to Maggie. She earns the gold for I-told-you-so's. Is that what you want to hear? Do you want to fulfill some sort of self-inflicted prophecy? Or would you rather do something different and prove everyone wrong?"

Everything. Is. Temporary! she thought as she stared him down.

Death. Death. Death.

Life circumventing death until it lunged from the shadows and stabbed her in the fucking heart. All of it one big three-ring circus coming to town for a night. Only to pick up and leave the next morning.

I can't do this. I can't do this. I can't do this.

Annie walked over to the sink with the noisy dishes, set them down, and stood with her hand under her nose, the ugly souvenir finger sticking out, as she tried to pull herself together.

"Annie, don't clean up or your cut might start to bleed again." His voice had switched. Undeniable concern threaded through his tone, feelings she knew he felt in his soul — not only for her souped-up finger, but for all of her.

"What do you care?" She turned on the faucet.

Cal was at her backside in an instant, warming her. He cut the water, but she wouldn't turn around. Biting the insides of her cheeks, she attempted to suck back the sobs along with everything else: the temporary, the bullshit, the summer that was supposed to be *hers*.

Mine.

And now it was over.

Cal put his hands on her waist, but she pushed them away and crossed her arms. Reaching for them, he gently tried to pull her limbs down by her elbows, but she stiffened, fought him, so he returned to her waist and gripped her there harder.

She kept her chin to the ground, her eyes on the floor. Annie wanted him with the same intensity with which she despised his behavior — his harshness, his conflicting bullshit, his need. Maybe she needed him to bury himself so far inside her, she wouldn't be able to breathe or cry or fight.

Then those magical hands spun her around to face him.

"Look at me."

It never got old. The "look at me" shit. Yet those three words, full of weight and substance, were unable to stop the tears tonight. If anything, the drops fell faster, streaming from her eyelids like hail.

Cal lifted her chin.

Their eyes locked.

His Adam's apple bobbed.

He saw the devastation he'd caused.

The aftermath of the storm.

As he stared at Annie's face, at the way her bottom lip trembled, the way her eyes glossed and glossed, Cal transformed, his own eyes morphing into a million different shades of only one man, a chameleon, a man on a journey from king to asshole. A prick with his foot shoved so far up his ass, he apparently couldn't speak. His hands dropped, and he stepped away. After taking out a bottle of Crown and a glass, he poured himself a drink.

Great, she thought, her bandaged finger jutting out, her stomach a pretzel. *No talking. No angry fucking.* She could've used a drink as well. God, even the whiskey looked appetizing to her parched throat.

"Don't you have anything else to say to me?"

Cal slammed a shot. "I have plenty to say to you," he replied, disguising his true hurt, his real fear as he avoided her gaze, her watery eyes, her truth.

If he couldn't drown his emotions in her pussy, he sure as fuck wanted to drown them in the drink.

But Cal went quiet.

Silent.

His lack of words had never been more deafening.

Cal picked up the bottle in one hand, the glass in the other, and went toward the stairs. Alone.

Like a drone, Annie stood motionless, watching as he shuffled along, as if treading up the steps against his will. After he disappeared into the loft, she remained in the kitchen, her stomach churning, the room spinning as though she were drunk or inside a kaleidoscope.

Everything was clear.

And everything was hazy.

Her feelings for Cal became clearer, the way a blue sky appears after fog parts. Cal... He... He belonged to her. His understated ways, his concern, his regrets. Hers. They fit together, Cal and Annie. Somehow, they fit. Being with him never got old.

Old... He wasn't old. Not to her. Ever. They could talk about anything. He supported her. He listened. He made her feel safe. But he wouldn't let her in. Not all the way.

Still... She loved him.

And what was she supposed to do with that? Deny it. Forever.

Call it temporary, Cal. Go ahead ... take the Crown. No amount of alcohol will change it.

No more doubts.

No more fucking running, Annie. Or hiding.

Truly.

Then what am I doing? Leaving. Working. Living.

I'm done running. He can follow.

I've loved him all along.

From the beginning.

From the very first time he kissed me in the rain ... on the sidewalk.

Annie could no longer pretend she didn't want more of Cal, that she didn't want all of Cal, that she didn't want to really be with Cal for more than their *one* summer of whatever, no plans, and what-ifs.

Annie knew now she could no longer pretend she didn't love Cal.

But she knew she would continue to pretend on the outside, in front of Cal, for as long as she could stand. Because what would he do with her words if she proclaimed them aloud? Squash them? Pulverize them?

They were her words. Hers. She owned them. She could love him quietly — for a few more weeks at least. Until her heart became a grenade.

Cal held the pin.

FORTY-FIVE

Agitated, Annie awoke in the middle of the night, unsure if Cal had even come to bed. She'd had a rather difficult time falling asleep. The anger had dissipated some after their argument, but she hadn't been able do a thing about the aching hollow in her chest.

Apparently, there was a reason for the sage advice: *Never go to bed mad.*

And so, it was with great relief when she flipped over and saw Cal lying beside her, a book open, its pages flat against his bare chest, glasses at the tip of his nose, the book rising and falling with his exhalations.

After watching Cal sleep for a few minutes, Annie climbed out of bed and made her way to his side. She removed his glasses, careful not to wake him, and closed the novel — the same one he'd started reading a couple months ago: *Infinite Jest.*

The ache wasn't only in her chest but her throat. A nonsexual, but sensual, be-my-companion aching. The feelings attempted to claw through skin. And they hurt. Old hurts mixed with new ones, all of them utterly distasteful, yet never more appealing.

Hurt and healing.

Pain and pleasure.

Perfect partners. Opposites. Yin and yang.

This man was her partner. Him. Calvin Warner Prescott. The sleeping, beautiful man. The chameleon — a million shades of everything she never knew she wanted.

I'll always feel the ache to feel the love. I'll always feel the hurt to find the cure. I'll always desire pain when you give me pleasure. She looked at his golden eyelashes, touched his sugar-soft hair. She inhaled his breath, wishing to stay in the quiet moment forever.

I love you...

FORTY-SIX

Sunday morning, after the sun had risen, Annie sat up in bed and yawned.

She glanced over at Cal's side, but he wasn't there now. She reached for her phone, but before picking it up, something underneath the device caught her attention: a piece of copy paper folded in half with her name neatly written on the upside.

Annie's heart sank, slithered off the sheets, and fell flat to the floor as she rubbed her eyes, scooted to the edge, and planted her feet on something solid.

She opened the note.

Annie Rebekah Baxter

I'm sorry. You know I care about you. Deeply.

-Cal

Annie blinked back tears.

Short, sweet, and to the point, the words confirmed what she knew in her heart.

It was true.

This wasn't only sex.

They had feelings for each other.

Real feelings.

The emotion she usually heard in his tone, the vulnerability she often saw in his eyes, the note solidified what she intuited. Poured concrete into the cracks of her doubts.

Cal did care. Deeply, monumentally, wholly. He cared more than he could bring himself to verbalize. The pen had done the talking for him, speaking what he never could seem to say aloud.

But he'd been saying it all along. With his eyes and lips and hands. His actions. Since the beginning.

God. What were they doing? This was still only one summer.

But it had never been *just* anything.

The note wouldn't change their circumstances. Annie was still leaving soon. And she couldn't tell him she loved him. Because in a few more weeks, they would move on. She would start over, lost or stronger or sick to her stomach. She would keep going.

It was fine.

Fine, fine, fine.

"Good morning," Rosa chirped as she entered the bedroom, causing Annie to nearly jump out of her skin. The woman continued right on into the bathroom, probably set to retrieve the hamper while Annie's mind fell back to the note, to the words, to the man who ... must've been out on his morning run. She stared at Cal's handwriting until her eyes blurred.

"*Mi amor...*" Rosa took a seat next to Annie, waving a hand in front of her face. "You are awake dreaming? *Perdido en un sueño.*"

Annie forced a smile. "Morning." She folded the paper and set it on the nightstand. Letting out a shaky breath, she grabbed a swath of hair and began to twirl it. She'd since put a new bandage on her finger — a regular one.

Rosa waited.

She waited longer.

"Cal's not here," the woman finally said. "He's on his run. If you want to talk to me, now is the time, *mi querida.*"

Shifting her upper body toward Rosa and bending her left leg over the sheets, Annie traded hair for fingers, making a these-are-my-hands-and-the-steeple-and-the-church-full-of-people — or whatever the hell that was.

Rosa lifted Annie's chin. "What is it, child?"

"I told him"—Annie swallowed—"that I'm leaving in a week to go home ... to schedule work. But I might move back home. I miss the West Coast." She looked across the room, bit her lower lip, and sighed. "We fought. He won't tell me how he feels about me."

Rosa cupped Annie's busy hands. "And *you*, did you tell him how you feel about him?"

"I can't." Annie stopped breathing, her eyes flicking to the note. "I need to hear it from him first."

"Maybe he needs to hear it from you." She exhaled. "You're both foolish in love... You are so young, and he is so scared."

"Of what? I've given him all of me."

"*All of you?*" Rosa's brows knitted. "Did you tell Cal that you love him?"

Annie's gaze dropped to the floor.

"No," Rosa snapped, and Annie looked up. "Then you have not given him everything."

"I'm scared too."

"No, you are strong." Rosa squeezed the photographer's bicep, and Annie managed a little laugh. "You can risk giving your love to him, without expectation. You've made this risk already, so tell him so. He needs your love."

The front door opened and closed. Annie whipped her head in the direction of the sounds, feeling like a child who had done something wrong.

"Don't worry." Rosa stood, peering down at Annie with a twinkle in her eyes. "I will not tell him we spoke of such things." She nodded. "You think about what I said, though. *Tiempo es precioso.*"

The moment Annie came out of the bathroom, Cal stepped into the bedroom, swinging the door nearly shut as he held onto the jamb and slipped off his socks and sneakers. Still donning her sleeveless nightgown and sleepy disposition — despite the morning's sobering conversation with Rosa — Annie stared at him.

The sorry he'd written in his note was scribbled in his gaze. His *I care for you* was in ballpoint pen — no, Sharpie — across his face.

Smiling, she made her way over to him and immediately buried her face in his chest. His arms went around her.

Flashes of relief pulsed through her, head to toe. She let go and relaxed. Hurt found healing. Annie found Cal.

It is love.

But it would be a quiet love, an unspoken love, and it would be displayed in the way Cal preferred: through the coming together of their physical bodies.

Annie lifted his shirt over his head, tossed it aside, and put her hands on his waist, pressing the tips of her fingers into his skin. It felt and smelled destined, meant to collide with hers, the way it always had. Taking her time, she trailed her palms up his abs, smoothing her nails through the hairs on his chest.

"I'm sweaty, baby..."

She kissed his stomach, his pecs, tasting his salty skin, turning her head side to side, aching, needing, wanting this "sweaty" man inside her body.

Now.

"Annie..."

"What?" she whispered against his neck.

"Let me shower first," he uttered without much protest.

As Annie stood tall, she stopped kissing him and met his gaze — like she needed to do so to breathe. Tucking her fingers into the elastic of his shorts, she pulled them down while keeping her eyes centered on his, making sure he heard what the green of her irises spoke.

Love.

"No shower." Annie's voice melted against him, a promise, a vow, her desire for him full, cresting. "I want you now. Like this. *Just as you are.*" She choked out the last words and the next. "Make love to me."

Cal slammed the door shut with the back of his hand and locked it, his eyes remaining fixed on Annie, his hands now tangled in her hair. She used her toes to finish removing his shorts. Then, the moment she pulled her gown over her head and dropped it, Cal spun her around, pushed her against the door, and kissed her mouth like he'd been starved.

She started to cry, her chest shaking, because she fought it. Not the kiss, but the weeping. Disavowing the sounds, she let the sobbing get swallowed by his mouth, his tongue ... his love.

She risked. He devoured.

She needed this man.

And he needed her.

Holding her hand, he led her to the bed, then pushed her hair behind her neck, staring into her eyes and cradling her jaw.

There. He said it. Now. Quiet and in his breath. In his eyes. And Annie spoke those three words in reply. Also without sound.

After putting on a condom from the bedside drawer, he climbed onto the sheets, sat back against the headboard, and gave her hand a tug.

"You want me on top?"

"Are you wet?"

Her palm skirted to her sex. "Yes."

Cal pulled on her fingers again and said, "Show me," as she straddled him. "I want to see you." Hands on her waist, Cal glanced down as she spread herself open, his eyes darkening, his chest constricting. "Touch yourself."

Her middle finger slipped between her seam as she listened to Cal make beautiful noises. Vowels and breaths. Groans. The single digit trailed up and down her slit, stopping at her clit each time to circle it as she attempted to take him inside her body. But he would not allow it.

"Not yet," he would say, his breath shaky. "Not yet..."

"I need you."

Cal pushed the tip of his dick into all the places her fingers had roamed.

"Yes," Annie moaned, the momentum increasing. "Mmm..." She tried to sit on him, but he took what she wanted from her grasp. "Let me have you."

"I said not yet." Lines stretched across his forehead. His thighs tensed.

Practically out of breath, Annie rode him anyway, swaying and grinding and shifting her hips, fucking every surface of his skin she could.

"Cal..." she whimpered, then shoved her middle finger into his mouth. "Now."

Gripping her waist, Cal buried himself inside her warm body. She took him, head back, rode him more violently. The love they made not gentle, but harsh. A need. A want. A necessity.

"You have all of me."

"No." She shook her head, pinching her eyes shut.

"Yes." He thumped her womb, not once but three times. And she bloomed.

"Please..." she pleaded, writhing on top of him, her upper body and hair moving like those of a woman at a rock concert. "Hurt me."

"Make love or hurt you?"

"We do both." Dropping her head, she grabbed his biceps. "It. Isn't. Just. Fucking," she panted into his ear.

In a split second, Cal flipped her over, stood, and pulled her to the edge of the bed. Her shins dangled off the mattress, feet not touching the floor. "Arms up," he demanded. "Hands above your head."

She submitted. Loved it. Needed it.

Lips trailed from her shoulder to her waist, kissing and biting as they went, softly at first. On the return trip, he bit harder, and she squirmed and wailed. Cal did the same to her breasts, nibbling, licking, and biting, tweaking her nipples until tears slid down her cheeks. Until she begged him to take her to the place where she could erase pain with pain, like with like. The horizon. Where she could see the love in his eyes, feel it with each push, own it with every cell in her body.

"Open." He bumped her entrance. "Show me your cunt."

Stretching her knees wide, she made garbled sounds, everything feeling stretched and perfect.

"Wider," Cal commanded, shoving open her thighs.

Inimitable sweet pain blossomed, filling all the available space inside her tissues, her muscles, her veins. She cried out in broken syllables the second he shoved back inside. Several times. Each thrust to the hilt. In, then out. Again and again.

"Say my name," he breathed out, voice frayed.

"Cal," she whispered, her throat raw, past words and sense as he slid in and out slowly now, torturing her again with his lack of movement.

Then he flicked her nipple. "Louder."

Keeping her arms and hands above her head, Annie winced, shuddering in that special way, the way that let Cal know she liked what he inflicted upon her. Arching her back, she offered herself to him.

To make love.

To hurt.

Everything.

All at once.

As he flicked the other nipple, twisting them in tandem, she found she couldn't speak. Not his name. Not anything. Wrapping her legs behind him, her hips rose off the bed, devouring the fuck, the love, the slow, slow sex.

Then she locked onto his gaze, suddenly finding words, not the ones he'd asked for, but what she needed to utter. They must've been there all along, waiting ... for weeks.

"Say my name," she whispered, blinking up at him.

Cal stopped, keeping his full length deep inside her. Then he pinioned her to the bed, gripping her waist. Neither of them moved for several seconds. He hung his head.

"Do you know what you have?" He glanced up, tripping into her eyes. "What you give? Do you know your own strength?"

"Not now." She tried not to sob, not to lose the moment.

"Yes, now," he growled as he flung one of her legs over his shoulder.

Her breath shook. She swallowed. Then she repeated herself... "Say my name."

"Come for me first." He touched her clit. "Are you close?"

"Uh-huh."

He began to move fast, those fingers, that cock, then faster. With the perfect pressure. The assurance in his eyes an agreement. A shake of the hands.

She would come. He would chant.

As she released, her jaw tightened, her toe knuckles bent. Her thighs trembled. And her eyes... God, her eyes, seemed to exorcise from her head.

"Annie..." Cal began, whispering, choking on her name. Their eyes remained locked as he shook. "Annie... Annie..."

Pushing forward one, two, three more times into her warmth, each of his exertions carrying her name, a promise, a prayer, until the last thrust. The final one hit her cervix as he cried, "Annie," the last two vowels morphing into a long, satisfied groan.

Collapsing against her chest, he buried his face into her neck and strummed one of her nipples. "What do you do to me?" He bit her collarbone, then trailed a thumb across her cheek.

Annie couldn't see his face, but she knew what he meant. She understood.

"What do you do?" he repeated.

What do I do? she thought. *It's called loving you. For one more week, at least, you fucking bastard.*

Words she couldn't express out loud formed in her head — the way they usually did...

I want to remain here ... against his chest.
breathe his every breath
I want to die a million deaths
with him
resurrect me
save me
pull me back
when I try to escape
keep me
from the nothing
hold me
inside
the wordless silent void
where passion
is center stage
where love speaks silently
through our bodies
where our lives
come together
like two vines
twisting
wrapping
climbing
a tree
a sequoia
we'll lie on the branches
we'll dream
we'll sleep
we'll harness a supreme energy
then we'll lie awake
dreaming of a place
where
time
or death
or circumstance
no longer exist

THE PUSH

FORWARD MOVEMENT APPLIED BY FORCE; OR
PERSUASION

resist
surround myself
with music
out of my comfort zone
into the walls
of your chest
I find
a healing
in lyrics
in hard to define places
and spaces
of time
running
ahead of me
with guardrails
blow up
imaginary parts
I come
apart
you rip me
I hold us together

you are the needle
I am the thread
what you push
out of me
shoves its way back in
a water jar
drought takes
rain replenishes
culminating
where we are joined

FORTY-SEVEN

Late Saturday night, Cal and Annie rode together to their destination in the heart of South Beach with Carl at the helm of the eco-friendly white sedan.

In two days, she would leave for Seattle.

Neither Cal nor Annie spoke of the plane, the trip, or the future, avoiding the conversation as usual, causing the tension of the last week to mount like bricks creating a castle to the sky.

Cal kept his hand over Annie's thigh for much of the drive, but his thoughts were elsewhere...

Perhaps going out tonight would ease his mind.

Dancing surely wouldn't.

The activity was something he did not enjoy. Ever. It was rare any woman — no matter her beauty, brains, or wit — could coax him out onto a dance floor, and Annie was no exception.

Except, Annie was the exception to every rule known to man.

Cal swirled his hand over the goose bumps cemented on Annie's skin, the pimples reminding him of the first time the two of them had been together in the Tesla: she'd been cold.

As he asked Carl to turn the A/C down again tonight, Cal smiled.

It was a bittersweet memory now.

Each day of the last week had been that way.

After the fight on the night she'd cut her finger — her insistence on talking of the future and his stupid denial — here they were, going on as always. Not even the feelings they'd silently shared all week could usurp the hurt swelling within him.

Nothing could stop the hundreds of thoughts he entertained about his mother. The guilt of leaving Constance behind last spring had increased with each passing month since he'd arrived in Florida. Another month not taking care of her, being there for her, never being what she needed. Forty-five years of not living up to her ideals.

How ironic.

Three thousand miles away, sick, and unable to comprehend the simple fact that it was her eighty-third birthday, and the damn woman still lived under his skin. Somehow, her presence mixed with Annie's in the backseat of the Tesla until the two of them formed a strange concoction.

Absinthe?

Funny he should think of that now. His grandfather used to talk about the bitter drink. Spoke of women and books ... of Hemingway. His grandfather had turned him on to music and reading.

Women, Cal found in time.

"When is the last time you went dancing?"

Turning from the window, Cal smiled tightly, then said, "I don't go dancing" as he ran an index finger over her thigh.

"You're impossible." Annie smiled and squirmed. "So, you haven't been to a club in South Beach?"

That question garnered his attention.

"The elusive non-dancer has gone to a club?" She pinched his quads. "To get laid?"

"I didn't get laid." He crossed an ankle over a knee. "You notice my eagerness to return."

"Maybe you'll get lucky tonight." She bounced her brows, and he grinned.

"Why haven't you wanted to go dancing before now?" he asked. "Not because of me?"

"No." She shrugged, releasing a loud breath as she dropped her gaze. "Crowds are sometimes hard for me. I haven't been to a club since before..." She swallowed, twirling the bracelet on her wrist. "Since Peter died."

"You benchmark a lot of things in your life by that day."

Annie glanced out her window, grabbed a spool of hair, and began to twirl it.

Touching her wrist, he stopped her telltale sign. "I didn't mean to upset you, baby."

Annie caught the driver's eyes in the rearview mirror. "I wasn't myself for a long time after..."

"Carl, can you please find a place to—?"

"It's fine, Cal," Annie clipped, playing with the hem of her skirt — the shiny, silver dress barely covered her thighs — bending the edges up and down.

"We're only a few blocks away, sir."

"Good." Cal's eyes never left Annie's, watching and observing her with his usual intensity. "Park and give us privacy. Please."

"Tell me," he said the moment Carl pulled over, stepped out of the car, and shut the door. Cal's fingers slid down the strands of hair Annie had been fiddling with, then he tucked them behind an ear.

"Tell you what?" she whispered, staring into his eyes, narrowly able to breathe. "You've heard all this."

And more.

She'd finally told him about the night she'd overheard — from her hiding place on the staircase — Maggie, Cal, and John speaking of the accident. The night the four of them had enjoyed dinner together.

Not long after returning from New York, shortly after giving Cal those gifts, she told him what she'd witnessed. Or he'd guessed. During an evening they'd spent walking on the beach, the activity quickly becoming a regular pastime between them.

It seemed Cal connected to the ocean the way Annie did.

Both of them had strolled barefoot, hand in hand, under the stars and on the sand — the practice akin to a confessional. But better. More spiritual. More sacred. A place for telling secrets. Except, Cal held onto his, and Annie talked in a string of nonsense.

"You're different," he said as they walked, both looking ahead. It was cloudy. The moon was huge. One of those supermoons, close to the horizon and painted by the hand of God a fantastic orange — Annie itched to photograph it.

"What do you mean?"

"Since you've returned from New York." They stopped. Cal pulled a piece of hair from her lips and watched it get taken by the wind.

"No, I'm not."

They started to walk again, but as she took hold of his hand, she noted the tension in his palm. The knots twisted and spiraled up his arm, making his jaw tic.

"Say it."

She sucked in a breath of salt and exhaled denial. She had waited long enough to confess what she'd overheard. "I heard you all..."

They came to a halt. Footprints in the sand. The waves crashing a few feet away. She watched his eyes flicker in the glow of the super moonlight, his hair blowing, his face indestructible. Like a rock remaining after a hurricane, holding himself there, steady and sure, waiting for her to continue, to take whatever she offered.

As he cupped her cheek, she nestled her face against his hand. "The night before I left, I heard the three of you. Talking about—"

Cal cursed as he jerked his gaze toward the ocean and dropped his hand from her face.

Taking her bottom lip between her teeth, Annie bit into it, trying to stop the pain, trading one hurt for another. There hadn't been a right time to tell him. Maybe this wasn't it either.

There would never be a perfect moment for it.

But the ocean and the breeze and Cal's strength... She touched his bicep, bringing his gaze back to hers.

"Maggie shouldn't have been the one," he said, pulling her into an embrace, "to tell me how it happened."

Annie wept against his chest, her head buried in his soft shirt. She inhaled the cotton and beach of his skin. Which was stronger? The Atlantic Ocean or Cal?

She would've put her money on him.

He held her tight and fast. Let her cry. He didn't try to fix it with words. He didn't taint the effect his secure hands wrapped around her body procured.

He. Just. Let. Her. Cry.

As they sat together in the back of the Tesla now, it didn't seem he would allow her that privilege. He wanted her words.

"Then why do I get the feeling there's more?"

"I stopped seeing people." She paused. "Daniel left, and I didn't want to go out with any guys after that. This part you—"

"I know."

"Well, I stopped doing things, like I said, crowds. I couldn't even shop for food like a normal person." Her eyes bounced around. "I stopped taking pictures. For fun, I mean. The way I always had. I completed my assignments, but it ... school was the only thing keeping me functioning. Breathing."

Her hands became fish out of water, flopping in her lap, one over the other, gasping for oxygen. She wasn't ready to tell him about the pills.

"I..." She stuttered the single vowel repeatedly. "I wasn't me."

Cal's eyes hadn't left Annie's face. If possible, he peered into her insides deeper. Farther.

"You're beautiful," he whispered. *"Just like this."* Opening her skin, he climbed in and lay down, becoming an integral part of her body. "You are always you. Don't you know that?" His fingers combed through her hair, scratching and massaging the back of her neck. "No matter what happens in your life, baby, it's you."

Annie dropped her head on his shoulder and cupped his cheek.

But Cal looked away, lost again in his own plight, unable to keep it hidden. "I'm sorry, Annie. I just have a lot on my mind."

Eyes glued to his profile, she sat forward and took his hand again. "What? What is it?" She searched his face despite knowing the answer might not come.

They were so fucked.

She still couldn't tell him certain things about herself either. Cal seemed to live at the edge of some sort of cliff, always deciding whether to jump or back off. *Jump, Cal. I'll catch you...*

"Thank you." Annie squeezed his palm.

"For what?"

"For taking me here, tonight, even though you didn't really want to," she replied, watching him smile. "Thank you ... for always listening to me."

"Not always."

"Yes, always," she whispered, her throat tightening.

Cal placed his thumb on the hollow of her neck. His index finger he stroked along her jawline. Annie glanced down, her eyes glossing.

"No tears tonight." He leaned in and kissed her forehead. "Come on." He tugged on her hand and opened the car door.

"Mmm. I can't make any promises, Prescott." She beamed. "Tears are my specialty."

FORTY-EIGHT

Annie held onto Cal's hand tighter than ever before as they entered the club on Washington and made their way through crowds of people.

"Finger out of your mouth." He tapped her wrist and put his lips to her ear. "Stand up straight, show off your tits. You're so fucking sexy, Annie."

The beat already rocked Annie to her core, thumping her chest from the inside out, as though the DJ spun records off her heart as Cal dragged her forward, closer to the main floor.

Resembling the shape of a box, the room was one huge square filled with people. Lots of people. A few lavender couches decorated the outskirts, a stage of some sort occupied the south end, and women swung on over-sized Hula-Hoop rings high above them. Behind the scantily clad acrobats were large screens playing all sorts of things, sensual things, erotic images flickering on and off in tandem as neon lightsaber-like beams cut through the air, causing everyone to glow in an array of colors.

Annie remained fastened to Cal's arm *and* the roller coaster of her emotions as they now wandered in the direction the bar. Gripping Cal even tighter, the two of them weaved in and out of people, some looking Annie directly in the eye, others only staring at her from head to toe, seeming to size up her dress, her hair, her shoes, critiquing the gorgeous man on her arm.

But she didn't give a fuck.

She was here to dance. To divert attention from her trip, to distract herself from acknowledging this night could very well be the last time she would stand alongside Cal as she did now. Today. As she had since first setting eyes on him.

Several minutes later, drinks in hand, a whiskey neat and a glass of champagne, they stood near the edge of the dance floor, watching the people. As far as Annie was concerned, they resembled a moving pack of penguins, flippers up and out, waving, squished together, gesturing and swaying, back and forth, up and down, side to side.

Hoping she could change the obstinate man's mind, Annie gave Cal the eyes — the ones that had worked that time she'd managed to get him up and dancing to Louis Armstrong. Tonight, he wouldn't budge.

Too bad.

She couldn't wait any longer.

The beat called.

Emboldened by her single glass of champagne, she slipped her fingers out of Cal's, gave him the empty flute, and joined the pack of flightless birds.

A song or two later, Annie spotted him, relaxing on one of the purple couches, ankle over a knee, a palm curled around his glass, staring at her. Straight at her. Or through her.

Lifting her hair off her nape, she imagined Cal against her as she moved, his pelvis meeting hers, her breasts bouncing, all while she gazed into his eyes across the space like she wanted to be the one to eat him alive for a change.

It didn't matter how many people were present.

It never did with them.

Cal enjoyed observing Annie as much as she seemed to adore the dancing. More than he'd anticipated. Watching her dance took him away from reality: of her leaving, of his mother's illness, of their impending moves, of his life changing as he'd gloriously known it these last two months.

Annie was an antithesis to it all.

Free and uninhibited as she expressed herself to the music.

A few people took turns approaching Annie, mostly men, *young men*, an occasional woman or two, all near enough to touch her body, close enough to feel her breath, to slide against the sweet surface of her skin, to practically taste the perspiration surely beaded across her upper lip and décolletage.

But it was the look on her face that really did it for him.

Lust.

Power.

Freedom.

She liked the attention. Or seemed to anyway. She didn't bask in it over-long nor reject it. Placing both feet on the floor, he tried to hide the rise behind his zipper, but he was unable to peel his eyes from the photographer in the silver dress.

The creature.

The woman.

Annie.

Wasn't that how it had always been? From the beginning. Commanding him, paralyzing him. With those fucking forest-green eyes and whatever magnets constituted her skin.

Like a voyeur, he stared, turned on to the maximum by her flirtatious manner and independence. The girl who had gripped his hand like a little mouse on the way inside the club now showed her true colors.

Her wings.

She owned the fucking floor.

He. Watched. Her. Every. Move.

The reflection from the lights flickered on and off her skin as her hair tossed about like choppy waves in the ocean on a blistery day. Skirt inching up her thighs, calves perfectly accentuated from the strain of the high heels, nipples pointing through the silk of her dress—

Fuck.

Cal swiped a palm clear across his face, unable to think of anything but touching her, having her, of finding some dark, out-of-the-way place to sink his cock so far inside her, neither of them would be able to find their way out.

He needed Annie.

Now.

She would take his ache, his pain, his fears. Cal needed Annie in a way he needed no one.

———————

Several drinks and songs later, after finishing an entire bottle of champagne, Annie began to tire. Her red stilettos had taken their toll. She plopped down next to Cal, massaging her calves, her whole body warm and slick with perspiration.

"I'm thirsty," Annie yelled, even though Cal sat only inches away. She blew air upward, trying to move the few damp strands stuck to her forehead.

Smiling, he waited a second or two, then pushed the matted pieces off her face. "Don't you think you've had enough to drink?" He signaled a server. "You need water."

Ignoring his steady, paternal gaze, Annie squeezed his leg, right above his knee, but he shoved her hand off. With a grumble, she leaned back against the couch, sinking into the cushions like a sullen teenager, and stared at the sweaty penguin people flipping and bobbing across the dance floor.

Time seemed to stand still as she waited for the water to arrive. Or it spun. The ceiling and room spun too. The women in the hoops ... and the lightsabers ... all spinning as she glanced toward the stage and let the champagne buzz take her...

The big-boobie-showing ladies ... ladies, ha ... they spin, spin, spin, doing splits and whatever-whatever all kinds of shit-stuff ... they must have rooms here where people fuck after all this shit ... they must have places spots holes to pee or puke ... I need to pee or walk or fuck ... I need water or maybe a drink or a pill ... yeah, I bet I can slip into one of those hoops and spread my legs and show myself out there — here for everyone to see and clap and dance for my vagina ... ha, vagina ... it would hurt to split open like that ... I am surely not that flexible unless Cal spreads my legs to infinity and fucks the shit out of me quite good ... ooh, my boobies are nice too ... he likes mine-mine-mine ... I would need a sexy bra to swing in one of those hoop thingies ... a push kind of bra to shoot my puppies up and out so people can watch and see ... what would Cal think of people staring at me? ... no more drinking for his Annie ... he says I need water ... no, I'll go dance some more, show him what he's missing ... I'll show you, Calvin Prescott fucker ... fuck, I love him ... fuck, I'm his baby...

what am I
who am I
who are we...

Cal touched a cold bottle to her leg, and Annie sat forward with a start, swatting a hand toward him. Missing the water, she only grabbed at air.

He laughed.

She stepped on his foot.

His gaze got all shitty, paternal again, as he twisted the cap off, handed her the drink like a gentleman, and watched her finish it off in one continuous swallow.

"I need to go to the bathroom." Annie burped and slammed the empty bottle onto his lap.

"Drink this one too."

Wobbly, she stood. "I need to pee."

He yanked her down. The position exposed her undies. He slid the dress over her thighs, but she brushed away his concern and took over fixing her skirt.

The other bottle was already open and at her lips. "Drink."

As she swiped it, drops flew out, splashing them both. She guzzled the entire thing, the same as before, then she crushed the plastic in her fist and handed it to Cal.

"Done, *Daddy*." She smirked, got up, and smoothed her palms over the dress. "This material is sooooo soft."

Strange. She didn't seem to have knees or feet.

Cal stood and took her palm. "I'm coming with you."

She burped, covered her mouth, and grinned. "*You're* coming with *me*?" She stabbed a finger into his sternum. "Into the ladies' room?"

Cal's oh-so-delicious devil-of-a-grin appeared as he removed her finger, stared into her eyes, and held her arm against her waist with an exquisite, annoying pressure.

Fuck him.

Annie was torn between feeling pissed Cal took care of her and happy Cal cared for her. Pissed and happy. It was a coin toss in her alcohol-riddled mind. And per usual, he got his way...

Cal waited for Annie across from the entrance to the bathrooms, his left leg bent as he leaned against the wall and scrolled on his phone. A few minutes later, Annie joined him, one hand on her hip as she looked toward the dance floor, the lights and images and people blurring in her vision.

"We're leaving." Cal pocketed his phone.

"I don't want to go." She twisted a heel into the floor. "I'm having a good time. I'm the one actually dancing."

Cal touched the small of her back. "We're leaving."

"You're not my father. You can't order me around like a..." Folding her arms under her breasts, she swayed a little to the side, looking like the Tower of Pisa. "Like a some sort of business transaction."

Cal squared her shoulders, met her eyes, and grinned.

"Don't you dare laugh at me."

Pausing, he looked down and erased the smile. When he glanced back up, he had everything under control. The chess face in place. She wouldn't rile him anymore tonight. Still, he trailed his fingers down her sides, shoulders to waist, sliding over the contours of her body — the places he desperately needed to taste.

She swayed again. But not because of the alcohol.

"No, Annie," Cal began, slow and certain, gazing into her eyes. "I'm not your father." His fingers smoothed up her arms as he observed her reactions. Goosepimples. Shivers. Eyes dilating. "I'm telling you I'm ready to leave because it's late," he whispered in her ear, "and because we're both tired. And because you have to pack tomorrow."

Annie tensed. The last thing she wanted to be reminded of was packing. Taking a step back, she placed her hands on her hips and glared at him. "You're just jealous."

"Of what?" Cal laughed, stood in her space again, and tugged on her sides. "Ah ... of the boys who danced with you?" He tapped her waist. "Annie, I'm the one who gets to have you."

She pushed his hands off, then shook her index finger around. "You think you can have ... and get ... and have ... whatever you want." She bit her lower lip, but it couldn't stop her from grinning.

Cal smiled too, exposing those dimples to die for.

"Fuck you." She smiled wider.

"Do you want one of those boys?" Cal nodded toward the dance floor.

"Is everyone under twenty-whatever a boy to you?"

"You want one of those men to, what?" Cal managed to step even closer. "Press their bodies against you again?" His shirt met her breasts, her heaving chest. "You think I'm jealous? The opposite. You make me so fucking hard, I can't think. Who do you want, Annie?"

She sucked in a breath and gripped his shoulders. "You, you bastard. I don't want any of those boys." She exhaled against his neck as she played with his collar, her nails grazing his skin. "I want you."

"Good." He squeezed her ass, took her hand, and tried to stuff away the craving he had to have her *right now*.

Tons of people stood around them on the busy sidewalk as they exited the building, many still lined up to get into the club.

Crowds, noise, distraction.

Cal wanted quiet.

Cal wanted Annie.

His impulse to fuck her was as strong as it had ever been, and he wasn't going to ignore it. He wasn't going to wait.

"Aren't you going to call Carl?" Annie scratched the nape of her neck. "I'm hot. Call him. Please. God, my feet."

"I want to walk." Cal pulled her along.

They rounded a corner into an alley that stretched between the two buildings. After walking a little more than halfway, far from the shadows of people and their chatter, they finally stopped several feet from a back door, near a dumpster full of bottles and boxes.

Neither of them spoke as Cal led her to the side of the building and placed a hand on her cheek. Neither of them needed to. They communicated so well without words.

Annie's heart dropped hard and fast, like a two-hundred-foot waterfall over the side of a mountain. She was more nervous now than she'd ever been at the idea of his insatiable appetite for having her, and she knew right now, at this moment, this was indeed happening.

The energy between them choked her. Her throat pulsed.

Would she cry or vomit or burst?

Please.

God.

The shaking started. The adrenaline rush could've surely enabled her to lift a car, superseding any effects the alcohol may have still had over her person. The only heat running through her veins now was the anticipation of Cal. His warmth. His certainty. His safety.

Nudging her back against the concrete, he wrapped his fingers behind her neck and pulled her hair, gazing at her face, her skin.

Studying her willingness.

The surrender in her eyes.

Could she see how much she meant to him? Could she see it all over him? The passion, the necessity, the need.

His fucking emotions.

This might be the last time he would find a home inside her body.

Annie touched his face and nodded, certain she couldn't think or speak or swallow. Then Cal kissed Annie with a fervor that lit her lips on fire ... her belly ... her thighs. God, she burned. Ached. Butterflies swarmed everywhere. Trapped under her skin. Unable to escape.

Cal smashed her into the wall, causing her back and shoulders to scrape against the concrete with each forceful movement, with the weight of his kisses and hands. His body. Swirling his tongue around hers, he fucked her mouth as he bunched the hem of her dress at her waist.

Annie kissed him with the same intensity, barely breaking to breathe or moan or reach down and unbutton his pants.

Yanking her fingers from his zipper, he shoved her wrists over her head while attempting to slow the pace, tasting each lip in turn, until he could no longer tell where she began and he ended. Until they felt like one gigantic heart beating against the wall of the building.

Annie attempted to deepen the kiss as she whimpered, almost sobbing, the urgency never more than it was right now, but Cal held her back, her hands into the concrete, scratching, rough, his fingernails biting into her wrists as he nibbled her lips, her face, her neck, her forehead, her cheeks, teasing, caressing, tasting, out of breath, pushing against her, solid like hard-packed sand, his lips grazing her repeatedly again and again, her head moving side to side, drowning, unable to contain the sensations for much longer, trapped and full, gushing, until he released her wrists and arms, their hearts opening, their kisses growing more intense, keeping his tongue in her mouth while pushing her underwear to the ground and unzipping his pants, Annie helping to shove them down, wasting no time, Cal pulling her legs up and around him as he furiously began to penetrate her against the wall in the dark alley.

Annie cried out with each thrust.

He didn't stop.

Didn't tease.

Didn't speak.

He only held her in place, pinioning her between the wall and his body, fucking a million reasons into her soul like a madman — a man who could only show feelings with action.

Annie's lashes fluttered as she took in their surroundings, the sensations. The vibration coming from the club, the sticky humidity, the sweet taste of his skin, the intense scratching on her backside, his breath on her neck, sweat dripping from his face to her tits, the push of him inside her — pushing and pushing and pushing.

Annie closed her eyes, forgetting the world. The only world existing contained the two of them.

She let go.

She forgot about death and pain and sadness.

She entered some sort of nirvana.

Each pulse, each scratch, each breath hurt. A terrible hurt. A wonderful hurt. One she wanted to feel forever. With him.

"Fuck. Fuck. Fuck..." Cal groaned as he held himself deep inside her and began to release. "Annie..." The tip of his cock bumped her womb as he took her hand and slid it between them. "Touch yourself, baby."

And that ... was the end.

She made little shaky, breathy sounds, and they only increased with the strokes she gave herself.

"Yes?" He started to pound her again.

"Yes!" She bit his neck, scratched her nails through his hair. "Yes, yes, yes." She cried his name over and over as she started to pulse around him, each contraction a beginning not an end.

The moment was over as fast as it had begun.

Cal swiped the back of his hand across his forehead, tucked himself away, then buttoned his pants. As Annie grabbed her underwear, her hands shook. Steadying her, Cal took over, watching her face as the hem of her dress fell over her thighs.

Their eyes locked.

Their breathing continued to even out.

Cal touched her face, brushed his fingers along her cheek, speaking words again without sound. After kissing her lips, he smiled. Then he stepped aside, took out his phone, and typed out a text message.

Annie shook. Uncontrollably. Everywhere. Her head fell into her palms, her fingers resting on her temples and grabbing at hair. Her eyes must've looked like spheres, leaking loads of tears. Two seconds later, she sucked in several ragged but quiet breaths as she wiped a finger under her nose, then across her cheeks, destroying the evidence. She covered her mouth with one hand and her eyes with the other.

Cal shoved his shirt into his pants and slipped his phone into his pocket.

"Are you okay?" He walked up to Annie and moved her hands from her face. "Did I hurt you, baby? Is it your back?" He swallowed. "Turn around."

"No, no. You didn't hurt me." She choked back more tears.

"Then what is it?" Touching her chin, he forced her eyes to remain on his.

As she stared at him, seconds turned to hours. Days. Annie fell into him more, further, deeper.

"What is it?" he repeated.

"I love you."

Cal didn't speak or move.

The impact of her words showed up in his gaze as he attempted to pull the emotions back inside, looking as though he asked how or why, the shock of her declaration crossing every inch of his face.

He aged.

Cal touched her cheek, kissed her upper lip, her lower. Then he inched back and peered into her eyes again. The quiet man actually became mute while Annie's heart turned to skin.

She would rip and burn and bruise. Her heart would die. Again. All conscious thought fled. Only the thunderous roar of those three heartfelt words remained...

I love you. I love you. I love you.

Cal slipped his fingers through hers and pulled her away from the wall — from the concrete, the moment, the awake, the dreaming, the magic — and guided her toward the street. They held hands the entire walk back to the Tesla.

Annie waited.

She waited between breaths and heartbeats for Cal to say something, anything, a single word, but the quiet man didn't speak. Other noises increased, becoming louder and louder, people talking, murmuring, music playing, horns honking, but Annie — she only heard the sound of Cal's silence and the clank of her heels on the concrete.

FORTY-NINE

"I'm going to start a bath for you," Cal said as they entered his apartment.

Annie nodded, holding her heels in one hand by their straps, and went toward the kitchen to grab a glass of water. By the time she entered the bathroom, steam had fogged the mirrors, creating clouds in the atmosphere. While the taciturn man sat on the ledge of the tub, still dressed, his fingers in the stream.

Their eyes met, then departed.

After removing her clothes and using the toilet, she stepped foot into the warm bubbles, focusing only on the sound the rushing water made as she sank neck-deep into the welcoming heat. Skimming her palms over the soapy foam, she closed her lids.

But the moment the washcloth grazed her skin, her eyes popped open.

Cal had shut off the tap, scooted to the rear ledge, and positioned himself behind her.

Instinctively, she sat forward and hugged her knees while he pressed the wet cloth over her shoulders and down her sore backside. The care went on for some time. Tears built in the corners of her eyes. Love caught in the tangled net of her throat.

But it couldn't last forever.

Nothing did.

Cal stood. And as Annie watched him undress, she found herself admiring his form. Tall, strong, defined back muscles. Rock-hard hips, a posture an artist would beg to sculpt — every inch of his physical body an open book.

Why couldn't his heart be the same?

Then he entered the shower. Because of course, it would've been too intimate to join her in the bathtub, especially after tonight. But the washing had been intimate. Cal Prescott was still ever the enigma Annie had encountered that very first night. A chameleon.

Oh, what had she done? Had she made a mistake telling him what she felt? Maybe there wasn't such a thing as a mistake.

Timing, Cal often said, emphasized. Timing and choices.

Annie hadn't planned on saying I love you in the alley. But she could no longer deny it, and she didn't want to. He needed to know before she left Miami.

No mistakes.

No denial.

It had to be said. Expressed. No matter the consequences — *he won't say it back* — she didn't regret telling Cal she loved him.

After finishing her bath, Annie stood near the mirror in front of the bathroom sinks, drying off. Alone. Cal had gone to the kitchen.

Glancing over her shoulder, she eyed her backside. The evidence of their joining, seeing those scratch marks and bruises — the pleasure they took in hurting — had her closing her eyes and recalling the frenzied moment leading up to her confession...

The warmth and tingling, the sweat and need.

Why was it all such a need?

Right now, it was still one. But it stung, leaving her feeling a different kind of warmth. Chills. A feverish energy slowly warming her, creeping into her veins. She relived the moment again and again and again: the push of him inside her, the drive for life, death, reason, his breath on her skin, the way he'd held her there, as if what they did together had both a beginning and an end.

Goosepimples formed over the whole of her skin.

The poison running through her veins a high.

She turned around, stepped closer to the mirror, and peered at her reflection. Staring into her green eyes.

Awakening replaced innocence.

Freedom replaced repression.

She'd come to South Beach to heal and had found some missing pieces. But where would she go from here? Home?

Home was in Cal's smile...

Would he ask her to stay? To move? Was it the end?

She didn't want to feel things, but she did.

Annie looked away from the woman who had changed, who loved, who lived, who didn't give up, and swiped Cal's robe off the hook from behind the door. After slipping it on, she tied the string and inhaled a deep breath. His smell encapsulated her. The scent time in bed on a rainy day under the covers with a good book or a movie playing on Netflix — time without worry or concern.

Could she fit his robe in her suitcase? Or him? She could box him up or tuck him into her sleeve.

The wasp-like poison in her veins moved to the pit of her stomach. Rocks rolled around in her gut.

Unsure.

Sure.

Hope.

Annie went into the empty room, snuggled into the bed, and within minutes, fell asleep, Cal's scent both a protection and a barbiturate.

Wearing a pair of comfortable sweatpants and no shirt, Cal entered the bedroom. The bathroom nightlight gave the otherwise dark space a little glow. The aroma of rose bubbles permeated the air, the soap he knew Annie preferred. Nothing could mask her natural scent, though.

Tangerine blossoms.

Oh ... Annie.

Cal leaned against the dresser, crossed his ankles, and rubbed a few fingers over his chin, wondering if Annie was really sleeping.

Or was she pretending and avoiding and running?

They'd both done enough of that.

Cal should've known better than to have allowed it all to happen. The summer spent with a woman twenty years younger than him. Age didn't matter, but it would once her clock began to tick. Or once she tired of his bullshit.

Sighing, he made his way to the bed and sat beside her, his breath catching in his throat as he wiped a palm clear across his face — unable to move a single muscle as he watched her dream. As he shaded her in, etching her into the corners of his mind.

Asleep and beautiful and his. *Just like this*, he thought. Smart and strong and talented and ... what? A comfort. A place to keep his secrets and hang his head. Was she even ready for all that bullshit? Was he?

And what would Constance Prescott think of Annie Baxter? He laughed to himself. If only they could meet. They could not.

Cal's first responsibility would have to be to his mother. He'd avoided her for too long. Too many years spent searching for something he would probably never find. The strength he normally drew upon to handle most situations in life seemed dull. Annie couldn't see him weak or his mother sick. Nor could she be privy to the life he had to lead. Summer had been like a tropical paradise. What would reality do to them?

Flatten, destroy, and change their relationship. An atom bomb exploding over loveliness.

Calvin Prescott ... falling in love with a girl of only twenty-five.

What was his excuse?

Misguided loneliness?

No. Excuses weren't for him. He made things happen. Controlled his destiny. Besides, he'd known what had been in store for them. He could decipher lust from connection. Loneliness from desiring true companionship. The night they'd met, his throat had turned raw, his mind had gone into overdrive, and his self-control had vanished.

Annie had never been a conquest or a fling. Or a distraction. She'd never left his thoughts. She made him better. Stronger.

Then why was he weak?

Because he wouldn't allow her to tie him off.

He hadn't summoned the courage to be the man she needed — the one he needed to be.

What could he offer her anyway? Twenty or thirty good years. No children.

And he'd done nothing to stop any of it — except live in denial. Maybe he could still do that. Sure, he could be with her, fuck her and spend time with her, he could even talk to her — although he still held back in that department too. But now ... she was leaving and deserved far more.

Running off to Florida to escape Reegan had been one thing, the summer an entirely different thing, but taking care of Annie, being responsible for her, building a life with her — stealing her youth from her — those were other things entirely. Did she even understand what that would mean? A life *with* *him*. What she would give up. The sacrifices.

Cal's pride told him he should push her away, to do what was best for Annie in the long term, but his heart — his fucking heart — had fallen in love. Hard.

FIFTY

The next morning, as Cal stepped outside his bedroom door and started to pull it closed, a cheery voice interrupted him.

"*Buenos días.*"

He'd forgotten Rosa was coming. She often popped by early Sunday with fresh produce, pickings from the local farmer's market — seasonal fruits and veggies she would prepare meals from in the days ahead.

After wiping her hands on the kitchen towel, Rosa made her way over, the chunky curls of her short, dark hair bouncing with each step. The two of them met around the dining table, Cal already doing his best to avoid her infamous stare, the one now combing every inch of his face.

"This one," she whispered, pointing toward the bedroom door, "she loves you."

Cal gripped the top of one of the chairs. "What makes you think she loves me?"

Already clucking her tongue against the roof of her mouth, Rosa squinted and shook her head. "I'm an old lady. I know what love looks like, and I see it in Annie's eyes when she's with you ... this whole time we've been here. You can't play me for a fool. I know you feel this from her. I know you feel it for her. *Usted no puede ocultar de mí.*"

Cal swallowed. He squeezed the back of the chair a little harder.

"She's leaving," Rosa continued, still scrutinizing him, smothering him with those onyx eyes and that tender voice. "We will be moving soon too. Do you want things to end this way? You're going to break her heart. Annie knows you love her even if you don't say it. So, tell her so. *Dile a ella todo lo que pesa sobre ti*."

Cal's eyes held a sheen or a film. His throat hurt. *Fucking ridiculous*, he thought as he stood stock-still, trying to focus on something concrete. Something physical. Things he could name and label.

"I don't think it will ever be enough," he finally uttered, turning his attention to Rosa, attempting to empty his eyes of the bullshit he wanted no one to discover.

"What won't be enough? What are you talking about?" Rosa's forehead crinkled. Her eyes narrowed. "You have more than enough of everything to give her for the rest of your life."

"You cannot possibly know ... I can't possibly know all she wants. One day, she'll want to be a mother. She'll want things she doesn't even understand at her age now." Cal flinched, his past playing on a large movie screen behind his eyes. "She'll change her mind."

Stepping closer, Rosa glared up at him. "You're afraid of giving this beautiful woman a baby? A strong man like you?" she scoffed. "A love like this ... you should give her everything."

"I would be fooling Annie, leading her to believe I would ... that I want ... that I would ever have children."

"No! You have been a fool to lead her on this long, then!"

"I told myself I wasn't going to do this again. She's young, with so many possibilities. I'm not—"

"You're not, what? Opening yourself up? Don't talk to me about age *no more*." Rosa sliced a hand through the air. "This love you feel for Annie is different than what you have felt in the past. Annie is different. She will support you. Grow with you."

"Women change their minds. And one day, whatever this is between us, it won't be enough."

"You're right," Rosa said, and Cal's mouth opened. "No, you listen. It wasn't enough before, but now you see that it's different. Now you know it's different." Her index finger stabbed his chest. "*Right here*. That's why you could never give Samantha a baby. Not because it isn't in you, *mi hijo*. Sam was not the one. But it is in you to be a father, a real father, one like you never had. You can't deny this. It's different with Annie, and you know it. This love is like nothing you have ever seen before." She snapped her fingers. "From the beginning you understood that. This kind of love ... it's scaring the shit out of you."

Rosa made the sign of the cross, looked heavenward, and mumbled, "Oh, *perdóname, Padre*," then she turned back to Cal. "This is more than love. It's more than sex. You feel this with her, yes?" The R's rolled off her tongue with such emphasis, such love. "It's more."

Cal's face heated and his throat swelled with all the things his mother had taught him were bullshit. Or maybe his father had taught him that as well ... when he'd left. *This kind of love...* He could no longer swallow as he imagined the possibilities — for a split second — of all he'd denied.

"I never thought I could love her the way that I do."

"What are you doing, Calvin?" Rosa placed a palm on his bicep, soothing him with the warmth in her eyes, with her touch. "How many more times must I ask you this question? Stop living in the past. This is the life God gave you. It's all we have. Share your life with this woman ... in every way."

Noises came from the bedroom. The toilet flushing. The faucet running. Cal composed himself, standing taller, and cleared his throat.

Rosa grabbed his chin. "Love is so hard for you, no? I love you, Calvin Warner Prescott. Don't take that from me."

Cal's eyes washed clean, but his throat remained a goddamn knot.

"Love her or let her go. You can't—"

"That's enough." His voice trembled. "*Ya has dicho suficiente.*" He stared Rosa down. "*Suficiente.*"

Dragging several fingers through his hair, Cal let out a deep breath and pinched the back of his neck. *Think.* Summer was over. *Think, goddammit.* What was the plan? There was always a plan.

Well, apparently there was a first time for everything.

He had no plan.

Cal didn't know what he wanted to do. But he did know what he had to do. He always knew. He always had to make hard choices.

His plan had been chosen for him.

A few seconds later, Annie appeared from behind the door fully dressed. She placed her bag at the desk and glanced toward the kitchen. Rosa folded a paper bag. Cal stared at the cabinetry like it held a solution to a problem. The atmosphere could've been sliced with a feather.

"Good morning, *mi querida*," Rosa called out on her way to Annie, purse hanging off her shoulder.

"Are you leaving?"

"Mmm." Rosa's onyx eyes lit up. "Yes."

"I'm going to miss you." Annie swallowed.

"I will see you again, child." Rosa pulled the photographer into an embrace.

But even with her head resting on Rosa's comforting shoulder, Annie couldn't help but absorb Cal's tension as he stood ramrod straight in the kitchen, staring at the photographs on the refrigerator.

"Believe, risk, *amor*," Rosa whispered, sliding her arms to Annie's biceps and sighing. "*Adiós.*"

"*Adiós,*" Annie replied, her face flushing.

Before opening the front door, Rosa peered across the room, directing her next words at Cal. "*Es suficiente. Tú eres suficiente.*"

Cal stole a quick glance at Annie, then his gaze settled back on Rosa.

"*Más que muchos gorriones.*" Rosa nodded as she opened the front door and stepped outside.

"I already sent for an Uber," Annie said as she made her way to the table. "No need to bother Carl."

Cal joined her, standing at the opposite end. He inhaled a deep breath, then released it with his next words. "My mother is sick, Annie." He hung his head, then lifted it. "She has Alzheimer's."

Annie couldn't feel her feet. Her heart started to thump against her chest.

"She... She's been sick for a long time." He scrubbed his cheek with his knuckles. "At least... God, at least ten years." He glanced to the right, looking at that painting on the wall. "I shouldn't have left her."

"You didn't." Annie tiptoed closer to him.

"I did." Cal met her gaze. "She needs me."

"Cal..." she uttered, placing a palm on his back, "I'm sorry she's sick."

"Annie, don't." He stepped away.

"Then why did you leave?" she asked as more pieces of his puzzle came together. Reasons why he never spoke about his family. About his hurt. "There must've been another reason, and don't say John." Annie waited several seconds for a reply to the question she'd never asked but had wanted to. Then she supplied her own answer. "A woman."

"I made a bad decision..." Cal exhaled. "The only way to rectify it was to put distance between us." His eyes bounced around the room. "I had a lot on my mind last night. It wasn't fair to you." He inhaled a sharp breath. "Yesterday was Constance's birthday."

"Baby... Why didn't you tell me?"

Glancing at the floor, he shook his head. "The same reason I don't *tell* anything." He looked up. "I was a dick last night ... after you... I'm sorry."

Annie wrapped her arms around his waist and held him for what felt like several minutes, then she finally said, "I'm sorry your mother is sick." Her lips moved against the crook of his neck. "I'm so sorry."

Cal met her eyes. "How do you do that?"

"What?"

"Put others' needs ahead of your own? Without crushing your spirit or losing yourself?" Both of them smiled. "Believe it or not, that's why I'm about to say this." Cal swallowed, his face losing some of its color. "I think ... while you're away..."

"Yes?"

"I think you should take some time to think about what you want. While we're apart."

"What do you mean?"

"Maybe I'm not what you really need right now. I have a responsibility toward my mother. I don't know how to do both. Be in a relationship and be a caretaker."

"This is a relationship. I'm not something you just 'do.' You can lean on me, Cal."

But he turned his entire body around.

"Are you breaking up with me?" She stepped into his space and stared at him. "Is this your polite way of saying, 'Oh, I'm sorry, Annie, but I don't want to see you anymore'?"

"Annie..." He sighed and peered into her eyes. "You're twenty-five."

"Yeah. And you're forty-five, Cal." She gently pushed on his chest. "We've covered this. At the beginning of our 'relationship.'" She made air quotes. "So. What!"

Cal grinned.

"Don't. Smile. At. Me," she growled. "It's my age, really? After all this — everything — you're worried about my fucking age?"

"You have a lot of changes ahead of you. You want to see the world. You really should give this more thought."

Thought, thought, thought. Thinking.

No. Not today.

Not this summer.

Not anymore.

Feeling like she might puke, Annie bent her upper body over a chair and placed a palm on the table, trying not to hyperventilate. Kicked in the teeth, ready to vomit, and sucking air into her lungs while finding herself wandering around inside the eye of a hurricane — that was where the *I love you* had brought and left her.

"Annie..." Cal uttered as he approached.

She stood tall, composing herself. "We can see the world together."

"You want to talk about our future? Yes?"

"Yes!"

"Then can you honestly say you've given meaningful thought to what a future with me would really be like — a man almost twice your age? I don't want children, and when I'm older and retired, you will still be young, vibrant, and in your prime. Is this what you really want? Or are you only going off your feelings — right now, this instant? That will not be enough to sustain a relationship."

"Do you hear yourself?" Both her eyebrows arched. Lines formed across her forehead.

"What?"

"You, of all people, *apparently*, should know what. You know I'm not on birth control. Have you not even thought for one second about that fact since last night?"

"Fuck." He pinched his nose.

"That's right. Fuck!" Annie covered her mouth, her palm shaking.

"God, Annie, the only thing I've been able to think about is what you told me afterward. Why didn't you stop me?"

"Me? When? When you held me against the wall? When you fucked me within an inch of my life?"

"I lost myself." He turned and stepped away again. "I lost control."

They both looked around the space. Annie let out a quiet puff of air.

"All I was thinking about..." he began a few seconds later. "All I was feeling..."

Standing at his profile now, Annie touched his back and searched the side of his face.

"I did too, okay?" She swallowed. "I lost myself. Or I..." *Found myself.* "It was..." *Fucking amazing.* Their eyes met as she blew out an exhausted breath. "My period should start any minute." Annie hadn't had to think about this shit in so long, coming off months of abstinence. And Cal had always been careful until he wasn't. Between the *I love you* and their impending moves and now this fight, the sticky semen still plastered to her skin on the ride home last night had been the least of her worries. "We're good."

Cal folded one of her hands between his palms. "I'm sorry. I wasn't..." He shook his head. "I wasn't thinking."

"Neither of us were thinking. And now," she said and inhaled, "it seems it's all we can do."

A couple seconds later, Annie let go of Cal's hands and strolled over to the refrigerator. A photo of Rosa and her children caught her attention. *Rosa was right...* In the short time Annie had known Rosa, she'd learned she was often right. Annie never should've waited so long to tell Cal how she felt.

But Cal Prescott had considered the future?

Of course he had. He wasn't shallow or nearsighted, but what an excellent job he'd done at being aloof, acting immune to necessary conversation.

No, Annie hadn't considered what having a real future together might actually look like. Or a lifetime. She hadn't thought seriously about having children — not even after the scare of last night. Right now, only three things seemed certain:

1. The sun was going to set, then rise again tomorrow over the horizon.
2. There was no one else on earth like Cal Prescott — the man was one of a fucking kind.
3. And she loved him; she loved him so much, she couldn't see straight.

Folding her arms across her chest, she ran her palms over her biceps, over and over as she contemplated ... *Cal.*

His delicious smell, especially after a hot shower — the beach, the cotton, the clean. His lips when they first made contact with her skin, along her neck or against her thighs. His tongue, harsh yet delicate, the finest eraser of thoughts she'd ever known. *Perfection*. His hands, grounding her to the earth in a split second. His arms, branches of a sequoia tree. The crinkle between his eyes — astounding. Mad, happy, or serious, the vertical lines appeared. His ears, listening endlessly, to anything and everything Annie said — each whim, every story.

His patience.

His commands.

His safety.

She closed her lids.

Mmm...

Then there was the ultimate feature. Her favorite. The thing she'd first noticed about him...

His ocean eyes.

Like waves, pulling her under, the man peered into her soul — as if he'd always known her since the beginning of time. Annie squeezed her biceps, wanting to love him. Wishing Cal would let her love him. Not wanting to do anymore pretending.

"Maybe I shouldn't come back," she said, thinking aloud while glancing over at him. She planned on returning to Miami to finalize a few things, but now, packing up her work seemed futile. Seeing him again an exercise in heartache. "I bought my flight out. Maybe Maggie can box up my stuff from the gallery."

Cal stood at the back of one of the chairs. His knuckles practically white. He wouldn't meet her gaze. Or give anything away. Or push back. Or fight.

Annie wanted him to fight *for* her, push her to be stronger, better, to challenge her, not push her away.

"So..." Annie marched toward him, wanting to shove him again. "You're pushing me away for my own good." Fists balled at her sides, she gritted her teeth and glared up at him. "Don't. Fucking. Push. Me. Away."

And...

Nothing.

The air crackled with his stupid silence. Cal had gone all mute again. Except, right now, his no-talking shit was anything but sexy.

Fine, she thought. *If he's going to push, I'll push right back.*

"Do you get that I want to be with you? That I want to really know you?"

"Damn it, Annie, you do know me. Stop throwing that in my face."

"Then, what?" She tossed her hands into the air. "Why?" Her voice cracked, resembling a boy going through puberty. "How badly have you been hurt? Who hurt you?"

Cal only stared at her, his eyes wormholes of hurt, his face losing more of its color.

"No, you don't understand, do you?" Annie shook her head. "I don't need time, Cal. I don't need to think! Fuck thinking. I want you." For a moment, she eyed the ceiling. "How ironic." She placed her hands on her hips and looked at him again. "Those words." She swallowed. "That's what you said to me." She took a few steps until she stood only inches from his face, his chest, his eyes. "That's what you told me that first night." She played with his shirt collar. "You said..." Perching up on her tippy-toes, she put her mouth near his ear and whispered, "I want you."

Nothing followed but the sounds of their bated breath. Their hearts beating in rhythm. Like his skin had become hers. They were so close. So intertwined.

Then Annie dropped her head, let go of his shirt, and sighed.

"Baby," he uttered, pulling her back against him. He nestled his face in her hair, moving his lips over the strands. "Annie..."

"You knew I loved you before I ever said those words." She hiccupped, then sniffed.

Tangling his fingers through her hair, he peered deep into her eyes. "Have you not known the way I feel about you every time I touch you?"

"That's the only way you show me."

"Annie, that's not true."

"Isn't it?"

Cal let go.

Annie did too.

"Why can't you feel this?"

"I feel this," he replied, a nervous tic in his tone despite the lick of confidence registered there. "No one has ever made me feel the meaning of those words the way you did last night. The way you've made me feel them all along..." His palms met over his lips and nose, forming a triangle, then he pinched the bridge. "Fuck."

"You're right," Annie blurted, and their eyes locked. "I haven't thought about a future that includes children, dogs and cats or picket fences." Annie paused and inhaled, trying to stop that annoying prepubescent boy from fiddling with her voice box. "But I want you, Cal ... Calvin Prescott."

Taking a few seconds to gather her thoughts, she attempted to swallow. But it was no good. Her throat seemed to have razor blades in it.

"I need you to tell me how you feel and often," she continued. "I need to hear those three words said out loud. I don't need time to know I would go anywhere with you. I'll stand by you." She shook her head and grinned. "Sounds cliché, right? I don't care. I will stand by you. I do. Maybe you're the one who needs time, but I... I only need you. All of you. I don't want there to be any more restraints or what-ifs."

"Promise me you'll come back to Miami." Cal stepped closer, cradled her jaw, and stared into her eyes like he didn't know how they'd gotten here or where they were going. He only knew this moment, and he wanted to live in it forever. "Promise me, Annie." Cal pushed strands of hair from her face and searched her eyes.

She swallowed, blinked. "I promise."

Dropping her gaze, she somehow managed to separate herself from his magnetic hold. But the second she started to walk away, he grabbed her hand and pulled her close again. Annie put a thumb on her temple, fingers on her forehead, and tilted her face to the floor, fighting tears. Her chest shook as she took in a breath.

They communicated so well without words.

"Cal ... please ... don't touch me," she whispered and stepped back, her heart sick, melting, her stomach knotted — the wanting always at an apex. No matter what. "Don't even look at me like you want to touch me. Don't tell me you want to touch me. Don't put your hands on me."

Cal released a loud breath.

He didn't like what Annie said or how sad she looked as she'd said it, but he understood her pain and accepted it. He ached to hold her and kiss her, to make love to her. And he refused to hide it. This was the way he preferred to show what he felt. And, now, she denied him. Cal would try his best not to actually put his hands on her body, but he didn't think he could ever look at her like he didn't want her. He would always want her. Always.

"You're asking a lot."

"Asking you to love me ... asking you to be with me. Yes..." She swiped her fingers under each eye, still hoping for those three words to part from his lips. "I suppose it is a lot."

But he remained silent. So, Annie turned, picked up her bag, and walked toward the front door.

"At least wait for the car inside."

"I can't," she replied without a glance in his direction.

As Cal watched Annie depart, it seemed she moved in slow motion, dragging his heart along by an invisible string.

Cal loved Annie.

He loved everything about her, and he truly wanted her to be happy. Even if that meant being without him. *Another fantastic lie*, he thought. Still, that falsehood was the only bright spot sitting in the shade of his heart.

The door shut. His *heavy* left.

"Why can't you feel this?" she had asked. Fuck, if he had any more feelings, he would be a walking stick of dynamite.

Of course he could feel this.

He'd just never really allowed it. Not completely. And now, after having heard those three words come out of the mouth of a twenty-five-year-old — a woman who *would* one day want a child — eventually, most all of them did — Cal was afraid to feel it and accept it. Perhaps, that was how the lies began. First, telling himself this relationship would be temporary. Now, trying to convince himself he only wanted her to be happy.

Annie wanted him.

Sure.

In this moment.

But in the next, she might be ready to move on — the way he always had to.

She would be uncertain. She would change her mind. She was young and would want a little taste of everything — the world, the moon, the stars. And he could only give her ... what? Himself.

A middle-aged man whose life had become his job.

Standing in the center of his kitchen, his feet cemented to the floor, Cal overlooked all he could give Annie, forgetting he'd already been giving many of those things to her, blind to the lessons he'd been taught, only seeing his hurt, his fears. The Lonely. And he did want Annie to be happy. But her happiness depended on being without him. Cal always had to leave the good, give up truth, let go of beauty.

Or people left him first.

He ran a palm down his face.

Why couldn't he at least have said it, though?

Because *I love you* wouldn't keep her here.

For a while. Maybe.

But that would be all. A moment.

Then she would tire of him. Leave. Move on. She'd said she needed him, but needs changed. Her age didn't matter to him, but it would still affect her choices. From the start, he'd known it was wrong to expect a girl of her age to want to be with him. She would eventually want more. Need more. And who was he to provide it?

They should never have waited so long to discuss all of this.

This last week, since the note and the fight and the bleeding finger over the kitchen sink, they'd been fucking. Like animals. Like two people who couldn't get enough expression out of skin or touch or lips or hands.

And he'd been unwilling to bring it up again.

Rosa had been right. Cal wasn't just scared — he was fucking terrified.

Cal moved to Miami to get away from examining his life. And Annie had caused him to look at himself in a way he hadn't for years. Perhaps in a way he'd never been able to. Annie saw things inside him he refused to acknowledge existed.

His thoughts drifted to her gifts. To the antique handheld mirror. To what he'd seen in that reflection. The one she'd forced upon him at first glance. On the fucking staircase.

The challenge.

The rising.

The rebirth.

Now, it was truly upon him. He had nowhere to run or hide. Except he was still running. This time, he'd be going home. Back to California.

Annie was home.

And he was a fucking prick.

Enough of this conjecture...

Cal had to push Annie away to keep her safe. He'd kept her close as long as possible because she was real, comfort and truth. But for her own good, he had to leave her alone.

Could he? It didn't matter.

He had an obligation to Constance. And no twenty-five-year-old would want to move to Ojai to help him play nursemaid to his mother. Annie would think he was weak. She could never see that side of him. No one did.

No one needed him.

A need was a few blissful moments in the sun.

The sun eventually set, though, went down behind the horizon. And when it came back up, people started something fresh and new. The ritual ushered in change, a coming and going. There was no such thing as forever. One day, even the star heating our planet would die. Cease to exist. Explode.

Like Cal's heart.

No amount of sky, or sun or light or warmth, could keep him from drifting about in the cold, immeasurable ocean.

FIFTY-ONE

Later that afternoon, Annie hoisted her red, hardback suitcase onto the window seat in her room, flipped open the locks and lid, and stared inside the empty shell.

She may as well have been looking into a mirror.

Except, she wasn't empty anymore.

She was full.

Of Cal.

Of feelings.

Of her heart beating once again.

The sensation in her stomach remained as well, the one that hadn't dissipated since this morning. Or perhaps the butterflies had made a home inside her belly much, much sooner.

Like last night when she'd uttered those three words aloud after they'd peeled themselves off the wall, away from the passion and the heat and the nirvana. Then in the car on the ride home, and again later, while floating in the bubbles in the bathtub. Or how about when Annie had tossed and turned through the night in his bed?

No.

The butterflies had arrived the second she'd said hello to him at the party in June. Actually, everything shifted off its axis when she'd first spotted Cal standing in the corner of Maggie's living room.

The next thing she knew, their summer zoomed by in a blur of kisses and caresses, holding hands and embraces. Sleeping beside a man she wanted to know forever. Or had known forever. Memories flooded her mind like a tidal wave. A deluge of things finished, completed. Or a dream.

As Annie stood in front of that empty suitcase while staring out at that beloved ocean, she replayed the morning's events.

His admissions.

Her pleas.

His denials.

The moment she'd stepped foot outside Cal's front door, after stubbornly refusing to wait for the driver inside his apartment, she'd broken down. Unable to look into the man's eyes any longer, to share air, to smell him, to imagine things he maybe didn't want or couldn't let inside.

Trailing the tips of her fingers over the door, sweat mixed with tears as Annie realized it would probably be the last time she would be in that space with Cal. Or it might be the last time she would be in *Cal's space*. She wondered if he was on the other side of the door doing the same.

Shutting her eyes from the bright of the sun on the warm, windy morning, she slid down the wall until her bottom met concrete, not opening her lids again until she heard the car pull up to the curb.

"Peek-a-boo." Maggie popped her head through the crack in Annie's bedroom door. "How's it coming?"

Shaking herself from the morning's recollections, Annie sighed, shifting her gaze from the ocean back to the empty suitcase. She surveyed the thing as if it held something she'd been searching for and couldn't find.

"That good?" Maggie joined Annie near the window seat, wrapping an arm around her shoulder. "I'm going to miss you."

Annie was certain she'd probably heard those words at least a dozen times in the last week, but she feigned a smile. The ceiling suddenly looked friendly, so she tilted her head up and stared at it, wishing her bottom lip would stop quivering and her mind would stop the stupid thinking.

Maggie dropped her arm. "What's wrong?"

"I'm fine. It's nothing." Annie went to the dresser and took out some shirts. "I'm tired." She shrugged.

"Don't give me that. You're not fine." Maggie plopped onto the bed and leaned back on her elbows.

"I can't get into it with you. I'm not going to listen to you say 'I told you so.'"

"I won't judge you." Maggie sat forward, but Annie wouldn't meet her gaze. "I love you."

Practically choking on the words Maggie uttered, on how easily the sentiment had passed her friend's lips, Annie peered out the window again at the water. "Last night..." Annie inhaled. "I told Cal 'I love you' ... for the first time."

Maggie planted her feet on the floor and stood. "He didn't say it back?"

Annie shook her head, then began to dart from dresser to suitcase, gathering more clothing.

"Stop, sweetheart. Please. Sit down."

"No." Tears leaked from her eyes, but she didn't make a peep, the only sounds the shuffling of her feet, drawers opening and closing, and a suitcase being packed filled the room.

"Annie..." Maggie began, but the photographer wouldn't stop zipping back and forth. "Cal tries to protect himself."

Annie stopped dead in her tracks and merely stared at the pile of denim in her hands, the insides of her cheeks raw from being bitten so much. "I bought too many clothes this summer."

Maggie took the jeans from Annie and guided her to the bed, patting the comforter. They both sat down.

"He's..." Maggie swept pieces of hair behind Annie's ear and gazed at the side of her friend's face. "He can be difficult."

As Annie eyeballed Maggie, a funny garble-like noise burst from her lips: a sob mixed with a *humph*.

"He doesn't say what he feels, like that, easily," Maggie continued.

"Yeah... Well..." Annie cleared her throat and rubbed a finger under her nose. "He's very open in the way he expresses himself ... physically. More than anyone I've ever met." She bit her bottom lip. "Fuck..." She dropped her head to Maggie's shoulder. "I love his stupid, annoying difficultness." Annie stayed there a moment, only breathing, then she lifted her head and wiped beneath her eyelids. "Maybe not so much right now." She laughed a little through her sniffles.

"Oh..." Maggie wrapped an arm around Annie's waist and squeezed. "I didn't expect you to fall in love, sweet girl."

"Didn't you?" Annie stared out the window. "Sometimes I forget how long you've known him. My God…" She glanced back at Maggie. "I must look like a fool. You told me I would hurt from this. From him. You did know I would fall for him."

"Anyone who doesn't love you is the fool, Annie."

"I know he loves me." Annie stood, giving Maggie her profile. "I'll keep fighting him … even while he's pushing me away. For as long as I can stand." She turned and met The Cat's warm brown eyes. "He expects people to give up on him."

Maggie sighed. She played with one of the buttons on her shirt. "I suppose, these last few years, I might have given him the impression that I've given up on him." She glanced at Annie, then away. "He's such a pain in the ass sometimes." A smile spread across her face.

"Were you ever in love with him?"

"Annie. Jesus."

"What? He's quite a lovable asshole, and he is sexy as fuck."

Maggie laughed and shook her head. "No. I've always loved him. Not in love…" She paused. "But there was a time … I fancied him. In college. But no. Never with what's in your eyes when you look at him. Or talk about him."

"'Fancied' him?" Annie grinned.

"John's influence. His word." She laughed. "Maybe my husband's right." Maggie paused, and one of Annie's eyebrows shot up. "John says Cal needs time. I don't know why, after a million years of brooding, but maybe he still needs it."

"That's what Cal said too. Time. *Tiempo*," Annie added as Maggie cocked her head to the side. "Yeah, that's Rosa's influence."

"You'll come back to pack up the rest of your new wardrobe and your photographs in a few weeks?"

"I don't regret it, Maggie."

"The clothes? Honey, I wouldn't regret them either." Maggie smirked.

"No. You know what I mean."

"I know, sweetie."

"You couldn't have warned me enough to stay away from him. I would've found him." *He would've found me.* "I don't regret a single minute of my summer."

Of being with her friends, the ocean, the sun. The gallery. She would never regret Cal. Or regret loving Cal the only way she knew how. She would never regret feeling *his* love exactly the way he'd said he showed it — *every time he touches me*. Over her, inside her, swimming through her, allowing that love to heal her wounds rather than infect them, drawing strength in the comfort, in the sadness, in the way they both had an equal give and take.

There were no regrets.

The summer didn't break their afraid-to-feel hearts after all.

The sun had shined down upon them, the ocean had watered them, and their hearts had opened. Blooming like that beautiful little sunflower Cal had plucked from a beach in Key Largo and planted in Annie's hair.

DISTANCE

THE SPACE BETWEEN TWO PLACES OR BETWEEN
PEOPLE OR THINGS; OR EMOTIONAL SEPARATION

a memory
a day trip
fog
on
the glass
of time
a breath
scattered
forgotten
my toes
point me
in every direction
I sway
with the wind
like a dandelion
I feed
off sun
and water
wind accelerates
my forward movement

I'm unbreakable
nothing
will keep me
from what I pursue

FIFTY-TWO

The moment Annie stepped out of the Seattle-Tacoma International Airport and into the somewhat cooler, definitely dryer, Pacific Northwest air, she immediately spotted the two-door, champagne-colored convertible Saab. Its top down. A pug roaming the backseat, pacing and panting.

"Did you have to bring Barney, Mom?" Annie dropped her backpack onto the seat next to him, smiled, and gave his goofy chin a good rub. "Pop the trunk, please."

"You know I twake him everywhere," Beverly cooed in her best baby-voice as Annie briefly met her mother's eyes in the rearview and hoisted her red suitcase into the trunk.

"You look fine," Annie droned, seconds later, after plopping onto the front passenger seat. Her mother traded a tube of lipstick for a cigarette, continuing to finger her wavy, cropped copper hair as she inspected her face in the mirror. "Absolutely presentable for picking your daughter up at the airport." Annie rolled her eyes, then laughed. "Are you meeting a man?"

"No." Beverly smacked her lips together, spreading around the red, then slipped on her sunglasses. Her eyebrows arched above the rims. "But you have."

"What are you talking about?"

Annie fastened her seat belt. Beverly lit the cigarette, then tossed the BIC, still fidgeting with her pixie cut.

"You're going to play innocent with me?" Exhaling, she put the car into drive and stepped on the gas. "You stopped being innocent when you stayed with that boy after he fucked another girl."

"For God's sake." Annie looked to the sky, wondering why they couldn't be normal for once. Start the conversation off with a *"Hi, how are you?"* Hugs. Or an *"It's good to have you home, Annie."* No. They were doing this shit-shit bullshit during their thirty-minute drive to her mother's cabin located in a small town east of Seattle.

"He played you," Bev continued, the cigarette dancing between her fingers. "Is that what this man is doing, too? Playing you?"

Annie pinched her eyes shut, bit her bottom lip, and silently prayed to a god she wasn't sure existed.

"I have to do all the talking?"

Extending her right arm outside the open window, palm facing forward, Annie ignored her mother's barbs, letting the breeze beat against her flesh, concentrating only on the wind. The pounding. The throbbing. *It will be fine,* Annie thought. *Fine. She'll be fine. She's not drinking. Not yet.*

"I spoke with Maggie last night." Beverly took a drag. "Do I have to spell it out?" Smoke whirled toward Annie's face as her mother gunned the accelerator and took the next curve sharper, her knuckles turning white over the steering wheel. "Maggie said the man you're fucking is old enough to be your father."

Annie's thumbs pressed into her jeans, nearly poking holes in the fabric. Her eyes stung. Her stomach turned to washboard, the kind people used to scrub dirty clothes on.

"Well..."

"I suppose those were Maggie's exact words." Annie glared at her.

"Why didn't you tell me about him? For God's sake, I'm your mother."

"This! This is why I haven't told you about him."

"Puh-leeze. Come on, you can talk to me."

"And he's not as old as Dad."

"No, he's not." Beverly laughed. "But he's still old enough to be your father."

"And *you* are in a position to give me advice about men. Really?"

"Do you want my advice?"

"No." Annie folded her arms across her chest while kneading the soles of her sneakers into the floorboard. An uncomfortable silence took over the car. Sans Barney. The dog continued to pant and snort.

"I'm going to give it to you anyway."

"Of course you are."

"You're young in his eyes," Bev began, her tone eerily soothing. "A plaything. You must know a man like that only wants one thing from you."

"A man like what?" Annie balled her fists. "What did Maggie tell you?" Her nostrils flared. "You don't even know Cal. Maybe he's *my* plaything."

"I don't know him. You're right." Beverly put her hand on Annie's knee and squeezed. "But I know you." She rattled her daughter's kneecap. "And I know you give your heart *fully* in everything you do."

"Can we talk about something else? Please." A few tears paraded down Annie's cheeks. She quickly wiped them away and composed herself. "I'll tell you about him later." She dropped the back of her head against the seat. "Just not now. I'm exhausted."

And in love...

Annie *had* given her heart. Fully. Cal had her. And it. No matter where she went. Three thousand miles of not far away. He resided in the pit of her stomach, the claw of her throat, her core.

"Of course, honey." The final bit of smoke snaked from Beverly's lips as she flicked the butt out the window.

Grateful for the silence, but annoyed her mother had tossed the cigarette outside, Annie shut her eyes for the remainder of the drive. The constant battering of the wind did little to block out her feelings, though — even with its exquisite pressure against her skin. The pounding and the throbbing.

Then her thoughts were back to Cal...

He gave the exquisite pounding and throbbing.

Wait.

No.

Cal Prescott had run out of things to give.

FIFTY-THREE

"I'm going out back to smoke." Beverly cradled the dog under her arm while making her way through the kitchen, past the dining area, and toward the sliding glass door, a pack of cigarettes poking out of the pocket of her white slacks.

"You just finished one." Annie stepped inside the rustic home for the first time in months — for the first time in over a year. The holidays had become a blur she'd avoided since her brother's death.

"Are you going to start treating me like a child in my own house?" Beverly unlocked the patio door and rubbed Barney's chin. He made a happy cry, curling his tail over his behind. "I'll smoke until my heart's content."

"I'm sure you will." Annie stretched her arms up, looked around, and inhaled a deep breath. The house smelled like cedar with a hint of pug. A nearly empty bottle of red sat on the island in the kitchen, and a few dirty dishes lay in the sink, mostly glasses and lipstick-stained coffee mugs. "I'm going to go lie down."

"I'll call you for dinner." Her mother started to close the slider.

"Are you actually going to cook?"

"I am." Beverly peeked through the tiny opening between the door and the jamb, pushing on her bangs with the hand holding the lit cigarette. Barney tinkled in the grass a few feet away. "Don't look so shocked, young lady."

Annie smirked. "Has hell frozen over?"

"I forgot what a little smart-ass you are," Bev replied, smiling as she closed the door.

Everything Annie had been attempting to avoid for over a year, met her head-on the second she entered her childhood bedroom.

The past.

Memories.

The handmade quilt covering the bed caught her eye first, reminding her of things that seemed to have occurred in another century or lifetime.

She smiled as she strolled alongside the four-poster bed, trailing her fingers over the soft, patchy material her grandmother had pieced together by hand, getting lost in the blanket's circular patterns and colors — lilac, white, and hints of mint green, the shapes spinning in her gaze like pinwheels. Lily Baxter had sewn quilts for all her grandchildren, and Annie considered hers a most prized possession. When Peter died, she'd been given his quilt too. It was in a bag stowed away in the closet.

Next, Annie wandered over to the large window and placed her elbows on the ledge. She stared outside, the backyard being one of her favorite features of her mother's home. No neighbors, only woods as far as the eye could see. Large pines, luscious and green, along with native firs, were scattered and abundant, some tall and pointy, others wide and fat. A couple patches of yellow and gold grabbed Annie's attention, popping out in the distant forest, the colorful leaves hanging from the branches of the vine maples.

She *had* missed the trees back home. Like she'd once told Cal.

And then there was Barney.

Walking below amongst the chrysanthemums. The white, pink, and astounding yellow flowers met the rear wall of the house, and wrinkly and adorable Barney was busy smelling and exploring them. The silly thing, he brought another smile to Annie's face.

Several minutes later, Annie pulled the shade down and yawned. Settling into the place she'd once called home, she snuggled beneath her grandmother's special quilt and fell asleep, and she didn't go downstairs again until her mother woke her up. For "dinner."

"I want to buy a car," Annie blurted a few minutes into their meal. She'd slept, regrouped, unpacked. The bottle of wine she'd noticed earlier on the kitchen island was gone, and another, somewhat fuller red sat in the center of the table. Water and salad and linguini also garnished the tabletop, the noodles lathered in butter and garlic, the lettuce in a rich, creamy Italian sauce.

"Oh, look at wittle Barney."

Annie followed her mother's gaze to where the dog slept a few feet away in his beige bed, snoring, in the Grand Room. Beverly had named all the rooms in the log cabin. The living room was grand because Beverly deemed it so — not because it was exceptionally large or grand. But Annie had to admit it was a little grand. With floor-to-ceiling beams in the corners, two skylights, built-in bookshelves, a fireplace, a television above the hearth, a luxurious brown leather couch, two matching recliners.

And ... Barney.

Apparently, the room was also a perfect place for sleeping. The pug obviously thought so, drool pooling from his lips.

"Did you hear what I said?" Annie tapped her fork against the side of the plate.

"So..." Bev smirked, meeting her daughter's gaze. "You *are* planning on staying out here, then?"

Annie shrugged. "Maybe."

"Huh..." Beverly chased some of the salad with a gulp of red. "I didn't raise you to be uncertain."

"No," Annie bit back. "I raised me." She pointed a finger toward her chest. "Remember?"

Wrinkling her nose, her mother sniffed. "You're not indecisive. Or unsure." She blinked. "Will you be staying in this house? And for how long?"

Annie stabbed at some lettuce. "I am going to move, but am I going to live here ... with you ... in the meantime?" She cocked a brow. "That remains to be seen."

"You can stay here as long as you need to."

"Thank you."

"That money won't last forever."

"Don't talk to me about *that* money, Mom." Annie pushed her plate aside. Peter's money. Annie had refused to spend it. Not a dime. She would buy her car with it, though. She couldn't let it keep forever. She hoped to invest it or donate it or forget it. Spending what he'd left her in his will meant parting with him. Again.

"What's wrong? You're not going to eat now because of what I said?"

"I... I'm just tired." Annie began to play with the wineglass, tilting the stem, hypnotized by the way the robust red slid up and down the sides.

"Bullshit." Bev chugged the remaining contents of her own glass, then started to fill it back up again. "You've slept half the day."

"Top mine off, please." Annie moved her glass toward Beverly.

They sat in silence a moment, only sipping cabernet.

"Did Maggie also tell you"—Annie looked off into the distance—"that I'm in love with Cal?"

"Maggie didn't have to tell me." Beverly stretched an arm across the table and touched her daughter's wrist. "I can see it all over you. I saw it in your eyes in the car when you spoke about him."

Annie retracted her hand. "But Maggie did tell you, didn't she?" Her eyes glossed. "Why did she have to go and tell you all my business?"

"I think she assumed I knew about him. She's very worried about you."

"Maggie makes it her job to worry about everyone. You know that." Annie wiped a few tears from her cheeks, brought her plate closer, and picked up her fork, ready to attempt some more mixed greens. "I'm fine." *Fine. Fine. Fine.* "Let's talk about something else, okay? I came out here to work."

"That's right. People who are *fine* always cry at dinner." Bev rolled her eyes. "I thought you came out here to see me."

"I did. I came out here for both reasons." Annie managed a bite and a slight smile. A few pieces of hair found their way around the tip of an index finger.

"That reminds me, I have a job for you."

Annie let go of the strands and blinked.

"Auntie Ingrid wants you to take pictures of her grandkids."

"I don't do that."

"Oh, I'm sorry." Bev patted her chest. "You take *photographs* — not pictures. I forgot." She fingered her copper bangs. "Auntie Ingrid wants you to take *photographs*. It could be fun. She wants to pay you."

"That's not what I meant." Annie fiddled with the wineglass again. "I've never really done that kind of photography. Not for money."

"Then it will be good for you and your portfolio. This could be something new and exciting you could do out here for work. If you stay. Are you staying?"

Annie's attention turned to the strips of linguini she now pulled from her mouth, staring at the matted ribbons in disbelief as they came out.

"What?"

"These noodles." Annie continued peering at them as she placed the clump to the side of her plate. "They're, like, stuck together. Why can't you cook pasta?"

"This is how I cook pasta." Beverly laughed, years of junk crackling in her lungs. "Have you forgotten?"

"Maggie taught me how to cook ... a little. I can teach you."

"You *are* a little smart-ass," Bev said as she began sucking strips of linguini into her pursed lips. "Besides, I know that too."

"God, Mom, is there anything Maggie didn't tell you?"

"Well, I am relieved this man of yours is a longtime friend of Maggie's." Beverly placed a palm flat on the tabletop. "I mean, that is something, after all. You didn't just pick any older, random, complete stranger to fu—"

"I'm going to bed." Annie pushed her half-empty plate away and stood.

"Did I say something wrong?" Beverly batted her lashes.

"No." Annie swiped the 1.5-liter bottle of cheap wine and refilled her glass. To the brim.

"You've been in that damn bed since you got here."

"Now, I'm going back. Is that okay with you?"

"You're not spending this entire vacation in bed." Beverly stood, cleared their two plates, then grabbed her cigarettes off the counter. Barney followed, wriggling near her feet.

"It's not a vacation. I'm—"

"You're working. I know." She made her way to the back door. "Call Ingrid."

"I will."

"Oh..." Bev glanced over her shoulder. "Don't forget your father is picking you up tomorrow night."

"I know, Mom."

"Why don't you come out and sit with me and this wittle guy?" Beverly opened the slider.

"You're going to freaking poison him," Annie said as she placed the two bowls of leftovers near the sink.

"No, no. He only wuns around and pways. Don't you? Oh, Annie, look at his wittle face."

Annie did look at his wittle face. For a few seconds, she merely stood at the island watching the two of them. Funny, how they'd started to resemble each other. The unlit cigarette hanging from Bev's mouth, the little pug shaking near her feet, her mother seemingly possessed by the anticipation of nicotine, endlessly distracted.

Whatever.

Annie had her own distraction. Cabernet. Cheap, yummy Trader Joe's cabernet. She'd missed that too. So before making her way upstairs, she drank a healthy dose.

The tannins were good for her. And the smooth taste drowned out the sounds of Barney's snorts along with her mother's monotonous baby talk. But the wine couldn't drown time. Annie wished she could jump in a time machine. Go back. She wished she could be in Cal's arms, resting, soothed, safe, never tired, always warm.

The alcohol was warm.

It made her feel warm, anyway. But its effects couldn't hold her to its chest and rock her back and forth. It couldn't truly keep her safe. The bed was safe. The bed was warm. Sleep took worries and pain. Sleep was safe.

The safest.

After making her way to the staircase, Annie grabbed at the railing, pulled herself along, and began to climb. The steps moved or shifted. Or she weighed a thousand pounds. The healthy, yummy, cheap wine hit Annie all at once.

Steady. She giggled. *Hold the rail. Up, up, up. Don't cry, pussy. Isn't alcohol supposed to make you numb? I want to numb.*

It's a depressant.

She slapped a palm to her flushed cheek.

Am I naked?

I'm hot.

Something was naked. And alive.

Her mind...

Riveting and terrifying, reminding her of everything she hoped to forget, the buzz bringing it to the surface, leaving it there to fester and pus.

Fuck alcohol. This house. My bed.

Finally, she reached the top. Everything still seemed so heavy. Like miles of ocean she had to tread through.

The hallway. The doorknob. Her memories.

She lost the now empty glass on the dresser — or somewhere — fell onto the bed, and sank into the feathery quicksand sheets.

Swallowed whole.

She spun.

Sank deeper.

Maybe she would puke.

That would be fun.

Not on Grandma's quilt.

What was a spiderweb like?

This.

Now.

God.

She ached.

How could she ache? Right between the legs. Her body deceived her. Her heart needed mending, and her pussy ached. The room tilted. She pulled her knees toward her chest, assuming a fetal position.

I hope he's curled up in a little ball too. I hope he has blue balls.

Longing for his touch, his warmth, for his magic skin and body to spoon against her, leaving no space between them — aching and spinning, spinning, spinning — Annie fell asleep beneath the beautiful handmade quilt, fully dressed, the need for the man she wanted and couldn't seem to reach reverberating through her body's speakers, blasting love-sex-time-static through her alcohol-riddled chest.

FIFTY-FOUR

Annie sat across from Albert in an oversized green booth inside one of his favorite downtown restaurants, The Metropolitan Grill, a renowned steakhouse in a building old as fuck.

Resting comfortably against the plush seats, she stroked the velvet with one hand while placing her other palm on the mahogany tabletop. Bottles were stacked neatly behind sheets of glass to her right. Booths and tables full of diners to her left. But mostly, Annie watched her father.

"Stop looking at me, for Christ's sake." Albert Baxter eyed his daughter over the top of the menu, the frames of his glasses as she remembered, round and wide and black. Sandy-gray hair fell across his lined forehead. "Pick up your menu and figure out what you're going to have."

"I've missed you."

Lowering the bill of fare, Albert gazed at his daughter, his hazel eyes sparkling some due to the glare coming from the upside-down, umbrella-shaped lights hanging along the center of the dining room.

"I'm not going to cry until I at least eat," he mumbled.

Annie laughed, then the waiter appeared, placing fresh dirty martinis with extra olives in front of them.

"Get a steak," Albert said after thanking the server and letting him know they needed a minute to decide. "That's why I brought you here."

"You brought me here because you love this place."

"You do still eat red meat, don't you? I hope Miami hasn't changed you into some sort of health-nut vegan or some other new-age bullshit."

"I eat meat." Annie laughed again while going over a few of the selections in her head, her mouth watering as she eyeballed some of the other customers' plates.

"Good." Albert nodded. "South Beach must've been good to you, then. You look beautiful. Radiant. The sunshine must've been what you needed."

Leg crossed over a knee, she swung a foot side to side under the table, blushed, and tugged at the hem of her skirt. She felt beautiful. Wearing a brand-new black shift dress, hair pinned up, lost pieces falling out and framing her face. She started to fidget with the silver feather dangling from her ear.

"Did Mom tell you I want to buy a car?" Annie asked several minutes later, after the two of them had made some small talk, precisely as their dinner arrived.

"No, she didn't tell me, but I think it's a great idea." Albert tipped his head at the waiter, dismissing him. "I would like to buy it for you."

"I can afford a car." She took a sip of her stiff drink.

"Annie…" Fork and knife in hand, crisscrossed over his prime rib, Albert sat forward, glaring at her. "You went to college on scholarship. You worked your ass off at that restaurant. Let me buy you a goddamn car. Enough with the humility. I don't know where you get that from. It's certainly not from me, and we know it isn't from Beverly."

"I get that from Peter," Annie replied, her heart lodged in her throat. "He taught me."

Albert glanced at his daughter. Quickly. "It's been a hell of a year." Picking up his martini, he stared off into the distance. "I should say"—his brows pinched together—"this last year has been hell."

Annie swallowed only hurt and pain — months of grieving she didn't know how to keep in motion without dropping all the death balls on the floor.

"How are you doing"—she reached out a hand—"really?"

"You know…" His gaze shifted back and forth. "I think of Peter every five minutes of my day instead of every minute. So, it's getting better." Wrapping a palm around the stem of his glass, he nodded at its contents. "I keep a bottle of this stuff at my desk."

"Dad," she said as she watched his eyes darken. She'd given up trying to hold his hand.

"That damn kid..." He shook his head, ruffing fingers beneath his chin. "That damn bike."

"He rode because he loved life." Annie sighed, trying to duct-tape herself together for the both of them. Always. "He wouldn't have lived any other way."

Albert looked away.

Fine, she thought. *He won't meet my gaze now. Fine.*

They began to eat. In silence. A couple minutes later, Albert ordered a second martini. Annie declined. Only one drink, and she could feel the Grey Goose in her legs.

"Your mother tells me you met some guy in Miami." That twinkle lit her father's hazel eyes again, making them look both brown and green.

"Since when do you talk to my mother about stuff like that?"

"We've talked more since Peter— We talk. We're friends."

"I did." Annie couldn't help but grin. "I met someone." The bastard and his need for *time,* and Cal could still make her grin. "I'm in love with him."

Her father only stared at her, cross-examining her, studying her. Annie swung her foot around. She began to perspire. Waiting for him to reply. To say something. Anything. *Come on, Dad.* The piece of meat she'd decided to stuff into her mouth finally went down.

Swiping his napkin across his lips, Albert picked up his fresh drink, the one the server had just dropped off, and took a sip.

Here it comes...

"And this man..." He cleared his throat, set the glass back down, and peered into her eyes. "Does he love you?"

Annie crossed, then uncrossed her ankles while fidgeting with the freaking earring. She shuffled the food around on her plate. Then she glanced up and met her father's discerning gaze.

Which was a mistake.

"Ahhh, Annie, there should be no hesitation. *Does he love you?*"

Annie swallowed and swallowed. "I thought he did." She exhaled, chewing on her bottom lip. "I-I don't know."

"Well, he's one lucky bastard to have your love." Her father stared at her for a few seconds, then he shook his head and smiled. "I hope he at least knows that."

"He knows." Annie deflated and grinned.

"Love isn't easy, is it, doodlebug?" Albert sighed, let go of his fork, and peered at his plate. "I'm getting a divorce."

"What?"

"Christ." The napkin crinkled in his fist. "Number three."

"What happened?"

"I'm surprised your mother didn't tell you. I think she's enjoying watching me squirm." He took a generous sip of his drink. "Monica said ... ahem ... a part of me died ... with him." He coughed. "Maybe she's right." Albert shrugged. "All I know is we've been miserable."

"I'm sorry." Annie touched his wrist, rubbing her fingers over the veins there. "I guess we're both unlucky in love." She raised her water glass, sporting a smile — because she didn't really believe that. There was nothing *unlucky* about giving her love to someone else. Even if it hurt. The pain taught her things as well. About herself. About what it was like to let go of expectations and surrender to the unknown. "Shall we drink to that?"

Her father smiled wider than she'd seen all night. "You really are something, Annie Rebekah Baxter." Albert chuckled. "Damn! It's good to see your face." He smoothed his fingers over his clean-shaven chin, a glimmer in his eyes as he reached across the table and took her hand. "I love you."

"I know, Dad." Annie squeezed his palm. "I love you, too."

Albert removed his jacket and placed it over his daughter's shoulders along with his arm as they walked to the car.

"You look so grown."

"I'm done growing, for God's sake, and you just saw me in June."

"I know. But I think I'm going to see my little girl and I see a woman instead."

"I'm still your little girl." She leaned her head against him for a moment and took in a deep breath. "You can actually smell the fall, and it's barely September. God, I've missed home."

They stopped in front of the vehicle, but instead of unlocking the door, Albert scratched his temple with the key.

"What is it?"

"What does he do, Annie?" Her father's tone changed. He stood taller, stiffer, wearing his face that brokered no time for sass or shit.

"What?" Her brows pinched together. Her eyes narrowed.

"The guy. What does he do? For work?"

"He has a name."

"I don't know it," Albert strained, then clapped a hand over his mouth.

"Must you always be so concerned with work?" She slipped off the wool jacket and held it out by a finger.

Glaring at Annie, he wrapped the blazer around her again. "I'm concerned about *you*." He tugged the lapels closed. "What's his goddamn name?"

"Cal. Calvin Prescott."

"What does Cal do for work, Annie?"

"He buys things and sells them."

Albert palmed her biceps, smirked, then looked to the sky.

"It's not like that."

"How do you know?"

"Because I trust him."

"What kinds of things does he sell?"

"He deals mostly in commercial land development. He puts together real estate contracts, the financing. He scouts and networks with potential clients. It's tedious, really, Dad. He's partners with John Allen. I can't believe Mom didn't tell you that. She seems to know everything."

"No." He shook his head; his posture relaxed. "No, your mother didn't tell me much. Only his ag—"

"Dad..." Annie could feel her Go-Go-Gadget eyes pop out of her head.

"I've not said a word..." Albert kissed her forehead and opened the car door. Annie took a seat, but her father only lingered, cradling the doorframe of the SUV, his chin tilted toward the concrete, his eyes remaining fixed on Annie.

"What is it now? Do you want your jacket back?" She shoved off her heels and ran her soles over the tops of her feet.

"No, silly." He moved a strand of hair from her eyes.

"It's Cal's age?" she whispered.

"No." He smiled and shook his head.

"Then what? What is it?"

"*Your work*, Annie. How is it going?"

"I told you..." She rolled her eyes. "I'm going to California to meet—"

"I know, I know," he replied, scrubbing a palm under his chin.

"Then what?"

"You're not losing interest in photography ... because of this relationship?"

"No." She tensed, stopped moving her feet. "You know me better than that."

"Yes, I do. But I've never seen you like this."

"What are you talking about?"

"What you feel ... for this man. It's different?"

Planting her elbows on her thighs, she dropped her face into her palms.

"Annie..." Albert touched her back.

"I feel..." She lifted her head and stared outside. *Crazy. Mad. Sick. Elated. Home. Safe.*

"It's okay. Take your time."

Relaxing her shoulders, Annie peered at her father as she pondered Cal, preparing to exhale truth and feelings and the *different* everyone she loved seemed to notice.

"I feel like I've always known him," she began in a hush. "Or I want to always know him. He... Cal sees me so clearly sometimes it scares me." Annie swallowed. "Yes, it's different. I love Cal in a way I didn't know existed."

"Oh, doodlebug..." Albert sighed, taking his daughter's hand.

What's next? she thought. *Fairy-tale princess forever, white picket fences, dogs and cats. Babies Cal said he didn't want to make.*

What did Annie want?

A million reasons to go on.

Beauty, love, her camera.

What did she need?

True friends, her family, a shoulder to rest her head on.

Me.

Annie couldn't keep running from her demons or her strength or her own needs.

Being afraid belonged to yesterday.

Maybe love could be forever. It didn't have to die. Death might take away a body, a beating heart, a life, but it couldn't kill love.

Ever. Ever. Ever.

FIFTY-FIVE

Day four. Scene twenty-six.

Quiet on the set.

Action.

Another day in Beverly's house, and if it hadn't already been difficult enough living with an alcohol-dependent narcissist, missing Cal made it worse. Actually, Cal made it worse with his incessant messages. Or maybe he made it better. Annie didn't know anymore.

She felt unhinged. On a table, ready for open heart surgery without the anesthesia. Her mother held the gas mask, and Cal held the scalpel. The man had been tearing her heart up with each text he'd sent. With each fucking song. He'd started blowing up her phone on Tuesday morning.

So much for time and distance.

Annie: Don't text me again while I'm gone. You said no phone calls or messages. You asked for time. Take it.

Cal: I miss you.

Annie: I can't.

Cal: You can. Do you have any idea how strong you are?

Annie knew she was strong. But when Cal posed the question, it changed something inside her. Or lit her on fire. Or his words gave her the permission she needed to fully realize who she already knew she was. Except, Cal didn't get to play the boyfriend or cheerleader.

He held the scalpel.

But didn't the person wielding the instrument in the operating room usually save the patient? *I don't need saving.* She needed loving.

This was one of the ways he showed it, though. Through music.

Annie: You don't get to do this.

Cal: ???

Annie: Send me songs. Tell me stuff about me. Don't play dumb. Doesn't suit you.

Cal: Did you purchase your return ticket?

Annie: Don't ask me any more questions either.

Cal: You made a promise.

Annie: Don't!

Cal: What DO I get to do?

Annie: Miss me. Take your time. Miss me.

Cal: Are you drinking?

Annie: Go away.

Cal: I'm calling you.

Annie: I won't answer. Stop texting me.

Cal: Another rule to add to the no touching or looking or wanting?

Annie: Please. No more songs. You're pushing AND pulling. Which is it? Love me or time?

Cal: I won't text you.

Of course, give him an ultimatum, and he can make a snap decision no problem.

Annie scrolled through his older texts, the songs. She'd been trying to ignore them. They were both unexpected and expected, and they tore her wide-open-operate-on-me-on-the-table heart right out of her chest, serenaded it, then set a flipping match to it.

He'd said he needed time. But time meant thinking and deciding, not suffering or drowning or ripping or pulling. Not surgery. It wasn't tug-of-war. It wasn't red-rover-red-rover-send-Annie-right-over.

The last song he'd sent — *right now* — was Bruno Mars. The fucker. Not Bruno — Cal. Choosing a song he didn't know very well or like. He knew she liked it. Had set her ringtone to it. Well, thank you very much, Cal Prescott. She wouldn't be able to hear "Just the Way You Are" again without thinking of him. She wouldn't be able to listen to any of the songs they'd shared since "She's So Heavy" because they all wailed, "Cal, Cal, Cal!"

Enough.

She shut the phone off.

Off!

If he called, he would get voicemail. He would get...

Wait for it...

Time.

Jim Croce understood.

Put that in your bottle, Cal. See how far it takes you.

FIFTY-SIX

The bright-red car Albert had bought his daughter shined in the middle of Beverly's gravelly driveway. The trunk open. All four doors ajar.

Annie's mother stood a few feet away, sporting an oversized bathrobe and holding a lit cigarette, habitually flicking the ashes and mussing with her hair while Annie secured the last few essentials she needed.

"I don't want you to drive at night." Beverly smashed the cigarette beneath the sole of her white shoes and came closer. "And don't go off alone, wandering and daydreaming."

Annie rolled her eyes, set her camera on the front seat, and closed all the doors to the car except her own as she mentally ticked off the items she'd packed, making sure she had everything.

"Have you decided if you're going to move in with me?"

As the sunlight made its way between the branches of the trees and around the variety of greenish-amber leaves, Annie shivered. The morning was unusually cool. Or she'd spent a summer in humidity and heat and had forgotten real cold. Or perhaps she'd adapted to being a Floridian — a person who thought sixty-five degrees warranted pulling out a fleece sweater and a pair of boots.

"I'm sure I will be for the time being." Annie took her place in the driver's seat. "You know we can talk about this when I get back."

"You'll be flying out to Miami when you get back."

"So, *now* is a good time? When I'm leaving?" Annie gripped the steering wheel and gazed straight ahead. Everything *was* packed. Ready. She was finally going, doing exactly what she'd wanted to do for so long. This should've been a happy moment, an easy one, but whatever she felt — frustration or resentment or lack of contentment — Annie seemed incapable of expressing any other emotion besides apathy or anger. "Right now?"

"Annie..." Beverly fluffed her copper bangs. "No time has felt like a good time to talk to you ... about anything."

The hold Annie had over the wheel softened. She glanced at her mother. "I'm sorry." She sighed. "I know, and I'm sorry." She started the engine. "I'll call you tonight once I get settled."

Bending forward, Bev planted a kiss on her daughter's forehead. "I love you."

Annie looked up, blinking, seeing only the trees and that light and those golden leaves.

FIFTY-SEVEN

Previously undefinable emotions morphed into things Annie could actually name as she drove south on I-5. Like peace and happiness. Bliss. Even the way the wind blew over her skin felt sensational, especially against her left arm, which freely floated out the open window near the side mirror, dancing and bobbing to the beat of "Everyday is a Winding Road."

The song quite appropriate at the moment.

Driving transported Annie to a place where not much else existed, making her aware of only herself and the earth, the road and the tress. No time. No Mom or Dad or Cal or aggravation or voices. No one to tell her what was wrong or right. Only the crisp Pacific air and Sheryl Crow keeping her company inside the brand-new Volkswagen Jetta.

A couple hours later, Annie ignored her mother's well-intentioned advice and decided to wander off and daydream. She detoured off the interstate toward the 363-mile stretch of coast in Oregon, beginning in Astoria. First, she climbed the town's famous Column, walked breathlessly to the top of the circular staircase, and was rewarded with a spectacular view: the Columbia River, Young's Bay, evergreens and spruce trees, and an incredible vista of the Pacific Ocean.

She took pictures that looked like postcards.

Next, she headed south along the 101, stopping at a few seaside towns, searching for the unique, the unseen, the forgotten.

Daydreaming. Wandering. Loving life.

She trotted along pathways near water, photographing lighthouses, boaters, tourists, children, and hundreds of inanimate objects. Taking the ordinary and making it extraordinary, she filled up a hole inside her soul that could only be sealed by spending time with her herself and her Nikon.

Wednesday, Annie arrived at her intended destination, Carmel-by-the-Sea, California. A lovely, tucked-away village located right off the Pacific Coast Highway.

Carmel stood out like Venus next to all the other stars in the sky.

The town had attracted artists for decades. Now, Annie would be counting herself amongst them. One of the creatives, the people searching for a little bit of heaven, a slice of peace.

After checking into her room, Annie walked over to the beach and took a stroll near the shoreline, the ocean always being a place she felt understood and comforted.

Waiting for the sunset, she plopped onto the sand and cradled her camera. Getting lost in the orange and purple horizon and melting yellow sun, the breeze was all she felt — that and the way she curled her toes into the warm dirt. Taking pictures and observing nature until the white sand became part of her skin, until all thoughts slipped beneath the water alongside the last trickle of daylight.

Back at the inn, after looking over her portfolio for the hundredth time, Annie fell asleep in the king-sized bed, nestled up beside her catalogue and aspirations, dreaming of moving forward, embracing her strength, facing fears and life and people and curators ... because tomorrow, a new day full of possibilities would begin.

FIFTY-EIGHT

The next morning, Annie stepped from the car, wearing a sleeveless gray dress and a pair of pink heels. Cradling a portfolio under her arm, she made her way toward the gallery, a striking building on a corner in downtown Carmel.

"Hi," Annie said to the woman she encountered after entering, "I'm here to see Mr. Turner." Her pulse raced. Perhaps, she'd waited too long to do this — meet people, move forward, show her work. She swallowed, stood straight, and held her chest out. "My name is Annie Baxter."

"Hello, I'm Janet," the woman replied, slicking her silver bob back as she extended a hand. "I'll let him know you've arrived."

Sunlight streamed through the large, arch-shaped windows making up the storefront, shining across the bamboo floors, causing much of the art inside to glisten, illuminating what the common observer might not otherwise notice: shading, textures. The start of something magnificent. Annie did a full three-sixty, taking in as much of the unique space and its contents as time would allow.

"Hello," came a deep voice from behind. The photographer shook some and turned around. "You must be Annie."

A smile on her face, she stuck her palm out. "You must be Mr. Turner."

"I'm Brian." He took her hand, his grip delicate, his tone not only deep but laced with a hint of Irish ... or something. "Please, don't call me Mr. Turner."

Annie's smile stretched a bit wider as she peered into his brown eyes, meeting the carob color perfectly level thanks to the height of her pink pumps. The curator had a ruggedly handsome face, a jaw filled with stubble, and crinkles stretching outward from the corners of his eyelids.

"I see you've been admiring the art," he went on and glanced over the room. "I didn't mean to stun you."

Annie dropped her chin and laughed a little. "It's the pieces that are stunning." Her gaze traveled to a nearby painting, the one she'd been examining when he'd approached. Reds, greens, and yellows along with an obscene black all raised off the canvas, a topography to rival a planet's terrain.

"Do you like abstracts?" Mr. Turner asked, and Annie could feel his eyes combing her profile. The side of her face.

"I like everything." Stepping back to gain another perspective, Annie tilted her head to the side, watching the non-uniformed formations, bleeding and dripping. The way the light danced with the colors, kissing the textures.

The undefinable piece dominated her senses, causing her to feel things she couldn't articulate, euphoria being the only word she could translate. She wanted to reach out and touch the painting or climb into it, the way she had wanted to jump into Dimitri's cherry trees.

"The artist is a woman," Brian said, interrupting her internal musings. "Most of our pieces right now, in fact, are by women."

"The sex doesn't matter to me." Annie pulled hair from her lips and glanced at him, then she looked at the painting again.

"Excuse me?"

Annie found herself foolishly attempting to name the nameless even though her heart accepted the abstract at face value, as it was, without border, without demarcation. Presence needed no labeling.

"The sex of the artist," Annie continued, as if there hadn't been a pause or an *excuse me*. She turned toward him, her portfolio still tucked under her arm. "The sex doesn't matter. Not to me. I think art should be valued the same whether it was created by a man or a woman. It should be viewed without filter."

The curator, Mr. Turner, Brian — the man with the accent and the stubble and the few stands of coal-colored hair that kept falling across his forehead — looked Annie right in the eye, viewing her the same as before when he'd stared at her profile.

She smiled.

He cleared his throat.

Then he invited her to his office, and they took a seat.

"You have an interesting point of view," he began, thumbing through her photographs one by one, his attention split between looking at the originals and glancing at Annie. She sat across from him. "You capture truth."

Leaning closer to the desk, Annie peered into the file, scanning images she'd seen hundreds of times. The sides of her high heels met the wood flooring, her feet flexing awkwardly, her cheeks taking a bruising as she bit their insides.

"I think we can exhibit you in the winter, maybe mid-January," he said, his expression giving nothing away as he closed the book and handed it to her over the top of the desk. "Will that work for you?"

"Yes. Perfect," Annie replied, contemplating for a split second where she might be in January. Her bottom lip may have been between her teeth.

"Are you sure?" Now, his face read scrutable. He smiled, his carob eyes lighting up.

"Yes." Annie grinned and deflated.

"I'll have Janet email you the paperwork." He offered her his card. "Look over the agreement and call with any questions." As he stood, he grabbed a pack of cigarettes off the paper-strewn desk.

"Thank you." Annie joined him, and they once again shook hands. This time, his grip was firmer. "I'm looking forward to it."

"Do you mind if I walk out with you? I want to have a smoke."

"Sure." Annie glanced at him as they made their way through the gallery. "You can tell me more about Carmel."

"You mean you've never been to our world-renowned, little tourist mecca?" He held open the front door.

"No." Annie laughed. Her cheeks were probably red. The color of her car, the one they made their way closer to as they strolled along the sidewalk, beneath the bright sun, chatting.

Between puffs, Brian told Annie about some of the sights to see and places to eat. He told her how long he'd lived here. He also informed her the town frowned upon public smoking while he repeatedly tucked the falling strands of his wayward hair back into place.

"Actually, I would like to take you to dinner." He extinguished the cigarette beneath his shoe, then picked it up and tossed it into a trash can. "How long do you plan on being here?"

Annie glanced at his stubble-covered chin but wouldn't meet his gaze, the sunshine blinding her. "I don't know."

"You don't know how long you'll be in town?" He grinned. "Or you don't know if you want to have dinner with me?"

Two simple questions — and Annie thought of Cal.

Well, she didn't actually have to *think* of Cal because he was always there, never leaving her mind or heart, reminding her of who she was and challenging her to go forward rather than backward.

Annie knew the time Cal needed included not speaking by phone — no texting, no email, nothing — a complete separation. By choice. His choice first, the decision he'd obviously ignored. And now, hers, after she'd told him to stop sending songs. Despite this mutual understanding of sorts, a sharp pain rushed through Annie's entire body from head to foot, stabbing her all over.

She met the eyes of the curator, trying to ignore the light, squinting. "I'm leaving Saturday. I can do dinner."

"Where are you staying?" he asked as she looked past him and gave him the name of the inn.

"I'll pick you up at eight."

"Tonight?"

"Yeah." He smiled, peering at her the same as before. The way she'd viewed the abstract. Like she was the art and he was the patron, waiting to dive inside the frame and explore the canvas.

Fifty-Nine

Throughout most of dinner, Annie listened while Brian talked about his life, his ex-wife and his mother, his old jobs and his new one, his conversation heavily peppered with what seemed to be his favorite word: fuck. The curator paused only when needing to take in more air as a chunk of coal hair repeatedly fell across his forehead, covering his eyes, and Annie found herself hypnotized by the way he pushed it back into the crowd — over and over.

After about an hour or so of this routine, Annie appreciated more than ever the security she felt whenever she was near Cal. Never before had she respected the understated, quiet man's fierce need for privacy quite the way she did right now.

"You don't have much to say," Brian said after paying the check.

Annie thanked him, then shrugged. "You seemed like you needed to get some things off your chest."

"It's been an interesting year, to say the least."

Annie struggled to keep her mouth from hanging open. She merely blinked.

"Let me walk you back." He stood, then pulled out her chair. "It's not far, and it's nice out."

The moment they stepped outside, a light breeze danced with the hem of Annie's skirt and mussed her hair. Brian's locks surely had fallen out of place again too. But she only looked ahead as they strolled down the sidewalk. Her inn was only a few blocks away.

For several minutes, Annie enjoyed the quiet. Only the sound of the ocean, a few cars, and the noise the BIC made as Brian lit a cigarette. Apparently, the curator had finally run out of things to talk about. Which felt a little weird. But then he surprised Annie by taking her palm and threading his fingers through hers.

Annie's heart thumped in her ears.

This was wrong.

Felt wrong.

It was so fucking wrong.

Still, they said nothing. Neither of them. For the duration of the walk.

"This is me." Annie stopped a few feet shy of the cottage door and removed her hand from his, feigning a smile.

Brian gazed into her eyes.

She swallowed.

"Thank you." Annie readied her key and turned toward the door. "I had a good time."

Brian followed her up the single step, leaned into the wall like he was James Dean, and stared at her profile, smelling of the cigarette he'd smoked on the way and the tequila he'd swallowed with dinner. The same piece of wayward hair fell into his eyes. *Pick it up, man. Cut it.*

"Annie..." he whispered, trailing an index finger down her arm.

"Brian..." Annie exhaled, turned, and met his eyes. "I'm not available."

"I thought you said you weren't married." He smiled.

"No." She held her breath. Cal filled her vision. "I'm not married."

"Then invite me in."

"You don't understand." Her gaze combed the concrete, her shoes, then his face. "I'm..."

"Hung up on someone."

"In love with someone."

"You didn't mention him." He coughed. "At dinner."

"You didn't ask." Annie managed a slight grin. "I'm sorry if I gave you the wrong impression. I wanted to go out. But only as your friend."

Brian took the Newports from his pant pocket and shook a smoke out of the pack. "You're right." He tapped the filter against his thigh. "We'll be working together. It's not a good idea." He met her gaze. "I'm sorry, too. I guess I got a little carried away."

"I'm really looking forward to January." She smiled. "This is a lovely little — what did you call it? Tourist mecca."

After stashing the unlit cigarette over an ear, Brian came closer and took Annie's hand. She could feel him peering at her profile, making those Bambi eyes again.

"Can I kiss you goodnight?" he uttered. "Just a kiss."

The inflection she heard in his tone had her aching ... but not for him. Or his touch. Or his kiss.

Annie ached for only one man.

"You're so beautiful," Brian whispered as he turned her head toward his and cradled her jaw.

Before Annie could make sense of what was happening, his lips touched hers and his beard scratched her skin. His body was close, too close, uncomfortably close, everywhere she didn't want him.

Pressing her hands against his chest, Annie shifted her face to the side and pulled away. Her eyes wide. Her heart frantic.

"I guess that was a bad idea too." Taking the cigarette from behind his ear, Brian shoved it in his mouth, lit it, and stepped back.

Annie watched a trail of smoke leave his lungs and get taken by the wind. Pieces of hair fell into his eyes as she placed the key into the slot and opened the door to her room. After stepping over the threshold, she glanced over her shoulder and looked at Brian as he exhaled and stroked his beard.

"This won't affect January."

"I'm not that kind of guy," he replied with a faint smile.

Annie nodded and said, "Good night," as she closed the door, locked it, then immediately sank all her weight against it.

Fuck, Annie. What were you thinking?

Raising a shaking palm to her lips, she began to cry. Silently. Then she started to bite the skin of a finger until her teeth left marks, until she could feel something other than the pit in her gut and the hole in her heart. Sniffling, she wiped beneath her nose and tore off her shoes. After throwing them across the room, she made her way to the bathroom, now sobbing uncontrollably but quietly — the emotions behind a dam.

As she leaned over the bathroom sink, hands on the countertop, she stared at her face in the mirror, her breathing shallow, her eyes red, her palms shaking more than at the outset.

The stain of that kiss had been wrong.

His lips, his touch…

Everything about him — wrong.

Her stomach churned as she peered past the girl whose summer had begun with so many promises, her sadness being replaced with anger. Fear. Then she dropped to her knees in front of the toilet, gripped the bowl, and vomited. Violently. Crying and shaking, she puked until she dry heaved, until she was an eye-watering, nose-running, hair-knotted mess.

Several minutes later, she flushed the toilet, wiped her mouth, and swallowed some tap water from the sink. Sitting on the floor and resting against the outside of the tub, she stared at the outdated wallpaper, thinking of Cal.

Was he kissing someone else as well?

Grimacing, she shifted her head, realizing what she'd told her father last week had been true. Annie did trust Cal. She was the one acting like a fool. She regretted telling Cal not to message her anymore. She could've used a song right about now.

Annie got up, removed her clothing, and started the shower. Before stepping into the warm water, she retrieved her phone, realizing she could pull up any one of Prescott's handpicked selections at any time. She chose one of the most recent ones, a link he'd sent prior to the texting ban. Annie could stand to hear it — the way Bogie had managed to listen to Sam play "As Time Goes By" in *Casablanca*.

A favorite of his, Cal had said, referring to Billie Holiday's version and not Eddie Vedder's. However, he'd sent both songs, explaining their differences of course. Right now, Annie preferred Vedder's take on the classic, off his album *Ukulele Songs*.

The man's unique voice echoed throughout the bathroom, proclaiming love, a haunting, profound love. Steam fogged the glass, wet the wallpaper. Yet, as Annie stood under the balm of the steaming hot water, listening to "More Than You Know," she only heard Cal.

His voice. His sentiments. His love.

The best things in life were meant to be felt, not understood. Like getting caught in a rainstorm on the streets of South Beach during the summer. Or the way the water felt now. Beading over her skin, creating a myriad of sensations, a multitude of emotions.

Annie *felt* Cal wherever she went.

And that was the one thing she did know. For certain.

PROCRASTINATION

THE PUTTING OFF, INTENTIONALLY AND
HABITUALLY, OF DOING SOMETHING THAT
SHOULD BE DONE

too early
too late
live
without regret
fears
sidestepped
no waiting
only now
sky sun clouds
ocean eyes
forming words
your lips won't speak
making
silent promises
to me
us
making life
I have every intention of keeping

SIXTY

Annie sat at the Allens' table in the nook across from Maggie, nauseous and exhausted and drinking hot tea on a Friday morning.

Which wasn't unusual — not this week, anyway.

The photographer had felt sick and sleepy for days, especially since arriving back in Miami on Tuesday. Initially, Annie assumed her symptoms had been due to the anxiety she felt in preparing to move away.

But.

First impressions were often wrong.

She lifted the mug of chamomile to her lips, her hand starting to slightly shake, as she attempted to decipher exactly when she'd first started to feel sick.

Translation: to precisely when she'd had her last period.

Fuck.

Still cradling the mug, now nibbling its rim, her stomach clenched, then dropped. She couldn't remember her last period. The entire summer seemed to have flown by in a blur, more so after returning from New York City in July.

Maybe her cycle was only late.

Well, it was always late. Never on time. Always irregular. But now, the atypical made her heart skip a beat. Or two or three. Or several. It had been too many days. How many? *Count. Count. Count. Goddammit*. Her breasts had hurt for, what? Two weeks.

Exhaustion, sore breasts, nausea.

Annie set the mug down and looked toward the window, her upper body twisting most awkwardly in the chair, one of her hands cradling the top rung, as she met her reflection in the glass.

Becoming acutely aware she'd begun to visibly change — ironically, like a chameleon — she turned a variety of shades before finally settling on pale. Her eyes stark, almost blank, she peered out at the ocean but only saw fog.

An early morning one.

She couldn't see anything else.

But herself.

Every muscle in her body went limp. Except one. Her heart. It beat faster, vehemently. Acid shot up her esophagus.

"Are you okay?" Maggie asked, sounding far away, like in a dream. Or in a tunnel. "Is the tea helping to settle your stomach?"

Annie continued to stare into the distance, thinking about the last time she was with Cal — the only time he hadn't worn a condom.

The. Only. Time.

The night he'd pinned her against the wall in the alley, mad with passion.

How could she be pregnant?

Annie shouldn't have even been ovulating then. Fuck. Not that she'd ever been an expert at tracking her cycle.

But come on. One time.

One fucking time they'd had sex without a condom — the entire summer. This could not be happening. Besides, she'd reassured Cal that this wasn't a possibility. They'd discussed it — children. God. Right. Children. Cal had said he never wanted any. He'd also said one day Annie would want to be a mother.

Did she want to be a mom?

Out of all the things Cal had told her that day, all she could focus on — besides the possibility of a pregnancy — was the one thing he hadn't said to her. Yet she trusted all the ways Cal had spoken those three words to her, anyway. The way he'd made her *feel* them over and over and over.

Don't you know how I feel about you every time I touch you? She knew how he felt. Just like she knew she was pregnant.

Instinct.

And she could not be pregnant. Not now. Not at twenty-five, ready to travel the world. She was merely irregular ... like always.

Suck it up, she thought. *Mask on your face. Breathe.*

"Annie," Maggie said and reached a palm across the table. "Are you okay?"

"What day is it?" Annie glanced over her shoulder.

"It's Friday, sweetie."

"No, what's the date?"

Maggie touched her phone screen, staring at Annie like she had two heads. "It's the twelfth."

Annie got up and stepped closer to the window. Her eyes became slits, peering out at nature. The morning sun had disappeared. Ominous clouds filled the sky as far as she could see, the impending storm matching her mood. An eerie stillness, the calm before the necessary intrusion.

Annie inhaled, her hands again beginning to tremble. Had her last period started the night the four of them had dinner here?

"I realized I have some shopping to do." Annie faced her friend and tried to smile, but instead twitched. Taking air deep into the pockets of her lungs, she swallowed several breaths. She hadn't had a panic attack since that evening at Cal's. "Tab's anniversary is coming up. I want to find her something before I leave."

"Do you want to go out today?" Maggie asked, her brows pinching together. Maybe Annie had grown a third head by now. "Let me take you. I have some things to pick up too."

Annie managed an "Okay," even though she really wanted to politely say, "No, thank you."

Lunch. Shopping. And a pregnancy test.

Another normal day.

The sky inferred it was anything but.

Annie remained for a moment at the large window in the nook. She heard the rain fall before she saw it. It seemed to drop faster than she could process thoughts, spilling from the melancholy clouds in sheets. Buckets.

Mesmerized, Annie squinted toward the sea, the ocean barely visible amidst the onslaught of rain. But she knew it was there. The wind blew fast and hard, replacing the haunting stillness of moments ago. The pressure beat against the windows, tapped the glass, whipped violently through the palm fronds. But the sounds of the storm and the crack of thunder couldn't drown out her thoughts or fears.

I'm pregnant. I know I'm pregnant.

Her inner voice became a loud whimper as lightning struck and thunder cracked.

She had no doubt.
Flash. Snap. Crack.
She was pregnant.

The rain had come and gone, but the peculiar mood remained as the two women returned home, shopping complete, test bought discreetly. Annie told Maggie she was going upstairs to rest.

And so, she went upstairs to do anything but that.

Once in her bedroom, Annie stopped, twirled some hair, and glanced around the space. It looked the way it had when she'd first arrived in Florida. Devoid of self, except for the picture frames sitting on the floor, leaning against the walls, even lining the walk-in.

Everything felt different as well. Would pregnancy make her different? *Had* Miami changed her — the way her father had inferred?

Like a man loosening a tie in a haste, Annie began to claw at her neck as she placed her purse on the bed. After finally unzipping the main pocket, she stared down at its contents as though looking at a grave. Her heartbeat slowed then climbed its way up toward her throat and tapped the veins.

Stroking, grabbing, and pinching the skin there, Annie couldn't get the necktie loose enough.

A pregnancy.

A baby.

No.

Not a baby.

Work.

Not a baby.

Photography. Carmel. Her life. Her plans. What plans? There were no plans. *I'm not Cal. I don't master plan. I don't play chess.*

Nine months of a new plan. Eighteen years of one.

Annie kept looking down at the purse, glaring at the test, continuing to think yet drawing blanks, ready to burst into flames. By the time she finally grabbed the box, her entire body had begun to shake. She would combust. Actually fucking combust.

Once she made it to the bathroom, Annie carefully read the directions: Two lines equaled pregnant. One line equaled not pregnant.

She took note of the time on her phone — 2:56 — and sat on the toilet, wet the strip, and waited. 2:57. 2:58. Annie stood, buttoned, washed. She wouldn't even glance at the damn thing until the time on her phone allowed her. Instead, she looked in the mirror.

She didn't see herself, though.

Annie saw a girl who should've taken a morning-after pill. She wouldn't have swallowed one anyway. Looking away from the eyes of the unknown, she waited. Her palms pressed into the countertop, her toe knuckles bent, beads of sweat gathering at her armpits.

Annie waited, suffocating.

She waited.

Waited.

The five minutes an eternity.

Then the clock struck 3:01.

She looked down at the obtrusive, plastic stick where it rested comfortably against toilet tissue on the countertop, picked it up, and held it closer to her face, confirming her eyes hadn't deceived her. But there was no mistaking it. Two pink lines shown in the window.

Two lines. Not one.

Pregnant.

Annie was pregnant with a baby she wasn't ready for by a man who had said he never wanted to be a father — by a man who wasn't man enough to tell her he loved her. Out loud.

Terrified, she set the stupid thing back on the counter and shook. Uncontrollably. Violently. Shaking more than she had in the kitchen. More than in the bedroom or on the toilet. Annie shook. Shit, she might puke.

Taking one last look at the two lines — one solid pink and the other faint but present, definitely present — she crumpled all the evidence up while uttering quiet, broken sounds. Then she stuffed it all down into her bathroom trash can — the fucking test, the panic, the tears she forbade release.

The anxiety wouldn't fit inside the cylinder. A square peg in a round hole.

She heaved, beginning to hyperventilate.

No. No. No. No panic attack.

Annie sat on the closed lid of the toilet and leaned forward, lifting her heels off the floor and curling her toes forward. Elbows resting on her knees, she put her palms on her forehead, her hands in her hair, and concentrated on breathing.

Breathe.

Fuck.

Breathe.

She pulled on the strands harshly, grabbing them, wishing to feel something, anything but the sensation of doom. Of death. Of dying. Of her head starting to pulsate. Of her face catching fire.

Annie sat there on the edge of the toilet, on the edge of no-fucking-reason, pulling her hair, breathing and breathing and breathing, and she remained there for several minutes — until she was so weary and exhausted from the aftereffects of the panic attack, the only thing left whirling around inside her brain weren't thoughts of a baby but the need she had to climb beneath the sheets and dream.

SIXTY-ONE

The sun set on the other side of the Allens' home. The ocean was calm. And the nook was wonderfully cozy as usual, the glow from the chandelier casting shadows and shapes along the only wall in the room without a window. Annie glanced intermittently at the gray spots dancing across it as they discussed their plans for the evening.

Her last evening in Florida.

It was late Saturday afternoon, and tomorrow, Annie would leave at noon. Tonight, would be a farewell meal for the three friends. For now, though, they enjoyed conversation, wine, and a snack. Maggie had melted a wedge of brie. Apricot preserves and oval crackers sat beside it. The heavenly ensemble was nearly gone.

Talking, laughing, and munching, Annie took turns eyeing the speckled wall and the ocean, the other friend she couldn't bear to leave, while trying to ignore the stinging in the pit of her stomach.

She was doing a marvelous job.

Emotions wrapped.

Pregnancy a secret.

Eating crackers and cheese and smiling.

It was the finest performance she'd ever given. Tabitha would've been proud. But alas, the feat was interrupted by the old-fashioned ringtone coming from John's cell phone.

Apparently, he couldn't hide *his* feelings. John's jovial expression changed the moment he swiped the screen and said hello.

"No," John said into the phone, and Annie's face fell. Cheese, crackers, apricots, nor Maggie's good intentions were unable to stop it. "We're goin' out. It's not a good time." He shook his head. "What happened?" John paused while Maggie and Annie hung onto every word of the one-sided conversation. "I don't think that's a good idea." A half second passed. "I told you. We're gettin' ready to go out." Pause. "Yes. With Maggie. What the hell is goin' on?"

If Annie thought John's face had changed before, she'd been wrong. Now, it transformed into something ugly, something she'd never wanted to witness again:

Shock.

"What?" Annie blurted, then covered her mouth.

John eyeballed Annie, then nodded. "Yes." A blip of a second passed. "A couple of days." Five of his fingernails danced across the tabletop. "Fine." John punched the red button on the screen.

Annie stood, her chair tipping backward as she went, but John caught it and called out, "Annie," as she clutched her stomach and rushed toward the kitchen.

"You told him I was here?" Annie cried the moment she reached some sort of safety, keeping her back to both of them.

"He asked." John met her at the countertop near the sink, his voice like a lullaby. "I'm not goin' to lie."

"Let's go out *now*," Maggie interjected loudly from the nook. John glanced over his shoulder and gave her the stink eye.

"Why did he call?" Annie muttered.

"I'll let him tell you that."

A thick lock of hair was wrapped around the end of Annie's pointer finger, twisting and looping without her consent. A baby was in her uterus without her consent. A man was on his way over. Without her consent.

She couldn't tell him. Not tonight.

The pounding in her throat started. Maybe she was coming down with something. It hurt to swallow. Rubbing her damp palms on her jeans, she looked around the kitchen for relief but found nothing.

Fridge. Stove. Dishwasher. Nothing.

And she couldn't look at John. Or she might burst. The hand he'd placed on her back for comfort was enough to make her feel like she would start to hyperventilate.

She certainly couldn't see Cal's face. Not tonight. She couldn't smell him. Couldn't be within reach of him. Couldn't swim inside his ocean.

The pain of the last few weeks had been enough to remind her she would rather leave Miami keeping the knowledge of the baby to herself. She didn't need any more heartache. No gravitational pull. No weak knees. No raw throat. No pushing *and* pulling.

Annie had nine months to work up the courage to tell Cal the baby news, and she needed all the time she could find. It would work out perfectly for Cal because time was exactly what he'd said he needed.

Now. He would have it. Plenty of it.

SIXTY-TWO

An hour or so later, the doorbell rang.

John looked at the face of his watch, then at Annie. She simply nodded, inhaled, and stood from her seat in the nook. Maggie said nothing. Surprisingly. For once.

Seconds later, the moment Annie swung open the front door, everything stopped. Only her heart beat, thumping like crazy against the walls of her chest.

Before her now.

A man stood.

In the flesh.

Hands at his sides, his fingers looking like they didn't quite know what to do with themselves. Cal didn't appear angry or proud as she'd imagined he might. He looked lost and hurt, yet he still managed to peer so far inside her, beyond the formalities, past all the bullshit, defining in an instant everything Annie had difficulty bringing to the surface.

"What ... uh..." she began, faltering over practically every letter in those two words. "What are you doing here?"

"Did you think I would let you leave Miami without saying goodbye to you?" Cal never broke contact. That damn crinkle between his eyes stood out like a firecracker. "Annie. You promised."

"I-I'm sorry for breaking it. I thought..." She bit her tongue. Hard. As she looked away, her eyes glossed. "I thought you would understand."

"No." His fingers finally found purchase. The trim of the door. He stroked the wood there. "I don't understand."

"How could you just show up here?" She swallowed, her tongue tingly and heavy. Her heart much the same. "I don't know what more you want from me."

Cal took a step forward.

Annie took a step back.

Her entire head shook as she gaped up at him. Eyes possessed. Wide. Her skin flamed. She opened her mouth, but instead of speaking, she snapped her jaw shut, turned, and rushed up the fancy staircase.

"Annie!" Cal yelled the moment he stepped over the threshold. By the time he shut the front door, she'd already met the top of the landing. Grabbing hold of the railing, Cal took a deep breath, attempting to gain some sort of composure before ascending.

What composure? he thought. He had none.

Cal Prescott, the man who always had the upper hand, a plan, *control*, failed to gather his wits about him. Fuck, he'd failed at that task since the very first night he'd met this woman. This creature. This photographer. This daydreamer.

"I think you need to leave," a familiar voice said, interrupting his conjecture.

Perfect, Cal thought, pinching the back of his neck as The Cat rounded the corner and joined him in the foyer, her eyes narrowed, her nostrils practically flaring.

"John didn't tell you why I called?"

The last thing Cal had expected to find on the other end of the line was Annie. Home from home. Breaking her promise. Sure, Cal feared he'd fucked everything up by pushing her away, but he didn't break promises — he fulfilled his end of bullshit.

"Please leave," Maggie replied. "Annie doesn't need this right now."

"When are you finally going to understand that *this* is none of your business?"

"You're in my house."

Cal dropped his chin, pinched the bridge of his nose, shook his head a little, and smirked. *Fuck.* He didn't want to see Annie off like this, in this way, in his friends' home, full of news he didn't want to deliver. Why hadn't John told Maggie why he'd called? Probably because he didn't want to be the one to tell Annie. What a fucking disaster. Lifting his head, Cal tossed one final insolent glare in Maggie's direction, then he proceeded to walk up the glossy, white staircase.

"Cal!" she yelled, striking a fist on the railing.

"Enough, Maggie," John said as he entered the room. Cal had already reached the top and disappeared from view. "Let them be."

"I can't."

"Come here." John opened his arms, and his wife fell into them.

"Annie has been off since she's been here," she muttered against his shirt. "Yesterday she was like a..." Maggie waved her hand around behind his back. "Like a statue."

"Cal's hurtin' too."

"I wish they'd never met."

"I don't think you really mean that."

Maggie picked her head up and gazed into her husband's eyes. "She loves him, you know?"

"I know," John whispered, playing with his wife's curls. "He needs her love, Mags."

"Even at her own expense?"

"We don't always choose," he said. "She needs him—"

"Like hell she needs him."

John smiled and shook his head. "She needs his love too." His gray-blue eyes looked mostly blue and a little wet, and they shone across Maggie's face like beacons.

"Maybe..."

"Wow. A maybe?" He tugged on her hair. The flattened curl straightened, then sprung. "That's progress." He smiled. "Come on, my Maggie the Cat." John slipped his fingers through hers, his drawl thickening. "Let's take a walk on the beach. They need privacy, and I have to tell you why he called."

SIXTY-THREE

The moment Annie exited her bathroom, she sucked in a sharp breath. Cal had entered her bedroom without bothering to knock, looking the same as when she'd first opened the front door.

Lost. Vulnerable. Hurt.

Their eyes locked.

"Why would you leave without seeing me?" he asked, standing about a foot away. He swallowed and swallowed. "You promised."

"The three of us were getting ready to go to dinner." Keeping her back to him, she went toward her favorite window. "I can't do this. I can't do this right now."

Cal followed, stood behind her, and peered at her reflection in the glass. "Do what?" His words spilled into her ear as his arms slipped around her waist.

Goosepimples popped all over her skin. Muscles ached. Limbs wilted.

The sound of his voice had already worked its magic downstairs, practically paralyzing her. But now, she could smell him: freshly-laundered-clothing-after-a-day-spent-at-the-beach.

Now, he used touch.

Glancing down, she considered placing her palms over his hands, her fingers through his. She felt his energy balloon around them, becoming a canopy, enveloping her soul, keeping her safe from harm and cold — a protection she longed for yet had refused for three weeks. Maybe she'd refused it all summer.

Bringing his head a little lower, he moved her hair some using only his face and nose, then he softly kissed her neck and earlobe.

"Please..." Her voice cracked. "Cal." She pushed his hands off her waist and stepped forward. "Go."

"When are you leaving?" Their eyes met in the pane.

"Tomorrow."

"It's been weeks since we've been together." He paused. Swallowed. Looked around. "Jesus Christ. You can't just—"

"I can't just, what?" Annie spun and glared at him. "I asked you not to touch me, Cal. I asked you not to look at me. Like ... *like this*. Don't you remember? You can't push me away, ask for time, send me love songs in Seattle, and now, *now*, bust into my bedroom ready to rip my clothes off. You can't have it both ways."

Cracking a smile, Cal reached for her palm, but she brushed him off, rolled her eyes, and folded her arms across her chest.

"Do you not feel the least bit of guilt coming here, to your friends' home, charging up their stairs to screw me in the middle of dinner?"

"Is that why you think I came here?"

"I don't hear you asking about my trip or my work or about me."

"You've had since, what? Wednesday, to call me. We've had plenty of time to talk. We could've spent the last few days—"

"What? Doing this? Fighting? Or fucking? I thought you needed *time*."

"I told you I wanted to see you when you returned."

"You came here for one reason." Annie pointed an index finger toward the ground.

Shoving a hand in a pocket, Cal inhaled and shook his head.

Annie began to pace in front of the window seat, her mind a pigsty of thoughts. Muddy, muddled, mud. All their time together — the summer, the carefree days, the beach, the talking, the sharing of meals, the making lov— the fucking — all of it flashed before her eyes, ending on the wall.

The concrete wall.

The no-bother-with-a-condom-fuck-the-life-out-of-Annie wall outside the South Beach club. Her stomach churned as if she'd consumed a bunch of scorching-hot chili dogs and beer and cheese puffs.

Well, at least the nausea wasn't because she was pregnant.

Are you there, God? It's me, Annie. I'm pregnant.

Maybe she would hurl after all. Wrapping an arm around her waist, she willed herself not to throw up or shake — to hold it together. How was she ever going to tell him, Mr. I-Don't-Want-To-Have-Children, that she had a living creature growing inside her body — his-his-his — and it was a life she wanted to keep?

My God. She was keeping it. Had it ever been a question? Or a decision? She didn't know. *Whatever. I'm fine. Fine.* Pacing beside her favorite window. In love. Uncertainty climbing. A pea in a pod. *I'm fine.* She scratched the back of her neck like a cat clawing at fleas. Her lips started to move in a monotone of a mumble.

Cal grabbed Annie's hand, stopping her frenetic pacing, and pulled her toward him until no more space existed between them.

"Baby," he uttered and lifted her chin.

Despite the confusion, the anger, the frustration, despite the tiny little thing-creature-life inside her womb, despite the muddied-up pigsty that was her mind, she still wanted Cal with a motherfucking passion. She wanted him to rip her clothes off. To erase. To go forward. To hurt. To expand her horizon.

"Is this all we are, Cal?" Annie pinched his shirt and blinked up at him. "A good lay?"

"Baby," he repeated, wiping a tear from her cheek, "this has never only been about a good lay. Ever."

"I know." She stared at his chest and exhaled several breaths. "I know."

"But it is pretty fucking good," he whispered.

She kneed his thigh, and he laughed. She let out a little laugh too, then sniffled. The two of them held each other tightly. Longer. Until Annie settled some more, until her breathing returned to normal.

"Have you had any more panic attacks?" he asked, and she stiffened and looked away. "When?"

"Um..." She chewed on her lip. "Yesterday."

"What happened?"

Their eyes locked. But for once, Annie gave nothing away.

Cal pushed some of her hair back and cradled her jaw. "I have to tell you something."

"The reason you called John." She sighed. "I'm being such a pain in the ass. I forgot to ask."

"Annie. Shhh. No." Cal surveyed the room a moment, his hands still on the sides of her face, then he glanced back and fell deeper into her astonishing green eyes. "I'm flying home Tuesday. For good."

She grabbed his wrists. "What?"

"Michelle, my cousin, she called today. Constance is..." He dropped his hands, deflated, and inched away. "She's dying, Annie."

She reached for the small of his back.

"She's barely eating, and she is..."

"Cal..." Standing at his profile, she touched his waist. "I... I'm so sorry." She eyed the side of his face. Words formed in her mind but they wouldn't exit her mouth.

"We'll figure this out." He exhaled, then kissed her forehead. "I'll call you when I get settled in Ojai."

"That's it." She swallowed. "You're leaving? Right now?"

"Annie, I'm simply following your commands. You asked me to leave."

They stared at each other a moment, then he turned and walked toward the door.

"Cal..." Annie choked on his name. "Don't," she clipped the second he reached for the handle. He froze, his hand on the knob, his back facing her. "I do..."

"You do what?" Shifting, he gave her his profile, watching her out of his periphery.

"I do want you to say goodbye to me. Now. Today. Please," she uttered, her throat aching, her heart full and mended and whole, her entire body filling with everything they ever were and could be. "I'm glad you came. I'm asking you. No, I'm telling you." She stepped forward. "Touch me. Take it all away. Everything. Please."

Three huge strides, and Cal met Annie near the foot of the bed and cupped her cheeks. "God, I've missed you." He nibbled the corners of her eyes, her jawline, her neck.

"It's been more than ten days," she whimpered, fumbling with his belt.

Threading his fingers through the back of her hair, Cal held her there, yanking her gently by those caramel-colored strands until he exposed her neck. "You understand I still need time."

She slid a palm past his waistband, inside his pants. "I said make me forget."

Cal grabbed her wrist and grinned. "Take off your clothes."

"I want to touch you."

"And I want you naked."

The power pendulum swung. Left. Right. Cal. Annie.

"Do you have condoms?" he asked as she finished removing everything. The tank. The shorts. The bra. The panties.

She bit the insides of her cheeks, then tipped her head toward her purse.

"Why are you nervous?" He slid his belt out of the loops, took off his shirt and shoes and pants, then he grabbed the bag off the window seat.

"I'm not nervous." Palms shaking a little, she found what they didn't actually need and placed it on the nightstand.

Cal steadied her hands, swirled the folded belt across her spine, and whispered, "You lie."

Annie shivered. "I expected you to have something."

"I told you — that's not why I came here today." Cal tossed the belt onto the bed and nudged her against the wall, his *I love you* on the tip of his tongue, in his gaze, across the lines of his forehead.

"Give me your will, Annie." He lightly tugged on a few strands of her hair. "Tell me you understand I need some time. Alone."

"I do," she replied and blinked.

"That's not good enough." He kicked open her legs, and she gasped. He rested a finger over her clit. "Say all of it."

Annie's knees went slack as she closed her eyes and bit her lower lip. "I missed you too."

Cal trailed fingers along her folds, up and down. "Do you understand me?" Two went inside her body. "Open your eyes."

"Yes."

"Do you?"

She nodded. He stroked.

"I... I understand you."

"When I leave and—"

"Not now." She jerked her head to the side.

"When I leave, Annie." He squared her chin. Brought it back, front and center. "I need to know you understand the reasons." His fingers slid out. "I need your will." He flicked her clit.

"Ow," she cried, then moaned.

"You will wait for me." He flicked her again and again, and she wiggled, groaned, and yelped. "You will be patient. Yes?"

"I'll wait," she choked out, scarcely able to breathe.

"Do you know your own strength?" Cal cradled her cheeks, neither of them blinking or barely moving. "Annie. Rebekah. Baxter."

Grabbing his face, she shoved her tongue inside his mouth, wrapping a leg around his waist, her center rubbing against his thigh.

A couple minutes later, both of them short of breath, Cal pulled away and said, "You wouldn't answer me the last time I asked you."

"Maybe because you're always torturing me when you ask."

Cal flipped Annie onto the bed. She landed on her stomach and laughed, propping herself up on her elbows. He wasted no time taking the belt and raining it down against her ass cheeks.

"Do you want me to ask you that question again when I'm inside you?" Leather met skin over and over. "Do you?"

Annie grunted, eyes rolling into her head as he snaked his fingers to her clit and rubbed her into a delirium.

"Did you hear me?" Yanking her by the hair, her face rose off the mattress. "What-what-what?"

Cal pulled her body to the edge of the bed, put his mouth at her ear, and clenched his jaw. "You need to know you're strong." He lifted her ass, positioning her on her knees and elbows, then he rolled on the condom. "More than just the two of us."

With his feet planted firmly on the floor, he gripped her hips and pushed into her. All the way. Filling her completely.

"Cal..." She swallowed his name before it ever left her lips. "Oh ... God..."

"I can't go home without hearing you say it." He pulled out. "Tell me."

"Please," she begged, flicking her tailbone, reaching behind her and grabbing on to him.

"That's a good effort." He laughed a little and removed her hand. "But that's not what I want, baby."

Shaking, near tears, Annie bunched the sheets and growled, "I am strong!" as she pounded the mattress with her fists.

"Yes!" He inched inside. Slowly. "What else?"

"Please," she repeated, and he pulled out again. "*Fuck...*"

"Tell me what you know."

"I will wait," she strained, glancing back at him, sweating, aching, exhausted. "I. Understand. You. You have my fucking will."

"I need to see you ... your face." He sat on the bed and pulled her toward him. "Come here."

She climbed on top of him, wrapping her arms and legs around him, and sank down, their skin slicked with sweat, their bodies melding together perfectly as they quickly found a rhythm. Foreheads touching, eyes roving into each other's souls, finding a home, an understanding, a comfort and an escape, a way to both forget and remember.

They stared at where they joined.

"Annie," he whispered, his voice sounding parched. So parched. She was his water, and her eyes were that desert he would gladly walk across all day — if it meant the reward was this. To know this moment. To feel this love.

"Cal," she said right back, squeezing his biceps as she swallowed and swallowed and swallowed.

"Please," he said, and their eyes locked, their jaws shook.

"Yes," she whispered into his ear as she threaded fingers through his hair.

"Please," he repeated.

"I love you."

"Yes."

"Yes."

"Fuck..." he groaned as she finished and he began.

Torn apart, then put back together. They fell against the sheets, narrowly breathing, fingers and limbs and hearts intertwined, absorbing the comfort they both feared would eventually abandon them.

Sixty-Four

Cal held Annie close after making love, the way he'd wanted to all those weeks she'd been away — he held and caressed her as if it might be the last time.

"You're still trembling, *heavy*..." Touching her cheek, Cal tried to meet her gaze. But she closed her eyes instead.

The words *I love you* were on the cusp of their tongues, but they didn't utter them. Neither Cal nor Annie could comprehend how she would actually board the plane in the morning, how they would wake up and spend every day without each other.

Propping her head up, her chin on his chest, she smiled, finally looking into his eyes. "Then you must be really good."

"You're the one," he whispered and swallowed. "You're the good one."

Annie is the one, Cal thought. She made him feel the way no other woman had ever made him feel — physically, emotionally, concretely whole. A man in every way. Not because he was incomplete without her. No. Being near her, listening to her simply breathe, had him intuiting what he must've always known.

That he was already whole.

Complete.

And never broken.

In the three weeks without her by his side, Cal hadn't forgotten the sensation. But now, as he peered into her soul, he solidly remembered. Annie's eyes unmistakably told him everything — the way they always had.

With a reluctant exhale, Cal broke contact first, wriggling out of Annie's grasp. After using the bathroom, he grabbed his clothes and sat on the bed facing the window seat, his back to Annie.

She reached an arm around his waist, her hand grazing skin beneath the blue shirt he'd started to button.

"Where are you going?" she moaned. "Stay with me tonight."

"I can't." He stood. Finished dressing.

Annie's eyes met the ceiling as she twisted the edges of the top sheet between her fingers.

Cal picked up his shoes, sat on the bench, and put them on. "I've already disrespected Maggie by coming upstairs when she asked me not to, and I can't..." He looked across the space and winced. "I can't be here in the morning when you leave."

"I want to be with you."

"You want to be at home too. For more than a couple of weeks. You've talked about how much you miss it there. We both need this time apart. I have no idea what's in store for me. I have a responsibility."

"I don't know how to do a long-distance thing." The sheet now appeared wrung out like it had just come out of a washing machine.

"Neither do I." Cal sat beside her on the bed. "It's only some time apart, baby."

"Fuck. Time."

Cal grinned. Annie sat forward, trying not to return the smile but failing.

"You'll be happy in your own space. Admit it."

"With my mother?"

"Are you going to move in with her?"

"I am right now. It's easier for the time being." *Easier for the duration of the pregnancy*, she thought. *Oh. My. God.*

"I've completely disrupted your life," he said, and she eyeballed him. "I have."

Cal had no idea how much he had indeed disrupted her life, and he would soon find out.

Would he?

Would she tell him?

Cal would probably end up hating her either way. Or resenting her. Or what?

What?

Define it.

He may never want to be with me again. He may never trust me again. I broke my promise. I'm keeping a huge, life-altering secret.

Cal kissed her cheek and said, "I'll message you," like he was sealing a business deal with a peck instead of a handshake.

Annie only nodded.

The entire scene played out in slow motion, her nod lasting centuries. Like the two of them were underwater. Cal standing, ready to move toward the door. Annie holding back this pivotal piece of information.

Leaning down, Cal kissed her cheek again, then he made his way across the room. As Annie quietly watched the father of her unborn child walk toward the door in underwater slow motion, she braced herself for the inevitable.

He reached for the handle.

His fingers grazed the knob.

Annie inhaled. She exhaled. She exhausted all her breath. "I'm pregnant."

Cal paused. For what felt like an eternity. When he finally turned and looked at Annie, his eyes pierced a hole straight through her skin.

"That's why I was nervous," she started rattling off, her gaze bouncing around, her fingers playing with that stupid sheet again. "Before..."

Cal started rotating his thumbs. Twiddling them? Then he took a seat at the foot of the bed.

"When?" He peered at his fingers. "How?"

"The last time we were together. Before I left." Annie watched him go through what she'd gone through yesterday. "The night we went to the club."

The street. The alley.

Cal recalled the wall. The sex he couldn't wait on.

Why hadn't he waited, pulled out, or stuffed a condom in his fucking pocket before leaving his apartment? He always took care of things. Always. He was responsible. He couldn't remember the last time he'd been so careless. Since practically the middle of August, though, it seemed everything had unraveled — his mind a haze, his mother sick and dying, Annie leaving. Cal now going back to Ojai earlier than he'd intended. *Wait...*

"We talked about this," he began, his eyes narrowing. "You said your peri—"

"I know. I thought... My period, it's ridiculous. I'm sorry."

"Sorry?" He shoved five fingers through his hair and pulled on the strands. "Who else knows about this?"

"No one knows. Jesus, Cal. I just found out yesterday."

"And you're sure?" He lifted a knee to the mattress and turned his upper body toward her. "You're positive you're pregnant?"

"I took two tests. They were both positive. And yeah, I've been sick to my stomach ... okay. I'm exhausted. My breasts hurt. I'm a classic case."

Cal stared in the general direction of Annie, but not at her person. He ran his fingers through his hair over and over. Seconds passed. Then something clicked. He looked her dead in the eye.

"If I hadn't found out you were here, *after I called John*, you were going to leave without telling me this?" He stood, pinched the back of his neck, and towered over her. "You were going to get on a fucking plane tomorrow without telling me this?"

"I'm sorry, Cal." She pulled the sheet up and wiped her cheeks. "I wasn't ready. I'm still not ready. I'm in shock. Don't you understand?" She swallowed. "You're not the only one who has a hard time with words."

Everything about Cal softened, his posture, his eyes, his shoulders, but he still looked over the room like it contained answers to his concerns. Her open suitcase on the window seat. Frames against the walls. The dresser. The mirror.

There were no answers. Only questions. And doubts. And fears.

"Have you been with anyone else since me?" Annie blurted, and Cal glared at her. "I mean, have you always used protection? Have you been tested?"

"You really pick the best times to have a conversation." He sat beside her and drew in a deep breath. "This is something you should've discussed with me from the start if you're so concerned about my history."

Strands of hair found their way around her right index finger. Her gaze wandered.

"Look at me, Annie," he said, his stare nearly blinding. "It's been years since I made the mistake of not using condoms — even in relationships. Okay?" Cal touched her waist, gently shook it, and she dropped the tangled pieces of hair. "I'm clean. I had a physical before I moved. It's only been you since the day we met. It's only been you since I've been in Miami. Fuck, Annie, you know that."

Her stomach flipped and flopped. Her palms began to sweat. Her upper lip did too.

"Has..." she began, feeling her facial muscles pull back in anticipation of his next reaction. "Has this happened to you before?"

"Has what happened to me before?"

"This." She pointed all ten fingers at her stomach. The sheet fell in her lap.

"Annie," he strained.

"Please, Cal, answer me."

"I think I just did." Swallowing, he looked at his hands. "Once." Cal glanced up, his Adam's apple bobbing.

"And?"

"And ... I'm not a father. I don't have any children."

Even though he'd replied without much inflection, she could decipher the *once* he'd spoken about had been a decision — and not his. The pain of the remembrance bloomed all over his face, his expression changing, becoming quite the opposite of his tone. Annie reached for his hand and squeezed.

"That's not me, Cal. I'm having this..." She eyed her stomach and covered her mouth, her forehead forming frown lines.

"Annie, I would never attempt to make that choice for you. Ever."

"You said you never wanted to be a father."

Cal brushed hair from her eyes, tucking a few wayward pieces behind an ear. "Not by choice, but now... Now, it's..."

"Now it's what?" Annie cocked her head to the side.

Cal's typical quiet became rather loud as he extended an arm over her legs, glancing down at her body and the way it was neatly wrapped in the sheet.

"Now, it's different," he said with a special kind of delicacy she didn't think she'd ever heard pass his lips. His gaze wandered from her stomach to her eyes as he stroked her cheek. "I lost my mind with you. No woman has ever made me so crazy." Playing with her hair, he rubbed the strands between his fingers.

"Don't, Cal, please." His underbelly was almost more than she could stand. "Maybe... Maybe that night in the alley we ... maybe you should have—"

"What are you saying?" Cal searched her face. "That I should've pulled out? That I shouldn't have fucked you? I don't take anything back about that night with you. No." He shook his head. "No. I wouldn't change any of it."

Annie sucked her bottom lip between her teeth, her eyes glossing again.

"Would you?"

"No."

Because not only had they conceived a child — a child who obviously already meant more to the two of them than they could even begin to articulate — it had also been the night she'd first told Cal she loved him.

They tangled their arms around each other and embraced.

Annie had wanted Cal as much as he'd wanted her that night, and in that brief moment of ecstasy, she'd wanted him inside her for all of it — from start to finish. She didn't regret the way it had all happened, and she didn't regret the life growing inside her now.

A minute or so later, Annie flung her legs to the side of the bed, stood and dressed while Cal stretched his entire frame across the width of the mattress, feet toward the floor, arms overhead, groaning.

"Will you come to dinner with us?" she asked after combing her hair in front of the mirror.

Cal stared at the ceiling, appearing mesmerized, lost. Uncertain.

"Did you hear me?"

"No," he said as he sat upright.

Annie picked up one of his hands and played with his limp fingers, bending the knuckles up and down. "It's not enough." She sighed. "How are we going to parent this child? God, Cal, together, we're only masters of fucking."

Cal stood and scoffed, tired of listening to the same words bubble out of her mouth over and over. This move, their separation, it would be painful for him too, despite what Annie thought about his decision. It was clear now, no matter how many times Cal reassured her that what he felt for her wasn't only about sex, she would not believe him. Or she refused to. If she really loved him as she said she did, she would let him go. Freely. She would give him the time he asked for. It wouldn't be for an eternity.

"When will you trust that our relationship is more than sex? Why can't you see the difference? Do you even know what it feels like to be with someone in the way you think I am with you?" He walked over to the bench seat and stared outside the window. "I asked for your will." He glanced back at her. "Your understanding. Was all of that bullshit?"

"No."

"I can't keep having this conversation." He took his hands from his pockets and turned around. "Why do you think I keep reminding you of your strength? Of what you know? You have to trust me. You have to trust the fact that my physical need to have you doesn't take away from my emotional need for you. Stop measuring everything by our physical attraction. I need you, Annie. *All of you.*" He stepped into her space, took one of her palms, and placed it over her own heart. "I need this." Cal's eyes ticked back and forth as he pressed their fingers against her chest. "But I also need time. You gave that to me when I was inside you ... a little bit ago."

Their hands fell to their sides.

"Do you realize how much has happened in the last few weeks? To both of us?" He searched her gaze. "It was enough hearing you say those words to me that night in the alley, and aside from worrying about my mother, my work, it's practically all I've thought about. *You* have been all I've thought about. And now ... now I find out you're pregnant."

Annie looked off into the distance.

Cal pinched the back of his neck, then inhaled a sharp breath. "Baby, I have to go to California ... alone. If you really love me, it won't fade away. It will still be there—"

"When will it be there?" Annie glared at him, her voice nose-diving while her hands flew into the air. "When? When you decide it's convenient for you? I don't want you to be there for me only because of the baby. This is about us. You and me. If you can't stand here right now and tell me ... and tell me—"

"Tell you what, Annie?" Cal grabbed both her wrists in midair. "That I love you! Damn it, Annie!" Cal released her arms in a huff. "I've loved you from the start. I've loved you since the first time I kissed you in the fucking rain. The thought of you leaving has made me feel like I'm not whole. If I give you any more of myself, I'll implode. I've told you how I express myself. You know how I express myself. I fuck." He pinched his nose. "We fuck!" Cal shoved his hands into his pockets and started to pace. "No woman has seen the side of me you see. Not completely." He stopped and pointed a finger at her. "I don't look on anyone the way I look at you. I'm sorry if I can't say those three words as easily as you, but if you don't know I love you when I look at you, if you can't feel it when I'm with you, then I don't know how else to get it through to you. If you love me..." Cal slowed down, took in several breaths, and reached for her hands, asking her to finally-finally-finally understand him, to trust him, to accept him as the man who stood before her now — the way he'd asked her to when he'd made love to her only moments ago. "God, baby, if you love me, then you'll give me the time I need."

Annie stared into Cal's eyes, her throat raw, everything aching.

Pushing her hair over her shoulders, Cal put his hands on her waist and inhaled. "These last few weeks without you made me realize how foolish I was to push you away. I was miserable without you here."

She dropped her gaze.

"Hey." He nudged her hips, and she glanced up. "I'm not pushing you away, Annie. We'll have to be apart, yes, but it's only distance, miles. Not our hearts.

"These last few months of knowing you have been like a storm. My life has changed more this past summer with you than it has in the last twenty years. I can't give you everything you want — right now, this instant."

"No." She smiled. "You just gave me the one thing you said you never wanted."

"I hope you understand what I said before — *this is different*. I do want this baby." Cal nodded. "I do. Or I will. I'm still in shock too." He cupped her cheeks. "I will always be there for my child." Cal gazed past Annie.

"What is it?" She searched his face. "What are you thinking?"

"I never thought I would say those words." *Like that. Out loud.* "'My child.'"

"Those aren't the only words you thought you wouldn't say tonight."

Annie stood taller and peered into his eyes. One of those amazing, full-body sensations ran through her muscles, her nerves, her veins as she slid her palms up and down his biceps, holding onto the safety and comfort of his sequoia tree for one more night.

Smiling, Cal massaged the back of her neck, bunched her hair, and placed his lips centimeters from hers.

"I love you, Annie Rebekah Baxter." His breath shook as he exhaled those words ... and the next. "*My heavy.*"

Annie rested her head on his chest and listened to the sound of his gentle, stoic, open, naked heartbeat. Seconds passed, then she whispered a promise of forever...

"I love you, too."

PART THREE
CONTINUUM

CHRYSALIS

PUPA OF A BUTTERFLY; PROTECTIVE COVERING;
SHELTERED STATE OR STAGE OF GROWTH

take me with you
where
will you go
I am not alone
you will never know
the inner workings
of my heart
the chains the gears the buttons
I am not alone
you will never know
me
unless
I let you
I say
I give permission
unless
I change my perception
unless
I give up my stronghold of unreason
I am not alone
I'll go forward

pretending
you understand me
believing
you can help me
until I believe
in me

SIXTY-FIVE

Beads of sweat tickled Cal's nape as he grabbed his luggage from the back of the rental and closed the trunk. It was the middle of September in Ojai, and the weather was seasonably warm. The air smelled like the valley too, crisp and dry, with a hint of citrus blossoming.

The citrus reminded him of Annie.

The house reminded him of everything he'd chased, caught, and brought to his mother's doorstep. For years.

His eyes scaled the walls of the pale two-story brick home — its color like that of a fresh tortilla off the press — stopping on a window on the second floor.

His window. His room.

The window on the left, not the right. Although, they both appeared the same from the outside: white shutters, flower planters below them, buds blossoming.

Always shiny on the outside.

Everything always perfect.

Shaking his head, Cal slipped the keys into the pocket of his black pants and wheeled his luggage along the stone path weaving through the front yard. As he did, a butterfly flew by, reminding him of days past. Times when a well-read book about the insects could most often be found on his nightstand or in his hands. Along with a jar and a net.

Feet bare, parading through the grass, a smile on his face, six- or seven-year-old Cal chased butterflies. Despite wanting to capture them, he also wished he could turn into one.

Because he wanted to fly.

Sometimes, he mused he actually could fly, and on some of those long-ago days, that same precocious little boy was secretly convinced he had flown.

"How do you know?" Rosa asked one evening, tucking the covers beneath his chin.

"Because I can feel it." Seven-year-old Cal grinned, rather sure of himself. He had flown.

Rosa pushed his bangs back and smiled. "Lo que sientes es real, mi niño," she soothed. "Sigue siempre a tu corazón."

"One more story..." Cal sighed, his eyes starting to close, his breathing slowing. He loved when she would stay over. It wasn't often, but when she did spend the night — usually whenever his mother had to be away — Cal looked forward to the attention Rosa paid him. The stories she would read, the way she would smile at him. Like he wasn't here to make sure she was happy, but he existed to simply be happy.

"One more, mi hijo. This one is about a boy who fooled a giant," she began, then recited the entire tale from memory.

Cal grinned, and in the blink of an eye, in the breadth of his smile, the beautiful swallowtail disappeared, its yellow, black, and astoundingly blue wings becoming camouflaged in his mother's garden.

After passing under a tall, white, vine-covered arbor and climbing the four steps toward the porch, he stopped at the entrance. Unable to camouflage himself like that butterfly, Cal couldn't deny his feelings or mood.

Perhaps he had wings.

But he couldn't fly.

Or he'd been afraid to try.

But he had followed his heart as Rosa had often admonished him. Except it didn't seem to have brought him where he thought he was supposed to be.

Today, it brought him here.

To Ojai.

In silence, he stood, wondering what it might be like inside. His cousin, Michelle, had said his mother could no longer talk. *Or perhaps she just didn't want to...*

Dropping his head, he shoved a hand in his pocket and fiddled with the keys.

God-fucking-dammit.

Not even inside the fucking house yet... How could he already feel so weak?

And he wasn't weak.

Ever.

It had to have been the flight.

Sitting on the plane had given him time to *think*. For several uninterrupted and undistracted hours. It had been too much time. More than he'd wanted. Now, standing at the front door of his childhood home — his ailing mother only steps away, reminders of a life he'd fled from time and time again — he didn't know what to do with himself or his hands. Or his five million fucked-up thoughts and feelings.

Gathering a deep breath into his lungs, Cal finally managed to open the front door. The hinges whined, but he stepped inside without making a peep and placed his things in the foyer.

The curtains were drawn in the room to his left. The sitting room — his mother had always called it that, tradition rendering it so. The elephants on the corner shelf remained visible despite the gray taking over the space. Some big, others little, all of them pointing toward the two front windows, displaying strength and pride. She had collected them for years.

Then a sliver of light meeting the floor of the hallway caught his attention. As did the low hum of a woman's voice. He began to walk toward it — the noise and the light — making soft strides without causing the old wooden floors to creak. Once he made it to the door of the guest bedroom, he stopped, but didn't enter. He couldn't. Holding his breath, he peered through the hair-line crack between wall and jamb, glancing around the room as best he could.

Until his eyes landed on her.

Propped up a few feet away in a double bed: Constance Marie Prescott. *A fucking guest in the guest bedroom.*

Michelle stood at her side, combing her aunt's gray-streaked hair, still humming a familiar song, one Cal couldn't place. His mother's pale blue eyes focused on nothing. Her gaze blank.

Cal gripped the trim with one hand while making a fist with the other. His entire body filled with tension. He was tight. Rigid.

Fuming.

His mother — always bold, opinionated, always full of her version of life — was dying.

Fuck... Cal pinched the back of his neck. He thought he'd seen the worst of this fucking disease before. But this wasn't his mother, the woman who'd raised him. This wasn't Constance Marie Prescott. The person in the guest bedroom had no spark. No spunk. It seemed an old, weary creature, inhabited her body.

Heart pounding in his throat, Cal inched away from the door. But he couldn't seem to stop clawing at the nape of his goddamn neck. Seconds later, he dragged himself back down the hallway and entered the kitchen, shoving a hand through the Old West-style doors on his left.

Constance might've changed.

This room had not.

The kitchen had always, unequivocally, belonged to his mother.

Boxed in on all sides, a single window positioned above the sink, the room showcased a perfect view of the yard and porch. A second set of swinging doors, opposite the first, led to a formal dining room that had long ago been converted into a den. And in the center of it all was an antique oak table and six chairs — the hub — where family and close friends gathered to share home-cooked meals, sarcasm, and stories.

Cal rested a palm on the top rung of one of the rustic, ladder-back chairs as he continued to survey the room. Copper ladles and pans dangled off a rack above the light in the center. Jars for sugar and flour were on the counter next to the toaster. Fresh flowers bloomed in a nearby vase. But his mind wasn't on any of those things.

Cal wanted a drink.

And it wasn't water.

His eyes roved over the fronts of the cabinets, wondering if any of them contained what he sought.

Ode to the liquor. Ode to the drink.

It had become the one constant in Cal's life on which he could fully depend. Faithful and loyal, never disappointing him. He craved a swallow now more than ever, but instead of lingering on his thirsty palate, he opened the fridge, shoving his true appetite aside ... to a place he could revisit later.

"Calvin Prescott," a voice sounded from behind.

Standing tall, he shut the door and turned around, managing a slightly amused grin. "Hello, Michelle."

In the center of the swinging doors, a single arm over the top of the partition, stood his cousin — his older cousin, a fact she never let him forget. Tall and stout and sporting mid-length, bleach-blonde hair, Michelle was smart and tough and had a heart as wide as the ocean. Right now, she looked like a cowgirl ready to barge into a saloon.

"Why are you dressed like you just came from a funeral?" The slatted doors creaked, flapped, then stilled as Michelle entered.

Two more steps, and Cal pulled her against him, wrapped his arms around her, and squeezed. Like he was that boy who had gotten lost in the fields again and she was the first one to have found him.

"Jesus, don't kill me."

Cal only sighed, attempting to release whatever had consumed him since arriving.

"Really, Cal"—she pulled away, tugged his shirt, and rolled her eyes—"all black."

"I saw you," he began, shifting his eyes, clearing his throat, "in the room with Mom a few minutes ago. She looks..." Gripping the nearest chair, his knuckles went white, his entire body filling with the same anger that had seized him prior. "She looks ... gone."

"It has been more than six months since you were here last." Michelle touched Cal's back, making soft circles over the material of his shirt.

"I know how long it's been."

"She barely eats. She doesn't speak anymore." Michelle rubbed a few fingers beneath her nose. "Well, I suppose I told you all that on the phone." She paused, then inhaled. "It's more than I can handle."

"You have help." Cal's brow furrowed. "No one quit?"

"Yes, of course. That's not what I meant." She smacked his bicep. "You're here five minutes and you already have me about to cry. I meant that it's..." She sighed, looking away. "It's more than my heart can take." Michelle leaned her head against his shoulder. "I'm glad you're here now." She glanced up at him. "*Home*."

"You want that hug now?" Cal wrapped his arm around her.

She smiled, sniffled, and gave him a little shove.

"I'm not going anywhere." He met her gaze and swallowed. "I'll be here," he clipped, not wanting to utter the words *until the end*.

Sixty-Six

"Where do you want this to go?" Rosa tilted the contents of a cardboard box toward Cal.

But he was distracted, catching up with work on the cream-colored settee in the sitting room, scrolling through several messages on his phone, laptop at his side, glasses at the end of his nose. A few papers were strewn across the entire length of the coffee table. An additional settee was angled to his left — that one bold, red, and velvet and also holding some of his paperwork. Both pieces of furniture were original, well-cared for, and pristine. Traditional and picturesque — typical Constance.

"Should I leave it in the box for now?" Rosa continued, the large turquoise stone hanging by a silver chain around her neck swinging as she spoke, catching the sunlight. Her hair-sprayed curls barely moved, though.

Raising a palm to shield his eyes, Cal blocked some of the sharp light beaming in the two front windows. The sunshine splayed across the floors, splashing the walls of the room — so bright, he could hardly see a thing. He didn't know why he'd chosen to work in this goddamn room. Or why Rosa had insisted on unpacking his things.

"No, I'd like to find a place for that today." Cal stood, slipped his phone in his pocket, and removed his glasses.

"Your mother ... she would like this music." Rosa tipped her chin toward an adjacent box, one holding some of Cal's vinyl. There were three or four boxes full of LPs scattered about. "You should put something on for her."

"That's a splendid idea," Michelle said the second she entered the room.

"*Splendid*?" Cal deadpanned while sliding his hands inside the box. He lifted his most prized material possession out of it, then set the player on the coffee table behind him. On top of his papers.

"I have lunch almost ready." Michelle smacked his shoulder.

"I'll come help you in the kitchen," Rosa offered as she removed a few records and set them on the table as well.

"It's okay. I have it almost finished." Michelle glanced at the vinyl and picked up the album on top. "Oh my gosh, Cal. I can't believe you have this. I haven't listened to Nat King Cole in years."

Cal eyed the tattered jacket in her hand, took a seat, then he glared at the mess around him. "Rosa, please don't set the records on the table where I'm working." Affixing his glasses to his face, he wrestled with the papers he'd trapped under the old machine.

Hands on her hips, Rosa tapped her fingernails against her capris, glaring at him.

Michelle picked up the LPs, intent on moving them. "You set the player on this table. Don't be an ass—"

"I'm not being an ass." Cal stacked the papers, then his gaze traveled to his cousin's shoes. "When was the last time Mom's floors were waxed?"

"Oh, he's not being an ass," Michelle mocked. "Do you hear this bullshit, Rosa? Are you kidding me, Cal? I don't know when the floors were waxed."

"Someone still comes in to take care of the house?" Cal peered at her through his readers.

With a heavy sigh, Michelle turned and tossed hair from her eyes. "No."

"No?"

"I've been taking care of it."

"That's ridiculous."

"I can help while I'm here," Rosa interjected.

"I pay someone to take care of this house. It's not your responsibility, Rosa, and it's not yours either." Cal eyeballed his cousin. "What happened, Michelle?"

"I wanted to do it. I want to take care of some things myself."

Fidgeting with the frames of his glasses, Cal grumbled, shifted, and gave his attention again to the documents.

"How long will you be staying?" Michelle asked Rosa while adjusting one of the window shades.

"Why are you closing that?" Cal snapped.

Michelle squinted at him, then she opened the blind back up.

"Mmm ... I'll be leaving tomorrow." Rosa stepped behind the settee and rested her hands on Cal's shoulders.

"And you're staying with Miguel?"

"Yes." Rosa began to massage him. "They surprised me yesterday," Rosa cooed. "They're having another baby."

"Congratulations," Michelle gushed, and Cal stood bolt upright, unsure what to do with his hands — an affliction that seemed to have cursed him since arriving. "What is Elena's due date?"

Cal wandered toward the fireplace, keeping his back to the two women, wishing he could crawl inside the brick hearth.

But he had nowhere to go.

No escape.

He had to be here.

In this fucking house.

But he certainly didn't need to hear the words *baby* or *due date*. He had too many responsibilities. The kind he wasn't used to. And even though he didn't do nauseated, his stomach turned.

"In April," Rosa replied with a strange lick to her tone. Before, Cal had noted pride in her voice, happiness. Now, he heard pity. Or concern.

"That's wonderful news." Michelle cleared her throat and eyed Cal. "I'll... I'll call you when it's ready."

"Thank you, love," Rosa said to Michelle while making her way toward Cal, past the two old rocking chairs near the fireplace. "I had forgotten about this too." Rosa tapped the jacket of the Nat King Cole record she'd grabbed on her way over. "I didn't know you had this in your collection."

"Several of my albums were Mom's. Or E.W.'s."

"I had forgotten this," Rosa repeated with a fond smile. "She would love to hear it."

"How do you know that?"

"Because she loves this album."

"*She* is not there."

"She is," Rosa insisted.

"Have you been in that room?" Cal's hands flew from his sides. "Have you seen her? *She is not there.* I thought she was gone before. But now, she is…"

"She is there," Rosa replied. "Give yourself time and you will know this truth."

Cal snickered, tilting his head toward the floor. "That's all I have here." He glanced up. "*Time* … and waiting."

"You shouldn't think of it that way."

"I mustn't think of anything." He stood taller, colder, nothing would penetrate him here. Ever. "Isn't that the 'Constance' way?"

"That's impossible, my love." After setting the album on one of the rocking chairs, Rosa placed a palm on his back, leaving it there for several breaths, for many heartbeats.

Then Cal moved his forearm to the mantle, resting it near several photographs. Pictures of family. The one he couldn't tear his eyes from was an old black and white of his mother. Young and staring back at him.

Had she always been so menacing?

He dropped his face into his palms.

"I'm leaving tomorrow, *mi querido*," Rosa whispered, moving her hand over his back in slow, steady circles. His lungs rose and fell across the tips of her fingers. "Please talk to me. I know what's troubling you is about more than your mother's illness."

"If I tell you, you'll only give me hell." Cal met Rosa's eyes, trying to silently communicate: *Annie's pregnant. Jesus Christ, I made a mistake. Annie's pregnant.* "And I'm already in hell, here, in this house."

"It doesn't have to be that way."

Eyes glossing, he pinched his nose, removed his glasses, then ran a palm clear across the entire surface of his face.

"Oh, *mi hijo*." Rosa sighed, touching the ends of his hair. "You have much love here." She glanced around the room. "Here … in this house."

"Love is the last thing that exists in this house."

"No," she soothed. "It is here."

Cal inhaled, and when he finally released the air from his lungs, his chest shook. He could feel Annie over him and through him. Right now. He could see her eyes peering into his guts.

"What are you afraid of, Calvin? It's me, your Rosa. Tell me what's bothering you."

"It's not the right time."

"Ah, *tiempo*." Arching up on her tippy-toes, she kissed his cheek. *"Un tiempo para todo."*

Feigning a smile, Cal started to speak, but then he pressed his lips together instead.

"I am hungry..." Rosa sighed, turned, and picked up the record, ready to return it to the pile. "I skipped breakfast."

"I couldn't have done all this without you." The words flew from Cal's mouth. The lump in his throat ballooned, and the forty-five-year-old man held his breath again like he was twelve.

Rosa smiled, her beautiful onyx eyes lighting up like shiny black marbles over a sunlit ocean.

"Vamonos," she uttered and gently smacked his cheek three times in succession. "We'll find a place for this old turntable in your mother's room after lunch." She nodded at the album cover. "Then we'll play her that song she likes so much."

SIXTY-SEVEN

After dinner, Cal sat with his mother, attempting to relax or read or listen to music while sitting in a bamboo folding chair he'd placed near her side. He'd spent every evening with her since arriving.

Rosa had left over a week ago, and Michelle was currently busy cleaning the kitchen, the dishes she washed clanking in the sink. Another type of noise rolled in over the mountains, a rare storm. The thunder roared louder than the dishwashing but not louder than Glenn Miller.

Lightning flashed outside the window, over the tops of the pale, yellow curtains, striking every couple of minutes as Cal moved his feet to the beat of "In the Mood," his thumb marking his place inside the book on his lap.

The moment the song ended and the needle stilled, Cal immediately lost his spark as well. Moving the record player into this space had been a *splendid* idea, as Michelle and Rosa had implied. Yet the music could only take the thoughts for a time. Nothing could ever really erase the reality he sat amongst night after night.

Half the room had been taken over by nurses, the workers coming and going at varying hours, their supplies and his mother's medication amply strewn about. The flowers on the chest across from her bed, next to the spot they'd found for the record player, were the freshest and brightest thing in the room, but despite the assortment of multicolored roses bursting from the vase, the space smelled and resembled a fucking hospital room.

His mother was here.

But not.

The spare bedroom didn't even contain *her things*. Only some of her clothing and her antique dresser. No other personal effects. Nothing highlighting her authenticity. Things she'd sewn, made, toiled over, knickknacks she'd chosen and carefully arranged.

The choice to utilize this room had been a difficult one, decided upon once it had become nearly impossible for Constance to walk up the stairs without assistance. The move had also proved to be more convenient for the caregivers and Michelle.

Ironically, this room had always been designated for strangers. Now, it seemed Constance was one as well.

"This bedroom is for the guests," his mother said upon finding Cal traipsing through the home's only downstairs bedroom yet again. They rented it out often, usually to traveling artists, people coming to Ojai for a glimmer of sunshine Hollywood could never truly provide. His mother desired the extra money. Constance always was interested in making a dime.

"How many times have I told you this room is off-limits? Can you not follow my simple instructions?"

Cal, eight or nine or ten, could only stare at her, mouth open, eyes wide.

Secretly, he'd wanted to get caught.

Again.

And he would continue to explore this room, the way he did the butterflies and the fields and all the things she labeled "time-wasters" simply because he wanted to. Cal enjoyed meeting the people who stayed with them too. They seemed so different than her, full of mystery and life. Not rules.

"Must you always be off in another world?" she scoffed. "Men must be certain, Cal. They must know what they want. Men must listen. Do you understand?"

Cal nodded, feeling like all he ever did was listen. He excelled at listening. It was obedience he struggled with. He'd heard every word his mother rattled off her cold, unforgiving tongue.

And he was rewarded for the practice.

Besides basking in the astonished looks he witnessed on her face whenever she would discover his nonsense and scold him, there was something else, another prize for listening. Something inside him she could never take:

The utter joy he felt when he decided not to follow through.

Cal set the book on the dresser, leaned forward, and placed his elbows on his knees. Dropping his chin onto his clasped hands, he moved his eyes over his mother's frame, following the lines on her face, pausing at her eyes.

A lump formed in his throat. His chest felt tight.

The woman he once knew didn't seem to be present behind those blue, blue eyes. He peered deeper, hoping to find what Rosa had insisted was true the other day...

But Cal couldn't find her. Or see her. She couldn't even speak to him.

Constance stared straight ahead, gazing at Annie's photograph of Pfeiffer Beach. The large glossy picture was actually the brightest and cheeriest spot in the otherwise bleak space, not the music or the flowers. Annie usually was the brightest anomaly in any room, but Cal refused to acknowledge those feelings too. Especially in this confined box of a room.

There wasn't enough space for the both of them.

Constance *and* Annie.

After tugging at his collar, Cal pinched the back of his neck, released a sigh, and stared at the photo too. At the beach his mother had once known, the photograph supplying the room with sunshine despite the rainstorm. His mother always had been good with the old memories — at least during the early stages of the disease — and now she had nothing. Not even words.

Could she remember the cove? Was she at that California beach now inside her imagination? Was she a middle-aged woman, making sandcastles with her son, spending time with her father and sister?

Thunder cracked, startling Cal.

And then the rain started to come down harder, sounding like hail over the metal roof. He stood and placed the needle back on the circle to compensate, then he stepped over to the side of the bed and caressed his mother's forehead and cheeks.

The quiet rage returned. Thinking of all she couldn't do. He had to stop himself from foaming at the mouth. From shaking.

Nothing was the same.

She couldn't speak, didn't know him. And she never would again.

Cal swallowed.

She couldn't feed herself. She couldn't even use the bathroom in a dignified manner.

Fuck me! Fuck this! The voice inside Cal's head began to taunt him. *She can't speak. She can't speak. She can't speak.*

The thoughts marched on like a million soldiers ready for battle. *She can't speak.* Despite the muteness she'd been struck with, he still heard her voice clearly in his mind as he recalled more of her constant demands and tart speech...

"What do you want to be when you grow up, Calvin?" This seemed to be one of her favorite questions as of late. She'd started asking it once he'd entered school. Cal wanted to chase butterflies. Capture them. He wanted to fly. But she'd wanted him to be something else. Something he couldn't understand back then, at the tender age of seven. Yet he'd felt it. Sensed it.

"It's never too early to give thought to this matter. What do you want to be?"

"A veterinarian."

Constance scoffed. "Are you copying other children in your class? That's the answer every little child gives, Cal. Are you like all the other children?"

"Did you know?" he asked, and she did a double take, shaking her head. "What you wanted to be?"

"Of course," she replied, her face rigid, her eyes stern, "but now, I am a seamstress. I make clothing for people who don't know how to make things for themselves. Sewing is a lost skill. I provide a service. I want more for you."

"Why?"

"Because..." She grazed the top of his head, and he leaned into her touch like a cat pushing against its owner's palm. "You have something special. And because you are a man. You're destined for more. You will not serve people, Cal — they will serve you."

However, Cal didn't understand what she meant. Not at seven. He only wanted her hand on his head, the softness in her voice, her blue eyes to look upon him forever the way they did in this moment when it seemed he could give her everything — things she'd wanted for herself but had never found.

Cal smiled. His eyes glossed. There were certainly times, he laughed to himself, that he'd wished she didn't have the power of speech. For her to be quiet and leave him alone. To not nag him.

The absurdity of it now, he thought. The disgust with himself.

What he wouldn't give to hear her one-of-a-kind voice, the one he heard now playing inside his mind over and over like a broken record. The way she often tried to disguise her love through her prickly tone, attempting to mask emotion with lessons about how he ought to live life.

Cal's pulse rose.

He scratched at his forehead.

Now, she was stuck in this room, in this bed, and it wasn't even her own bed. Or her own room. She was a shell. A hull of her former self. Every last bit of freedom she surrendered to this disease. *Everything*.

Pulling at the collar of his shirt, he tugged the material back and forth, then he undid the top two buttons. Placing his palm behind his neck, he rubbed his skin raw.

Being in this house had always been hard. Always stifling.

Constance and Cal were too damn alike. Both strong-willed, opinionated, wanting things their own way — or no way. Constance was old-school, old-world, and she'd raised her son under that impervious thumb.

But now, being here, felt impossible.

Squeezing his thumb and first finger into the corners of his eyes, Cal resisted the tears he could feel beginning to slide down the mountain of his grief. He refused them, the way he refused love — his mother's, Annie's, anyone's — as he touched her shoulder and trailed a finger up and down her arm.

Touching her was odd too.

Arguing wasn't.

And he wanted to fight with her. He wanted to argue.

To scream.

Right. The. Fuck. Now.

He didn't know if he'd ever felt anything as strong.

The need to push back against her tempestuous nature, to see a knowing glance in her eyes, to watch her sit up in bed, raise her fists or yell. To see the emotions she thought she could hide swim through her eyes. The looks implying she loved him, her stark blue eyes being the only way she ever told him.

He wanted to see it now. He *needed* to see it now.

Fuck. Fuck. Fuck. Where was she? In the water at Pfeiffer Beach?

Silently, he called out to her, imploring her with his own eyes. He squeezed her frail palm softly, but of course she didn't respond.

Seconds later, Cal let go, stepped away, and turned around. Never had he been more aware of his breath, of the way his lungs moved up and down as he caught his gaze in the mirror hanging over the dresser. After staring at his pained expression, he glanced at his mother's sterile one.

The definition of torture: to watch someone you love die.

The situation seemed worse knowing things between them had been left unsaid, words they both were too stubborn to utter, thousands of *I love yous* that had never been spoken. Still, it didn't matter how strained their relationship had been. She was his mother. And she'd raised him to be a man, an honorable one.

That was why he always eventually came home. Even when he protested or complained.

Cal tilted his head toward the floor. This fucking disease was unfathomable. Being with her was unfathomable.

His eyes watered.

His throat ached.

He cried.

Goddamn tears leaked out unbidden. Shit he hadn't wanted to deal with for years. The helplessness he feared. The weakness that had been following him around for weeks suddenly swooped down like a hawk, capturing him, pinning him to the ground and entangling him.

The tears took away his power.

But when had he ever had true power? Not over death.

Money couldn't save her. Everything she'd scrimped and saved. Everything he'd worked for — his pride — none of it could reverse what she'd become — a goddamn shell — or where she was headed.

How ironic.

All the money in the entire fucking world couldn't stop the disease from progressing. It couldn't speak his love, his regret, his struggle. Money was empty. Like the room. A piece of paper. Nothing. The only thing that would take away her pain now was death.

Cal dried his eyes, shielding his tears from his mother. She wouldn't be able to ridicule him if he hid them. *She is in there*, Cal thought. So he disguised his tears. Because by age three, Cal had been forced to stop crying over spilt milk.

Old habits die hard... he thought.

Turning, he glanced over the tops of the pale, yellow curtains. The rain had slowed to a pitter-patter. The music played on. Annie's photograph vibrated. The roses opened their petals a little wider. While Cal hummed along to the song under his breath and sat down on the edge of the bed in a trance.

Sixty-Eight

A brisk and bright October morning, Cal sat in his room atop his bed, one leg over the blanket, a knee bent, while the other dangled over the edge. His glasses were on, and his laptop rested next to him, open.

He attempted to write Annie an email, the cursor blinking as he stared at the blank space on the screen. Cal had emailed her a few times over the last several weeks, but he hadn't heard the sweet sound of her voice in a while. They missed each other's calls sometimes, or he avoided them. It became easier to make excuses as the days wore on.

The tone of her voice reverberated through his mind now, though, distracting him from typing. Cal grabbed his cell phone, then set it down.

Annie...

With a dramatic sigh, he dropped his head and covered his eyes.

Fuck him.

Picking up the phone again, he opened the last text message Annie had sent.

Annie: I know this song but hadn't ever really paid close attention to the lyrics. They're beautiful even though they're somewhat melancholy. Reminds me of you, Cal. Things can be easier ... if you make allowance.

Why did she always have to be so fucking kind? Even when he was acting like a dick and wouldn't call her. He hadn't responded to that text yet either, the one referencing "Everlong" by The Foo Fighters. He'd shared the acoustic version. A few of those lyrics seemed quite applicable to him now...

His thumb remained over the iPhone's home button — the damn laptop cursor still blinking. Knowing he wasn't giving Annie everything she deserved. Or needed. Trying desperately to believe he was what she truly wanted. He clung to that thought — *do you get that I want to be with you? That I want to really know you?* — the way he clutched his phone.

Cal regretted not being able to text more often. He regretted not being able to call right this very moment. But hearing her voice on the line would probably crack him wide open. Which in turn would make him act cold. Well, colder. And then he might drive her away for good. That was why she wasn't with him now. He didn't want to end up treating her the way he'd been treating Michelle — he'd been acting like a fucking asshole.

Communication would have to be mostly via email. At the very least, he could type. That was what he would explain to Annie now. Because if they spoke, she might pick up on the constant stream of vulnerability dripping from his weary tongue. Surely, she would make note of the weakness in his tone the moment they would say hello.

Sticking to email meant Cal could build her up with words, ask about the pregnancy, discuss baby names, encourage her work, suggest she send photos. Anything to avoid what was happening inside the walls of this fucking house.

If he let her in too much, he would break. And he had to stay strong for his mother. For Michelle. He had to stay strong for Annie. He had too many things on his plate.

Fuck, you're an asshole. She's pregnant.

Cal set the phone down and wiped his damp palms over the bedspread, trying like a fool to push his love for Annie aside, never wanting to allow it to envelop him completely, feeling as though he never deserved the love she offered. He attempted to keep her at arm's length.

Finally, he started to type.

Dear Annie,

I'm sitting in my room, thinking of you. I'm always thinking of you.

"Damn it," Cal whispered, giving the laptop a shove. He cradled his head in his palms.

Cal Prescott, always more than capable, could no longer pretend. He could no longer hide the frailty in his eyes. His voice *was* weak.

Grabbing at his T-shirt, he wrestled the cotton away from his chest. Then he rubbed a few fingers over his forehead, over and over and over, waiting for more words to come — any fucking words — but they didn't. Thinking of Annie was all he could do — needing her and pushing her away, a constant tug-of-war.

Cal wanted to give Annie all of him, more of him, but he couldn't.

What are we doing? she'd asked in her last email. He pushed, and she pulled. That was what they were doing.

And per usual, a woman needed to define everything. Except this was Annie, and she deserved the whole fucking dictionary. But what could he give her?

Nothing.

Emails. Sure. Great. No phone calls.

She was only carrying his baby ... alone. Or with her mother. Or perhaps those two things were one in the same. But Cal couldn't be in two places at once. And she couldn't be here, not after the death of her brother. Could she even handle this house, his fears, his anxieties? Being here made him impotent. Obstinate. She *was* better off with her mother.

Fuck.

It was all about timing.

For once, maybe it would be right, even though it wasn't right right now. Constance came first. No. There were no firsts. Only priorities and necessities.

Annie was strong. Her love would endure. Her patience was unlike anything he'd ever encountered. And he refused to ask her to share in his pain when he felt he'd already given her too much of a burden all her own to bear.

But he needed her — he needed her to share in his pain — and so the contradictions festered. Grew. The thoughts always with him. Annie was with him as if she'd always been with him. Always. There had never been a time without Annie.

His heavy.

Cal looked over the room, blankly at first, like the cursor, attempting to settle his restlessness. Then his gaze fixated on something else. Something old.

Next to a chest of drawers across from his bed, propped up against the wall in a corner was something he'd been trying to ignore. The way he'd been trying to ignore everything lately. But the fucking thing stared at him, whispering, taunting him — its voice so loud now he was distracted from trying to type an email.

After removing his glasses, Cal ran his palm over his unshaven face and made his way across the room until he came face-to-face with his surfboard. The board he'd bought when turning sixteen.

He touched it.

Skimmed his fingers along the edges.

And as he did, his breathing calmed.

His expression changed.

Morphing from a blank slate to a man on the verge of endless possibilities.

Even though Cal had been aware of its presence since arriving, he had disavowed himself the pleasure of imagining his body over it, fearing he would face massive guilt for wanting to spend time with the ocean. Time away from his mother. From Annie.

But now, as he held his beloved board in his hands, he realized how much he missed it. How much he needed it.

The water.

The ride.

The rhythm of the ocean beneath him as he stretched across the board, the gentle current as he anticipated the wave. The peace. The connection he felt to everything when drifting about in the endless ocean. The epiphany that came sudden and often in the vast, watery deep:

Most everything he'd been taught by society to value wasn't what truly mattered in life.

Out there, his mind blanked. And not the way it had when trying to type Annie an email.

The ocean didn't care how much money Cal had or what kind of car he drove. It didn't care about his designer fucking clothes. The ocean would pick him up and spit him out. Surfing would remind Cal of the important things: people, kindness, giving. Feeling.

The sun shining.

The gentle breeze.

Were those the true reasons he'd avoided the activity for so long?

Absorbing the water, the energy, the salt, the sun. Feeling himself in his own body. Feeling alive. He'd forgotten what that was like. Burying himself in work, drowning himself in drink, pleasing everyone but himself, he'd forgotten what it was like to be twenty-one.

Annie had been helping him remember.

Holding the board with both hands in front of his person, he smiled and dropped his chin, fondly recalling Annie's gifts: the surfboard wax and the antique mirror, the words she'd expressed in those handwritten notes. The strength he needed to value that ride *had been* inside him all along. She'd been right. It had never left him. He only needed the courage to let go.

To set aside his work.

To feel all his pain.

The courage to accept love.

To heal the things infecting his brain.

Allowing himself this nautical pastime wouldn't be an answer to everything beating against the walls of his heart, but it was a start.

A beginning.

It held promise.

Taking his surfboard out into the cold Pacific waters would offer Cal something nothing else in life could touch.

SIXTY-NINE

A few more weeks had passed. Constance appeared much the same. The medical staff couldn't predict how long she would hang on. Cal did his best to hang on as well, to cling to life as he'd once known it.

It wasn't working.

His life was changing.

It had changed.

He tried his best to keep up with business, but it suffered too. Everything in the old brick house suffered. The mourning left no one in its wake.

Resting in one of the rockers in the sitting room, facing the fireplace, Cal rubbed his fingers between the material of an old blanket his mother had crocheted. His thumb poked through its holes as he glanced at the large canvas hanging above the mantle.

His grandparents peered down at him from their place in the photograph, the glow from the flames intermittently lighting up their young faces. Cal rocked and stared, shifting his gaze between the fire and the canvas.

Everett approved of him.

He hadn't had to fight for that man's acceptance or chase it. It was just his.

And as he met E.W.'s bold, blue eyes, the only father Cal had ever known, it seemed he was still alive. Sometimes, Cal would nearly reach for the phone, ready to call and share a piece of exciting news with him. It had been years since he'd passed, Cal had only been sixteen, but it didn't matter — every so often, the urge to speak to his grandfather rushed over him...

"You were out again..." Grandpa E.W. glanced at Cal's feet and smiled. "In those fields. Barefoot."

Cal nodded, grinning as well. He was thirteen or twelve.

"You better go wash up, boy." Everett nodded toward the hallway. "Before she tans your hide."

Cal bolted toward the guest bathroom, scrubbed his feet, then joined his grandfather again in the sitting room. E.W. usually came over in the evenings, smoked his pipe, shared stories, listened to music. He had dinner with the two of them often. More often since his wife died.

"What do you find out there?" he asked the moment his grandson took a seat on the throw rug between the chairs near the fireplace.

Cal assumed a lotus position as his grandfather struck a match and lit his pipe. For a moment, Cal only stared at him. Regardless of how many times he'd seen him rock in that chair or hold that pipe, Cal was mesmerized. Like watching a beloved movie over and over.

And what Cal found in the tangerine fields was undefinable.

Peace of mind. Quiet. Only wind and beauty. Trees and endless opportunities.

"I like the smell," Cal replied instead and shrugged.

Everett chuckled.

Cal didn't just like the smell of the fruit and their blossoms, he liked the scent of his grandfather's pipe as well.

"Where is she?" Cal glanced around the sitting room.

"Upstairs. Sewing."

Her hands had grown more worn as the years passed. The way E.W.'s had. Only his were calloused from carving things he loved and Constance's from making garments she despised. For Hollywood. But she took the money. She never passed up an opportunity to earn a dime.

"I'm hungry."

"I bet." E.W. took a puff, blew smoke through the room, and rocked. "You should have heard her when you didn't make dinner."

Cal grinned.

His grandfather shook his head, but Cal could see the smile there, in the man's eyes, beaming with pride.

A few seconds later, the room went quiet. Too quiet. Cal could practically hear the sewing machine trudging along upstairs. Or his mother frothing.

"What's wrong?" Cal asked, never one to miss a tell or sign. Emotions.

Everett feigned a smile. "Thinking of your grandmother..." E.W.'s eyes glossed as he looked over the room. He tapped the arm of the chair. "Put on a record, Calvin."

Cal jumped up, made his way over to the old player his grandfather had lent them, and grabbed an LP.

He never needed to ask which one.

Cal's lips curved into a smile. He stopped rocking, sat forward, and looked around, stretching his legs toward the heat, crossing his ankles and warming his feet.

The house was quiet.

Michelle was presumably upstairs, and Constance was sleeping. Only the sounds coming from the fireplace crackled in his ears. Cal stared into the flames for a few more minutes, then he stood, stretched, and glanced at the bookshelf in the corner.

Those fucking elephants... he thought and shook his head. Their trunks pointed toward the front windows. They *had* to face the windows. He laughed as he ran a hand over his beard and made his way over to them. The moment he reached the knickknacks his mother had been collecting since she was a little girl, he touched a few. Turned them, inspected them, looking closely at the one Rosa had once glued back together...

After wandering into the sitting room one afternoon, Cal found Rosa carefully lifting each elephant on the corner shelf, wiping them with a towel, wiping the space they occupied as well, then returning them to the bookcase. He thought the task might take hours. And he wanted to help.

"Why do you do that?"

"They collect dust."

"So."

"So..." Rosa glanced at him and smiled. "We have to clean them."

"But they're not yours."

"Your mother asks for my help, Cal. You know this. It is my job to do these things."

"I don't like it."

"You think service is beneath you?"

Cal shrugged, picking up one of the smaller elephants. It was crystal, translu-

cent, a baby who had a mother. He examined it, then he accidentally dropped it. When it hit the floor, his heart followed. Only the trunk had snapped, one clean break, but knowing his mother and how much she cared for her elephants, that wasn't much of a consolation.

Rosa started to make sounds. Morse code for whenever she disapproved of his behavior. A noise emanating from her mouth. One Cal had probably heard hundreds of times before, but had never been able to successfully imitate.

After lowering to the floor, Cal picked up the glass, the body and trunk, then he stood tall and swallowed.

He wouldn't look at Rosa.

"Calvin," she soothed, no longer clucking her tongue over the roof of her mouth. "Look at me, child."

Cal thought he might be coming down with something. His throat hurt. Like he was ill. Or had a fever. He couldn't go to school tomorrow. Nor could he face her. His mother would kill him. When he finally glanced up, he met onyx orbs of light. Full of love, not disappointment.

He clutched the beloved pieces in his palm. Rosa opened his hand and lifted the trunk.

"This is the love," she began. "It is in here. In this part of the elephant." She placed both pieces of glass on the shelf and cupped his chin. "And even when we are broken, the love is always there." She nodded. "Do you understand?"

Cal's eyes glossed. The lump in his throat seemed to be shrinking. Perhaps he wasn't sick after all. Still, his mother would kill him.

"And ... there is superglue," Rosa whispered and grinned. "Do you know where she keeps it?"

Cal nodded and ran off, and when he came back they sealed the two pieces back together, making something whole that had never ceased to be perfect.

Cal grinned. His mother never found out. Or she never let on.

As he released the baby elephant, his gaze fell to the shelf below, his fingers already grazing several spines. Lots of them. Books, old books, ones he'd left behind when he moved to New York City, took up three of the shelves.

Cocking his head to the side, he scanned the titles, looking for a treat to take off to bed. The moment he hooked a finger into the spine of *The Sun Also Rises* and pulled it off the shelf, something fell out. Cal lowered to his haunches, smiled, then he laughed out loud.

Un-fucking-believable.

A joint had slipped from the pages. A very old one. He laughed again as he stood tall and rolled it between his fingers, his eyes wide and growing wider, the eagerness of wanting to read being quickly replaced with a desire to find out if his discovery would burn.

"What are you looking for?" Michelle flicked on the kitchen light.

Cal slammed a drawer shut and looked up. "Matches."

He'd spent the last few minutes searching every godforsaken drawer in the room, rustling through utensils and gadgets, clinking and clanging as he moved junk around in the dark.

"Matches?"

"Yes, Michelle. Matches." Goddammit. He wasn't a child. He didn't need to explain himself to her.

"Did the fire go out?" She yawned. "I could hear you banging around down here from upstairs."

"Is she still asleep?"

"Yes." She yawned again.

"Are you going to tell me where they are?"

"I keep matches on top of the mantle."

"I looked."

Tapping a bare foot on the floor, Cal followed her every move. After what seemed to be an eternity, Michelle retrieved a pack from one of the upper cabinets, then extended her hand. As he reached for the matches, she pulled them from his grasp and smirked.

Cal did not.

Fuck. Her.

"How do I know you aren't going to set us all on fire?" She raised her brows.

"Give me the goddamn matches." Cal felt like he was ten years old. Everything in this house seemed to be having that effect on him lately.

Fuck. Him.

"You really need to lighten up..."

That's exactly what I plan on doing, he thought as he swiped the pack from her palm. And he couldn't wait.

"Where are you going?" she asked the moment he reached the swinging doors.

"To bed." He paused but didn't look back at her. "Is that okay with you?"

"It's not even nine!"

"I'm tired, Michelle." Glancing over his shoulder, he rubbed his forehead. "I need to be alone right now. *May I please go to bed?*"

"Ever since you've arrived, you've wanted to be alone. I've given you your space."

Cal sighed, his posture softening some.

"We used to talk all the time," she continued as he made his way over to the table. "Don't keep avoiding me."

But Cal excelled at avoidance.

Since arriving in Ojai, the two of them had been skimming the surface of most matters, usually at dinner, making polite small talk, going over necessary details, schedules and finances, but they hadn't shared the bigger stuff.

The heart stuff.

Let's see... Where could Cal start?

His long-distance girlfriend, the woman he'd been shirking like the plague, was pregnant. Oh, yeah, and she was the Allens' surrogate child, and she'd recently graduated college, and he was a bastard. Well, the bastard part Michelle knew.

Fuck. Him.

"You've given me my space." Cal set the book on the table. "I'm sorry."

Sorry. That was all he was lately. *I'm sorry, Annie. I'm sorry, Maggie. I'm sorry. Sorry. Sorry. Sorry.*

"Well ... sit." Michelle tapped the top of a chair. "Let's talk."

"Not here." Cal slipped a hand into his pocket, pulled out the joint, then opened his palm.

Michelle slapped a hand over her mouth, smiling like Goofy. "Are you really going to smoke that ... in this house?" She glanced around. "Where the hell did you get that thing anyway?"

"I'm going upstairs..." He didn't grin, didn't flinch, didn't leave any room for argument. "To hopefully get high. If you want to talk"—he smiled—"it will have to be in my room. I found it in my book."

"That one?" She nodded at the old Hemingway novel.

"Yes, Michelle."

After putting the joint back in his pocket, he picked up Papa and exited the kitchen, the sounds of Michelle's footfalls not far behind.

The novel hit the bed with a soft thud.

As soon as Cal began to unbutton the cuffs on his long-sleeved shirt, the overhead light came on. *Christ*. Michelle was always turning the fucking things on and *leaving* them on in every room of the fucking house.

She wasted no time making herself comfortable, lying on her side on the bedspread, resting her head on an elbow, flipping through the pages of the book.

After hanging up his shirt, Cal cut the main light, the old switch snapping like one from a breaker box.

"Hey," she whined, and Cal wasn't sure which noise had been more annoying...

Sighing, Michelle dropped the paperback and glared at Cal. "I would like to *see* your face when we talk."

Cal had already clicked on the Tiffany lamp atop his nightstand the second she'd mouthed off.

"When are you going to shave?" Michelle eyed his jaw.

"You don't like it?" Cal stroked his beard, the color quite a contrast to his dirty-blond locks, the hairs on his face richer, darker. He hadn't bothered with shaving since arriving. Or having his hair trimmed.

"I don't know. I'm not used to it ... or your longer hair. It's not causing problems with work?"

"Fuck work." Cal opened the window closest to the bed, the one facing the side yard, and stood there a moment, inhaling the cool, invigorating air.

"What are you? Twenty?" Michelle scoffed. "'Fuck work,' grow your hair, and get stoned."

"Tonight, *I am me*." He glanced over his shoulder. "Do you even remember the last time you didn't care about a million different things?"

After taking the two items from his pocket, Cal sat in the adjacent antique chair, the one with the padded cushion embroidered with flowers, an old secretary next to it. Everything in the room was ancient.

Including him.

"Do you remember the last time you smoked?" Michelle asked.

Staring down at the joint, Cal rubbed it between his fingers. He couldn't recall exactly. But he was pretty sure it had been with Allison. However, that wasn't the time he was thinking of... His mind wandered to college. To Jocelyn

Ryan. To one particular night in her bedroom. Cal remembered the way the wind felt, the songs that played on her little radio.

Ironically, Cal was now the one in *his* forties about to get stoned after years of being someone he thought he needed to be in order to be happy. Or to appear happy. Fuck. When had life happened to him? When had Joe's prediction come true?

"One day you'll see what you really need..."

Well, right now, he needed this.

"I don't know," he lied, then put it between his lips.

After striking the match and bringing the flame to its final destination, Cal inhaled, then held his breath. Looking outside, his eyes narrowed, as he coughed, the sound mixing with his beautiful, carefree laughter. He extended his hand toward his cousin, but she politely refused. Stretching his legs and crossing them at his ankles, Cal sank farther into the chair while resting his other hand comfortably over his bare chest. Leaning his head back, he peered at the ceiling.

Michelle assumed a lotus position and swatted her hands through the air. Cal picked up his head and laughed, grinning until his cheeks hurt.

"I think this is the first time I've seen you laugh since you got here." She returned the grin. "In fact, come to think of it, I haven't even seen you smile that much either."

Their eyes met. Cal looked away first as he swallowed, then took another hit, resuming his stance in the chair. Beyond relaxed. His eyes closed.

Several seconds later, he cocked an eye open. "What's on your mind, Mishy? Come on." Cal patted the arm of the chair. "Talk to me."

Michelle sighed, paused, then opened her mouth. She talked and talked, telling Cal details of her grown children's lives, goings-on throughout the last six months, complaining heartily about her ex-husband, the father of her children. She gestured uncontrollably and spoke practically without stopping for air.

Cal knew better than to interject. He listened patiently and quietly, following the stories as best he could.

None of it mattered, though.

Michelle did, but the bullshit — none of it mattered. Safety mattered. Peace mattered. Every muscle in Cal's body felt like it had been massaged. Time became suspended ... like watching dandelion seeds blowing in the wind.

Everything Michelle said floated up and over his head like a beautiful butterfly, several of them, all flapping their wings, coming at him in 3-D.

He only had to nod and smile and inhale marijuana.

A few minutes later he stood, leaned closer to the window, and blew the last bit of smoke from his lungs. Then he snuffed out the joint on the ledge of the sill and stood very still, gazing out into the darkness, the cool outside air enveloping him while the tip of his nose touched the screen. He genuinely tuned out Michelle's chatter now. He wasn't even pretending to listen. Finally, he felt freedom. No more morbid thoughts. No responsibilities.

He could think of Annie.

He felt Annie.

Freely.

He had thought of Annie often, constantly, but now he was free. He didn't feel the tug or the war. Or the guilt. The contradictions. He didn't feel the dull ache, the push or the pull. Just her. On the beach with her camera. A flower in her hair. Her hands. Her skin. The sound of her voice.

He allowed himself to feel something other than sadness. Cal finally gave himself permission to feel the one emotion he so desperately needed to cling to — the one he usually avoided and refused to acknowledge.

Love.

Love made the baby, he thought. *Fuck ... the baby.*

Annie had a child inside her body. Growing. His. The reality of it hit him hard and fast, threatening this newfound sense of security he was basking in. Sliding his fingers through his hair, he combed them all the way to the back of his neck and pulled on the strands.

He would be a father. A father. A father!

Cal's eyes started to ping-pong across the yard.

Who the fuck was he to take care of a child?

What did he know?

He needed to get a book or two or three. He needed to gain control. He needed Annie.

He needed...

Home.

Home was wherever Annie Rebekah Baxter happened to be. Home was balls deep inside her body. Holding her hand while watching her fall asleep. Home was listening to her breathe.

"What is it, Cal?" Michelle asked, startling him from his stupor.

Putting a thumb and first finger into the corners of his eyes, he dropped his head. No longer able to keep up his staunch display of what he thought was the definition of masculinity. Not in front of his cousin anyway. Not high. The shit he'd swept under the rug unfurled. Tears filled his eyes.

Michelle stood and went to his side. As she rubbed a hand over his bare back, he turned and embraced her. She held him like a mother, and he sank into her body like a son. A few seconds later, Cal lifted his head and smiled.

She put a hand on his cheek. "I've been talking so much. I'm sorry."

"Don't be." He cleared his throat, stepped back, and glanced outside. The cooler air now gave him goose bumps. "You needed to talk." He cleared his throat again. "I'm sorry I haven't been here for you."

Michelle squeezed his bicep, gave him a tight smile. The moment she opened her mouth to speak, he uttered, "I met someone."

"Damn it, Cal!" She shoved him. "And you waited all this time to tell me."

"I didn't want to overwhelm you."

"*Overwhelm me?*" She slapped him playfully again. "You've been away too long if you think you can't talk to me."

Cal's gaze shifted, his eyes bouncing around the room.

"I didn't mean it like that." She bumped his arm. "You had every reason to go to Miami. You had to. It took me a while to realize it. And you met someone. So, it must've been a good decision. Right?"

Cal smiled, recalling Annie on the porch and in the sand the night they'd met, remembering her face with the single pink rose in the picture he kept on his phone.

"Well. What's her name?" Michelle's eyes lit up. "How did you meet?"

"Her name is Annie." Cal combed every inch of Michelle's face, trying to gauge what her response might be. He paused. "She's twenty-five."

"You always cut right to the chase." Michelle laughed. "I don't care how old she is. Tell me something else."

"I'm in love with her."

"Oh..." Michelle's mouth opened.

"What? Is *that* so surprising?"

"Yes. Actually."

"So, I can *meet* someone who's twenty-five, but I can't fall in love with them?"

"You've never been serious with someone so young, and after what you went through with Sam, I guess I didn't think—"

"Michelle, don't."

"Is she... Is Annie in love with you?"

"Yes." The tightness in his throat pricked him like the spines of a cactus.

"Are you sure you're not confusing love with great sex?" Michelle grinned.

"Do you really want to have that conversation?" Cal smirked. "You want to talk about sex? *With me?*"

"No." Michelle sliced a hand through the air and smiled.

"You should sit down." Cal cleared his throat.

"Okaaayyy..." Michelle took a seat in the chair he'd formerly occupied.

For a moment he only stared at her, running fingers over his beard.

"Cal..." She blinked.

"Annie's pregnant."

Michelle said nothing. For several minutes. So Cal decided to look out the window. Insects made calls. The wind rustled through the leaves of the trees.

"I need to go to bed," he finally said, the last word stretching with his yawn.

After taking one last long look outside, Cal closed the window, locked it, then scratched his fingers over his chest as he arched his back.

Michelle stood, locking eyes with him.

"Ahhh ... I did overwhelm you." He laughed. "I've never seen you speechless before."

"We can talk about this in the morning." She started to walk toward the door.

"I don't need a lecture, Michelle," he replied, and she faced him. "It's done. She wants the baby, and I want her. It's done. I don't need you passing judgment on me in the morning. I've got enough shit going on around here without you scolding me."

"I'm not scolding you."

"Bullshit." Cal placed the book on his nightstand and dragged the blanket down to the center of the bed. "Let's finish this now, or I won't be able to sleep."

"I've always supported you. With everything."

"With *everything*? Your tone right now says otherwise."

"Fine. It's because I'm shocked. Okay? You've never wanted children. Am I not supposed to be a little bit surprised you absentmindedly impregnated a twenty-five-year-old after running off to Florida to get away from a married—?"

"Watch. It."

"What the hell happened?" She tossed her hands into the air. "I mean, it's not like you to be so ... so..."

"Arbitrary?" He laughed again.

Michelle rolled her eyes and grinned.

"And I don't know what happened." Cal shrugged.

"See!" She pointed a finger at him like they were kids. "That's not even like you. '*I don't know what happened*'?"

"I'm stoned, Mishy. Give me a fucking break."

"Well, stoned or not, you *know* what happened."

"Yeah, but when it happened ... it was..." Cal trailed off, at a loss for words, seized with the taste of Annie's skin, concretely remembering the way he'd held her against the wall that night in the alley, the way he'd wanted and needed her, knowing he hadn't had protection but drowning out the voice telling him it was wrong, subconsciously intuiting she was the one. The memory now heightened knowing the urgency and love they'd expressed had made a baby.

She was the one.

It was over him now. It was what he'd always felt but couldn't bring to fruition.

"Nothing like that has ever happened to me before." He shook his head as though waking from a dream.

"I know."

"Everything about her has pushed me off the rails. I think about her, and I can't think." He stuffed fingers through his hair. "I've always been able to think. No woman's pussy has ever made me incapable of thinking."

"Cal..."

"You wanted to have this conversation."

"Not *that* conversation." She wrinkled her nose. "I thought it wasn't just about great sex."

"It's not, Michelle. That's my point. It's more than physical. *I want all of her*. I want to take care of her. I would give her anything. I simply want to hear her breathe."

"Did you ask her to come to California with you?"

"No." He rubbed a palm across the sheets, smoothing out some lumps. "She supported my decision. Annie understands me."

"God, I hope so. Because sometimes I don't even understand you. I still can't believe you waited all this time to tell me news like this."

"You're the first person I've told." He glanced back at her, his eyes glossing over, and it wasn't because he was high.

"Holy shit..." Michelle joined him on the other side of the bed. "You're going to be a father, Calvin."

Smiling, he let out a shaky breath, one he hadn't realized he'd been holding.

Michelle peered into his eyes. "When is Annie due?"

"In May."

The two of them only stared at each other a moment in silence.

"It is different this time," Michelle muttered, looking at his face the way a psychic might read a palm.

"What?"

"I see something in you." She looked deeper into his eyes. "I never saw it when you were with Samantha. I've never seen it before..." Michelle continued glaring at him like he was the most fascinating thing on planet Earth. "I'll be damned..."

"Rosa said something similar." Cal swallowed, cleared his throat, and looked away.

"Bring Annie out here."

"I can't." He glanced around the room. "Not with Mom dying."

He gazed at the floor, concentrated on breathing, then pushed his hands into the pockets of his jeans.

"I love you." Michelle tugged on his elbow. "I'm here for you in every way. You know that."

"Thank you..." He looked up. "For everything. Always."

"I wanted to be here and live with your mom. You know that."

"I know. But thank you."

"Thank you." She beamed.

"For what?" He grinned, the beard unable to hide the adorable dimples on his cheeks.

"I'm going to be an aunt."

"You're going to be a second cousin."

"No, no, no. I'm going to be an aunt!"

SEVENTY

Cal sat with his mother after dinner, reading a book aloud, the sound of his voice a touchstone to her silence. But on this particular December evening, Cal felt restless.

More than usual.

Even his mind wandered as he read. Drifting to the ocean...

Although he'd been reading about a young boy and his summer, Cal couldn't help but reflect on a different boy, a man, and his autumn.

Cal had braved the cooler waters several times over the last month, taking his surfboard out to Ventura. It had taken plenty of patience and endurance to get up, stay up, and not fall off his board. Thank God he was a runner, but he still awakened muscles that had apparently gone dormant.

Each and every wave had been worth it.

Like Annie had said.

Peace seemed elusive tonight, though. He would stop and reread paragraphs in his head as it became increasingly more difficult to concentrate. After a while, smack in the middle of a poetic passage, Cal abruptly shut the book and stood. He set the old Bradbury novel on the nightstand and glanced at his mother — she was awake and sitting up in the bed — then he turned and stepped toward her dresser.

Cal removed his glasses and stared at his reflection.

Dark circles under his eyes, age lines, a beard.

Scratching his jaw, he turned his head side to side, inspecting the length of his hair and the situation on his face. Not since college had his hair been longer than any "respectable man's" should've been.

Mom would hate it.

That thought alone filled him with bliss.

He glanced at her again — the owl, the hawk — then he turned back to the antique dresser. Walnut wood with batwing handles. Wide and rectangular. The only thing in the room that had come from her original bedroom besides her clothing. The space she'd given up when walking up the stairs had proven too difficult.

Cal began to open the drawers. Starting with the shirts, he ran his fingers over them one by one, lifting up each piece and inspecting them. Her whole life seemed to be confined to the fucking guest room. Nothing personal. Nothing unique. Nothing screaming, "I am Constance Prescott!" — until Cal opened the bottom drawer.

At first glance, it looked like all the others, holding clothing, but lo and behold, peeking out from beneath the underwear, was something different, something that didn't belong:

A manila envelope.

He stood tall, undid the clasp, and looked inside. It contained photographs. A thick stack of them. She had never bothered making picture albums or displaying too many frames. So Cal wondered what made these special and worth keeping. And he wanted to know why they were hidden.

His gaze moved to his mother. He peered at her reflection in the mirror. Had she lost the ability to recognize a loved one in a photo? Cal had sent her Annie's photograph of Pfeiffer Beach. She couldn't talk, but maybe she could remember ... something. Did the picture of the alcove hanging across from her bed give her comfort? Would these photos?

He shook the contents of the envelope into his hand. *At least a few dozen,* he thought as he fanned them out, pictures he'd never before seen.

The first one was of Constance. An old, square black and white with deckled edges. She looked no older than thirteen. His eyes were her eyes, his stance hers. He smiled and went to the next.

The jovial expression left him.

He held the print out from the rest.

A photo of his mother *and* his father. Together. He quickly shuffled through all of them. Practically every single one contained his father. At least

Cal *thought* it was his father. It had been so long since he'd seen the man's face he'd forgotten what it looked like.

The bastard had left when Cal was five. He had virtually no memory of him. A fuzzy recall. A dream image. A faint outline of a man's jawline, his eyes, and a still frame in his mind of the way he walked. The only actual tangible thing that remained of Cal's father was the Prescott name...

"Do not say his name again in this house."

They were in her kitchen. At eighteen and ready to leave for college, Cal had become curious. Wiser. Ready to take on more of her bullshit. He'd also grown taller. And much more confident.

"Why?" He stepped closer.

His mother folded her arms across her chest, nostrils flaring. "If you repeat that name, I will not speak to you again. Ever. Mark my words, Cal. Don't test me."

Cal scoffed. "All I've ever done is test you."

She smirked.

"Why did you keep his surname?" Cal's posture relaxed. His mother's did not. "At least tell me that, Mom? I want to know before I move away." His chest started to hurt, to ache, growing tighter and tighter. "Why did you keep the name of a man you can't even bear to—?"

"Because of you, Cal," she began, sounding softer, lighter, but looking the same — like an owl on a rooftop ready to snatch prey.

Still, Cal had never heard her like this, not even at his grandfather's funeral. On the verge of tears, holding something back yet offering it to him freely.

"I wanted you to grow up with the same last name as your mother. To feel that you belonged to me." Her blue eyes shone, but her lips remained a hard-pressed line. "That I wanted you."

Cal's throat swelled to the point of pain. He knew why she'd kept the name. Now, he wondered why she'd kept the pictures. Or why she'd never shown them to him.

Spreading the photographs out on top of the dresser, Cal stared at them, his eyes darting back and forth from one to the next, over and over. Then he started to pace. There wasn't much space in this part of the room — in any part of it. Nevertheless, he paced, scraping knuckles across a cheek, taking his hands in and out of his pockets.

He didn't belong.

That was it.

That was what had always been missing.

The thing he couldn't find and always searched for.

He didn't belong.

Anywhere.

Not in the photos, this house, or in this goddamn claustrophobic room. He didn't fit or belong. No one understood him.

Cal's eyes moved faster than his thoughts, bouncing around like a pinball. The temper he'd masterfully controlled for most of his adult life was about to turn green. Like The Hulk. Snatching one of the pictures off the dresser, he pinched it between his thumb and two fingers and stepped closer to the side of the bed.

First, Cal stared down at the blanket, at her body, then he looked at her face, feeling enormous shame for what he was about to do. But the emotion was heavy, thick, and he couldn't tamp it down.

Waving the picture in front of her eyes, his nostrils flaring, his jaw practically shaking, Cal cried, "*Who was he?*"

Those three words were the first personal ones he'd spoken out loud to his mom since coming home. Sure, he'd read books, played music, he'd even sung along to some of the tunes. But he hadn't spoken to her personally or asked her questions, telling himself it was because she couldn't answer him.

He was such an asshole. A huge, fucking asshole.

The disease.

The loss of speech.

The lack of recognition.

The non-belonging.

The photographs.

The guilt.

All of it serving as a stark reminder that he'd never been able to bridle the endless searcher who lived inside him.

"Why did he leave you?" Cal continued, much louder, tears beginning to form.

What did it matter if she couldn't talk? Constance had never satisfied his curiosity about his father while Cal was growing up — when she could talk — and one day, Cal had given up asking. All he knew about the man were the things his grandpa E.W. had told him.

"Was it because you couldn't love him the way he needed to be loved?" Cal set the print on the nightstand, then brought a hand to his forehead. He was sweating. Everywhere. He was angry. Pissed. At himself. At those pictures. He felt both guilty and relieved.

Rubbing his eyes, he looked back at his mother. His tongue weighed a thousand pounds. His throat was full of knives. "You couldn't love anyone, Mom."

"She loved the only way she knew how," Michelle said as she entered the bedroom.

Whipping his head around, Cal narrowed his gaze. "And what way was that, Michelle?"

"You shouldn't speak to her like this." She adjusted Constance's pillow and stroked her arm. "*Shhh...*" Michelle glanced at him. "You'll agitate her."

"*I* will agitate *her*." Cal was riddled with pain. Bullet holes. He didn't know what he was saying anymore. Or he didn't care. No, he did care. Too much.

"No, I shouldn't speak to her like this. I could never speak to her about anything personal." He looked at his mother. "Maybe that was the problem." He stared at her, some sort of wet filling his eyes, then he glanced back at his cousin. "Look at her, Mishy. This is all I have left of the past. This is it. I feel like I never even knew who she was." Cal took a seat at the edge of the bed and nodded toward the dresser, a lump forming in his throat. "Why did she keep those pictures?"

"You knew who she was." Michelle sat on the other side, continuing to brush her fingertips over Constance's arm.

"She showed me what she wanted to."

"Cal, have you ever considered that what she gave you was all she knew? All she had to give. And that it was enough. That she loved you."

Cal scoffed, turning his head. Michelle touched his arm now too.

"She loves you."

"She never said it."

"Did you?"

Cal shifted his body toward them and gazed down at his mother.

"Let go of the past, you stubborn man." Michelle jiggled his wrist. "You have a future now. You have a family."

Cal blinked. His eyes opened wide. Then wider. His throat felt parched.

"A family," he mouthed, touching his lips, needing to feel the words as they exited.

Something clicked. Connected. And for the first time, Calvin Prescott felt

like a father. A real father. He was finally ready to let Annie in. Fully, unequivocally, unconditionally.

Forever.

"Did you tell her?" Michelle asked, nodding at her aunt, and Cal swallowed. "Did you tell her about the baby?" Michelle's blue eyes twinkled. She
wiped under her lids and sniffled. "Tell her she's going to be a grandmother."

Cal peered at them, looking from his mother to Michelle. Then he started
to cry. He made no sound. Released only a few tears. But his chest shook. The
whites of his eyes turned red.

He took his mother's hand. "Mom," he said, peeking at the side of
Michelle's face, "I'm going to be a dad."

Cal dropped his head and sobbed. When he finally glanced back up, he
gazed into his mother's eyes, searching the blue, until he was certain he saw her
in there. Until he witnessed a flicker of acknowledgment.

And he hadn't imagined it. It was present in her stare.

"You're going to be a grandmother." Cal smiled through his tears.

Sitting on each side of Constance, the two cousins looked like sturdy little
bookends to one of the greatest stories of their lives.

Nodding, Michelle encouraged him to continue.

"I met someone." Cal tripped over his breath as he exhaled. "Her name is
Annie. She's..." Turning his head away, he smiled, then he looked back and
stared directly into his mother's bright blue eyes. "She's young." He laughed a
little. "*Younger than me*, and you probably wouldn't like that." He scrubbed
beneath his nose. "But I don't give a damn because I love her." He squeezed
Constance's hand. "I love Annie, and I want to marry her."

Michelle's eyes popped from her head, but she merely glanced at him and
smiled.

"You would like Annie." Cal swallowed. "She's kind. Generous. But she's
also tough as nails. She doesn't let other people make decisions for her." Now,
he didn't think he could swallow at all. "She's... She's amazing."

And beautiful. And his. And he wanted to marry her.

Choked up and unable to utter another sound, Cal stood and cleared his
throat. Twice. Turning toward the dresser, he dropped his palms on it and
hung his head. A minute or so later, he looked up into the mirror and wrestled
with the collar of his shirt.

He needed her words.

He thought he could do without them. He thought his mother's eyes would've been enough. The acknowledgment. The something in her stare. But it wasn't.

Sliding his palm to the nape of his neck, he rubbed and rubbed. The control was slipping again, and it was too late to stop it. For the second time tonight, he didn't want to stop it. He didn't care about consequences. He only knew he had to release the throbbing pain in his chest.

"Fuck!" He threw a hand in the air. "Speak, Mom, *please*. Why can't you talk? Say *something*!" He stood at the edge of the bed. "Anything! Tell me what a disappointment I am. Tell me I fucked up. *Again*!"

Michelle stood and made her way over to Cal. The second she touched him, he pushed her hand off.

"This disease is bullshit. Utter. Fucking. Bullshit!" Cal inhaled a few sharp breaths and paced, waiting for Bruce Banner to return so he could calm the fuck down, turn from green monster back to human.

How much longer could he stand to watch her slowly die?

That was the worst of it right there.

All she needed now was support. And he had to give it, endure it. Trouble was ... he had tired of climbing the mountain, of being the mountain. Of being the rock. The protection. A summit. He wanted to drop to the floor and crumble.

"The best thing about Mom was what came out of her mouth," he managed a minute or so later with a faint smile. "You never knew what she might say, and everyone around her braced themselves."

"That's true." Michelle grinned.

For the next several minutes, Cal and Michelle shared fond memories, including Constance in the conversation as well. After a while, they quieted.

Michelle yawned and looked at Cal. "Do you want to be alone with her a bit longer?"

"Yeah." His eyes never left his mother's face. He sat beside her on the bed again.

"The nurse will be in soon. Good night."

"Thanks, Mishy."

The second his cousin left, Cal folded his arms across his chest, rubbed his hands over his biceps, and stared into Constance's eyes. Strange ... *her* life started to flash before him in stages.

She used to climb a ladder to pick fruit from the trees.

She loved to cook.

She wore aprons. Every day and always a variety.

She shook her index finger when rebuking him.

She made him stand in the corner, and she made him scrub floors with a toothbrush.

She danced, twirling really, to her father's records.

When she smiled, the lines it made swelled all the way up to the corners of her blue eyes, and when it went extra wide, he saw her dimples. The ones she'd given him.

Cal took the brush from the nightstand drawer and began to comb his mother's hair for the first time in his entire life.

Each stroke giving him peace. Comfort.

They didn't need words.

After setting it aside, Cal gazed at his mother for a long time, peering at her in a way he'd never dared to before.

"Mom," he whispered as he pressed his fingers into hers, staring back and forth into her eyes.

Then a nurse entered the room, breaking his concentration. He asked for another minute or two.

Cradling his mother's face, he tried not to cry, but failed. Leaning closer, he kissed her softly on the forehead, then the cheek. He started to stand, but something wasn't quite right.

The something always missing nagged at him. The voice inside his head pulled on his sleeve.

Smiling, Cal put a hand on her cheek and peered into those unforgettable, haunting blue eyes, certain he saw tears forming.

"I love you," he choked out, "Mom."

He trailed a thumb beneath her eyes, wiped a tear from her cheek, and smiled. He gave her another kiss, and then he stood tall and proud.

A man.

He played with her fingers, but before he let go, he felt something. A gentle squeeze.

Cal gazed into her eyes, unable to breathe.

"You're a beautiful dancer," he muttered.

Another squeeze.

Cal smiled so wide his cheeks nearly burst.

She still looked beautiful in his eyes. God, she would always be beautiful. She would always be his mommy.

She was more than enough.

Despite all the helplessness and powerlessness he'd felt over the last several years of her disease, Cal finally realized he could give his mother what she needed most. What he needed most.

Love.

They'd been giving it to each other all along.

A wise woman once told him love didn't have to look like a picture-perfect postcard. It had only taken him twenty-four years to understand what that meant. It didn't *look* perfect. But it was.

Love looked like Constance Marie Prescott.

After giving his mom another kiss and repeating the words, *I love you*, Cal left the room and went upstairs, intent on writing Annie an email. It was late, and he was tired, but the urge to write her was strong.

The words came easily this time.

Dear Annie,

The last several weeks, I've missed you more than I thought possible. It shouldn't surprise me, but it does. Not because of you. You're beautiful, Annie. God, you're so beautiful. Any man would have to be fucking insane not to miss you. Maybe I am actually fucking insane. This house is about to make me insane...

It's me, though. Not you. It's always me. Fighting myself. For reasons you wouldn't understand. Or maybe you would. Because you've always understood me more than anyone I've ever known, more than I've been able to give you credit for. You've understood me better than I sometimes understand myself. I didn't know that existed in this selfish, fucked-up world.

I'm tired of apologizing for my behavior, for my lack. I want you to see me for who I am. I want to give you all of me.

My mother is at peace. That's what I meant before. I feel a change. A shift. I spoke with her a little while ago. I mean, I really spoke with her. I told her about you. I told her about the baby. What I wouldn't give to see a smile cross her face. But nothing I have can bring her back.

I told her I love her. Maybe that sounds simple to you, but to me, it's huge.

My mother never told me she loved me. Never. I never said it to her either. It was a habit. A horrible one. I regret it now, but she probably still wouldn't hear of such foolish talk in her home. How ironic that I can only tell her I love her when she can't possibly say it back. Nor can she scold me. I never thought I would miss the scolding.

I miss you, Annie. Your eyes. They're like a mirror, showing me what's really inside me. I've never seen myself as clearly as I do when I look at you. I need you, Annie Rebekah Baxter. I need you. That's something I've never told a woman. It's harder than saying I love you. For me anyway. But then again, that isn't saying much. The truth is, Annie, I never did need a woman the way I need you.

I'm going to bed. It's late. I'm tired.

I feel a strange peace too. A calm. One I haven't felt in a long time. I don't know if I've ever felt it quite like this. I hope you can have some of my peace too, or I hope you're finding your own. And I hope you're feeling better and aren't as nauseous as you were the last time you messaged. Please let me know ... everything.

I love you, baby.

– Cal

Constance Marie Prescott died later that night, in the early morning, only hours after Cal left her side, passing in her sleep. Her struggle had ended. Her suffering had ceased. Cal chose to think that his mother had not only heard every word he'd uttered that evening, but that she'd understood.

She had understood. He'd wiped a tear from her cheek. She'd squeezed his hand. She loved him.

Cal hoped she'd truly felt his love as well. He hoped she'd felt it all along, from the moment he'd been born.

Cal desperately wanted to believe the silent final conversation Constance had had with her only child, her son, meant she could finally let go. She could be free. She didn't need to hold on anymore. Or wait.

She could release.

Like a butterfly, slipping from its chrysalis, ready to fly away, to begin a new life.

Constance *had* loved him in her own way, and Cal knew it.

Believed it.

Accepted it.

Her blistering love, her strong sense of self, her hard-knock ways — it all reverberated through every part of his being.

At long last, Cal had had the courage to give his mom his love in a way he thought she never wanted. He braved giving her all of him. And with that love, with her passing, came a peace.

Cal could finally let go too. He had to.

Her death freed him. Relieving him of his own pain. The control he'd held over his soul for so long ... he could let go now. His own struggles had been dying a slow death right alongside his mother.

What he'd once thought was broken, but now knew had always been whole — like the trunk and body of that little baby elephant — finally made complete sense.

It was a boy who'd entered that cocoon, but it was a man who exited.

SADDLE UP

READY TO RIDE; COURAGE; RISK

I climb
inside
the walls
you erected
long ago
I tear them down
with my bare hands
with my womb
my strength
with a gentle persuasion
we craft a house
made of bricks
not cards
where promises
which began
as whispers
become a lion's roar

SEVENTY-ONE

Annie didn't know how long she'd been sitting on the couch in the grand room, the fire roaring across from her — the view spectacular, the photos and flames competing for her attention — editing pictures of a wedding she'd photographed on Bainbridge Island when she heard a rap on the front door.

For a split second, Annie wondered who would've been crazy enough to venture out into the cold December Washington weather besides her cigarette fiend of a mother — who was currently out back and smoking — as she glanced in the direction of the foyer.

After setting her things aside, Annie made her way to the door, her softest slippers shuffling against the hardwood, her blue jeans hugging her hips and resting below her blip of a belly. Her black, long-sleeved sweater covered the bump, the lamb's wool clinging to her skin.

The moment she reached the foyer, she cracked open the front door, then she opened it wider and sucked in a sharp breath.

Calvin Warner Prescott.

Looking fresh.

Gorgeous.

Like he belonged to her.

The man was clean-shaven, had his hair trimmed much shorter than when she'd met him in June. He wore a black, wool coat, the collar up and around his neck, dark-blue jeans, and boots. Looking hot despite the cold, he caused a wonderful sort of stinging to begin dancing across the back of her neck, the hairs there standing at attention as if they knew who was in their presence.

Her whole body did.

She hummed.

"Hello, Annie." Cal didn't miss a beat or bat an eyelash.

His voice still sounded like sex. But Annie didn't flinch. Didn't move a muscle. She didn't even blink. Until finally forcing herself to speak.

"What are you doing here?"

"You didn't reply to my email." He glanced up, flicking his bold eyes in her direction. He fingered the door trim. "You haven't been answering my calls either."

"So, you just show up here ... after, what? Three months. Without a word."

"No. I called. Several times. You refused to answer."

"Would you like a medal for your efforts?"

Cal let out a long, shaky breath while continuing to fiddle with the wood. Annie folded her arms across her chest.

"Constance died..." He sighed, shifting his gaze. "A few days ago."

"Oh, Cal..." Annie stepped toward him, but he pulled back. It was subtle, but he pulled back.

"I'm so sorry," she continued, wanting to reach out and grab him, to bring his body flush against hers, but after weeks and weeks of not touching him, it seemed he didn't want her embrace, and so she held back as well, jamming a thumb inside a front jean pocket as she inched away.

"How are you?" Cal glanced at her belly. "How have you been feeling?"

"I'm fine. The baby's fine." Her eyes darted around his face while her palm instinctively cradled her stomach. "I felt it move."

"Right now?" Cal swallowed.

"No." She smiled. "Last night. I felt it ... for the first time. I think."

Cal's eyes traveled from her belly back to the cedar trim. He couldn't seem to stop fidgeting with a splintered piece, smoothing his fingers over the sharp edges.

"Are you going to let me in?" Warm air from Cal's mouth mixed with the cold, and clouds blew toward her face. But Annie could only stare at him. *Let him in...* She did that months ago. "It's freaking cold out here."

Annie moved aside.

Cal stepped over the threshold.

Then she helped him remove his coat, pulling the sleeves down his arms and off his person. She inhaled his ocean, the cotton, his fresh-laundered scent. Her knees nearly buckled.

"You ignored my calls," he repeated as he glanced around the house.

Annie hung the garment on a nearby hook, avoiding his gaze, his words, that smell. Everything that would render her incompetent.

"Why didn't you answer?"

She opened her mouth, closed it, then breezed past him, making her way to the table, and picked up her water glass.

"Do I not even get so much as a hug from you?" Cal asked as he joined her. They stood at opposite ends, facing each other. "After all this time."

Annie lowered her glass, her hand now shaking, her heart taking over her throat. She glared at him. Lost her breath. Her eyes shrank to the width of dimes, her nostrils flaring like those of the bulls running down the streets in Pamplona.

"What? Are you afraid to touch me?" Cal smoothed a palm over the table-top, and she guffawed. "Do you think if you touch me, I'm going to just fuck you, right here ... on the kitchen table?"

"You never hesitated before." Annie matched his gaze, his posture. Her feet were firmly planted on the floor.

"I can recall a time when you needed to be ready."

"And I can recall that never stopped you from trying." She rolled her eyes. "Did you come all this way for a freaking hug?"

"I ... uh..." Cal flinched, breaking character a moment, his eyes softening, his voice cracking. "I have something to give you. Something that belonged to my mother."

Annie's stomach tingled. Her crown tingled. Her palms began to sweat. "Don't you think that's something personal ... that you should hold on to?"

The slider opened, and they both turned.

"Oh," Bev cooed as she entered, Barney trailing not far behind, "I didn't know you were expecting company today." She removed her jacket, draped it over a chair, and stood near the center of the table, Cal on her right, Annie on her left. "It's cold out there today."

"Neither did I," Annie mumbled, feigning a smile. "Mom, this is Cal. Cal, this is my mother, Beverly."

"Cal..." Beverly nodded, picking up the pug and introducing him as well, scratching the dog behind his ears as he snorted.

"It's nice to meet you both." Cal stuffed a hand in and out of his pocket.

"Would you like something to drink? I see my daughter hasn't given you anything." Bev glared at Annie, then she set Barney down. "We have water and juice. Or I can make coffee."

"Do you have any Crown?" he asked as though he'd been in the home a hundred times, as if Beverly weren't an alcoholic.

"I have Jim Beam." She grabbed the bottle from an upper cabinet and proceeded to pour him a small glass. "How long will you be staying?" She handed him the drink.

Cal took a sip, those green eyes still roving the walls, his hand still entering and exiting the pocket of his jeans.

"Mom," Annie interjected, clearing her throat, "I think we need some privacy."

"Oh ... well, I need to go to the market anyway." Bev rummaged through her purse, coming up with a set of keys. "Is there anything I can get for you?"

"No, thanks."

The moment her mother left, Annie realized she didn't know what to do with her hands either. Keep them at her sides? Twirl pieces of hair? Shove them into her pockets? Use them to rip Cal's clothes off, then slide them all over his body?

The second the automatic garage door finished shutting, Cal moved closer to Annie. They both stood near the sink. Then he finished the Beam, set the glass down, and turned toward Annie.

"My mother," he began with a sigh, giving her his profile, "was worse than I ever could've imagined." Palms on the countertop, he hung his head. "She couldn't speak. She wasn't..." He lifted his head, then shook it. "While I was there, in that house, I dealt with feelings I didn't even know I had. Or feelings I pretended not to have. Things I tried to deny for years.

"I wish you could've met her." He squeezed the back of his neck and inhaled. "I'm so sorry I didn't take you out there." He glanced out the kitchen window. "Even though she wasn't the same woman I once knew — the person who raised me — I still regret not bringing you there. I... I didn't want you to see me..." His voice shook. His head shook. "Like this..." He gestured at his body. "Every fucking day."

Cal put so much weight on the countertop it seemed he might dislodge it from the cabinetry.

"You were a good son, Cal," Annie whispered as she studied each vein.

Each muscle. Each intake of breath. For the first time, she understood — truly understood — why he'd needed time away in California. Alone. She made circles over the back of his shirt. "Your mother loved you." Electricity ignited on the tips of her fingers, bouncing back and forth between the two of them. "Even if she couldn't say it ... she loved you."

Cal glanced up, sucking in a deep breath. "You read my email?"

"Of course I did."

"You wouldn't ... you didn't reply. You wouldn't answer my calls."

"I needed time." She dropped her hand and sighed.

"Haven't I given you enough of that already?" He laughed a little.

"Cal..." Annie fingered his collar, then the shorter hairs meeting the nape of his neck. "I would've been honored to know your mom."

"This is what you do," he whispered, placing his hands on her waist and staring into her eyes. "How...?"

Annie's eyes closed. She swayed her head gently from side to side. Everything seemed to move in slow motion as Cal pushed the tips of his fingers through the back of her hair, pulling at the strands, holding her there. Then her eyes popped open. She inched from his grasp. "You said you had something from your mother."

Cal looked across the kitchen toward the table, his lips curving upward, dimples forming. He leaned his ass against the counter, crossed his arms, and peered at her. "Have your feelings for me changed?"

"What?" She practically choked on the word. Her hands flew to her hips. "I still want you. Which is why I don't know how *this* is going to work."

"I can see in your eyes that you want me." He smirked. "I'm asking if you still love me."

"No! I mean yes. No, my feelings haven't changed." Her nostrils flared. She pinched her nails into her waist. "God, I'm the one who should be asking you that question. It's not a switch I can just turn off and on, you know?" She flung a finger up and down, then started to pace. "So..." She stopped and smacked a hand on the countertop. "You flew all the way out here to ask me stupid fucking questions?"

"No," he said and grabbed her wrist. "I came all the way out here to ask you something else."

Cal stepped into her space, stepping so close to Annie she thought she would become a part of him. But she'd become a part of him long ago. Maybe before she'd ever met him.

"I never thought I could love someone the way I love you." Cal picked up Annie's left hand and played with her fingers. He stared at the side of her face. "I'm sorry I couldn't be everything you needed ... when you needed it." He lifted her chin. "But I'm ready to be with you now." He took in a deep breath. "If you'll have me."

Annie's heart thumped outside her chest. She could hear the beating everywhere like a loud drum. Tears started to slide down her cheeks.

"Don't cry, baby." Cal wiped away the drops, then he put a hand in his pocket and pulled out a ring. "I came all the way up here to give you this." He paused, his own eyes starting to water. "It belonged to my grandmother and then my mother." Cal slid the band onto Annie's finger. "I want to marry you." Their eyes locked. "Will you marry me, Annie Rebekah Baxter?" He cupped her cheek. "*My heavy.*"

She smiled through fresh tears while gazing down at the solid platinum band. An ornate carving encircled it. As she turned it over and over, she began to shake. Everywhere. Then she squeezed Cal's hand, buried her face in his chest, and concentrated on breathing. Deeply and slowly. Willing herself not to hyperventilate.

Cal wrapped his arms securely around her. The two of them remained like that for several minutes, only holding each other and breathing.

After a while, Annie let go and peered at him, looking at him the way she had the band. She swept away more tears, then walked back toward the table and swallowed the rest of her water. Her eyes bounced around the room.

"Annie..."

She looked square at him. "Having a baby isn't a reason to get married."

Cal glanced off into the distance, made a noise, and pinched the bridge of his nose. "God, Annie..." He took a few steps toward her. "Why do you do it? Do you think this is something I haven't really thought about?"

"I don't know what you think or want half the time. I haven't seen you in forever, Cal." She stepped toward him as well. "You didn't want me with you in California. You hardly called or texted me while you were there. Not until ... until ... you wait until now to let me in, to tell me everything. I understand why you needed time, but it still hurts. I'm still scared. My mind is still spinning from that email you sent. I'm still soaking those words into my heart. I'm trying to accept them. How do I know *this* is what you really want?" She eyed the ring, twirling it around and around. It was loose on her slender finger.

"Because it's who I am." Two more steps and he was inches from her again. "You know who I am. You've always known. And because..." Cal glanced away, then back again. "Because I'm not afraid." He lifted her hand, touched the band, and swallowed. "I know what I want. *Do you?*"

"I don't know," she whispered. "Everything has happened so fast."

"Bullshit," he replied, and Annie twisted the ring again. "You do know." Cal touched her chin. "You aren't the kind of girl who doesn't know what she wants. You know, Annie. You know exactly what you want." He grinned.

She tried not to follow suit, but his smile was infectious. She did want him, this, all of it, but she never wanted to hurt again the way she had these last few months without him.

"Do you remember what I told you the night before you left Miami?" he asked as she gaped at him. The quiet man wouldn't shut up now. "I said if you really loved me, it wouldn't fade. It would stay. It would last. I'm not fading, Annie. I'm staying. I've. Never. Left. You." He held her gaze. "Being away from you has been unbearable for me too. I've wanted you more than I thought possible."

Annie eyeballed him.

"No, baby." He slipped his fingers into hers and peered into her eyes. "I'm not talking about the sex." He kissed her cheek. "Although I did miss it." He ran a knuckle over her jaw, and she shivered. "I need you in a way I've never needed anyone. I missed having you in my bed ... asleep next to me. I missed talking to you over a meal. I missed your laugh. I missed listening to you, hearing you, the sound of your voice. But I think what I missed most," he said and paused, brushing his thumb near the corner of her eye, "were your eyes. When you look at me..." Cal trailed off, turned his head, and squeezed her fingers. "When you look at me, I'm the man I want to be." Their eyes locked. "Baby or no baby, *I want you, Annie.*"

Running her fingers up his chest, she stopped upon reaching his shoulders, then she pulled him against her, nuzzling her nose into the nape of his neck.

"I want to marry you," she whispered, a smile taking shape on her lips. "I love you."

Cal cradled her face and kissed her, tasting her upper lip, then her lower, Annie already moaning and deepening the kiss. Her hands ran through his hair, his tangled in hers, until they were both a mess of limbs and teeth and tongues. And love.

"Jesus, baby," Cal panted, inching back some, palms on her cheeks.

Annie smiled. She nipped his lower lip, sliding a palm to the zipper of his jeans and rubbing him over the denim. "Fuck," she whispered, watching how she touched him, her eyes wide, her heart rate increasing.

"Keep that up..." Cal began, still out of breath, kissing her neck and jaw as he removed her hand. "And I'll come ... right in my fucking pants."

Their eyes met.

Their lips crashed.

Her nails scratched up his backside.

"You smell like home," Cal muttered as he trailed his nose over her neck until hundreds of goosepimples formed. He bit her skin. "And you taste like home."

"I love you," she said again, and Cal swallowed her words with another kiss.

Annie whimpered, wrapping a leg around his thigh, clawing the skin of his neck, moaning and kissing him, keeping her other hand on his hip, trying desperately not to go for his zipper.

Then Cal's tongue became fierce, licking and tasting her with more vigor, more and more and more — until Annie forgot where she was.

But not what she wanted.

"Maybe we should wait," she heaved, pushing against his chest, but he didn't stop. The fantastic pressure. His mouth on hers. A hand on a tit, squeezing and squeezing, continuing to bring her to the place where the rest of the world erased.

"We should wait," she repeated, trying to catch her breath.

"For what?" Yanking on the back of her hair, he caused her head to tilt up. The man stared at her lips. "We're alone." He bit her neck, sucked on her skin. "We can go upstairs."

"Cal..." she moaned, still rocking her hips. "Maybe..." She exhaled. "Maybe we should wait until *after* we're married."

Standing tall, Cal gently pushed her off him, then squared her hips. "We've waited months already."

"I know..." Annie slipped a thumbnail into her mouth.

"You're serious?"

"I'm serious."

Cal pinched the back of his neck, stepped aside, and glanced at the empty liquor glass. "Annie, you're being ridiculous."

"It's not ridiculous. It's romantic."

Scoffing, Cal tore his gaze from the highball, and moved forward. Calm. In control. Eyes like laser beams. Nudging her backside against the countertop, placing his hands on either side of her waist, he hemmed her in. The tent in his pants made contact exactly where it was supposed to, pressing ever so gently against the triangle between her legs.

"Since when do you want romance?" Cal studied her face, combing every feature there until Annie cracked a wide smile. "Huh?" He trailed his nose along her jawline. "I know what you want, baby, and it's not romance."

Cal tried to kiss her, but she turned her head to the side.

"This is different." She grinned, daring a glance back at him. "Maybe I do now."

"*Really*?"

"Really," she squeaked.

"You said this is different." His eyes moved back and forth. His jaw clenched. "Why is this different?"

Annie swallowed, gulping really, as she blinked and blinked.

"Why?" he repeated.

She tucked her bottom lip between her teeth. She itched. Burned. She wanted Cal to flip her around, strip her bottoms to her ankles, and fuck her — now and hard. The pregnancy only made it worse.

God, God, God.

Why had she suggested such a foolish thing when she couldn't follow through? Now she had to tell him something. And it had to sound mildly convincing.

"The waiting," she began, chewing more on her lip, shifting her head, "would make that night, our wedding night, that much more special."

"Annie..." He pulled her chin back front and center. "The day we get married couldn't be any more special if I waited a year for you." Cal met her eyes, innocent as a dove yet sly as a fox. His fingers found the belt loops of her jeans and tugged. "That night, that entire day, will be special because I'll promise in front of our families to love you and hold you and to be with you always."

Then he went in for the kill. He put his lips to her ear. "So, you're telling me, after all this time, your body isn't *aching* with any desire?"

Annie wouldn't meet his gaze. She pushed his wrists off her jeans.

"Look at me, Annie."

She locked onto his eyes. Green to green. Ocean to sky.

"Tell me, Annie." He paused. Waited. He picked up strands of her hair and played with them. "Tell me you don't want me to fuck you, *now*, in the kitchen. Bare," he whispered in her ear, and she shivered. "I'll tear your jeans off and bend you over that table." He nodded across the room. "I'll fuck your sweet little pussy so hard — until you remember who we are and forget all this fucking bullshit."

Heat filled her belly. The space between her legs throbbed. Her mouth opened, but no words followed. She touched his cheek and simply let out a breath, a long jagged one — one she'd apparently been holding for several weeks.

"Yes?" Cal cupped her over her jeans, and Annie gasped. "Tell me, Annie."

"Oh, God," she moaned, "you're such a bastard."

Smiling, Cal bunched as much of her hair as he could in his palm, pulling and pulling, until her head tilted toward the ceiling. "Unbutton your fucking jeans."

She fiddled with the zipper. The moment she was free, he slipped a hand past the elastic of her panties.

"Fuck..." she uttered, scarcely able to breathe as his fingers met flesh.

"Tell me what I want to hear." He stroked her perfectly. "God, I've missed your voice." His lips were at hers. "You're so fucking wet." He rocked their bodies in rhythm, caressing her until she was a fucking mess. "I need to hear you say it, baby. What you want. *Please*."

Cal pushed his nose past the scoop neck of her sweater, breathing all over her skin, then he began biting her breasts over the material, pressing his face into her tits, his head moving side to side while continuing to massage her clit.

"Say it, Annie."

"I want you," she burst, quivering, closing her eyes and pulling on his hair so tight she thought it might rip from his scalp. "God... Fuck me, Cal." Beginning to cry, she grabbed at the shoulder seams on his shirt, pinching the cotton, bunching it and squeezing him. Tears of pleasure slid down her cheeks. "*Fuck me. Take me. Please.*"

The automatic garage door rose. Annie tried to shift her head, but Cal wouldn't allow it. He shoved two fingers into her hole and yanked on her hair harder.

"Give yourself to me right the fuck now." Cal continued touching her the same way he'd spoken. "Give me all of you. Don't worry about the goddamn door."

"You have me."

"Show me," he bit out. "Let go. Let go now. I have you. Let go of everything and come. Come, Annie. Here. Now."

Cal's fingers curved, hitting the spot that made her instantly cry out. Letting go of her hair, he covered her mouth.

Annie looked into Cal's eyes as she whimpered behind his palm, as she clutched his sweaty neck, as she rammed her body against his touch, as she obeyed and released, going limp, relaxing — everywhere.

Head to toe.

Muscles to jelly.

She peeled her fingers from his body and gripped the counter while her head fell back as far as it would go. Cal put his face in her neck, smiling, and ran his nose along her jawline, toward her cheeks, sweeping away a few of her tears using only his face, then he zipped and buttoned her jeans.

Annie's chest rose vehemently, her insides still tingling and pulsating, the sensations running through her, dripping like honey.

"You're beautiful," he whispered, kissing her cheeks over and over. *"Just like this."*

The handle turned on the door.

Annie stood tall as Cal stepped back. Both of them looked wildly into each other's eyes, grinning and ready to burst.

"Hello." Beverly set a couple of bags down on the island behind them.

Cal and Annie made no reply.

Bev looked at her daughter. Annie looked at the ceiling. While Cal stood with his back to them. No one spoke but Barney. He waltzed into the kitchen, grunting and snorting.

"Oh, well, wittle Barney will twalk to me, won't you, boy? Mommy has a treat for you." Bev pulled his favorite from one of the brown paper bags.

Annie glanced at Cal's zipper, then she clapped a hand over her mouth and stifled a giggle.

"Are you okay?" Bev eyed her daughter as she placed her purse on the counter.

Annie laughed. Beverly rolled her eyes and started to put away the groceries.

"I picked up lunch too." Bev opened the fridge.

Annie ignored her mother, focusing instead on Cal and his protrusion. He stood very still, facing the sink, palms on the countertop. Because it was all he could do.

"Are either of you going to fucking talk to me?" Beverly snarled, turning around with a block of cheese in hand, pointing it back and forth between them.

"Yes, Mom, God." Annie tucked her messy hair behind her ears. "What did you get for lunch?"

"Pizza and salad. It's still in the car."

"I'll get it," Annie offered.

"Cal can get it. Please, Cal, would you mind?" Beverly batted her copper lashes.

"I don't know if he can." Annie laughed.

"The car is open?" he asked as he washed his hands at the sink.

"Yes, thank you." Beverly glared at Annie.

She giggled while Cal stepped into the garage.

Beverly took a large jug of Chablis out of the fridge. "What the hell is going on with you today?"

"Nothing. Everything."

"Is he staying here?"

"I don't know where he's staying." Annie giggled as she took out three plates.

Beverly placed her hands on her hips and raised her brows. "Did you have a drink while I was gone?"

"No."

"Well, I'm having one."

Annie set the table while Beverly chugged half the contents of her freshly poured glass. Cal returned, minus his hard-on, holding a large cardboard pizza box and a Styrofoam container. Delightful smells filled the air.

"This isn't your food, you wittle spoiled baby," Beverly said to Barney as she bent down and scratched his back. Then he followed Cal to the table, paws tapping the flooring.

"Thank you for picking up lunch," Cal said as he placed the takeout down.

Annie stood in the kitchen, still giggling, interrupting the exchange between her mother and her lover — fuck, her fiancé — forgetting why she'd come back into the room in the first place.

"Of course," Bev replied, eyeing her daughter again.

Annie held a palm to her mouth. She laughed and laughed.

"Annie, for God's sake." Beverly glanced at Cal, and he made his way over.

The moment he reached her, Annie stopped cackling. Then on a dime, she began to cry. The crying like the laughing: steady, rising, falling, out of control. Whooping and sobbing.

Cal put his arm around her. "Come on, baby. You need to eat." He moved pieces of hair from her eyes.

"I can't." She began to hyperventilate. "Oh ... fuck."

"Shhh." He kissed the top of her head and stroked her cheek. "Breathe, baby." He held her close for several minutes until she calmed, until her breathing slowed. "Come on." He took her hands away from her face and led her to the table. "Sit down."

"I want my water," she said, sniffling.

"I'll get it." Beverly sighed. "I want my jug."

Cal stood behind Annie's chair, gathering her hair and pushing it over her shoulder toward the front of her body. He began to massage her neck and back. "Keep focusing on the sounds of your breath."

Annie closed her eyes, only inhaling and exhaling for what felt like days. Once she settled, Cal lowered to his haunches and looked up, brushing the corners of her lids with his thumbs. She stared fervently into his eyes.

"I love you," he whispered, placing both palms on her face, cradling her cheeks.

Annie's eyes filled with tears as she nodded, her head moving in unison with Cal's strong hands. He kept peering at her, assuring her he was going to be there for her.

He wasn't leaving.

Or going anywhere.

Ever again.

Beverly breathed another sigh of relief as she carried her jug and a glass of water to the table. Cal stood, kissed Annie's forehead, then sat down beside her.

"You don't eat pizza?" Beverly asked Cal a moment or two later, staring at him and his plate full of salad from across the table. He'd placed strips of salami off to the side.

"I do."

Beverly held her hand out to Barney, feeding him some meat.

"I'll take a piece now, please." Annie extended her dish toward Cal, and he put a slice of sausage and mushrooms on it.

They ate. No one spoke. Beverly drank. Cal and Annie chewed. Barney sniveled. After Bev drained her glass, she hoisted the jug up, ready to pour.

"Do you really need more, Mom?"

"I don't recall hearing any protest out of your mouth when your boyfriend asked for a drink *this morning.*"

Cal took the bottle from Beverly and finished filling her glass. After setting it down, he grabbed Annie's hand and gave it a firm squeeze.

"So. Cal." Bev batted those lashes, her tone the same as when she'd asked him about the pizza. "How long are you planning on being in Washington?"

"I'm not sure yet." He cleared his throat. "I arrived this morning."

"Oh..." Bev cooed as Annie eyed her mother cautiously. "And ... where are you staying?"

"Mother..."

"It's okay, Annie," Cal replied, glancing at her, then back at Beverly. "I actually haven't made any plans yet. I have to—"

Beverly slapped her hand on the table, interrupting him. "Well, you can stay here! Right, Annie?" Beverly brought her glass to her lips, ready to take a drink.

Annie looked at Cal's profile. He eyed Bev.

"I don't want to impose on you, Ms. Baxter."

Beverly began to choke on her wine. She patted her chest. "Cal..." She snorted and grinned. "My name is *Saint* not Baxter."

Cal glanced at Annie, and Annie rolled her eyes.

"Besides," she continued, "I'm only nine years older than you ... so you don't need to call me *Ms. Anything.*" She tapped her nails on the side of her wineglass. "Call me Beverly." Her smile now looked fake. "And you're not imposing. I mean, you already knocked up my daughter. I don't think it matters much, then, if you fuck her upstairs in her own bedroom. That is why you came here, yes? After all this time?"

"Jesus Christ, Mom." Annie stood and glared at her mother, nostrils flaring.

Beverly looked at her plate and stabbed her salad.

Cal grabbed Annie's hand, pulled on her arm, and nodded. "Sit, baby. It's okay."

"I'm sorry, Cal." Annie winced, scooting the chair toward the table with such force that the bottom of the legs made a horrible noise against the flooring. "My mother is..."

"Oh ... your mother is...?" Beverly mocked. *"Concerned for you."* She impaled the lettuce with her fork again.

"She has every right to be upset," Cal interjected, tossing Beverly a curt glance.

Annie played with the half-eaten piece of pizza on her plate.

"That's right. We're all adults here." Beverly twirled the stem of her wineglass. "We can say what we think."

"Would you like to know what I'm thinking?" Cal asked with a bluntness Annie wanted to kiss him for displaying.

"I would love to know." Bev leaned forward, squinting at him from across the table.

"I did come here to sleep with your daughter," he said, and Beverly's eyes bulged. "But it's because I'm in love with her. It's because I don't want to be without her."

Silence descended over the room. Even Barney was quiet.

"I... I asked Annie..." he started but stopped. Gazing at his heavy, he nodded.

"Mom..." She took over, stretching her left hand across the tabletop. "Cal asked me to marry him."

Beverly's jaw dropped. She looked at her daughter, then at the band. Back and forth.

"Son of a bitch!" Bev finally exclaimed. "My God." She put a palm near her chest and fanned herself. "My God," she repeated. "No wonder you were emotional, sweetie. Is this what you want?" Beverly leaned forward, speaking as if Cal weren't even in the room, getting a better look at the ring. "It's a big deal. This is your life. Your goals."

"It is, Mom." A beautiful confidence colored Annie's cheeks, lighting her eyes like a rainbow shooting across the sky. "It's what I want."

Beverly grinned like a fool and stood, glancing at the two of them, her nearly empty plate in hand. Pausing, she peered at Cal. "Well, you most certainly better stay here. Annie doesn't even know how badly she needs to be fuc—"

"Mom!" Annie interjected, holding a palm near her forehead, covering her eyes. "For God's sake."

Beverly laughed and set her dish by the sink. "What? Everyone knows how horny pregnant women are. Now you can—"

"Stop, Mom. Please."

Grabbing her coat, Beverly jammed a smoke in her mouth and went toward the slider, the unlit cigarette jiggling between her lips as she mumbled to herself, Barney not far behind.

"I'm sorry, Cal," Annie said as soon as the slider shut.

"Annie, if my mother..." he began, his eyes starting to water as he looked away. "She'd be raising plenty of hell too." He gained his composure, feigned a smile, and met her gaze.

"Your mother wasn't an alcoholic." She eyed the jug of wine.

"Does she drink like this every day?"

"Yes," she whispered, trying to swallow another bite of pizza past the gigantic lump in her throat. "I didn't know... I didn't know if you wanted me to tell her right away about your mom."

"I'll tell her ... when she comes back in." His hands curled into fists. "It was probably better that we waited."

After wiping her fingers on her napkin and taking a sip of water, Annie touched the back of Cal's head. "Your hair is so short." She toyed with the razor-clipped pieces. "I barely have any to hold on to."

"You didn't have a problem in the kitchen." He grinned.

"Neither did you." She smirked while bumping his shoulder.

"I wanted it short. I grew it out while I was at Mom's."

"What?" she stuttered. "What do you mean you *grew it out*?"

"I never had it cut."

"Holy shit." Annie tried to imagine what he must've looked like, and she wished he'd sent a selfie. "That must've felt good."

"It did, actually. I grew a beard too."

Annie laughed. "You're a wild and crazy man, Calvin Prescott." She trailed her knuckles along his jawline, becoming mesmerized. "Grow it again."

"The beard?"

"Yes." She smiled, grabbed her plate, and stood.

"I don't think so." He laughed.

"I remember..." She swallowed, staring at him. "I remember when I first came back from New York. I remember your face ... your skin." She closed her eyes, shook some, then opened them. "And your scruff against my thighs..."

"Do you want to go upstairs now?" He smacked her butt cheek.

"Stop it." She grinned and began to walk away, but Cal snagged Annie's hand.

"You really felt the baby kick?"

"Yes..." She stared into his eyes. "Well, not kick exactly. It was more like a flutter. A swoosh." She smiled.

Cal pulled her toward him and set her plate aside. Slowly, he rolled her sweater up her abdomen, one centimeter at a time. Until the hem rested below her bra line. Putting a hand on the small of her back, he brought her navel closer as Annie's eyes filled with tears. She ran her hands through Cal's short hair over and over, her nails pricking his skin.

Placing an ear against her stomach, Cal listened as her insides made sounds. Digestive ones. Annie made sounds too. Sniffling, crying happy tears. Warmth traveled through her entire body as she rocked a little in his hold, Cal's head moving with her gentle motions.

Then a hiccup or a flutter passed through the walls of her uterus.

She stilled. Went silent.

Didn't move a muscle or breathe.

"Shhh," she whispered.

It happened again, and she grinned.

As Cal tilted his head up, a smile wider than one found on a jack-o-lantern spread across his face. Tears wet his eyes. He swallowed past the lump in his throat as he rolled her sweater back down and kissed her tiny little baby bump.

"You really don't have any plans?" She ran a finger along his jawline. "You just showed up here unannounced with no idea what was coming next?"

"You're my plan, Annie Baxter." He gazed at her smiling face. "We do have to go back down there in the next day or two. I still have to make additional arrangements for the funeral."

"*We*?"

"Are you free?" he teased.

"I've never felt freer." She glanced at her mother and Barney on the porch. "And you're sure ... you're sure you still want to marry me even after witnessing that brand of crazy?" She nodded, and Cal smiled, and it warmed her from the inside out. "You're smiling now, but you still have to meet my father."

"Come here." Cal scooted his chair from the table and patted his thigh.

Annie sat on his lap while Cal put a hand on her waist and looked into her eyes, sporting the most earnest gaze she'd ever seen him display.

"I'm sorry I wasn't here for you."

"You already apologized. It's okay."

"No, Annie." He wiggled her hips. "It's not okay."

Annie's eyes ticked back and forth. She swallowed.

"I'm sorry," Cal repeated, pressing his fingers deeper into her waist.

They stared into each other's eyes. Then Cal leaned his head against Annie's chest. She rubbed her fingers through his hair, holding him to her.

He breathed her in. Soaked her in. He was full of her.

Cal was the ocean.

And Annie was the sky.

He was home.

Running through the tangerine fields.

Finally.

SWIM

MOVE THROUGH WATER; NOT GO UNDER; SINK OR
SWIM; LIVE OR DIE; SURVIVE OR PERISH

learn to swim
butterfly
backstroke
breaststroke
freestyle
please everyone
please
no one
drown
Olympic judges waste my time
I am drowning...
in amniotic fluid
or I am
flailing
in the ocean
surrounding your heart
and mine
drown wade drown paddle
DROWN
fuck
come up for air

toss me
your circular-shaped preserver
or I'll give you mine
and we will share
the orange ring
and find safety
riding the tides

Seventy-Two

Annie should've been happy Cal had brought her to the beach, ready to do something she'd suggested, but the drive to listen and learn and surf wasn't in her today. Or it had left her.

The anticipation of the week's upcoming event kept her on the edge of sorrow. If she climbed on the surfboard, if she pushed herself, she might slip. Not into the ocean. She could handle crashing into the floor of the sea. What she couldn't do was slip over the precipice of memories. That cliff was at least twenty or thirty feet deep...

Straight.

Down.

They found a spot several yards from the shore, dropped their things, but held their boards. A few people were in the water. Some on the sand.

"The first thing I want you to do—"

"I've done this before." Annie cut Cal off with a smile, arching a brow. "Remember?"

The sun hid behind a few white clouds, but it couldn't trap the bright rays of light. Or mask the insistence on Cal's handsome face. "When?"

"I was sixteen."

"Who taught you? One of your boys?"

"No. Yes. Not really."

"Show me what you remember."

Annie marched toward the water.

"No." Cal took a few giant steps, blocking her from moving forward. "Here." He pointed at the ground, then he grabbed her board and placed it on the sand.

"You want me to get down ... on the sand and—"

"And show me the moves."

"Oh. I'll show you the moves." She lifted a brow.

Cal placed his own board beside hers, crossed his arms, and waited, his chest inflating like Superman's.

"For God's sake, Prescott..." She rolled her eyes, but Cal only stared her down, waiting for her to comply.

Annie scoffed, then stretched out on her board facedown, head up, looking like a penguin ready to glide across sand.

Cal walked around her, doing a complete three-sixty, whistling. "Sexy, baby."

"This is my eyeline," she interjected, slicing the air with a palm, indicating where her eyes should rest. "This is my middle." She wiggled her torso over the imaginary line she drew in the center of the nine-foot-six board. "It's coming back to me."

Cal lowered to his haunches. "Knees and feet together." He brought her ankles closer until they touched. "Good. Now show me how you stand and balance."

"Really?"

"Annie..." Cal said as he stood. "Since when do you have a problem listening to me?"

"This board is not your bed."

"No, but you're making me want to spank the living fuck out of you."

Whipping her head around, she squinted up at him. But then she cracked a smile. He looked so freaking beautiful. Dressed in a wetsuit and backlit by the sun. Annie stood, grabbed the board — without showing him how she would balance, and she would balance — and jerked her head in the direction of the Pacific. "Let's go."

"Are you always this impatient?"

"I'm restless."

"The ocean will calm you." He played with her ponytail as they made their way to the water.

"The ocean calms you." She bit her lip. "It makes me nervous."

"Nothing makes you nervous. Doing this is going to settle you. I know the water makes you feel good."

"Do we have to?" Annie stopped a couple feet from the shoreline.

"What's going on with you?"

Change. Stuff, she thought.

Where were they now?

Thirty minutes from Ojai at Mandalay Beach. Miami to Seattle to California. Where would they live? When would they actually get married? And would they marry? Or would this be one of those long engagements ending when someone inevitably backed out?

"Maybe surfing isn't safe for the baby."

"We've talked about this." Cal studied the side of her hardened face. "I researched it."

"Google is not my doctor."

"Do you want me to call your doctor?" Cal stepped in front of her until they stood chest to chest, toe to toe, heart to heart. "That's not what this is."

She gave him her shoulder and made her way toward the water.

"Damn it, Annie," he mumbled as he followed, his footfalls pounding the wet sand, his board in hand.

Several wipeouts and dozens of waves later, Annie's body gave new meaning to the word tired. Not merely pregnant-tired, but exhausted and sore. Leaving him to it, she carried her board over her head and came back to their blanket to rest. With a large towel draped across her shoulders, she spent the next thirty minutes or so digging her toes into the sand, sunglasses on, watching Cal.

In the black wetsuit.

With those defined muscles.

His hair slicked back.

Water beading over his exposed skin.

His ass looking particularly delectable as he paddled against the waves, turtle-rolled, and hoisted his spectacular forty-five-year-old body on top of his twenty-five-year-old board.

The man was in the zone.

Annie also spent time picking over the details of the week. The thirty-foot precipice of sorrow — the funeral and the rest of the family she had yet to meet. She hadn't been to a service since... She had to bury that thought —

along with her feet under millions of inconsequential but essential grains of sand.

They'd scattered her brother's ashes in the Pacific Ocean...

Cal trotted toward her, wet hair matted to the side, surfboard in hand, a satisfied smile on his face. A peace in his eyes he had at one time misplaced.

"I need a date," she yelled as he closed the distance between them.

"We can go out tonight." He dropped his board, then took a seat beside her on the blanket. Grabbing a towel, he wiped his face. "Where do you want to go?"

"A wedding date." She eyeballed him.

"Write it in the sand." He nodded toward the ground as he took a bottle of water from the cooler. "We do good things in the sand."

"I can't be waddling down the aisle." Annie grabbed the bottle and took a few sips.

"Let's wait until after the baby is born, then."

"No. Life will happen. The baby will happen."

He swiped the water and guzzled it. "Have you thought of any other names?" He burped.

"You still haven't told me if you want to know the sex." Annie shifted, lay down, and rested the back of her head on his lap. He was cold and wet. She blinked up at him.

"Sure. You?"

"Maybe." She fidgeted with the zipper on her suit, pulling it up and down. The noise and sensation pacified her the way a strand of hair around her fingers did.

"It will be fine." He touched her wrist, putting a stop to her telltale sign. "Either way, it will be fine."

Annie sighed several times.

"Do you want to tell me what's going on?" He glanced down at her, then removed her shades. "I do have ways of finding out." He bounced his brows, laughed a little, then swallowed some more of the water.

After another exhale, she started again on the zipper.

"Annie." He grabbed her hand.

"It's like..." She huffed and puffed. "If I make a bad choice now, it will ruin things later." She covered her eyes, then peeked through the web of her fingers. "I have pregnant-brain."

"Is that a real thing?"

"Oh, you have so much to learn." She smiled but then turned pensive again. Her breathing slowed. "One decision changes fate, Cal."

Dropping his chin, he peered down at her, not looking a day over thirty-five, sun behind him, green eyes changing to the color of a gem, damp bangs dangling over his forehead despite the shorter cut.

Touching her cheek, he smoothed his fingertips over the contours of her face. "You can't go through life without choices."

"I know." She swallowed. "But what if I do something wrong? What if one of those *choices* accidentally hurts the baby?" She cradled her stomach. "What if something happens if I choose to find out the sex? If I change an appointment? He wasn't supposed to work late. *He made one choice.*"

Peter would never meet their baby. He had wanted to have his own baby. He had been too young to die.

Cal glanced out at the ocean, wiggled his toes, and exhaled. "Superstitions be damned, Annie. We have a funeral to get through this week." He drew lines in the sand with one of his fingers. "I should've given this more thought before I asked you to come here with me."

"I'll be there for you." Annie sat bolt upright and stroked his cheek. "It's all I've ever wanted. I'm fine."

Cal leaned closer, grabbed the back of her neck, and planted kisses all over her salty skin. "All"—*kiss*—"you"—*kiss*—"ever"—*kiss*—"wanted."

"Yes," she groaned, and their lips met. He tasted like salt as well, like the complete opposite of superstition. She held both his cheeks and stared at him. "I can handle it. I've handled *you*." Then her tongue slipped into his mouth.

Annie would swim with the big fishes. Make choices. Have a baby. Bury sadness. Inch away from the cliff that called out to her in the early morning hours, waking her up at three o'clock in the morning.

After breaking the kiss, Cal pulled back, hugged his knees, and looked out into the distance. He flicked pieces of nothing off his wetsuit.

"My mother hated surfing." He smiled tightly.

"Really?" Annie glanced at him. "No. She probably—"

"What the fuck am I going to say?" He sighed. "At the funeral?" Cal met her gaze. "To the people?"

"You're good with people."

"Constance wasn't always so good with them." Cal shook his head and smiled. "People will be there who knew my grandfather. He was the one who loved Ojai. She moved us here to be closer to them."

"I'm sorry." Her throat bobbed as she swallowed. "This week. I don't know..." She shrugged. "I'm supposed to be the one making you feel better."

"You make me *feel.*"

The air hung like static between them, their eyes speaking millions of miles of everything the silence wouldn't say.

"What else do you remember about her, your mom, from when you were younger? C'mon. Something positive."

"The light catches your eyes," he said instead.

Annie had never seen him so serious — and this was Cal — the definition of concentration and intensity.

"I see myself in there."

"What do you see?"

Cal glanced again to the ocean — a straight line of depth and courage all the way to the horizon. "Both of us chase death."

Both of us demand a reason for it when there isn't one, Annie thought.

The baby would replace the grieving. Was that how it would be? One thing replacing another. Distractions.

Did she chase death?

It didn't matter.

Everything would be all right.

Annie would be what he needed.

That was, after all, what she'd wanted all those weeks without him. She didn't need to drain him. She wished to be the stars he saw inside her eyes. The flashes, the flecks, the comets. The reason one stayed up late toting a blanket to recline in the grass and stare at the blinking canvas. Hoping to catch one swoosh, one brilliant streak as it zoomed across the night sky.

To replace empty with hope.

The way the baby would.

Cal and Annie would ride the cosmic wave together.

Wherever it might take them.

SEVENTY-THREE

Annie stared at the animals arranged on the corner bookshelf in the sitting room, inspecting each one's size and strength, wondering where and when Constance had collected all of them.

Which ones might have been gifts?

Which might have been purchased when traveling?

No two elephants were alike — except for a beautiful solid crystal mother and baby. As Annie reached out and touched the smaller one, the light coming from the front windows illuminated its rotund shape, making the glass sparkle, creating a rainbow.

"Are you hungry?" Cal snuck up behind Annie, touching her waist.

She shook, letting go of the little elephant, the motion causing it to clank against the mother. Cal laughed.

"Shut up." She glanced over her shoulder after tucking him back in place. "You scared me."

"Michelle is making lunch." Cal played with the tips of her hair.

"Can you get my camera?"

"You want to photograph my mother's old relics?" Cal's eyes roved over the statues. "You do see beauty in everything..." Then his breath caught as his gaze landed on the books on the lower shelf — one book in particular.

"How did I miss this?" he mumbled.

"What?"

Cal pulled the hardcover from the shelf. The corners of a photograph stuck out of the top of the dust jacket. He grinned.

"Are these all yours?" Annie eyed the row of novels neatly arranged below the elephants along with the two rows above them.

"Most of them," he replied, his gaze still stuck on what he held. "I reread quite a few while I was here."

Annie ran her hands over some of the spines.

"I've been wanting to tell you..." He looked up, clearing his throat.

"What?"

"I came across ... well, something fell out of one of the books I grabbed to take to bed one night."

"That one?" Annie tipped her head toward the novel he held.

"No, not this one." Testing its weight in his palm, Cal peered at it. The feel of the edges and even its smell, all transported him back to his twenties. "Apparently, sometime, a long time ago, I tucked a joint into that other book, and I—"

"You..." Annie interrupted, placing a hand over her belly, practically tripping over her words. "Don't tell me you smoked it?"

Cal glared at her, unflinching. But then he cracked a smile, showing teeth and dimples.

"I had a hard enough time picturing you"—she scratched his chin—"with a beard and the longer hair, but..." Annie clutched her stomach, unable to contain the laughter.

"I'm glad you find me so amusing."

"Oh, I always find you amusing."

"The point is—"

"There's a point." She giggled.

"After I went upstairs—" he began, but she laughed again. "Michelle asked me if I remembered the last time—"

"You got high?"

"Yes, and I said I didn't, but I lied."

Cal pulled the photo from the book, without glancing at it first, and showed it to Annie. She blinked, several times, alternating between staring at the picture of Cal and *at* Cal as he stood before her now.

In the photograph he had blond-blond hair and the face of a boy who hadn't quite grown into a man. His features were somehow softer, his lips curving into a mischievous grin, his eyes haunting the way they'd always been.

The person next to him, a woman, perhaps in her late thirties, sported a wide smile while peering at Cal instead of into the lens.

"She was..." Cal flipped the photo around and stared at it. Then he looked away, shaking his head. "She was the first woman I ever loved."

Annie swallowed, watching his face carefully, before her gaze combed the two people in the picture again. "I can see by her expression that she loved you too."

"Well," he said and inhaled, starting to stuff the picture back into the novel, "that was a very long time ago."

"I want to know more, Cal." Annie touched his waist. "I've never pressed you about your past. But now, we're getting married, and I want to know everything. Who was she?"

"You've always wanted to know everything." He ran a knuckle along her cheek, his eyes twinkling.

She smiled, sighing. "And I've waited."

"You've been more patient with me than anyone I've ever met." Cal's eyes moved back and forth for what felt like an eternity, then he cracked that devious smile again and said, "She was my teacher."

Annie's mouth dropped open. "In high school?"

"No." He laughed and led her to the red settee. They both took a seat. Cal placed the book on the table and held one of her hands. "I was a senior in college." His eyes bounced around the room before settling again on Annie. "She was... She was beautiful."

"She is..." Annie swallowed, glancing at the novel.

"No, I mean beautiful ... like you." Cal squeezed her hand, his Adam's apple bobbing. "Inside and out." Pausing, he grinned. "I didn't know what the fuck I was doing."

"*You*?" She studied every inch of his face. "You always know what you're doing."

"I was twenty-one when it began. We were together ... if you can call it that — because our relationship had always been clandestine — but we were together for most of my senior year. Then I moved to New York after graduation."

"You never saw her again?"

"Once. About ... sixteen or seventeen years ago." Cal ran a finger over Annie's skin, tracing the lines on her palm. "She taught me how to love, and then I guess I forgot..." His voice shook. "Or I didn't think I needed it. I was afraid to receive it." Cal glanced up. "Even from her. Back then."

"Cal..."

"She gave me that book." He eyed the hardcover on the coffee table. "Have you ever read it?"

"No."

Smiling, Cal peered at the novel as if acknowledging a long-lost friend, then he exhaled a big, shaky breath.

Annie took his other hand. "We'll have to thank her—"

"Jocelyn," he interrupted, looking as though he could see parts of his first love in the eyes of his Annie.

"We'll have to thank ... Jocelyn," Annie continued, cradling his jaw. "She apparently taught you things about life, about yourself. You didn't really forget. The love, the acceptance, it's all in your heart, Cal — along with her ... and me." Annie smiled. "Your heart is bigger than you ever could've imagined."

"You've made me remember." Cal tucked hair behind her ears, staring at her until she gulped air. Or forgot how to breathe.

Then he pressed his lips to Annie's.

"I love you," she uttered between kisses, running her hands through his hair.

"I love you, baby." Cal pushed her back flat against the cushion of the settee and hovered over her, his arms on either side of her waist, his face inches from hers.

They stared at each other.

Annie's chest began to ache.

Then Cal moved pieces of hair from her mouth and kissed her. Stronger than before. More insistently. Giving her all he had, allowing the comfort he'd tried for twenty years to erase. He swallowed it up in her taste, in her soft whimpers, knowing he would grow old first, wishing the beauty of Annie would last forever, wanting to never have to leave her, wanting this love, their love, to outlast death.

Death...

That's why we're here... he thought. *In this house. Fucking death.*

It would come for everyone eventually. Not Annie, though. Never Annie. She was forever. Her love was forever.

At one time, that had been a word hard to come by. A word Cal never used. Or believed in.

Nothing was supposed to be forever.

Certainly, not this ... not relationships.

Forever hadn't existed until he met Annie. The word had been meaning-less. Now, Cal wanted there to truly be a forever so he could live there with Annie, in the solace of it — where time didn't exist.

Forever to listen to her breathe, to hear the gentle sound of her voice, to feel the familiarity of her skin. He needed forever, not merely half a lifetime to love her while attempting to give her everything she deserved. Cal could only hope to live another forty-five years alongside his Annie.

Michelle cleared her throat.

Cal lifted his chest, placed an arm around Annie's back, and guided them up to a sitting position.

"It's okay, Michelle," Annie called, her hair mussed, her lips tender. "Come back."

Michelle peeked around the corner of the room she'd begun to exit. "Are you sure?"

"Yes." Annie waved her hand.

"I wanted to show you a couple of photo albums." Two were in her hands. "I thought we could look at them before lunch."

"Since when did Mom have photo albums?"

"I put these together. I've been digging through her pictures, mine and yours too these last few days ... for the service. Barbara helped me." Michelle placed both books on the table but opened the larger one first.

Perched on the edge of the settee, Annie couldn't wait to see their contents. Ready to marry a man she'd always felt she'd known, yet she didn't even know what he looked like as a baby.

The pages turned slowly in Annie's hands as she sat between them, Cal on her right, Michelle on her left.

He was adorable. Blond-blond hair. Green eyes lit from within. Determi-nation abundant in the shape of his chin and the squaring of his hips. She studied the photos and asked questions. Even Cal perked up and joined the conversation, answering without hesitation.

Constance came alive as well. Her beautiful, thick, auburn hair. Blue eyes. A jaw set in stone. Like Cal's. His entire childhood seemed like a dream sequence. There were plenty of photos of his grandpa E.W. and other relatives too. Michelle had tagged them all with actual handwritten script, below each photo, indicating something memorable about them.

The second book contained pictures from what seemed to be the last twenty years or so. Cal graduating college, his friends, an antique car. A woman appeared in several of the prints — not his mother. An athletic girl with wavy brown hair and stunning dark eyes.

Annie took note of Cal's many expressions as they thumbed through this album — he wasn't talking as much as before. But his eyes, as usual, displayed whatever emotions he held back. Or wished to share.

Disappointment? Regret? Love.

Before Annie had a chance to ask questions, his phone rang. He answered the call and stepped outside.

"It's a lot to take in." Michelle sighed and shut the album. "Family. A funeral." She eyeballed the closed front door. "*He's* a lot to take in."

Annie laughed a little. "Has he always been such a mystery?"

Michelle brought her thumb and forefinger together, leaving only a small space between them. "A little bit." Then she smiled, lifted Annie's hand, and glanced at the ring. "He must've shocked the hell out of you with his proposal." She fingered the band. "He told his mother he wanted to marry you ... the night before she died." She exhaled. "I've never seen him like this. Do you have some kind of superpower?"

First, they eyeballed each other, then they laughed.

"Are you ready to eat?" Michelle asked as Annie stood and stretched.

"I'm always ready to eat." But Annie made her way to the mantle, not the kitchen, and began to rub a petal belonging to a beautiful arrangement of flowers between her fingers. "We should wait for Cal."

"He might be a while..." Michelle peeked out the front window. "And the baby won't wait."

Annie barely registered those words. She was too busy staring at the card sticking out from the bouquet, remembering what she'd heard the two of them discussing earlier...

"Samantha sent flowers," Michelle had said as Annie remained in the hallway, listening.

"How does Sam even know?" Cal replied.

"I told her."

"Why would you do that?"

"She cared a great deal for your mother. I've had to contact people. You still need to make some phone calls too."

And that was all they had said about a woman named Samantha before moving on to the topic of Rosa. Now, Annie's fingers had a mind of their own. Massaging the little white card, the same way she'd stroked the tulips, she flipped open the note and read it.

My deepest sympathy to you both, Cal and Michelle, and your family. Constance was a force to be reckoned with, and I imagine God has his hands full in heaven.

Love always,

Sam and family

Sam. Samantha. Mad love number two. She had to have been the pretty woman in the second book.

"You read the card, honey?" Michelle asked, and Annie shook. "That was Sam ... in the album. You know, when Mr. Mysterious got all quiet."

"I heard you mention the flowers ... before. When I came downstairs. I didn't think ... well, it didn't seem like the time to interrupt."

"To interrupt what?" Cal asked, stepping foot inside the room.

"Annie asked about these flowers." Michelle cocked her head to the side.

Glaring at his cousin, Cal grumbled and made strides toward Annie. "Let's open the book again." Taking her hand, he led her to the antique sofa.

Annie chewed on her thumbnail. "We can go eat. It's okay."

"No. You know I've loved two people." Cal and Annie sat down. "I should've explained earlier."

"You never told her about Sam?" Michelle asked, standing a couple feet away. "No wonder you think he's a mystery, honey. Truth is, he's just a big scaredy-cat." Michelle laughed.

Cal had barely found the page he wanted when Michelle took a seat beside them and said, "She has two kids, you know."

"Who?" Cal said.

"Samantha. Don't be a dick," she replied, and Annie stifled a laugh.

"She didn't waste any time."

Michelle took out her phone and slipped on her eyeglasses, the ones hanging from a string around her neck. "Her children are adorable."

"How do you know?"

"I'm still friends with her on Facebook."

"Did you tell her I'm going to be a father?"

Michelle glanced down her nose through her readers. "Damn these phones sometimes. Where is she? Come on..." She tapped the screen.

"Did you hear me, Mishy?"

"What? Ah, here they are."

"Did you tell Samantha I'm going to be a father?"

"Why don't you want her to know?" Annie asked, an eyebrow shooting up, her bottom lip twisting between her teeth.

"It's complicated," Cal replied.

"No, it's not," Michelle said. "She's happy for you."

"Right."

Michelle patted Annie's knee and whispered, "He wants everything complicated. He's not a mystery — just a goddamn complication."

Cal scoffed. Annie laughed. Michelle smirked.

"This is Kyle, and this is Alyssa. Two and one."

"Aww. They're cute," Annie said.

"Are you friends with the babies too?" Cal asked, and Annie laughed.

"Seriously, look." Michelle wiggled the phone. "Soon you guys will have one of these. You have no idea what you're in for." She snickered and closed the app. "Come on. I want to eat."

"We'll be along shortly," Cal said.

"And that's my cue." Michelle stood.

"Don't leave me alone with him," Annie cried.

"You're already pregnant, honey. I don't know how much more damage he can do."

Annie linked her arm through Cal's and smiled as his cousin exited the room. They sat in silence a moment, the album open to a photo of Cal and Samantha. Sun on their faces, wearing T-shirts tagged with numbers.

"You don't have to talk about it today, baby. I—"

"I lived with Sammie for seven years," Cal began on a sharp inhale, leaning forward, fingers now stuck in his hair. "I loved her." He flicked his eyes to the picture. "I probably still do." Cal sighed. "She met someone, left me, married him, and apparently had two children. The family I didn't want to have. The kids I refused to—" He stopped abruptly, then blew out a breath. "I was the bastard who wouldn't get her pregnant."

Annie touched the small of his back, waiting a moment, but he said nothing further.

"How much longer will you beat yourself up over stuff like this?" she whispered, making circles over his shirt. "You're a good man, Cal."

Standing, he dragged a palm over his jawline, then pinched his neck. "Don't you want to ask how someone can spend seven fucking years of their life with someone who they know isn't right for them?"

Annie stood and grabbed his waist, squaring his hips. "That's what she did?" She touched his chin, and he glanced up. "She pressured you?"

His shoulders relaxed, his eyes softened. His entire expression changed.

"She never let you forget it either." Annie ran a hand up and down his arm. "Oh, Cal..."

"How do you do that?" He brought her closer, suffocating her inside his arms, putting his lips to her ear. "Are you real?" He poked one of her hip bones a few times until she giggled. "You're the most real person I've ever met. The most patient, understanding."

"Stop it..." Annie buckled as he continued to tickle her. After shoving his hands away, she straightened, and held his face in her palms. No longer laughing. Or smiling.

"A bastard would walk away from his child," she began, staring up at him. "A bastard wouldn't know how to love someone the way you love me." She kissed the tip of his nose, then his upper lip. "You deserve this life, Cal. You deserve to be a father to this baby. Our baby."

A smile spread across his face. "I love you."

Annie smirked, her palms sliding lower. She cupped his ass. "I can tell." She glanced down at the tent in his pants.

Cal's hands met her bum as well. He squeezed her cheeks. "I've never fucked on one of my mother's beautiful settees."

"And you won't be doing that now either." She laughed.

"Tonight..." Cal nibbled the skin of her neck. "We can sneak downstairs and christen it."

"You're horrible." She slapped his chest. "Like a horny teenager."

"You're the horny one with your crazy pregnancy hormones."

"I'm not crazy."

"But you are horny?" Cal laughed, and she shoved his chest again. "No..." He kissed her cheek. "You're sexy and beautiful and amazing. Did I mention sexy?" He bit her earlobe.

"Stop," she moaned but pulled him closer, her pelvis meeting one of his thighs.

"You stop. You're the one already rubbing your goddamn pussy all over my leg, making me fucking insane."

Annie looked up at him, chewing on her bottom lip, her eyes wide and begging.

"Fucking Christ…" After pulling them to a settee, Cal hoisted her body over his until she straddled him in her jeans. Her tits in his face. Her breath on his skin. "Fuck," he uttered, beginning to bite her nipples through the material, gently bouncing her up and down. "Do you want to come?"

"She's right there," Annie panted, gripping the tops of his shoulders, pinching her eyes shut, "in the kitchen."

"But you want to come." Cal cupped her over her jeans. Hard. "You want to come. *Like this*…"

"You're the worst…" Groaning, she tossed her head back, moving faster and faster.

"I'm the best," he whispered, fingering the denim, trying to put a hole through the seam.

Annie matched his rhythm, squeezed her tits, bit back screams. "God…" She rubbed, bounced, grinding herself against him until she burned and burned. "Mmm…"

"Quiet."

Her nails clawed at the nape of his neck. Her eyes expanded. Then her body went slack, boneless, emptying of anxiety, as she rested the side of her face against his, clutching his biceps, enjoying the safety of his sequoia tree.

Cal smelled like a wonderful, clean T-shirt and the salt at the beach.

"I could feel you releasing through your jeans," he muttered. "I love it when you let go, when you fucking forget everything."

Once she caught her breath, Annie glanced up and licked his face, chin to temple, and laughed. "That's what's in store for you." She moved her lips to his ear. "After lunch, I'm going to put my mouth on your cock." She reached between them and gave it a good squeeze. "I'll make you *let go* and lose your everything."

"A blow job … on the settee?" He raised his brows.

"You're awful." She smacked his shoulder, and they both laughed.

"Indeed," Cal said and lifted her up. "And I'm hungry." They stood. He smacked her butt cheek. "Let's go feed my baby."

Annie rolled her eyes, but the second she realized he'd noticed, she took off, running toward the kitchen and laughing.

Cal wanted to chase her, catch her, and ply her with kisses. Or perhaps he wanted to fuck her so hard she wouldn't be able to walk or breathe. But he couldn't do any of those things. His dick was still hard. So he waited. In the sitting room. With the photo albums, *Siddhartha*, and the elephants.

Seventy-Four

"What's going on with you?" Rosa asked.

Two days until the funeral, and she'd arrived in Ojai this morning. Had been in the house all of about two seconds when Cal cornered her and dragged her over to the red settee in the sitting room.

"I don't like this sitting down for news. It's enough that your mother has passed..." Looking heavenward, Rosa made the sign of the cross. "*Que ella encuentre la paz.*"

Cal stared at her, his chest puffing up, holding back a grin, then he glanced toward the hallway and called out, "Annie..."

Rosa's eyes expanded. She patted her breasts and coughed. "You've kept this from me..."

Annie appeared from behind the corner, hands clasped below her stomach, a grin on her face, as Rosa slowly stood.

"*You* ... you rotten boy," Rosa cooed, eyeballing Cal as she strode toward Annie, her arms wide and open. "*Mi querida.*"

Annie fell into them, breathing in Rosa's perfumed scent. A moment later, Cal joined them. Taking Annie's palm, he glanced at her belly, then his gaze met Rosa's.

He nodded.

"No..." Rosa cried, covering her mouth, shaking her head. "*No...*" Her onyx eyes glossed as she lifted Annie's other arm and stared at her somewhat expanded waistline. When she looked up, both women leaked tears.

Cal put a hand on Rosa's back, but she waved him off.

"You truly are rotten." She gave him the stink eye, then peered at Annie and smiled. "How far along are you?"

"I'm due in May." Annie cradled her belly and bit her lower lip.

"Oh my..." Rosa fanned herself. "*Dios mio. Tu me has dado un regalo especial hoy.*"

Annie looked to Cal. He tucked hair behind her ear. "She said you have given her a special gift."

"You have given her this gift." Annie squeezed his palm.

"*We,*" he choked out, and Annie nodded.

"I will have two new grandbabies." Rosa's hand shook as she made a V with her fingers. "*Dos.*"

Sniffling, she wrapped her arms around them, squishing them inside her petite embrace. A moment later, she stepped back, wiped beneath her eyes, and glared at him.

"You kept this from me." She pointed a finger at Cal. "You are so bad." Then she laughed. "This..." Her eyes grew wide. "This is a miracle."

Cal guffawed as he led the two of them to the cream-colored settee. Rosa sat between them. Cal and Annie each placed a hand on the small of her back, exchanging a glance.

"There's more." He swallowed.

Rosa stared at each of them in turn until Annie blurted, "We're getting married," and extended her left hand.

Rosa gasped, looking back and forth at the two of them again, fanning herself and blinking — several times. Finally, she held Annie's fingers and inspected the ring.

"This is your *abuela's,*" Rosa said to Cal as she sucked in a shaky breath. "You're giving me too many heart palpitations. More than my other children." She shooed him away. "Get me a drink, Calvin."

He laughed under his breath and left the room.

"Oy..." Rosa sank against the cushions, her gaze bouncing around. "Oh, *mi amor,*" she continued, cupping Annie's cheek. "You both are so good for each other. I knew this." She patted Annie's thigh. "Is this right for you?"

"Yes." Annie smiled.

"I knew when we met." Rosa nodded. "You have an old soul too. He waited for you. Ah, I might weep again." She pressed her lips together and stopped on a dime. "I never cry."

Annie retrieved a tissue box from the corner table as Cal returned with a glass of something red.

"Oh, this is good." She cleared her throat and stared ahead after draining half of it. "This is good, *mi hijo.*"

Cal laughed and sat on the coffee table, facing the two women. Annie grinned. Rosa put her glass down and grabbed each of their hands.

"This moment where you bring new life into the world..." Rosa paused and shook her head.

"Rosa..." Annie soothed.

"No. No." Rosa swallowed, squeezing their palms. "I must say this, and then we will talk and laugh." She gazed at them. "Your mother breathed out her last breath in *this moment* where you have new life." She tripped over the last word. Fresh tears formed in the corners of her eyes. "It is ... something found. Something you were not looking for. What is the word?"

"Serendipitous," Cal and Annie replied at the same time.

"Jinx," Annie said, peering at Cal. "You owe me—"

"Oh, I owe you something." Cal smirked.

Rosa swatted him. "You owe her a wedding. Getting her pregnant first..." She shook her head as she began to make her famous sound, her tongue clucking against the roof of her mouth.

"Oh, *mi amors...*" Smiling, she sighed. "You made me a happy woman today. Your mother..." she choked out, glancing at Cal, "*she is very happy ...* and she is with you now."

SEVENTY-FIVE

Annie stood near one of the two windows in Cal's upstairs bedroom in his mother's home in Ojai and looked outside. A light sprinkle fell over the yard. It was late, the evening of Constance's funeral.

Coming up behind her, Cal removed her jacket and kissed her neck. "Are you okay?"

"Yes."

Cal sighed. "It rained the day of my grandfather's service."

Peter's too, Annie thought.

She didn't know what it was about funerals that seemed to agree with rain but they did. Despite the cheery association she had with one particular downpour — the night she'd told Cal she would sleep with him; truly, the night she'd realized she'd fallen for him after that magical kiss on the sidewalk, in *that* rainstorm — there still might always be a sadness mixed with this kind of weather too. A welcomed sort of gloom.

"It's been a long day." Cal started to undress.

Annie almost didn't want him to. He looked so beautiful in his black suit, white shirt, and Everett's floral tie.

"You handled everything so well." Annie slipped off her dress and pantyhose. "You were worried."

Cal shrugged, draping his garments over the back of the nearby chair, standing in his boxer shorts.

Now, he glanced out the window.

"Baby..." she uttered, and he turned his attention back to her. "Why didn't you ever tell me your mother was a seamstress?" She unhooked her bra. "You knew I made a lot of my clothes too..." Annie found one of his comfy T-shirts and put it on.

"I want to brush my teeth."

Annie smiled and scoffed and followed him to the hall bathroom.

A few minutes later, after they'd both cleaned up and climbed into bed, Annie pressed the front of her body against the side of his, snuggling up to his bicep.

"It was her story to tell," he began, clearing his throat while staring at the ceiling, "not mine. And she couldn't tell it..." Cal swallowed. "She didn't talk about what she did, Annie. Not often. She didn't like the people she worked with."

"I'm sorry." Her fingers threaded through the hairs on his chest.

"People think Hollywood is so glamorous." He eyeballed her. "It's an industry. And my mother tried to get away from it, but they sought her out, and she wanted the money." He paused. "I think that's why she didn't like to talk about it." He sighed. "I've carried that torch for her."

"Along with many others..." Annie whispered, draping a leg over his thigh.

"Yes." His hand found her cheek, but his eyes went back to the ceiling. "I want to tell you something."

Annie peered at the side of his face, waiting for the words to come, but the man only kept looking upward, his breathing growing shallower by the second.

"Baby..."

Cal turned his entire body toward hers. "The night before she passed, I found some photographs." He inhaled, his eyes darting around some.

Annie stroked every line on his face. His lips, his cheekbones, the wrinkles. "Yes," she whispered.

"Of my father."

"Oh..." Annie's hand stilled over his jawline as she stared into his eyes, but his gaze bounced around again. She kissed his lower lip, and he came to.

"I've never had much desire to find out who he is... Perhaps, I carried that as well, doing it for her because she wouldn't have wanted me to look for him. She wouldn't say his name." Cal met Annie's gaze. "Kept his fucking last name but wouldn't utter his first." Cal shook his head.

"What is it?"

"Harrison."

Annie peered at him for a heartbeat or two. "You could have siblings."

"I know." His voice trembled. "Or he could be gone as well."

This time, when Cal swallowed, his throat felt like it had sprouted razor-blades. He could be an orphan. His child was coming into this world and his mother was no longer here and his father was anywhere. Or dead.

"I'll wait until after the baby comes, then I think I want to hire someone to find him."

"Okay." She nodded. "But you don't have to wait."

"I want to." He gave her a tight smile. "I need some time too."

"I love you so much." Annie nuzzled her nose to his, closing her eyes and inhaling his fresh clean scent.

"Thank you for being here this week." Cal cradled her cheeks. "It was a lot to expect."

"No." She kissed him. "This is what you deserve. What you need."

Cal is many waters, Annie thought, and she would swim inside him until she grew sea legs and built a home there in the depths of his ocean.

SEVENTY-SIX

If he looked over the edge, he would fall straight down the steep cliff.

And Cal would not go down into that pit again.

Not when Annie was next to him, at his side as his partner. The shoulder he'd never needed to lean on — but did — rubbed against his, inviting him to relieve his burdens.

His sadness.

The cliff they stood on looked out over the valley. The pink moment would happen at any minute.

Later, they would gather with close family and friends, but this ritual was only for the two of them. The four of them actually. The baby growing inside Annie, and Constance. Soon, they would cast his mother's ashes into the place she'd called home for forty years.

The breeze brought a slight chill with it. Cal wrapped his jacket across Annie's shoulders and stared at the Piedra Blanca. Despite what they were doing, what they were about to do, his thoughts kept bringing him back to one word.

Baby.

"I'm pregnant," Annie had said to him last September. That declaration meant he could go forward, stop living in the past. Stop regretting. Stop searching for what wasn't there and start realizing the thing he'd chased had been inside him all along.

What you need is within you, he thought, remembering Joc's words. *It's in you.*

What he needed also stood next to him, and what he had needed as a boy was now in a vase, awaiting release.

Constance would mix with nature, the wind, and blow over the edge of the cliff through the valley. She would become part of the tangerines and rocky places, birds' nests and leaves. Constance would be everywhere all at once, the way she'd always been.

"It's happening," Cal said with no inflection, something fantastic and terrifying mixing in his stomach as something spectacular and out-of-this-world changed the color of the sky and mountainside from gray to golden and pink.

He opened the lid of the urn.

Annie palmed the small of his back.

"It's beautiful," she said, gazing at the Topatopa Bluff. "Magical."

Cal waited for the wind to change direction "People say it's the hand of God." The moment the breeze shifted, he emptied the urn, watched the ashes of a beloved woman toss and swirl as sunlight painted strokes of unimaginable pink and peach and lavender across the sky and up sides of the mountains.

"You'll regret not bringing your camera," Cal said as the last bit of Constance "The Owl" Prescott faded away.

"Did you ever see *The Secret Life of Walter Mitty*?" Annie asked.

Cal only stared ahead, into a void, eyes stuck on the past, maybe on a remembrance.

"You probably saw the 1940s film," she went on, and that got a reaction out of him. Annie smiled. "I know it's silly to mention now, but there's this one scene..." Setting the vase on the ground, Cal gave her his full attention. "Maybe I shouldn't ruin the movie."

As he touched her cheek, she focused on his grief and vulnerability. The latter being something rare — a privilege he shared with few. Today, he shared it with mountains and wind and a one-of-a-kind view.

"One of the characters in the film, Sean Penn plays him, he's a photographer."

"Like you."

"Mmm. He's an adventurous photographer."

"Like you."

"He flies over volcanos."

"He's fictional."

"So, anyway, he's on this mountain..."

"Like you."

"Cal ... stop..." She grinned a mile wide, not knowing whether to keep smiling or to cry.

Running a hand through his hair, he smiled and asked her to continue.

"Well, Sean Penn is stationed on a mountain, in the cold, waiting for the appearance of a rare snow leopard. He has his camera set up and ready. And then ... after a lot of time passes ... when the leopard finally crosses his lens"—Annie swallowed as she glanced over the valley, then she looked back at Cal—"he doesn't take the picture."

They stared at each other for several heartbeats, cold and wind and death nonexistent. Only the three of them.

"Look." She tipped her head toward the view.

They gazed at the pink moment. The hand of God. The magic. And like that — just like that — it faded. The sun went down. Disappeared. The colors dulled.

"Some moments are meant to be experienced without any barriers," she continued, "not even a lens. Without any distractions."

Tears slid down Annie's face as she dropped her cheek against his chest, feeling the rise and fall of their lungs. She could feel everything all at once.

His sadness.

His relief.

Their love.

"Tell me something you remember." Annie popped her head up.

Cal pinched his thumb and first finger into the corners of his eyes.

"Please," she went on. "A happy something about her."

"We went to Big Sur a few times." He sighed. "Maybe when I was eight or nine. We camped and hiked. My grandfather, Michelle, her mom, and mine."

"*Yours*," Annie said, linking her arm through his.

"My mom..." His breath contained all his sensibilities — every bit of control he'd ever tried to bridle. "She was often distant, always seemed far away, but her eyes, if you looked closely, told a million stories. You could see things in them. Sorrows and lessons and love. They were blue."

He inhaled and started fresh. "Whenever we went there, she seemed more relaxed. Freer. As free as Constance could be... It's why I love your photograph. The one I sent home. She would sit in the sand and build castles with me." He shifted his gaze. "We would tell stories at night, and she would sometimes dance." Cal scrubbed a finger beneath his nose, then smiled. "She taught me."

"But you don't dance."

Hand around my waist, palm on my shoulder, Cal recalled his mother's words, trying not to laugh. *Look me in the eye and lead. A man must lead. He must be in control of the movement at all times. Relaxed but in control. Guide her. Direct her. And never — ever — step on her feet.*

"Precisely." Cal smirked.

Annie kissed his temple. "I love that story, Cal. I want to come here again, another time, with my camera. We can bring the baby."

"Jackson," he quipped, peeking at her out of the corner of his eye.

"Maybe it's a girl."

"Jackson." He smiled.

"I'm not naming my baby after a popstar or a city." She rolled her eyes.

Cal picked up the urn and took one final look at the valley below, the glow of dusk still highlighting the magnificent features of the place he also gladly called home.

"Is she free, Annie?" His shoulders appeared stern and tense and masculine, holding the weight of the world there.

"They both are..." She exhaled, peering at him. "Now, we have to learn how to be without them. We have to learn how to live free."

SEVENTY-SEVEN

Talk turned to the funeral as Cal, Annie, and her father relaxed in a booth at Albert's favorite restaurant in Seattle, sipping cocktails and water, nibbling on an appetizer, waiting for their food to arrive. Cal spoke of Constance's service as though it were a distant memory, not something that had occurred only weeks ago.

"It smells good," Annie said the moment the waiter arrived, hands full of their dinner plates. She squeezed Cal's bicep, nuzzling her cheek against his shoulder.

"She smells everything now with some sort of superpower." Cal glanced at Albert. Albert eyed the food.

"Can I bring you anything else?" The server gave the table a once-over.

"No, thank you," Annie replied.

"Another drink, please," Albert interjected, feigning a grin, holding up his empty martini glass. The moment the man left, Albert looked square at Cal. "You never married, then?"

Annie eyed her father, her face heating, her spine stiffening.

"No," Cal replied, squeezing Annie's palm, never breaking eye contact with his future father-in-law.

"And what makes you think it's right? *Now*." Albert grabbed a steak knife while pointing his fork at Annie. "With my daughter?"

Annie bit the insides of her cheeks as she gripped Cal's hand hard. So hard, she couldn't believe he didn't react to the pressure. From her *or* her father.

"It's right. This is right." Cal glanced at Annie and smiled. She relaxed, let go of his palm, and started to cut her meat. "I knew the moment I laid eyes on her."

Albert's own eyes widened, slicing Cal in two, telling him he knew what he'd seen the first time he'd *laid eyes* on his daughter, and it had nothing to do with love or marriage.

"No..." Cal laughed. "I mean ... I knew Annie was different."

"Damn straight," Albert mumbled around a mouthful of food.

"You both are talking about me like I'm not here."

"Annie saw something in me that first night," Cal continued, smiling and eyeing her in his periphery. "She's shown me what it is to truly love."

"Reminded you." Annie bumped his shoulder.

"Reminded me," Cal conceded. He finally began to eat.

"Well, Annie has always known what she wants." Albert took a sip of his fresh drink.

"I know." Cal wiped his mouth with the napkin.

"And if she wants this—"

"Dad..."

"I'm sorry, doodlebug. If she wants you, Cal, then she must, as you said, see something very special in your heart."

"I do, Dad. Can we please keep eating?"

"I'm not stopping you from eating. Eat."

Annie tapped the toe of her boot to her father's shin, rolled her eyes, and took another bite.

"You will buy a house soon, then?"

"Really?" she blurted, the tender morsel of filet going down her esophagus with a hiss.

"We're talking, Annie."

"You're grilling."

"Imagine that little baby—"

"Imagine *him*..."

"Yes." Albert coughed and fidgeted. "Imagine him, that little wiggle worm in your womb, all grown up, bringing a man to you out of thin air." He snapped his fingers.

"Not a woman, Dad?" Annie gushed.

"Christ, Annie Rebekah, you know what I mean."

Annie giggled. "Calm down. I've never seen you so worked up."

"I've never had to meet the man who wants to take away my baby."

"I'm not a baby."

"No, but you're having one, aren't you?" His voice broke into several little pieces, then he cleared his throat, focusing a moment on his food.

"He's right," Cal piped up, eyeing Annie and grinning. "To ask us questions."

"I'm glad someone thinks I'm right," Albert huffed. Annie folded her arms across her chest. "So, you are looking for a house?"

Cal's mouth was now full. Annie took a sip of water.

"You can't keep her tied down to some hotel room forever," her father continued. "I don't care how nice—"

Annie started to choke, her eyes watering, as she patted her chest, coughing and coughing.

"Are you okay, baby?" Cal touched Annie's back.

"Wrong hole," she managed, shooting him a mischievous grin, the sparks between them crackling like bugs caught in a powerful watt of voltage.

"What's so funny?" Albert asked.

"Nothing," she spluttered.

"Drink some water," her father insisted.

A minute or so later, once Annie had settled, Cal placed a forkful of salmon in his mouth, turning his attention back to Albert the second he swallowed. "We've been looking at houses."

"Where?"

"Here," Annie interjected.

"What neighborhoods?" Albert asked as Annie rolled her eyes while Cal tried not to laugh. "Who's your realtor? Have you spoken with Susan?"

"We're using someone Maggie recommended." Annie squeezed Cal's thigh as Albert grumbled. "Thank God we kept eating, baby." She peered at Cal. "Because he will just go on and on and on..."

"Very funny, Annie." Albert grinned, his hazel eyes twinkling.

"Funny, but true." She smiled, splayed a palm beneath her belly, and gazed at her father.

Fixating on the creases edging the corners of his eyes, hypnotized for a moment by the gentle lines he'd passed on to his only son. She sighed... At least this dinner was turning out better than the disastrous lunch at Beverly's.

God, a meeting with a two-headed alien would've turned out better than anything at her mother's house.

Her father was steady.

His word a promise.

A little worse for wear perhaps, especially over the last year and a half, becoming less and less a reliable safety net — even before Annie had left for college. Still, he was like a beloved teddy bear. *And a grizzly bear...* she thought. Appearing rough and gruff on the outside, but on the inside, soft and gentle and with a heart bigger than Mount Rainier.

SEVENTY-EIGHT

Annie stood in the kitchenette of their hotel room, drinking a Perrier straight from the bottle, one hand around the green glass and the other cradling her tiny baby bump.

She hadn't stopped scowling since they'd arrived home. Home but not home. The hotel, where apparently, she was being tied down. Actually, she'd been tied down here on many occasions. In fact, being tied down was one of the things that made the swanky downtown room feel like home, that and the man who now stood across from her — the man who did the tying, the sexy man's jacket, belt, and shoes already removed.

"Are you going to tell me what's wrong?" Cal asked, and Annie jerked her head in his direction. "What? I can tell when you're upset." He joined her near the countertop. "Was it your father? He was a little—"

"It's not him. I mean, yes, he can be a little temperamental, but no. His intentions were good." She drank more fizz, trying to evade Cal's questions.

"Do you want to tell me?" Cal grabbed the bottle from her and took a swig. "Or do I have to drag it out of you?"

"And how might you *drag* it out of me?" Annie bounced her brows, stepped closer, and put her hands on his shoulders.

"*Now* you would rather fuck than talk?" Cal shook his head. "Your libido is out of control."

"I'm pregnant."

"Yeah, and I've fucked your sexy, pregnant body all over this place since we arrived. Between that, meeting your family, and work, I'm exhausted."

"Not Cal Prescott... And besides, since when do you prefer *talking?"*

"Annie, what is it?" He set the glass down. "You barely spoke on the ride home."

"It's..." She shifted her eyes, capped the bottle, and sighed. "It's something you said at dinner."

But she didn't elaborate. Instead, she bit her lip and walked farther into the suite, stopping in front of a mahogany desk and removing her heels.

"My father said it first," she finally went on as Cal came up beside her. "Then you repeated it."

Her earrings came off next, then her bracelet.

"What, Annie?" he asked when no words followed. Placing his hands on top of her shoulders, he began to massage them.

"You said, 'It's right. This is right.'"

"Well, isn't it?" He turned her around to face him.

"It wasn't what you said." She wouldn't meet his gaze. "It was the way you said it." She glanced up. "Like you were convincing yourself to do the honorable thing with me. The *right* thing."

"Annie..." He squared her hips. "We've been over this. I don't need to keep reassuring you. I want you in my life with or without the baby." He kissed her cheek.

"Forever?"

"Yes, Annie. Forever. That's what's right, okay? *Please*, put this to bed."

"'To *bed*.'" She bounced her eyebrows again.

"You don't stop, do you?" Cal started to unbutton his shirt.

"Take me to bed..." She pushed the garment off his shoulders, down his arms, and thumbed his nipples. "Calvin Prescott..."

"Don't beg, baby." He removed her hands from his chest, then threw his shirt over the chair. "It's not very becoming of you."

"You love it when I beg you."

Grabbing her by the arm, Cal spun her around until her pelvis met the front of the desk. Her eyes met the wall. And her heart met the top of the roller coaster ready for a fall. Lifting the hem of her black wool skirt, he breathed against the back of her neck.

"Do you want me to spank you?"

"Fuck..." she hissed, dropping her head, trying to catch her breath.

After parking her skirt above her waist, Cal stripped her tights and panties off. Then he grabbed her ass cheeks. He smacked them. Several times. Until she was panting and writhing. Nearly crying.

"Jesus, Cal," Annie groaned, gripping the corners of the desk. "I thought you said you were tired."

"You need to understand me." His palm slid toward where she ached, stroking her folds, drawing her out slowly, listening for the sounds, watching her head lull side to side.

"I love you," he whispered.

"Fuck," she choked out, her hips shifting. She was unable to speak any other word. Or make any other sounds.

"You're not going to come yet." He slapped her ass again. "You need to listen to me first." *Smack, smack, smack.* "Do you hear me, Annie?"

"Y-e-s."

Cal yanked on her hair. "Do you want more?"

"Uh-huh."

"What?" He shoved two fingers inside her cunt. "What was that?"

"Yes!" She slapped the desktop.

Cal struck her cheeks harder. Fingered her faster.

"Oh ... God..." Her voice shook as she twisted her lower lip between her teeth, practically bruising it.

After several more seconds of that routine, the slapping, the fingering, the begging, Cal stopped.

All of it.

A loud hiss passed her lips.

"I'm going to marry you, Annie." Cal's fingers slid back inside her, his digits moving perfectly against her waves and her tide. "Because I want to. *Not* because you're carrying my baby." Now, he moved those same two fingers so agonizingly slow, she thought she might die. "Do you understand?"

"Mmm..."

"I want you." He swallowed. "Forever. This is only the beginning of our life together, and it is right. Say it's right."

"It's right," she moaned, writhing against the desk and his palm.

"Again," he repeated, thrusting his clothed erection against her butt cheeks, his digits in and out of her warmth.

"It's right."

"Again."

"It's right," she cried, circling her hips in perfect rhythm with his fingers.

"Fuck, Annie," he heaved, his voice splintering. "I need you." Cal turned her around, one of his hands gripping her shoulder, the other a hip as he stared into her wild eyes. "Nothing has ever been this right for me, and nothing or no one else ever will be." His pants were open. Her ass was on the desk. Her knees spread. Cal's eyes glossed as he entered her greedily, sealing up any remaining space with every inch of his fucking cock.

Annie scratched behind his neck, narrowly breathing, drunk on how he'd filled her so deeply, so tightly, so immediately.

"I need you too."

"Good." He watched the way they made love.

"Good?" she burst, laughing a little.

"Is it too much?"

"No."

"I mean, am I hurting you?"

"No." Her eyes rolled far, far, far into the back of her head. "Show me, Cal." She pinched his skin and glanced up. "Like always. Fuck forever into me."

Staring into her eyes like a madman, the desk rattled as he drove his love, his lust, his fucking out-of-this-world need for her that would never die into her body.

His home.

His forever.

"Oh God…" Annie cried a couple minutes later, her legs wrapped securely around him, her ankles meeting the small of his back. She'd fallen into another state of consciousness.

"I need you," he dinned as he held himself deep inside her, holding, holding, holding.

Cal peered at their centers. At where they joined. He kept his chin down. His eyes hooded.

"I need you, Annie Rebekah Baxter." His voice cracked. "God, you're so beautiful." He glanced up and swallowed. "*Just like this…*" His tip, he ran over and over her clit and her slit, then he filled her up again. Completely. "Come, baby. Come all over me."

Annie shook, impaling herself against Cal, twisting and rocking as she looked toward the ceiling, screaming out several broken sounds, her entire body trembling uncontrollably. Then she became limp.

Something motionless.

A thing without sorrow.

Only bliss.

Cal waited until the pulsing stopped, then he pushed her knees up and took her deeper. She sucked a sea of air into her lungs, gaining a second wind, and moved in tandem with him, crying out again and again, lost in a blur of the *it's right* and wanting none of it to end. Ever.

"Look at me, baby," he heaved, peering into her eyes, swimming in the green. "It is right." He pushed up and into her, holding the reason tightly against her cervix. "I love you, Annie."

She cradled his face. "I love you, Calvin Prescott."

Right after her beautiful whisper, Cal began to shake, shaking with almost as much violence as Annie had displayed. He released deep into her core, loving the feel of her insides and the sweat and the cum, loving the smell of their sex. The two of them had made a fucking baby with that smell, with that love. With that everything.

"Fuck ... Annie." Cal dropped his head, exhausted now in the best of ways. "I want to do *this* with you forever."

She giggled. "I think I understand you now." She lifted his chin, using only her index finger. "You made your point."

Cal smiled as he carried Annie over to the king-sized bed. They removed the rest of their clothing and relaxed together beneath the covers. Stroking her face, he wiped a single tear from the corner of her eye.

"You have no need to doubt our love ever again," he whispered. "It's right."

Annie nodded, holding onto more tears as she pulled his face toward hers and kissed him. "I'm yours."

"You are," he said, nuzzling her cheek. "Mine. Forever."

"Forever," she repeated and rested her head in the crook of his neck — the place where she had always fit. Perfectly.

FASTEN

ATTACH OR JOIN TWO PARTS OF SOMETHING;
MAKE SECURE; FOCUS ATTENTION

I'll warm you
on cold nights
keep you safe
from harm
smooth out your wrinkles
like the pages of a beloved book
to read
cherish
savor
as the words parade across the beautiful green screen of your eyes
alongside the ocean
and blue, blue sky
the place where we meet
near the horizon
bound by promises
new life
magic
and God

SEVENTY-NINE

As Annie made her way down the Allens' simple staircase, she became acutely aware of the life jostling around inside her body, aware of how the gorgeous, champagne-colored satin gown clung to her buttocks and belly, causing a mild constriction with each step.

One that felt good. Necessary.

The dress she had carefully chosen, the garment rumpling at her bosom and back with a fancy swoop scooping low near her tailbone. Its only intricacy a unique embroidery — shining like the silver jewelry dangling from her ears — banding above the waist of her protruding stomach and forming thick straps over her shoulders. The skirt pleated at her thighs. And the hem hit the ground in the front, stopping near her bare feet, but still covering them, leaving a slight trail behind her.

The wedding gown shimmered like a newly formed pearl. The star of it, though, was Annie. The bride filled it out beautifully. Wore it to perfection.

Grasping the rail with the hand holding her flowers — roses, pink and pearl — her other hand cupping the edges of her round stomach, she attempted to hold the weight of the baby as she finished making her way down the wooden staircase of the Allens' home.

"I hope that lucky bastard makes you as happy as you've made me all these years," Albert said as she reached the ground floor, his hazel eyes glistening.

Her father looked polished in his best suit. Checkered wool. Almost too fancy for the casual beach affair.

"You don't need to worry about me anymore."

Her father held her wrists.

They blinked back tears.

Then Annie stepped aside, lifted the bouquet, and ran her free hand over a hip, checking behind her and all around to see if everything was in its rightful place.

Maggie and Beverly had made a fuss earlier. It all had to be proper. Old and new, borrowed and blue. The dress was new. The ring was old. The earrings borrowed. And the bracelet Peter had given her on her sixteenth birthday was blue.

The two mothers, along with Tabitha, had thoroughly examined Annie's makeup (minimal) and hair (a braided crown with wispy soft curls around her ears), after which she'd kindly shooed them out of her old bedroom. Even Tess, her friend and their wedding photographer, had been asked to wait outside. Only Annie and Albert and the little wiggle worm in her womb — the baby they'd still not chosen a name for — occupied the house.

Still, Annie knew the three of them shared the room with a ghost.

"Tell me ... not to worry," Albert replied with a shake of his head and a scoff. "Bunk, Annie. You wait until you hold that little baby in your arms for the first time."

She fanned out the pleats near her thighs.

"You look fine. Your dress is fine," he grumbled. "Have you heard a word I've said?"

Annie stopped fiddling with the gown and gave her father her full attention, sporting a lopsided grin.

"Good." He sandwiched one of her hands between his. "You'll learn that a parent's concern never ends." He rubbed her palm as if it needed warming. "No matter how old they get, you'll worry." Albert squeezed his daughter's hand and sighed, looking through the glass wall of windows, past the white chairs full of guests and arbor Cal stood under. His eyes began to foam like the salty bubbles hitting the shoreline.

Placing her other palm on top of their hand sandwich, she squeezed him too, the specter in the room suddenly discernible in the kaleidoscope of her father's eyes. In the lines of his forehead. Across the breadth of his shoulders.

"He's with me, Daddy." Annie shook their palms. "In my heart." Albert stared at Annie. "He's here ... with me. With us. Now."

Albert smiled, but it was fake, his gaze full of the ambiguity he must've felt in giving his daughter away, unable to accept that his only son hadn't lived to see the day. In the midst of her own wedding, Albert Baxter managed to make Annie feel like he was temporarily the bride, his worn face showing his love and sadness like a mixed-up Picasso canvas.

"You look beautiful, doodlebug..." he said several seconds later.

Annie linked an arm through his, smiled, and took his hand. "Are you ready?"

"I know you're ready." He nodded. "You were born ready." His smile was sincere now. And expansive. "You came into this world with magic, Annie Rebekah. Never forget it."

She exhaled, grinning a mile wide. "Let's do it."

The second he opened the French doors, the salty breeze hit their faces and blew their clothing back, drying any remaining wetness around their eyes. After glancing at each other one last time, they stepped onto the deck, ready to walk down the aisle toward Annie's new life.

EIGHTY

A strange glow lit the March sky. The deeper parts of the water shone a gorgeous turquoise, the color matching some of the beads on Annie's bracelet. Patches of beautiful aqua blue were scattered amongst the darker spots of the Atlantic too, places where one couldn't see past the surface.

Nothing else was needed.

Not when they had the ocean.

The sky.

Their hearts.

And love.

Everything Annie could ever want was here. On Golden Beach.

Except Peter.

And Constance.

And perhaps Cal's father was missing too. Or he had been for forty years.

Strolling alongside her dad, down the sandy path towards Cal, Annie tried to imagine the three of them were here in spirit. But a larger part of her had always thought that sentiment was bullshit — despite having reassured her father only moments ago that her brother was present.

Albert squeezed Annie a little harder, and she smiled, her eyes stinging from the salt floating through the breeze. Or perhaps they stung due to the sight of the man standing up ahead under a handmade wooden arbor. Smiling like an idiot. His eyes glistening the color of the ocean.

Pulling her under. Making her forget the dozens of guests, the ones rising and staring at father and daughter sashaying down the makeshift aisle to Pachelbel's "Canon in D."

Right now, it was only Cal and Annie. The way it had always been. Annie and Cal and music being played by a string quartet ... alongside the waves. Under a sky painted pink by the hand of God himself. Taffy clouds peeked out behind a few dark gray ones as those stunning rose hues slid across the horizon. The wind blew. Birds intermittently flew overhead, flapping their wings, unaware of the spectacle below.

Annie's the spectacle, Cal mused, standing tall, his hands clasped, the ocean's swoosh sounding like clockwork several yards behind him as he waited in keen anticipation for his heavy.

God ... she's beautiful, he thought. *Just like this.*

Feet bare.

Dress hugging her curves.

Her fingers beneath her belly.

That smile lighting her eyes.

A few tiny moles sparsely scattered across her face — one near her lips and a couple on her cheekbones, insignificant and hard to see from a distance, but up close, they dotted the landscape of her face like neatly placed sprinkles on a cupcake.

Each graceful step brought her closer to him.

He could've waited forever, though.

Time had lost its meaning. Lost its depth.

The only perception Cal measured was the distance between their eyes, their beating hearts, and their intertwined souls. Time wasn't a bitch as he'd often assumed — it was a fool.

Cal was no fool.

Mesmerized, he continued to gaze at Annie. The nearer she came, the more he realized he couldn't fucking move.

Only his clothes shifted, the breeze blowing his beige jacket up in the rear, the tails splitting open, the lapels spreading apart in the front, revealing the crisp, aqua-blue button-down shirt tucked into his pants. The top two buttons of that shirt open.

He didn't need a tie.

Annie was his tie, binding him, fastening him, his life ready to meld with hers. Completely.

The violins ceased. His thoughts evaporated. And the photographer who'd occupied his thoughts since he'd first laid eyes on her last June arrived at his side.

Albert let go of his daughter's hand and kissed her cheek. Then after being asked who gives this woman away in marriage, he replied, "Her mother and I do," as he took a seat next to Beverly.

Cal placed a palm on Annie's back, grazing the tips of his fingers across her skin while they both turned toward each other and grinned, her adorable belly fitting snugly against his lapels and belt buckle.

Then the ceremony began. There was no wedding party. Cal's friend, Christian, officiated. A few well-chosen opening words were spoken, then Christian instructed Cal to recite his custom vows first.

After taking a gigantic breath, Cal exhaled, then smiled. "I never believed in forever until I met you..." He peered into her forest-green eyes, then cleared his throat. "I searched for things I could never find, and when I least expected it"—his voice cracked—"I found you." Brushing wisps of hair from her forehead, he stroked her cheek. "I love you." He swallowed. "I want to spend every day of my life with you, to see you smile, to hear you breathe. To make babies with you ... and chase them *and you* all over the goddamn earth." He grinned, then blew out a breath. "I do, Annie."

She wiped beneath her eyes. Cal smeared a thumb in the corner of his. Then they smiled and gripped each other's tearstained hands again.

"I don't think I believed in forever either," Annie began with a gentle shake of her head. "I didn't believe in the fairy tale." She giggled. "I said I would never get married."

"She did say that," Cal called out, lifting her left hand into the air.

The crowd laughed.

Annie blushed.

"But here I am..." She placed his palm on her belly and stared at their intertwined fingers, at the way they cradled her there. "Here we are..." Nodding, her eyes glossed as she glanced up at him and smiled. "I want to hold your hand every day." She gently swung their palms between them. "I want to share my everything with you, tell you stories, inhale your breath. I want to hold you tight in the rain..." They grinned, both remembering the night thunder had cracked on a particular South Beach sidewalk. "...catch drops with you, and frogs, chase rainbows and stars. And when you're old..." She smirked, winked, and paused. "You can show your young, sexy wife off."

A few guests chuckled.

Cal put his lips near her ear and whispered, "I already do that, baby," as he wiped a tear from her cheek.

She pushed against his chest, then took his hands again. "I want you forever. I do, Calvin Warner Prescott." She squeezed his fingers in time with each forthcoming promise. "I do. I do. I do."

Cal leaned toward Annie's lips. But Christian cleared his throat and shook his index finger. "*Not yet.*"

People laughed.

Cal and Annie grinned.

After exchanging rings, they waited for the final announcement.

"Ladies and gentlemen, friends, family, loved ones," Christian declared, "it is with great pleasure that I introduce to you for the first time, Mr. and Mrs. Calvin Warner Prescott. Now"—he smiled—"you may kiss the bride."

Thank fuck, they both thought.

Cal tucked loose wisps of Annie's hair behind an ear, stared into her eyes, and cradled her beautiful face. He pulled her body, baby-belly and all, against him. Then he put his lips on Annie's as if no one was watching.

Because that was how it had always been with this chameleon called Cal and a photographer named Annie: despite being in a room full of people, only the two of them existed.

Nothing else.

Except the magic.

And now a little baby growing inside her.

Annie melted into him, their tongues twisting with their oaths.

They were one.

Two distinct people coming together, preserving their individuality while standing in front of the sky and the ocean.

They were one.

EIGHTY-ONE

Cal held the French doors open for Annie as they stepped inside the house full of waiting friends and family. Tess had taken pictures of the newlyweds near the shoreline, the water leaving Annie's dress damp and sandy at the bottom. Some of her caramel-colored hair had come loose from the braid. Those pieces looked a little tattered by the wind, but her face was in bloom and glowing. As was her skin.

People clapped the moment they entered, a few even hollered, while the first to receive them were John, Christian, and Albert. The men fawned all over Annie, then John turned his attention to the groom.

"Congratulations, old man." He smacked Cal on the back.

"I didn't think we'd live to see the day," Christian added with a grin while shaking his friend's hand.

"Careful," Cal joked, showing teeth.

Annie laughed, but then her father pulled her aside, leading her to a private corner of the living room.

"What is it?"

Albert only sighed. Staring at his daughter, his eyes filled with tears.

"I'm still Annie, Dad," she reassured him, resting a hand over his heart. "I'm still right here."

Albert kissed the tip of her nose. "And there's only one like you." He exhaled as he looked over the three adjacent rooms. "Your mother is anxious to see you. I don't know where she went off to."

"I'll find her. Don't worry." Annie lifted the hem of her dress and made her way to the kitchen.

"You did great, sweetie," Maggie said a few seconds later, sneaking up beside Annie. For once, the photographer didn't jump. "How do you feel?"

"Fine." Annie opened a bottle of water and took a few generous sips.

"Really, honey?" Maggie tugged on the pleated parts of Annie's shimmering gown.

"Yes. Really."

"Well, you look fine." She fanned out the silky material. "Are you sure you don't want to change out of this thing before we start the show?"

"I already told you—"

"What did you tell her?" Beverly interrupted, batting her lashes as she joined them at the countertop.

"That I'm not changing."

"Let her be uncomfortable..." Bev rolled her eyes. "It's her choice."

"I'm not uncomfortable." Annie guzzled more water. "I'm fine."

Funny how *fine* never meant fine. It didn't actually mean anything anymore. It was a word, and it had lost its power. And its curse. Cal had taken control of it. She had him, and he had her. *Fine.*

"Well, are you ready for the rest of the evening to begin?" Maggie asked, appearing prepared to summon the crowd.

Annie took a deep breath, set the bottle on the counter, then glanced over at Cal. He still stood near the rear windows, talking to the men, his fucking dimples never sexier, his face fixed with a charming grin.

She *was* ready for the rest of the evening to begin. *I do. I am.*

"Okay, everyone," Maggie announced over the buzz of conversation, without waiting for Annie's reply, then she motioned for Cal. "Now that the newlyweds have joined us, it's time for them to enjoy their first dance as husband and wife."

The room quieted as Cal took Annie's hand and led her to the center of the living room. The space had been temporarily transformed into a ballroom. The furniture had been removed, string lights hung, and a globe dangled from the ceiling, creating glorious speckles across the wooden floors.

Cal splayed a palm across Annie's bare back while her hand came to rest on his shoulder, the two of them skirting the floor the moment the Dave Matthews song began.

"I didn't think you liked to dance, Prescott." Annie's eyes widened. Her cheeks hurt from smiling.

"I've danced with you before," he replied, and her brow arched. "At my apartment in South Beach. After we went to Key Largo. We danced to Satchmo."

Annie tossed her head back and laughed. "That hardly counts. I had to force you." She met his eyes and smirked. "Well ... you are quite good."

"Did you expect me to be bad?"

"No." She blinked up at him, shivered, then rested the side of her face against his chest, sinking into his solid branches. They remained like that for several verses.

"How are you feeling?" he asked as the song neared its end.

"Tired." She lifted her head. "But I feel good."

"I want to take you back to the room and get you off your feet."

"I'm sure you do." Annie grinned, almost snorting.

"I'm serious, Annie." He met her gaze. "It's been a long day."

"Don't keep treating me like I'm breakable goods." Her brows pinched together, causing him to laugh. "*I'm serious*, Cal." She pushed on his chest. "I'm the same person I was when you barged into my bedroom last September." She nodded toward the staircase. "I can handle it. I need it. I need you."

"Where is all this coming from?"

Annie bit her bottom lip and peered at him, blinking like that deer caught in headlights again.

"You've been different with me," she uttered. "Even before I left for Miami."

Cal swallowed.

He didn't know what Annie wanted.

He'd never wished for time apart before the wedding. But he'd agreed. And so it had been two weeks since Cal had held her close. No fucking. No kissing. No touching. No joke. At Annie's insistence, he'd stayed behind in Seattle as she traveled to Florida early to finalize the wedding preparations. He'd obliged her ridiculous notion of having a little separation in the name of romance, anticipation, and delayed gratification.

So, not only had they not been in the same house for two weeks, or in the same bed, but they hadn't even shared so much as a kiss — until today, on the sand, after they were pronounced man and wife.

"What do you want, Annie?" Cal stared into her eyes.

"I don't know."

Cal laughed a little as he palmed her cheek. "We know that's not true..."

"I want..." She exhaled. "I want you to—"

But then "Crash Into Me" ended, another song began, and Annie's father and Rosa appeared at their sides, ready to cut in.

After sharing a mother and son dance with Rosa, Cal made his way to the kitchen and grabbed a glass of champagne. Leaning against the countertop, he finished the contents of the flute as Maggie joined him.

"You couldn't have asked for a more perfect day," she mused. "The weather..." She glanced at Annie. "Everything."

Cal cleared his throat and looked over the room until his gaze landed on Annie too. "Thank you, Maggie ... for all this." He met The Cat's chocolate eyes. "Perhaps I'm not the bastard you thought I was all these years."

"Oh, Cal..." She sighed, linking her arm through his. "I never thought you were a bastard."

"Bullshit." He laughed, placing the empty glass down. "You always thought I was a bastard."

"Well..." She shrugged, her eyes twinkling. "I guess you've finally proven me wrong."

"I never had anything to prove to you."

"Let's not fight."

"Are you challenging that statement?"

"A little." She laughed.

Cal shook his head and smiled.

"Maybe..." She shifted her gaze. "Maybe I was hard on you because I always wanted what was best for you."

"And now I've found it." Cal nodded at his wife.

"It's more than Annie, Cal." Maggie turned and faced him. "I couldn't see the better parts of you. Ever. I refused."

"*Not you*," Cal teased.

Maggie grinned, the light from the ceiling's ball finding its way to her brown eyes, and Cal followed the speckles.

"Dance with me," he said out of nowhere, deepening his tone as he bent an arm behind his back and bowed. "Dance with me, Ms. Oppenheimer."

"God," Maggie choked out, "you haven't called me that in—"

Cal had already taken her hand, guiding her toward the renovated living room. Before they joined the others, though, Cal looked around the space full of loved ones. At Annie. His eyes glossed.

All he could ever need was inside this house.

Except Constance.

He should've been preparing to have a dance with his mother, but she was missing it, and he was missing her. Still, he was thankful she no longer suffered. Content he felt his mom's blessing, certain he heard her approval in his mind — an approval that would've sounded more like disapproval — Cal dropped his chin, bit back a laugh, and smiled.

Actually, it was Maggie's words that had made him acutely aware of his mother's absence. Constance was the one Cal had always been trying to prove something to. Maggie might've reminded him of the absence but Rosa had reminded Cal of something else. As they'd danced this evening, only moments ago, she'd repeated what she'd told Cal after E.W. passed: no one was ever really gone.

Taking their place amongst the other guests, Cal swallowed past the lump in his throat, feeling his mother and somehow even his father, definitely feeling his grandfather, as he pulled Maggie toward him and rested an arm across her shoulders.

Cal Prescott held Margaret Jaqueline Oppenheimer close as they skirted the dance floor.

The way he always used to.

Only now, he didn't feel that pressing need to prove his worth. Not to anyone.

His mother smiled.

Still imparting lessons from wherever it was she'd gone.

EIGHTY-TWO

Maggie moved the evening along effortlessly, taking full charge of the festivities. Food, cake, and champagne had been consumed. A couple hours had passed.

"Your wife is tired, Cal," Rosa said as he entered the den. She played with a few pieces of Annie's hair. The bride had since taken the braid down. Caramel-colored strands hung over her breasts and across her backside. "You need to get her off her feet."

"Be careful, Rosa." He smirked. "My wife won't like that suggestion."

Annie rolled her eyes but didn't move. Keeping her weary head against Rosa's shoulder, her gaze blurred at a painting on the wall, one she could see perfectly through the gap created between Michelle's and Sophia's bodies.

"Suggest what, *mi hijo*?"

"That she rest."

Rosa playfully slapped his arm, and he grinned. Then the women started to make noise again. A hand in his pocket, his eyes straight ahead, Cal tuned out their chatter and began to daydream, mentally counting back the months since he'd met Annie. Until he reached June 2014.

My God, he thought. It had only been nine months since he'd first beheld Annie's quintessential face.

Nine. Months.

In a trance, Cal ran his hand over Annie's back, recalling the way her skin had felt then, the way her eyes had radiated truth, luster. Specifically when he'd told her he wanted her on the porch in the moonlight. He'd had no idea how much he would want her.

Now, he not only wanted her, he needed her and loved her. Cal was fucking consumed. Annie had never left his mind, and now she would never leave his heart. He couldn't imagine his life without her, not seeing her face ... her eyes, her smile.

He couldn't believe how much things had changed.

His world was different.

Better.

Astounding.

"What are you thinking?" Michelle asked, breaking into his thoughts.

"He's thinking about taking Annie home." Tabitha smirked.

"Mmm..." Annie began to yawn. "I can't wait to go home-home. To my own bed."

"I forgot you've been here two weeks. Then Cal must really be ready to take you home." Tab waggled her eyebrows.

"Stop it," Annie groaned as a limb traveled across the wall of her uterus. The body part could be seen through the satin of her dress, poking and prodding. "The baby's really moving a lot. You should feel it, T."

Smiling, Cal removed his hand from his wife's back while Tabitha put hers on Annie's rotund belly. The second a firm thump grated against Tab's palm, the other women in the room became quiet, watching the exchange.

"You're going to be a mommy." Tab beamed.

"You've said that to me, like, a million times."

"I can't help it."

"I'm going to miss you." Annie sighed, tears pooling in her eyes.

"Don't you start on me." Tab pointed a finger. "I don't want to end this wedding business crying like a big sissy."

"You are a big sissy." Annie squeezed Tab's hand. "You're my big sissy."

The friends embraced.

"Promise you'll call as soon as you go into labor," Tabitha said as she inched back and stared into Annie's eyes.

"We have some time—"

"Promise me!"

"Okay, I promise. Jeez."

"I think we're ready to leave, ladies," Cal announced, and surprisingly,

Annie didn't protest. She wiped beneath her eyes and took her husband's hand.

The women hemmed and hawed and doled out hugs and kisses, one by one. Beverly took hers last, a palm around the back of her daughter's neck, gripping harder than Annie could ever recall her doing in the past.

"I love you," her mother strained.

"I love you too."

After bidding the other guests a fond and personal farewell, they sought out Albert and John. Even though Cal and Annie had requested a quiet departure without the typical post-reception fanfare, the two men insisted on walking the couple to the front door.

"You'll message once you get settled?" Albert asked, flanked by the spectacular staircase and his daughter.

"Yes."

"You won't forget?"

"I'll make sure she doesn't forget." Cal smiled.

"Good."

"Thank Maggie again, John." Annie's cheeks warmed. "For everything."

"It's chilly out tonight," Albert interrupted. "Do you have a jacket?"

"I'll be fine, Dad. Cal has a jacket."

"Maggie has been consumed with this thing for weeks," John said, looking back and forth between them. "You know she loves it, Annie." The blue gray of his eyes twinkled. "And she loves you."

"I love you both," she uttered and leaned closer, planting a kiss on John's cheek, his finely groomed silver mustache tickling her skin.

She turned to her father. "I love you too, Dad."

He kissed her temple. "Ah, there's so much love here tonight." Albert peered at Annie, his eyes glossing. "You better get out of here, doodlebug, before you make us all weep."

"Too late for that." Cal extended a hand to his father-in-law, giving his palm a firm shake.

The men smiled, patted Cal on the back, and gazed again at Annie.

Then the newly minted couple opened the front door of the Allens' home and stepped outside, ready to start their married life together.

Or perhaps Cal still planned on getting his bride off her feet.

Eighty-Three

The second the door closed, Cal carefully pushed the front of Annie's body against it.

Goose bumps formed over her skin.

Her father had been right.

The night was unusually cold.

The temperature had dropped some since the ceremony. Low humidity. A soft breeze. The leaves rustled in the palm trees. Parts of Annie's dress and strands of her hair caught in the wind.

"If you don't think I haven't been anything but mad for you these last few weeks," Cal began, his voice gruff and hoarse, "then I don't know what else to say." All ten of his fingers skated down her bare back as though skimming the surface of the ocean while lying on his board.

Annie glanced over her shoulder, met his gaze, and smiled.

The way Cal felt when pressed against her from this position was indescribable. Hovering behind her, his front to her back, arms on either side of her waist, he warmed her instantly. The magnets of their skin twisted and pulled, attacking nerve endings, the fatigue Annie felt moments ago having been replaced with an invigorating excitement.

This was exactly why she'd wanted to be apart before the wedding.

Delayed gratification.

An orgasm to follow that would rattle the universe off its axis.

"I don't know what you want..." Cal sighed. "You asked me not to touch you for two fucking weeks."

Annie turned around. "You've always known..." Her throat went dry as she stared into his eyes. "I want you as you've always been with me." She palmed his cheeks. "I'm the same."

Dropping his forehead against hers, Cal gripped her waist and moved his hands to her butt cheeks, cupping her over the dress as he gently pushed her backside against the door and kissed her lips — slowly and multiple times.

"Fuck, Annie"—he pulled away and gazed into her eyes—"don't keep looking at me like that. It's our wedding night. I want to do this right."

"What does that mean?" She laughed a little. "Since when do you care about some outdated, misguided version of sexuality?"

Cal swallowed and glanced down at her belly. No smile, eyes full of inexplicable love and tenderness, he put a hand over her gown, and as he did, the baby kicked against his palm.

Annie swallowed too. And it hurt.

God ... this man, she thought. *He would walk through fire for his family.*

The love in his heart moved her beyond words. Still, she wanted those feelings to translate into action — the type of action Cal usually displayed. She didn't want the baby to circumvent the forwardness, the brazenness, or utter haste they always had to be together. She wasn't ready for the dynamic between them to change.

Lifting his chin, she repeated, "I'm the same, Cal."

The words barely passed her lips when his mouth hit hers. Explosively. Two weeks' worth of pent-up passion lighting her up on the porch, Cal pushing her entire body practically through the door, much harder than before.

"Fuck..." she breathed out, her nails scratching through his hair, narrowly able to move in the tight dress. Annie felt constricted, perfect, her bare back rubbing against the unforgiving grain. The slow suffocation of his touch, the feel of his weight against her.

On her way to that place.

Where nothing else existed.

But the two of them.

Grazing his nose along her jawline, he wet her cheeks, her forehead, moving his head side to side, whispering "I love you" over and over. Then Cal inched back and peered at her lips. He touched them, swallowed, and when he glanced up and met her eyes, the slightest hesitation crossed his face again.

"Cal," she whispered, nodding, cradling one of his cheeks. "Please..."

One of her arms he shoved above her head, slamming her wrist against the door as he kissed and bit her neck. "You want this now, Annie?"

"Yes..."

"Where?" He brought her other arm up to join the first, applying more pressure, threading his fingers through hers. "Where do you want to be fucked, Mrs. Prescott?"

"Kiss me," she panted instead.

Like a bolt of lightning, his tongue went into her mouth. The moment he released her wrists, she reached below his belt and touched him.

"Oh, God, I need you now." Trembling, she buried her face in the crook of his neck while making a fist around him over his pants and squeezing. "Now, Cal, please..."

"You're so beautiful, baby," Cal whispered, leading her across the driveway, bunching strands of her hair inside his palm as they went. *Just like this.* He kissed her cheek. "I love you."

"I love you too."

Seconds later, the two of them stood at the rear passenger door of the limousine, Carl at the wheel, when Annie reached for the handle.

"Wait."

Annie stopped and stared at him. "What? Did you want to be the one to open it?"

"No." Cal squared her hips, tugging the sides of her satin dress. He smirked. "I want you to take your panties off."

Annie flicked her eyes to the front of the vehicle.

"He can't see us."

She glanced back at Cal and grinned. "You take them off." She palmed her belly. "I am, like, a million years pregnant and can't bend in this thing."

"You insisted on keeping it on."

"Because I'm insisting on you being the one to take it off ... later." She bounced her brows.

Cal grinned, but as he began to gather up the material of her skirt, Annie pushed against his wrists.

"What?"

"Come here." She wiggled her index finger, then pulled his shirt from his pants as he stood tall again. Running her fingers beneath the cotton, over his abs, she arched up on her toes, put her mouth near his ear, and hummed, "I want you to take my panties off the way you did the first night we were together."

Cocking his head to the side, Cal smiled and replied, "You're insatiable," as he dropped to his haunches and slowly trailed his face down the front of her body.

Annie trembled.

His hands on her bare thighs.

His warm breath over her skin.

She placed a palm on the car to steady herself.

Memories of how it felt standing in his kitchen last June took over her psyche. The anticipation. The heart beating out of her chest. An immaculate, crushing need.

Many moments they shared together over the last several months flashed before her, and a series of several different, tangling emotions hit her like a brick falling from the top floor of a skyscraper. The feelings were almost indescribable. Hard to articulate.

Define it, Annie.

Not. Now...

Yes, now.

Her life had transformed so much over the past two years. The man before her new and fresh. And old — not in age or mind, but an old soul to her complementary spirit. Old as a symbol to the way she felt she'd always known him.

Annie became transfixed by his face, his mouth, his eyes while the thoughts continued pouring over her like cool rain on a hot summer day.

A death.

A lover.

A husband.

A baby.

A best friend.

One best friend lost and another gained.

A baby, a baby, a baby.

That particular word replayed multiple times, her body reminding her of him with the gentle pull she felt in her abdomen, between her thighs, the ache in her perineum.

Annie's throat swelled the way it had on the porch in the moonlight at Maggie's. The first time Cal had said he wanted her. It swelled the way it almost always had whenever he was near. Except now, the wanting, it was so much more.

She wanted Cal now. Always. She wanted him forever.

The want was more than physical. It *was* a need. A part of her very being, transcending anything she'd ever known or experienced.

Cal stood tall, panties in his fist, an accomplished smile across his face while Annie wore a very different expression. Tears welled in her eyes, puddles, like change in a pocket about to overflow.

"Annie, what is it?" Cal whispered, his voice cracking. He shoved the underwear into his jacket pocket and placed his hands on her hips. "What is it, baby?"

Annie twirled the jewelry on her wrist, the beaded, aqua-blue bracelet Peter had given her.

The gift usually gave her courage.

She carried it everywhere.

But the talisman didn't seem to be working now. The strength Cal liked to remind her was an integral part of her seemed absent.

Annie focused on the way the beads glistened in the moonlight, how they complemented Cal's shirt, and the way they looked as she turned them round and round and round.

Cal knew what it meant. He knew Annie. He'd always known her.

Placing a hand over her wrist, he stopped her incessant twirling. She met his eyes for a beat, then she abruptly burst into tears and put her face against his chest. Cal stroked her hair with one hand and her bare back with his other, his eyes wide, staring off into the distance. The darkness. Absorbing all the pain in Annie's heart.

The death of his mother.

Her brother.

Would it ever stop?

Her crying slowed. She tilted her face up. He pushed her hair back and gazed into her green-lollipop eyes.

"Oh, Annie..." He exhaled. "Your love will never die. Your love lasts forever. Let it fill you up. Let Peter's love fill you. Don't fight it."

The vigor she'd felt earlier with her father at the bottom of the staircase had left her. Now, she desired Cal to put her back together. Annie was worn from being the pillar Albert always needed. She was worn from feeling the constant sadness of Peter's death.

"I didn't want to feel any pain tonight." She sniffled. "Not tonight."

"I know." He palmed her cheek. "I didn't want to either. This night is special even with the pain, though. I miss my mother too."

"I know. I'm sorry."

"This night will always be ours, baby. Nothing can take that away."

Wincing, she bit her bottom lip. "Do you know what people said to me after he died?" She shifted her gaze. "*Right after he died*. They probably said it to you as well..." Annie inhaled, shaking her head, her hands starting to tremble. "They said, 'I'm so sorry, dear. It was just his time. It was his time to go.'"

Annie glared at Cal. "It wasn't his time! He was only thirty-six. *It wasn't his time*. He was supposed to be here, Cal. He was supposed to be alive!"

"Peter was supposed to be here, and he is," Cal soothed, wrapping his arms around her waist. "Not in the way you want. I know."

"You think your mom is here?" She swallowed.

"I hear her goddam voice in my head," he replied, laughing some, "that's for sure."

"Maybe you're crazy."

"Peter's here, Annie. And you know it."

Although Annie had spoken those same words to her father before the start of the ceremony — the same words she often spoke to him — she knew they'd been lies. She didn't really believe them. Maybe she never really had.

But Cal had uttered them so seriously, full of such assurance, Annie almost believed him. Or she wanted to. But nothing could take the place of Peter — his love at her heart, her throat, the way he occupied her thoughts.

None of it would bring him back.

Annie feared if she allowed her brother's love to fill her up, if she allowed the sound of his voice to play inside her mind, she might break into a thousand little pieces.

"Don't give me that bullshit," she finally uttered. "That same bullshit I've heard over and over. I've had to listen to it come out of my own mouth for a fucking year. God, for almost two years now. I can't do it anymore. I can't say it anymore." She started to hiccup. "He's not here. There's no reason. There's nothing."

Both of them stood stock-still. Annie trembling. Cal holding her securely.

Then she looked across the yard. "I'm cold."

After trailing his hands up and down her biceps, Cal removed his jacket, placed it across her shoulders, and sighed. "He must've loved you like there was no tomorrow." He ran his knuckles across her cheekbone. "You were probably the last thing on his mind, the last thing from this earth he could take with him before he died."

Annie hung her head and started to shake and cry. Cal pulled her tighter against him, holding her in his arms until she settled, one hand on the back of her head, the other around her waist.

He could feel her heartbeat.

He could feel their baby moving around inside her womb.

And he hadn't been lying.

He could feel his mother.

Here. Somewhere.

And he had no doubt Annie could feel her brother too.

One day, she would tire of denying it.

"What do you think Peter would've thought about his little sister falling in love with a man like me?" Cal smiled.

Both of them pulled their heads back and stared at each other.

"At first..." Annie sniffled, dragged a finger under her nose, and looked at the trees, at the palm fronds still blowing in the wind. "Oh, God." Turning her gaze on Cal again, her eyes twinkled. "At first, he would've wanted to kill you." She smirked. "He would've come around, though." Annie wiped beneath her eyes. "Eventually..." She cupped his cheeks. "He would've come around ... once he knew you really loved me."

"I do really love you."

"I know..." Annie sighed, relaxing, and it felt like they were dancing again. So comfortable they were, lulled by the wind, each other's eyes, their skin.

"He would've approved," she continued, puffing up with pride, "of this night, of us, the baby."

"Annie, you are—"

"Shhh." She covered his mouth. "I'm your wife! That's what I am."

"You're so much more," he mumbled, removing her palm.

"I want you," she burst. "I want all of you."

"I know." Cal grinned, and Annie nudged his shoulder. "You have all of me ... forever."

"Kiss me before I explode, Prescott. I might actually spontaneously combust right here, you know?"

Cal laughed. He thought Annie had never looked sexier. Leaning his forehead against hers, he gently rocked her entire wonderful, amazing, pregnant body with his to the beat of the breeze, to the rustle of the leaves, to the drum of the ocean. He cupped the back of her neck, slid his fingers through her hair, and kissed his wife.

He kissed Mrs. Prescott.

Softly, wholly, full of love.

Then they took their seats in the back of the limo.

"We're ready now," Cal said to Carl.

"Very good, sir," the driver replied. "And congratulations again."

"Thank you," Cal and Annie said at the same time as Carl raised the partition.

"Sir..." Annie rolled her eyes.

Cal smirked and lifted her onto his lap, bunching her skirt as she straddled him.

Annie brushed invisible nothings off his shirt. "Not so fast. *Sir*."

"Have you changed your mind again, my dear wife?"

"No." She giggled. "I like the sound of that. *Wife*."

"I love you. Wife." Cal nipped her earlobe, and Annie squirmed as he began to slide a hand up her thigh.

"Don't," she said, grabbing his wrist, grinning. "I want to tease you tonight, sir."

Dropping her gaze to his waist, she unfastened his belt buckle and the button of his pants. As she lowered his zipper, her eyes lit up like a stick of dynamite.

"Have you been good?" she whispered, making a fist around him. "Did you have *needs* while I was away these last two weeks?" Her palm slid up and down, getting him harder. "Did your hand meet them for you?"

"My hand"—he cleared his throat—"could never meet the needs you satisfy."

Annie tossed her head back, laughing. "Good answer."

"What about you?" He gripped her waist, pressing his fingers into her sides. "Did you touch yourself while we were apart?"

"I was busy planning our wedding." She batted her lashes.

"God, Annie," he hissed as his head fell against the cushion, "I've missed you."

"Where are we going?" she moaned a few seconds later, her face in his neck, her hand sticky with precum. "How much time do we have?"

"I want to wait." Cal clutched her wrist, his jaw practically twitching. Their eyes met. "For the bed."

"Where are we going?" she repeated instead, bucking her hips against him as she continued to jerk him off. "How long is the ride?"

"You know it's a surprise."

"When, Cal?" She squeezed and squeezed. "When will we be there?"

"Fuck, Annie..." Cal let out an elongated moan and looked up at the ceiling. "Forty-five minutes."

"Well..." She ran a thumb over the tip, licking her lips. "It may seem longer."

Cal gripped her hips — much harder than before. Now, his jaw resembled steel. His green eyes appeared black as night. "I don't want a fucking mess all over the back of the car."

"I'll make sure you come inside me. But you can't touch me." She pushed him away at his biceps. "Put your hands away."

Cal smirked.

"I'm serious, Prescott. No touching."

He placed his palms flat on the seat. "This I have to see."

"I can manage."

"What are you up to?" He raised his brows.

"This is my wedding gift to you. I've been thinking about it for two weeks."

"You're my gift, Annie." Unable to help himself, Cal reached up and stroked her cheek.

"Yes, and tonight, I'm fucking you. So, keep your hands away, sir." She swatted his arm. "Very good, sir."

"If you keep calling me that, I'll have to take you over my knee and spank the fuck out of you."

"Oh, you will?" Annie arched a brow as she gathered the hem of her skirt, lifted her hips, and positioned herself closer to his erection.

The flesh of her clit rubbed against him, and he dropped his head back and groaned as she began to rub herself all over him. His dick between them, painfully hard, Annie panting, still holding the material up so that she could see them. Her eyes wide, her tongue between her teeth. Cal's throat bobbing. His chest looking like it might burst.

"Fuck me now, baby," Cal strained, pinching his eyes shut, his knuckles turning white against the leather seats.

"I thought you wanted to wait for the bed." Annie unbuttoned the rest of his shirt, spread it open, and ran her hands all over his chest.

"This is all I've wanted for two weeks." He thrust up against the silk of her dress. Against her belly. His palms twitching next to his thighs. "*You*. To be near you. Inside you."

"Not yet," she whispered, threading her fingers through his hair while continuing to writhe all over him. She kissed his neck, his cheeks, his mouth.

Annie closed her eyes and let go.

The way Cal always asked her to.

They both let go.

Of the pawn, the queen, the king, the knight.

Annie forgot.

Forgetting the backseat of the limo, forgetting the seven-month-old heaviness in her womb, the Buddha belly, the shadow of death circling around them, forgetting and forgetting to the point of being unsure if she could continue to play Cal at his own game.

Fuck, she thought. He always was better at it. Cal had the self-control. What did she have? A wet pussy and pregnancy hormones. A few more minutes of this, and she would be done.

Two weeks of waiting and anticipating, and the thirty minutes of playtime she'd hoped for would explode into an unruly orgasm in a matter of minutes. Or seconds.

"If you missed me so much," she panted, her eyes on where they met, how they touched, "then why have you been hesitating with me?"

Cal stilled and strained, "I told you..."

"No, you didn't." Annie stopped moving. She swallowed. "You haven't said the words out loud." Their eyes locked. "It's been like this for weeks. I'm not talking about only tonight."

"I..." Cal glanced to the side, his Adam's apple bobbing. "I don't want to hurt you..."

"Baby," she whispered, bringing his face back front and center, "you could never hurt me." She kissed him. "I'm pregnant, not breakable. The only thing hurting me right now is knowing you're afraid to be yourself with me."

Annie rose up and then sank down. Until he filled her completely.

Cal groaned, trembled. His palms were still flat on the seat.

"Fuck me, Cal." Taking his hands, she placed them on her hips. "Touch me. *Now*." Their eyes met. "I'm yours to do with as you please. Like always. Don't hold back with me anymore." Annie was drunk on him. Gone. Hazy. "This is what I want. You. The way you are." She nodded. "*Fuck me. Hard*."

"Lift up," Cal instructed as he slipped off his shoes, his pants, then pulled her atop him again. Several wonderful sounds filled the car as Cal found a home inside her body for only the second time in almost two weeks.

"Fuck..." His eyes rolled back into his head. "Ride me, Annie. Fuck me, baby, like you wanted to. You. Show. Me." The straps of her dress came down. He folded the scoop neckline beyond her breasts and began to trace the peaks that seemed to have swelled even more since they'd seen each other last. Leaning forward, he took a nipple into his mouth — sucking, biting, licking — until she pushed against his chest and nearly screamed.

"Fuck me, Annie," he repeated. "Show me your gift."

Wrapping her fingers around the back of his neck, Annie picked up speed and bounced, rising all the way up to his tip, then sitting down, squeezing her thighs, rubbing her clit against him, moaning and moaning, crying out each time he hit her cervix.

"Give yourself to me, Annie." Holding her hips, Cal gripped her, his nails digging into her skin as he guided her body to do as they wished.

He controlled the rhythm, the need, the fuck. It was him, pushing her far, far, far into that place, the abyss of bliss where nothing — nothing — could come for her. The place of safety ... home.

Where they belonged and always wanted to roam.

"I am." She was his gift. He was hers. "I am... *Fuck*..." His eyes and body possessed her. She was his. Always his. Never another's. No one else's. Annie held his face. "I have given myself to you." She hiccupped. "I've always been yours. From the beginning."

The next time she rose up, she stopped, resisting the strength of his hands, the way he attempted to push her back down over him.

"Say it to me," she cried, her voice shaking. She coiled her fingers around the back of his slippery neck as she inched her groin farther from his desperate tip.

"I love you." He started to kiss her but she pulled away.

"I know," she said, fighting tears. "Say ... tell me..."

"What, heavy?"

"Tell me that I am yours."

"Fuck, Annie. *I am yours*. Let me inside you."

"Fill me up with it, then, Cal." She sat back down, swallowing his dick completely. "Say it again."

"I'm yours..." Cal thrust upward with such force, he nearly knocked the breath from her lungs.

"Oh fuck!" she cried and moaned. "Forever..." Annie tossed her head, biting her lip, exhausting herself. "Say it."

"I'm yours." Cal held her face. Stared into her eyes. "Forever, baby."

His tongue went into her mouth, making love to her the way he'd originally said he wanted to. Sucking up her whimpers and cries.

Everything hurt, a good hurt, a satisfied hurt.

Tears dripped from the corners of her eyes, her muscles tightening as his tongue continued to explore her mouth, loving and devouring her. The moment her body finally started to convulse, exploding into a million pieces of whatever it was they shared or were made of, Cal froze, his eyes locking onto Annie's. Then he groaned and twitched, jerking as he filled her with cum.

Sweating, shaking, and still pulsing, bound and together, they remained lost in that forever — in the sealing of their union.

Annie's fingers wound through Cal's hair. His face pressed against her cheek. Both of them struggling to breathe.

Undying.

Breathless.

Winding.

Close.

Tight.

Complete.

Their souls tangled, mingling and running through each other. The uncomfortable dress, the tight position, the Buddha belly, the sleepiness, death, heartache, pain — nothing could lessen it. The force, the need, the want, the paralyzing desire all became sealed on this day. With vows and kisses and rings. Then with the ultimate consummation in the backseat of the limousine.

It was made official.

Tied up and bound.

Fastened.

Now, afterward, at the end of it, when their bodies, hearts, and minds were utmost sated, Cal and Annie Prescott kept each other close the remainder of the ride to the hotel.

stay near
never far
be the bridge
to my heart
keep me safe
heal our wounds
go to battle
for you
for me
always
and forever
together
wielding magic
as we sleep beneath the stars

WARNING

THERE'S STILL TIME TO TURN BACK...

THE PARADOX

A SEEMINGLY CONTRADICTORY STATEMENT
OPPOSED TO COMMON SENSE, YET IT MIGHT BE
TRUE; SOMEONE WHO DOES TWO THINGS
SEEMINGLY OPPOSITE TO EACH OTHER

two hearts
equal one
and three made us stronger
until
I became weak
chemical dependent worthless nothing
suffering
on the inside
where no one sees
the wounds
my scars
had only recently started healing
and now
there is a fissure
where instead
there should be
bond
glue
the opposite of apathy
a smile
a Mary Poppins disposition

when I couldn't fall in line
I fell behind
and the life
I had been given
the life
I'd chosen
the things I said I accepted
I doubted
questioned
I was confused
until
up became down
right became wrong
and the beautiful little boy
we created
-    deserved better
than me
and the man
I loved
maybe
he didn't need me
the rules shifted
the universe spun
while I hung from a string of burned-out stars
and the open window
allowing a safe return from space...
appeared to be closing

EIGHTY-FOUR

"I'm thinking of our wedding night."

"What, Cal?" Annie mumbled, half-asleep, the two of them lying side by side in their king-sized bed at their home in Seattle, her back to his front.

The clock on the dresser screamed 11:13 in bright red numbers.

A masculine hand grazed her waist, and she tried to pull away from its warmth and safety. But he didn't let go. She clung to the pillow, not moving a muscle, wishing he would roll over and pretend to sleep.

"It feels like only last week," he whispered on a sigh.

But it had been over two months since they'd exchanged vows on the beach, since they'd combined their lives, sealed heartbeats.

It had been weeks of being unable to sleep.

Oh, she slept some at night. But her adrenaline was locked into overdrive, or her hormones were shifting. Or something. She hadn't even been able to take a nap since the baby had been born. Their baby. Their son.

Benjamin Everett Prescott.

It had all happened so fast ... not long after the wedding night.

Ben had arrived early. Married in March. A baby by the end of April.

Mother's Day had come and gone...

"Annie..." Cal's nose pressed into her shoulder blade, trailing over skin, breathing against her as he came to a stop at her jawline. "The doctor said it's okay."

The prescribed six weeks of abstaining from intercourse had passed. Except they'd abstained from everything, including some of the nightly cuddling.

"I'm not ready," she replied, and his body tensed. His hand remained wrapped around her waist, now a fist.

"Just let me love you." His chest expanded, then deflated.

"I'm so tired. I've hardly slept."

"Rosa will fly back out here in a heartbeat."

"I want to be with Ben. Only the three of us for a while. I don't want someone here every night."

"Okay." He kissed her in all the places his nose had caressed, holding her tightly.

But there was nowhere to go.

She couldn't get away from him.

Practically since the moment she'd given birth, she had changed. Again. And this... Touching, the thought of sex...

She never felt the least bit of excitement at the prospect of an orgasm. She didn't fantasize. Or crave her husband. That part of her seemed dead. The memory of their wedding night wasn't enough to rouse her mood, the evening Cal had just referred to...

Flowers, rose petals minus stems and thorns, had been strewn across the floors and bedding of the bridal suite — red and pink and yellow and white — symbolizing the ones she'd once drowned and the ones Carl had peeled apart and thrown into the Tesla.

If only things could be that simple.

And at the time, those things had seemed hard.

Hindsight...

It was a dream.

The last two years seemed that way. First, a nightmare, then a dream. She didn't know how to plan for anything or what to expect. Each day brought something new. The baby had thrown Annie into a tailspin. Lack of sleep made her unreasonable.

The way Cal's body pressed against hers now hurt. His kisses felt like weight. Every time he'd tried to touch her these last few weeks, she'd recoiled like a snake.

All she wanted was sleep.

She daydreamed about lying on a beach in the sun. The heat warming her head to toe until she could relax and drift off...

And she wished Cal wouldn't try to love her because each attempt made her feel pressured, then ashamed. Failing to be what he expected. Miserably. His patience only reminded her of the things she wasn't and may never be.

Was that how he'd felt when they'd been dating?

Inadequate.

"What can I do for you?" Wet, open-mouthed kisses peppered her shoulder, her collarbone.

"Let me sleep." She clutched the pillow harder, hoping it would provide relief. If she could just sleep soundly and for hours on end, this bleakness she felt might cease. Things would go back to the way they'd been before she went into labor.

Once-magical fingers trailed down her arm, and she pretended to be pacified by their spell. She attempted to warm to his ministrations, even letting out a little sigh, snuggling against him, her hips meeting his thighs.

Seconds later, the baby began to cry.

Eighty-Five

Some days later, Annie strolled down the hall, following the sounds of music drifting through their home.

It seemed Cal was always playing this particular record.

Annie crept into the room, the downstairs bedroom they'd converted into a study-library-office, wearing her gray sweatpants and soiled top, a few buttons of the latter still undone at the collar. He'd shut the speakers off everywhere else but hadn't bothered to close the door.

"I just got him to sleep," she said, eyeing Cal's backside. His fingers flew at a frenetic pace across the keyboard. "Finally..." Annie slouched. Her stomach felt hollow. "He cried all morning."

She was about to turn to leave when he closed the laptop and patted his knee. "Come here."

"Honey..." Her eyes bounced around the room.

Cal stood.

Annie tripped backward, looking like a frightened bird as Cal took a few tentative steps. Until he was close enough to smell her: breast milk, tangerines, and the calendula from the baby cream. His nose fell against her hair. His hands touched her waist.

"Dance with me." Cal lifted her limp arm and placed her hand on his shoulder. He found a familiar spot to rest his palm: the small of her back.

His feet began to move, but Annie was a statue. "La Vie En Rose" wasn't having the effect it used to...

Cal had his record player brought to the bridal suite. The one his grandfather had given him. A few choice albums were there too.

Annie didn't ask questions. She only followed his lead, seeming to relish being surprised. She trusted him.

It was the first song he played. The first they danced to after the wedding ... when they were completely and utterly alone, rose petals scattered across the floor and bedspread, her dress rumpled and dragging on the floor. She leaned her head against his chest, content to let him guide her in this start of their new life as man and wife.

And he'd never felt more honored.

This is a privilege, *he thought.* To be entrusted to care for this woman, someone who could certainly survive without him, but she'd chosen — she wanted — his guidance and partnership.

She needed him. And he needed her.

Her skin felt like satin, like the dress.

It would be a shame to take it off. Maybe she could wear it indefinitely. And they could dance like this forever and only to this song. Louis made him feel things too. Satchmo's scruffy voice was pure soul and magic. And he hadn't even begun to sing yet.

Cal had turned into a fool.

"I love you," he whispered, his throat swollen and tingly, like shards of glass piercing skin.

"Mmm," she replied.

"Do you want to just go to sleep?" He kissed the top of her head.

Pulling back some, she peered up at him. "I want you to make love to me."

"The backseat wasn't enough?" He grinned.

"Nothing is enough. Love isn't enough. I want everything."

"And you shall have it. You'll have to help me figure out how to get you out of this fucking thing." He began to fiddle with the contraptions holding it together.

"I know this song," she moaned against his shirt, her head resting on his chest again.

He stopped fingering the back of the dress and concentrated on holding his wife. "You probably know it from a movie."

"But it's familiar, like from something else too."

After over a minute of only melody, the voice they knew well began to croon.

Annie's smile was so huge it broke Cal wide open. His heart belonged to Annie. His body and soul too.

"Is this the romance *you claimed you wanted tonight?" he whispered near her ear, and she shivered.*

"You're pretty good, baby." She glanced up at him. "The flowers... The record player... But don't get a big head."

"Too late." He pressed his groin to hers, then they both threw their heads back and laughed.

"I've got you. Lean on me," Cal said as they continued to skirt across the floor of the study to Louis — such a contrast from the night they'd shared in the hotel room.

They could've spent a week there and foregone a honeymoon ... and food ... and sunlight.

Why is it different now? Annie wondered. When would it feel like it used to? Even her bones felt brittle from climbing up the hill of an endless mountain. She wanted to reach the summit.

And if she could, this would be over. Things would be as they should: complete. Perfect.

"When will I stop being so tired?" she mumbled against his neck.

"Don't be so hard on yourself. This is an adjustment."

But she hadn't showered again in days. She could barely stand upright. And the heather sweatpants she wore had become a second skin. She didn't even take them off to sleep. She hardly looked in the mirror. She never combed her hair.

"I'm a mess, Cal."

"Let me take you to bed."

Annie stopped dancing. She dropped her arms to her sides.

"I meant only you." He wiggled her hips, willing her to smile by giving her one of his own, dimples and all. "To sleep."

The song ended. Something else was ending too.

Or beginning.

"I'm sorry I haven't been able to..." Her gaze wandered around the room. "You know..."

"Don't apologize." He grinned. "I can go without sex."

Annie guffawed and shook her head.

"I can." He tugged on her hand. "Come on..."

"It won't matter. I won't be able to fall asleep."

"You should try." He pushed back some of her hair. "Have you eaten?"

"Crackers."

"Annie..."

"*Please* don't scold me." Tears filled her vision.

He ran his knuckles along her cheek. "Can I give you a bath?"

"No." She took in a sharp breath and stared into his eyes. "I'm fine."

Eighty-Six

Cal loved to watch Annie with Benjamin.

Right now, he watched from the hallway. She sat in the companion rocking chair in their son's bedroom, one of the two they'd brought from his mother's. The little man nestled across her chest.

Cal loved gazing upon them, especially when she nursed him.

Today, tears fell over her cheeks as she glanced out the window, seeming to look for something in the glass the way Cal used to look for things in the ocean.

He assumed this behavior was normal postpartum. The crying. The moodiness. And it wasn't always difficult. There were good days too.

Or maybe Cal had chosen to be optimistic. To see the glass half-full.

It had only been a couple months, maybe twelve or so weeks, and birthing babies was traumatic. Her body had gone through an event most men wouldn't have been able to accomplish. Correction: zero men. And now she lacked sleep, a schedule, friends, spending time with her camera. And she was feeding an infant from her breasts, giving their son precious nutrients.

It was beautiful to witness.

The tears had a beauty all their own as well.

Cal had to stop himself from wanting to erase them. To do away with them. He'd learned they were sometimes necessary — a part of the grieving and healing process. He was learning not to default to feeling helpless.

Right as he was about to fully open the bedroom door, something happened. Benjamin's mouth was still fastened around his mother's nipple, but he had broken suction. It caught Annie's attention too. She gazed down, a smile taking shape across her face, a few tears in her eyes ... and then she looked up.

"Cal," she said in amazement as he entered the room. She glanced back down at Ben. "He knows me."

"Of course he knows you, Annie."

"I mean"—Ben squeezed her pinky, still smiling—"it's ... it's the way he's looking at me. He's smiling. It's in his eyes too." She peered from Benjamin to Cal. "He knows who I am."

"Oh, Annie..." Cal dropped to his knees, placed his head on her thigh, and a hand on her waist. "*My heavy.*"

He remained there with the two of them as Ben resumed nursing, both boys starting to nod off, Cal feeling and not thinking. Absorbing love — the kind only one woman could provide.

EIGHTY-SEVEN

Mozart spun on the record player. Cal had found the perfect spot for the turntable in their living room. Near where Annie sat now. Speakers had been placed strategically throughout the house too.

Benjamin liked music. Especially Mozart. Annie was starting to tire of noise, though. Even her head buzzed. Her muscles wept. Her armpits smelled.

She slid her fingers through her greasy, uncombed hair and peered down at the sleeping baby on her chest. Four months old, and he was still so tiny. His head rested in the crook of her neck, his knees hit her breasts, and she had to resist the urge to stroke his long, wheaten eyelashes...

At least he was asleep.

Finally.

He'd cried for most of the day.

As she swayed in the rocker Cal had brought from his mother's, this one placed in their living room, she continued to study Benjamin's adorable little face. He had his father's lips and dimples ... and maybe her smile. And deep insights could be seen in his blue eyes for miles. His forehead crinkled as he dreamed, his eyes twitching underneath their delicate lids. His lungs made a beautiful sound, and she could feel the rise matching her own.

"Do you need anything at the store?" Cal interrupted, his hand caressing the top of her head.

His touch startled her. Her breast was still out. Her eyes stung like she'd swam in the ocean with them open for hours. A tremor passed through her, a chill.

"Annie," he whispered, reaching out an arm. "Let me put him to bed."

"He'll wake up." She shifted. "No."

"Did you hear me before?" he asked, and she shook her head. "Do you need anything? I'm picking up diapers and fruit."

Ben wiggled. She patted his bottom, tapping it lightly, willing him to stay asleep. Because the sleeping was a reprieve. He cried. A lot. He nursed. A lot. And she still couldn't sleep well even when he did.

Annie shook her head again.

The market didn't sell what she needed. A hydrocodone ... maybe a bottle of them. An injection of something to knock her out cold. Sometimes she empathized with Michael Jackson. Which should've scared the shit out of her, but in this moment, tired and exhausted and still unable to sleep like a normal person, those thoughts made her fearless. Invincible. On top of the world.

Then...

...her head tingled, and her throat turned to sandpaper.

Shame settled into the pit of her stomach.

"Let me put him down. Then you can shower."

Tears welled up in her eyes as Cal reached for their son. But Annie gave him the cold shoulder.

He sighed, walked away, grumbling as he grabbed his keys and went out the front door.

Annie sat there, barely rocking, thinking of nothing, only feeling hurt clawing its way up the walls of her chest. Until the record stopped, the needle skipped, and the baby woke up.

EIGHTY-EIGHT

Memories of the birth came to her at night in flashes.

The pain — exactly where she'd felt it in her body, nowhere and everywhere all at once — she welcomed.

Then and now.

Because thinking about childbirth gave her something to do between nursing and burping and changing, between washing clothes and struggling to maintain a sense of anything.

ANNIE: It's happening.

The phone rang immediately after she'd sent Cal that text — the morning she went into premature labor.

"How often?" he said the second she swiped the screen.

Still in the throes of one, she panted into the receiver, groaning.

"I'm ten minutes away."

"Hurry."

"Should I call an—?"

"No ... just hurry."

Cal arrived home within minutes and transported her to the hospital faster than any emergency vehicle could have. The labor was short in duration, or so she'd been told. She opted not to have an epidural.

It was good to feel pain. Always had been.

Pain was better than what she felt right now, lying in the king-sized bed she shared with her husband in their home in Seattle, the baby monitor on, its Darth Vader-like static singing a melody she wanted to squash.

Because she was supposed to feel love, elation, the joys of motherhood.

But as Annie lay there in the dark, Cal and Benjamin sleeping, she felt ... nothing.

Still.

For weeks.

Annie had felt bleak before. Depressed. She had changed after Peter's death. But this was different.

Her moods felt darker, scarier. Like something she couldn't see her way through. A fog. Like The Nothing from *The Never Ending Story*.

She'd gone into the hospital as Annie and come out a misfit, a freak, someone unfit for the job she was supposed to be intuitively made for.

Annie had come home with a baby she thought she knew how to care for. But every feeling was new. Each day a surprise. Depression had only taught her acceptance was hard. Being responsible for an infant was climbing a mountain, not a fucking molehill.

Thinking of the labor made her feel strong. And so, unable to sleep, she clung to the memories...

"I need to push." Her teeth clenched. Her belly was tight. So tight. Her midsection, her lower back, her womb and thighs, ached violently.

Cal glanced at the monitor and its spiky green lines.

"Get someone," she screamed.

He went into the hall and started cursing and yelling as Annie rode the wave of the contraction, her eyes closing, her nostrils stretching just to breathe. She had to resist the urge to push with all her might.

He was coming. He was coming. He was coming.

"Cal," she moaned. Her head fell against the pillow, rolling to the side as she shut her eyes in exhaustion.

In an instant, he was there, wiping sweat from her brow and whispering words of praise and love into her ear. Then a nurse strolled in, attaching gloves to her hands.

Annie hated the smacking sound the latex made when it hit skin. Hated fingers probing inside her body — for the hundredth time — especially when she was about to push a human through her opening.

"You're not quite ten centimeters."

"I need to push." Annie closed her eyes again, suppressing the urge with a grimace. Another contraction about to crest. She didn't think she could hold on.

"Where's the doctor?" Cal barked.

"He's coming," the nurse replied, and Annie knew he was coming, but she was beginning to doubt the doctor would. "I'm going to stretch you a little so you can start to push. Okay?"

Annie nodded and winced while Cal stroked her hair and face.

A man in blue scrubs burst through the door three contractions later. Annie had already begun to push, Cal and the nurse holding her knees, encouraging her.

"He's crowning, Doctor."

Tears were in Cal's eyes. But Annie couldn't see anything past the sensation of wanting to bear down and squeeze and squeeze and squeeze.

A burning sensation and a pinching followed, like she was being stuck with a big fat syringe, then it felt like something astronomical slipped through the eye of a needle. Seconds later, the sounds of a baby crying filled the room.

They placed him on her chest, his cord still attached to her body. His face red and gooey.

The little boy smelled like he belonged to her, his eyes struggling to open. His mouth wasn't having any difficulty, though. It was wide, and he was crying.

His father was too. Quietly, though.

Cal touched his son's head — a small swath of dark hair covered it — and cupped a hand over his own mouth.

The parents' eyes locked.

So much passed between them in those seconds that Annie's heart practically stopped with the connection she felt fusing the three of them together.

"Benjamin," Cal whispered, and Annie nodded, smiling, cheeks hurting from the pure joy radiating from her heart. "I love him."

"I love him too."

EIGHTY-NINE

Annie pushed open the door to the study, Benjamin against her chest, his head and neck arching backward, her hand trying to hold him steady while he wailed.

"Hold on a minute, please." Cal spoke into the cell phone from where he sat at the desk, his face toward a window and a wall, then he pressed a button on the screen and turned around.

Pools filled his wife's eyes, ready to overflow at their edges. And the whites looked red, like she'd spent half the morning already consumed by the activity.

"He won't stop."

"Annie"—he removed his glasses and pinched fingers into the corners of his eyes—"I'm in the middle of an important call."

"Sometimes..." she began, her voice quiet and trembling, her gaze bouncing around, "I need your help."

Cal stood and gripped the back of the chair until his knuckles turned white. "I offer plenty of help." He glared at her. Her nostrils flared. The baby hadn't stopped fussing. "You refuse me. You can't come barging in here in the middle of the day and ex—"

She turned and marched toward the door.

"Annie!" he cried, but neither of them stopped, Ben wailing, Annie stomping. "Goddammit. Don't walk away from me."

"You said you didn't want to be interrupted."

"Fuck." He pinched the bridge of his nose.

"Stop cursing. You're going to upset him."

"I'm going to upset him?"

Cal's phone danced across the desk. The caller must've hung up. They both turned to look at the noise, Annie's expression a challenge and Cal's showing he didn't care if he failed the test.

"You're in this room all day long."

"I work, Annie."

"And I don't."

"That's not what I said. Don't put words in my mouth. I'm trying to avoid having to leave the house. That's why I'm in here. I'm avoiding going out of town, meeting clients."

"I need you."

"You need things I'm not sure I can give you." His voice calmed. Lowered. He took three tentative steps forward. "You want me to remove a burden ... but some hurts never leave us." The distance closed between them with two more strides. "And it's okay if they don't."

Cal placed a palm on his son's back while he wiped newly formed tears from the corners of his wife's eyelids. Then he whispered, "I love you," and took Benjamin from her arms.

His phone vibrated again, but he ignored it and left the office, patting Ben's bum and humming a tune as they exited.

NINETY

Many days later, as Cal walked up the stairs toward their bedroom, he heard Annie in Ben's room crying quietly. Hesitating in the hallway, he watched as she pulled the string and closed the slotted shades over the window.

Cal wasn't immune to whatever the fuck was happening in their household. Maybe he had been living in denial, though. He used to think this kind of bullshit didn't sprout wings overnight and soar. But fuck him if the two of them hadn't just up and decided to run to the edge of a mountain and jump off a cliff.

Days had turned to weeks and weeks to months. Nights had become a reason to roll toward the edge of the bed and ache for the comfort only one woman could give but refused to grant.

She no longer wanted what he offered.

Touching and kissing and holding hands had morphed from hardly ever, to almost never. Talking usually meant arguing, nagging, or playing a game of blame. Sometimes all three. So, Cal kept himself busy with work and Benjamin, pretending to have plenty to do … even when he did not.

But he couldn't carry the weight of Annie's sadness much longer.

His back was about to break.

Annie shook upon noticing him, then she wiped tears from under her eyelids and straightened her spine.

Cal stared at her, glaring really.

However, the puddles about to overflow from the ridges of her red lids had him softening. He moved toward her, but the second he stepped a couple paces forward, she stopped crying on a dime while maintaining the same ramrod posture.

Ignoring her stance, he closed the distance between them, wrapped an arm around her waist, and cradled her head to his chest. Surprising him, she released a few puffs of air, exhaling loudly and deeply, sinking farther into him, her nose near the crook of his neck.

But then a moment later, she pulled back.

"What is it?" he whispered, palming her cheek, staring into her eyes.

You want something from me, she itched to say but didn't. Besides, the baby took up that space: the needs, the contact, the skin. She was burned out on giving everything to Benjamin. There was nothing left for Cal.

"What is it, Annie?" he repeated.

"Nothing," she replied as she took one last look at Benjamin sleeping in his crib before exiting the room.

"It's been five months," Cal said with no inflection as he joined her in the master bedroom a few minutes later. But his tongue felt heavy. His throat starved. "What do I need to do? Tell me, Annie. Anything, and I'll do it."

Arms folded across her chest, she stood by one of the windows, peeking through the open slots of the wooden blinds, gaze blurring over the deciduous trees and their red, orange, and yellow leaves.

What did she need?

Red leaves. *Anything.*

Orange leaves. *He wants sex.*

Yellow leaves. *Sex...*

Sex. Sex. Sex.

They still weren't having it.

And it was the big, fat elephant in the room, following her around wherever she went. Upstairs, down, to bed, in her dreams. And now, she wasn't sure which had come first: the depression or this crack in their marriage. The egg or the chicken. The thought or the motherfucking feeling.

Her chin dropped, and her bottom lip trembled. Why didn't she want him?

Because she was different.

Her body had changed. Her mind played tricks.

Would she ever want Cal again?

The guilt made it ten times worse, knowing she couldn't satisfy him.

"Just find someone else," Annie mumbled, lips barely moving, her eyes glued to the landscape of her grief and no longer on the backyard. "Go meet your needs. It's fine. I know you need to have sex." She swallowed and looked over at him. "I want you to have that. Even if it's not with me."

Light crept through the blinds, hitting Annie's features, and Cal could see the exhaustion, the blank stare, the numbness all over her face.

"Do you actually think I would do that?" He pinched his nose, biting his tongue to keep from saying what he really thought. "Fuck. Do you think that's what I want to do?" He stepped closer. "Look at me."

"Don't order me," she spat. Besides, she couldn't *look* because the energy emanating from him felt weightier than the sun bouncing off the trees and peeking through the blinds. "I'm not a child."

"Christ, Annie, you know this isn't just about sex. This is about you."

It was enough she'd literally denied him access to her body in the simplest of ways, to hold her hand, to touch her face, but now to tell him he should go out and fuck whomever ... whenever. A stranger. That was absolutely fucking unacceptable. This quagmire they found themselves in was about much more than the absence of sex.

Annie had always liked to make their relationship about sex, though. The things they hadn't fully worked through when dating were coming back to haunt them.

"I need you," he pleaded, staring at the side of her obstinate face. "I want to be able to touch you without you thinking I want more. I want to hold you in my arms. Don't keep pushing me away."

Annie crossed to the other side of the room, passing him without a glance, and folded her arms across her chest. "Then don't keep pressuring me to give you something I can't."

Cal took two big strides, pulled her hands to her sides, and laced his fingers through hers. "I don't understand. What's different?" Cal swallowed. "Help me understand you, baby. Is it me?"

"No," her voice squeaked as she turned to fully face him. The connection between them was still strong. Not a cord — the way it had been on Maggie's staircase or during the kiss in the rain or with their son on her chest in the hospital bed. Maybe it was only a piece of yarn or string. But it was still holding them together, and it was electric. "It's not you."

"I think you should talk to someone." He peered into her eyes. "I'm not capable enough anymore, and I'm ... I'm too close to the situation. I'm biased."

After waiting several seconds for her to speak, he deflated and glanced around the room. Annie wandered to the bed, sat at the foot, and began playing with her fingers mindlessly. He made to exit.

"Cal..."

At the sound of his name, he stopped and turned, looking at his wife in the dark of the room, gray except for the beams of light shining between the slots covering the window, streaking across the floor in a pattern of fine, broken lines.

A rainbow of promises.

"Don't be with anyone else," she began, tripping over her words, choking. "Don't. Don't."

"Annie..." Cal joined her, sitting beside her, fingering the tips of her hair. "I only want you."

She dropped her head to his shoulder, and he made circles over her back.

"Baby, when I promised to love you, I meant it. I'm not going anywhere ... with anybody else." He kissed her forehead. "We'll get through this."

Annie wondered if she would get through it. Maybe being depressed was an integral part of her very being. Intertwined with her soul the way the earth needed water, the way the plants needed sun.

The way her sky needed his ocean.

She remained seated on the bed, head on Cal's shoulder, somewhat willingly allowing him to hold her for several minutes.

She didn't push him away.

Cal rested his chin on the top of her head.

Everything about Annie felt so good against him. A current he didn't ever want to swim away from.

Then the baby started to cry. Annie jerked upright.

My God, he thought. She'd actually lost herself for a minute in his embrace, and it was one of the most beautiful things he'd experienced with her in weeks.

Before turning to leave, she gave him a slight smile, and even though it didn't reach her eyes, it showed promise. Her intrinsic magic.

The smile was a beginning.

A start.

Hope bloomed fresh in Cal's heart.

NINETY-ONE

Cal sat, legs crossed, wearing only bathing suit trunks and holding a washcloth, in the garden tub in their master bathroom.

Ben was in his own tub — the kind made for infants — situated in front of his dad. The big tub had no water in it. The little one did. Benjamin didn't much enjoy getting wet. But he loved his father's attention.

This was how Annie found them.

She smiled upon entering, then skirted to the walk-in and began to change clothes. She wanted her sweatpants. The things that made her feel comfortable and most like herself.

"How'd it go today?" Cal called, his voice echoing a little off the tiled walls.

"Fine," she said when she popped back out.

She began replacing nursing pads while standing in front of the double sinks, swapping wet for dry. Ben whimpered, though, and so soon she would be soiling the fresh ones.

"I know what fine means with you: bullshit." Cal rinsed Ben's hair.

"I don't want to talk about it."

"Did you like her?"

"It's a him. And no."

Their eyes met in the mirror, tangling, then untangling. Cal's were stern, unyielding.

Case in point.

One reason why she wouldn't discuss what had happened at the office of the therapist this afternoon. It had only been the first visit. But Annie had a feeling something was off. Or she couldn't open up.

How could she share intimacies with a stranger when she could barely talk to Cal?

The girl with the heart on her sleeve resided somewhere else. Or maybe her feelings were obvious, but she wasn't vocalizing them. She knew she held back with Cal ... with everyone she loved. And the shame of knowing it and being unable to conquer the bullshit was debilitating.

She was slowly suffocating.

But she had her comfy clothes on now. Her hair was still somewhat combed from having gone out. She'd had a shower earlier, and what she wore had been laundered — by someone else.

She resented the help.

Rosa having done it occasionally in the past was one thing, but not being able to perform a basic function for her family like washing the fucking clothes — Cal had taken that away from her and was paying someone to do it — was humiliating.

The only consolation was the scent it bathed her in: Cal's. Coconut, beach, a clean T-shirt.

After wrapping the baby in a beige towel, the one with ears on its hoodie, the two boys joined her near the sinks.

"Don't hold him like that." Annie eyed her son, his little mouth trying to latch on to Cal's nipple, his fingers treading chest hair. "He wants to nurse."

"I'll dress him," Cal replied, lifting Ben upright so he could look over his father's shoulder, "and then bring him to you. I know he's hungry."

Annie waited in the rocker in their bedroom, a few buttons of her shirt open. No lights on. In the dark room. Outside the skies were gray too. Rain started to pelt the windows.

"Tell me about the first time you recall feeling depressed," the therapist said earlier.

"Are you saying I'm depressed now?"

"You told me"—he looked at his notes—"you feel sad all the time. Sometimes nothing at all."

"I..." She played with the hem of her skirt. "I don't want to talk about it."

"But the first time was prior to having a baby?"

"Yes."

He scribbled more things down. The writing made her uncomfortable. He was judging her. And now he wanted to label her. Why had she come here?

For Cal. For Benjamin.

An olive branch to show her commitment to improvement. To make things go backward in the name of moving forward.

"What can you tell me about being a mom?"

"What do you want to know?"

"How has it exceeded your expectations? How has it failed to meet them?"

"I fail if I admit failure."

"Parents are often surprised to find the reality of parenting doesn't always meet the ideal."

"He cries a lot. He's ... colicky." Annie sighed and twirled a whole mess of hair between her fingers. *"Nursing is harder than I imagined. It's demanding ... time consuming."*

"Have you tried supplementing with formula?"

"I didn't ... I don't want to."

"I see." He made more notes. *"And name some things which have exceeded your expectations."*

"Do you want a light on?" Cal asked, interrupting Annie's thoughts as he placed their son in her arms.

Ben latched on. Cal went to the window, shoving his hands in his pockets. The wind had picked up, and the rain struck the glass harder.

"Should you find a different therapist?"

"I don't know." She stroked Ben's hair. It had changed color but hardly grown. Darker than Cal's, lighter than hers. His eyes remained blue ... like Cal's mother's.

"Why did you make the appointment?"

"Because you wanted me to."

"I'm not an expert"—he strolled over to Annie and sat on the foot of the bed—"but I think you should be there for *you*."

For me... she thought. But every waking moment was about Benjamin. *Waking* being the operative word.

Her throat tightened as she shifted her eyes from Cal to Ben.

"I'm going to order dinner." He stood and wiped at the tear sliding down her cheek. "What can I get you?"

"I'm not—"

"Don't tell me you're not hungry."

Her bottom lip trembled, and she nibbled it as she switched Ben to the other side.

"What can I say to make you happy?"

"Annie..." Cal's palm seemed fixed to the back of his neck — squeezing and squeezing. "I want *you* to be happy."

"You want someone else."

He narrowed his eyes, and the pain she saw etched in them hurt her greatly.

"I mean"—she recoiled—"you want who you thought I was when we met. Not who I am now."

"I want you. Period. End of fucking discussion." Cal pinched his nose and went toward the door.

"I..." she began, and Cal stopped. "The doctor asked me about expectations."

Turning, he fixed his gaze again on Annie. She held Ben in a way which never ceased to move him. Like her body had been created to cradle his son. There was something rhythmic about the rain too, mixing with the quiet noises Benjamin made. It was relaxing despite the tension.

"What expectations?"

"About being a mom. He suggested I make a list."

Silence swallowed the room when she failed to elaborate. The rain continued.

"Where are you going?"

"To order food."

"Cal?"

"Yes, Annie."

"Will you sit with me a little longer? The rain ... it makes me feel things I don't want to."

But downpours made her cognizant too.

Aware of what she would put on that list, she glanced down at Benjamin. His eyes closed. His lips pursed, intermittently sucking. His lungs perfect.

1. *I didn't expect him to feel like an extension of me. So much so and so fast. Instantly.*
2. *His skin is familiar. The way Cal's was ... is. Different but the same.*

3. *I didn't expect to feel this kind of love, love that suffocates me and invigorates me all at once.*
4. *I had no idea I could love anyone this much.*

NINETY-TWO

The two of them sat at the table in the kitchen, Annie spoon-feeding Benjamin, Ben strapped into his booster seat, smiling, avocado smeared all over his face and tray while Annie placed her phone on the tabletop and selected the "speaker" button.

She'd been talking to Tabitha for several minutes. Actually, the three of them had been talking. Prattling really. Her next sentences ran together.

"I've done everything I went to see someone Cal suggested I talk to someone." She bit her lip and forced a smile for the sake of Benjamin.

"You mean ... like a therapist?" Tab asked.

"Yes," she replied, and Ben grabbed the spoon, then he slammed it and his slimy hand down repeatedly and delightfully. "Mommy's okay, Bennie boy." She smiled again, but now fat tears pooled at the bottom rims of her eyelids. "Talking to him wasn't any better than talking to my mother," Annie huffed. "If you can imagine..."

"Has your mom visited lately?"

"Uh-huh." She wiped her son's fingers with a damp cloth.

Both her parents had visited. Several times but not at the same times. Thank God.

Cal and Annie had chosen to buy a house in Seattle to be near her father. Her mother still lived forty minutes away. Nevertheless, Annie was of no use to either of them. They didn't know how close to the bottom she'd once fallen. Nor her propensity for pills. They didn't know how much she'd suffered after Peter died. And they wouldn't know any of those facts now.

"Have you talked to your regular doctor?"

"*Yes* ... but I don't... I don't want to be on medication." Annie glanced around the room. Blues and whites and grays. Fresh flowers in a vase on the table. "Why doesn't anyone talk about this?" She stood, shifting her gaze from Ben. "Why do people only ever tell you how great it is to be a mother? People lie." She winced, pinching her eyes shut. "I feel like shit."

As Annie opened her lids and peered at her son again, her heart filled with his beauty and wonder, but her eyes filled to the brim with salt water.

"Benjamin deserves more than I can give him. I don't have anything. And I certainly don't have anything left to give Cal. There's nothing. Don't you see? Nothing!" Annie paused, sucked in a breath and snot, and gave Ben a kiss on the forehead. "Are you there, Tabitha? Don't leave me. Don't hate me."

Annie plopped down and planted another spoonful of smashed avocado into Ben's mouth. He slapped his hand onto the tray and cooed.

"Yes..." Tab cleared her throat. "I'm here."

"Say something, then."

"I'm going to fly out, and this time, I won't take no for an answer."

"When?"

"Before the end of the week. Oh, and, Annie-pie?"

"What?" She sniffled.

"I love you."

NINETY-THREE

The girls took turns pushing Benjamin in his stroller around the winding streets of Annie's neighborhood. He was layered and bundled, a blanket stretching out across the carriage. The girls were in full gear too, covered in coats and scarves and boots, pounding the asphalt and talking.

"When was the last time you took pictures?"

"I took some yesterday of Ben." Annie moved wayward strands of hair from her lips.

"No." Tab put a hand on Annie's shoulder. They came to a stop. "When was the last time you were *inspired* to take pictures? I know this little guy is inspiring." She nodded at Benjamin. "But I want to know when you last experienced that feeling"—Tab smiled—"deep in the pit of your gut?"

Annie gripped the bar of the stroller while looking off into the distance.

"I've seen you get lost doing your thing," Tab continued. "It never mattered if it was a tiny creature crawling on the ground or a giant cloud in the sky. You were always mesmerized."

Annie kept peering down the road, beyond the curve, staring at the mailboxes lining the street, then at the trees, the cars — until her eyes burned. She couldn't remember the last time she'd noticed the small things, the big things, the meaningful things ... things other people usually took for granted.

Had she been missing the point, the rainbows, the clouds, the silver lining? Had she misplaced her magic? Again.

"I don't know." Annie shifted her gaze, grieving what she'd never truly lost. The passion remained within her ... somewhere.

They started to walk again. Tab's long raven hair blew in the wind. Annie's remained bundled beneath her hat, but for the wisps catching between her lips.

"Have you thought about having someone come in during the week?" Tab asked a couple seconds later, not missing a beat. "Regularly?"

Tab had been at Annie's a few days, this being the second visit with her friend in Seattle, the first having occurred shortly after Ben was born. This week she'd spent time making the family several meals — some they could eat immediately, others they could freeze and easily reheat. She plied Annie with water by the gallon. Bought her a new bottle, a rather large one, and told her she had to fill it every day to the brim, then consume every last drop. Tab shopped, cleaned, and opened the windows, letting in the cold, pristine Pacific air and some fucking sunlight. She gave Annie massages every night and took walks with her daily, sometimes twice a day. Things she knew Cal had offered and Annie had stubbornly refused. The way she was just about to...

"Absolutely not."

"Annie, Cal said Rosa is—"

"He talked to you?" Annie stopped and glared at her friend. "He talked to you about this?"

"He wants to help you." Tab placed her hand on Annie's bicep, her blue eyes filling with love, her brows pinching together. "You won't let him. You won't let anyone help you."

"That's not true. Cal helps. And Rosa lives far away."

"She would stay with you, Annie. Besides, the help you do accept, it's not enough. I know Rosa did things for you both *before* you had the baby. What's the difference now?"

"What do you think you know?" Annie narrowed her gaze. "About any of this? About taking care of a baby?"

"When are you going to realize if you don't give up this self-righteous, control-freak bullshit, you may never come out of this ... this depression?" Tabitha paused, took shallow breaths, then settled some. "Annie, if you can survive what I saw you go through after Peter died, then you can get through anything. You're so strong."

"No." She shook her head. "No, I'm not."

"Yes, you are. You're one of the strongest people I know."

"This is different. It's like..." Annie swallowed. "It's like I have no control over it. It has control of me."

"Well, while I'm here"—Tab smirked and bounced her eyebrows—"*I have control of you.*"

NINETY-FOUR

Several mornings later, Annie strolled into the kitchen wearing her gray fleece bathrobe.

"You look good," Tab said.

"Yeah."

"Yeah. Your eyes aren't all puffy, and you have color."

"Gee, thanks."

"I'm gonna take you to get a facial before I go."

"Tab..."

"He's sleeping better?"

"Seems to be. Did you work your magic on my son too?"

"I'm very magical." Tabitha laughed while scraping oatmeal down the sides of her bowl. "Cal left for his run. And you ... you are going to be a photographer today." Tab waved an imaginary wand. "I'm casting my spell."

Except no one could force Annie to be a photographer. Cal had tried and failed. He'd mentioned it plenty, and each time, Annie had scolded him. She regretted having done so. But neither of them had a right to make her *be creative.*

It was a job, but it was also a feeling.

Annie balled her hands into fists inside the pockets of her robe while Tab continued to eat as if what she'd said was no big deal. *Cast a spell... The witch... Go be a photographer. Whatever...* Annie didn't say a word, but her body language spoke volumes — stiff spine, eyes looking everywhere but at Tabitha, palms starting to perspire.

"You are, Annie. Wipe that fucking look off your face and go get dressed." Tab nodded toward the staircase. "I'll make you something to eat that you can take with you."

Annie inhaled a sharp breath, watching as Tab finished her breakfast in peace, jealous of her friend's ability to start every day fresh without a dark cloud hanging over her ready to unleash rain and snow and sleet.

"I don't know..." Annie exhaled, dropping her chin, shoulders slumping.

"I can manage this." Tab lowered her head, trying to meet her friend's downcast gaze. "Ben will be fine. You're going."

Annie sighed.

"Go."

"Fine."

Annie headed upstairs and dressed, then she pulled her camera off the top shelf of the closet and set it on the bed beside her — without looking at it.

She had taken a million pictures of Benjamin.

But.

This.

Now.

It was different.

And terrifying and exciting.

The prospect of both failure and success.

A knee on the bed, Annie shifted toward what was once one of her most prized possessions. She held its weight, reacquainting herself with her companion in this new way, rubbing her fingers over the black, coarse body, recalling the years they'd spent together.

Then Annie heard Benjamin. As his cooing and babbling grew louder, she was struck with fears. Lots of them...

People might make fun of her silly manner, positions she would get into for a shot, things she would need to capture.

Not to mention ... she feared leaving the house ... alone. Driving in the car ... alone.

Could she handle being alone?

Ben was always with her now.

Could she own the space of solitude with no noises, responsibilities, or distractions?

The idea was mortifying.

Her normal, shining confidence — whatever Cal had been attracted to — was barely at an ebb. There was no ebb. Only a jagged cliff.

Feet pounded up the staircase, breaking Annie's daydream ... her nightmare. But they stopped her fears from escalating. She stood, placing the strap of the camera over her head and across her chest as she made her way to Ben's room.

"Good morning," Annie said to her boys, her voice somewhat shaky.

Back from his run, Cal stood in the center of the room, holding Ben, grasping his tiny fingers, bouncing him a little as they spoke to each other. He didn't even seem to notice Annie, so engrossed in conversation he was with his son.

"Good morning," he finally replied without bothering to look over at her. Nor did his tone carry any inflection.

"I'm going out." Annie tried to sound certain, but she knew the words tumbled out frayed. "I'm going to..." Her heart pounded. "I'm going to look for things to photograph."

"Good." Cal placed Ben on the changing table.

"Tab will watch him."

"I'll take care of him." He readied a clean diaper.

Annie moved closer, studying every move Cal made, then she leaned over and kissed her son on the cheek. He smiled. "Hi, Bennie." She tickled his belly button. "Mommy's going out."

The baby babbled, toes in the air, fingers holding onto them. Annie grinned. Cal continued wiping and cleaning, talking to Ben, virtually ignoring his wife's presence. Annie glanced at Cal's profile, then she turned to leave.

"Have fun," Cal said as she reached the door, this time with a genuine smile lighting his face, the sound of it filling his voice as well.

"Thank you." She nodded, then swallowed. "I love you."

"I love you too."

NINETY-FIVE

Cal entered the kitchen, holding Ben in his arms. Annie had left with her bagel and camera. Tab was at the sink, washing dishes.

"Are you hungry?"

"I'll make something." Cal set Benjamin down in the Pack 'n Play and put a toy in his hands.

"When did Rosa stop coming?" Tab dried her hands on a towel.

"I've had someone coming in to do the—"

"I know. You told me someone helps with the laundry. You know that's not what I mean."

"Rosa visited after Ben was born. She offered to stay."

"You mentioned that. I guess I didn't realize that was the last time."

"Annie wanted it to be the three of us for a while."

"And you agreed?"

"Rosa agreed. I agreed. We all agreed."

"What about Maggie?"

Cal shot Tabitha a look that could've only been described as "Are you fucking kidding me?" They'd made their peace at the wedding. But Maggie and a new baby and Annie and anxiety ... those things didn't mix. Not for days or weeks at a time. Although, her and John had paid a visit within the first month of Ben's life also.

"Why did you agree? Why...?" Tab folded her arms across her chest. "How did you let it get this far?"

"Neither of us knew how this would turn out." He glared at her. "And it wasn't like this in the beginning." Or it was and Cal had been living in denial. "This isn't the time to pass blame."

"I'm sorry." She sighed. "But it's been over six months. Did you think it was going to fix itself?"

"This isn't anyone's fault, T. This whole thing is a fucking mess. I don't even know how it got this far."

"I'm sorry," Tab repeated on an exhale, her gaze bouncing around the kitchen. "You're right. It's just hard for me to see her like this. I know it's been hard for you too."

"I almost don't remember her any other way." Cal's eyes blurred. "I don't know who she is anymore. I don't know who I am half the time. She isn't the person I met."

"She is." Tab squeezed his bicep. "She's in there. I told you before... I read up on it. We're going to figure this out. She'll come out of it. We need to find her a new doctor too."

"She doesn't want a prescription. I've tried talking to her about it. She's like the fucking Berlin Wall sometimes."

"No, I know. She won't take it. She... She can't."

"What do you mean, 'she can't'?"

"She just can't."

"Don't give me that bullshit answer."

"Pills fuck her up, okay?"

"What pills?"

"All pills. I don't know." Tab shrugged. "She never does well with them. Why do you think she never took birth control? God, I shouldn't be telling you this."

"Of course you should be telling me this. My wife should be telling me this. I'm her fucking husband. I'm here. I'm not going anywhere. I'm not some jerk-off boyfriend who—"

"I know. I know." She scratched her forehead, then she glanced back at Cal. "She never told you? About any of it?"

"Not the finer details apparently," he replied. "*Please enlighten me.*"

"Well ... what do you know?"

"She took anxiety meds after her brother died. She told me she didn't do birth control. I never asked why."

"She reacted pretty badly, like crazy side effects, to both those things, and then, after Peter died, she started taking prescription pain medicine."

"For pain?"

"She had her wisdom teeth pulled." Tabitha wouldn't meet his gaze.

"For pain?" he repeated louder, his jaw clenching.

Their eyes locked.

"Not physical pain." She swallowed.

Cal ran a hand clear across his face, forehead to chin. His breath hitched. His eyes fixated on a particular corner of the floor where tile met cabinetry. Was there dirt there, crusty food, or leftover conversations?

"She won't touch it," Tab continued. "Any of it. It all scares the shit out of her."

Benjamin began to fuss, banging the plastic teething toy into the floor of the pen. Cal turned to him, but he didn't really look *at* his son. He peered through him, completely stupefied by Tabitha's revelations about his wife — a woman he should've known much better than this.

"I've already started to work on her about Rosa." Tab picked up Benjamin, breaking Cal's stare. She planted a kiss on the baby's chubby cheek. "I want you to take her out tonight."

"On a date? The two of us?" Cal grabbed a container of homemade baby food from the fridge. "Good luck getting her to agree to that. I've tried."

"Oh, she'll agree. Trust me." Tab smirked, placed Ben in his booster, and strapped him in. Benjamin arched his back, squirming and protesting. "It's coming, big boy. Daddy has your food."

NINETY-SIX

Annie and Cal sat at a small table in a dimly lit restaurant directly across from one another, together but alone, the distance in their hearts vast.

The waitress approached and asked for their drink order. Annie studied the menu, not answering the question. Cal lowered his and looked at Annie through the lenses of his glasses.

"Do you want something to drink?" he asked.

"I'm sorry." She cleared her throat and glanced at the server. "I'll have a water, please."

Cal eyeballed Annie, his feathers already beginning to ruffle. Tipping his head at the server, he declined alcohol for the moment. Then the woman departed, off to retrieve two iced waters.

"Don't not drink because of me, honey," Annie said after deciding what she wanted to eat. Cal continued to read the selections. "If you want to have a drink ... then get a drink."

Cal closed the menu. He removed his glasses. He pretended to clean them.

"You know you want to," Annie teased.

His eyes narrowed. "You think you know what I want?" He slid his glasses into his shirt pocket. "I didn't think you gave a fuck."

Annie's smile disappeared. She ran her fingers through her hair, then crossed her arms over her chest. Shifting her gaze, she bit the insides of her cheeks.

"If I want a drink"—he leaned forward—"I'll have a fucking drink."

"Mmm ... I forgot." She rolled her eyes. "It's always about what you want."

"I don't want to do this, Annie. Not now." Cal shifted in his seat. "Not here."

"Do what? *Talk*?"

"Don't bait me in the middle of a fucking restaurant."

He sat back.

Annie deflated.

Neither of them spoke again until the server set their waters and a basket of bread on the table.

"What you chose sounds good," Annie said shortly after they'd placed their order.

"I've never had it here before."

"Everything is always good here."

"I can't believe it's been so long since we've been."

Annie picked up her glass, looking anywhere but at him.

"I mean that I like this place, all right?" Cal reached a hand across the table. "It's okay."

She glanced at his palm.

"Hold my fucking hand."

Rolling her eyes, Annie swung her boot, narrowly missing his shin. "Well, when you put it that way, how can I resist?" She dropped her palm on top of his.

Cal brushed his thumb over her knuckles, watching the way he touched her skin. "I have to go out of town next week."

Annie stared at him. Her palms began to sweat. "How long will you be gone?"

"A few days." He cleared his throat. Cal hadn't been away from his family since Benjamin had been born. "Maybe a week."

"You have to go?" She removed her hand from his.

"Yes." He sighed. "I've put projects on hold for you. I've turned projects over for you. I've—"

"Did I ask you to do any of those things?"

"Why?" Cal turned his face to the side. "Why do you do it?"

"I don't know." She smeared condensation up and down her water glass. "I don't want to."

"Don't cry."

"Don't tell me not to cry."

Leaning back in his seat, he pressed the tips of all ten fingers together, forming a collapsing triangle. "Well, so far we've established neither of us wants to be told how to act or what to do."

"We established that long ago," she replied with a smile as she dotted below her eyelids with the napkin.

"Come with me to California." Cal braved extending a hand across the table again, his eyes twinkling.

But Annie wouldn't reach for him. "And leave Ben?"

"Excuse me," Cal called out to a passing server, flagging him down. "I'll take a drink from the bar, please. A Jameson neat."

"Who would he stay with?"

Cal looked at her curtly, gave her a tight smile, refusing to answer her asinine question.

The two of them sat in silence again, waiting for Cal's drink to arrive, waiting for dinner, counting down the minutes until their forced interaction would be over.

"How did it go when you went out today?" Cal asked several moments later, after swallowing most of the whiskey, attempting another go at civilized conversation.

The waitress interrupted them, placing their plates down.

"It went fine," Annie replied, once the woman departed. Holding her fork, she stabbed at the field greens mixed with strawberries, chicken, and pecans.

"It went *fine*?" He smirked, then held a spoonful of his dinner toward her, wiggling the utensil some, but she hesitated. "Take a bite. You said it sounded good."

"Don't you want a bite first?"

"Damn it, Annie. Take a bite." He pushed the spoon closer to her lips.

As soon as she opened, Cal inserted creamy grits and a single plump shrimp covered in homemade sauce into her mouth. Annie waved a hand in front of her lips and chewed.

"I want to hear more than 'It went fine.'" Cal refilled his spoon. "I want to know how it actually *felt* to capture things ... the way you used to."

"It's hot," Annie warned.

"The pictures?" He grinned.

"No." Her cheeks flushed.

"It's hot, but it tastes good, right?"

"It's amazing," she replied, her eyes lighting up.

"And today, earlier, was that amazing as well?"

"You really want to know about my day?"

"Baby, I always want to know ... everything."

"It felt..." She shrugged her shoulders. "Forced. The way it did once before..." Her eyes combed the restaurant. "Like I'd lost something I never had to think twice about before. Like losing a finger."

"Like losing a finger?" Cal stopped chewing and gaped at her.

"Yes..." She smiled. "Haven't you ever imagined what it would be like to lose a finger?"

"No." He laughed. "I can't say I have."

"Well ... not allowing myself to take pictures of anything besides Ben, it made me think about what it might feel like to lose a limb or a finger."

Mesmerized, Cal only stared at Annie, holding his spoon in the bowl, not moving or blinking.

"I never realized how much I needed it or how much it meant to me until it was gone," she went on. "I mean, I always knew I loved it. But I never really lost that spark of creativity ... some after Peter died. But this..." She shook her head. "It scared me." She swallowed past the lump in her throat and put a forkful of lettuce and nuts and fruit into her mouth.

"You'll get it back. Your finger will grow back."

"What if it doesn't?"

"It will." Cal didn't flinch. Didn't mince words. He only continued gazing at Annie, love filling him to the brim. *She's opening herself up to me again*, he thought. And he wanted all of her to come back. Right now. Every bit of depth he'd ever seen in those forest-green eyes. And for the first time since their son had been born, Cal believed it truly possible. "I see it in you."

"What do you see?"

Cal smiled and wiped his mouth with the napkin. "I see you, Annie." A glow lighting her face like a rainbow appearing after a rainstorm. Colors he could see and taste. The inexplicable magic. "I see a woman who loves so much she sometimes forgets to love herself..." He grinned a little, the pain of that statement lodging in his throat. "I see a woman with a passion for everything close to her heart. A woman who is a wonderful mother, far surpassing anything I ever could've imagined. I see a woman"—he paused, inhaling a sharp breath—*"who's not afraid."*

Her lips parted, but she didn't speak.

Or move.

Annie appeared to stare straight through him.

Reaching a hand across the table, he touched her forearm, and she came to. Their magnets connected, causing their skin to heat and prickle, causing goose bumps to form.

"What you don't realize, Annie..." Cal peered so far inside her she wanted to both crawl away and run to him. "About that night ... at the gala, when we first met, when you told me you were afraid of everything..." He swallowed. "Only someone who actually *has* courage can say something like that. The rest of us are merely lying to ourselves."

NINETY-SEVEN

Cal stood in front of one of the two sinks in their master bathroom, brushing his teeth, wearing a pair of blue sweatpants as he gazed at his wife's reflection in the mirror. She stood on his right, combing her hair, dressed in an adorable knee-length nightgown, the kind that opened at the front for nursing.

The couple had found Tabitha and Benjamin sleeping when they'd returned from their date. Now, it was quiet, but for the sounds of the brushing — the hair and the teeth. Not to mention the sounds of their breathing.

Annie looked at Cal as well. Out of her periphery. Specifically, at his chest, his arms, his shoulders. At his skin. She blushed, wondering if it would still feel amazing: the slightest kiss of his skin against hers. If it would be magnetic.

It had felt like that for a moment at the restaurant.

Never more aware of every move she made, completely conscious of the lack of space between them, she lost the hairbrush, stepped behind him, placed her hands flat against his bare back, and began to drag her fingers up and down him.

Cal spit, rinsed, then pressed his palms against the countertop, every one of his muscles tightening.

Annie peeked around his torso and into the mirror. He'd pinched his eyes shut. His chest slightly shook. The man appeared to be in great pain. Fantastic pain.

His breath quickened.

Hers did too.

The air between them faltering, like it had tripped over a cord or a string.

Even though Annie barely moved, only her hands and the tips of those magical fingers still sliding up and down him, she started to pant as though she'd been jogging.

Cal's knuckles turned white as he opened his eyes and studied her face, her movements, the way her fingers trailed to the front of his body, making their way through his chest hair and over his nipples. He closed his eyes again, clenching his jaw as Annie shifted her head side to side over his shoulder blades several times, then she rested a cheek against him.

A moment or two later, Cal woke from a dream.

Turning around, he leaned his back against the countertop, gripped the edge of the vanity from this new position, and stared into her forest-green eyes — woods he would gladly get lost in. But Annie glanced down at their feet, her hands lightly holding his waist.

"Look at me," he whispered.

Annie swallowed, lifted her head, and peered into those eyes. The feel of his skin felt so right for the first time in a long time. It *was* magnetic. A pulse she could feel tapping against her pores.

Cal didn't move.

His hands remained attached to the ledge of the countertop.

Annie eyed his fingers. His lips.

She wanted to kiss him but was afraid.

Would they have sex?

What if it hurt?

What if she couldn't give herself to him fully?

What if he wanted more than she could handle?

Pushing the nagging thoughts far from her mind, Annie moved her hands to Cal's cheeks and leaned closer, putting her mouth to his. She kissed his upper lip, then his lower. The taste, the texture, it tickled, and at the same time, it seemed … weird.

Her eyes popped open. His face felt and looked huge.

Stepping back, her pulse sounded off in her ears with a great charge, a pounding. As much as she wished things could be as they'd always been between them, she knew they weren't the same for her.

Not completely.

It wasn't because she didn't love Cal — she did. More than she thought possible. But her sexual feelings had disappeared after the birth of Benjamin. Every touch, every kiss, took effort. And sex ... well, sex seemed like an obstacle needing to be overcome.

God ... how she wanted to overcome.

It wasn't like riding a bicycle. Pedaling was easy. Marriage and babies were the Tour de France.

Annie put her head on Cal's shoulder and her face in the crook of his neck.

His fingers remained glued to the countertop.

Annie thought about those hands and those fingers and all the places on her body they'd been. Her need for his touch was almost vanity. A test.

She knew why he wasn't touching her, and she wasn't physically aching for him to actually do it either, not the way she had in the past, but it frustrated her that he wasn't doing it, nonetheless.

Seconds later, Benjamin's cries interrupted their attempt at halfway. They could hear him through the crackly monitor. Annie's entire body tensed. She looked up at Cal, then began to step away. But he yanked on her fingers the moment she turned to leave.

"Wait," he whispered.

Annie stood at arm's length, holding his hand, then she pinched her fingers into the corners of her eyes. Cal pulled her against his sequoia tree of safety and wrapped his arms around her. Her ear to his chest, she released her breath, relaxing as he stroked the back of her hair. A few seconds later, Annie tilted her head up, stared at his lips, then kissed him.

It didn't take long for Cal to reciprocate, sliding his hands through her hair and returning the kiss with grave intensity. Not faster or harder, but with a magnificent insistence she could feel attacking every one of her nerve endings.

Ben's cries became background fodder.

Annie kissed Cal more and more and more, wetting his cheeks with her tears, and then she cracked a smile, eased back, and gazed at him. Cal returned the grin.

They both knew someone had to go to Ben, and so she went.

A couple minutes later, Cal followed Annie down the hall, remaining right outside the door of Ben's room, watching his beautiful wife with his beautiful son, observing her without them noticing as she held Ben against her chest, patted his back, and moved slowly across the floor, dancing and humming.

When Annie finally saw Cal, her eyes opened wide and she smiled.

Two outstanding qualities were now fixed in her husband's gaze: love and patience. The replete look of a man who had gained an existential satisfaction in being a first-time father. A man falling in love with the mother of his child all over again.

Later that night, after falling asleep in their bed, Annie dreamt about Cal in a way she hadn't been able to for months — with a smile on her face and a man's arm wrapped around her waist.

NINETY-EIGHT

Cal stood in the lobby of a hotel in LA, talking business with a few of the people he'd traveled there to meet. The week had passed rather slowly. Tomorrow, he would get on a plane, and then he would see his family.

The men had eaten dinner, and it was late, yet their conversation dragged on and on.

Cal's mind wandered. As did his gaze...

A woman strolled by the circle of suits.

White dress.

Long legs.

High heels.

Shoes that made her the perfect height to hold a man in place while he buried his loneliness inside her.

Then she entered the bar. It was visible from where they stood. A few other patrons lined its counter.

Cal wasn't thirsty, but fuck him if he wasn't suddenly inventing a million fucked-up reasons why he needed to have a drink.

And now.

The men finally bid one another goodnight. Cal rode the elevator up to his room. Once inside, he stood in front of the huge window, hands raised overhead, palms on the glass, and looked down at the city below. Nighttime, but full of flickering lights. While coming up with more excuses to visit the bar...

I can't sleep. I'm thirsty. Maybe I left something downstairs.

Until he actually believed he wanted a drink. Needed one. Deserved it.

Sure. He deserved it.

After shoving all the thoughts telling him it was a bad idea aside — *one choice can fuck up your life; haven't you learned that lesson a thousand times by now?* — he went down to the lobby intent on having

Only. One. Fucking. Drink.

His heart raced. Perspiration slicked the back of his neck. But before entering the space, he looked around.

Noticing a loneliness.

A sadness.

The energy vibrated all around him, yet it was disguised as something else. People attempting to mask pain with alcohol. Wanting to leave with a stranger. Wishing to fill a hole in their soul that could never truly be filled — not with a million drinks, not with an orgasm.

Cal dragged a palm over his face. What the fuck was he doing here? On the outskirts. The fringe. He didn't belong here. But he was here. And he wanted a fucking drink. He also desperately wanted to run his hands over a woman's body.

But mostly he wanted a drink.

After making his way to the counter, Cal took a seat. The woman who had passed him earlier sat a few stools to the right. Her short, straight, dark bangs partially covered her eyes and her legs looked even more incredible from this angle, winding down to the floor like marble pillars, satiny and smooth.

She turned her head in Cal's direction between sips of wine. But he pretended not to notice as he swallowed Crown.

It isn't her face, he thought.

She wasn't the most attractive woman he'd ever been with, but she had an air about her. Or maybe she faked confidence. Most importantly, though, she was a woman. Which meant she had a body with everything Cal needed. Tits and ass and legs. *Fuck*. He hadn't even realized how much he missed the contact. How much he needed a woman beneath him, spread out and open, wet and ready. Fuck. This was a bad idea.

Still, a part of him felt flattered. Because, after all, he did want attention.

He did need some fucking attention, and he'd come down that elevator knowing damn well the kind of attention that might be waiting.

Miles of legs. Lips willing to suck and give. Someone who would say nothing. A girl who would only listen.

Something else lurked beneath the surface, though. Beyond his vanity and needs.

He eyed his nearly empty glass, tilted it forward, and stared at the minuscule amount of liquid left, watching the amber slide around the edges.

Sure. The something else...

Shame.

He felt it creep over him slowly, heating the back of his neck again for even considering the idea of fucking another woman. Had he considered it? Really? Sure, he'd toyed with it, and he didn't play fucking games. He either did something, or didn't. He made choices.

Cal *chose* to order a second drink, hoping to drown out her legs and the way they looked in his imagination wrapped around him. But as he did, she stood and moved closer. No matter, he would continue to ignore her. He wouldn't glance in her direction. He would act as if she weren't even here. Except some women liked that kind of bullshit.

"I saw you earlier," she said, taking a seat beside him. "I was hoping you would come ... but I didn't think you would."

Yeah, he cleared his throat, she'd uttered the word *come* exactly the way she meant to. This was too easy. Cal was slightly amused at how simple it would be to bed her, but he didn't let it show on his face.

"I came back down to have a drink." He finally looked her right in the eye, trying to keep the smile from his own eyes and the tent from rising in his pants. "I was thirsty."

She smirked.

Apparently, he hadn't managed to say those words like that — as if he really needed a drink and not her. He needed to fuck.

Now.

And not his fucking hand again.

Looking back at his glass, he finished its contents as the woman leaned forward some, causing her tits to spill out of the low neckline of her white dress.

"Really?" She hadn't lost the grin. "It's almost midnight. You left. Came back. You expect me to believe a man like you rode the elevator back down here because you were thirsty?" She eyeballed him. "You don't have water up in your room?"

Cal wanted to wipe that smirk off her goddamn face with his cock.

And maybe she was right, but that was the man he used to be. Hearing those words out loud made him feel strange. Tingly. Warm. *A man like you.* He stared straight ahead at the bottles lining the shelves.

"You have no idea what kind of man I am." Even his feet burned inside his shoes.

"You're the kind of man who isn't getting laid." She came closer, brushing her shoulder against his. "Or you wouldn't be here right now, having a drink with me." She set her glass down and turned until her entire body faced him.

Cal shifted too, meeting her calculating eyes, but what he really wanted to do was put his hands on her knees and spread them. *Fuck. Fuck. Fuck.* He could feel the beads of sweat on the back of his neck, the twitch of his cock, the whiskey coating his veins — all of it telling him it was okay to take her upstairs and fuck the shit out of her.

"You're married, right?" She glanced at his ring.

Fuck. God. Yes. He was married, and he wanted to be married. He wanted his fucking wife. Not her. Not an impostor. Not a predator. This woman would say anything to get what she wanted.

Cal was pissed. Pissed for wanting her, pissed she threw herself at a stranger. Pissed at the emptiness driving them both to this moment. To these choices.

Ignoring her question, Cal motioned to the bartender for his check. Then he pulled out some cash, slapping the money onto the countertop.

This was it. Do or die.

Fuck. It would be so easy. She would give him something. He could be rough with her. Bruise her. Take her cunt every which way. She would allow it. He could drown out the reasonableness of no reason. There wouldn't be any bullshit between them.

It could just be sex.

Except...

It could never be only sex.

Not anymore.

It didn't matter if it was different. It was the same.

Sex was never the panacea Cal wanted it to be, no matter how good it felt, how much he needed it, no matter how beautiful the girl or even how much he loved her.

The panacea was love. Real love. Unconditional love.

The kind that gives without asking and refuses to take. The pill he'd chosen all those years had been empty. A placebo. Like the feeling in him when the sex was over, carving out a hollow inside him. Empty like the feeling inside him now.

At one time Cal thought sex could fill up that place inside him where he felt he lacked something, the thing he thought he was missing, but it never truly did. The emotions he tried to free himself of always came back to haunt him. He mistakenly thought he could simply have sex and not feel, and that used to be part of its appeal, but now Cal wanted nothing more than to feel it all. Everything.

If it meant he could feel the love, then he also wanted to feel the pain.

"First of all," Cal finally said in reply to her query, "I am married. And second, I'm not here *with you*." But he had to stop himself from growling the words into her ear.

As the woman put a foot on the bottom rung of his stool, her skirt inched higher and her fucking legs jumped out at him.

"No..." She tossed some of her black hair over a shoulder. "But you could be with me. *Now. Up in my room.*"

Cal dropped his chin and grinned.

"Is there a third?" she asked, placing a palm on his bicep.

That did it.

Her touch.

It was the opposite of comfort.

No spark. Nothing. And even if there had been one, it wouldn't have mattered. Only one woman could set him on fire and breathe life into him all at once.

Cal's lips formed a hard line. His face became stolid.

The woman turned and went back to her wine. Cal to the lobby.

He rode the elevator up to his room. Alone.

Without a hard-on. Or a guilty conscience.

God, how he'd wanted Annie to come to LA with him. Placing a hand on his forehead, he stared blankly at the ground.

How could he have come so close to fucking a complete stranger?

The idea repulsed him.

It could never fill a void.

Fucking her would've only driven him further from Annie.

Oh, Annie...

Cal loved her. Needed her.

He wanted to take away all her pain. He needed to take care of her, but she wasn't letting him.

When would this nightmare end?

Cal rode the elevator up, up, up, feeling down, stinging, raw. He wanted nothing more than to be with his son and with his Annie.

His *heavy*. His family.

Cal *was* married. He touched the band on his finger, smiled, and exhaled a shaky breath.

This was only a rough patch. On the other side of the storm the two of them would find the sunlight. The rainbow.

The sky and ocean.

The magic.

All the things that had never truly left them.

NINETY-NINE

When Cal walked through the front door the next morning, his record player blared, the speakers seeming to sound from practically every room of their house. The voice of Michael Hutchence even traveled down the stairs.

The girl who hadn't been wanting noise stood in their living room, Ben on her hip, spinning in circles to the beat of INXS.

Ben giggled repeatedly, and Cal's heart swelled.

After another twist and turn, Annie almost tripped as she met his eyes from across the room. Cal wore a grin. And a suit...

Dark gray. A white button-down shirt underneath the jacket. A vest and tie. Her breath caught at the sight of him. She didn't think she'd ever seen him look so sharp. Even at their wedding, he'd pulled off casual ... with his open blazer and no tie.

"It's Daddy, Bennie boy." Annie lowered the volume while bouncing him on her hip. "Never Tear Us Apart" had ended. "Mystify" was starting up.

Cal joined them, the widest smile still on his face, and took his son — who had been stretching his arms outward, pinching his fingers, and squealing with delight — from his wife. He plied Ben with kisses over the entirety of his little face, then he lifted him in the air and attacked his tummy.

Benjamin's sounds were the best music.

"You've been dancing," Cal said, a glint in his eye. He kissed Annie's cheek, then eyeballed an end table where her Nikon sat. "And taking pictures."

"Yes." She kissed him back. "You're home early."

"I changed my flight."

"Why?"

"I needed to see the two of you."

"Something went wrong?"

"Not exactly."

Cal sat on the love seat, placing Ben on his lap. Annie planted her bum on the rug in front of them and crossed her legs.

"I was reminded of someone I used to be and never want to be again."

She opened her mouth to speak, but Cal interrupted.

"Leave it at that, Annie."

Clearing her throat dramatically, she raised an eyebrow, trying not to giggle. "A woman ... came on to you?"

Cal did a double take. His wife's eyes were wide and sparkly. She wasn't blinking. He fought a scoff or a scowl, scratched his head, and bounced Ben on his knee.

"You think you're so hard to read." She laughed.

"You think it's funny?"

"You're funny ... and apparently hot."

"Annie..."

"I like your outfit."

"My outfit?" He looked down at himself like he was an alien from another planet.

"That's probably why you got hit on."

"Fuck," he mumbled.

"What was that?" She cupped a hand to her ear, grinning.

"So..." He glanced at his son. "You've been playing my records, huh?" Ben babbled and smiled. Cal kissed his chubby cheeks.

"You like this music, Bennie? It's Daddy's," he went on, "and it's old ... like him."

"Your daddy's not old, little man." She pinched Ben's waist, and he laughed. "He's still getting attention from women."

"Dammit, Annie."

She smirked, rolled her eyes, and stood. The tripod leaned against the wall by the back door, and she grabbed it and set it up.

"I'd like to get some pictures. Of the three of us."

"Let me change." He stood.

"Cal ... you look handsome."

"I haven't even showered."

"Please. It will always remind me of us. Of this moment. Our clothes and everything."

Annie wore an aqua cardigan and jeans. Gone were the sweatpants and soiled nightgowns. She'd even put on a pair of earrings, but she had to be careful — Ben liked to yank on them.

After they'd taken a few photographs — Benjamin loved the countdown, and each time Cal made it a challenge to see how much he could make his son laugh — Annie readied the space.

For just one more.

It would be of the three of them sitting together on the floor. Cal had been making funny faces and connecting Mega Bloks with Ben while pointing out each and every color of them.

"Okay. Ready." Annie pushed the button, raced over, and sat down, Ben in the middle, Cal leaning toward her with a palm flat on the rug.

"Look at the camera," she said through her teeth, trying to maintain her photogenic smile. But Cal didn't take his eyes off her face as she counted, "Five ... four..."

Ben banged two blocks together.

Annie pulled hair from her mouth and turned toward Cal. And when their eyes locked, the camera made a click and Ben made a coo.

The Nikon captured what they'd seen on the staircase. That very first night. Their souls were speaking to each other. And nothing could've interrupted the connection.

Not depression. Or panic attacks. Not worry or pain. Or death.

They were forever.

A family.

Lovers.

Parents.

Partners.

Friends.

Soulmates.

Now they had tangible evidence.

ONE HUNDRED

Cal woke in the middle of the night to a familiar sound. One he wished would soon be a distant memory. But he knew life meant tears. And for some, it meant many.

"Annie," he whispered, and she froze. The shaking subsided, but the tension she now held made her look like a statue. "What is it, baby?" It was exactly three o'clock in the morning. "Have you slept?"

She exhaled. Her body trembled. Her back was to his front.

"I'm a good listener ... remember."

She nodded and swallowed, then took in a deep breath. "He's growing up so fast." She hiccupped. "I'm missing it."

Cal reached out a hand, almost grazing her backside, then he retracted it, doing so several times.

"You're not, baby. You're with him every day."

Labored breathing and sniffles were her only response.

Cal pressed a palm to his forehead, his eyes going wide at the ceiling.

The day had gone so well.

But Cal was still adjusting to the concept that depression could be one step forward and two back. Like climbing an icy mountainside in high heels. Not that he'd ever tried to walk in the damn things. But he had an imagination.

An excellent one.

A few seconds later, Annie shifted so that they were both side by side, flat on their backs, looking up at the knockdown. Annie laced her fingers through Cal's and squeezed.

"You've been doing really good." He peered at her. "What's happening?"

She turned her face away from his kindness. Tears slid past her closed lids. She waited a minute.

"This thing ... these feelings..." Her chest rattled with her exhalations. "They don't go away in an instant."

"I know..." He turned onto his side and pushed pieces of hair away from her face.

"I realized something today." She angled her body his way as well. "The song. The one we were dancing to when you got home..."

"It's a good one."

She smiled. "The lyrics are for us ... and me. I know why I have wings." She pinched her eyes shut and started to cry again.

"You need sleep." He stroked her face. "I've been gone too long. I won't leave again for that many days. I promise." He braved placing a palm across her waist, keeping it there until she calmed.

"He's teething. He's been up a lot."

"I'll get him tonight if he wakes up. Please, Annie," he whispered. "Open your eyes. Look at me. That's better." His fingers trailed up and down her arm. "Why do you have wings?"

"I used to think I needed permission to fly. To be free." She gazed upon him. "I have wings ... so I can fly away from the sadness. It's the only way." She swallowed. "It's better than jumping."

His Adam's apple bobbed. He brushed a single tear from her cheek. "Can I make wine from these?"

"I love you," she uttered in the most heartfelt voice he'd ever heard.

Cupping her jaw, he stroked his thumb over the contours of her beautiful face. "I love you."

"I need to tell you something."

"I'm listening."

"There's a reason I wouldn't take birth control pills." Her gaze bounced around the room. "I've never told anyone this but Tabitha..."

"What is it, Annie?" Cal asked even though he knew what she was about to say. He was proud of her bravery. Her courage. His chest inflated. She trusted him. And he had no resentment over the time it had taken her to give him this precious gift.

Annie scooted closer, placed her head in the crook of his neck, and sighed. Then she told Cal the rest, sparing no details. And he held her tight and listened, loving her, caressing her ... letting her cry. When she finished, the three o'clock in the morning had passed, and she lay in the safety of his arms as his mate in the branches of his sequoia tree.

And that was where they fell asleep.

ONE HUNDRED ONE

"I miss you telling me what you want to do to me."

They'd been sitting in a restaurant, rekindling the flame, trying to start a fire for over an hour. It had taken Annie the entire length of their meal to muster up the courage to say those words to Cal. They'd flown from her mouth right after the check had been paid.

"Baby..." He reached an arm across the table and took her hand. "I haven't stopped wanting to give that to you."

"Then show me you're the same." She squeezed his palm and exhaled, her eyes flitting about. "That you haven't changed."

"I thought I had to." He let go of her hand. "I thought it was what you wanted." Cal swallowed. "Do you have any idea what I've stuffed aside? What I've turned off?" He inhaled. "I didn't want it this way." He met her gaze. "This was your choice."

"God, Cal ... you know this wasn't a choice. I didn't wake up one day and wish this upon us."

"I stopped being my— initiating because you pushed me away, not because I don't want you."

Silence fell over the table.

"You've barely even let me touch you," he began several seconds later as he reached a palm out again, "just to hold you, to cuddle you in the bed. Have you forgotten?"

"No, no, I haven't forgotten," she said, the sound of tears crackling in her voice.

But Annie wanted to forget.

All of it.

She wanted him now.

To hold her. Pin her. Bruise her. Claim her.

She needed to feel his naked body pressed against her skin. Or at least ... she thought she did.

"What do we do?" she pleaded. "How do we go back? I want to go back now. I want you the same as you were the first day I met you."

"Annie, we can't go back." He shook his head. "We have to go forward."

"Your eyes," she whispered as she gazed into them, her throat tightening, "they followed me around Maggie's house..." She swallowed. "And it felt like..." Her irises twinkled like the wings of an emerald swallowtail shimmering in the sunlight. "...they undressed me." Her cheeks flushed, but the warmth traveled everywhere. "You could've had me that night, Cal. I wanted you so much."

"If you were ready."

"I'm ready now." She threaded her fingers through his.

"Annie..." He blew out a breath. It had been so long since he'd heard that inflection in her tone. Since he'd seen that look in her eyes. Cal thought he was ready to be with her too, but now that the moment had arrived, he knew it couldn't be in the way she'd asked. "I switched a part of myself off. I..." He ran a hand clean through his hair. "This almost feels..."

"Don't say it."

"Forced."

"I want to go."

––––––––

"You didn't unlock it yet, hun," Annie said the moment she reached the passenger side door of the vehicle.

Cal slapped a palm on the roof of the car, trapping her between the Tesla and his body while Annie jumped, a rush coming over her like a tsunami on its way to the shoreline. Her knees faltered as he nuzzled her hair, pushing the strands away with his nose and cheeks. His lips, so close to her ear, gave her goose bumps.

"The moment we return home," he uttered, placing his palms on her waist, "we'll turn back into pumpkins."

"It doesn't have to be that way." She put her hands flat against the vehicle's window, responding to him in all the ways she knew he wanted, but something still felt off.

Cal lifted his head toward the sky.

A few seconds later, he exhaled, then released her. "I'm not the only one who needs to flip my switch back on."

Annie turned and faced him. "What do you mean?"

"Baby, you won't accept help from anyone." He moved hair from her eyes. "You still resent someone doing our laundry."

Annie scoffed, and Cal laughed.

"I want to do it."

"No one wants to do laundry."

Annie rolled her eyes and folded her arms across her chest.

"You barely accept help from me."

When she tried to look away, Cal searched her eyes until she held his gaze steady. "Let Rosa come to the house. She can stay for a few weeks. Let me take you out on a date ... like this ... several times a month." He inhaled sharply. "Let someone else take care of Ben sometimes, Annie, just a little, so you can keep taking good care of yourself."

"I did tonight. And Tab helped."

"Yes, but we have to keep going forward." He pulled her arms down and held one of her hands. "More changes..."

"But what about...?" She swallowed. "What I said after we finished dinner."

Cal glanced away.

"You won't..." She hiccupped. "You won't be with me until I have Rosa come to the house ... until I agree to *your* terms?"

"I won't take you to bed the way you asked until I have *you back full-time*." He tucked strands of hair behind her ear.

"How can you say that? How can you do that?" She wiped beneath her eyelids. "You can't hold that over me."

"I'm not, Annie. But I want—"

"What?" She placed her hands on her hips. "What do you want? What do you want it to be? *Perfect*? This coming from the man who was ready to fuck me the first minute he ever saw me."

A smirk curled the corners of his lips.

"Don't smile." After kneeing his thigh, she began to grin herself. "God, you and your damn smile."

"This is different. I want to wait because you've been sick."

"Don't say that." She shook her head. "Don't say it like that."

"Why, baby?" he whispered, brushing bangs from her eyes, pressing his body closer to hers. "There's nothing wrong with that word. There's nothing wrong with you."

"I'm getting cold."

"I'm not finished." He tapped her waist. "Look at me."

Annie met his eyes.

"You're an amazing mother."

"Cal..." she said in a hush, stretching his name.

"You are." He tugged on her sides, on her heartstrings. "You make Ben's food from scratch, always have actually, manufacturing it from the finest breasts I've ever seen."

Annie smiled and pushed on his wrists.

"And you've done it without complaint, getting up with him at night, night after night, meeting his every need, willingly and patiently. And the way you look at him..." Cal glanced away, swallowing, his eyes glossing. "When you look at our son, I've never seen such love."

"You can stop now."

"I'm not done. You won't even give yourself credit. You're doing it right now. You won't accept more than half of what you actually do and have done because you've been—"

"Depressed," she interjected. "You can say the word. It sounds better than sick, for God's sake."

"It doesn't take away from you. *You, Annie*. It doesn't change who you are."

"How can you say that?"

"Because the depression doesn't change you. It doesn't make you a bad person or an unfit mother. It doesn't define who you are."

Cal watched his words hit their mark while trailing his fingers across her tearstained cheeks, loving her more today than he ever thought possible.

"I want to get to know you all over again," he uttered as she stared into his eyes. "I want to be slow ... with everything. With all of it."

"Holy shit..." She palmed his cheek. "I never thought I'd hear those words come out of your mouth." Her thumb stroked his lips. "Hasn't it been slow enough already?"

"I would wait forever for you." He slid fingers down strands of her hair. "For it to be right ... for both of us. Completely, absolutely ... right."

"It's not for you?"

"I thought it was," he replied on an exhale, voice shaking. "I want you... God, Annie, I want to fuck you." Cal stared deep into her eyes. "But it's not the answer. I used to think sex was an answer to everything. But if all the pieces aren't right, then it's only a moment, and then that moment is replaced with a bitter you don't want to taste." He winced and looked away. "For the first time in my life ... I don't want sex to be a Band-Aid." He met her eyes. "And I want to be able to be myself with you in every way. I want to be everything you need me to be."

"You are." Her hands circled his biceps.

"No, baby." Cal smiled. "I mean the way we always were with each other *sexually*. The way you asked me to be at dinner. I can't be that man tonight."

"Why?"

Cal smirked, giving her the ruler-of-the-fucking-world eyes. "Put your hands under your dress." He nipped her earlobe, and she giggled. "And then slip them inside your panties."

"What?" She laughed again.

"You're not ready."

"Because I won't put my hands up—?"

"You never hesitated before. You never laughed."

She brought her thumb and forefinger nearly together and said, "Maybe a little."

"Are you playing with me, Mrs. Prescott?"

"Will it get me a spanking?"

Cal dropped his chin, grinned, and shook his head, wanting nothing more than to flip her around, shove her against the car, and smack her ass. Hard. Hard enough to make her gasp and heave and beg for more — the way she always had — but he knew it wouldn't go well. Not tonight. Despite the fact that she'd teased him and pleaded with him, it wasn't right.

Not yet.

Cal wouldn't have mediocre sex just to get the wheels turning. He wouldn't give audience to her giggles or lack of trust.

"Baby," she began much more seriously, "I don't expect you to always be—"

"But it is what you need." He stared into her eyes. "Breathe..." He smiled as he fingered a piece of her hair, twirling it the way she usually did.

Annie exhaled loudly and grinned. "How could it have been so much easier when I hardly knew you?"

"You've always known me," he replied, not skipping a beat. "And it wasn't that it was easier. It was timing. It wasn't forced. It happened naturally. Don't you want it to be that way again?"

Annie inched her fingers toward his collar and began to play with it, folding it up and down.

"And I want to wait for you to get better, baby." Cal spoke against the top of her hair. "And better and better. I want you whole."

"I'll never be completely whole." Her voice cracked.

"You're always whole," he said and paused, palming her face and meeting her gaze, "but you need to know it. You and I will both know when it's right, when it won't feel forced, and you can't look me in the eye and truthfully say it's now. Even that first night at Maggie's, we wanted each other, but it wasn't right."

As Annie shoved her hands inside her coat pockets, a grin spread across her face while she peered at him and shook her head. "Calvin Prescott ... always a riddle." She spread her jacket open and enveloped him with it as best she could, her arms around his waist. "You still manage to surprise me, you know that?"

"Good." He smiled. "Now, get in the car. I'm freezing, I'm tired, and I want to go home and give my son a kiss goodnight."

Annie rolled her eyes and grinned. "Give me a kiss goodnight."

"My lips are cold."

"I don't care if they're blue. Put your mouth on me."

ONE HUNDRED TWO

"You shouldn't have your work here, Calvin." Rosa indicated the papers scattered across the dining room table.

She'd been in the Prescott home a few days. A couple of weeks had passed since Cal had made the suggestion, and Annie had finally agreed.

"I like the light in this room." Glancing toward the front window, he squinted into the late-morning sun through his lenses.

"But now you have a family to share this space with. And you have an office for these things. Yes?"

Tapping a pen against his thumb, Cal eyed Rosa and smiled. He began bunching the papers into a neat pile. She looked pleased as she made her way to the sink. Then the front door creaked open, and rubber wheels rolled across the wooden floors.

"Did you get to take some pictures?" Rosa asked Annie as she appeared in the kitchen, resting the stroller near the table.

"Yes." She pushed the hood of her jacket down and mussed her hair.

"Oh, he's sleeping." Rosa peeked under the canopy, her enthusiasm at an all-time high. "I love his chunky little face."

"He fell asleep almost as soon as I hit the pavement. I found a spot I'd never seen," Annie began but stopped when she noticed Cal's expression. "What?"

"Nothing," he said, but his eyes, as usual, gave everything away. "I'm proud of you."

Annie was proud too.

She'd finally given herself permission to be a photographer again, to make it a priority in her life — daily. She was taking pictures and editing and had even scheduled an upcoming wedding. Although the work didn't come first in her life, and it may not for a long time, the freedom she felt when cradling the camera in her hands — when discovering the unknown — couldn't be replicated by any other pleasure in life.

The change wasn't lost on either of them.

Before leaving the room, Cal backpedaled, coming to a stop inches from Annie's body, the smell of winter and tangerines already consuming him.

Their gazes locked. Cal kissed her cheek. She smiled. His mouth hovered over hers, his grin spreading as he paused, not kissing her lips, only lingering and peering at them.

"Go." Annie smacked Cal's hip.

"You look happy, *mi amor*," Rosa said once Cal finally made his way to the office. "Content like that sleeping baby boy."

Annie peered at Benjamin and smiled.

"You know ... I've been waiting for you to talk to me since I arrived."

The photographer took a bottle of water from the fridge and undid the cap.

"Are you happy?" Rosa asked.

Annie took a sip. "Happy isn't a state of constancy."

"True. But you have a glow about you. One that was absent the last time I was here. Are you expecting?"

"No." Annie laughed.

"Do you want more children?"

Annie shrugged, sat next to Rosa, and glanced at the stroller. "I'm still getting over the shock of this little man."

"Motherhood brings about many changes ... for the husband and wife's relationship too. The first year of marriage can be very hard. And you both had no time to settle in. Benjamin Everett came right away. Oh, I love his name."

Annie fiddled with the label on the bottle, peeling the paper away from the plastic.

"Annie..." Rosa touched her wrist. "What is it, child?"

"I know Cal has already told you everything."

"A woman's courage is in her own voice. That's where the strength lies. It returns from your voice. I want to hear what you have to say."

Annie kept her gaze on the table, still playing with the paper, trying to avoid grabbing pieces of her hair.

"Your strength has never left you," Rosa continued.

"How do you always know exactly what to say?"

"I'm *viejo*. Old." She chuckled.

"No. It's more than the right words. You make it easy to share. I can't talk to my mother like this."

"Like what?" Rosa patted Annie's forearm. "Tell me."

"I'm ashamed." She made a noise, almost choking on the sound as she turned her head to the side. "I'm ashamed to say it aloud."

"Of what? Why, sweetheart?" Rosa tucked strands of Annie's hair behind an ear. "You have nothing to be ashamed of. You're a beautiful mother."

Annie stared at Rosa, blinking.

"I felt this too, you know?"

"No, I don't know." Annie swallowed. "What do you mean?"

"When my second came along..." Rosa sighed, then wiped Anne's cheeks with her thumbs. "It hit me very quickly. It was unexpected. The pregnancy and the sadness. I didn't even know what it was. At that time, not many people talked about this. There was no computer for information. There weren't even very many books, and yes, there was shame."

"Why didn't you tell me this before?"

"Mmm ... because I trust you. And I trust Cal. I waited for the right time, and now it's here." Rosa nodded, exhaling. "It's good. This was the time for us to talk. A time for everything."

She made the familiar noise, her tongue clucking against the roof of her mouth. God, how Annie had missed that sound.

"I didn't want to push myself into your heart," Rosa went on. "I wanted you to ask me here." She glanced around the room. "And here..." She held a hand over her own heart and lightly tapped the muscle.

"I love you," Annie whispered as she leaned closer and wrapped her arms around Rosa. "I do feel happy. I'm happy you're here."

ONE HUNDRED THREE

"You're still tinkering with this thing?" Annie said as she walked into their garage, hands on her hips.

Cal slid out from under the Land Rover Defender, his back flat against the creeper. He'd bought a '97 when he'd returned to Ojai. He wanted something he could play with, fix up. He wanted something practical for surfing.

He'd kept the Tesla. Because he liked it. And because he could.

"Dinner is almost ready."

"Did you cook it?" Cal grinned.

The whites of his teeth were even more of a contrast when he had grease on a cheek. His dimples ever present ... and fucking adorable. A forty-six-year-old man shouldn't be adorable. But he was.

"Yes. I know how." She smiled. "And maybe Rosa has been helping me."

"We should take Ben surfing when the weather changes."

"I think he'll need swimming lessons first."

"I hope he takes to the water."

"Like you," she said.

"You aren't so bad yourself."

"Please..."

"You were..." Cal's hands surrounded his stomach, mimicking a balloon.

"Don't you dare," she teased, her eyes wide and shining.

"I liked you big and pregnant."

"You liked my boobs."

"I still like those." He bounced his brows and flung the towel he'd wiped his face with toward her shin. It cracked like a whip against her jeans.

Annie tried to grab it and failed, then she raced toward him, straddling him over the thingy on wheels. It sailed a little across the floor the moment she sat on top of his thighs.

"Careful." He placed his hands on her waist and stared into her eyes. And for once, she pinned him with her gaze. He couldn't move. Didn't want to.

"You missed a little." She took the cloth and wiped at the corner of his eye, so close to him that her breath caressed his skin; her chest heaved near his chin.

Then she set the rag aside and kissed him. Pulling his lower lip into her mouth, she slid her tongue past his teeth and moaned, gasped ... sighed. Then she relaxed against his chest and inhaled the ocean.

"You still smell like the beach even when you're dirty."

"I'm always dirty." Cal laughed as he stroked her hair. "Did I ever tell you what I smell when I'm near you?"

She lifted her chin and gazed at him.

"*Home...*" he uttered, moving his thumbs over her abdomen. "You smell like the trees in the fields I ran around in. In Ojai. Right as they start to blossom. It's the sweetest thing. There's nothing like it ... except you."

Keeping his hands exactly where they were, Cal didn't move a muscle. He hardly blinked.

"You never told me the meaning." She brushed hair from his eyes. He'd been growing it out. Strands fell past his ears and over his forehead. His face had scruff too. "You only ever said 'home.'"

Her fingers found their way to his lips, and she traced the shape, the edges, as she stared at his pout a good long while — until she could feel him growing antsy beneath her.

"I want you to listen to a song."

"Are you sure you don't want to text it to me first?" she asked, and he smiled.

"'Still Remains.'"

"I don't think I know that one."

"It's Stone Temple Pilots." He patted her thigh. "Up you go."

"I'm hungry." She stretched as she stood.

Those were two words Cal never thought he'd miss hearing...

"Pull up the song first. Read—"

"—the lyrics." She rolled her eyes.

In a heartbeat, Cal was up, the cloth in his hand. He slung it toward her ass. The second it made contact, he laughed, then he made for the door.

Annie chased him into the house, cursing and smiling.

She was coming after him.

ONE HUNDRED FOUR

"What are you up to?" Cal asked a few days later upon entering their living room.

"Shhh," Rosa reprimanded while rocking a snoozing Benjamin in her arms. The boy's mouth was open a smidgeon, and Cal had to resist the urge to smother his face with kisses.

Annie glanced over her shoulder. "I'm hanging pictures."

"I see that. I like the frames."

They were made of wood, raw-looking and jagged. She liked them too, the way the color of the pink pearl roses and Atlantic Ocean complemented the splintering of the trees.

"Where have you been hiding these?"

"I never printed them."

"Why?"

She shrugged. "I never got around to it. I have so many to choose from."

"These are special, though."

"These are the flowers you thought would get you laid."

"It worked."

"Oy," Rosa said, placing a palm to her forehead. "*No necesito saber estas cosas.*"

Cal and Annie looked over at her and laughed, then they returned their attention to the three pictures, staring at the eleven-by-fourteen glossy prints, the ones showcasing the roses she'd drowned many moons ago on Golden Beach. In one photo, several petals were floating in the sea. In another, the flowers were partially covered in sand, thorns and stems still visible. And in the third, they were everything — in the ocean, some on the sand, some whole, others broken.

"Where's the fourth?"

"What?" Annie dragged her gaze back to Cal. He held his phone near her eyeline.

Cupping a hand to her mouth, she suppressed a squeal, her eyes lighting up as she grabbed the device. "Oh my God, you still have this selfie on your phone."

"Of course." He smiled, puffing out his chest. "If it had been on film, I would've slept with it under my pillow."

"You lie."

"Look at your face there, Annie."

She swallowed as she stared into her own eyes.

"That's the girl I met. It's who I fell in love with..."

"Stop it." She bumped his hip, and he wrapped an arm around her waist.

"It's what I see when I look into your eyes every day and what I want to see for the rest of my life."

After placing the phone aside, he squared her hips so she faced him. "I see depth there. Emotions beyond my imagination. I see *my heavy*."

First, Cal kissed her cheeks, then he pressed his lips to hers until they became one, tongues mingling, breathing growing labored, hands beginning to search for body parts.

"Ahem," Rosa muttered. "*Por favor, ve a tu habitación. Hay un niño y una anciana presente.*"

They both smiled and pulled away, holding very still, until their heartbeats regulated.

Except they wouldn't regulate.

They beat too hard and too fast.

Then Benjamin began to cry, his neck arching backward, his eyes closed.

Cal kissed Annie's cheek and whispered, "I'll get him."

"I think he needs to be changed." Rosa wrinkled her nose.

Annie stretched her arms toward the ceiling. "I'm going to go upstairs and change too. I need to go to the store."

"You are stinky, little man," Cal said as he took him from Rosa. Ben's cries calmed, sounding more like whimpers. Tiny tears fell from his cheeks.

Annie grabbed her camera from the coffee table — she'd been out earlier taking photos, this time alone — and followed the boys up the staircase. Cal split off into the baby's room while Annie continued down the hallway.

After setting her Nikon on top of her dresser, she stepped into the master bathroom, unzipped her jacket, and gazed into the mirror. Starting at her forehead, she went over her profile, her eyes drifting down her body until she faced forward again and leaned closer to the glass. Pressing her palms on the countertop, she looked into her eyes the way she'd looked at that photograph on Cal's phone.

Her eyes were so green.

Greener than she'd ever before fully esteemed. She relished the color: subtle green, fresh-forest green, dark emerald. She continued to stare into her own eyes for several minutes as though she'd never met this person. Mindful of her breath, trying to see into her own soul, validating a place inside herself no one else could touch.

Then she shook her head, broke the gaze, and took off her jacket.

The moment she finished removing the garment, she peered intensely into her eyes again, suddenly struck by her expression: conscious awareness. She was mesmerized.

"Look at Mommy." Cal swung Ben beneath the center of the doorframe, holding him like Superman.

"Oh my God." Annie brought a hand to her heart and jumped. "You scared the shit out of me."

"Look at your beautiful mommy," Cal repeated, swinging his son back and forth. Ben giggled, infectiously, laughing and laughing.

Annie stepped toward them with a huge grin on her face. "There's my boy." She kissed Ben's cheek. "Are you flying? Are you flying, Bennie?" She tickled his sides as Cal swooped him through the air. "You smell better. All fresh and clean, huh? Did Daddy change your diaper?"

"He was a mess." Cal placed him on the ground and held his palm.

Ben stood, wobbly on his feet, fussing and stretching his free hand upward, pinching his fingers, asking to fly again.

"A stinky mess." Annie took her son's other hand.

Benjamin waddled between his parents, holding onto their fingers as the three of them went toward the full-length, oval-shaped mirror outside the bathroom. The antique had been Constance's, and its place was now in this home in a corner of the bedroom.

The second Benjamin spotted his face in the mirror, he seemed to forget about flying. Now, he was consumed with his reflection. Letting go of his mom, he slapped his hand against the glass, but he continued holding onto Dad. Otherwise, he might fall down — he was still new to this furniture walking business.

"He likes looking in the mirror almost as much as you do." Cal eyeballed Annie and smirked.

"How long were you standing there ... watching me?" She hooded her gaze some. "I can't believe I didn't even hear you come in."

"Mmm ... you must've been in deep thought."

"I was feeling."

"Did you like what you *felt*?"

She sighed, dropping to the floor beside Ben. The little boy smacked at her reflection now, babbling, saying his gibberish word for Mommy.

"I did." After kissing Ben's cheek, she tilted her head toward Cal.

He sat on the floor too, crossing his legs, never letting go of his son's fingers. Ben let out a wonderful sound of surprise — a laugh mixed with a loud, joyful cry. The noise tapered off as Benjamin looked back and forth at his parents' reflections, dancing and slapping, leaving prints on the glass and laughing.

"Who's that?" Cal moved closer to the mirror, opening his eyes wide. "Who is that? Is that Bennie?"

Annie held onto her son's waist, watching the three of them, their faces, comparing their features, amazed this sweet little boy was all theirs.

"He grew inside you, baby," Cal said, voicing what she'd been thinking. "He grew inside your body."

"I know." She stared into her son's blue eyes.

Annie's face and eyes shined as she continued to look at Benjamin, fully contemplating the import of what that meant.

"Come here." Cal tugged on the sleeve of her sweater.

After scooting closer, she leaned her head against his shoulder, placing her hand on Cal's face. Resting her palm along his scruffy jawline, she stroked his magnetic skin. Benjamin turned around and fell into them.

Cal and Annie laughed as Ben pushed his face into Annie's chest, nuzzling her, patting her, and talking.

"Look at us." Cal glanced in the mirror. "Look at us, Annie. We made a fucking baby."

"Tell Daddy to watch his mouth." She met his reflection, rolled her eyes, and pinched her husband's waist.

"You watch my mouth." He stared at her lips, then kissed them while grinning.

Benjamin climbed up their bodies and put his face on his mommy's cheek, his mouth wide open in a complete circle, wetting her skin with his drool, making a soft humming sound.

"Kisses from both my boys," Annie exclaimed.

"Benjamin already knows how to get a lady's attention." Cal turned toward his son. "He knows what he's doing. Don't you, little man?"

Then Cal grabbed Ben's bottom and lifted him. And just like that, they were off flying again in an instant.

Annie laughed while wiping drool off her cheek.

"Get changed. I want to take us all out to lunch." Cal swooshed Ben through the room. "You can go to the store later."

"Let's go to the park too." Annie stood.

"It's cold out."

"He's used to the cold. And you know he loves the swings."

"I want to take you out."

"Just me, right now?"

"No, all of us now. Tonight, only you."

"Tonight?"

"Yes, tonight." Cal's throat began to close, knowing it was going to be *the night*, knowing he could be himself with her in every way, knowing Annie was herself. She was always Annie, but she was here and present and had returned from her own long and winding flight. Ready to descend into their hearts and land — forever.

Cal wanted Annie forever.

Any way he could have her: sick, depressed, exhausted, happy, exuberant, magical — anyway, anyhow, anywhere.

Even the air in the room had shifted. Changed directions. Gratitude circled the breaths they drew.

Cal was ready. Annie was too.

The window was open.

The landing imminent.

Sometimes holes needed to be patched before the rocket could return safely from space.

ONE HUNDRED FIVE

"Look at that couple over there." Annie glanced at two teenagers holding hands in a corner of the restaurant. "Aren't they adorable?"

"What's so adorable about them, Annie?" Cal looked casually to his right, relaxing back in his chair, wineglass in hand, and waited for his wife's reply.

The Prescotts were on a date. The one Cal had suggested earlier. Not their first outing alone this month. It was their third or fourth or fifth.

It was their fifth.

The two of them had ordered their meal — their fifth — when Annie became distracted by the arrival of that "adorable" couple.

"Maybe it's the first time they've been in love." She brought her head closer to the center of the table. "It's sweet."

"Annie..." Cal laughed a little under his breath as he moved closer to the middle of the table as well. "That boy over there is concerned about one thing and one thing only. And the travesty is that he doesn't have a clue how to get it, let alone how to do it correctly."

Annie smirked, twining some strands of hair around an index finger. "Maybe you're just too old to remember."

"No, I remember." Cal peered off into the distance and smiled, then he fixed his gaze on his wife. "What about you?" He lost his smile. Arched his brows. "You never told me about your first time."

"My first time what?" She batted her lashes. "You tell me about yours."

"I asked you first." Cal grabbed the bottle and topped off their glasses.

The second he finished the chore, Annie snatched the glass and swallowed chardonnay, her eyes dotting around the restaurant.

"Maybe I'm wrong..." He laughed. "If the memory is making you all warm."

Placing a palm on a flushed cheek, she rolled her eyes.

"Well..."

"I was sixteen," she blurted, and his eyes widened. "I... The summer I took surfing lessons... We..."

"Oh..." Cal grinned. "*A surfing boy*. How old was he?"

"Eighteen ... I think..." Annie smiled while swinging a leg beneath the table. "I was... We were friends really. Or I thought we were. But on the day of the last lesson, he started flirting with me, acting so different. He was really hot." She eyed Cal and almost laughed. The bastard hadn't stopped grinning. "You're the worst."

Cal cleared his throat and adjusted himself. "Keep going."

"We were rinsing off and getting out of our wet suits." She swallowed. "And he kissed me." Stopping short, she looked dead at Cal, then drank some more of the wine. "How much more do you need to know?"

"Oh, I need to hear more."

"We started to make out in his Jeep." Annie covered her eyes. "It's embarrassing." She peeked out from behind them.

"It's normal."

Exhaling, she wrapped her hands around the wineglass. "It wasn't..." She sighed. "God. It wasn't how I imagined my first time. Okay."

"My point exactly." Cal tipped his head toward the teenagers at the nearby table.

"That's different..." She glanced at them again as well. "They might be—"

"So, you think because they might be in love with each other that their first time will be exactly like they've imagined it? They're sixteen or seventeen, Annie."

"You're a killjoy." She shoved her foot against his shin and rolled her eyes again.

"Did you climax?"

Annie slapped a palm over her mouth. "No!" She stifled a giggle. "It was over too fast."

"Mmm..." Cal grinned. "Sounds like your surf-instructor boy was the killjoy, then."

"You think this is so funny."

"I'm not the one laughing."

Annie stopped on a dime, but her smile remained wide and impregnable. "Well, Mr. Prescott, now it's your turn."

Staring across the restaurant, he blinked a few times, then grinned. "I was older than you."

"No, you weren't."

"Yes, I was," he emphasized. "I was eighteen. The summer before college."

"And...?" Annie perched on the edge of her seat, a fingernail in her mouth.

"You find this amusing, don't you?"

"God, yes!"

"I wasn't always what you see before you now." The man gestured at his own body. His posture perfect. His teeth white.

"What do you think I *see*?" Annie teased.

"I was very studious." He smirked. "Sometimes to a fault."

"'Studious'? Is that code for geek?" Annie laughed, unable to imagine Cal any other way than as he sat before her now: self-assured and inherently masculine.

"No, but it was a little while before—"

"Before what?" She couldn't wait for him to finish, tapping the toe of her boot to his shin.

"Before I learned how to please a woman, Annie." Cal exhaled, picked up his glass, and guzzled wine. He might've even rolled his eyes, but he didn't take them off his wife.

"So ... you think you know how to please a woman now?"

"I think I've got a handle on it." Cal leaned forward and grinned.

"And what about at eighteen? You didn't have a 'handle' on it then?"

"You're so bad."

"You're not getting out of this that easily."

"The girl..." Cal stroked his chin. "She was an artist ... staying with us. I've told you how my mother rented out the downstairs bedroom."

Annie grinned.

"She, uh... She was a few years older. She knew it was my first time, that I wasn't going to last. But she did climax." He smirked. "That was also the first time I had my face in a girl's—

"Cal..." Annie exhaled, her pulse rising as the man stared into her eyes in that special way of his. Into her. Through her. Her throat went dry. It felt as though Cal had his face in *her* pussy.

"Well..." she managed a few seconds later, after clearing her throat and fiddling with her neckline, "when did you finally get a handle on it?"

"When I realized what the clitoris was," Cal deadpanned, and Annie nearly spewed wine. "I've always wondered..." Cal handed her a napkin, and she dotted her mouth with it. His gaze shifted. His tone had changed. He tapped five of his nails across the tabletop.

"What?"

"What you must've thought of me..." He gave her a tight smile. "The night we met."

"You mean, did I think you were a conceited asshole?" She eyeballed him and grinned. Then her demeanor changed as well. Exhaling, she paused and peered at him. "I wanted you like I'd never wanted anything in my entire life."

"Really?"

"Yes," she whispered, losing her breath again. "I'd never met a man like you. You already know that."

"You hadn't met too many assholes?" Cal cleared his throat.

Annie reached a hand across the table. "No," she uttered. "I'd met plenty of those..." She sighed. "But never a man who knew exactly what he wanted, who wasn't ashamed of going after it, and who at the same time seemed so alone ... even in a crowd of people..."

Cal tried to remove his hand from Annie's but she wouldn't let him.

"I was drawn to you," she went on. "You were a force when I met you..." She smiled. "Actually, when I first saw you in the living room from where I stood on that staircase, watching you—"

"And blushing." He grinned.

"It was like *nothing* I'd ever felt." A chill ran through her entire body. "By the time you kissed me in the rain on that sidewalk, I felt like I'd always known you. Like there was no time in my life without you there." She swallowed. "I fell in love with you, Cal." Their eyes locked. "You always made me feel safe, and you always supported me, never judged me, and you listened to me like you are now — quiet and strong, safe and comforting. And when you do make a point to speak, you usually have exactly the right words to say."

"Jesus, Annie." Cal wiped a palm clean across his face.

"I'm not done." Taking both of Cal's hands, she turned them over, palms up, and ran her fingers along the lines. "And your skin..." She turned her head away for a second. Her throat closed up, stinging her. When she met his gaze again, she almost faltered. "From the first time your skin touched mine, it was... God, it was more than—"

"Just physical," they both uttered.

Electricity coursed through Annie, down her arms, to her fingers, over her thighs. She shook a little as she began to brush her thumbs over the veins on his wrists.

"In the beginning," she continued, "I was afraid... I was afraid it was only me feeling it — all of it. I thought..." She shrugged, her stomach filling with butterflies. "I thought I was simply another girl you wanted to fuck."

"Mmm..." Cal stared at her for a long time. "I did want to fuck you." He leaned forward, his gaze so piercing, so intense. So everything. "But you were never just 'another girl,' Annie Rebekah. *Ever*. I saw my reflection in your eyes."

Annie shivered. Cal squeezed her hand.

"You were different." He started to twist the two bands on her ring finger around and around.

"How was I different?"

"Because you care." His eyes moved from his grandmother's keepsake to Annie's precious face. "I could sense it before I even came to know it." He tapped his temple. "Up here." Then he tapped his heart. "But here..." He inhaled. "It was obvious immediately. The way you care ... about yourself and other people."

She shook her head.

"It's true. You look at the person, the whole person, and I mean you really see them, not what they have, the things they possess, or even what they look like on the outside, but you see their insides.

"And when I saw that you wanted to know me — and I wanted you to know me, but I didn't think you could love me if you really knew me — I tested you." He grinned. "You were something ... this relationship was something I realized I did not want to screw up."

"Well, you did a fine job ... *testing me*," she joked. "I think I'm more screwed up now than ever before."

Annie laughed but Cal's expression remained. That same primal intensity was written across his entire fucking face along with something else. Vulnerability.

"I don't know what every day of our married life is going to be like, but I know what I feel for you hasn't changed." He sat forward in his chair and took a deep breath. "I feel closer to you now, more than I ever did. And I always felt close to you." Cal's eyes glistened. His throat stung. "I want to make love to you. I want you tonight."

Annie peered at Cal, his stare so penetrating, so blinding. A sharp feeling ran through her entire body, slicing her in half, making her ache in places that had gone dormant.

"I've never stopped wanting you, Annie." His Adam's apple bobbed. "I only wanted you to feel better. To feel good about yourself again. And I wanted to be able to be myself with you ... in every way."

"I was a mess for so long..." She dropped her gaze. "I'm sorry." She looked up. "I'm sorry I didn't want you to touch me." She swallowed. "*Ever*. It wasn't you."

"I know, baby." Cal trailed a finger over her forearm, tickling her. "That's the past. This is now. Rosa will take care of Ben. I want you with me all night tonight. Without leaving our bed. Without distraction."

"Yes," Annie replied, gazing into his eyes, wondering if he could hear her heart thumping against the walls of her chest.

"We're leaving."

"Now? We haven't even eaten."

"I'm only hungry for you." He grinned. "We can take it home."

"And eat in bed." Her eyes opened wide. "Like on our honeymoon."

Cal smirked and tapped her wrist with a single finger.

"The food!" Annie quipped.

"You're beautiful," he whispered. "*Just like this*." Pulling her hand away from her earring, he held her palm, running his index finger slowly up and down the tendons on her wrist. "I want to taste you."

The server appeared with two plates of hot food, and Annie nearly fell into a fit of laughter.

"We're going to need that boxed up, please. And bring the check back with you too."

Annie giggled as soon as the man departed. "Do you think he heard you?"

"Did you hear me?" Cal replied, his voice deep and low, his eyes matching the tone. "I want to put my mouth on you. All over you..." Cal's words were like cinders floating through the air in the middle of a forest fire. "I want to hold you down and lick your cunt..." They wrapped around her body like silk, tying her up. "And kiss you. *Everywhere.* All over your fucking skin until you scream my fucking name and come. *Over and over and over.*"

Annie stroked her throat. Repeatedly. She couldn't move or talk or breathe. Her nostrils flared. Her face flamed.

"Have you forgotten what that feels like?"

"No," she squeaked.

"Are you ready for that, Annie? Are you ready for me?"

Shaking her head as though waking from a dream, she clasped her fingers around his and stared at their fused hands.

"Look at me," Cal whispered.

Annie swallowed with great difficulty, then she looked up at him keenly, feeling nude in the middle of the restaurant.

"I love you," he uttered.

Annie's eyes began to water as she squeezed his hand. He squeezed back and wrapped his feet around her ankles. She tilted her head down and squinted, causing tears to drip from her lids.

Cal lifted their palms and wiped the moisture away with their fists. "You know I always wanted you, Annie. I never stopped wanting you, loving you, or needing you."

"I know," she replied, fighting more tears. "You told me."

"I'm telling you again. You deserve to hear it again. And tonight, I'm going to make you feel it — *again and again and again.*"

ONE HUNDRED SIX

Hand in hand, Cal and Annie left the restaurant, each stride in unison, pulses vibrating against each other as their coats flapped in the wind.

Upon reaching the Land Rover, Cal opened Annie's door, holding her palm as she sat down in the passenger seat and placed the takeout bag in the back of the car.

He paused. Smirked.

Then he began to undo the buttons of her coat. One by fucking one.

Pushing the lapels open, he slid his hands down the edge of the garment until he reached the hem, watching her figure materialize as he raked his gaze over her beautiful body — the soft, black dress, her swelling breasts, her curves — and then he peered into her eyes again.

"Take off your boots."

Annie dropped her head on the rest, releasing her breath as she set her foot against the dash, wondering what the hell he was doing. But he'd spoken to her so straightforwardly, so *Cal*, she desired to do whatever he commanded.

The moment she placed a hand at the top of the black, high-heeled boot, he took over, pulling the zipper toward her ankle, watching her skin unfold little by little through the fishnet of her stockings. Then he did the same with her other shoe.

"You're so sexy." He ran his fingers up her tights, stopping at her thighs. "Put both feet on the floor."

Annie swallowed, touched his cheek, and looked at Cal — the way she had that very first night on Maggie's front porch.

And reminiscent of that night, the man wouldn't give her the kiss she silently asked for. Instead, he removed her hand from his face and placed it above her head, over the seat, then pressed his palm flat against her thigh. Her eyes closed. Her heart pounded against the walls of her chest.

Then he slid a hand under her skirt.

"Cal..." Annie whispered as her eyes popped open.

He lifted her other arm, joining her hands behind the headrest.

"Take me home..." Closing her eyes again, her heart pumped faster and faster. "The bed is warm."

"You're warm." Cal pushed two fingers into the center of her tights, fingering her through the nylon all while peering at her face — the way he always liked to. God, how he'd missed seeing that expression, the one he saw now with her arms above her head, wrapped around the seat, her head tilted back, chest out, whimpering, looking fabulously out of her fucking mind.

"Oh, God..." She moaned. "You're going to make me come. It's been so long."

"Good." He put his lips near her ear while ripping open the tiny holes of the fishnet, wasting no time wiggling two fingers inside her panties. "I want to watch you come."

Then his flesh met hers.

For what felt like the first time.

It was so electric, Annie nearly burst.

"Fuck," he hissed as he continued to touch her, his face the perfect picture of concentration, strain. Beauty.

"Take me home, Cal," she dinned several seconds later, shimmying her hips, glancing into his eyes. "Not here." Her chest rose. "I want to wait until we're home. I want to feel you inside me. God, I just want to feel *you*."

"You're so warm," he repeated, his fingers pulsing in and out of her slowly, "so fucking wet."

"I can't, Cal..." She gulped and shook her head. "I want to wait."

His digits no longer moved, but he kept them inside the torn fishnet of her stockings, inside the lace of her panties, inside her body. "Do you want me to be myself with you?"

The universe ground to a halt.

Annie stared at him, blinking, her mouth open and parched.

"Yes," she finally choked out.

"Then listen to me. Now." It sounded as though Cal couldn't breathe. "I want to feel you come. I want to keep my hand on you. My fingers in you." He pressed his thumb against her clit. "*Right. Here.*"

"People will hear us."

"There are no people." Cal wandered into her woods, getting lost in the deep green forest of her eyes. "It's only you and me." He swallowed, never breaking eye contact. "Give yourself to me, Annie. Like always. All over again. *Now.*"

Annie bit her bottom lip, pinching her eyes shut. Fighting it, him, this — the habits of her depression hard to scorn.

"We'll have all night to be in our bed. In our warm bed. I want this for you," he said but removed his hand, and the loss registered across every line on her face. "Here..." Cal dragged those same two fingers over her bottom lip, then he slipped them inside her mouth. "That's it, taste yourself."

Annie whimpered and sucked and moaned and squirmed against the seat.

"Tell me to touch you." He removed his fingers from her mouth. "Beg me, Annie."

Her heart beat faster, harder, as she peered into his eyes, leapt into his ocean, and fell under his magical spell.

"This is a new start for us." He cradled her cheek, gazing into her eyes. "Tell me. *Please.* I need you, baby."

"Touch me," she burst and shook. "I need you too, Cal. Put your fingers inside me ... where they belong. You belong with me. Inside me."

"So fucking sexy," he bit out as he cupped her harsher than before, sliding the same two fingers up and forward, leaving his thumb to circle her clit.

Her breathing hitched. She closed her eyes. "Oh, God." She dropped her head against the seat and heaved. "Fuck..."

Cal nibbled her bottom lip, tasting the arousal he'd painted there as he continued bringing her closer and closer... "You've always been mine, baby."

"Yes ... please." Annie joined the motion, fucking his palm.

"But I wish..." He turned his head away, wincing, slowing down the finger-fucking. Her eyes popped open once she noted the break in his tone. "I wish you had never left me."

"No, no, no." She palmed his cheeks. "I never left you."

But she had.

She had left him.

Not intentionally.

She hadn't wanted to.

"You did, Annie." Cal's Adam's apple bobbed. He brushed strands of hair from her eyes.

"Please, don't stop touching me." She pressed her thighs together and shut her eyes.

"Look at me," Cal choked out, and the guttural tone she heard in those three familiar words both scared and ignited her. Her eyes opened. His jaw clenched. "Don't. Ever. Leave. Me. Again."

"I won't." Annie pulled his face closer and kissed him. "I'll never leave you again."

"Never..." he uttered, nuzzling his nose with hers.

"Never." The salt of her tears mixed with their kisses, swirling around their tongues.

"Show me your never." He picked up the pace, tapping his fingers over and over her G-spot. "Let me hear your never."

Arching her hips forward, Annie moaned and moaned, yanking on the lapels of his coat as though she clung to life itself.

And she did.

Her life.

His.

Theirs.

They were one.

Inching his head from her beautiful face, he echoed her favorite edict, "Look at me."

Biting back tears, she nodded, speaking the *never* as a solemn pact, one between their eyes, their hearts, his fingers, their sounds.

Their souls.

"Never," he repeated like an oath, his breath shaking.

"Never," she whispered.

"Louder."

Everything the two of them ever were, charged through Annie. The feeling often in her throat — the throbbing, the aching — ripped through her stomach, her legs — *fuck* — her thighs, her chest, tearing her apart, inflicting her with a pleasurable, tingly pain.

Like he'd become an actual part of her.

"Never," she burst. "I love you."

"Again." His fingers pulsed as he circled her clit, then he pinched it unexpectedly.

"Never!" She sobbed.

"Come," he ordered.

He didn't need to say it twice.

Annie's muscles tightened around his fingers, and as they did, Cal's eyes glossed. He watched her come. He felt her release and surrender, and with that trust, a safety returned. *Her* eternal comfort. Her magic. Her love, her lust, her passion became one with his.

They became one.

Now.

Today.

Again.

The woman who had been his from the start — his always, his forever, *his*, tied to him and bound — spoke new vows.

He inhaled the breaths she exhaled. His body contained her soul, and hers contained his.

This new beginning was the new forever.

She would never leave him again.

UNDEFINABLE

She no longer needed to be a square peg trying to fit into a round hole

ONE HUNDRED SEVEN

Benjamin was twelve months old, but Annie felt a year older for each month he'd lived.

Her world had changed as everyone who knew her — everyone who really knew her — had predicted. It had changed in ways she never could've imagined, and now she'd finally settled and embraced it, and with this change, she knew there would still be more to come ... and more ... and more and more.

She couldn't stop it, and she no longer needed to fight it, and the strength she'd once poured into her struggle now poured into her very bones, carrying her up and over every hurdle with a new sense of ease.

An appreciation. A deep sense of gratitude.

It wasn't only Annie's world that had changed. She had changed.

Just as it had been after Peter died, so it was now.

Annie couldn't be the same. She had to move forward. She had to surge ahead. She was different. Annie had, at last, come out on the other side of a many-months-long depression amazingly unscathed — but she had changed.

It would've been impossible for Annie to feel what she'd felt, lose what she'd lost, and gain what she'd gained without metamorphosis.

New life after a fire blazing through a vast forest.

Without the burn, without the flames, there could be no new growth — there could be no creation. Or rebirth.

From the ashes rose life.

ONE HUNDRED EIGHT

Cal and Annie walked up to the door of a sprawling estate located on the beach in Malibu one beautiful late afternoon in May of 2016. Cal had business in Los Angeles, and this time Annie accompanied him — without Ben and with no regrets.

The wind whipped Annie's white hippie skirt up her legs and blew caramel-colored strands across her face. Her hair had been recently cut. It curled at the ends, falling a little over her shoulders.

Something else had fallen over one of her shoulders too.

Eyeing Annie's bra strap through his aviator sunglasses, Cal tucked the pink piece of lace under her top the moment a wobbly and giggly stranger opened the beast of a front door.

"Oh," the faltering guest said as he passed. "Excuse me."

Annie and Cal exchanged a smirk as they stepped over the threshold.

Less than two seconds inside, and already Annie gave the immense room a once-over. Like an observer behind a sheet of glass — that girl on Maggie's staircase who thought no one could see her — she peered into a secret world the likes of which she'd never before seen. Not up close, anyway.

Enormously high ceilings climbed to a second story. Museum paintings covered the walls. A grand chandelier hung above them. Clusters of people floated about. And then there were the floors. Blotchy, nonuniformed patterns made up the beautiful slatestone, the color matching the rocks found in the

Petrified Forest. Cal had recently taken Annie and Benjamin to Arizona where she'd captured photographs of that forest, the Grand Canyon, and plenty of sights in Sedona.

It was a dream.

Like this house.

Everything here seemed huge, larger than life — even Cal.

But none of it made her feel small.

Wearing confidence on her sleeve — the way she wore everything on the freaking thing — her sense of belonging-anywhere-she-damn-well-pleased shined like a fresh, glossy coat of lipstick ready to smack against anything that breathed.

After removing his sunglasses and placing them over his shirt collar, Cal nuzzled Annie's neck. "Are you ready?"

She squirmed from the contact, the sun-on-the-sand warmth of his breath, and the magnets of his skin. Threading her fingers through his, she glanced at the makeshift bar located along the rear wall of the Hearst Castle-esque living room.

"I am." She smiled as they began to move forward. "I'm ready for a drink."

"Cal," a man interrupted, slapping Cal's shoulder, an unlit cigar wedged between his fingers. Another man approached as well, and so the four of them stood, forming a circle.

"Bill." Cal took his hand and shook it. "Good to see you."

"Did you just arrive?"

"My wife and I arrived last night." Cal tipped his head toward Annie.

"I was wondering when I was finally going to meet this mysterious bride of yours," Bill replied with a wry smile while yanking his pants toward his protruding waist. "I was beginning to think she might be only a figment of your imagination."

"I'm real." Annie reached out her hand, but Bill surprised her by lifting her fingers and kissing them instead of gripping them.

"Bill, this is my wife, Annie." Cal then caught the eye of the other man, the unfamiliar one. "I'm sorry. I don't know your name."

Bill dropped Annie's palm and cleared his throat. "I apologize." He shoved a hand in his pocket, beginning to jingle keys or change or something rattling and distracting. "I thought the two of you had already met."

"No," the other man said in a thick Southern accent. "I never forget a face." He smoothed his tanned fingers over the tips of his salt-and-pepper mustache. "My name is Beauregard. Beauregard Templeton."

"Hmm," Cal muttered, the Rolodex of his mind flipping through card after card. "That name's familiar."

"Like I said," Templeton grumbled, fingering the hair over his upper lip again. "I don't forget a face."

"We've done work for Beau, Cal," Bill said.

"Here, in Malibu?" Cal asked.

"Yeah." Bill fidgeted. "Ahem... It's been a few years."

"Bill said you're here for the merger," Templeton interjected, "and he tells me you're the best."

Cal found the card.

The one in his mind.

His veins filled with sand as he stared into the imperious man's bulging blue eyes.

The reason the name Templeton was familiar infiltrated every part of his body, traveling at a rate faster than the speed of sound, shutting down his ability to make conversation.

Fuck. Him.

Annie took note of Cal's face — the color had vanished — and grabbed her husband's hand and held it, squeezing his fingers.

"Cal is the best," Annie gushed, extending her free hand toward Templeton.

"I'm sorry, sweetheart." Templeton grasped her palm. Annie thought his handshake had too much sugar and spice and everything nice and not enough backbone. "You must think me to be rude. It's nice to meet you, Mrs....?"

"Mrs. Prescott."

"That's right," he said with a snide bit of laughter. "Prescott... Bill told me that. You'll both be here all week, then?"

"Yes," Annie replied.

"Well, it's too bad my wife isn't here," Templeton went on. "I think the two of you would probably get along fine. You could shop and gab and do whatever the hell it is women like to do. I'm sure all this man talk bores you to tears."

"Not at all." Annie smiled despite the salmonella the man's presence gave her gut. "Will she be here later in the week?"

Cal clamped down on Annie's hand, his palm now damp. Bill shifted his gaze.

Templeton's eyes opened wide like an eagle's. "My wife is ill," he said with an oddly bitter tone as though her illness had offended him personally.

Cal cleared his throat and looked at Annie, his cheeks regaining some of their color. They actually appeared a little blistery.

"I'm so sorry." Annie touched Templeton's arm, but he only peered down at her fingers, his gaze swimming with something rather disgusting.

She removed her hand and glanced at Cal, willing him to speak. Bill coughed and stood on the balls of his feet, rolling the unlit cigar between his fingers.

"Beau, you old devil," a man interrupted. "How's Reegan?"

"She's fine," Beau replied gruffly as he turned and stepped away with the other man. "She's off getting treatment," they could still hear him saying. "The best. You know it's nothing but the best—"

"Excuse us, Bill," Annie said politely while eyeing Cal. "If you don't mind. I think we're thirsty."

"No, of course. Get yourselves a drink. I'll be over shortly. I want to start on this bullshit tonight." Bill turned from Cal and faced Annie. "It was nice to finally meet you, Mrs. Prescott."

"It was nice to meet you as well."

Annie took a seat on one of the bamboo chairs at the end of the bar while Cal stood next to his wife and played with the tips of her hair, a drink in his other palm.

She peered at Cal, waiting for the words he held back to roll off his tongue — to choke off — but she realized they may never come out of the quiet man's voice box.

After stirring the olive-coated toothpick around her triangular-shaped glass for several more seconds, she tilted the rim to her lips and took a few sips of the dirty martini. The Grey Goose couldn't do a thing to ease the burn or swell in her throat, though.

"Did you love her?" she finally asked as she set the drink down and waited for Cal's wandering gaze to meet hers.

"No," he replied, then downed half the whiskey in his glass.

"You cared for her."

"I felt sorry for her." His tone held no pleasure, only a dull knife of regret.

"When did you know her?"

Palm around the highball, he exhaled. "I met her," he faltered, recalling Reegan's kinky, waist-length blonde hair, the empty in her pale blue eyes, "close to a year before I met you."

"She was the distance you needed from LA?"

Cal nodded and looked to the drink, wishing the alcohol could swallow him whole instead of the other way around.

"Why did you—?"

"Have an affair?" Inhaling the shame, his eyes bounced around the guests, the room.

"Yes." She fidgeted with the toothpick again. "I'm sorry. I have no right to judge you."

"The loneliness in her was..." Cal began, trailing off.

Annie never took her compassionate gaze off him. Cal held up the empty glass and signaled the bartender.

"Jameson neat, sir?"

"Yes, please." Cal cleared his throat and feigned a smile, thinking of Reegan sick and possibly dying, the memory and unknown of it all causing an unusual floundering within him.

A moment later, the bartender handed Cal his fresh drink.

Annie watched him take a sip, and then she reached up and touched his face, giving him her love and strength through the tips of her fingers.

"Her loneliness was more than mine," Cal said, his voice still a little shaky. "Nothing took it from her. *Nothing*." He looked at Annie, his gaze sharp and keen, while removing her hand from his cheek. "Her husband's a—"

"I noted that..." She shifted her eyes to where the arrogant caveman formerly stood. "Had you really never met him?"

"No." Cal ran a palm over his jaw and released his breath. "No."

"You gave her something, then."

"Annie, don't."

"What?"

"Don't be so fucking kind." He glanced away.

Standing from her chair, Annie grabbed the sides of Cal's shirt and pinched her fingers toward his collar.

"She's lonely," Annie uttered, "not you. Not anymore. And she chose to stay with that man." Annie smoothed her hands over Cal's shirt. "And I do have to be so fucking kind. His wife is sick, and I wouldn't wish that on anyone, not even someone you—"

"Annie..."

"What?" she asked, the familiar ache in her throat.

"That's all it was."

"No, it wasn't, Cal."

Feelings rushed over him as he plunged down the rest of the whiskey, resisting the emotions, both fighting them and needing them.

Annie took Cal's hand, kissed his cheek, then moved her lips toward his ear. "You're not alone anymore," she whispered. "You are loved."

Cal captured the words off Annie's tongue and stored them in the safety-deposit box marked Annie Rebekah Prescott. The risk he'd taken not to be lonely had finally rewarded him with a wife, a son, a life, an antidote for the empty, a reason for the struggle and the fight.

Reasons to live.

Not reasons to exist.

To live.

And he felt it. Cal felt it. He trusted it.

Bill approached — unaware he was blatantly interrupting — ready to whisk Cal away to talk of the merger, to talk of things no longer pressing in on Cal's soul — necessary things, but nonessential to what Cal called *life*.

Annie pressed Cal.

She held her hand against his chest, his heart beating at an incredible rate, speaking to him without words, pressing, pressing, pressing, making sure he would still feel her long after Bill pulled him away.

ONE HUNDRED NINE

Finding herself alone in a sea of unfamiliar faces and in a room full of grandiose things, Annie held her dirty martini glass by its stem in one hand and a bunched-up section of her full, embroidered skirt in the other, swinging the material back and forth between sips.

Like George McFly on the 1955 dance floor when noting the time, Annie's gaze came to a halt on the windows. The walls. The floor-to-ceiling view of the Pacific Ocean.

Even though Annie lived in Seattle, she hadn't seen much of Washington's coastline, and it certainly hadn't been the same way she'd seen the Atlantic in Miami — every single day, greeting her with a kiss and a smile, a roar and a handshake.

Moving closer, she took up residence near the center of one of the windowed walls, a childlike urge taking over her psyche, a voice asking her to do something other people might call silly. And as with most times in Annie's life, she followed her whimsy, doing what made her happy without regard to who might be watching.

She pressed a palm and nose to the glass and peered at the crowds of people gathered on the outside deck.

Annie itched to photograph them. But she hadn't brought her Nikon. It was back at the hotel. On the bed. Annie felt naked without it by her side, hanging from her neck. And she found it hard to believe not much time had passed since she'd drifted so far from being a photographer — the kind who sees the possibilities everywhere, beauty in everything — when now she wanted nothing more than to have the camera with her always.

Like an extension of her.

Still, even without it, she was mesmerized, eyeing dozens of shots, framing them up in her mind's eye...

The habitual flick of the cigarette in the hand of a blonde-haired starlet. The stem of a red-pumped heel grinding its tip into a crack in the concrete. Three bearded men in a circle, one of whom sported a huge, brown bowtie. A pink carnation in the pocket of an older gentleman's jacket.

Without her camera, though, Annie was forced to make an imprint on only the film of her mind. Walter Mitty-style.

Her phone rested in one of her skirt pockets, but taking a picture with it could never compare to looking through the viewfinder of her Nikon, studying a person or thing in its lens, that perfect other side of the rainbow where artist meets subject — and it could never take the place of the weight of the camera in her hands.

Sighing, she watched her breath fog up the glass. Then she observed the steam as it vanished.

Annie vanished.

She lost her nearly empty glass, then stepped out onto the enormous deck — the wind blowing her hair and skirt, the smell of salt tickling her nose — and made her way through crowds of people. The guests resembled dozens and dozens of lily pads strewn across a pond.

As she met the southern edge of the deck, she noticed steps. Several of them. Made of stones. The path appeared to lead to a garden. Following her whimsy again, she removed her shoes and descended, feeling a little like Dorothy beginning to skip along the yellow brick road.

And what met her at the bottom seemed just as fantastic as The Land of Oz. A garden. A beautiful secret garden.

One she could get lost in.

The soles of her bare feet caressed soft blades of grass while the tops of her fingers grazed foliage. After stroking the flowers and leaves and shrubbery, Annie found a spot on the ground and relaxed. She observed lizards, insects, the blue, blue sky. The rhythm of her heart beating against the walls of her chest.

A few minutes later, she noted a different sound.

She stood, strolled to the edge of the ledge, peered around some vines, and looked over the side.

A little boy played a couple of feet away. Six or seven. Impeccably dressed. Nutmeg hair falling across his forehead, strands pointing close to his dark, chocolate eyes, he hummed a tune. Dancing around a circle of people, he swung from their legs like the limbs were monkey bars at a park.

The song was familiar.

The hairs on the back of her neck perked up the moment she noticed he'd spotted her. After wandering over, he lowered to his haunches, attempting to peek around the leaves and vines.

"I'm Annie."

"I'm Peter."

Annie sucked in a breath and almost tripped backward. She gripped the concrete ledge.

The little boy cocked his head to the side, slid an arm past some branches, and touched Annie's aqua bracelet, playing with the shiny beads between his fingers.

"Peter ... huh?" she finally managed, smiling wide. "That's a strong name." Her eyes glistened. "My brother's name is Peter."

"Where are you?" Glancing around, he let go of the jewelry and tried to peek around her again, but there was too much greenery, a wall of plants meant to disguise the natural oasis from everything fake.

"It's a secret," she whispered.

Peter smiled, exposing an adorable gap where he would soon grow two upper front teeth, and went back to circling the legs of the people.

Annie couldn't take her eyes off him.

She tried to imagine Benjamin older.

But it was nearly impossible for Annie to construct a kindergarten version of her son, hard to imagine him any different from the buoyant one-year-old he was now. Yet she knew one day — and with each passing day — Ben would grow bigger, taller, and stronger. He would grow into a boy like the one standing a few feet away, and then he would grow into a man.

She couldn't wait to experience the journey with him: temper tantrums, potty training, teaching him to read, taking hikes and surfing, riding without training wheels, Disney.

Annie was ecstatic she would be Ben's mom forever.

Forever existed.

It did.

Fuck depression.

Sighing, she climbed the steps, making her way out of the hiding spot, but before she got very far, she bumped smack into that little boy.

"I'm sorry." Glancing down, she steadied his arm.

"Peter," his mother snapped, joining them. "I apologize," she said to Annie, then turned her attention to her son. "I told you to please look where you're going."

"It was my fault," Annie said, grinning. "I don't think I was looking where I was going."

The women smiled at one another.

"You have something on your skirt," the mother said as she started to grab the leaf off the photographer's clothing.

"Oh." Annie laughed. "Thanks. I was just down in this garden." She nodded at the ledge a few feet away as she smoothed out the material.

Peter held on to his mother's legs, humming again, not looking at anyone.

"I'm Annie, by the way." She stuck out her palm.

"I'm Eda." They shook hands. "And this is Peter."

"Hi, Peter," Annie said with the widest smile plastered across her face. "Hey…" She knelt, looking at him. "Would you like to see the garden?" Annie glanced at Eda. "If it's okay with your mom."

He peered up at his mother, his brown eyes twinkling. She patted his head and nodded. After Annie gave Eda her phone number, Annie and a boy named Peter made their way down the stone path and landed in a garden.

A secret one.

As Peter looked around, he started singing the lyrics of the song he'd been humming: "We're Off to See the Wizard."

Of course, Annie thought and grinned.

"Do you like that movie?" she asked as they began to explore.

"It's my favorite."

"What's your favorite part?" The road didn't need to be yellow or brick. It only had to lead her where she wanted to go.

"When she goes home," he replied, and Annie only stared at him. She wasn't expecting that answer. Perhaps the witch melting or the cowardly lion scaring Dorothy or even the tornado. But…

"Why?"

"Because it's where she belongs."

Annie swallowed. "With the people she loves."

"Yeah."

Peter started to hop around like a frog, bursting with enthusiasm. Then he looked back and took her palm, and Annie followed.

At one time, her brother had led her everywhere, literally by hand and by example with his heart — he'd shown her everything.

Suddenly, Annie couldn't breathe.

The sky seemed dark.

Her palms began to sweat.

The boy let go of her hand and searched the ground, the leaves, the trees for signs of life. His eyes sparkled like diamonds when he found lizards and butterflies, ants and dragonflies. Peter's delight in the simple, unnoticed, and truly vital matched her own.

Nothing should've been easier than being in the moment with him.

To be present.

The way she'd been a few minutes ago when alone.

Annie stared beyond the garden, past the beautiful little boy who couldn't get enough of the scenery, and was hit with a barrage of emotions, sensations, feelings people usually attempted to hide from — the ones Annie used to try to run and fly away from.

They tripped her up.

Choked her up.

She had nowhere to go. Nowhere to run.

A little boy needed her.

Annie allowed the can of worms to open, the shit she'd been trying to bury for the last three years, and the contents weren't as ugly as she'd imagined.

Glancing over at five- or six-year-old Peter, Annie remembered how she felt when her brother would wrap his arms around her. How he smelled like sandalwood and Celtic sea salt. Closing her eyes, she tried to hear his voice. His tone was faint and not nearly as loud as it had once been, but it was present...

Always look for what other people don't see. Find that place that makes people uncomfortable and capture it. Don't exploit it, Annie, but harness it. You're a natural. Your smile lights your eyes. You and me, Houdini. Anybody ever tries to hurt you — you come to me.

Peter had treated her like an adult from day one. Never a child. His confidence had been infectious. God... One day, she might forget. One day, she might not be able to feel him anymore. Or hear him.

This was too much. The feelings. The can of worms. The indescribable need to escape. But she needed to feel...

Because...

If you can't feel ... how can you heal?

Peter called her name, breaking up her incessant musings, and then a few minutes later, she led him back up the path to his mother.

"Well, buddy"—she mussed his hair and smiled—"I hope you have fun tonight."

Peter looked at Annie as he held his mother's hand. Grinning through those missing teeth, his eyes beamed. Right as Annie started to walk away, he leapt forward and wrapped his arms around her waist.

Annie's eyes enlarged to the size of lollipops. Her chest inflated. The ease with which Peter showed what he felt — without holding anything back, not asking any questions, not overthinking — enveloped her.

And as a result of this little boy's gift, or because Annie had finally let her guard down, Peter Baxter was here with his sister now. Present in her mind and alive in her heart. In all the ways she'd ever wanted him to be. In all the ways she'd been refusing to let him be.

He's free, she thought. *So am I...*

Annie rubbed Peter's back, swallowed past the throat-scratching lump in her throat, and uttered, "Goodbye" with a tear in her eye, then she turned to face the sea of lily pads, ready to reenter the world people mistook for reality.

ONE HUNDRED TEN

The bounce of Annie's skirt made her feel as though she walked on puffy little clouds as she strolled across the expansive deck, barefoot — intent on gazing at the ocean.

The sun.

The way the fantastic early evening light caused the surface of the Pacific to still sparkle like jewels.

Before she met the edge of the deck, that perfect spot, something tickled the nape of her neck.

The hairs there stood up again.

She whipped her head around but no one was present. Placing her elbows on the ledge, she leaned back and scoured the crowd, looking for the man who commanded her attention, the one causing all the goose bumps to erupt.

She couldn't see him.

But her body let her know he was near.

While sliding five fingers through her wind-battered hair, resisting the urge to twirl some of the pieces, Annie followed another whim and stared straight ahead.

A few people parted like that sea.

Exposing someone very familiar.

Someone very handsome.

Someone resembling a sequoia tree.

Annie smiled.

Wearing a dark-gray suit and a fuchsia button-down — because, fuck, it was Malibu — Cal owned the deck. His chess pieces in place as he attended to polite conversation. A hand in his pocket. A smirk on his face custom-made for Annie. And like a shy schoolgirl at a dance, she waited for the boy standing several feet away to ask her to be his partner.

The saying must be true, she thought, *some things never do change.*

The weight of his stare blew over her body as the California breeze did. Encompassing her, warming her, calming her.

She felt the same way she had the first time Cal spotted her on Maggie's staircase — a girl at a party. Hot and bothered. Warm with nostalgia. Nervous. The first time he'd peered into her eyes, the first time he'd held her attention. Right in the palm of his hands. That look and those eyes crossed Maggie's house in a wave, the way they traveled across this deck now: the same *and* different.

Both.

Because it was better.

His gaze held treasure, open chests, valued at more than Annie ever thought possible. The night they'd met, Annie never could've imagined a more intense stare beaming from his eyes, but it was here. Now. Like a laser attacking her senses.

Better, more, and different because those fucking green pools spilling over their sides overflowed with unconditional love. And Cal Prescott wore love better than any clothing he would ever buy.

A moment later, Annie's view became obstructed. She twirled the bracelet on her wrist. A woman passed offering hors d'oeuvres.

"Trisha," Annie choked out to the blonde-haired server sporting a white shirt, black vest, black pants, and a bowtie.

Upon catching sight of Annie, the woman nearly tripped over her own feet.

"Oh my God." Annie covered her mouth, her gaze flitting to Trisha's belly, her eyes filling with tears. "You're pregnant."

"Annie," Trisha whispered. "Honey..." She passed the tray off to another worker and led Annie to a concrete ledge where they both took a seat. "What are you doing here?"

"My husband..." Annie glanced up and looked around. "He's doing some..."

"My God..." Trisha beamed, moving pieces of Annie's hair off her forehead as she eyed the photographer's aqua bracelet. "You're married..."

"And you're having a baby." Annie swallowed. "When...?"

Trisha cradled her stomach. "In August. Where are you living now?"

"Seattle. But ... we're thinking of moving."

"Where? Here?"

"Yeah. Near LA."

"God..." Trisha exhaled. "We'll have to get together. I'm in Ventura. I'm sorry we've lost touch." Trisha met the gaze of another worker and stood. "Shit, I have to—"

"I know." Annie nodded, joining her. "It's okay."

Trisha pulled out her phone. "Do you still have the same number?"

Annie rattled off the digits as a man approached.

"Hi," Cal said, a hand in his pocket, a grin on his face.

Trisha looked from his waist to his lips to his eyes. She squinted, then stuttered, "H-hi."

Annie laughed. "This is Cal." She tipped her head toward him. "My husband."

"Oh, fuck..." Trisha smiled. "I'm sorry." She patted Cal's bicep. "Are you an actor?"

"No." Annie laughed again.

"Huh," was all Trisha said as she stared at him. "Well, there are a lot of them here tonight..." She rolled her eyes. "Anyway ... I have to get back." She kissed Annie's cheek. "So good to see you ... *Houdini.*" Trisha nodded. "You still taking photographs?" she called out after stepping away.

"Yes," Annie yelled, grinning.

"Houdini?" Cal asked, raising his brows, squaring Annie's hips, then wrapping his arms around her waist.

"Yeah... Peter... He liked to call me that."

"You never told me that."

"It was because..." Annie swallowed. "You know my dad liked to say I was magical."

"You are magical." He jiggled her hips and met her gaze.

"I haven't heard that name in..." Annie dropped her forehead against Cal's chest, and he caressed the back of her head, rocking them a little in his embrace.

"That was Peter's wife?"

"His girlfriend." Annie lifted her head. "They were trying to conceive when..."

"Now she's pregnant... She'll want to meet Ben."

Annie looked frantically around the open space. "I forgot to tell her—shit! I was just so shocked to see her."

"You'll bump into her again."

"She has my number."

"See..." he said, peering into her eyes. "I want to show you something." Cal led her to the edge of the deck. The sun was flush with the horizon. Any moment now it would disappear. He gestured out to sea and squinted. "Do you see that point there?"

Annie narrowed her eyes.

"Where the ocean meets the sky?"

"Yes," she whispered, wrapping an arm around his waist. They both faced the Pacific, standing in profile.

"I used to think it was an impossible place to reach. I didn't think I could make it there. And I tried..."

The sun was falling fast, collapsing. The colors going with it too.

"Now I know that it's right here." He squeezed her waist. "The light never leaves me." The sun went down, and Cal turned Annie toward him until she faced him fully. "The sky is always with that ocean." Cal swallowed, held her hands, their foreheads meeting. "It never leaves."

"No," she uttered, on the verge of weeping.

"Dance with me, *heavy*."

Annie already swayed along with him. "There's no music."

"There's always music," Cal said, and they both smiled, thinking of each and every song they'd ever shared. "It's here." He tapped his chest, rocking them some more. "Listen to my heart," he whispered. "It beats for you." Cal didn't take his eyes off her, or his hands, or his breath. "You're beautiful." Cal cradled her face, peering only at Annie, never breaking gaze. "*Just like this.*"

They skirted the deck for several minutes, dancing to their own music, making it up as they went along, taking a cue from fate and winks from the stars.

"Look at me," he said a few minutes later, and Annie glanced up into his beautiful eyes, green as a sea ... and wet like one too. "I love you, Annie Rebekah Prescott." He swallowed. "Forever."

"I love you, Calvin Warner Prescott," she replied, her heart full beyond measure, her mind clear as a crystal.

Life's a series of snapshots, she thought. *A variety of still frames. Endless waves. Perpetual motion.*

A continuum.

As Annie stared up at her husband — suspended in his gaze, his grasp, his energy — she realized out of all the words Cal had ever said to her, out of all the words he would yet say to her, none could be as potent or as beautiful or ever take the place of those three simple words.

In her mind, nothing — *nothing* — could cut straight to the heart of a matter like the words *I love you*.

Annie always liked simple.

She always liked truth.

And the truth was, Annie Rebekah Prescott no longer needed to be a square peg trying to fit into a round hole.

The photographer, the mother, the lover, the wife, the sister, the daughter, the friend, the daydreamer, the girl with magic in her heart no longer needed to define herself.

Ever.

Keep reading to sample an excerpt from *The Ocean in His Veins* — the companion novel to *Where the Ocean Meets the Sky*, featuring Cal from age sixteen to forty-five.

THE OCEAN IN HIS VEINS
EXCERPT

Part I

Two Dancers

The Doors

"For man has closed himself up, till he sees all things thro' narrow chinks of his cavern." – William Blake

The door opened.
Because he turned the handle.
And he walked through it.

CHAPTER ONE
October 1990

"There are lots of things I can teach you—"

"What? You don't knock when you enter a house you've never been in before?"

Two steps into her kitchen and Cal was already amused. He wanted to smile but didn't. And no, he hadn't knocked, because tonight he planned on making himself at home.

First, she gave him her backside, then her profile while busying herself with a cluster of red grapes she'd pulled from the fridge — arranging them in a glass bowl. Cal had a pretty good idea why she avoided his eyes, but he had no trouble taking in the view. She looked the same as when he'd seen her hours before:

Red dress, tanned legs, caramel-colored hair cascading across her backside, brown eyes still pretending not to notice him. Still ... she pitched herself a certain way, angling her body toward his — and tells often spoke louder than words.

"Didn't your mother teach you any manners?" she teased when he gave no reply.

But Cal always had answers. He just chose his words carefully. And Calvin Warner Prescott did have manners. If his mother had taught him anything ... it was manners.

"You lowered the garage door?"

"Yes."

"But you left the light on," she said after opening the door leading to the garage anyway.

He had shut the automatic one. He wasn't a liar. Nor had he driven all the way across town to be doubted ... or checked up on. He didn't play fucking games. "Didn't you hear it close?"

"Do you always drive that thing?" she asked instead, referring to the road-ster now parked in her two-car garage, the space otherwise full of art supplies, empty frames, boxes.

"When she runs."

Flicking the light off, she closed the door and faced him, head-on, a hand on her hip, a wide smile on her face. "Your car has a sex?"

"Yes."

Inches apart, they stared at one another, both grinning, a lush hue brightening her cheeks. Making the few seconds suddenly feel like days. But she broke gaze first, heading back to the boomerang-decorated countertop where she proceeded to make a drink.

A precise number of ice cubes, alcohol poured without a shot glass, and a few splashes of orange juice were all added to an iced tea glass — a ritual she could probably perform in her sleep. Or perhaps the motions were a diversion, allowing her the pretext of keeping the evening superficial.

Or maybe she was nervous.

Cal smirked, stepped closer to the Formica, and reached a hand into the bowl, breaking off several grapes. Without asking. Because, as he'd mused to himself earlier: *tonight, he planned on making himself at home.*

He would take his time.

Not rush.

The best was yet to come.

Starting with her scent...

Lemon zest, a flower that bloomed in spring, and sex. Maybe she'd been touching hers—

"What year is it?" Her question broke into his thoughts, her brown eyes studying what he hoped was confidence plastered across his chiseled face. "Your car?"

"A '32."

"You're not worried your board will get stolen ... hanging out of the back like that?"

"You worry about too many things." His eyes drifted from her girly, motherly, sensual gaze — a trifecta — to the glass in her palm.

"Do you want a drink, Cal?" She dipped the tip of a finger into her freshly made one.

"No." He leaned against the counter, crossed his ankles, and popped a couple more grapes into his mouth.

"You don't drink?"

"I don't want a drink *tonight*."

"What about water?" She retrieved a glass from the cabinet anyway. "You might get thirsty."

"You haven't changed your clothes."

Grinning, she fingered the top two buttons of her red dress. "No, I've been working."

"Still?" He glanced at the clock on the wall.

"Yes, *still*." The maternal tone he'd heard many times in the classroom made itself known, but her eyes twinkled less like a mother's and more like those of a girl in line for a Ferris wheel. "Do you have a job?"

Cal surveyed more of the modest house — the staircase, the adjoining living area with its open windows and their curtains blowing in the wind — then he pinned his gaze on her again. "Yes."

She cleared her throat, then offered him the glass of water, but Cal refused. "Well ... what do you do?"

"I work on cars, old cars, antiques."

"Really?" Her hips swayed, the gentle motion like a sudden breeze over the ocean — something one felt but might not bother to notice. Cal noticed. "Like the one in my garage?"

"Yes."

"You don't seem like the type." She smirked, her cheeks still appearing flushed. "You don't seem like the type of guy who likes to get his hands dirty."

"Mmm, you don't know me, Ms. Ryan. There are lots of things I can teach you—"

Her laughter interrupted what he thought had been a cunning attempt at acting like a grown-up. "You think you're going to teach me things?"

"Yes," he assured her once the laughter died down. Because no one teased him. *No one*. Except for perhaps Michelle, his cousin — and she didn't count.

"There's more to it than knowing where it goes."

"I know." Cal stepped closer, then ran an index finger down her arm.

"You're so cocky."

"You're so cocky."

"I'm not cocky."

"Why did you even pick me, then?" He stood tall, straight as his surfboard. Their eyes locked. "Is this your *thing*? Selecting young men in your class to fuck?"

She coughed.

"Don't tell me you're not cocky."

"I'm *not* cocky." She mirrored his stance, not bending or backing down. "And I don't prey on my students. I've never invited a student here before." Her voice didn't match her body language, though. "I've never done anything like this."

"What exactly are we doing?" His palms met the counter, one, then the other, boxing her in at the waist. He glanced up.

"I thought you didn't need a teacher."

"Maybe I do."

"Your *peers* haven't been teaching you anything?"

"I learn on my own."

"Oh." She laughed.

Tilting his face toward the floor, Cal grinned and shook his head. "That's not what I meant." Her chest rose and fell as he made her wait an eternity for an explanation.

"I watch. I listen," he finally said, each word tumbling out with the skill and intention of a much older man. "I learn what a girl likes and doesn't. I'm very perceptive."

"Well," she began after slinking beneath his bicep, "I'm not a *girl*." Once several feet away, she peered over her shoulder. That same fucking smirk lit her beautiful face. "I'm a woman."

Cal folded his arms across his chest, relaxing against the counter she'd vacated. But he didn't smile or give anything away.

"You don't intimidate me, you know." Her ass met the edge of the breakfast table. "With that arrogant posture"—she rattled the ice in her glass— "those green eyes ... with that voice and your choice of words."

"Then why?"

"Why what?"

"Why me, then?" Puffing up his chest, he glanced around the room. "If this isn't your thing? *Boy chasing*."

"Go to hell, Cal."

There wasn't a piece of the floor he didn't own as he stalked toward her now. His nostrils practically flaring. His brow crinkled.

"Why me, then, *Professor*?" he asked the moment he reached her.

"Don't call me that."

"I'll call you what I like." Barefoot, she was maybe five or six inches shorter than his six-foot stature. And he liked the way her head tilted back when she looked up at him. "We're not in the classroom."

For a moment, neither of them moved. Or blinked. Only their lungs laboring to breathe. Their hearts beating erratically.

"Where's the painting?" Cal asked as he wiped perspiration from his forehead using a wrist.

But she made no reply.

The two of them only continued peering at one another, Cal thinking of the note she'd slipped him earlier in the day, at the end of class. Hiding precise instructions, her address, and the following invitation beneath another paper she'd distributed to all the students.

I have a piece of art I want you to see. It hangs on a wall in my home.

Cal began to wonder if there was an actual painting.

There were paintings, of course.

She was an art history teacher, an enthusiast, a misplaced dreamer. There were lots of paintings and drawings and sketches in her charming house stationed near the ocean in Santa Cruz. Covering the walls, lining the staircase, canvases on shelves. But he also noticed, by her prior inflection and still-flushed complexion — by the way she'd been eyeing him for the past several weeks — that what she'd invited him to her home to see was far more than a painting.

The professor swallowed — not her vodka with the bits of ice and the splash of juice, but saliva. And when it passed her throat, Cal noticed that too.

"Where is it?" he repeated, his throat thick with something he couldn't name. Nor did he care to.

"In my room."

"Show me."

"No."

"You expected a different kind of college boy?" Cal began to play with the skirt of her dress, dancing the hem toward her thighs.

"Yes," she choked out.

"I'm not like other..."

Download The Ocean in His Veins here

RESOURCES

**If you or someone you know are experiencing any form of mental illness, please reach out to someone.
You are amazing. And you are not alone.**

https://www.marielhemingwayfoundation.org/

https://drjoedispenza.com/the-mission

https://edenenergymedicine.com/about-us/about-donna-eden/

Also by A.R. Hadley

THE OCEAN SERIES

Where the Ocean Meets the Sky

The Ocean in His Veins

THE STANDALONES

Bodhi

The Flyaways

The Truth in the Lie

Moonlight Drive

THE PHYSICAL COLLECTION

Perfect Circle

The Peacock

Fireflies

Love the book, please consider leaving a review!

Check out my website!

And join my newsletter!

Thanks so much for reading!

XO

Amber

PLAYLIST

PART I
"Paralyzer" – Finger Eleven
"Ocean Eyes" – Billie Eilish
"(Sittin' On) The Dock of the Bay" – Otis Redding
"Let's Dance" – David Bowie
"I Want You (She's So Heavy)" – The Beatles
"Wildflowers" – Tom Petty
"Then I Kissed Her" – The Beach Boys
"Alone" – Heart
"The Dummy Song" – Louis Armstrong
"One" – U2

"Crash Into Me" – Dave Matthews Band
"I'm on Fire" – Bruce Springsteen
"Hurt" – Nine Inch Nails
"Hurt" – Johnny Cash

PART II
"Miss You" – The Rolling Stones
"Ain't No Sunshine" – Bill Withers
"Stay" – Maurice Williams and The Zodiacs
"Magic Man" – Heart
"November Rain" – Guns N' Roses
"Stand By Me" – Ben E. King
"Breaking the Girl" – Red Hot Chili Peppers
"Mother Mother" – Tracy Bonham
"Just the Way You Are" – Bruno Mars
"Time in a Bottle" – Jim Croce
"Everyday is a Winding Road" – Sheryl Crow
"As Time Goes By" – Dooley Wilson
"More Than You Know" – Billie Holiday
"More Than You Know" – Eddie Vedder

PART III
"Love is the Thing" – Nat King Cole
"In the Mood" – Glenn Miller
"Everlong (Acoustic)" – Foo Fighters
"Maybe I'm Amazed" – Paul McCartney
"Canon in D" – Johann Pachelbel
"Crash Into Me" – Dave Matthews Band
"La Vie En Rose" – Louis Armstrong
"Requiem In D Minor, K 626" – Wolfgang Amadeus Mozart
"Never Tear Us Apart" – INXS
"Still Remains" – Stone Temple Pilots
"We're Off to See the Wizard" – Judy Garland and Ray Bolger
"All I Want Is You" – U2

END CREDITS
"Beautiful Day" – U2

About the Author

A.R. Hadley writes imperfectly perfect sentences by the light of her iPhone.
She loves the ocean.
Chocolate.
Her children.
And Cary Grant.
She annoys those darling little children by quoting lines from *Back to the Future*, but despite her knowledge of eighties and nineties pop culture, she was actually meant to live alongside the Lost Generation after the Great War and write a mediocre novel while drinking absinthe with Hemingway. Instead, find her sipping unsweet tea near a garden as she weaves fictional tales of love and connection amid reality.

https://www.arhadley.com

facebook.com/arhadleywriter

instagram.com/arhadleywriter

amazon.com/A.R.-Hadley/e/B01J7WHH16

bookbub.com/profile/a-r-hadley

Made in the USA
Columbia, SC
15 December 2024

47783268R20428